THE GOLDEN MILE

ALSO BY JOHN SHERLOCK

The Ordeal of Major Grigsby

The Instant Saint

The Hiders and Finders (with Eugene Burdick)

The Dream Makers

J.B.'s Daughter

The Amindra Gamble (with David Westheimer)

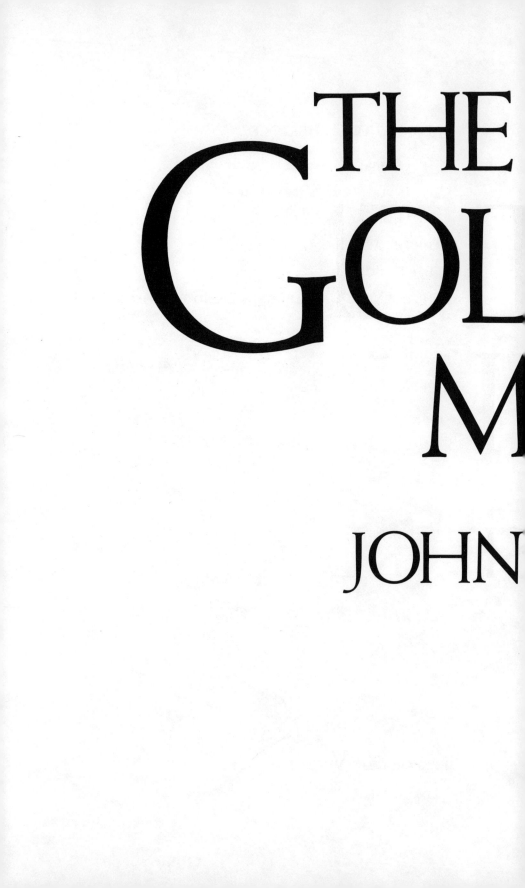

THE
GOL
M

JOHN

DEN
LE

SHERLOCK

 VIKING

VIKING
Viking Penguin Inc., 40 West 23rd Street,
New York, New York 10010, U.S.A.
Penguin Books Ltd, Harmondsworth,
Middlesex, England
Penguin Books Australia Ltd, Ringwood,
Victoria, Australia
Penguin Books Canada Limited, 2801 John Street,
Markham, Ontario, Canada L3R 1B4
Penguin Books (N.Z.) Ltd, 182–190 Wairau Road,
Auckland 10, New Zealand

First published in 1986 by Viking Penguin Inc.
Published simultaneously in Canada

LIBRARY OF CONGRESS CATALOGING IN PUBLICATION DATA
Sherlock, John, 1932–
The golden mile.
I. Title.
PS3569.H3997G6   1986   813'.54   85-26459
ISBN 0-670-81067-3

Printed in the United States of America by
The Book Press, Brattleboro, Vermont
Set in Garamond
Designed by Sharen DuGoff Egana

For Peter, my son,
also Patty Ecker, Joseph Benti, and family,
with fondest love.

"The Gods visit the
sins of the father on the
children."

    —Euripides

I would like to express my gratitude to Marilynn Saunders and her associates at the Beverly Hills Public Library for their gracious help and endless patience in assisting me during the research phase of this book.

THE GOLDEN MILE

1

LOS ANGELES: June 3, 1985

The shrill yelp of an injured animal jolted Anna Maxell-Hunter awake. She had taken a sleeping pill before going to bed, and at first she was unable to decide whether the anguished cry was real or part of a nightmare. Glancing at the illuminated dial of the digital clock on her bedside table, she saw it was 1:27 A.M. The silence in her bedroom encouraged her to dismiss the noise she thought she'd heard as part of a bad dream, and she settled back against the pillows. But no sooner had she closed her eyes than she heard the animal again. This time it was a whimper that slowly grew fainter and finally ended in a low gurgle.

"Shep!"

Anna's voice trembled as she called her daughter's Yorkshire terrier, which always slept in a basket in the kitchen. When the dog didn't respond, Anna got up and tried to open the bedroom door, but it was locked from the outside. She heard footsteps crossing the living room floor and then the sound of objects being smashed and fabric ripping. Tiptoeing to her dressing table, she flicked on an intercom that was linked to her daughter's bedroom in another wing of the penthouse, but the red light indicating it was live did not come on.

Consciously striving to control her rising panic, Anna lifted the receiver of the telephone that was a direct line to the night clerk in the Wellington House lobby, thirty-five stories below, but the connection was dead. She crossed quickly to an emergency button set in the wall above her bed and pressed it. Each room in her luxurious 9,000-square-foot condominium was equipped with one of these devices, which were designed to trigger the beeper alarms carried by the many security guards who patrolled the high-rise around the clock. This time, no one responded.

Beyond the door, Anna heard labored breathing and guttural mumblings. The light at her bedside suddenly flickered and went out, plunging her into a darkness that was total except for the faint glow cast by blinking indicators on a panel that was built into the wall near the panic button. On it was a plastic overlay representing all eighteen rooms in the penthouse, each of which was equipped with security devices: infrared sensors in the ceilings, ultrasound detectors in the walls, microwave scanners, and pressure-sensitive pads under the carpets. They all clearly indicated the presence of an intruder moving between the living room and library.

She was still gazing at the blinking lights when an ultrasensitive detector over the fireplace in the living room suddenly clicked on, adding volume to the sounds that had previously been muted, making them seem just inches away from where she stood. It was as if the intruder was in the bedroom with her. She instinctively tensed in readiness for his touch, but seconds later the sounds abruptly stopped.

After a moment's hesitation, she crossed to the door and pressed her ear against the wood paneling, straining in vain to hear the footsteps and muttering that had been so clearly audible a short time ago. Placing her hand on the doorknob, she started to turn it but felt an opposite pressure from the other side. Somebody was trying to enter the bedroom. Her breathing became shallow and strained, and for one terrible moment, as the door started to open, she thought she was having a stroke similar to one she had suffered years earlier, but then she heard her daughter Janna ask softly, "Are you all right?"

"Thank God it's you!" Anna gasped. "What on earth . . . ?"

"Somebody's broken in," Janna whispered. "I was locked in my bedroom until a few moments ago. Whoever it is may still be out there."

"I tried calling security" Anna said, "but the lines are dead."

Janna reached for the phone, put it to her ear, and heard a continuous buzz. "It's working now," she replied, audibly relieved as she heard the night clerk's voice at the other end of the line.

Frank Kershaw, manager of Wellington House, arrived at the penthouse at 1:44 A.M. A tall, thin man in his late forties, he wore a morning coat and pin-striped trousers and was impeccably groomed despite the late hour. With him was George Harris, chief of security, a heavy-set man with a florid complexion, whose belly bulged over a wide leather belt from which hung an assortment of objects, including a flashlight and holstered revolver. Summoned by the night clerk, the two men had met in the lobby and discussed the situation as they rode up to the penthouse in the small private elevator. The report of an intruder on the condominium's thirty-fifth floor was almost impossible to believe, even though it came from Janna Maxell-Hunter, who, as co-owner of

Wellington House, was also their boss. As far as they were concerned, the high-rise, and particularly its penthouse, was impregnable. In addition to the security guards who patrolled the premises twenty-four hours a day, the building was equipped both inside and out with strategically placed closed-circuit television cameras that were constantly monitored on numerous screens at a central desk. Should any of the security areas have been breached, alarms would have sounded and integrated microcomputer processors would have immediately warned of an intruder. "Even if somebody managed to sneak past the guard in the lobby," George Harris argued, "the only way to reach the penthouse is by using the private elevator, and that can only be activated by a magnetically coded pass card."

When Kershaw announced their arrival into a small speaker set to one side of the massive copper-sheathed front door of the penthouse, a voice he recognized as Janna Maxell-Hunter's told him to come through to the bedroom in the east wing. There was a quick buzz, followed by a click, as the electronic lock was activated and the door opened. The two men stepped into the penthouse and were surprised to find the living room in darkness. Harris unclipped his torch and shone its beam in a wide arc, revealing ripped furniture, slashed drapes, scattered books, and smashed glass coffee tables.

"Holy Christ!" He slid his gun out of its holster.

"Check all the rooms," Kershaw ordered.

Harris cautiously began his search, while Kershaw picked his way over piles of debris to the bedroom in the east wing. Tapping lightly on the door, he identified himself and went inside. As he entered, the lights suddenly flicked on. The two women were standing near the window.

"Harris! Thank goodness. What on earth took you so long?" Janna demanded sharply.

"I came as soon as the night clerk—"

"Why wasn't there any response to the panic button?"

"No alarms sounded, ma'am, and the guard at the desk swears nobody without the proper identification has entered or left the lobby since he came on duty four hours ago," Kershaw answered stiffly.

"Well, you can see from the mess out there he was wrong," Janna said.

"I'll have the whole security system tested—"

"The sooner, the better," Janna said, "but I want you to use the utmost discretion. If word of what's happened up here gets out, it could be disastrous. My company has invested over a hundred million dollars in Wellington House, and the primary reason we've succeeded in selling these condominiums at such high prices is that we've guaranteed our tenants protection against exactly the kind of thing that's just—"

She halted in mid-sentence as George Harris, his face ashen, appeared at the bedroom door. "There's something I think you should see, ma'am," he announced hoarsely.

Janna hesitated a moment, then followed the security chief into the library. The mutilated corpse of her dog, Shep, lay in a pool of blood on the Aubusson carpet.

"Oh, no!" Janna gasped.

Her eyes remained fixed on the slaughtered animal for a full minute, then slowly shifted to a place on the wall where Shep's blood had been used to paint a huge Nazi swastika.

At 9:45 A.M., Anna Maxell-Hunter sat at her dressing table putting the finishing touches to her makeup. Her face mirrored the tension she'd been under. Her pale skin was drawn tightly over gaunt cheeks, and the dark circles under her eyes were the result of not being able to sleep despite the assurances of both Kershaw and Harris that the intruder was no longer in the penthouse. Janna had offered to stay up with her, but Anna knew that her daughter had an early board meeting at the company she owned, Star Industries, in Century City, so she insisted that the younger woman get at least a few hours' rest.

Before going back to bed, Janna had put through a call to Lieutenant Joe Dawson, an old friend who worked out of Central Station in downtown Los Angeles. He had been out on an assignment, but she left a message asking him to call her back as soon as possible. Dawson still hadn't phoned by the time Janna left for her office at eight thirty.

In the hours Anna spent alone waiting for daylight to come, she tried to will herself not to think, but she was unable to block out images of the past: the Warsaw ghetto in flames, children perched on the window ledges of burning buildings, used for target practice by German soldiers; a mother smothering her baby to keep it from crying and betraying the hiding place of other Jews concealed in an underground bunker.

She stared at herself in the mirror of the dressing table. For a woman of sixty-five who had suffered a stroke, she was still attractive, with high cheekbones and taut, supple skin that was virtually unwrinkled except for fine lines under her eyes and across her forehead, which only became noticeable when she was worried or under great stress. After the night of terror she had just experienced they had deepened to rifts, and there was a profound weariness in her dark brown eyes that pads of cotton wool soaked in witch hazel had failed to erase.

After brushing her shoulder-length hair—which, thanks to a weekly touch-up by Kieko, her Japanese hairdresser, showed no sign of gray —she got up and went into the living room. There, the corpulent black cook-housekeeper, Sarah, was supervising a small crew of maintenance men who had been sworn to secrecy by Frank Kershaw before being assigned to clean up the wreckage.

"The rate these folks is goin', this is gonna take all day," Sarah announced in her throaty Southern drawl.

"They know what they're doing, Sarah." Anna said. "Stay out of their way, and if Lieutenant Dawson calls, tell him Janna's at her office, that I'll be back in a couple of hours, and we'd appreciate it if he can come by as soon as possible."

"Yes, ma'am," the black woman replied, shaking her head as she looked at the swastika, which still hadn't been cleaned from the library wall. "Ain't nowhere safe nowadays."

Anna continued to watch the workmen clean up the $20-million condominium that had been her home for almost a year. The most expensive dwelling of its kind in the world, it had ten bedrooms, a climate-controlled wine cellar, crystal chandeliers (one of which had been smashed by the intruder), a private screening room, a landscaped terrace built around a swimming pool, a sunken video-stereo center, a sauna, a foyer filled with art insured for over $8 million, and twelve bathrooms with dolphin-shaped faucets plated in 24-karat gold.

With a last look around, Anna let herself out of the penthouse and walked slowly down a short carpeted passageway that led to her garage. It was located alongside the condominium and was equipped with an oversized elevator designed to lift cars the 35 floors from street level to the top of Wellington House. It was a feature that was unique to the building, and one which had received considerable publicity when the high-rise was under construction eighteen months earlier. Many of the wealthy tenants who had purchased condominiums in Wellington House had done so because the automobile elevator allowed them to drive to within a few steps of their front doors without ever having to leave the safety of their cars. After the numerous muggings that had taken place in subterranean parking lots, it was a feature that ensured the ultimate in personal security, one for which they were willing to pay highly.

The chauffeur, standing by the open door of Anna's Rolls-Royce, put a supporting hand under her elbow to help her into the back seat. The stroke she had suffered many years earlier had paralyzed her right arm and left her unable to speak clearly. Only intensive physical and speech therapy at UCLA had enabled her to regain a reasonably full range of movement and turn garbled utterances into haltingly spoken sentences.

She tensed as the elevator began its smooth descent and automatically braced herself for the slight bump when it reached street level. Traffic was light for a Monday morning, and much less congested than it had been a year ago when the Olympic Games were under way in Los Angeles. Smoggy heat had settled in a brownish haze over the city, but the whisper-quiet air conditioning in the Rolls made it bearable as the chauffeur guided the car along the section of Wilshire Boulevard that linked Westwood with Beverly Hills. This strip had become known locally as the "Golden Mile" because the high-rise towers that lined it on each side contained condominiums that outpriced any concentration of privately owned apartments in the world, including the Avenue Foch in Paris and the moneyed battlements of Manhattan's Park and Fifth avenues.

"Shall I wait, ma'am?" the chauffeur asked as he slowed the car to a stop in front of the Simon Wiesenthal Center on West Pico Boulevard, a few blocks south of Beverly Hills.

"No, I don't know how long I will be," Anna replied. "It'll be easier if you come back for me in an hour."

After the chauffeur helped Anna out of the car, she paused for a moment; the event she had come to attend was an annual one, yet despite the number of years she had taken part in it, she'd never quite overcome the feeling of trepidation she always experienced when it was time to put in another appearance. Mentally bracing herself, she started up the steps of the building.

Deborah Epstein, Coordinator of Holocaust Activities, was waiting for her on the steps. "Anna! How well you look! Rabbi Hier is down at the Convention Center, but his assistant is expecting you."

Anna followed the other woman down a flight of stairs, which led to the section of the building that housed the Wiesenthal Center. It was crowded with visitors from all over the world who had come to Los Angeles for the annual gathering of Jewish Holocaust Survivors. Even though it was now over forty years since the horrors of the Nazi persecution, the chance of finding lost families and friends still drew over 10,000 people, far too many to be accommodated by the limited facilities of the Wiesenthal Center. This year the focus of the gathering was the huge Convention Center in downtown Los Angeles, where banks of computers were putting together fragments of information gleaned from throughout the world in an attempt to provide answers to the questions that still lingered in the hearts of those who had survived.

As Anna made her way slowly toward the administrative offices in the basement of the building, she saw elderly men and women embrace and passed others wearing T-shirts emblazoned with such messages as *Have you seen my brother?* with a name and last known address in Poland. She knew their hopes were higher this year. The computers at the Convention Center contained the names of 350,000 holocaust survivors cross-indexed with fragments of information from Jewish communities around the world. Memories of shared bunkhouses at half a dozen different concentration camps; a month of trench-digging detail in Russia; the conversation of passengers shivering through bitter nights in freight cars bound for Treblinka and Bergen-Belsen—all were now recorded on magnetic tape in the most sophisticated electronic memories available. By opening doors that had remained closed for half a lifetime, computers had given new meaning to bits and pieces of information that had previously seemed unrelated.

Before entering Rabbi Hier's office, Anna paused in front of the doors to the permanent exhibition memorializing Jews who died in the holocaust of World War II. It was a display she had looked at many times in the past, and yet she suddenly experienced an overwhelming need to see it again.

"Do you mind?" she asked.

"Of course not," the other woman replied with an understanding smile. "I'll wait for you here."

As Anna pushed open the doors she felt again the same sensation she'd had the first time she visited the exhibit: anxious anticipation combined with a familiar sense of place. The interior was lit in a dim, almost theatrical way that created the impression of entering a grotto, but instead of glittering stalagmites and stalactites there were drab, lifeless reminders of the unimaginable horrors of the systematic persecution that had taken so many lives.

Considering the enormity of the atrocity, it was an understated display. There were photographs of Auschwitz inmates who had committed suicide by hurling themselves onto high-voltage wire fences surrounding the concentration camp; pictures of the piles of corpses found when the British Army liberated Bergen-Belsen; drawings depicting the nightmare of daily existence in a concentration camp by a young girl who lived through the horrors of Dachau; and a photo of members of the Jewish Fighting Organization who waged a heroic battle against the Nazis during the final days of the Warsaw ghetto, being forced out of fire-gutted bunkers.

Anna gazed at this last image for three or four minutes before finally turning away. Although moving, the rest of the exhibit, which included the striped suits concentration camp inmates wore, the crude implements they used as part of their daily existence, the empty cylinders of Zyklon B gas, the photographs of mass executions, seemed secondary. She had images of her own indelibly etched in her memory. It was these specific recollections she had needed to verify.

"Ready?" the waiting woman asked when Anna emerged from the exhibit.

Anna nodded and followed as Deborah Epstein led the way to Rabbi Hier's office. A tall, thin young man was waiting for her, an assistant to the center's Dean. He had an easy, outgoing charm and was obviously aware that, as somebody who had contributed millions of dollars over the years to support the Wiesenthal Center, Anna merited VIP treatment.

"Please sit down," he said, escorting her to a sofa and handing her a large manila envelope. "Rabbi Hier asked me to give you this."

"What is it?" Anna asked.

"The material you've been trying to find since the first day you came to the Center."

Anna experienced a quick surge of excitement but hid it behind an expression of careful composure. "Everything?"

"Not quite," the young man replied. "There are still a few pieces missing. It's possible we'll come up with the rest when the information we're receiving from survivors at this year's meeting is programmed into the computers."

"May I take this with me?" Anna asked, tapping the envelope.

"Of course."

"Thank you." Anna got up from the sofa. "Now, if you'll excuse me, I have some important reading to do."

The maintenance crew was leaving when Anna returned to the penthouse. There was no longer any sign of glass from the smashed coffee tables or shattered crystal chandelier, and the only visible evidence of the vandalism was a damp spot on the carpet in the library, where one of the men had removed the bloodstains of the slaughtered dog, and the fresh paint on the wall where the swastika had been daubed.

"They comin' back to give it another goin' over jus' soon's this coat dries," Sarah said, "though the good Lord alone knows why they couldn't have used thicker paint."

The Nazi symbol was still faintly visible beneath its white covering. "Tell Mr. Kershaw I want the whole wall redone," Anna said brusquely.

"Lieutenant Dawson was here while you were gone," Sarah said. "He looked around plenty but had to leave. Said he'd be back in a little while."

"Show him into the library when he gets here," Anna said. "And if the phone rings let the switchboard get it. I don't want to be disturbed by anybody but Lieutenant Dawson."

Anna closed the doors of the library and settled into a deep leather chair near the window. She gazed out at a panoramic view that encompassed a 180-degree sweep from the Pacific Ocean beyond Malibu to the glass-paneled skyscrapers glittering in downtown Los Angeles, and included the whole of Beverly Hills, with its scores of swimming pools hidden in the lush greenery of mansions like tiny beryls of the palest blue. What she saw was so breathtaking, its vibrancy so dazzling, it might have been created with a painter's palette, yet Anna was unmoved by it all. In her mind's eye she was still seeing the pathetic relics displayed in the exhibit at the Wiesenthal Center.

Switching on a reading light, she pressed a button and waited as silk-lined draperies automatically slid into place across massive picture windows, before turning her attention to the envelope. In it were three manila folders, each of which contained the picture of a young woman, along with copies of original documents, and a collection of grainy photographs taken in the Warsaw ghetto by a German war correspondent whose name and newspaper affiliation were still visible on the back. They showed bearded old men being kicked by German soldiers; groups of emaciated children hunched in the gutter with outstretched hands; corpses charred beyond recognition; rows of houses in flames; and, on the walls of a gutted synagogue, a crudely scrawled swastika.

Anna gazed at the photographs, focusing her attention on those of the three women, but looked up when she heard the door open. Joe Dawson entered the library. He was wearing jeans and an open-necked work shirt, an outfit that signified he was off duty from his job as commander of a SWAT team in the Los Angeles Police Department.

"You all right?" he asked.

Anna nodded. "Sarah told me you were here earlier."

"I saw the mess."

"Then you know what happened here last night."

"I talked with Janna. She was in a meeting and couldn't say much, but the manager and the chief of security filled me in. Now I'd like to hear more about it from you."

Anna remained silent for a moment, then said, "I think it's time I told you the whole story—from the beginning."

Dawson crossed to a chair, sat down, and waited for Anna to begin. It was two or three minutes before she spoke. Her eyes were glazed and she appeared lost in her own thoughts. Dawson didn't try to hurry her, preferring to let her find her own way of reaching back across the years. His patience was rewarded when Anna finally began to talk, hesitantly at first, and then with increasing certainty as she parted veils of memory that had remained untouched for over forty years.

2

WARSAW: April 18, 1943

A shaft of sunlight streamed through a shattered window in the basement of a fire-gutted building on the corner of Zamenhof and Wolynska streets in the central section of the Warsaw ghetto. It had once been a bakery, and the room that the brilliant golden light illuminated was lined with ovens, but the huge barrels that had formerly held flour were empty, and there wasn't a crumb of bread or any other food to be seen. The last remnants of anything edible had disappeared two and a half years earlier, in October 1940, soon after Nazi troops stormed into Poland and herded all the Jews of Warsaw into 840 acres of slumland in the northern section of the city, which the Germans had then surrounded with a ten-foot-high, eleven-mile-long wall containing fourteen tightly guarded gates. An official food ration of under three hundred calories a day had been imposed, ensuring slow starvation, the evidence of which was all too visible on the pallid, hollow-cheeked faces of the children clustered on the brick floor.

Anna's heart ached every time she looked at them. It was two mornings before Passover, but she knew that few if any of these youngsters would sample the hard-boiled eggs, matzos, and bitter herbs that were a traditional part of the seder.

"That's enough for today, children," she announced with a brightness she didn't feel. "Now I want all of you to go straight home. Is that understood?"

"Yes, Miss Maxell," the youngsters chorused, wiping their slates clean with scraps of damp cloth before quietly filing up the debris-strewn steps that led to the street.

Anna watched until the last of them had gone. Instead of the sudden outbursts children normally make on getting out of class, there was only an empty silence. Life in the ghetto had made these youngsters old long before their time. It showed in their vacant eyes, stooped shoulders, and weary shuffle. For the umpteenth time she wondered if continuing their classes in secret after the school at Okopowa 55-A was closed by the Germans had been a good idea. Teaching them was illegal, and many members of the Judenrat, the community council that had become an instrument by which German authority was imposed on the ghetto by the Jews themselves, had condemned her actions. Despite the fact that it was now common knowledge that over half a million men, women, and children taken at systematic roundups had been shipped like cattle in closed boxcars to near-certain death at such concentration camps as Treblinka, Buchenwald, and Dachau, more than a few members of the Judenrat still continued to believe that by cooperating with the Nazis they would receive favorable treatment.

When the Judenrat members questioned Anna about continuing to teach the children in secret, she had argued that attending classes gave a semblance of structure to the youngsters' fractured lives. It was a place to go, something to do, an illusion of normalcy. Now, as she stood alone in the cellar of the bakery, she realized that what she had been describing were her own needs as much as those of the children.

Almost twenty-three, Anna was dark-haired and, according to the yearbook of the Manhattan Academy of Fine Arts, the school she had attended while her father was practicing medicine in New York, "beautiful in a refined, somewhat ethereal way." That was in 1935, only eight years ago, but it seemed an eternity. An advanced student, she had graduated when she was barely fifteen. She tried to remember what it was like to wear a white dress to the prom, to gorge herself on ice cream at Coney Island, to picnic with her family at Jones Beach, but the closed oven doors in the walls around her denied such flights of fancy.

Her father, an Austrian Jew with a medical degree from Heidelberg University, had emigrated to the United States in 1919 with Rachel, his Polish-born wife, and set up a small practice in New York. Anna was born a year after her parents' arrival in the country they had chosen as their new home. But her father, a sensitive, highly cultured man, had found it hard to adapt to the materialistic American way of life, and when he was offered the post as Director of Warsaw's Bauman-Berson Hospital in 1936, he accepted and, despite the growing political unrest in Europe, returned to Europe with his family. It had proved a fateful decision. When German troops occupied Warsaw in September 1939, Dr. Maxell, who had never even applied for American citizenship during his stay in the United States, was arrested with his wife and daughter, had his Austrian passport stamped with the word JUDEN, and was imprisoned behind the walls of the ghetto along with over half a million other Jews.

Anna picked up a broken piece of chalk from the floor and placed it on a table where bakers had once rolled dough. As she did so she caught a reflection of herself in a fragment of mirror that was still attached to the wall over a cracked sink. She looked older than her years. The strain of merely staying alive in the ghetto had taken its toll, heightened by the additional risks she had exposed herself to by smuggling weapons in from the Aryan side of the wall.

Her parents knew nothing of her activities as a courier for the Jewish Fighting Organization (ZOB). If they had known, they would have done everything in their power to stop her. The risks were extreme, and the penalty on being caught was immediate execution. But she had continued to take money out through the sewers and bring weapons back via whatever route the Germans still hadn't uncovered, because she believed it was better to die fighting than to be led passively to slaughter in a concentration camp.

She had been recruited as a courier in August 1942 by Josef Kandalman, a section commander working under Mordechai Anielewicz, the twenty-four-year-old commander-in-chief of the fifteen hundred Jews who comprised the Jewish Fighting Organization. Kandalman, a man in his early thirties, had owned the Club Warszawa, a small night spot on the Aryan side of the wall, prior to the Nazi decrees requiring all Jews to move inside the ghetto. Rather than sell out for a pittance to unscrupulous Polish speculators (who were making quick fortunes by appropriating property Jews were being forced to abandon), Kandalman had transferred ownership of his property to Genevieve Fleury, a strikingly attractive twenty-five-year-old Frenchwoman who had worked for him as a hostess before the war.

Even after Kandalman was imprisoned in the ghetto, he continued to prosper by setting up clandestine trade links with the Aryan side. He did this by organizing a complex operation whereby dozens of smugglers, many of them children, crawled through sewers and small breaches in the wall to exchange precious family possessions for food and medical supplies. On the Aryan side of the wall, Genevieve Fleury used contacts she made at the nightclub to keep her former boss supplied with whatever items he could sell at a profit inside the ghetto.

Anna had met Genevieve a number of times and been greatly impressed by her. The petite Frenchwoman had a perfectly proportioned body and long auburn hair that fell almost to her waist, and she exuded a sexuality that was almost tangible. It had triggered a spark of jealousy in Anna, but she couldn't help admiring Genevieve's intelligence, which, though street-learned, served her well in her dealings with black marketeers.

Helping Genevieve run the nightclub and buying goods on the Aryan side of the wall for Kandalman was a woman called Keja. Although nearly twenty years old, she appeared much younger; her blond hair framed a face that was dominated by huge, ingenuous blue eyes. The daughter of a Gypsy who had been sent to a German concentration camp in early 1937, Keja had escaped the roundup and fled to Warsaw with half a dozen other members of her tribe, where she found work as a dancer in Kandalman's club.

He had obtained false papers for Keja, capitalizing on her blondness to pass her off as a Swedish citizen, an identity that gave her the protection of that country's neutrality and allowed her to continue working as a dancer at the nightclub after her mentor was forced to move into the ghetto.

Anna had never understood the exact nature of the relationship between Kandalman and the two women who continued to serve him so faithfully. Both of them often stayed with him in his bunker on Franciszkanska Street when it was unsafe for them to return to the Aryan side of the wall, but whether or not either of them were Kandalman's lovers was a mystery Anna had never tried to solve. She had learned first-hand that the former nightclub owner had a dangerous temper and, when provoked, could become extremely violent. He was also a secretive man and didn't share information about himself with others.

The one exception was Pan Halevi, a huge, muscular ex-wrestler who had worked for Kandalman as a bouncer at the nightclub before being ordered behind ghetto walls with his boss. The two men shared quarters in the bunker on Franciszkanska Street, and it was quickly apparent to anybody who came into contact with them that Halevi was devoted to Kandalman. He carried out unquestioningly whatever orders the other man gave him; there were persistent rumors that Halevi had killed more than a few men who Kandalman felt had crossed him.

By the end of 1942, Kandalman's smuggling operations had prospered to the point where he was able to live in considerable comfort in the private bunker he had constructed for himself. Although he had profited from mercilessly exploiting less resourceful fellow Jews, more than a few secretly admired him for the cunning he displayed in setting up his organization. Even his enemies—those who condemned Kandalman as a ruthless profiteer—still grudgingly admitted that his knowledge of the ghetto labyrinth, including both the sewers and the interconnecting attics made by knocking down walls to create a maze of hidden passageways linking whole blocks of houses, was unequaled.

Because of Kandalman's ability to move with such ease between the ghetto and the Aryan side of the wall, Mordechai Anielewicz invited him to join the Jewish Fighting Organization. The ZOB desperately needed arms, and the organization Kandalman had created to conduct his smuggling operations was the most obvious way to get them. There was no shortage of money. The ZOB had assigned "tax collectors" to squeeze cash for arms from rich ghetto residents, by force if necessary, and additional millions of zlotys were available in the form of valuables donated by those singled out for shipment to concentration camps. These included some men, wealthy jewelers before the war, who had managed to smuggle hundreds of their finest gems into the ghetto. Diamonds, rubies, and emeralds—a vast treasure that was easily portable and virtually beyond value—were put at Kandalman's disposal on the condition that he use the fortune to purchase weapons the ZOB badly needed for their final stand against the Germans.

When Kandalman accepted Anielewicz's offer there were many who claimed that his only interest was in the profits he stood to make, but events had proved them wrong, and by mid-April 1943 even the most outspoken of these doubters had been obliged to admit their fears had been ill-founded. For as SS Major General Jurgen Stroop stepped up his annihilation of the ghetto Jews by the use of tanks, armored carriers, and flame throwers, the daily atrocities seemed to trigger a change in Kandalman. Anna, whose work as a courier brought her into almost daily contact with the ex–nightclub owner, sensed that being accepted as an important member of the ZOB had caused him to undergo some kind of deep personal catharsis. This man, who had spent his life living by whatever means were expedient, now found himself suddenly respected. People admired his skills, applauded his cunning, and marveled at his audacity, and in response to this, he worked even harder for the resistance. . . .

The sound of gunfire jolted Anna out of her reverie, and she hurried up the stairs from the basement of the bakery to the street. It was late afternoon and sunlight illuminated every corner of the ghetto. The air was sweet with the scents of spring, and amid the rubble of shattered buildings flowers swayed in the warm, gentle breeze. It stirred the mantle of down and feathers from bedding left behind by those taken at selections and thrown out of windows by Nazi scavengers, creating a snowlike swirl in strange contrast to the mildness of the day.

The courtyard of the old gray-stone Czyste-Bauman-Berson Hospital was shrouded in silence. The place had once catered exclusively to children, but they were long gone, taken at the earliest selections to the furnaces at Treblinka. Because there were so few youngsters left to treat, the Bauman-Berson and Czyste hospitals had merged, and the building was now filled to overflowing with adults, few of whom were elderly, as they, being the least mobile and therefore expendable, had been among the first to be massacred by the Germans.

Anna started up the stairs toward the second floor, climbing over piles of plaster and masonry that had fallen during her absence. The echo of her footsteps merged in her mind with another sound—the screams of patients in their beds being shot by German soldiers in retaliation after the January revolt, when Mordechai Anielewicz and nine comrades, each armed with a pistol or grenade, had opened fire on SS guards leading a terrified procession of Jews to boxcars waiting at the railhead in Umschlagplatz. It had been the first show of armed resistance on the part of the Jews in the ghetto, and even though German vengeance had been ruthless, the ZOB action had sparked the sentiment that, if death was inevitable, perhaps it was best to fall proudly in battle.

Pausing at a ward on the second floor, Anna stood at the door watching her father move between beds long since stripped of pillows and linen, on which lay huddled shapes wrapped in stinking rags. She heard him try to comfort the dying in soft, gentle tones. Solace was all he had left to offer them: there was no more medicine and little food, but he still felt a duty toward them, both as a doctor and a fellow human being. Tears welled up in Anna's eyes as she saw her father doing what he could to make his patients' suffering more bearable. His stooped shoulders and waxlike pallor mirrored the toll such care was taking on him, and she wondered how much longer he could endure the strain he had put himself under in recent months.

Yet his belief in the essential goodness of man continued undiminished. It was as much a part of his being as the tenets of his religion, which, as an orthodox Jew, he considered as essential to life as breathing. In spite of the horrors that had become part of his daily existence, he still couldn't believe the Germans intended to annihilate the entire population of the ghetto. "They need live Jews to work their factories and mills," he reasoned. "What good to them are we dead?"

Anna could have answered him, but she didn't; he was too old and set in his ways to even begin to comprehend the horror she saw all around them, and there was nothing to be gained by challenging the principles that had been the very foundation of his life for sixty-three years. That was why she hadn't told him about her work as a courier; violence of any kind, even armed resistance against Hitler's storm-troopers, was antithetical to the values he cherished.

He looked up and saw her standing inside the door. For a moment their eyes met. His face was etched with fatigue, but he still managed to smile, half raising his hand in greeting, before turning his attention back to the patients.

He was accompanied on his rounds by his nurse, Janet Taylor, a plain-featured Englishwoman who was wearing what had once been a starched white uniform but now looked more like a gray shroud. She had started working for Anna's father in the late summer of 1939, soon after arriving in Warsaw with the young Polish man to whom she was engaged. He had been killed in one of the first border skirmishes against the Germans, but instead of returning to England, the English-woman had stayed on as a surgical nurse at the Bauman-Berson Hospital.

In the months that followed, Anna had come to know Janet Taylor well enough to realize that she was a dedicated socialist. During her stay in the ghetto she had become involved with a Communist-oriented group of intellectuals who distributed propaganda leaflets aimed at stirring the Jews to active resistance. The bond between the two women was strengthened by the fact that both had been required to cloak their activities against the Germans in secrecy: Anna to avoid upsetting her parents, Janet because many Jews still didn't trust Communists, even though Stalin's brief honeymoon with Hitler during the early months of the war was long over. Yet Anna still didn't feel as if she really knew Janet. She rarely spoke about her family, and on the few occasions when Anna had probed, Janet had retreated into her natural shell of shyness.

Turning away from the ward, Anna continued up the stairs until she came to a small alcove that had once been used for storing mops and brushes. Pausing in front of a dust-filmed mirror, she waited, and moments later a panel slid open to reveal a stairway which led to a series of small, interconnected rooms. It was guarded by a fourteen-year-old boy wearing a frayed cloth cap and holding a 9mm Weiss pistol. He nodded and said, "Your mother's frantic with worry. There's been another roundup, over near Halman's clothing factory."

"Was there any fighting?" Anna asked.

The boy, Jacob, shook his head and slid the wall panel shut. "They let themselves be taken like sheep." Anna heard the bitterness in his voice, but instead of replying turned toward the inner room, where her mother was hunched over a small stove on which was a saucepan filled with thin, watery soup. When she saw her daughter an expression of relief crossed her face, quickly replaced by one of feigned anger.

"I think you enjoy hurting me," she said, continuing to stir the steaming liquid with a wooden spoon.

Anna put her arm over the other woman's shoulder. "You know that's not true, Mama."

"So why do you go out without letting me know where you are?"

"You know I teach the children—"

"Against your father's wishes."

Anna didn't answer. She was too tired to argue and knew her mother's words were prompted more by worry than anger. Instead, she hugged her from behind, then crossed to what had once been a walk-in closet, but now served as a sleeping area she shared with Janet Taylor, and wearily slumped down on a straw-filled mattress.

The room, originally built as a resting place for half a dozen doctors, now provided sanctuary for eighteen people, and there was barely enough space to turn around when all of them were present. Privacy was the one thing Anna missed more than anything else. While others in the garret wove fantasies around food, she recalled memories of the summer afternoons she had spent walking alone in Lazienki Park, under a cloudless sky, her hair stirred by a warm breeze heavy with the scent of roses.

"Anna."

It was Janet. At twenty-four she was only a year older than Anna, but her quiet self-confidence made her seem much more mature. This impression was heightened by the plainness of her features, although she possessed an engaging smile and calm, hazel eyes.

"There's a meeting tonight," Janet murmured, keeping her voice low so as not to be overheard by others in the crowded room.

"Where?" Anna asked.

"At the bunker on Franciszkanska Street. Kandalman ordered me to pass the word. He wants us both there."

"My mother's already worried sick—"

"I've told her I need your help with somebody who is ill in another part of the ghetto."

"And my father?"

"He will be with his patients the rest of the night."

Anna hesitated, then slowly got to her feet. She had almost reached the door when her mother called after her, "Are you in such a hurry that you can't eat the soup I spent all day fixing?"

"It's an emergency, Mama," Anna said.

Her mother looked at the broth, which was little more than a few cabbage leaves floating in greasy water, and tears welled in her eyes. "Keep it warm," Anna said gently. "I promise to eat it the moment I get back."

Kissing her mother gently on the cheek, she pulled on her threadbare coat and hurried with Janet to where Jacob was still guarding the door.

"There's word the SS has thrown up a heavy cordon just outside the wall," the boy said. "And the seder planned for ghetto leaders has been canceled."

Anna glanced at Janet, seeking confirmation of what she'd heard, but the Englishwoman's expression remained blank. As they hurried down the steps to the courtyard, Anna said, "You knew, didn't you?"

"Yes," Janet replied.

"Why didn't you tell me?"

"There wasn't time."

Anna started to protest but checked herself and went out into the street without speaking. Darkness had fallen, but there was a moon, and its pale light accentuated the bleak outline of the ruined ghetto buildings against the night sky. There were no lights at any windows, but Anna could see shadowy figures heading for bunkers and other places they considered safe to hide. As they walked Janet confided that soon after noon a Jewish policeman secretly working with the ZOB had passed along word that the Germans were planning something big for early next morning. This had been confirmed by a worker at Walter Tobbens's factory on Lesno Street, who had seen SS troops gathering just beyond the wall.

When they reached Franciszkanska Street, Anna followed Janet down dusty, plaster-strewn stairs to a cellar, where they crawled through an opening behind a big stove and entered Josef Kandalman's bunker, which now served as one of ZOB's temporary headquarters.

The meeting was already under way, and Mordechai Anielewicz's second-in-command, Pavel Sokolczyk, a thickset man with a scraggly beard, was in the middle of an impassioned speech when the newcomers made their appearance. He paused, waited for them to find places to sit on the floor, and continued to address his audience with undiminished zeal. The room, a large cellar that had been reinforced with steel beams and equipped with concealed ventilators, was crowded with ZOB fighters, who listened intensely to every word Sokolczyk uttered.

"We don't have to convince anyone of our will to fight," he said, "but we must have weapons we can depend on. In the last shipment alone more than a third of the pistols had defective firing pins."

An angry murmur stirred in the crowd.

"The only way to be sure this doesn't happen again," Sokolczyk continued, "is to convince our thieving suppliers they are not dealing with fools."

A chorus of assent echoed around the bunker.

"We must teach them a lesson they won't forget."

Sokolczyk didn't specify what he had planned, but quickly moved on to giving each group commander detailed orders for the coming battle. The strength of SS troops readying themselves beyond the wall had been estimated at 850 men commanded by 16 officers—Waffen SS, police, Wehrmacht, and Askari units—backed up by a tank and two armored cars. An additional 2,000 German soldiers had been readied should they be needed.

"I don't know how long we'll hold out," Sokolczyk concluded, "but at least when the end comes we will die with pride."

Mordechai Anielewicz nodded his approval as those who had heard the speech clustered around Sokolczyk, shaking his hand and wishing each other luck in the next day's fighting. Only one man remained apart from the others: Josef Kandalman. He continued to stand at the back of the bunker, his arms folded, his brooding eyes taking everything in but showing no emotion.

He was solidly built, and had thick black hair, a thatch of which protruded through the open front of his partially unbuttoned shirt, forming a cushion between his skin and a gold medallion he wore on a fine chain around his neck. It had a striking design, a circle with intersecting lines that resembled Leonardo da Vinci's sketch of the divine proportions of man.

The bunker emptied rapidly, but when Anna and Janet started toward the exit they found their way blocked by Kandalman. "You were both involved in buying those defective weapons."

Anna tensed. It was true that she and Janet had taken money out for the purchase of guns, but the transaction with the suppliers of the arms had been handled by Genevieve Fleury.

"We only worked as couriers."

"But you saw who supplied the pistols?"

She nodded.

"And you can identify him?"

"His beard was streaked with gray."

"Come with me," he ordered. "Both of you."

Kandalman checked his Mauser, slid the gun into his belt, and put a grenade in each pocket. Then he loaded three Molotov cocktails—glass bottles containing gasoline with rags taped to their necks—into a canvas knapsack which he handed to Pan Halevi, who strapped the load over his massive shoulders. Without any further explanation, he led the way out of the bunker, motioning the others to follow.

When they reached the street Anna once again became conscious of the preparations taking place under cover of darkness to counter the impending German attack. The air was filled with tense expectation and fear, sensations Anna shared, but for different reasons.

She had no idea where Kandalman was leading them, or for what purpose, but she'd heard that he was a man who exacted a terrible vengeance from those he believed had betrayed him, and she had every reason to believe he now considered herself and Janet in that category. This suspicion increased as she realized that Kandalman was leading them toward the Wild Ghetto, a no-man's-land that had been uninhabited since the first deportations in the summer of 1942.

When Kandalman suddenly ducked into a doorway at the corner of Smocza and Dzielna streets, Anna recognized the house as one under which a tunnel had been built by professional smugglers soon after the wall was erected three years ago. She had used the route several times in carrying out her duties as a ZOB courier and admired the skill with which the tunnel had been constructed. In its crude way it was a triumph of engineering, ingeniously bolstered by a forest of props that made it strong enough to support the weight of traffic using the road to the Catholic cemetery on the Aryan side, where its entrance was cleverly hidden inside an elaborate marble crypt.

"Keep your heads down and mouths shut," Kandalman said.

They crept down a steep flight of stone steps that led to a damp cellar, their way lit by the beam from a large flashlight Pan Halevi carried, but the moment they reached the tiny subterranean room he snapped the torch off, and they were abruptly enveloped in total darkness. Anna experienced a sudden wave of panic and struggled to overcome it by taking a series of deep breaths.

"All right?" Janet whispered.

"Quiet!" Kandalman snapped.

Footsteps, muffled at first, then louder, sounded from below where they stood, and there was a metallic clink as a hinged flagstone in the cellar floor was slowly eased open. An arm holding a flickering candle emerged, followed by a bearded face that Anna immediately recognized as belonging to the black marketeer who had sold them the defective guns. He was followed by a boy of thirteen or fourteen lugging a heavy wooden crate, which he dumped noisily on the floor before straightening up.

"Stay right where you are!" Kandalman said.

His voice echoed in the darkness, startling the newcomers, and the man with the beard started reaching for a pistol that was stuck in his belt, but before his hand reached the weapon Halevi flicked on his flashlight and warned, "Try that and you're a dead man!"

"What the hell's going on?" the smuggler demanded hoarsely. "You ordered weapons and I've brought them."

"Guns that work?" Kandalman asked.

"Still in their grease wrappings."

Kandalman took the flashlight out of Halevi's hand and motioned the ex-wrestler toward the box. Taking a large knife from a sheath strapped to the inside of his leg, Halevi knelt down and expertly pried the lid open. Laying his knife aside, he reached inside the box and took out a package covered with thick grease.

"Schmeissers," the smuggler said. "Straight from the factory. I checked each one myself."

Kandalman crossed to where Pan Halevi was still kneeling next to the open case of weapons and took the unwrapped gun out of the big man's hand, first balancing it in his palm, then expertly slipping a clip of bullets into the chamber. Suddenly, in a movement that was so quick it blurred against the beam cast by the torch, he grabbed the smuggler's beard, forced his jaws open, and stuck the barrel of the Schmeisser into his mouth. There was a loud click as Kandalman pulled the trigger. When the weapon failed to fire the smuggler struggled to pull his head back, but Kandalman tightened his grip, forcing the barrel of the automatic even deeper into his throat.

"Jews are no longer going to eat your shit," Kandalman said. His finger started to tighten on the trigger again, but just before firing the gun he eased off and slowly took the barrel out of the bearded man's mouth.

"For God's sake!" the kneeling man pleaded.

"Tie him up," Kandalman said.

Halevi secured the smuggler's hands behind his back and forced him down onto the slime-covered flagstones. Kandalman watched him squirm, then took a Molotov cocktail out of the knapsack, unscrewed the metal cap, and poured the contents of the glass bottle over the man's head. The pungent odor of gasoline filled the cellar. It caught at the back of Anna's throat, but before she could cough, Kandalman lit a match and tossed it in front of him.

A whoosh of flame erupted, engulfing the smuggler's upper body. His screams echoed from the seeping walls of the cellar as he writhed in agony, repeatedly banging his head on the floor in a series of futile attempts to extinguish the blaze. After about ten seconds Kandalman nodded to Halevi, who used his jacket to smother the fire.

"It would have been kinder to shoot him," Janet announced bitterly.

"But not as effective." Kandalman crossed to where the burned man was whimpering in a stupor of pain and cut the rope holding the smuggler's wrists. Looking at the boy, who stood trembling against the wall, he said, "Tell your Polish friends what happened here, and why. We Jews are still willing to pay well for weapons, but God help anybody who tries to play us for fools."

Anna watched as the youngster guided the burned man down

through the trapdoor and into the tunnel. She heard the shuffle of their footsteps, and the anguished moans of the injured man, but they gradually faded away, leaving only a sweet, sickening stench of charred flesh. It filled the cellar, and Anna began to retch.

"Better get used to it," Kandalman said. "We're going to be down here awhile."

She didn't ask why. Nor did she attempt to explain that her need to vomit wasn't attributable only to the nauseating smell. Kandalman's cold-blooded brutality was equally to blame; it made a mockery of the very ideals for which the ZOB fighters were prepared to die.

An hour before dawn, Kandalman issued the order to move out and led the way up to the street. It was still dark, but searchlights the Germans had mounted on towers beyond the wall in front of the Catholic cemetery, whose beams swept the rubble of the Wild Ghetto throughout the night, had been switched off, allowing Kandalman and his group to slip unseen through a gap in the barrier to the Central ghetto.

When they reached Franciszkanska Street, Kandalman and Halevi disappeared into their bunker, leaving Anna and Janet to find their own way to the posts they had been assigned by Pavel Sokolczyk at the previous evening's meeting. They walked together in silence to the corner of Nalewki and Gensia, where Janet nodded toward a house bearing the number 33. "That's my post," she said. "Yours is across the street."

"I'm going back to the hospital," Anna murmured.

"Your orders are—"

"Orders? After what happened in that cellar I'm no longer sure what I'd be fighting for."

"You sound like your father," Janet said.

"Do I?" Anna was silent for a moment, then added, "That might not be such a bad thing."

She leaned forward, kissed her friend's cheek, held her for a moment and hurried away into the first gray light of dawn.

3

Janet waited until Anna rounded the corner, then went into the house where she'd been assigned a post at a window in the attic, a position from which the Nalewki Street gate was clearly visible.

Half a dozen ZOB fighters were checking their weapons and talking softly to each other when Janet entered the small room under the eaves of the house. They looked up, nodded, and went back to preparing for the battle all of them knew was imminent. Mosher Pachter, who had once operated the bakery where Anna had set up her illegal classroom, handed Janet a pistol and grenade.

"Keep your eye on the gate," he said.

Janet took the weapons and crossed to the window. The pale, uncertain light of dawn emphasized the emptiness of the streets. She found herself wondering if Anna had reached the hospital safely and wished there had been more time to talk before they left each other. What she had said must have sounded harsh and unfeeling, perhaps even created the impression that she approved of Kandalman's brutality, when nothing could have been further from the truth. As a nurse her dedication was to the relief of suffering, not the creation of it, yet terrible though Kandalman's retribution had been, she understood the reasoning behind it. The ZOB's stand against the Germans was about to begin, and they desperately needed all the weapons they could get. The sight of the smuggler's burned face would serve as an effective deterrent to any others who harbored thoughts of selling Jews defective arms; not enough to dry up the supply completely—greed would ensure that—but more than sufficient to ensure that guns shipped through the sewers from the Aryan side of the wall would be in top working order.

She checked the pistol Mosher Pachter had given her, a Luger, raised the gun in her right hand, and aimed it at a manhole midway between where she stood and the Nalewki Street gate. Her grip was steady. She took a long, deep breath, held it for a second, then slowly expelled the air in a long sigh. Her finger curled on the trigger, lightly, because she didn't want to sound a false warning shot or waste a bullet, yet still with enough pressure to give her the feel of cold steel against her skin.

It was a familiar sensation, one she had first experienced when she was sixteen years old and her father had shown her how to cradle his shotgun against her shoulder and peer down the exquisitely engraved blued-steel barrel at pheasants rising with a clatter of wings on the family's thousand-acre estate near the Suffolk village of Weston, on the southeast coast of England. She hadn't fired the weapon, one of a pair her father had bought at Christie's for over two thousand guineas, because he was afraid the recoil might hurt her, but she had never forgotten the feel of the polished walnut stock against her cheek, or the coolness of the metal trigger.

That moment had been etched in her mind and absorbed into her subconscious, along with other unrelated incidents, to form the memories she now had of her childhood: the pony she received as a gift on her fourteenth birthday; the Christmas ball at which the staff that kept the estate running smoothly throughout the year were guests, sitting self-consciously at long tables in the banquet hall while her parents served them champagne. But her most vivid recollection was the sights she had seen in her eleventh year, when her father had taken her to Lancaster, an industrial city in the northwest of England, to visit the textile mills that were largely responsible for the family fortune.

It was 1930, a year after the Wall Street crash triggered a depression in the United States, an event that also affected England and paralyzed most industries, particularly the wool market, which was heavily dependent on foreign trade for its existence. She and her father had been met at Castle Station by the mayor and had driven in a venerable old Rolls-Royce through the cobbled streets to Moorland, a site along the banks of the canal on which factories had been built to take advantage of the cheap transportation available by horse-drawn barge to Liverpool, a port for oceangoing ships.

Everywhere she looked Janet saw the gaunt faces of hungry people: men in cloth caps, sullen and resentful at being thrown out of work when the factories closed their doors; women wearing wooden clogs and carrying babies who cried from hunger on their hips. Inside the few factories that were still operating, children of eleven and twelve—her own age—walked barefoot behind stretching frames, working twelve-hour shifts in a bedlam of earsplitting noise for subsistence wages.

She and her father visited the workers' homes, terraces of tiny stone houses linked by narrow back alleyways, where whole families huddled around meager coal fires in a pathetic attempt to warm themselves against the freezing rain that sheeted in from the Irish Sea. The mayor's aim in arranging the tour had been to persuade her father to reopen some of the mills he had ordered closed, but Mr. Taylor brusquely informed the mayor that such action was unfeasible and had cut short his tour of the workers' houses in order to visit the Ashton Memorial in Williamson Park.

Situated on top of a hill overlooking the city, this was an utterly useless edifice built at a cost of ninety thousand pounds by Lord Ashton, head of a local linoleum mill, as a memorial to his first wife. At the time Janet had been fascinated by the tropical birds that flitted about in a large cage surrounded by palm trees, but in later years the sumptuous shell, built by profits squeezed from workers who barely had enough to eat, had become a symbol in her mind of everything that was wrong with the capitalist system.

The awareness that her own family benefited enormously from this unfair distribution of wealth triggered a profound sense of guilt which, by the time she completed her first year at Oxford University, was sufficient to prompt her to join the Communist Party. Doing so was an act of contrition more than a statement of political belief, and it wasn't until she had earned a First in Languages and begun her nurse's training at Guy's Hospital in London that she became emotionally committed to the ideologies of the cause.

She had learned about them from Leon Rojek, a twenty-two-year-old Polish student attending the London School of Economics, whom she had met when friends brought him to the emergency room at Guy's for treatment of injuries received in a fight that erupted after he tried to shout down a Fascist who had spoken at Hyde Park's Speaker's Corner in support of Hitler's claims to the Sudetenland.

This encounter marked the beginning of a friendship that quickly deepened to love, and by the summer of 1939 they were engaged to be married. Janet's family strongly disapproved of the tall, thin, stoop-shouldered young foreigner and did everything in their power to persuade their daughter to change her mind, but she remained unmoved, firm in the belief that Leon was not only the man she loved but the one person who, through his political beliefs, had brought real meaning into her life.

To him communism was less a political dogma than a social cause, and he organized the collection of food for families in London's East End slums, many of whom survived by rummaging through dustbins. With Janet's help, Leon also recruited nurses from Guy's to hold free clinics at church halls for people who couldn't afford to pay for medical treatment.

In July 1939, Leon decided to return to Warsaw, where he was born, to urge his parents, both Jews, to leave before Hitler made good on his threat to invade Poland. He tried to convince Janet to stay in London, but she insisted on going with him and withdrew money from her trust at Rothschild's Bank to pay whatever bribes might be necessary to facilitate his parents' escape.

But Leon's father refused to leave Poland until he could sell his small garment manufacturing business and was still in Warsaw when German troops stormed across the border. Leon, who joined the Polish Army, was killed on September 2, 1939, and his parents were both sent to concentration camps eighteen months later.

Soon after her arrival in Warsaw, Janet had found work as a surgical nurse with Dr. Maxell, a pediatrician at the Bauman-Berson Hospital. When it was enclosed inside the ghetto walls in October of 1940 she continued working there, partly because of the enormous respect she had developed for Dr. Maxell, but more particularly out of love for her now-dead fiance, Leon.

After Russia joined the fight against Germany, Janet became a member of the People's Guard, the military arm of the Communist Workers' Party (PPR), which was supplying the ZOB with whatever weapons it could, while planning its own attacks on the Nazis. When Josef Kandalman suggested that Janet's Aryan features would make her an effective courier, she agreed to work for him.

The sound of hobnailed boots clattering on cobblestones snapped Janet out of her reverie, and she looked toward the Nalewki Street gate. Hundreds of German soldiers armed with submachine guns were pouring through the opening on Gensia Street, coming closer and closer, until a ZOB fighter hurled a grenade. Instantly the intersection of Nalewki-Gensia-Franciszkanska was transformed into a cauldron of death and destruction. Molotov cocktails and crudely assembled homemade bombs, which, like the grenades, had to be lit by matches, were hurled from windows into the street, where they sent up geysers of smoke and rubble mingled with human flesh.

As Janet watched, the attacking column crumbled into small groups, hiding in doorways and hugging the walls of buildings as they slowly began to retreat. When the invaders finally began to return fire, their exposure made them easy targets for concealed snipers.

When Janet had exhausted the bullets in her Luger, she tossed it aside, took up a primitive grenade, and attempted to light the fuse with a match, but gusts of wind kept blowing out the flame. After three abortive attempts she finally succeeded in lighting the fuse, and hurled the grenade into a group of German soldiers who were firing from the hip as they retreated toward the Nalewki Street gate. It exploded in a burst of orange flame, and the air was filled with cries as the soldiers raced for cover in the bombed-out shops.

"Juden haben Waffen!" one German yelled frantically as he scrambled into a doorway.

Half an hour later the attackers fled, leaving their dead and wounded where they had fallen. Not long after they vanished, a lookout girl arrived with the news that another battle, which had been raging at the corner of Zamenhof and Mila, a little square facing the Judenrat building, had also been won, and the ZOB fighters swarmed into the street, throwing their arms around each other in a wild demonstration of emotion that included both laughter and tears. But their celebrating ended abruptly when a German tank and two armored cars appeared at the Nalewki Gate and began rolling into the ghetto.

4

Anna heard the tramp of boots in the stone courtyard of the Czyste-Berson-Bauman Hospital at 8:30 A.M., less than half an hour after the first German troops poured through the Nalewki Street gate.

"Alle Juden herunter!"

The guttural order echoed from below. She lay on her straw-filled mattress in the tiny alcove of the hidden room on the second floor, to which she had returned after leaving Janet Taylor. Her mother had been waiting, visibly worried, but after one glance at her daughter's haggard face, instead of demanding to know where Anna had spent the night, she silently served the watery soup she had saved from the previous evening and went downstairs to help her husband on his morning rounds of the wards.

Although Anna was exhausted and tried to sleep, she found herself haunted by the scene she had witnessed in the cellar of the Wild Ghetto; images of the smuggler writhing on the floor, his head and shoulders engulfed in flames, made sleep or rest impossible.

"Alle Juden herunter!"

This time the sound was accompanied by the crash of doors being kicked in and the short, staccato bursts of submachine guns against a rising background of screams.

Memories of the January 18 hospital massacre flashed through her mind as she ran toward the door, but Jacob barred her way by standing in front of the sliding panel, his 9mm Weiss at the ready.

"There's nothing you can do," he whispered.

Another fusillade of shots reverberated through the building. Anna struggled with the boy, trying to force her way past him, but his slight body possessed surprising strength and he easily held her pinned against the wall, one hand over her mouth, until the firing stopped. Then he loosened his grip.

"I've got to go down there," Anna breathed.

"Not yet."

It was evident from Jacob's set features that he wasn't going to let Anna pass until he judged it safe, and only after hearing the crunch of boots receding across the courtyard did he cautiously slide open the panel.

"Wait here," he instructed.

Anna watched him inch down the stairs. Her impulse to stop the Germans from hurting her parents had been replaced by the dread of what they might find now that the sudden storm of violence seemed to have passed, and when Jacob beckoned her to join him at the door to the ward on the first floor she had to will herself to move.

"Bastards!" The boy uttered the word in a voice hoarse with emotion, and when Anna looked into the ward she saw why tears were streaming down his cheeks.

The room had been turned into an abattoir. Corpses lay at grotesque angles across beds and on the floor; blood was spattered across the walls and ceiling; men and women, about fifty in all, most of whom had been suffering from typhus, lay heaped in corners where they had been herded to be slaughtered.

"Oh, God—"

A muted sob stifled the rest of Anna's words, and for a long moment she remained motionless at the door, trembling as she watched Jacob search the carnage, but when he motioned to her from the far end of the ward she forced herself to step over bodies and hurry to where the boy was standing.

"I'm sorry," he muttered.

She followed his gaze. Her father was hunched in a corner, back against the wall and both hands crossed over his stomach in a vain attempt to hold back loops of intestine that had snaked out through a gaping hole.

"Papa!" Anna gasped.

There was an oddly bemused expression on his face. He looked at her through glazed eyes, then slowly turned his head toward an over-turned bed under which lay the body of his wife, her skull smashed by a rifle butt.

"Help me to lay him down," Anna said, kneeling next to her father.

"It won't help," Jacob replied. "And we've got to get out of here."

Anna started to answer, but stopped when she heard a smothered gurgle and saw bubbles of blood spewing from her father's mouth. Realizing he was trying to speak, she leaned forward and put her ear close to his lips.

"Far vos iz gevorn farendert die . . ."

She recognized his mumbled words as a fragment of one of the Four Questions traditionally asked at the seder meal: "Why is this night different from all other nights?"

"We don't have much time," Jacob warned.

Anna saw her father's eyes close and knew he was slipping away.

"He could go on suffering like this for a long time," Jacob said.

"I'm staying as long—"

Flame spurted from Jacob's gun as he fired a single shot into the nape of the dying man's neck. Deafened by the sudden roar, Anna instinctively closed her eyes. When she opened them, her father's body had sagged to the floor.

"Let's go." Jacob's face was ashen, but his mouth was set in a hard, thin line.

Their eyes met. Anna saw he was no longer a boy. After a long moment Jacob turned away, crossed the ward, and hurried back up the stairs toward the hidden room. Anna watched him go, too numbed by what had happened to think or feel. No anger or sorrow; not even tears. Just a void, and a terrible, aching weariness.

Finally, after more than half an hour of kneeling next to her father's body, she slowly got up and went down into the courtyard. It was a glorious day; trees with thin branches quivered against rose-tinted clouds, and birds were singing. Even the air was crystal clear, except for clouds of dark smoke over Nalewki and Gensia, where fighting was still taking place. But Anna was oblivious to the delights of the spring morning. Moving like a sleepwalker along the debris-littered sidewalk, she failed to notice a group of three helmeted German soldiers herding a small cluster of Jews along Zamenhof Street.

"*Halt!*" one of the Germans, a sergeant holding a submachine gun, shouted.

Anna froze.

"*Juden?*"

It was too late to run. All she could do was obey the sergeant's orders to join the other half dozen terrified prisoners and allow herself to be marched with her hands clasped behind her head toward Umschlagplatz, the great square on the northern edge of the ghetto that had become the railhead for boxcars being used to transport Jews to concentration camps.

As the column straggled past the corner of Zamenhof and Mila, she caught a glimpse of some German medics, who were loading soldiers wounded in the fighting earlier that morning into ambulances, while a wrecked tank smoldered in the background.

"The ZOB fighters were magnificent," the woman next to Anna whispered. "One of their Molotov cocktails did that." She nodded in the direction of the fire-gutted tank. "They're saying the crew burned to death."

German artillery outside the ghetto suddenly opened fire, making it pointless to attempt any further conversation, and throughout the rest of the march Anna didn't say anything.

The Umschlagplatz was packed with Jews. They stood in long, snaking lines that were kept moving by German soldiers using their gun butts and guard dogs to implement orders. Many of the prisoners had donned their best clothes for their final journey, and seeing their elegance made Anna conscious of her own garments, which were torn and bloodstained. But she didn't care how she looked. When the Germans herded them into a building that had once been a hospital, instead of loading her group into boxcars, she experienced neither relief nor curiosity.

The large, stinking room was filled with prisoners maddened by thirst. People screamed as Ukrainian guards indiscriminately beat heads with rifle butts; children pleading for water were given their own urine to drink by their mothers; a small baby was trampled underfoot as the terrified captives wildly milled around in an attempt to escape guards wielding whips. The sight of the child's mangled body triggered the scream Anna had been suppressing since the bullet fired by Jacob had slammed into her father's neck, but the sound was lost in the general tumult of the room, and nobody appeared to notice when she crumpled to the floor.

How long she was unconscious, and how long she slept, Anna never knew; the two had merged, separated only by brief moments when she opened her eyes to see a man peering down at her. When she finally emerged from her shock-induced state, the man, who identified himself as Dr. Stefan Arad, told Anna she'd been slipping in and out of consciousness for days, during which time he'd kept her alive by sharing his meager rations.

"Why didn't you let me die?" Anna murmured.

Before Dr. Arad could answer, she turned on her side and retched. It drained what little strength she had left, and for a long time she lay with her eyes fixed on the barred window in the nearby wall, oblivious to everything but the square of blue sky she could see beyond the steel grille.

"You don't remember me, do you?" the man seated next to her asked.

Anna shifted her gaze to his face. He had fine semitic features and a dark, scraggly beard.

"I served my internship under your father at the Czyste Street Hospital," he said.

Again Anna studied the man, trying to imagine him without his beard, and realized there was something familiar about his huge brown eyes.

"Weren't you at our seder last year?"

He nodded.

"Your wife helped my mother with the cooking . . ."

"And Dr. Maxell explained the Four Questions to my son Dolek."

"Is he here with you?" Anna asked.

"Dolek and my wife were sent to Dachau three months ago." He averted his eyes. "The Germans kept me here for interrogation. They seem to think I know where the ZOB bunkers are hidden."

Anna closed her eyes in an effort to shut out the anguish she saw on his face, but quickly opened them again when she heard a flurried disturbance among those lying on the floor nearby and saw a Ukrainian guard using his rifle butt to force a path through the tangled mass of prisoners.

"You," he shouted in heavily accented Polish, probing Anna's ribs with his boot, "come with me."

Dr. Arad helped her to her feet. "Courage," he whispered, as the guard hustled her roughly out of the stinking room, down a long stone-flagged corridor, and into what had formerly been the lobby of the hospital but now served as an interrogation room.

An SS captain with blond hair and blue eyes, who spoke Polish fluently, motioned her to a chair in front of his large wooden desk.

"If you are sensible this shouldn't take long," he said. "Tell me your name."

"Anna Maxell," she mumbled.

"Speak louder, please. Address?"

"Gensia Six-eight."

"The Czyste-Bauman-Berson Hospital?"

She nodded.

The SS captain looked at a sheet of notes. "We have been informed that you worked as a courier for the Jewish Fighting Organization. Is that true?"

"No," Anna replied.

The German got up, put on his cap, and beckoned Anna to follow him. They went into a courtyard where five men were being lined up against a wall by a sergeant commanding a squad of eight soldiers armed with submachine guns.

Anna recognized among the prisoners some Judenrat leaders who had recently been arrested. The SS officer crossed to where they were standing and called out their names. Then he nodded at the sergeant, who fired several short bursts that sent the five prisoners sprawling to the ground.

"I am tired of playing games with you Jews," he told Anna. "Either you tell me what I want to know by dawn tomorrow or you will be shot."

He stalked back to his office and motioned the guard to take Anna away.

Stefan Arad was waiting for her. He must have heard the firing and thought the worst, because he made no attempt to disguise his relief at seeing her alive. He wrapped her in his arms for a long moment before leading her to a spot against the wall that he had been saving.

He gave her some brackish water and a crust of bread. She told him about the SS officer's ultimatum, and he listened without saying anything. When darkness fell he took her head in his lap and talked about his family while gently stroking her cheek with the tips of his fingers. Neither of them slept. Just before dawn Anna got up and crossed to the window. The blue patch of sky had been replaced by a flickering orange glow from ghetto fires, but beyond them the moon was clearly visible.

"Too late for wishes."

She turned and saw Stefan standing behind her. "They gave you the same ultimatum, didn't they?" she said.

He nodded. "And the terrible thing is that if I'd known the location of those bunkers I'd probably have told them."

Anna didn't answer. When the final moment came, would she have the courage to remain silent?

5

The door slammed open. Three guards grabbed Anna, Stefan, and eight other prisoners and marched them down the long corridor to the courtyard. In the gray morning light it appeared smaller and more forbidding than it had the previous afternoon, and even though the early morning air was surprisingly warm for the first week in May, Anna found herself shivering as she was positioned with the others against the wall.

"I'm going to give each of you a last chance," the SS captain announced.

He took out his pistol, scanned the line, and moved to the left, positioning himself in front of a bearded old man.

"Name?"

"Israel Helman," the prisoner replied.

The German glanced at a sheet of paper containing a list of names, then looked at the man standing in front of him.

"Where is the headquarters bunker of the ZOB located?" he asked.

"I am a rabbi," the old man said. "I know nothing of the ZOB."

There was a loud crack as the German officer fired his gun, sending a bullet into the old man's forehead with such force that it slammed him against the wall. Without even glancing at the fallen body, the SS captain took two paces sideways and faced Stefan Arad.

"Do you wish me to repeat the question?" he asked.

The young doctor shook his head.

"And . . . ?"

"I have nothing to say."

The gun exploded again. Stefan spun almost completely around before falling to his knees. He steadied himself, and somehow managed to maintain his balance, but when the German fired another shot into the nape of his neck, Stefan sagged forward until his chest rested against the ground.

Anna closed her eyes. She felt only relief at knowing she would soon be released from a world gone mad. She heard the SS captain repeating his question to each of the prisoners, a litany followed by the explosion of his pistol. The ritual was repeated again and again as the German officer methodically worked his way down the line of prisoners to where Anna stood.

"Well?" he asked, his face so close to hers she could smell the brandy on his breath.

"I have nothing to say," she replied, keeping her eyes closed.

Instinctively, her body tensed. There was an unbearable silence, broken only by the click of the pistol being cocked, but the slam of the bullet she had expected never came. Instead, there was a loud explosion, and a blast of searing air lifted Anna off the ground and hurled her sideways, to land heavily on the body of one of the executed prisoners.

Rolling onto her side, she saw the three guards who had brought her to the courtyard sprawled with their limbs at grotesque angles, and a squad of German soldiers who had performed earlier executions were firing their submachine guns in frantic bursts at barely discernible shapes on top of the surrounding wall. As she watched, a grenade sailed into their midst, exploding with a blinding flash that sent a bloody shower high into the now-bright morning sky.

"Anna!"

The voice shouting her name was that of a woman, and vaguely familiar, but the cloud of smoke sent up by the grenade was still too thick for Anna to see who had called.

"Lie down and stay where you are!"

Still unable to grasp what was happening, Anna did as she was instructed, and seconds later another explosion rent the courtyard. Its blast hit German soldiers who had begun pouring out of the building and slammed them back into the doorway, forming a pile of corpses that blocked any exit by their comrades.

"Run to your right!" the voice ordered.

Anna tried to obey, but her limbs failed to react.

"Move!"

There was an urgency to the command that prompted her to try again, but when she attempted to stand her knees gave way under her.

"For God's sake!"

This time the voice was nearer, and when Anna looked up she saw Janet running through the smoke. The Englishwoman was accompanied by a man Anna recognized as a ZOB fighter. Both were armed with pistols and carried knapsacks filled with homemade grenades. They hauled Anna to her feet and half carried, half dragged her across the courtyard to where a gaping hole had been blown in the wall.

The first person Anna saw in the street was Josef Kandalman. He didn't speak, but after firing a last burst through the smoke into the courtyard, he slung his machine pistol over his shoulder, put an arm around Anna's waist, and helped her limp in the direction of his bunker on Franciszkanska Street.

The Germans had thrown up barbed-wire barricades at most intersections, and because of the constant threat posed by ambushes, Kandalman abandoned the streets in favor of the labyrinthine maze of attic passageways. It was a route that required them to constantly scale debris, and Kandalman frequently stopped to help Anna over the wreckage. Finally, when they came to a house in the middle of a block on Gensia, Kandalman called a halt, declaring it was too dangerous to continue until after dark. Anna gratefully collapsed onto a torn mattress, wondering if she would ever have the strength to rise again.

The attic in which they found themselves had no windows and was filled with a sweet, pungent odor. When Kandalman lit a match its flickering flame revealed three bodies staring up at them from among ripped bedding and scattered clothing.

"Wait here," Kandalman said, moving toward the next attic. Despite the corpses, Anna was relieved. The bed felt blissfully comfortable and her fatigue was so great that all she wanted to do was sleep, but as she adjusted herself on the mattress her arm brushed against something hard, and when she explored the object with her hand she felt the cold smoothness of human skin. With a gasp she sat bolt upright, lit another match, and saw a foot protruding through a tear in the ticking. Pulling the mattress covering back, she uncovered a body so completely covered with feathers that it wasn't until she had brushed them away from the face that she recognized the dead man.

"He used to work as an orderly at the hospital. . . ." Anna's voice trailed away.

"It was burned down days ago," Janet said.

The match went out, and silence settled between them. They could hear Kandalman rummaging around in the attic of the next house.

"He's an enigma all right," Anna murmured. "I never thought he'd risk his life to rescue me."

"He was trying to save Stefan Arad," Janet said. "Stefan knew the exact location of every bunker where ZOB fighters were hiding. Kandalman was afraid he might crack under torture."

Anna remembered Stefan's words before they were marched into the courtyard: "If I'd known the location of those bunkers, I'd probably have told them." God, she thought, he hadn't even trusted her.

"*Ist jemand da?*"

The phrase was repeated half a dozen times in a guttural voice from somewhere below, gradually growing weaker, until it finally died away.

"We'd better get out of here," Janet breathed.

She led the way into the adjoining attic, where Kandalman and the other ZOB fighters were peering through a small dormer window.

"Let's go," he said.

Again, Kandalman helped Anna as the group crept from one attic to another, until they finally found refuge in a cellar on Majzelsa Street that had once been an engraving shop but was now fire-gutted and abandoned.

"You two rest here until we get back," Kandalman said.

He didn't explain where he was going, or why, and neither Janet nor Anna asked; both were too glad of the chance to regain their strength. But the three other ZOB fighters weren't so lucky, for Kandalman beckoned them to follow as he started up a flight of stone steps leading to the street.

"He's a hard man," Anna said when they were alone.

"Driven would be a better word. He seems to have turned the ZOB fight into a personal cause. Maybe it's his way of making up for the years he denied he was a Jew."

"He told you that?"

"Pan Halevi did. He knew Kandalman before the war."

"It's the first time I've seen Kandalman when Halevi wasn't tagging along. Where is he?"

Before Janet could answer there was a sudden chatter of gunfire and a series of explosions out in the street, followed by German voices shouting to each other. Anna, who had dropped to the floor when the firing started, looked up at a shelf holding a row of large bottles encased in straw, which had been loosened by the explosions and appeared ready to fall. Quickly rolling to one side, she inched toward Janet, who was crouched facing the steps, a pistol gripped firmly in her right hand.

The Englishwoman touched a finger to her lips and nodded her head in the direction of the door. Anna heard labored breathing and the noise of something being dragged down the steps. Janet had started to curl her finger on the trigger when a voice called in a low whisper, "Jerusalem."

Recognizing the password, she lowered her gun, and seconds later Kandalman crawled into the basement, dragging his shattered left leg behind him. He lowered himself onto the floor. "Ambush . . . the others are dead. . . ."

Janet examined the wound. A grenade fragment had smashed his kneecap. "Lie still," she said.

"The Germans have—"

"Do as I say," she commanded brusquely.

The pain in Kandalman's eyes turned to a look of surprise, and the trace of a smile crossed his lips. It remained as he watched Janet use a strip of mattress ticking as a tourniquet to stop the bleeding, and wooden slats from a broken shutter to improvise a splint, which she secured in place with pieces of fabric torn from a charred curtain.

"You have clever hands—"

His sentence remained unfinished as, with a tremble followed by a roar, the gutted structure above the basement suddenly collapsed, sending an avalanche of brick and plaster cascading into the open well of the courtyard. Everything in the cellar shook, and the shelf that had already been loosened by the explosion fell, causing the bottles it had been supporting to topple. Despite their protective covering of straw, they broke when they hit the floor, spraying the liquid they contained over Kandalman's face and chest. A sharp acrid odor immediately filled the room, and even before the injured man began writhing in pain, Anna knew the liquid he'd been drenched with was sulfuric acid.

"Get some water," Janet snapped.

Anna ran to a lead-lined sink that was partially filled with scummy water, on the surface of which floated the bloated bodies of drowned rats. She had seen it earlier, soon after they first entered the cellar, but even though her throat was parched, she had left the water untouched rather than risk typhus infection. Now she took off her shoes, quickly filled them with the polluted liquid, and hurried back to where the Englishwoman was doing what she could to ease Kandalman's agony.

The acid had already eaten deep into his skin. His left cheek and jaw were a mass of blisters, but the worst damage had been done to his chest. The acid had turned the thick thatch of hair covering the upper part of his body into a steaming, pulpy mass, and had given the gold medallion he was wearing the appearance of a tarnished brand. Indeed, when Janet gently took it off and put it around her own neck for safekeeping in order to swab the area under it with water, Anna saw that the medallion had actually left an imprint lividly etched into the flesh on Kandalman's chest.

"We've got to get him to the hospital bunker, quickly," the other woman said.

"He can't walk on that leg."

"Then we'll have to carry him."

Kandalman was still conscious and in terrible pain, but he remained silent as the two women put together a crude stretcher from a broken bed frame and strips of canvas that had formerly been used by engravers to hold the plates they were working on. It was flimsy, but it held as the two women placed Kandalman on it and carried him up the steps leading to the courtyard.

It was nearly midnight, but there was enough light from the fires raging along Majzelsa Street, and throughout the rest of the ghetto, for them to find their way over piles of rubble and debris to the bunker that served as a hospital. They encountered no Germans; the Nazis disliked sending in patrols after dark, having learned from bitter experience that nighttime was when they were most vulnerable to attack by ZOB fighters hiding in ruined buildings. But the obstacles the two women had to surmount, and the difficulty of carrying Kandalman over them, made the undertaking a supreme test of endurance for both of them, and by the time they finally reached the walled-off area in the three-room flat that served as a hospital they were ready to collapse from exhaustion.

Yet, despite her fatigue, Janet still insisted on helping the young doctor in charge of the bunker perform an emergency operation on Kandalman, during which they reset the bone under his shattered knee and peeled away skin burned by the acid, all without benefit of anesthetic.

"You're lucky infection hasn't set in," the doctor told his patient. "It usually does with burns as bad as these."

"I had two good nurses," Kandalman replied.

His words gave Anna a sense of quiet satisfaction, and she felt pleased with herself as she flopped down on a mattress and immediately fell asleep. Her exhaustion was so total that when she awoke over twelve hours later, it was only to eat a small piece of bread and swallow some watery soup before slipping back into unconsciousness for another whole day.

"Come on, wake up!"

The voice seemed to be coming from a great distance away, but when she opened her eyes Anna saw Janet leaning over her.

"Do you know how long you've been asleep?" the other woman asked.

"Not long enough." Anna yawned.

"Nearly thirty-six hours."

"I could lie here forever."

"Not a chance," Janet said. "Pavel Sokolczyk wants us at Mila Eighteen. The messenger says it's important. We'd better get a move on."

Anna got up and wearily followed the Englishwoman down to the street. She hadn't changed clothes in weeks and they were filthy; the stench of them would have been embarrassing if everybody else in the ghetto hadn't been in the same unsavory condition. There was barely enough water to drink, let alone to bathe or wash clothes in.

"Do you know what he wants?" she asked as they hurried through the labyrinth of connecting attics toward Mila 18.

"No," Janet replied, "but things aren't going well for the ZOB fighters, and there are rumors they can't hold out much longer."

This was confirmed when they reached Mila 18, the bunker Pavel Sokolczyk had taken over from Shmuel Asher, a heavyset blustering man whose gang of professional smugglers and thieves had excavated a gigantic cavern under three large adjoining buildings. It contained numerous rooms linked by a narrow corridor and was equipped with electricity, a well, a kitchen, and even a recreation room.

The ZOB fighters lay stretched out in their underwear on mats of rags, sweating in the intense heat and nearly suffocating from lack of air in their stinking, overcrowded alcoves. Not only had their food almost run out, so had the ammunition with which to carry on the battle, and there was reason to believe the Germans knew the location of the bunker, even though they still hadn't found the entrances to it. The previous afternoon, occupants of Mila 18 had heard the Germans hammering heavy metal probes into the ruins above them, and bits of plaster had fallen from the ceiling.

Anna and Janet found Pavel Sokolczyk squatting on the dirt floor, surrounded by those of his commanders who were still alive, including Josef Kandalman, who had been carried from the hospital bunker by Pan Halevi. Sokolczyk appeared calm, and it was clear from his words that he was resigned to death, but the aim of all ZOB fighters, he still believed, should be to live as long as possible in order to exact every last ounce of German flesh. When they were no longer able to kill Germans in the ghetto, he urged his men to fight as partisans in the forests outside Warsaw, assuming they could find a way of getting there.

"There is another matter of great importance that I want to resolve now, while there is still time," he announced.

He summoned two ZOB fighters, who carried large canvas bags to where Sokolczyk was squatting and emptied the contents onto a sheet another man had carefully spread on the earthen floor. A murmur stirred through the onlookers as a stream of diamonds, rubies, emeralds, and other jewels poured from the bags like a shimmering multihued waterfall.

"This immense treasure has been contributed over many months by thousands of Jews who were taken at selections and wanted their wealth used to carry on the fight against the Germans," Sokolczyk said. "Until now we have used these jewels to purchase weapons, but the time has come when we must find another use for them. This fortune must not be allowed to fall into enemy hands."

Sokolczyk paused and looked at the faces of those gathered around him. They reflected the toll the struggle against the Nazis had taken: glazed eyes; bandaged wounds; ragged, stinking clothes. Over forty-five thousand Jews were known to have been captured or killed since the *Grossaktion* began two weeks earlier, and Sokolczyk knew that the life expectancy of these gaunt, hollow-cheeked survivors was a matter of days, maybe even hours.

"The question of what to do with this sacred treasure has been discussed at length," he continued. "And it has been decided that an attempt will be made to smuggle it out of the ghetto to Switzerland, where it will be kept in the vaults of the Credit Suisse bank in Geneva and used to aid whatever Jews survive this madness."

A murmur of approval stirred through the crowd.

"I am neither a businessman nor a smuggler," Sokolczyk concluded. "That is why I have assigned somebody who is an expert at both to make whatever arrangements are necessary for the successful completion of this vital mission."

He nodded toward Josef Kandalman, who was seated on the floor on the opposite side of the bunker, using the wall to keep himself propped in an upright position. His left leg was still sheathed between two splints and obviously useless as a means of support, but it was the upper part of his body where his injuries were most visible. His left cheek and jaw were one massive suppurating wound. From the pus oozing from it, it was evident that the doctor who treated him at the hospital bunker had been premature in saying Kandalman was lucky to have escaped infection. But most sickening of all were the acid burns on his chest, where the skin glistened raw and wet. An attempt had been made to bandage the injuries, but the strips of torn sheet had pulled loose during the trip between the hospital bunker and Mila 18, a journey Kandalman had made in Halevi's powerful arms, and the wounds were clearly visible.

"I originally intended to carry out this crucial task myself," Kandalman said, "but, as you can see, I can't take a shit without help."

A few in the bunker chuckled.

"I have written a letter to my personal banker at the Credit Suisse in Geneva, Pierre Chambord, instructing him how the treasure is to be disbursed. The qualifications are simple: the applicant will only be required to establish need and prove that he, or she, is a Jew who survived Nazi persecution. I know from my dealings with Chambord that he is a man who can be trusted. All that remains is the decision as to how this letter and the jewels can best be delivered into his safe-keeping."

Kandalman paused, his eyes mirroring the pain he was experiencing.

"My experience as a professional smuggler has convinced me that women make the best couriers," he said, "particularly during a war, when any man who isn't wearing a uniform immediately becomes suspect. And, as I'm sure most of you men know, women also aren't averse to relying on their feminine wiles whenever their well-being is threatened."

This time the laughter was more general.

"But this mission is too risky, and its successful completion far too important, to pick someone for this task who hasn't already proved herself," Kandalman added. "That is why I have chosen two women whose exemplary behavior under extreme stress I have witnessed at first hand. They are Anna Maxell and Janet Taylor."

Every eye in the bunker abruptly shifted to where the two women were standing.

"Step forward," Kandalman said.

Visibly surprised, Anna and Janet edged their way through the tightly packed throng as the others respectfully pulled back to give them room.

"This is the most important decision either of you will ever be asked to make," Kandalman said, "not only because of the immense value of the treasure you will be carrying, but also because of what it represents in terms of human lives. I want each of you to think very carefully before telling us whether or not you will undertake this mission."

The silence that followed was suddenly broken by a metallic tapping as yet another German patrol used steel rods to try and discover the hidden entrances to the bunker.

"Well?" Kandalman asked.

"I'll go," Anna said.

"So will I," Janet added quickly.

"Good, we don't have much time," Kandalman said. "You will have to use the sewers, and the only entrance still open is at Franciszkanska Twenty-two. You both know Genevieve Fleury?"

The two women nodded.

"She knows of my plan and will provide you with fresh clothes and whatever else you need for the journey after you reach the Aryan side of the wall. Expert forgers here in the ghetto have prepared false documents identifying you as volunteer laborers working in German war industries who are returning on home leave. Pan Halevi will also accompany you—"

"No!" The vehemence with which the big man uttered the word took everybody by surprise.

"The Germans have blocked the sewers in many places," Kandalman said, putting his hand on the other man's shoulder. "The women will need your strength to ensure they get through."

"I stay with you," Halevi declared firmly.

"The need for you to go with the women is greater."

Halevi still appeared unconvinced.

"We have been together a long time," Kandalman said quietly. "Now I am asking you to do this one last service for me, as a friend."

"If you put it that way," the big man muttered, "I'll go, but not willingly."

Kandalman issued orders to the two ZOB fighters who had emptied the jewels onto the sheet, and they quickly began loading them into five canvas knapsacks, one of which they handed to each woman, the other three to Pan Halevi.

"Here is the letter for Pierre Chambord," Kandalman said, handing

Anna a sealed envelope. "Under no circumstances is it to be given to anybody but him. Should you encounter a situation which makes it impossible to complete your mission, the jewels are to be hidden where they can be retrieved after the war. Is that understood?"

"Yes," she said.

Those gathered in the bunker seemed to understand that the transfer of the jewels out of the ghetto signified the end of their short-lived struggle, and they watched in silence as each of the couriers was given false documents, cubes of sugar, and a crust of bread. But as the women started toward the exit they reached out their hands for a handshake or final hug: "Good luck . . . think of us . . . we'll pray for you. . . ."

As the farewells continued, Kandalman beckoned Halevi close and whispered, "Don't let the jewels out of your sight. They represent a fortune I have every intention of putting to work for us both if I survive the war." The big man's hangdog expression was replaced by a knowing grin as he straightened up and hurried out of the bunker.

Led by Pan Halevi, the women walked quickly, feet wrapped in rags to muffle their footsteps, stopping abruptly whenever they glimpsed any movements in the shadows. A house nearby still burned, eerily illuminating the night. Anna breathed the night air in gulps; after the suffocating heat inside the bunker at Mila 18 she couldn't seem to get enough of its coolness.

It was nearly midnight when they reached Franciszkanska 22. Anna and Janet sucked on the sugar and nibbled their crusts of bread, while Halevi busied himself lifting a heavy iron grate. Before they left Mila 18, Kandalman had told them to leave the sewers at the exit in the middle of Bielenska Street and hide in some ruins from the 1939 bombardment, where Genevieve Fleury would meet them and guide them back to the nightclub.

"Ready?" Halevi asked.

The women nodded but avoided each other's eyes. Now that it was time to go underground, Anna's earlier exhilaration had given way to apprehension, and she gauged from the grim set of Janet's features that she was experiencing similar anxieties. As ZOB couriers, both of them had used the sewers many times before, but it was no secret that in recent days the Germans had erected barriers of various kinds to seal them off. They had even used gas to flush out Jews. The prospect of probing the foul-smelling darkness triggered a quick flutter of panic in Anna, but she steeled herself and followed Halevi through the hole in the bunker floor.

The big man carried a stub of candle, which he lit with a match he had been chewing since they left Mila 18. Its feeble flicker was reflected from the glistening slime-covered walls as they slushed through the foul water. In places it came to their chins, and the current was so strong they had to struggle against it to keep from being carried away to the Vistula River, into which the sewer emptied its stinking contents.

After about twenty minutes, Anna glimpsed a bright light in the distance and guessed it was a German patrol exploring the sewers, but it faded and disappeared.

"They've gone," she whispered.

"What if they're still waiting?" Janet asked.

Anna didn't answer. She knew they had no choice but to move on; they couldn't continue crouching in sewage up to their necks, and the water was ice cold. Finally, realizing that somebody had to take the initiative, she continued on through the narrow passage that grew smaller the farther from the river they got.

Soon the only way for them to move forward was by doubling over and holding on to each other for support. Halevi kept relighting his candle, but each time he stumbled it went out. In the darkness the sound of every movement seemed heightened, and they were constantly nudged by the floating corpses of others who had attempted the same journey.

They frequently became lost, so their odyssey continued for hours —longer by far than it should have taken to travel the relatively short distance between Franciszkanska 22 and the manhole on Bielenska Street. But finally, when they thought they could go no farther, they saw a faint yellowish-orange light coming through an overhead grating.

"It's Bielenska Street," Halevi whispered.

Climbing up on a ledge, he put his thick fingers through the iron bars and pushed, but the grating didn't move. He tried again, putting his huge shoulders into the effort and straining until the veins in his neck corded, but still the grating held fast.

"Shit," he muttered, lowering himself back down to where the two women were standing up to their waists in the ice-cold sewage. "There's a truck parked on the manhole. We're trapped."

6

Four hours earlier, at 12:30 A.M., Genevieve Fleury left the Club Warszawa in the city's business district on the Aryan side of the wall and made her way hurriedly toward Bielenska Street. She had been alerted by a message from Josef Kandalman late the previous afternoon to expect two couriers. Her former employer had instructed her to escort the escapees back to the apartment over the nightclub and provide them with supplies for a long journey.

His orders weren't surprising. Everybody in Warsaw knew the Jewish ghetto was being systematically reduced to a pile of rubble by the Germans. Indeed, as she slipped from doorway to doorway in an effort to remain unseen by German soldiers patrolling the streets to enforce the nightly 8 P.M. curfew, her way was lit by the flames of ghetto buildings burning against the night sky, and the roar of collapsing structures helped conceal the sound of her footsteps. But what had surprised her was the fact that Kandalman wouldn't be among those she was to meet.

He had been specific about this point but offered no explanation. She was puzzled. It was uncharacteristic of him to risk his life by staying in the ghetto to the bitter end. She could not reconcile such selflessness with the ruthless, mercenary man who had hired her as a hostess when she reached Poland from France in 1937, at the age of nineteen. There seemed to be no connection. She concluded that Kandalman must have hidden reasons for staying behind, ones that would produce a handsome profit, for he rarely did anything that wasn't going to enrich him in one way or another.

This had been clear from the beginning of their relationship. He had quickly established that, in addition to her duties as a hostess at the nightclub, he expected her to sell her sexual favors, and in order to facilitate this he had moved her into a small apartment over his club. She had agreed to his conditions because she needed a job, and she had learned long ago that every favor came with strings attached.

Since her childhood in the slums of Marseilles, where she was raised by her laundress mother along with five other children, all of whom her fisherman father had abandoned two or three months before Genevieve was born, she'd been obliged to survive by whatever means presented themselves. First she had begged for centimes from tourists visiting the colorful waterfront, then earned money as a street entertainer during the hours she wasn't delivering laundry to the homes of her mother's customers. There had been neither time nor money for much formal education, and most of the knowledge she possessed had been learned from living by her wits. At an early age she had concluded that what mattered most in life was money—regardless of how it was obtained.

Her body was fully developed by the time she was thirteen, a fact men were quick to appreciate and she to exploit, and by the time she met Josef Kandalman in the summer of 1937, she was sufficiently experienced at bartering sex for money to take his conditions of employment in stride. What she hadn't been prepared for was the relationship that quickly developed between herself and her employer.

It began by her simply wanting to please him and grew into a dependency on her part that was the closest she'd ever come to experiencing any kind of love. The fact that he didn't return her affections only added to his allure, making him different from other men she'd known, all of whom she'd easily manipulated through her overt sexuality. Their bond was sado-masochistic from the beginning, but it satisfied a need in her she didn't question, even when he moved another woman, a blond-haired Gypsy named Keja, into the apartment over the nightclub.

After Kandalman was imprisoned in the ghetto, both Genevieve and Keja had made frequent trips through the sewers to deliver goods they'd obtained on the black market, and they often remained overnight at his bunker on Franciszkanska Street. On these occasions, the Frenchwoman always slept with her former employer.

It was a practice that Keja neither understood nor condoned. Her mores were conditioned by the Gypsy code of ethics, which was extremely puritanical when it came to a woman's relationship with a man before marriage. Physical contact of any kind was strictly forbidden; if a couple was discovered to have had premarital sex, their noses or ears were cut off and they were banished from the tribe.

Yet it was obvious that Keja felt something for Kandalman—if not affection, then gratitude for letting her live in the apartment over the club. She expressed it by giving him a talisman, a gold medallion that, she assured Kandalman, would protect him against evil.

As Genevieve approached the ruined building where Kandalman

had said the couriers would be waiting, she moved with extreme caution. The huge pile of rubble was a perfect place to hide; she had met other couriers there on numerous occasions and knew the space in the basement where they invariably waited, but this time it was empty. Something had gone wrong. It was 1:45 A.M., forty-five minutes after the time Kandalman had said they would emerge from the sewers, but there was still no sign of any movement from the manhole.

She debated whether to stay or to return to the Club Warszawa. It was only a temporary haven, for the Nazis suspected it was a place where black marketeers gathered and had ordered it closed by the end of the month. She still didn't know where she would go after it was boarded up. Perhaps it wouldn't matter after tonight. She had risked her life in coming to meet the couriers; she could be shot on sight for being out after curfew, and the SS squads that patrolled the streets of Warsaw didn't hesitate to carry out these orders.

Immobilized by indecision, she remained crouched under a slab of concrete that had once been a balcony but now lay at a crazy angle between a pile of rubble and the street. Minutes ticked away in a silence that was broken only by the crackle of fires burning inside the ghetto. When the hands on her watch reached 2 A.M., she decided she had waited long enough, but as she was about to leave she saw an army truck turn onto Bielenska Street and come to a halt on top of the manhole through which the three couriers were scheduled to emerge.

She could see the driver drinking from a bottle in his cab and guessed from his mumblings that he was drunk. At the same time she glimpsed a hand protruding through the iron bars in the manhole and realized the couriers for whom she had been waiting had arrived.

What to do? If she waited and gambled on the truck's moving away, perhaps the best thing was to do nothing, but if the vehicle didn't move, the chances for those trapped below would get less with each passing minute toward dawn. Bielenska Street was a busy thoroughfare, and by daybreak there would be a steady line of traffic moving along it. The alternative was to try and lure the driver away from where he was parked, allowing those trapped in the sewer to climb out and find a hiding place in the ruined building, but if she did this she risked being shot by the driver, who was undoubtably under orders to kill anybody he saw breaking curfew.

A muffled explosion came from somewhere underground. She guessed German sappers were blowing up the entrances to the sewers on the ghetto side of the wall. If she didn't act quickly the couriers were going to die in the filth where they were trapped. Getting up from where she'd been hiding, she walked with uncertain steps toward the parked truck. She knew her first obstacle was going to be language; if the driver knew only German, a tongue she didn't speak, it was probable he would shoot her on sight.

"Good evening," she said in Polish, looking inside the cab with a bright smile. "I wonder if you can help me?"

The corporal inside was sprawled across the seat with his tunic unbuttoned. He looked up in surprise, and it was a second or two before his alcohol-fogged brain registered her presence. When it did he sat up and reached for a pistol he wore on a holster on his belt.

"Curfew . . . against law. . . ." He slurred the words and continued to fumble for his gun.

Genevieve breathed a sigh of relief. He had spoken in Polish; heavily accented and monosyllabic, but still Polish. So long as he understood what she was saying, she knew that manipulating him would be easy.

"My mother, an old woman, is sick," she said, infusing just the right degree of helplessness into her tone.

"Sick?" The German sounded puzzled.

"I had to go to her," Genevieve persisted, "it was an emergency."

"You should not be out after curfew," the German said, enunciating the words slowly, but with greater fluency than before.

"I know . . . that's why I'm glad I found an understanding man like you."

She wet her lips and pressed her breasts against the half-open window, moving them back and forth over the glass rim. The corporal's eyes fixed on her nipples, which had grown firm and were clearly visible through her thin blouse.

"What do you want?" he asked guardedly.

"Just a lift home."

"I don't know. . . ."

"I'll make it worth your while."

He wiped his hand across his mouth and took a long swig from the bottle of beer he was holding.

"It is against orders. . . ."

"But you wouldn't mind breaking them if I let you come with me?"

He chuckled drunkenly and leaned over to open the door on the passenger side. "Get in," he said.

"Not here," Genevieve said coyly. "It's after curfew and I don't want any trouble."

"Just money, eh?"

She nodded. "My apartment isn't far from here—"

"I have orders to stay where I am."

"How long?"

The driver shrugged. "Dawn, maybe later. It depends on when the squad I'm to pick up finishes their patrol."

The Frenchwoman realized her plan wasn't going to work, and the chances of being arrested were increasing with every passing minute. All she could do now was come back again the following night, which meant the couriers would have to remain in the freezing water another twenty-four hours. She doubted they could survive for that long.

"Another time, then. . . ."

In a movement that was swift enough to suggest he was less drunk than she'd thought, the driver reached out and pulled her halfway through the open window.

"Not so fast," he said.

Genevieve tried to shake herself free, but he tightened his grip.

"I can't make you happy when I know a patrol might come along at any minute!"

"Bitch!" He spat the word out, but she saw his expression and knew her words had registered. "All right," he said, after a brief silence, "I'll come with you, but we're going to walk to that apartment of yours."

Genevieve knew she was trapped, but still managed a seductive murmur. "Good, let's go."

The German, a fleshy man in his late twenties, with a nicotine-stained mustache, took another swig of beer, farted, and swung himself out of the cab. Genevieve hurried down Bielenska Street, walking as quickly as the man holding her arm would allow, trying to plan her next move. He moved with surprising agility for a man who was so overweight, and by the time they reached the Club Warszawa the exertion of the walk, combined with the cool night air, appeared to have cleared his head.

"How much do you want?" he asked the Frenchwoman as she unlocked the door to her apartment.

"Five hundred zlotys," she replied.

"You think I can afford that on a corporal's pay?"

"Four hundred, then."

"General Stroop may be able to afford that kind of money, but I can't."

Genevieve switched on the light next to the bed and saw it was already occupied by Keja. She stirred and opened her eyes. The sight of the German soldier didn't alarm her; she was accustomed to her roommate bringing customers to the apartment.

"Four hundred zlotys. Take it or leave it."

The corporal's gaze fixed on Keja, who was lying with one of her breasts partially exposed and her blond hair spread across the pillow. "All right, four hundred—for both of you," he said.

Genevieve saw Keja's concern and quickly said, "She's not for sale, but you can have me for three hundred."

The German grinned, took out his wallet, and laid three hundred-zloty notes on the table next to the bed. When he began to strip, Keja got up quickly, her body draped with a sheet, and disappeared into the other room.

"What's her problem?" he asked.

The Frenchwoman shrugged. "We came to fuck. Let's get on with it."

She undressed and lay on the bed next to the corporal. He reeked of beer and was still slightly drunk, but it didn't affect his erection.

"Now you know why we're called the master race?" he said, stroking his penis.

It was no different from the many others Genevieve had seen, but she said, "My God, you're huge!"

She took the head of his cock in her mouth, ran the tip of her tongue around it, and felt him begin to tremble. Hoping to bring him to ejaculation she quickened her stroke, but he pulled away and muttered, "Take it easy, I want this to last."

Genevieve glanced at the luminous dial of an alarm clock next to the bed. It was nearly 3 A.M. She wondered how much longer the couriers in the sewer could hang on. Taking hold of his penis she started to put it back in her mouth, but he slapped her hard across the face.

"Not so fast," he said. "First, I want to watch you play with yourself."

His blow hurt, but she was damned if she was going to let him know it, and sliding her fingers between her legs she pretended to masturbate.

"Spread your knees," he commanded.

When she obeyed he pulled her forward until she was in a kneeling position directly over his head, then put his hands behind her buttocks and pressed firmly. She felt his tongue on her clitoris and glanced at the clock again as his breathing quickened.

"You taste good," he murmured.

She felt behind her and grasped his penis, but before she could begin to masturbate him he squirmed out from under her, spread the cheeks of her buttocks, and rammed his cock into her anus. It sent a stab of pain through her pelvic area, and she gasped. He gave a deep, final thrust and erupted inside her. She felt his sperm pulsating in a thin, hot stream. When he pulled himself out of her, a trickle of it rolled down the inside of her thigh.

"All right," she said. "You've had your party."

"But the guest of honor wasn't here," he replied, getting up from the bed and walking naked toward the other room.

Genevieve scrambled after him, but by the time she reached the door he had come to an abrupt halt. And she saw why: Keja was pointing a small Walther pistol at the German's chest.

"Touch me and I'll kill you!" she said.

The corporal remained motionless, his eyes fixed on the gun.

"Keep him covered while I get dressed," Genevieve said.

When she returned to the room three or four minutes later, the tableau remained exactly as she had left it.

"Are the clothes we got for the couriers ready?" the Frenchwoman asked.

Keja had dressed while her roommate was with the German. She nodded, motioning to a pile of garments on the sofa.

"Put everything in suitcases, including anything you want to take with you," Genevieve instructed. "The Germans have ordered the club closed at the end of the month, and there's no reason for either of us to stay in Warsaw."

"What about him?" Keja asked, nodding toward the corporal.

"Leave him to me," Genevieve replied, taking the gun out of the other woman's hands and keeping it trained on the German while Keja quickly packed three shabby cardboard suitcases.

"Where are we going?" she asked.

"To rendezvous with the couriers at the ruined house on Bielenska Street. You go first."

"What about patrols?"

"Keep to the shadows."

Keja nodded, picked up two of the suitcases, and hurried out of the door. Genevieve waited until the sound of her roommate's footsteps disappeared down the stairs, then told the corporal, "Get dressed. Hurry."

He donned his uniform without uttering a word.

"Pick it up," the Frenchwoman ordered, motioning with her gun to the remaining suitcase. "Stay ahead of me and don't try anything, or I'll shoot. Understand?"

The corporal nodded, lifted the suitcase, and started down the staircase down to the street. There was no sign of any patrols, and they reached the gutted house after twenty minutes of brisk walking.

"Get in the truck," Genevieve told the driver.

He obeyed, first placing the suitcase on the passenger seat, then swinging himself behind the wheel. Genevieve climbed in after him, keeping the gun aimed at his head.

"Now start the engine and move the truck forward about ten feet."

The German looked puzzled, but he did as he had been ordered, while Genevieve instructed Keja, who was standing on the running board, to go to the manhole, help the couriers out, and load them into the back of the truck. Minutes later she felt the vehicle rock slightly, as the newcomers scrambled aboard, and heard Keja whisper through a small window at the back of the cab that they were ready to leave.

"Keep both hands on the steering wheel and do as I say," the Frenchwoman told the driver.

Glancing at her gun, he eased the truck forward. Genevieve crouched down in the well of the passenger seat but kept her pistol trained on the driver. Dawn was breaking and traffic got heavier as the truck rolled through the central part of Warsaw. From time to time Genevieve raised her head long enough to check their position and give directions to the driver. She had picked as her destination the Lomianki Forest about five miles north of the city, but when they approached the bridge across the Vistula River she saw several German guards standing at a roadblock.

"Stop!" she commanded.

The driver hesitated, gauging his chances of reaching the soldiers before Genevieve could shoot him, but decided the risk was too great and brought the truck to a halt.

"Turn around," Genevieve said, "and keep going until you find a bridge that isn't guarded."

The truck picked up speed as the driver obeyed the Frenchwoman's orders. She raised her head to check their location and saw green parks in spacious squares. About forty-five minutes later, the driver finally found an unguarded bridge, crossed the Vistula, and entered the Wyszkow Forest.

"Turn left."

The truck's suspension creaked as it bounced over deep ruts in the dirt road.

"Stop here," Genevieve ordered.

The vehicle trembled to a halt, and the tailgate swung open. Motioning with her pistol, the Frenchwoman ordered the driver out and marched him to where Keja was standing with the three couriers. The latter were still covered with slime, and their stench was overwhelming. For several minutes they remained motionless in the warm spring sun; then the two women fell into each other's arms and began to cry. Halevi, looking even more bearlike with his thick covering of filth, fixed his eyes on the driver. "What about him?"

The Frenchwoman shrugged. "We can tie him up."

"German patrols would find him in a matter of hours."

The corporal, who obviously understood the exchange even though it was in Polish, excitedly shook his head. "I will not tell them anything. I am tired of this war—"

Before he could finish his sentence, Halevi grabbed the German's head in a choke hold, and there was a sickening crunch as his neck broke. Without uttering a word, Halevi hoisted the driver's body over his massive shoulders and lumbered away to a nearby stand of trees.

Anna and Janet stopped crying. The sudden violence had stunned them. For a moment nobody spoke. Then Genevieve murmured, "There's a stream over there. We've brought clean clothes. You can pick out what you want after you wash."

Keja had packed a bar of soap in one of the suitcases, and she used it to wash the hair of each woman. She paused when she saw the medallion Janet was wearing around her neck—the talisman the Englishwoman had removed from Kandalman's acid-burned chest—but continued the shampooing without commenting on it.

Anna and Janet were still nude when Halevi reappeared wearing the driver's uniform, boots, and helmet. When he saw the women he quickly averted his eyes.

"We must get rid of the truck," he said.

Picking up the five canvas knapsacks containing the jewels, he loaded them into the back of the truck. The women dressed quickly and clambered aboard. Halevi got behind the wheel and started the engine.

They passed a convoy of trucks headed in the opposite direction, and when the SS soldiers waved to Halevi, he smiled broadly but didn't lift his foot from the accelerator. Genevieve opened one of the suitcases and took out a loaf of bread, some cheese, a large sausage, and a bottle of white wine. "It's all we've got," she said. "We can finish it now or try and make it last."

The others agreed it would be wiser to keep some for later, so she sliced small portions for each of them. She was in the midst of handing out the food when the truck suddenly slowed, throwing her to the floor.

"All out!" Halevi shouted, slapping the side of the truck as he walked back to the tailgate. "And bring the knapsacks with you."

Anna was puzzled by Halevi's order, but obeyed him, and watched as he returned to the cab, shifted into neutral, released the hand brake, and gave the steering wheel a violent twist. The vehicle picked up speed until it reached a sharp corner about fifty yards downhill, where it plunged over the edge of a cliff and hurtled hundreds of feet into the lake below.

"Now we walk," Halevi announced.

Shouldering his knapsack, he picked up two of the suitcases and started up a steep incline. Janet took hold of the remaining suitcase, slung a knapsack over her shoulder, and followed him. Anna, Genevieve, and Keja hesitated a moment before taking up their loads; it was evident from the sun, which had almost vanished below the horizon, that darkness wasn't far away, and all three were exhausted. But when Halevi summoned them, they wearily started up the path toward the trees.

There was a bitter chill in the air. It got even colder when darkness brought a dank mist, but they had continued to climb upward for almost an hour before Anna gasped, "I've got to rest."

"Not yet," Halevi said.

Anna slumped down on a rock.

"Come on, I'll help you," Janet said.

She grasped Anna's arm and supported her throughout the next hour until they reached another tree line, where Halevi announced the women could wait until he found a safe place for them to spend the night.

"Thanks," Anna murmured as Janet lowered her to the ground. "I couldn't have made it without you."

Genevieve opened her suitcase and divided what was left of the food into equal parts. "We might as well finish it," she said, passing around the portions along with a half-full bottle of wine.

Keja refused the food, saying she wasn't hungry, but when Halevi returned he wolfed down his share before leading the women to a small cave he had found a short distance away.

"We'll spend the night here," he said.

It was a natural alcove, sheltered by an overhanging ledge. The floor was covered with pine needles.

"I'll keep the first watch," Halevi said, "then each of you will—"

He stopped speaking as a metallic clink came from outside the cave. Pressing his ear to the ground, he listened intently for two or three minutes. Then he looked up at the women with a finger pressed to his lips. "It sounds like a German patrol," he whispered.

7

The sounds came again, this time louder than before and joined by a crunching noise. The women glanced at each other anxiously, but their tension eased as the sound lessened and finally faded away. All of them found it difficult to sleep.

Just before dawn, Halevi slipped out of the cave to see if the coast was clear. He had gone about a hundred yards when a voice warned, "Stay right where you are, or I'll blow your head off!"

Halevi froze.

"Put your hands behind your head and walk forward slowly." The instructions were issued in Polish, although it was apparent from the man's thick accent that Polish wasn't his native tongue.

Halevi followed a rutted path that wound between clumps of bushes and led into a grassy copse that was surrounded on three sides by tall trees. He was surprised to see a heavy farm cart piled high with cut logs on one side of the clearing.

"Turn around but keep your hands where they are."

Halevi obeyed. A dark-haired man was standing two or three yards away, a shotgun cradled in the crook of his arm. He wore corduroy pants, a bright collarless shirt, and a broad-brimmed hat. But what commanded attention were his eyes: huge and black, they were piercing, yet they possessed the restless, unstable quality of a wary animal. His face had strong, sharp features, high cheekbones, and skin the color of weathered oak.

"*Katar san tun?*" he asked in a language Halevi didn't understand. "Where do you come from?" he repeated in Polish.

"The city," Halevi replied.

"What are you doing here?"

Halevi looked across at the wagon loaded with logs. "Like you, I am cutting wood for fuel."

"With your bare hands?"

"I left my ax where I slept."

They faced each other in silence. The man with the gun kept glancing over his shoulder, and minutes later Anna, Genevieve, Janet, and Keja came into view, hands behind their heads, escorted by another man and a boy, both of whom carried guns. Behind them walked an old woman. Her long, braided hair was gray, but she moved with a supple ease that belied her age.

She spoke rapidly with the man covering Halevi in the same strange tongue he had used earlier, her voice getting progressively louder, until finally she stalked away, muttering to herself angrily.

"I wish I knew what they were talking about," Anna whispered.

"The old woman says we must be killed, and he can't make up his mind," Keja said. She faced the man and announced, *"Yekka bulisas nashi beshes pe done grstende."*

He looked at the blond blue-eyed woman in astonishment.

"What did you say?" Genevieve asked nervously.

"I told him that with one behind he cannot sit on two horses," Keja replied.

"San tu rom?" the man asked in Romany.

"My parents were both Gypsies," she replied in Polish. "They were both killed by the Nazis."

"I am Tibere" he said, lowering his shotgun. "Tell me about your friends."

"Gaje," Keja said.

The man looked at Halevi, then shifted his gaze to where the three women were standing. "Jews?"

"Only one of them. We're all from Warsaw."

"I have heard what is happening there. It is terrible. The Germans will not be satisfied until every Jew in Europe is dead."

"And every Gypsy," Keja said.

"True," the man replied, shaking his head sadly. "Many of my tribe have died at Dachau and Ravensbrück."

"Such shared misfortune should make us friends," Keja said. "As a *Rom* I ask your protection."

The old woman, who was at the far side of the copse, shouted in

Romany that he was a fool to believe that such a fair-skinned woman could be a Gypsy.

"Quiet!" he snapped, his dark eyes blazing angrily. "This is my *kumpania*. I make the decisions."

"Then be prepared to live with the consequences," the woman warned.

She continued to mutter as the others gathered armfuls of dried twigs and started a fire. Janet, who was numb with fatigue, tried to determine why the Gypsy men would scour the ground for firewood when their cart was loaded with freshly cut logs. The mystery was solved when the man who had spoken to Keja reached between two of the logs and stepped back as a hidden door swung open. It revealed a large area containing a pile of brightly colored eiderdowns, cooking implements, dry goods, and leather harnesses for the horse that stood quietly grazing at the far side of the copse.

Anna watched as the men unloaded a heavy cauldron which they suspended from a tripod over the now smoldering fire. After another raucous exchange in Romany, the old woman sullenly began preparing a meal: fried onions, tomatoes, red peppers, and a meat that was tender and delicate in texture, but gamy tasting and thick with fat. Anna was too hungry to ask what it was until she had finished eating, and instead of telling her, Tibere picked up what appeared to be a small rabbit, loosened its skin with a pointed stick, put it to his mouth and inflated the creature until its skin was taut. Only when the quills stood on end did Anna realize she'd eaten a hedgehog.

"Good, eh?" Tibere said.

"Different," Anna replied as Tibere deflated the hedgehog and hung it on a line strung between two trees.

While they were still eating, Tibere identified the other members of his group as Latso, a rail-thin young man in his mid-twenties; Andrei, a boy in his teens with curly black hair and a quick, ready smile; Jonitza, another boy, nearly nine years old; and Phuro, the old woman, who was the tribal grandmother.

The Gypsy leader concluded his meal with a loud belch. It seemed to please the old woman; her mahogany face creased into a smile as she took away the dishes, which she cleaned by scouring them with soil.

The horse stamped its hooves and shook its long gray mane as Latso slipped a bridle over its head. Far away, on some high pasture, Genevieve heard sheep bleating. Her head ached from the altitude and lack of sleep, but when Tibere continued to sit by the fire talking with his guests in Polish, she feigned deep interest.

The reason his *kumpania* was so small, he explained, was because most of his tribe had been killed by the Germans near Kielce a year earlier. The dead included Tibere's wife, a fact the Frenchwoman instinctively noted, as the Gypsy leader described how a total of over 600,000 *Rom* had perished at the hands of the Nazis.

As Genevieve listened, she found herself studying Tibere with heightened interest; he emanated a strength that attracted her. When he finally doused the fire and escorted the women to the wagon, she tried to hold his arm in such a way that he would feel the swell of her breasts pressing against his biceps and was puzzled when he shied away from her touch.

The women crawled into the hidden compartment under the logs, except for Phuro, who hautily selected a sleeping place under the wagon. Halevi started to climb in with them, but Tibere quickly stopped him, explaining brusquely that under Romany law a strict separation between the sexes had to be observed at all times.

"I'm no Gypsy—"

Before Halevi could finish his sentence, Tibere swung his shotgun into position and curled his finger on the trigger.

"That may be," he said coldly, "but in this camp you obey my orders."

Halevi looked at the gun. For a moment it seemed as though he was going to make a move, but then he shrugged and climbed up on the bench that served as a driver's seat. If there was going to be future conflict between the two men, Genevieve decided it might be in her best interests to curry favor with Tibere. He was a man who, like Kandalman, was experienced in taking care of himself and those who were closest to him. Even though he had pulled away when she tried to touch him, she knew enough about men to feel sure she could find a way to please him. When the wagon started to move, she turned to Keja. "Are all Gypsies really so prudish?"

"Touching any part of a woman to whom they are not married, even her clothes, is strictly forbidden under *Rom* law." the other woman said.

Genevieve didn't answer, but as she lay listening to the *clip-clop* of the horse's hooves on the dirt path, there was a knowing smile on her lips.

Days merged into each other as the journey continued. It seemed Tibere had only a vague idea about where he was headed, although he periodically declared that his ultimate aim was to cross the Pyrenees into Spain. He spoke of contrabandistas, professional smugglers who were willing, for a price, to guide people through the dangerous mountain passes, but they were at least a thousand miles away and he appeared to have no definite schedule in mind for reaching them. But he continued moving toward the southeast, a direction Janet assured them was daily bringing them closer to the Swiss border, so they decided to continue with Tibere and his *kumpania* until it was propitious to leave.

Little by little, the women fell into the rhythm of Gypsy life, though much of the time it was anything but easy. The horse was in poor condition and frequently needed rest. They were obliged to make detours when the forest growth became too dense for the wagon to pass through, and often they dared not stop to cook food for fear of their fires being seen by German patrols. Nor was the atmosphere made less tense by old Phuro continuing her long, moody silence, and insisting on sleeping apart from the other women.

When they finally emerged from the forest near the Czech border and stopped for the night at the edge of a marsh, it was apparent that the women's nerves were frayed. Living in such close quarters heightened even the smallest conflict, and though each of them made a conscious effort to control her temper, doing so became increasingly difficult. Genevieve's overt attempts to ingratiate herself with Tibere sparked bitter resentment in the other women, particularly Keja, who warned that breeching the Gypsies' rigid moral code could result in banishment for them all, but the Frenchwoman ignored the caution and continued to seek his companionship.

She made a point of walking with Tibere during their long daily treks and flattered him whenever she could. One way was by asking him to teach her the Romany language, and she mastered a few simple words. The Gypsy leader told her that *marhime* (unclean) was a matter of great concern to the Lowari. "The same word is used to describe someone banished from a tribe for serious misconduct," he said.

"Like what?" she asked.

"Premarital sex or infidelity," he replied.

Although Tibere seemed to enjoy talking with Genevieve, he never did or said anything she could interpret as an expression of sexual interest. Often while they chatted, young Jonitza would walk alongside them, adding bits and pieces of information he felt the Frenchwoman should know. The bond between the two Gypsies, who were not related, was like father and son, and Jonitza made no effort to disguise his worship of Tibere.

Their easy comradeship contrasted sharply with the conflict that had developed between the women traveling in the back of the wagon. As the trip lengthened, they engaged in frequent arguments as to how much longer they should stay with Tibere before breaking away to attempt the final leg of their journey to Switzerland.

"We'd be fools to leave him before we have to," Genevieve maintained heatedly.

"It's true," Keja agreed. "Tibere has lived in the open like this all his life. He knows how to keep out of the way of the Germans."

"But he's heading for the Spanish border," Anna said.

"And he doesn't seem to care how long it takes to get there," Janet added. "Our orders are to get the jewels into the bank in Geneva. That means we're going to have to rely on ourselves, and we might as well begin now."

The long rainy days when all of them had to share the cramped space inside the wagon were the worst: their clothes were damp, the heat became unbearable, and the stale air gave them all constant headaches. The acrid woodsmoke of the camp fires stung their eyes, and the ever-present reek of horse urine clung to everything. Tempers flared with increasing frequency, followed by long periods in which each woman lapsed into a prolonged silence.

"Tibere may know what he's doing," Genevieve snapped, when the Gypsy leader ordered her back inside the wagon to avoid being seen by a small group of refugees who were slowly making their way along a forest trail, "but I'm sick and tired of him running my life."

"He may be saving it," Keja said.

"If you don't like his telling you what to do," Anna added, "stop hanging around him all the time."

"Will you two stop bickering?" Janet interjected brusquely. "We'll all have to put up with Tibere for as long as it's necessary."

Tibere's decision to cross the border between Czechoslovakia and Austria was a welcome relief after days of being confined in the back of the wagon, even though he chose to make the attempt at night during a heavy rainstorm. Leaving the roads, they traveled cross-country through rugged terrain, at times slowing to a crawl and wading ankle deep in mud. The women worked alongside the men, pushing and shoving the wagon through the rain-drenched darkness. None of them were sure at what precise moment they crossed the ill-defined border; the strain they were under sapped every last ounce of energy, and after hours of backbreaking work the only indication that they had achieved their goal was when Tibere suddenly ordered a halt and unharnessed the horse.

During what was left of the night Phuro and the men sheltered under a tarpaulin, while the women lay in their mud-spattered clothes on damp eiderdowns inside the cart and tried to sleep. But it was impossible; they were too damp and cold.

"You couldn't pay me to go through that again," Anna said.

"There's still the Swiss border," Janet reminded her.

"It will be much more difficult, and we won't have Tibere to help us," Keja added.

"Couldn't we bribe the guards?" Genevieve asked.

"It would take a great deal of money," Keja said.

The Frenchwoman opened her knapsack, scooped up a handful of jewels, and let them trickle through her fingers back into the canvas bag. "We're carrying a fortune," she said.

"Not for our use," Janet reminded her.

"If we don't get them to the bank in Geneva they won't be of use to anybody," Genevieve reasoned.

"She's right," Anna said. "And to make sure we've always got a few when we most need them, let's sew some into the hems of our dresses."

When the other women voiced their agreement, Janet didn't protest. Keja found needles, thread, and scissors in a small compartment of the wagon, and they began to unpick their hems. The only illumination in the back of the wagon came from a single candle, but its fragile glow was enough to make the jewels glitter.

Each woman selected six stones: Keja, emeralds and rubies; Janet, diamonds; Genevieve, sapphires and opals; Anna, half a dozen perfectly matched pearls. As she worked Anna remembered how, when she was twelve or thirteen, her mother had taught her to sew. The memory triggered recollections of the last time she'd seen her parents in the ward at the hospital—her father propped against the wall with a gaping hole in his belly; her mother lying under an overturned bed with her skull crushed. She shuddered and, when the task of hiding the jewels was complete, blew out the candle and settled, still shivering, under the damp eiderdown.

Janet, too, was preoccupied with her own thoughts: the gold medallion she had taken from Kandalman when she treated his burns was no longer around her neck; she assumed she had lost it during the border crossing. She saw again the awful scar the acid had left on Kandalman's chest, then willed it from her mind and tried to sleep.

An hour later Genevieve was still awake. She was also thinking about Kandalman, but in quite a different way. Her memories focused more on their life together before he was ordered by the Nazis to live in the ghetto: of the wonderful meals they'd shared, the champagne they'd drunk, the expensive dresses he had bought her, and the weekend visits they had made to small inns in the countryside outside Warsaw. It all seemed to have happened long ago, but the details were etched in her memory, and because they contrasted so completely with the discomfort of the situation in which she now found herself, she relished every recollection.

It had started to rain when they awoke, but the day got warmer as they traveled along narrow, winding back roads lined on both sides by tall shady trees. At last Tibere called a halt in a lush green meadow through which a small stream ran. The women washed off the mud that still caked their arms and legs and did what they could to remove the previous night's grime from their clothes, but they were careful not to rub too hard where the jewels were hidden in the hems of their skirts. Phuro, not wanting to light a fire, prepared a meal of bread and slices of cold hedgehog, which they all consumed ravenously.

By afternoon they were on the move again, but when a German tank column rolled up alongside the wagon, headed south toward Linz, Tibere swung off the road onto a deeply rutted dirt track that led through weed-infested fields of sugar beets to the seclusion of a farmyard.

It was a fairly large farm, deserted and half collapsed, and they were greeted by scattering chickens and honking geese. But a brief exploration by Tibere and the other men quickly revealed that the birds were not the only inhabitants. A number of men, all of draft age, were encamped in the large hayloft.

Rather than join them, Tibere took over a large outbuilding, driving the wagon inside to keep it out of sight. Phuro went foraging for food, while the men joined some Polish coal miners and farmhands who had gathered in the main part of the farmhouse to listen to a radio. They explained that they had fled Poland to avoid being pressed into service by the Nazis, who were shipping all able-bodied men to work in factories in Germany. Instead, they were hoping to make it to Spain, where they intended to stay until the war was over.

The news they heard on the radio suggested that that day might not be too far off: British and American bombers were inflicting heavy damage on Germany's war industry, Mussolini's government had been overthrown, and the Italians under Marshal Badoglio were rumored to be discussing an armistice with the Allies.

About half an hour after they had arrived at the farm, a German armored personnel carrier drove up the dirt road leading to the outbuildings. It didn't enter the courtyard, remaining instead in a position that effectively blocked any possibility of passing it. Not long afterward, a tank rumbled to a stop on the opposite side of the courtyard.

"I don't like the looks of this," Halevi muttered, watching the Germans through broken shutters.

"They're just out on maneuvers," Tibere said.

Halevi wasn't convinced; he gathered the women together. "Give me your knapsacks. I don't want them falling into German hands."

Hefting the five canvas bags over his shoulder, he went into the main part of the farmhouse and disappeared down steps leading to a cellar.

"A typical *Gaje*," Tibere remarked to Keja. "His first concern is for your possessions."

She didn't answer, but she knew the Gypsy leader must be wondering what the knapsacks contained. Ever since the women had first joined his *kumpania* he had eyed the bags with undisguised curiosity, but his respect for the privacy of others had kept him from asking about their contents.

It was early evening, but still light enough for them to watch the Germans setting up a loudspeaker on top of the troop carrier. *"Achtung! Achtung!"* a voice announced. "Come out with your hands up. You have five minutes before we begin shooting!"

8

The silence that followed this announcement was absolute—no bird or insect sounds, just a void in which time seemed to stop. It ended when the door of the ruined farmhouse squeaked open, and a trickle of men slowly made their way toward the German personnel carrier with their hands behind their heads.

Tibere spoke rapidly to Phuro in Romany and helped the old woman climb to the driver's seat of the wagon. The horse hadn't been unharnessed yet, and it was only a matter of moments before Phuro started guiding it out through the wide double doors of the outbuilding. Tibere spoke briskly to Latso, Andrei, and Jonitza, again in Romany, and they hurried through a hole in the rear wall where part of the brickwork had collapsed, quickly disappearing into the waist-high grass that lay beyond.

"The Germans want only able-bodied men," Tibere explained. "Old Phuro will be of no interest to them, but she can get the wagon through safely, and we'll meet up with her later."

He started toward the hole through which the other Gypsies had escaped and the women followed, all except Janet, who hung back, her eyes on the cellar steps down which Halevi had disappeared with their knapsacks.

"We can't leave without . . ." She left the sentence unfinished, and the other women weren't sure if her concern was for Halevi or the treasure.

"Quickly!" Tibere urged.

As he spoke the Germans began shelling the farmhouse with salvos from both the tank and the armored personnel carrier. Shells ripped into the already ruined structure, sending walls crumbling in showers of bricks, while machine guns swept the area with bullets.

Tibere ran into the high grass, and because the outbuildings were between him and the Germans' line of fire he made it without their seeing him. The four women followed as shells continued to slam into the courtyard and flames belched from the hayloft.

The roar of gunfire was deafening, and it continued uninterrupted as the women ran at a crouch toward a thick stand of trees. The earth under their feet shuddered and the air was filled with the acrid smell of cordite, but they kept going until they reached the trees, where they sprawled under a layer of matted shrubs.

The firing stopped as suddenly as it had started, but by then the farmhouse was in flames. Twilight had fallen, adding an eerie half-light to the tableau. As darkness slowly settled over them the women heard gunfire again, a series of short bursts followed by the sound of the personnel carrier's engine starting and, moments later, the thunderous roar of the tank coming to life.

Genevieve started to her feet, but Janet grasped her arm. "If we try and make a break for it now they're sure to see us," she whispered.

Keja remained silent, her eyes fixed on the tank that was rattling forward on its steel treads, heading right at them. Then it abruptly changed direction and rolled directly toward the farmhouse. It plowed into the outbuilding and continued straight through the flaming wreckage. The women all watched, unable to turn away or close their eyes until the tank disappeared into the darkness down the same dirt road the armored personnel carrier had taken.

After waiting about fifteen minutes, Janet got to her feet and walked cautiously toward the outbuilding. She was joined by the other three women, who stood silently by her side gazing at the wreckage. The entrance to the basement where Halevi had gone in search of a place to hide the jewels lay buried under a massive pile of ancient stones.

"Maybe he got out before it collapsed," Janet suggested, her eyes searching the wreckage for signs of life.

"There wasn't time," Anna said.

"We can't be sure . . ." Genevieve's words trailed away.

"He moved too slowly to have escaped," Keja added.

They stood together in the darkness, the defeat on their faces visible in the glow cast by the flames of the burning hayloft.

"We've got to find Tibere," Keja said, finally breaking the silence.

The other women murmured agreement. At least it was an immediate objective, something on which to focus. None of them knew what to do. The Gypsy leader had told them he was going to cross the Pyrenees into Spain, but the women hadn't listened very attentively because their destination had been Switzerland, and they knew they would be leaving Tibere before he turned west to continue his long trek across war-ravaged Europe.

"Where do we start looking for him?" Anna asked.

"If he still lives," Keja replied, "he will have left trailside messages that I can identify when it gets light."

Turning away from the wreckage of the outbuilding, she walked back toward the bushes where they had hidden during the shelling. The others followed, all except Janet, who remained at the ruined structure as if hoping that some miracle might have saved Halevi and the jewels from entombment. After five or ten minutes she seemed to acknowledge the futility of her vigil and joined the others, but not before picking up the small portable radio on which the Polish coal miners had listened to the news reports, which had somehow survived the attack.

The night air, warmed by the still blazing fires, wafted over the women as they lay under the shrubbery, bringing with it the stench of burned flesh. Whether it came from the charred bodies of refugees who hadn't left the hayloft or farm animals caught in the flames was impossible to determine, but it lingered throughout the night and made sleep impossible.

As they lay with their eyes open gazing up at the stars, each woman found herself wondering what the future held now that the task of delivering the treasure had suddenly been taken away from them. They were left with a series of conflicting emotions. Uppermost was an overwhelming sense of failure, blended with memories of what they had left behind and the fearful uncertainty of what lay ahead.

"Let's go," Keja commanded as the first light of dawn seeped into the sky.

She crept out of their hiding place and motioned the others to follow her. They obeyed and for almost an hour moved cautiously through the forest, taking great care not to step on twigs or make any other noise that might betray their presence to German patrols. Then Keja raised her hand and signaled them to halt.

"Stay here while I check the trail for signs that they passed this way," she said.

The women sank to the ground, exhausted by their sense of failure as much as by fatigue, and watched Keja as she went off alone through the trees. During the weeks after their escape from Warsaw, she had undergone a change that was so gradual as to be barely perceptible, a change that had begun when they joined Tibere's *kumpania* and had continued as she slowly settled into the daily routine of Gypsy life. No longer a shy and diffident girl, she was now a calm, mature woman. Even her body was more womanly.

Nobody had been more impressed by this transformation than Tibere. Initially, even though she spoke Romany, he treated Keja with the same casual disdain he showed the other women, who, simply because they were non-Gypsies, seemed to be of less consequence to him than his horse. But as she underwent her metamorphosis, his attitude changed, first to interest, then respect. Genevieve, who had realized that her overtures were getting her nowhere, sensed that Tibere was sexually attracted to Keja. He took advantage of every opportunity to display his masculinity through body postures and over-stated hand gestures, though he pretended to ignore her whenever she was in his presence.

When Keja reappeared her face was flushed, and she beckoned the others to follow as she led the way hurriedly to where a shred of cloth was hanging from the branch of a tree.

"Tibere left this," she announced excitedly.

"How do you know?" Anna asked.

Keja pointed to a piece of wood that had been notched in a singular way. "It is his tribal badge," she replied.

Walking a short distance away from where the others stood, she cupped her hands and blew into the hollow, making a sound like the cry of a cuckoo. It was immediately answered by a long, low whistle that was repeated twice and then, after a short pause, once again.

"They are near," Keja said.

She walked along the trail with smooth, easy strides for about five minutes, followed closely by the other women, and then repeated the sound of the cuckoo. Moments later the low, deep whistle came again, this time from much closer.

Moving in the direction from which the sound had come, they found themselves in a grassy clearing. On one side, under the thick foliage of a tree branch, stood the wagon. Tibere was kneeling next to it, cradling Latso's head in his lap, and old Phuro stood a few paces away holding Jonitza's hand. All of them looked up, as the women crossed the glade, but immediately turned their attention back to Latso, who was moaning softly.

His face was ashen and blood flowed from his nostrils. Even though Janet was five or ten yards away she knew from the rattle in his throat that he was dying. Kneeling next to where Tibere crouched, she put her fingers on Latso's pulse. It was fluttering weakly. Blood seeped from a hole the size of a fist in his belly; he must have been hit when the Germans fired their first salvos ten hours earlier. She marveled that he had been able to hang on to life this long. He must be in terrible pain, but he showed little evidence of it.

"Andrei is also dead. . . ." Tibere's words trailed away as a series of spasms racked Latso's body and his head rolled to one side.

"He's gone," Janet said.

Phuro uttered a shrill wail and tore her dress from neck to waistline, but Tibere continued to hold Latso's body for at least another fifteen minutes. Then he got up slowly, took a shovel from the wagon, and began digging a shallow grave on the far side of the clearing.

Using a narrow piece of cloth that he tore from his shirt, Tibere first measured Latso's body, then broke the dead man's little finger and fastened some paper money to it with a ribbon from Phuro's hair. She took Latso's watch, stopped it at the exact moment he had expired, and crushed it under her boot. After burning Latso's few personal possessions, Tibere lowered his body into the grave and poured brandy over the corpse.

As he was closing the grave Phuro raised her face to the sky, her lips quivering, and broke into a lament for the dead. Her voice had a penetrating quality, and as her chant went on she seemed to gain in stature and presence.

Anna picked some wildflowers and placed them on the grave, but Tibere angrily hurled them across the clearing. Frightened and puzzled, she asked Keja what she'd done wrong.

"Gypsies consider picked flowers a symbol of premature death: not one that has already happened, but one that is still to come," the other woman replied.

9

In the days that followed, Tibere observed the Rom's strict rules of mourning; while the rest made steady progress south toward the border between Austria and Italy, he walked apart, refusing to either shave or comb his hair. The only food he would eat was black bread, which he swallowed with a cup of cold water. Each time he thought of Latso, instead of mentioning his name, he poured some water on the ground, or let fall some crumbs of bread.

Phuro also remained separate, walking with her head bowed and frequently uttering moans that were so full of suffering that the other women wanted to comfort her, but they were warned against doing so by Keja, who explained that such solace wouldn't be appreciated. Gypsy tradition required that she grieve alone, and as the same strict customs also forbid her to cook, wash, or clean up the campsite, these chores fell to the other women.

They were supervised in these daily tasks by Keja, who had taken up the Gypsy ways again so completely that Genevieve was obliged to admit that she had misjudged her former roommate. Gone was the shy, almost childlike insouciance; in its place was a mature competence that gave the other three women the reassurance they so desperately needed. Even her physical appearance had changed as her blond hair lengthened in a tangle of curls and her pale skin took on a deep tan from constant exposure to sun and wind.

Climbing out from under the huge eiderdown beneath which all the women slept, she was always the first one up in the morning, gathering twigs for a fire, grinding coffee beans in an ancient brass pestle, fetching water in enameled jugs from the nearest stream.

Tibere, although remaining apart, still managed to keep an eye on everything that was happening, and after his period of mourning was over he acknowledged Keja's contribution by making her a present of the strip of cloth he had used to measure Latso's body before putting it in the grave.

It seemed an odd gift until Keja explained to the other women that the length of cloth was believed by Gypsies to have potent magical properties. "It must be carried at all times but saved as a last resort, because it can only be used once," she said. "Afterward it must be thrown into flowing water as soon as possible, or whatever has been wished for won't happen." She tied the colorful piece of cloth around her neck, and the other women noticed that she was never without it during the weeks that followed.

As they neared the border between Austria and Italy, which Tibere planned to cross through the Brenner Pass, the women walked alongside the wagon, helping to push it when they encountered deeply rutted tracks that made the load too much for the horse to pull alone. They also began traveling shorter distances and kept to rural areas as much as possible. By listening to the small portable radio that Janet had taken from the farm, they were able to keep track of the war in Europe, where the Allied invasion of Sicily had begun and the Italian forces under Badoglio were on the brink of surrender.

But Tibere showed little interest in these distant happenings. He was more concerned with how to obtain fake identification papers, without which it would be impossible to continue their journey across Europe to the Pyrenees. He resolved the problem by bribing secretaries in a German military headquarters at a town near Innsbruck, who managed to procure documents identifying the members of Tibere's *kumpania* as French citizens, originally from Tarbes, who were volunteer laborers working in German war industries, returning on leave.

The secretaries, whom he paid with exquisitely wrought silver bracelets, also helped Tibere obtain old work clothes, which he insisted that everybody wear so they would look like the industrial workers described in their documents. Unfortunately, the sizes weren't always exact, and the women ended up with garments that hung on them so loosely the swell of their breasts was totally obscured.

Keja, who was by far the most petite of them all, ended up with a jacket and pants that were much too large but she didn't seem to mind, and the others guessed it was because she had recently put on considerable weight. The healthy outdoor life she had been living had improved her appetite, and she ate frequent samples of whatever she was cooking.

After supplying them with work clothes, Tibere ordered the women to throw their old dresses away, so that night, as Phuro carefully guided the wagon down the Italian side of the Brenner Pass, the women removed the jewels they had sewn into the hems of their skirts and hid them in the seams of their work trousers.

Once again days melted into each other as they journeyed across Northern Italy, crossing the border into France at Crissolo, always moving in a southwesterly direction toward the town of Tarbes at the base of the Pyrenees. They frequently passed military convoys heading toward the front the Germans had established in the Italian sector, but whenever they were stopped at roadblocks and checkpoints, the documents Tibere had obtained provided safe passage.

As weeks dragged into months, the daily pressure of living in such close quarters produced renewed frictions between the women. Janet, who was obsessively neat, was endlessly irritated by Genevieve's slovenliness, while Anna found herself resenting the Englishwoman's tendency to form quick judgments based on an assumption that she knew what was best for them all.

Genevieve, who by this time had abandoned her attempts to ingratiate herself with Tibere, was puzzled by Keja's reaction to the Gypsy leader's interest in her. She had repeatedly rebuffed his advances, but her doing so had only made Tibere increasingly persistent, and he continued to advance his cause at every possible opportunity, until it became nearly impossible for Keja to keep rejecting his attentions without offending him.

It was a dilemma Keja herself didn't know how to resolve: she knew, as did the others, that their tenure with the Gypsy leader depended solely on his willingness to accept them as part of his *kumpania*. He could throw them out at a moment's notice and leave them to fend for themselves, which meant they would no longer have access to the guides he intended to use to take them over the Pyrenees.

When they finally arrived in Tarbes, Tibere took matters into his own hands and, after making a formal proposal to Keja, set about arranging a wedding, even though she had asked him for time to think it over. She reacted to the pressure by turning in on herself, spending long periods of time alone, and refusing to talk when the others tried to discuss the matter with her. Janet grew particularly worried when, after Tibere began announcing to other Gypsies they met along the road that he was planning to take a new wife and inviting them to the wedding,

Keja began to show physical effects from the strain. She tired more easily, urinated frequently, got swollen limbs, and was only able to walk short distances without taking a rest.

"She can't go on like this," the Englishwoman told Anna and Genevieve. "It's making her sick."

"I can't understand why she doesn't just tell him she isn't interested in marrying him," Genevieve said.

"Maybe she feels our safety would be threatened if she did," Anna observed.

Tibere appeared oblivious to what was happening and made no effort to hide his pleasure as the day he had chosen for the wedding got closer. He had made arrangements to meet the contrabandistas, professional smugglers who made a business out of guiding refugees through the high mountain passes in the Pyrenees, at a small country inn on the outskirts of Tarbes, and he decided that was also a good place for the marriage to take place. Word went out to other Gypsies in the area, and they started gathering at the inn on the wedding day soon after it got light.

Improvised tables were set up on sawhorses under the arbor at the back of the inn and covered with checked tablecloths. The owner's wife allowed some of the Gypsy women to use her huge kitchen, and they vyed with each other in preparing foods for the guests. Great care had been taken to invite local farmers who were known to have abundant supplies of food, some of which they sold to the Gypsies and contributed the rest as wedding gifts.

Around the fires men talked and drank brandy as the day wore on. An old man played tunes on a concertina, and the others joined in clapping and singing. A group of younger men beat out the rhythm with their feet until one of them, more restless than the others, leaped into a small open space and started dancing.

In a small room at the back of the inn, where the sound of music and dancing was audible through windows that opened onto the arbor, Tibere sat at a bare wooden table with the contrabandista he had selected to guide his group over the Pyrenees. It was their third meeting and all the bargaining was over. Tibere had agreed to pay eight thousand francs for each member of his party, somewhat less than the going rate because there were seven of them and all, including old Phuro, were in good physical condition. Janet, whom Tibere had used as an interpreter at all his meetings with the smuggler because of her fluency in Spanish and French, wasn't so sure about Keja, but she kept her doubts to herself.

The smuggler, Casimir, was a Montagnard whose native tongue was Aragonese Spanish, but he also spoke heavily accented French. He attached great importance to the health of the people he would be guiding, repeatedly cautioning that he wouldn't even attempt the crossing with anybody who wasn't in top physical condition. "It can be hell up there," he warned, "particularly if the weather gets bad. I don't want anybody dying."

As if to prove there was no possibility of this happening, Tibere led the other man to the open window and pointed out those who would be making the crossing. Anna and Genevieve had joined the men who were dancing, following Jonitza's instructions as he tried to teach them the steps, while Phuro was helping another Gypsy woman lift a side of beef off a spit over an open fire. Only Keja wasn't involved in the activities. She sat apart from the others on the steps of a wagon, wearing a dress that some Gypsy women had made for her as a wedding gift. It looked as if she had been crying.

"Women!" Tibere shook his head in mock exasperation. "They dream of their wedding day, but when it comes all they can do is weep."

Casimir, who had established that he was a married man with four children, laughed and accepted Tibere's invitation to join the celebration. He had brought a pile of heavy clothing for the trip, which was scheduled to begin at dawn the next day, and he left the garments in a closet in the small room after being assured by Tibere that they would be distributed after the wedding celebration was over. The wagon, which would have to be left behind anyway, had been promised to Casimir as part of his fee, and he had made arrangements for it to be collected by members of his family after Tibere and his group embarked on their crossing the following day.

Janet followed the men out to the arbor where, when the guests saw Tibere, they applauded and offered toasts to him. He laughed and waved to his guests, most of whom had finished eating but still lingered at table, sipping their drinks. They belched politely, commented on the excellence of the food, and wiped their hands on the tablecloths. When the men finally got up to watch the dancing, an unruly mob of women and children descended on whatever food still remained on the tables, stuffing it in their mouths with both hands.

Tibere watched the melee. "Thank God the wedding isn't going to last the usual eight days!"

Smiling broadly, he stopped to talk with guests as he made his way to where Keja was seated on the steps of the wagon. When he reached

her he took her hand gently but firmly in his own and led her to where
the young men were still dancing. Grasping Keja around the waist, he
pulled her to him, and rapidly whirled her around on the already
well-trampled grass.

She hung limply in his arms and let him whirl her at a dizzying
pace. Tibere tried to mask her lethargy by quickening his step, but
when he stopped dancing she slumped to the ground. It was a moment or two before the onlookers realized that something was wrong.
Those closest to her laughed, thinking she had become disoriented
from being spun around, while Tibere picked up a glass of beer and
drained it in a single gulp. But when Keja didn't move, a murmur of
concern stirred through the crowd. Still the men made no attempt to
help her up, aware that it would be a serious breach of Gypsy law for
them to touch a virgin.

Janet, who had seen Keja fall, rushed to her side and felt her pulse.
It was very weak. The Gypsy women sensed something was seriously
wrong and crowded around to offer their help.

"Please stand back, she needs air," the Englishwoman pleaded, but
the Gypsy women ignored her, lifted Keja up, and carried her to
a cluster of wagons parked alongside a country road that ran past
the inn.

Janet followed them but wasn't allowed inside the caravan into which
Keja was taken. She was in good hands, the others assured the Englishwoman; the person attending her was famous for her knowledge of
herbal remedies. But Janet persisted and, after more than half an hour
of repeated requests, was finally allowed inside.

The caravan was slightly larger than that in which she and the other
women had spent the last five months, and lined with glass jars containing herbal potions. Light came through two small windows, and the late
afternoon sun shone in a single brilliant shaft on an old woman squatting in the corner. Her skin was cracked and her hair hung in oily
strands framing owl-like features, but there was an unexpected gentleness in her dark hooded eyes, and she spoke with the softness of a wind
lightly stirring.

"This woman isn't ill," she said, "she's pregnant. Her child will be
born six or eight weeks from now."

She addressed herself to Janet, but her statement was overheard by
the half dozen Gypsy women who had gathered at the open door of
the caravan, and a shocked murmur spread among them. Word quickly
reached the other guests that the bride was not a virgin, and many

immediately left the gathering, incensed by Tibere's attempt to trick them into condoning his marriage to a woman who was *marhime.* "How could he not be aware of her condition when the woman had been with child for almost seven months?" they asked each other angrily.

Janet knew the answer merely by looking at where Keja had been left inside the caravan after the old woman finished examining her. Now that she had been stripped of the voluminous skirt and many-layered petticoat of her wedding dress, the bulge of her stomach was obvious, but because of her small-boned frame and the oversized work clothes she'd been wearing, she had succeeded in hiding her condition.

It was impossible for the Englishwoman to explain all this to the offended guests, who stood in clusters angrily discussing what had happened. By knowingly harboring an unchaste woman, Tibere had not only broken the strictest law of the *Rom* but also, by making them accomplices, made them subject to the worst possible luck, which was the last thing they needed with the dangers of crossing the Pyrenees ahead for them all.

One of the older men, an elder in another tribe, issued commands in Romany to some Gypsy women standing near the caravan. They dragged Keja outside, stripped off what few clothes she still had on, and paraded her naked in front of the assembled guests. Some spit on her, others shouted insults in their own tongue, and when the procession reached where Tibere was standing, the old man who had issued the orders handed him a whip and a long-bladed knife.

The women who had stripped Keja forced her to kneel and held her firmly. A tense silence settled over them as they waited for their host to administer the traditional punishment of scarring Keja's face in such a way that she would carry the mark for life, but Tibere let the whip and knife fall to the ground and strode toward the inn.

An angry buzz flowed through the circle of Gypsies around Keja. When the old man picked up his whip and knife, it seemed for a moment that he was about to exact retribution himself, but instead he ordered the members of his tribe to leave and led them off down the road toward Tarbes.

Keja remained kneeling on the ground, eyes closed, body quivering. As Janet, Anna, and Genevieve helped her back to Tibere's wagon she moved like a sleepwalker. Phuro, who had watched from the steps of the wagon, turned away as Keja approached, and when Jonitza reached out a hand to help her into the wagon, the old woman, speaking in

Romany, angrily ordered the boy not to touch somebody who was unclean.

Janet and the other women did what they could to help Keja, wiping the spittle from her body with a damp towel and dressing her in the work clothes that had so effectively hidden her pregnancy during the weeks since they left Austria. As Janet was helping Keja into her shirt, an object fell from the breast pocket: the gold medallion Janet had removed from Kandalman's neck. She realized Keja must have taken it. Puzzled, but aware that Keja was in no condition to explain, Janet replaced the medallion in the shirt pocket and persuaded the other woman to lie under an eiderdown.

But Keja was finally speaking. "I should have told you I was pregnant. . . . I was too ashamed. . . . It went against everything I'd been raised to believe in as a Gypsy—but my life in Warsaw was so different from anything I'd ever known—"

Gently, Janet placed her hand over Keja's mouth. "Try and sleep," she said.

Keja was still awake an hour before dawn when Tibere appeared at the door of the wagon. He said, speaking in Romany, "The guide has come and we are leaving. You will understand why I cannot take you with me."

Keja nodded. "But you can take my friends," she whispered.

Tibere shook his head. "They must have known you were unclean."

"It was my secret."

"Then you must bear the responsibility for what happens to them," he said. "I have left money with the innkeeper. He will let you stay two or three days, but you must find another place because Casimir now owns this wagon and will claim it when he returns from guiding us over the mountains."

"I am sorry to have brought you such shame," she said.

"I forgive you," he replied, looking at her for a long moment, "but God may not be so understanding."

Before she could answer, he turned and strode away.

10

During the hours that followed Tibere's departure, there were strong autumnal winds and heavy driving rains. Cloistered inside the wagon, the women were tense.

"What happens now?" Anna asked, when Keja finally fell asleep.

"I don't know," Janet admitted. "We can't stay here, and the whole area is swarming with Nazis."

Genevieve looked at where Keja was huddled under the eiderdown, her face to the wall of the wagon. "Who could possibly be the father?" she wondered.

It was a question that was uppermost in the minds of all the women, but Keja hadn't volunteered the information, and because of her fragile emotional state the others hadn't probed.

"You lived with her during the time she must have conceived," Anna said.

"It must have been in March," Janet added.

"She never even got close to a man," the Frenchwoman assured them. "If there had been anybody, I would have known—"

Her sentence was interrupted by the arrival of the innkeeper bringing food. It had stopped raining, and the sky was marbled with rose hues. Even though he'd had to walk through inches of mud to reach the wagon, the innkeeper was in good humor because he had made a handsome profit on the previous day's wedding celebration. "Only bread and cold meat," he announced, passing a tray to the women, "but there's plenty of it, and I included a bottle of wine."

The women waited for him to leave, but he remained at the door, shifting his weight awkwardly from one foot to the other.

"Tibere left some money," he said finally. "Not much; enough to guarantee that you won't go hungry for a few days. But the Germans have begun making arrests in Tarbes, and after what happened here yesterday, you'd be wise not to hang around too long. Gypsies are a vicious lot, particularly to people they consider outsiders, and after the way they were shamed I wouldn't be surprised if they tell the Nazis where to find you." He glanced at where Keja was sleeping. "I can let you stay until tomorrow, but after that I want you out of here. Understood?"

The women didn't answer, and when the innkeeper left they ate their food in silence.

"I'll go into Tarbes," Genevieve said finally. "There must be somewhere we can stay."

"Not without money," Janet said.

"But we've got the jewels!" Anna exclaimed.

"If we tried to sell them, word would spread like wildfire," the Englishwoman said. "And the last thing we need is to draw attention to ourselves."

"It is my fault you are trapped here." Keja raised her head from where she was lying. "I want you to leave me and save yourselves."

"The Germans are already starting a roundup," Genevieve said.

"I will take my chances."

"They wouldn't add up to much with half the Gypsies in the area holding a grudge against you."

"My people are not—"

"Your people?" The Frenchwoman laughed. "I doubt if they count you one of them any more."

She hadn't meant her words to sound so brutal, but it was apparent from the way Keja averted her eyes that they'd hurt.

"Why don't we hire our own guide to take us across the mountains?" Anna asked.

"Because we don't have any money," Janet replied brusquely.

"If we showed a guide the jewels, then left immediately, and only gave them to him once we were in Spain, there shouldn't be any risk of drawing attention to ourselves."

"She's right," Keja said.

"What about you?" Genevieve asked.

"I'll stay here. It's all I deserve."

"You can't. It's too dangerous."

"And what about the baby?" Anna added.

"Anna is right," Janet said. "You have a responsibility to the baby."

Tears suddenly streamed down Keja's cheeks. "All right, I'll go with you."

"It won't be easy, in your condition," Genevieve cautioned.

"Don't worry, I'll make it," Keja said. "For the baby's sake."

Janet remained silent. She knew that Keja would be risking her life, but she was also aware that Keja's odds of surviving in Tarbes were no better.

Two evenings later the innkeeper, who had grudgingly allowed them to stay an extra day, knocked on the door of the wagon and announced that the new owner had come to collect it. Janet, who had been present when the deal was struck, expected to see a member of Casimir's family but was surprised when the smuggler himself appeared at the rear of the inn. It was only three days since he had left to guide Tibere, Phuro, and Jonitza over the mountains, far too short a time for him to have made the round trip.

"Where is Tibere?" she asked.

"There was an accident," Casimir replied, nervously running the brim of his hat through his fingers. "The weather got bad, but Tibere wouldn't turn back." He spit out a stream of tobacco juice. "There was an ice bridge over a crevasse . . . it broke, and they fell."

"All of them?"

"They were roped together."

The women looked at each other in stunned silence.

"It was not my fault," Casimir insisted. "I am a good guide."

"We're going to give you a chance to prove it," Janet said.

The smuggler looked puzzled.

"We want you to guide us over the mountains."

"Impossible! It is almost winter and the weather is too unpredict-able—"

"You will be well paid."

"Money is no use to a dead man."

"Ten thousand francs."

"It would be very dangerous."

"Twelve thousand."

"Each?"

Janet nodded.

"Tibere told me you have no money," the smuggler said.

"We can pay," the Englishwoman assured him.

Casimir ran his tongue over his weather-cracked lips. "Thirty-six thousand for three of you—"

"Forty-eight for us all."

The smuggler looked at Keja and shook his head. "Not her," he said.

"She can still walk." Janet said.

"But not survive the kind of hardships that exist up there." He nodded toward the peaks, which had turned pinkish-gold as the sun lowered in the sky.

"We will help her," the Englishwoman persisted.

"She is cursed and will bring bad luck."

"That is just silly superstition."

"Perhaps," Casimir replied, "but since it was revealed she is an unclean woman three people have died. I do not wish to be the fourth. If the rest of you are ready to leave at dawn, and will pay me in advance, I will take you over the mountains, but not the pregnant one."

He replaced his hat and disappeared inside the inn, leaving the women in the darkness of the wagon, silent and unmoving, until Keja struck a match and lit a candle.

"You must go without me," she said.

"We've already decided not to," Janet replied wearily.

"Maybe if we offered him more money . . ." Anna's voice trailed away.

"What if he will only accept cash?" Genevieve asked.

Janet took a pair of scissors and snipped open a seam in her work pants. Three diamonds fell into the palm of her hand, each about the size of the nail on her little finger, and glittered in the candlelight.

"You think he's going to refuse these?" She opened the seam on the other side and added three equally large gems. "They're worth far more than Casimir could make in ten lifetimes of smuggling."

The women slept fitfully, tossing and turning in the narrow space. On two occasions they were awakened by the roar of German convoys heading north, and another time by the sound of a Nazi patrol that halted near the wagon but quickly moved on.

When Casimir came at dawn, Janet met him under the arbor at the back of the inn and showed him two of the diamonds. The smuggler, obviously surprised, picked them up and examined each stone carefully.

"They are worth far more than the price we agreed on," she said.

"They are fine stones," Casimir agreed.

"Then we have a deal?"

"For three women I want three diamonds."

Janet took another diamond out of her pocket and showed it to him, but when he reached for it she quickly closed her fist.

"You get this one after we cross the border into Spain," she said.

His weathered face creased into a grin, revealing uneven, tobacco-stained teeth. "Don't trust me, eh?"

"Let's call it insurance," Janet replied. She dug into her pocket again and took out the last three diamonds, which she displayed along with the one still in her palm. "And you get all these if you agree to take Keja."

"All right." Casimir shrugged. "But it is very dangerous on the mountain."

"We're all willing to take the risk," the Englishwoman assured him.

"So be it," Casimir said. "But don't say I didn't warn you. That woman is bad luck."

11

Instead of leaving at dawn, as he had with Tibere, Casimir set their departure for after darkness, so the women spent another twelve hours hidden inside the wagon without knowing whether or not the smuggler would betray them to the Germans.

Casimir must also have alerted the innkeeper to what was planned, because about two hours before it got dark the women were taken into the small back room of the inn and told to get ready. They donned the heavy coats and sweaters the smuggler had left in the closet on the day of the wedding, and the innkeeper's wife, a thin, kindly woman, cooked them a meal, which she insisted they eat even though nervousness had robbed them of hunger, warning that it might be a long time before they got any more hot food. She also provided each of them with slabs of bread and a small flask of brandy as an added protection against the cold.

Casimir returned at dusk, and not long afterward the women found themselves under a pile of sacks in the back of a farm wagon. Casimir traveled up front with the driver, a young man barely out of his teens. He didn't say where they were headed, but it became obvious, from the endless twists in the road and the steepening incline, that they were climbing into the foothills at the base of the mountains.

It started to rain, and as they gained altitude the air became thinner. Suddenly the driver reined in his horse and spoke in low, urgent tones to Casimir, who jumped down from where he was seated and called for the women to follow him. As they ran up a slope a German personnel carrier roared into view. Casimir flung himself into a snowdrift and the women followed his example, obeying his whispered orders to keep their faces pressed against their hands. The German vehicle slowed, but didn't stop, and continued on its way up the winding mountain road.

When the sound of its engine vanished, Casimir got up and started walking. The women followed him, sleet going down their necks, clothing soaked, feet wet and freezing cold. As they kept climbing the sleet thickened, but Casimir went on, constantly squinting at the sky. He spoke to no one but Janet, and only rarely to her. In the beginning she forced herself to stay up with him but soon found the effort too great and gradually slipped behind. The other women found the going just as rough as they forced themselves upward, their limbs aching from cold, struggling to keep up but finding the gap between themselves and the smuggler constantly widening.

Toward morning Casimir stopped at a broken-down hut, and the women collapsed on its wooden floor.

"This is hell," Genevieve muttered. "I wonder how much longer the journey's going to take?"

Janet glanced at where Casimir sat hunched against the wall, but when he offered no answers, she turned to Keja and asked, "How are you feeling?"

The other woman's face was gray from exhaustion, but she still managed a faint smile, and when she spoke it was with a steadiness that reflected none of the suffering all of them knew she must be experiencing.

"Not being able to urinate is the hardest thing," she said.

"There's no shame in wetting yourself."

"I already have—twice."

The women tried to sleep, but the raw, damp cold made it impossible to get any real rest. Each of them dozed off for brief periods, only to wake suddenly as if warned by a sixth sense of danger. On the last of these occasions Janet opened her eyes to see Casimir hunched over Genevieve, holding a knife, but when he sensed he was being watched he raised a piece of bread he had cut off the Frenchwoman's slab and stuffed it into his mouth. His gesture was so obviously intended to allay Janet's suspicions that it made her uneasy, but Casimir just grinned and said, "It's getting dark. We must move on."

Keja struggled to keep up with the others, but the pain of doing it was so intense that she finally reached a stage where she ceased to care; it was as if she'd become detached from herself and was watching a stranger forcing a path through the snow. Her pants were drenched with urine and constantly chafed. Her feet were blistered, and even though she shivered from the cold, her forehead was filmed with sweat from a burning fever.

At the end of their second night's trek, under Casimir's supervision,

they burrowed into the snow and huddled together for warmth, trying
to find refuge in sleep. But for Keja this proved impossible: a strange
lassitude had settled on her, and she found her mind drifting peacefully
even though her eyes were wide open. Would her child be a boy or girl?
Images of her own upbringing filtered through her mind, of green
pastures and azure skies seen through a tracery of autumn leaves. . . .

"Keja!"

The voice seemed to be coming from a great distance, but when she
looked up she saw Janet standing over her.

"We have to move on," the Englishwoman said.

She grasped Keja's arms and pulled her upright. It was noon and still
snowing, but at least the wind had stopped. Casimir was taciturn as ever
and showed no signs of either hunger or fatigue. Nor did he show the
slightest compassion for his charges. Maybe, Janet thought, it was his
way of surviving.

As the hours passed it began to snow more heavily, and the resulting
lack of visibility made staying together extremely difficult. Whenever
there was a break in the weather, Casimir would stop, glance up at the
surrounding peaks, and, with a sense of direction instilled by hundreds
of crossings, get his bearings and move on.

Finally, when Casimir and Janet, who were in the lead, reached a tiny
lean-to that was used by shepherds for shelter during summer months,
the Englishwoman insisted that they stop and wait until the others
caught up. The smuggler argued that they must keep on, but when
Janet pointed out that Anna and Genevieve were barely visible on the
white slopes below and that Keja was so far behind that she was completely out of sight, he reluctantly agreed to wait one hour.

Squatting in a corner, he folded his arms across his knees, rested his
chin on his arms, and gazed into space. Realizing this was an opportunity to relieve herself, Janet trudged through the snow to the back of
the lean-to, where she found a small walled-off area which she imagined
was used during summer months to pen the animals of shepherds taking
shelter in the open-sided shack. As she started pulling down her pants,
she glimpsed Casimir watching her through a crack in the boards so,
seeking more privacy, she walked a little farther away, to where snow
had gathered in a deep drift against a rock face. It had once been much
higher, but the wind had sheered the top off, causing it to partially
collapse.

She had started to ease down her pants again when she saw what first
appeared to be a jagged branch. When she examined the object more

closely, she saw it was a human hand. Her heart started to thump, and its pace quickened even more when she glimpsed a marking above the wrist: it was of a bird, intricately detailed and once brightly colored, but now grayed by rigor mortis. She vividly remembered having often seen the tattoo on the lower part of Phuro's arm. Shoveling the snow with her hands, she uncovered the body enough to see that the old woman's throat had been cut.

Stunned by her gruesome discovery, Janet struggled to recall the exact words Casimir had used when she questioned him about his early return from the mountain: "There was an accident . . . an ice bridge over a crevasse broke. . . ."

She tried to focus her mind, but the bitter cold had so numbed her faculties that logical thought was virtually impossible. What, for Christ's sake, had Casimir to gain from killing an old woman and a boy? He might have murdered Tibere to steal his money, but that was no reason to kill the other two. What to do now? There was no point in telling the others. They all needed the smuggler to guide them across the Spanish frontier. Without him they didn't stand a chance. But how long could they expect to stay alive with him? If Casimir had killed three people for the relatively small amount of cash Tibere must have been carrying, he wouldn't hesitate to do the same thing to a group of women he knew were carrying jewels worth a fortune. The only question was when and where it would happen.

A movement below caught her attention. Anna and Genevieve were struggling toward the lean-to. Covering Phuro's body with snow, Janet felt in her pocket for the diamonds she had promised to give Casimir after he delivered her and the others safely across the border. They were gone. He must have taken them while she slept. What about the jewels the others were hiding in the seams of their clothes? If he hadn't found them yet, chances were he was just waiting for the right opportunity to make his move, as a thief—or a killer.

These thoughts whirled through her head as she stumbled back through the snow toward the lean-to. When she entered the small open-sided shelter, Casimir looked at her searchingly, but she met his gaze without giving an indication of having found anything out of the ordinary.

"Where is Keja?" she asked.

"Down there," Anna replied, pointing to where the other woman was just visible against the background of snow.

"She's in bad shape," Genevieve said.

"I warned you about the Gypsy woman," Casimir muttered gruffly. "She will bring us all bad luck."

It was late afternoon before Keja arrived at the lean-to, and she looked near the point of collapse. Her face was swollen, skin cracked and bleeding, and her breath came in labored gasps.

"She can't go on," Anna said. Instead of answering, Casimir turned and started out into the snow. It was falling rapidly and half an hour later had become a blizzard. Still Casimir urged them forward, using the shaft of his ice ax to probe patches he suspected of not being strong enough to support their weight. It was while he was doing this that he struck something that gave off a metallic ring, and falling to his knees he scraped with his hands until he uncovered an iron obelisk.

"We've made it!" he announced with unexpected emotion. "This marks the border between France and Spain. I didn't realize we were so close. There's a small hut not too far away where we can rest."

The Englishwoman nodded but didn't say anything. The prospect of spending hours in such close proximity to a man who was certainly a thief, and probably a murderer, was ominous, but she knew there was no other choice, and when he moved on she fell in step behind him.

The cabin Casimir had mentioned was similar in structure to the shelter in which they had spent their first rest period. It was not hidden under a snowdrift, as the other had been, and was clearly visible from quite a distance away, but between it and the place where the women stood was a deep crevasse, the blue ice of which glistened wetly in the rays of the lowering sun.

"We will cross there," Casimir announced, pointing with his ax to where a narrow ice bridge spanned the chasm. "It is quite safe. I have used it many times."

The women inched to the edge of the crevasse and peered into its depths. The sheer walls of ice narrowed from their broad opening at the top to a gap of two or three feet at a point about thirty feet below them.

"I hope he knows what he's talking about," Genevieve said nervously.

"He's been right about everything so far," Anna observed.

"What other choice do we have?" Janet asked.

Casimir uncoiled a rope he had carried slung across his shoulders throughout the crossing and tied it around his waist. Then he buried the shaft of his ax deeply in the snow and used it as an anchor around which to loop the rope. "I will stay on this side while each of you crosses," he said. "Then I will throw you the ax and you can use it as an anchor for me."

Genevieve was the first to cross, and she reached the other side without incident, as did Anna, but when Janet, who insisted on helping Keja, was halfway across there was a loud crack, and the ice bridge started to tremble. Banks of snow at the brink of the crevasse shook loose and fell in powdery showers into the chasm. The Englishwoman held Keja steady until the trembling stopped; then both of them slowly edged their way to where Anna and Genevieve were waiting to grasp them.

Casimir narrowed his eyes as he tried to gauge whether the ice bridge would take his weight: the ice was covered by a thick layer of wind-hardened snow that hid whatever fractures had occurred when the walls of the crevasse shifted. He turned and gazed in the direction from which they had come, as if considering retracing his steps, but the approaching darkness was heavy with clouds that promised another blizzard. As he weighed his chances Janet realized this was the moment she'd been waiting for: they could leave the smuggler where he was, separated from them by the chasm, and make their own way to the nearest village; but there was no guarantee that Casimir wouldn't attempt the crossing without their help, and if he succeeded his retribution was likely to be quick and violent.

She was still considering these options when Casimir tossed her his ice ax and shouted for her to anchor it in the snow. After a moment's hesitation, she buried the shaft and wrapped the rope that was still tied to her waist around it. Casimir eyed the bridge again, then started across it, placing one foot delicately in front of the other so as to disturb the hard pack as little as possible. He was almost across when they heard another crack—this one much louder than the first—and Casimir stopped moving. If he had quickened his step or thrown himself forward, he would have made it safely to the other side, but he waited a fraction of a second too long. The ice bridge collapsed with a roar into the crevasse, and the smuggler fell with it.

Janet closed her eyes to protect them against flying splinters of ice, felt the rope go taut, and was suddenly tugged off her feet. If it hadn't been for the buried ice ax she would have been pulled into the crevasse too, but it slowed her enough so that she was able to dig her heels into the snow and stop herself from sliding.

It was several minutes before the cloud of snow thrown up by the collapsing ice bridge settled enough for any of them to see into the chasm. Janet couldn't move—tension on the rope kept her pinned where she had fallen—but both Anna and Genevieve rushed to the edge of the crevasse and peered into its depths.

Casimir was suspended at the end of the rope about twenty feet below them, swinging in a wide arc that sent him crashing repeatedly into the smooth bluish-white walls of ice. His body was limp. From where they crouched it was impossible to tell whether he was merely unconscious or dead. Both of them grasped the rope in an attempt to pull him up, but it was futile. Even if they had been in good physical condition, lifting the smuggler would have been a herculean task, but weak as they were it was impossible.

Janet felt as if she were being cut in two by the rope, which had torn the flesh from her hands and now threatened to pull her into the crevasse. She braced herself in such a way that the tension of the rope was slightly eased by wrapping it around one leg, allowing her enough slack to untie the knot. Her fingers were numb and her palms slippery with blood, but she managed to loosen her link with the man in the chasm and let go. The rope flailed in the air and disappeared over the edge of the ice. Moments later there was a thud.

Janet limped to the brink of the chasm and peered down at where Casimir's body lay, about thirty feet below. It was trapped face down where the walls of ice narrowed, and the rope hung free in the greenish-blue depths below him. She stared down at the smuggler's motionless form, then got to her feet, aware that Anna and Genevieve were looking at her expectantly.

"There's nothing we can do," she said, and went back to Keja.

The other two couldn't seem to grasp what Janet had said and were slow in crossing to where she waited. Keja hadn't looked into the crevasse or uttered a word since the ice bridge collapsed. She was obviously in very bad shape, but none of them realized just how desperate her situation was until they finally reached the ramshackle shelter Casimir had pointed out to them earlier.

Once inside, Keja sat in a corner, her legs spread in front of her, rocking from side to side and moaning softly. Finally, after what seemed like hours, her cooing trailed away and she appeared to have fallen asleep, but was awakened less than five minutes later by an anguished cry. Amplified by the sheer walls of ice from which it rose, the voice was clearly that of Casimir.

"Oh, God," Anna said, "he's still alive."

She got up and started for the door, but Janet stopped her. "There's nothing we can do for him."

"There must be something—"

"Nothing," Janet repeated firmly. "And if it will make you feel any less guilty, I found Phuro's body in the snow back at the lean-to while I was waiting with Casimir for you two to catch up."

"But he told us they fell," Genevieve said, her face ashen.

"Her throat had been cut, and although I didn't find Tibere or Jonitza, my guess is they were killed, too."

Again, Casimir's voice echoed in the darkness, his words no longer discernible, his cry having become a high-pitched wail that continued for three or four minutes before finally fading away.

"Why would Casimir kill Phuro and the others?" Anna asked. "I mean, what was in it for him?"

"The same thing he wanted from us."

"I don't understand—"

"Show me your jewels," Janet said.

Anna appeared puzzled.

"The stones you hid before Halevi died," the Englishwoman added brusquely.

Anna felt along the cuffs of her snow-drenched work pants. "They're not here," she said.

"And you?" Janet asked, turning to Genevieve.

The Frenchwoman pulled her pants out of her soggy boots and displayed the seams, both of which had been sliced open.

"The only ones he didn't get were Keja's," the Englishwoman said, "and he was probably planning to steal those tonight."

All three of them looked at where Keja was hunched in the corner. They thought she had been sleeping, but now they saw that her eyes were open and filled with pain. A series of spasms racked her body.

"Christ, not here," Janet murmured.

"Is it time?" Anna asked.

The former nurse nodded. "She's going into labor."

12

The only light in the hut came from a candle someone had left there, stuck in an old wine bottle. Genevieve had put some matches in her pocket before leaving the inn at Tarbes, but she almost exhausted them trying to ignite the long-unused wick, and even after she got the flame going it sputtered and was constantly on the verge of going out. But the illumination, although faint, was still enough for Janet to take a closer look at Keja. Because of the difficulty they experienced in removing Keja's clothes, which were stuck to her skin with filth, the examination was perfunctory, but Janet was able to establish that her contractions were taking place at half-hour intervals.

"How long will it be?" Genevieve asked.

"It's hard to say," Janet replied. "Some women take ten or twelve hours; others start the delivery phase much sooner."

"Can we do anything to help her?" Anna wanted to know.

"Just keep her warm and hope to God she holds on until we get to the village Casimir told us about."

When they started to put Keja's clothes back on, she tried to cooperate, but each movement brought a gasp of pain. Yet, when Janet started to untie the strip of cloth from around her neck, Keja stopped her.

"If that thing really does have magical properties," Genevieve said, "now's the time for it to work."

"I'd settle for plenty of hot water, clean linen, and some antiseptic," Janet declared.

During the hours that followed, the women took turns sitting with Keja, each one watching her for as long as she could keep her eyes open, then awakening another to take over. Throughout the long vigil Keja made no attempt to speak and occasionally closed her eyes, only to be jolted awake by another contraction. They occurred every thirty minutes for about four hours, and then stopped. Just before dawn they started again, this time at ten- or twelve-minute intervals.

Anna, whose watch it was, awakened Janet. The nurse had just placed her hand on Keja's belly when the bloody plug in the pregnant woman's cervix burst out of her vagina, followed seconds later by a stream of pinkish liquid.

"Her water's broken," the Englishwoman said. "We've got to get her to that village as quickly as possible."

When they emerged from the hut it was dawn. There was enough light to see they were about a mile away from the village of Irati, which lay under a thick mantle of snow. Janet and Anna made a seat for Keja by clasping wrists, and slowly carried her to the closest building, a farmhouse with a huge overhanging roof. As they approached it dogs set up a howl from somewhere inside, and the wooden shutters swung open to reveal a grizzled old man in a nightshirt, holding a shotgun.

"Get out of here or I'll set the dogs on you!" he shouted in Spanish.

"This woman is having a baby," Janet replied in the same tongue. "Please help us."

"I'm warning you!" the man added threateningly.

"Without a doctor she will die," Janet persisted.

The man at the window looked at Keja, who was hunched over in pain, but the sight did nothing to allay his suspicions, and he was raising his shotgun when an old woman suddenly pushed him aside and peered through the open window.

"Idiot!" she snapped, the word distorted by her absence of teeth. "Go and get Dr. Dominguez. Tell him it's an emergency, and tie up those stupid dogs."

She waited at the window until her husband had secured the dogs and opened the door, then beckoned the women to enter. The old man, now dressed and wearing a beret, stood aside as they passed him at the door, then hurried into the village. They entered a large room with a stone-flagged floor, a huge fireplace in which a log smoldered, some crude wooden furniture, and various farm implements. Keja, who was now having contractions every two or three minutes, lowered herself to the floor and sat with her back against the wall trying not to give in to the pain that engulfed her whole body. The only sound came from the old woman moving around in the loftlike room overhead. When she finally came down a steeply angled ladder that served as stairs, she had unbraided her hair and put in her false teeth. She didn't ask any questions and, after assuring Keja that the doctor wouldn't be long in coming, she disappeared into a large kitchen and clattered some pots and pans.

"Can you hold on?" Janet asked.

Keja nodded.

The Englishwoman glanced quickly at the kitchen, then took a knife from a box under the window and crossed to where Keja was crouched. Without offering an explanation, she cut the seams of the pregnant woman's pants and took out the jewels Keja had hidden there: three large emeralds and an equal number of rubies. Hearing footsteps, she slipped them into her pocket and had returned to the fire by the time the farmer's wife entered from the kitchen carrying a tray of food.

"It isn't much, but at least it's hot," the old woman said, putting plates on the table.

All the women, including Keja, watched with wide eyes as she laid out a spread of boiled potatoes, blood sausage, bread, and hot wine flavored with cloves.

"And this is for the little mother-to-be," the farmer's wife announced, taking a bowl of warm milk to where Keja was seated with her back against the wall. "I put in some molasses, it will give you strength." She crossed herself and glanced up at a crude replica of the Virgin Mary hanging on the opposite wall.

"Is there anywhere she can lie down?" Janet asked.

The old woman nodded toward an alcove on the far side of the room. "It's where my son used to sleep," she said.

As she busied herself moving the sacks of onions and potatoes that occupied the space, Janet and Anna, assisted by Genevieve, helped Keja to her feet and guided her to where the old woman was arranging pillows and a once colorful but now badly faded quilt. When they undressed Keja, the stench of stale urine was overpowering.

"Is there some water we can use to wash her—and ourselves?" Janet asked.

"Of course," the farmer's wife replied. "Believe me, I know how terrible it can be out there on the mountain. My husband was once lost for a week, and when he came home he smelled terrible."

She hurried back into the kitchen, reappearing moments later with a large zinc-lined tub which she placed in front of the fire before vanishing back into the scullery.

"I'd forgotten that people like her exist," Anna said.

"We aren't the first refugees she's seen," Genevieve remarked.

"Meaning what?" Anna asked.

"Nobody does anything for nothing."

"Just once can't you believe that somebody might act out of human decency?"

Before the Frenchwoman could answer, the farmer's wife bustled in carrying an enormous black kettle, from which she poured a stream of steaming water into the tub. She handed Janet a bar of homemade soap. "I'll bring you some towels."

The Englishwoman had the uneasy feeling that Genevieve was right. The farmer's wife was being overly solicitous. Did she expect to be paid? There were still the emeralds and rubies. Converted into pesetas, they would be more than enough to remunerate the old woman, the doctor, and anybody else who contributed to their well-being, for weeks, possibly even months if the true value of the gems could be realized. But in using them they were confronted with the same problem that faced them in Tarbes: the moment it became known they possessed such wealth they would become targets for every unscrupulous person in the village.

Rather than think about the dilemma, Janet washed Keja and spoon-fed her the molasses-sweetened milk.

"There is something I want you to have," Keja murmured. Picking her shirt up off the floor, she reached inside the breast pocket and took out the gold medallion. "It is a talisman I gave to Josef Kandalman. Gypsies believe such things must always remain with either the receiver or the giver and can only be passed along to their children. If I die—"

"You won't!"

"I want you to keep the talisman and one day give it to my child." She pressed the medallion into Janet's hand. Before the English-woman could speak, the door opened to admit the farmer and another man.

"I am Dr. Dominguez," the newcomer announced in heavily accented French. "Manuel, here, tells me my services are urgently needed."

He took out a pair of wire-rimmed glasses, adjusted them on his prominent nose, and looked at where Keja was lying in the alcove. Janet joined the doctor as he examined the pregnant woman and saw immediately that he knew what he was doing. His manner was pompous, and his appearance an odd blend of shabby elegance, but his thin fingers probed with a sensitivity she hadn't expected to find in a village doctor.

"When did the contractions start?" he asked.

"About eight hours ago," Janet replied.

"And her water?"

"It broke soon after dawn."

"She is very weak." He shook his head. "I would prefer to deliver the child at my clinic in the village, but it would be dangerous to move her. Have you any experience in such matters?"

"I am a nurse."

"Is that so?" The doctor looked at Janet over his glasses, then turned his attention back to Keja. "I will need your help," he told the English-woman. "And there isn't any time to lose. Get me plenty of hot water and all the clean linen you can find."

The farmer disappeared through the kitchen door, muttering that somebody had to tend the animals, but his wife, who normally milked the cows, remained to help in heating water and readying sheets.

Keja remained with her eyes open, and when she caught Anna's glance, she called her over to the bedside. Unknotting the colorful strip of cloth from around her neck, she handed it to Anna and said, "Find some flowing water and throw it in. Only then will what I have wished for come true."

Anna hesitated a moment, but remembering what Keja had told her about the importance Gypsies attached to such talismans, she went outside and made her way toward a narrow gorge through which a mountain stream tumbled.

It was early afternoon, but the sun had vanished behind a bank of dark clouds, and the vast panorama they had seen earlier was now hidden by a dense, freezing mist. Leaning over the gorge she held the strip of cloth at arm's length over the roaring torrent and let it drop. It remained visible in the gushing, icy water for a brief moment, whirling like a fallen leaf, then vanished under a thick sheet of ice.

As Anna turned back to the farmhouse it began to snow and she quickened her step, but she stopped short when an anguished cry rent the air. It came from the farmhouse, and had an atavistic quality, like that of a trapped animal. When she stepped inside the house, Anna saw the others gathered around the alcove where Keja lay. Janet was crying, and Genevieve's face was ashen. Even the farmer's wife had averted her eyes, and when Anna joined them she realized why.

Keja lay with her legs spread wide, and resting between them, still joined by the umbilical cord, lay a newborn child. As Anna watched, Dr. Dominguez cut the cord, lifted the baby by its feet, and hit it across the buttocks. There was a long moment of silence, but when he slapped the infant again, it began to cry, and he handed the baby to Janet, who wrapped it in a towel. Then he felt Keja's pulse, looked into her eyes, and pulled the sheet up over her head.

"It was too much for her," he said.

"What about the child?" Anna asked.

"A little girl," Janet said. "Three or four weeks premature, but otherwise healthy."

Anna gazed in wonderment at the baby's tiny wrinkled face, as Dr. Dominguez washed his hands, put on his jacket, and looked down at the sheet-draped body lying in the alcove. "I don't know how she hung on this long," he said. "She was a brave woman. Crossing these mountains in her condition must have been very hard on her. She must have desperately wanted this child to live."

There was silence in the room after he left. When the women finally dried their eyes, Anna asked, "What will we call her?"

"Janna," Genevieve replied.

The others looked at her in surprise.

"A combination of Janet and Anna," she explained. "I thought about it a lot while we were on the mountain. The child should have a name that represents the spirit of those who fought the Germans during the final days of the ghetto. You two were a part of that, and naming the child after you both is a symbol of hope that what the others died for won't be forgotten."

Anna and Janet looked at each other, visibly moved, but before either could reply the farmer's wife bustled in carrying a bowl of warm milk, which she fed to the baby by dipping her little finger in the sugar-sweetened liquid.

"There is a woman in the village who recently lost her baby," the old woman said. "Dr. Dominguez is going to send her here. She will wet-nurse this little one and be glad to earn a few pesetas for doing it."

Pacified by the milk she received from the old woman's finger, Janna stopped squalling and remained quiet as the farmer's wife carried her up the rickety ladder to the loft.

"How are we going to pay the wet nurse?" Genevieve asked when they were alone.

Janet didn't answer. She had already given Dr. Dominguez the smallest of the emeralds she had removed from the seam of Keja's work pants, which left a total of five more stones. It wasn't something she had wanted to do, but the doctor had demanded payment before he would treat Keja, and the Englishwoman had nothing else to offer.

Sure enough, word must have leaked out, because when the wet nurse arrived within the hour she agreed to remain at the farm and provide the baby with nourishment from her own milk-swollen breasts but at an exorbitant price, obviously aware that she was the only woman in the village able to provide the service. And not long afterward, when the village barber, who also served as the local undertaker, arrived with a handcart in which to remove Keja's body in preparation for its burial the following afternoon, he also demanded payment far in excess of his usual fee.

Janet agreed to both their demands because the baby had to be fed and Keja buried, but she refused to hand over any more gems, which is what each of them wanted. Instead, she displayed a single ruby, told them it was the last jewel she possessed, and promised they would both be paid just as soon as she was able to use it as collateral to raise a loan at the village bank.

She didn't have to go in search of the banker; he sidled up to Janet while she was standing at Keja's open grave in the small cemetery at the back of the local church and introduced himself while the priest was still uttering his final benediction.

"I am Señor Ortega," he whispered, crossing himself as the priest sprinkled holy water over the grave. "Manager of the regional branch of Banco de Madrid."

Janet ignored him and continued to look at the crude rough-hewn coffin until the priest finally left and she was able to perform some last rights of her own. Taking out a bottle of wine she had brought from the farm, she poured its contents on the ground around the grave.

"This custom of yours," Señor Ortega commented, pointing to the bottle Janet was holding. "Is it a Polish tradition?"

She shook her head, realizing he must have guessed at her nationality from the conversation in Polish that she and the others had had in an attempt to assuage their grief before the funeral service began.

"I am English," she said. "My friends are French and American."

"I see." He nodded gravely. "And you know it is against the law for anybody to enter Spain without a passport and visa?"

"I'm aware of that," Janet replied.

"Then perhaps I should also tell you that I am a deputy to the Chief Judicial Administrator—"

"Then you won't mind contacting our respective embassies," she interjected.

"I'm afraid that is impossible." He spread his hands in a gesture of hopelessness. "We have been snowed in for over a week, and the telephone lines between here and Pamplona are down. But you must all consider yourselves our guests until the weather clears—"

"The way things have been going, that could prove expensive."

"I have heard." He shook his head sadly. "The people of Irati are kindhearted, but they live a hard life and have learned to make a profit from those who come over the mountains. Greed is a universal human weakness, is it not?" When Janet didn't answer, he added, "Dr. Dominguez talks when he drinks. It was a mistake to give him such a jewel."

"I had no choice."

"You could have come and seen me."

"And now we have found each other?"

"I would be more than happy to arrange a loan."

"Against what collateral?"

"My proposal is simple enough," Ortega said. "I will keep your valuables in the vault at my bank and in return will advance whatever pesetas you need while you are here in Irati."

"And when we leave?"

"Your belongings will be returned to you."

"Less what we owe you?"

"Of course."

"Plus interest?"

He shrugged. "I am in business to make a profit."

"All right," Janet said, realizing she had no choice. "Let's get on with it."

She accompanied him to a low one-story building with a huge over-hanging roof, across the window of which were stenciled the words BANCO DE MADRID. The offices, which were closed, consisted of little more than one room with a counter, behind which was an area containing a desk, some wooden filing cabinets, and a large old-fashioned safe. After ushering Janet inside, Ortega locked the door and led her to where a chair was placed in such a position that she couldn't be seen through the window.

"You have them with you?" he asked.

At first Janet produced only one jewel, the smallest of the remaining two emeralds, forgetting that she had already shown the wet nurse and the undertaker a ruby. Ortega sighed and looked pained. "I am an honorable man, Señorita, and it would be easier for us both if you trusted me. You will receive a receipt for any valuables left in my safekeeping."

She realized that he knew she had more jewels and decided it would be absurd, possibly even dangerous, to continue playing games. Ortega could easily have them arrested, and then they would lose everything. She placed three of the remaining four jewels on his desk. It was late afternoon, and a shaft of sunlight coming through the frost-hazed windows added fire to the gems, making them glow. Ortega appeared mesmerized by their brilliance; he stared at the jewels for a full minute before finally writing out a receipt and handing it to Janet, along with a thick wad of pesetas he took from a desk drawer.

Anna and Genevieve were waiting for her when she returned to the farmhouse, and together they counted the paper money. It amounted to less than one third the value of the smallest gem.

"At least we have enough to keep the wet nurse happy," Anna said.

"And the farmer's wife," Genevieve added. "She's been hinting all day that unless we pay her soon we can start looking for another place to stay."

"I managed to keep one ruby," Janet said wearily. "Maybe Ortega will extend the loan when this runs out."

Rather than discussing their dilemma any more that night, the women agreed to talk about it again in the morning, wrapped themselves in blankets, and lay down around the smoldering fire, in front of which the baby was nestled in a basket. A strong wind had come up and it whistled through cracked boards in the barn next door, setting up an eerie wail that made sleep impossible. All of them were still awake when, just after midnight, the door of the farmhouse was suddenly kicked in by four Guardia Civil carrying submachine guns, which they waved menacingly as they herded the women and the child into the back of an open truck.

13

The truck crawled along at a snail's pace through endless S-turns in its long descent from Irati to the foothills, beyond which lay its destination, the ancient city of Pamplona.

Two of the Guardia Civil rode next to the driver in the warmth of the cab, but there wasn't room for the other two, so they sat hunched in the back of the vehicle along with their prisoners, trying to keep warm in the thin, bitter air by wrapping themselves in their voluminous capes.

Sleep was impossible: the raw wind, added to the constant twists and turns of the truck, precluded resting for any of them except the baby, who snuggled under Janet's thick sweater. Janna slept soundly except when she was hungry, and she went back to sleep once she had been fed.

Janet accomplished these feedings by letting Janna suck on a strip of towel stuck into the neck of a wine bottle filled with milk. It was a technique one of the soldiers demonstrated to her when they had stopped at a farm to put water into the radiator. The farmer, angry at being awakened but impressed by the Guardia Civil's submachine guns, obeyed their orders to provide not only water but also milk, a bottle, and a towel, for which he received no payment. After they resumed their journey down the mountain the friendly soldier, a thick-set man in his early thirties, talked quietly in Spanish with Janet, telling her about his own family and his newborn son.

His friendliness surprised the Englishwoman, particularly after the force he and his companions had displayed in arresting them, but as the night hours passed she began to realize that in spite of his imposing uniform, with its theatrical cape and three-cornered hat made of stiff black oilcloth, he was just a simple man doing a job he didn't always particularly enjoy.

"The war has driven many refugees across the Pyrenees into Spain," he told her, "and the mountain villagers have made a business of cheating them. First they pretend to help, but only long enough to steal their valuables; then they inform us where the illegal entrants are hiding. We have no choice but to make arrests, but it is not always something a man feels good about, particularly when such a small child is involved. Are you its mother?"

Janet shook her head. "She died giving birth."

The soldiers crossed himself. "Things will not be easy for any of you in the days to come."

Evidence of this wasn't long in coming. The jail in Pamplona, where they arrived late the following evening, was filled far beyond its usual capacity by prisoners—men, women, and children—languishing in cells that were so overcrowded there was barely room to lie down. The only toilet facilities were a hole in the floor of each cell, and the stench rising from them was sickening. The women managed to stay together, but as they arrived too late for the evening meal they were obliged to buy bread and milk for Janna from the guards at exorbitant black market prices, using the pesetas Señor Ortega had advanced to Janet. During the ride down the mountain, the Englishwoman had learned from the soldier who befriended her that it was Ortega who had betrayed them, something he had done many times before with other refugees crossing the Pyrenees. This only confirmed what she had already suspected.

Once it became known that she possessed even a few pesetas the prison guards continually pestered her, offering to trade everything from pens to wristwatches, and charging the women for blankets and straw pallets. For a few additional pesetas they roughly cleared other prisoners from a corner of the cell so the newcomers would have enough space to lie down. This action didn't endear the women to their cellmates, who expressed their resentment in low, angry murmurs, but when the lights dimmed and many of the inmates found refuge in sleep, the tension gradually eased as the prisoners who stayed awake turned their attention to other problems.

Prime among these were the fleas that infested the straw pallets and left their victims with massive welts. Janet suffered from this more than either of the other women and was finally forced to hand the baby over to Anna, who rocked the child gently in her arms until she stopped crying. When Janna awoke again about an hour later and needed changing, Anna tore a piece from the bottom of her work shirt, fashioned it into a diaper, and fastened it with a safety pin the wet nurse had provided when she first started breast-feeding the child.

"I like your style," a voice said in English.

Anna turned. A lean blond-haired man in his early twenties was lying on a pallet about fifteen feet away. A stubble of beard on his chin lent a ruggedness to his otherwise sensitive features, the most striking of which were his blue eyes. Gaunt cheeks emphasized his high cheekbones, and he had a quick, easy smile, yet he projected an aura of toughness that made it seem as if his attractive physical appearance was only a facade that hid a much harder core.

"Beggars can't be choosers," she replied.

"They can if they're clever enough." He grinned.

"Well, this one can't anyway," Anna said as she finished diapering the child.

"Just wait till she grows up."

"After such a beginning she's certainly going to be a survivor."

"Sounds like this is your first experience with prison?"

"And my last, I hope."

He laughed. "This is a palace compared with Miranda de Ebro."

Anna looked puzzled.

"The internment camp where Spanish authorities send foreigners," he explained.

"Sounds like you know all about it."

"I ought to, after spending over eight months there."

"Why are you here?" she asked.

"I escaped. It's a hobby of mine. The Jerries had me in five different *Offlags* but I broke out of them all." He got up and offered his hand. "Derek Southworth, Pilot Officer, Royal Air Force. I was shot down over France in the summer of 'forty-two."

"Anna Maxell."

"Are you English?"

Anna hesitated. "I learned to speak English in school," she hedged.

Southworth motioned to where Janet and Genevieve were dozing fitfully on their pallets. "Are those two your friends?"

She nodded. "We crossed the Pyrenees together. The Guardia Civil arrested us at a village in the mountains."

"Illegal entry?"

"Yes."

"Like most of the others here."

"What will happen to us?" she asked.

"They'll parade you in front of a judge, go through the motions of a hearing, and bundle you off to Miranda de Ebro," he said.

"You make it sound awful."

"It's a hellhole." He saw her turn pale and added in a more upbeat tone, "But the place gets more tolerable once you learn the ropes."

Janna uttered a series of quick sobs but didn't open her eyes.

"She's dreaming," Southworth said, picking up the baby's tiny hand between his thumb and forefinger.

"Nightmares, more likely," Anna said.

Southworth stood looking at the sleeping child; then he returned to his pallet, put his hands under his head, and immediately went to sleep. The abruptness of his departure left Anna with a vaguely unsettled feeling, as if she'd somehow been dismissed.

An hour later she was relieved by Genevieve, who bundled the baby inside her sweater while Anna slept. None of the women seemed to possess maternal instincts, and the Frenchwoman was visibly nervous each time she handled Janna, yet she still did her best to care for the child, even though her diaper generally remained unchanged during Genevieve's watch.

Soon after it got light there was a commotion among the prisoners as the guards roughly hauled Derek Southworth to his feet, handcuffed him, and dragged him away down the corridor. When he saw that the Frenchwoman was watching him, he flashed her a quick smile and winked.

Not long afterward the same guards came for the women. With the baby, they were escorted to a van waiting in the courtyard of the prison and transported to an ancient stone building near the center of Pamplona. Three judges in black robes were holding court. Janet was carrying the baby in her arms as they appeared in front of the bench behind which the judges sat, and when they realized she was the only one of the prisoners who spoke Spanish, they addressed themselves directly to her.

"You are charged with entering Spain illegally," the oldest of the judges declared. "How do you plead?"

"I am English," Janet replied calmly. "My friends are French and American. We have been denied the opportunity of contacting our respective embassies—"

"That is a matter for the court clerk," the judge interjected. "He will take all the relevant details and convey them to the proper authorities. Now, how do you plead?"

"It is true that we entered the country without documentation, but—"

"I have no choice but to order you held at Miranda de Ebro until such time as there is a response from your respective embassies," the judge concluded.

He nodded to two Guardia Civil, who escorted the women to a small annex next to the court. There a fussy middle-aged man, who identified himself as the court clerk, carefully noted their particulars, assuring them repeatedly that the information would be passed along to the proper embassies. But when it came to Janna he looked puzzled. "You claim the baby was born in Spain?"

"At the village of Irati," Janet replied.

The clerk looked at Anna, who was now holding the infant.

"And she is the mother?"

Janet didn't answer immediately. She knew that if she said that Janna was the offspring of a Gypsy, this identity could harm her in wartorn Europe. Anna didn't understand Spanish and wasn't aware of what the clerk was asking, so there seemed little harm in bending the truth.

"Yes," Janet replied, "the baby's name is Janna Maxell. Her mother is an American citizen. I want the United States Embassy to be informed."

The clerk took another look at Anna and the child, then turned his attention back to his notes and recorded what Janet had told him with neat, careful strokes of his pen.

From the clerk's office the women were marched through the streets of Pamplona to the railway station, where they were put on a passenger train in a coach filled with peasants carrying bulky packages, baskets, crates, and hens with their legs tied. The two guards accompanying the women removed their handcuffs but chained their ankles, and then they settled back in the hard wooden seats with their three-cornered hats lowered over their eyes, as the train lurched out of the station.

◇

Their first glimpse of the infamous internment camp came in late afternoon when the train was between Burgos and Vitoria, and from a distance the neat whitewashed barracks didn't appear too daunting. Even after the train stopped and they shuffled off under the supervision of their guards, there was no immediate evidence to lend credence to the ominous description they had received from both Southworth and the peasants on the train.

The camp was flanked by a series of barbed-wire fences along which, at widely separated intervals, stood soldiers with submachine guns slung over their shoulders. The Guardia Civil troopers marched their prisoners through the main gate and didn't remove the women's manacles until they reached the administration building.

The Commandant, a tall, extremely slender man in his early fifties with carefully groomed silver-white hair and penetrating brown eyes, spoke both English and French fluently, a skill he took pride in displaying as he interrogated the newly arrived prisoners.

Opening a large envelope one of the guards had brought from Pamplona, he took out a carbon copy of the notes the court clerk had made and asked in slightly accented English, "Which of you is Janet Taylor?"

"I am," the Englishwoman replied, taking a step forward.

"You are a British citizen?"

"Correct," she said, "and I insist that our respective embassies—"

"That is a matter for the courts in Pamplona," he interjected curtly. "Meanwhile you will remain here at Miranda de Ebro." He returned his attention to the notes. "Genevieve Fleury?"

The Frenchwoman raised her hand.

"Parlez-vous anglais?" he asked.

She nodded.

"Then I will make things simpler by using that language."

"As you wish." Genevieve shrugged. Her English was more heavily accented than the Commandant's.

"And you must be Anna Maxell," he said, turning to Anna, who was holding the baby. "Are you the mother of that child?"

"She is," Janet assured him before Anna could respond. Anna glanced at her with a puzzled expression, but didn't say anything.

"And you claim the infant was born in Spain?"

"At the village of Irati," Janet replied. "This can be confirmed by Dr. Dominguez—"

"Perhaps," the Commandant said, "but it is of little consequence unless you can prove the father was a Spanish citizen."

"He wasn't," the Englishwoman replied.

"Then the child has no legal status in this country." When Janet remained silent, the Commandant asked, "Where is the father?"

The question was addressed to Anna, and she glanced quickly at Janet before saying, "He was killed."

"Where?"

"In the Warsaw ghetto."

The Commandant raised his eyebrows. "You are Jewish?"

"Yes."

"But it says here you are an American."

"It is possible to be both."

"And the baby's father?"

"It was possible for him too," she replied.

"That is why it is important that the United States Embassy in Madrid be informed," Janet persisted.

The Commandant slammed his fist on the desk and angrily summoned two guards, who marched the women to a small building with a corrugated iron roof, where another guard issued them eating utensils and thin blankets before assigning them to a barracks.

The women found themselves in a huge concrete structure containing a series of small cubicles which housed up to three people. The prisoner in charge of the barracks, called a *cabo,* was an obese woman with a frizz of blond hair that was constantly in a state of tangled disarray. She wore a loose-fitting garment that had been fashioned from a blanket and a pair of men's boots that were unlaced.

"I run this place," she announced, first in Spanish and then, when Janet began to translate, in guttural English. "What I say goes! Understood?"

The women nodded.

"If you've got money I can obtain anything you want."

"I'd like a place to lie down and some milk for the baby," Anna said.

The fat woman, whom the other prisoners had nicknamed "Countess de Cabo" because of the genteel air she often affected, held out her fleshy hand, rubbing her thumb and forefinger together. Janet handed her the few pesetas she still possessed, and the Countess ambled down the walkway through billowing woodsmoke to a small cubicle already occupied by three other women. Pulling aside the blanket that functioned as a door, she issued orders in Hungarian, and the other occupants sullenly gathered up their few possessions and abandoned the tiny space.

Anna, who would normally have protested such an unfair eviction, was too exhausted to care about ethics, and handing the baby to Janet she flopped down on one of the straw-filled pallets the other women had left behind. Still holding Janna, Janet settled on another, but when Genevieve tried to enter the cubicle the Countess blocked her way.

"Three to each cubicle," she growled.

"But there are only two," the Frenchwoman protested.

"Two adults and one child makes three," the fat woman said. "I'll make room for you with me."

Genevieve sensed that the other woman's interest in her was sexual but, after the briefest hesitation, decided she didn't care: she'd had sex with women before and would do so again if it would help them to survive. Clearly, there were advantages to being the lover of a woman who had some power in the camp.

She followed the Countess to the far end of the barracks where, as *cabo,* she was permitted to have a cubicle to herself. It contained two mattresses, and Genevieve guessed she wasn't the first prisoner to attract the fat woman's attention. What did surprise her was the elegance with which the space was furnished: pieces of faded silk draped the walls; three crystal wineglasses stood on a small table; and lithographs of paintings by several great masters hung over the straw pallets. There were also some photographs in glass frames, sepia prints blurred by age, all of the same woman but taken at different periods of her life.

The Countess noticed Genevieve's interest and handed her one of the photographs. It showed a young woman wearing a bathing costume posed on the steps of a wheeled hut on the pebbled shore of some seaside resort.

"It was taken at Sevastopol in the summer of 1923," the fat woman said, adding with a sigh, "How I loved bathing in the Black Sea."

Genevieve returned the picture and tried to hide her surprise by admiring the crystal wineglasses.

"They are all that is left from a house that was one of the most beautiful in all Russia," the Countess said wistfully. "It was destroyed in the revolution, as was my whole family." She glanced at the lithographs. "The originals were owned by my father."

"They are very lovely," Genevieve murmured.

"So are you, my dear," the other woman said.

The Frenchwoman readied herself for the proposition she was sure was about to come, but instead the Countess handed her an empty wine bottle and motioned her to follow.

It was dusk, and the camp had turned into a galaxy of lights: from the windows of other barracks, from searchlights sweeping the barbed-wire fences, from the tiny flames of hundreds of candles other prisoners had lit and were using to find their way along the slatted wooden walkways that linked the various buildings. The smell of hot olive oil hung heavy in the night air, and from one of the barracks came the wheezing strains of a Bach prelude being played on a concertina.

"Stay close," the Countess instructed, "and leave the talking to me."

They had reached a barracks that was known as the Hangar because it housed mainly pilots who had been shot down during Allied missions over Europe and had somehow managed to reach Spain. The man in charge was a tall fair-haired young Englishman wearing a faded blue RAF tunic with insignias on the epaulets that signified his rank of Pilot Officer. Genevieve immediately recognized him as the man from their cell in the Pamplona jail who had winked at her as the guards dragged him away. It was also immediately apparent that Derek Southworth remembered her, because he grinned and said, "A woman as beautiful as you doesn't need money to do business here."

The Countess waited as Southworth scooped milk from a galvanized steel cylinder and poured it into the empty wine bottle Genevieve was carrying. Then in spite of Southworth's insistence that the milk be his gift to Genevieve, she hurriedly paid him and hustled her charge out of the barracks.

"Be careful of that man," she warned as they made their way back along the wooden walkways.

"But, why?" the Frenchwoman asked, "He's so attractive,"

"Just take my word," the other woman snapped. "Stay away from him."

The anger remained in the Countess's voice as she described how the inmate hierarchy was structured: a group known as the Expatriates considered themselves rulers of the camp and controlled most of the worthwhile tasks, which they allotted to whoever was willing to pay for them. They were largely men who had fought in the Spanish Civil War and were still bitter at the harsh treatment they had received from the Falangists.

"They hate outsiders," the Countess warned.

She went on to describe how a man known as Patrón led the Expatri-

ates, assisted by an inmate referred to by the others as *la comadreja*
because of his reputation for ruthless brutality.

"They aren't passing through," the fat woman said. "This camp is
their home, and they run it their way. But Derek Southworth refuses
to accept their authority and has set up his own black market operation.
There are rumors that he escaped from camp a few weeks ago to avoid
being killed by *la comadreja*. Now that he is back, everybody knows that
sooner or later there will be a showdown between the two."

The Countess didn't explain why she'd gone to the Hangar for milk
instead of obtaining it from one of the vendors who hawked their goods
at the barbed-wire fences, and Genevieve didn't ask. Instead, she took
the milk to the cubicle, where Anna and Janet were trying to quiet
Janna's hunger cries, and watched as the Englishwoman transferred the
milk to a bottle with a rubber nipple that a peasant woman on the train
from Pamplona had given them. Minutes after being fed, Janna fell
contentedly asleep.

"God knows where her next meal's coming from," Anna said.
"We've used up our pesetas."

"We can always sell this," Janet said, taking out the single ruby she
had hidden from Señor Ortega.

"Can we risk attracting that kind of attention?"

"Don't worry," Genevieve assured them, "I'll make sure that we
don't go hungry."

Taking a long look at the sleeping child, the Frenchwoman turned
and quickly walked back to where the Countess was waiting in her
cubicle. She had undressed and was lying under a blanket on her
straw-filled pallet. Handing a small glass of cognac to Genevieve, she
said, "To a profitable future for us both."

"I'll be happy just to survive," Genevieve answered, clicking glasses
and sipping the brandy.

The Countess watched the Frenchwoman undress, taking careful
inventory of her firm breasts, trim waist, slender legs, tight buttocks,
and thick dark thatch of pubic hair. Genevieve felt herself being examined and when she was naked turned to face the other woman, expecting her to begin making advances. But the Countess merely said, "You
are going to make us both rich"—and, draining her glass, she blew out
the candle.

14

The schedule in Miranda de Ebro included a dawn roll call at the main parade ground nicknamed by prisoners "Plaza Generalísimo Franco," where prisoners were required to stand at attention as the Spanish flag was raised and join in singing a discordant rendition of the Spanish national anthem.

Janet learned from other inmates after her first of these assemblies that nearly fifty nationalities were incarcerated in the internment camp. Many of them were permanent detainees, like the Expatriates; others were transients who had entered Spain illegally and were being held until arrangements could be made to ship them back to their countries of origin. In some instances, such as with Gypsies and Jews, this involved their being returned to face almost certain death in German concentration camps, a fate that Janet realized might well lie ahead for Anna if she couldn't prove her American citizenship. It also dawned on Janet that she might unwittingly have made a terrible mistake in identifying Anna as the mother of Keja's child, for if Anna was returned to Poland, the baby would certainly be sent with her.

Anna must also have been aware of this possibility, but she made no mention of it, continuing instead to focus all her energies on caring for Janna, which was no easy task. The barracks were constantly filled with smoke from improvised stoves, about which the guards did nothing, even though it was against the rules to have them, and the camp was infested with all kinds of vermin, as well as numerous stray dogs, which many inmates kept as pets until hunger drove their masters to kill them for food.

Dog meat was considered a luxury by prisoners subsisting on a small daily ration of "roncho," a greasy mixture of cabbage and beans in lukewarm water on top of which floated a thick layer of olive oil. Daily consumption of this slop took its toll in the form of a diarrhea the inmates called "Miranditis," which both Anna and Janet began suffering from within days of being interned, and that necessitated hourly trips to latrines located in a building on the opposite side of camp. Both men and women used these facilities—holes cut in the stone floor—without benefit of any privacy.

Making matters worse was the incessant rain, which began at the end of their first week at Miranda de Ebro and continued unabated for weeks. It turned the already muddy camp into a swamp where the only means of getting around was by walking on the slatted wooden walkways—which actually began to float, but sank whenever more than one prisoner stood on the same plank. After a time this continual bending caused many sections of the wood to break away completely, leaving gaps that could be crossed only by wading through knee-deep slime.

Anna and Janet did what they could to care for the baby and also looked after each other. Because she existed almost exclusively on milk, Janna did not experience the gastrointestinal problems that plagued her guardians. Whenever one woman had to make the dreaded journey to the latrines, the other stayed behind with the baby, a system which ensured that Janna was never alone. On the rare occasions when both had to relieve themselves at the same time and couldn't wait, Genevieve was summoned to look after Janna.

The Frenchwoman, like the baby, was also immune to the acute diarrhea which afflicted her two friends and most of the other prisoners in camp, a resistance that she attributed to the fact that, like the baby, her diet also did not include roncho. From the first day she took the young Frenchwoman under her wing, the Countess had ensured this by purchasing all their food either from vendors or black marketeers, who had ample supplies of bread, olives, cheese, chicken, fruit, and milk but at prices that were so inflated few in the camp could afford them.

The fat woman bought these supplies with money from a thick wad of pesetas she kept in a money belt that was always fastened around her ample stomach. When Genevieve insisted on sharing her portion of the food with Anna and Janet, the Countess didn't object, particularly when it came to keeping the baby supplied with fresh milk, for she made no secret of the fact that she had a soft spot in her heart for all children. But when she bluntly informed Genevieve that it was time for her to start earning her keep, it was clear that the Countess's largesse wasn't born of charity.

"I've carried you until now, because even though you have all the right equipment for the job I have in mind, it wasn't in the best working shape," she said. "I knew that could be remedied with rest and plenty of good food, but getting you what you needed has cost me a lot of money, and it's time that I get a return on my investment."

"Don't worry, Madame," Genevieve replied stiffly, "you won't be disappointed."

The following afternoon Genevieve began "work" by strolling the Promenade des Anglais, an area of the camp where the privileged inmates congregated while buying assorted goods from the vendors— everything from food to cigarettes and rum. In a camp like Miranda de Ebro, "privileged" meant two things: the prisoners were not hard-core inmates serving sentences for either political or criminal acts, and they possessed enough money to exist on purchases made on the black market.

These perquisites included enjoying the services of prostitutes whom the guards brought in from outside the camp, an arrangement facilitated through bribes paid by the two groups competing for control of all black-market operations inside the camp. The guards didn't care whether their payoffs came from Patrón or Derek Southworth; even the Commandant, who received a percentage of all bribes, didn't seem to be concerned. He knew that it was easier for him to let the prisoners settle their own differences than attempt to defuse them and risk disrupting a lucrative source of illicit revenues.

Genevieve's appearance on the Promenade des Anglais was noteworthy in more ways than one: not only did it excite the ardor of prisoners who had learned to settle for the much-used local whores, it also attracted the immediate attention of both Patrón and Southworth.

The Countess had planned the debut of her protégée very carefully: not only was she in top physical condition, which immediately set her apart from all other female inmates, she was also beautifully dressed and immaculately groomed. This the Countess achieved by hiring two gifted prisoners to work their magic on Genevieve. One had formerely worked as a seamstress for a leading Paris designer; the other had been a much-sought-after hairdresser on the Côte d'Azur before the war.

Virtually overnight, the silk hangings in the Countess's cubicle were converted into a number of well-styled dresses that clung to every curve of the Frenchwoman's voluptuous body, and her hair was coiffed in a soft, lightly waved style.

Not only those strolling the Promenade des Anglais were affected by Genevieve's initial appearance. Word spread like wildfire, and men from half a dozen barracks hurried to the south side of camp for a glimpse of the phenomenon. They stood in clusters, some openly ogling her, other just silently staring, mesmerized by a sight they had been denied so long. They had forgotten a woman could look so beautiful. For these men Genevieve wasn't an object of sexual fantasy as much as a reminder of times they had once known but long ago forgotten. In passing, she left the faintest trace of a perfume the Countess had dug out of an ancient wooden box in which she stored her few personal possessions; the men inhaled its sweet fragrance with long, deep breaths. After the stench of mud and latrines, woodsmoke and unwashed bodies, the scent transported them for a fleeting moment to other places and happier times.

Derek Southworth was the first of the seigneurs to make his appearance. He sauntered up to the Countess, hands in his pockets, exuding a casualness designed to suggest that he was taking a stroll and had just happened by the Promenade des Anglais. "Not bad," he commented, watching Genevieve parading in front of the large crowd.

"Real class," the fat woman said. "Just what the camp needs."

"Maybe."

"They think so," the Countess said, nodding toward the men gazing longingly at her protégée.

"They can look," Southworth said. "But nobody touches until I say so."

"I've got a lot invested in her. . . ."

"You manage her, I take a piece off the top."

"Patrón might see things differently," she said, looking across at where the leader of the Expatriates was also watching Genevieve.

"Fuck him," Southworth declared. "Either she works for me or not at all."

Before the Englishman was out of sight, *la comadreja,* the thickset man who was Patrón's enforcer, appeared at the Countess's side. "The boss wants you," he muttered gruffly.

The fat woman followed him to where Patrón was standing apart from the rest of the crowd, a grim expression on his face.

"Your *puta* is on my territory," he said hoarsely.

"The Promenade des Anglais is neutral ground—"

"Don't give me that crap! If you want her to work anywhere in this camp, I get a commission."

"For what?"

"Protection."

"Can you guarantee it?" the Countess asked.

"You know the boss runs this place," *la comadreja* said.

"Southworth doesn't think so."

"Piss on him! His days are numbered. Count on it." The enforcer spit out the words with a vehemence that sprayed saliva.

"I am," the fat woman assured him calmly. "And the moment he's gone I'll start paying your boss protection money."

She turned away and motioned Genevieve to follow her.

"What was all that about?" the Frenchwoman asked when they were back in their cubicle.

"You'll see," the Countess said.

"But I had a lot of good offers."

"And they'll get better the longer we wait."

"I don't think—"

"You don't have to," the fat woman interrupted brusquely. "I'll do the brainwork for both of us. You just obey orders. Understood?"

The other woman's anger frightened Genevieve. While visiting the latrines she had overheard a conversation between two women inmates, one of whom had provoked the Countess's wrath a few weeks earlier. The Countess had used her influence to ensure that the woman was moved to a particularly unpleasant part of the camp, and away from her infant son. Remembering this incident, Genevieve murmured, "Whatever you say."

"It will all work out for the best, believe me," the Countess added in a softer tone.

Within hours the whole camp knew that a confrontation between Patrón and Southworth was imminent and that it was only a matter of time before the struggle for dominance finally erupted. Both men were known for their cunning, and each surrounded himself with aides whose job it was to protect him. Excitement mounted as everybody speculated on the outcome: most favored Patrón because they believed him more vicious, but a few gambled on Southworth because the odds against him were so great. All knew that, no matter who triumphed, they would still be left with a man whose greed ruled their lives, so neither man was the sentimental favorite.

When the anticipated showdown between the two still hadn't taken place by late the next day, the Countess instructed Genevieve to put on another silk dress, one with a neckline that showed her firm breasts, have her hair coiffed by the hairdresser, and take a second leisurely stroll along the Promenade des Anglais. By now everybody realized the fat woman was using her protégée to taunt Patrón and Southworth, but no one knew why she wanted to trigger a conflict between the two men. Some suspected her motive was revenge for excessive commissions she'd been forced to pay both men on her illicit dealings in the past, while others were convinced she merely wanted to force a showdown so she would only have to pay protection money to a single winner. All agreed it was brilliant strategy on the Countess's part—she would profit whatever the outcome—but nobody made any offers for Genevieve's sexual favors; they all realized that none would be forthcoming until the conflict between Patrón and Southworth was finally resolved.

That night the Frenchwoman visited Janet and Anna in their cubicle at the other end of the barracks. Both were still suffering from stomach problems, but their diarrhea was no longer acute, and they had been able to cut down on their visits to the dreaded latrines. She arrived bearing gifts of fresh bread, spicy blood sausage, goat cheese, oranges, a bottle of Anis del Mono, and some milk for the baby. Ironically, Janna had put on weight since arriving in camp and was no longer the undersized infant she had been.

"She's got the same hair as Keja," Genevieve observed, trailing her fingers through the child's fine blond curls.

"And her eyes are just as beautiful as her mother's," Anna added.

"One thing she hasn't inherited is Keja's passive nature," Janet said. "Less than six weeks old and she's already stubborn as a mule. This is one little girl who is going to be a self-willed woman. God help the man who tries to tame her!"

The Frenchwoman laughed, glad to be back with her old friends.

"You look pale," Anna observed. "Is everything all right?"

"Why shouldn't it be?" Genevieve said.

"No reason. . . ."

Janet was more blunt. "We've heard the Countess is using you."

"Only because I allow it," the Frenchwoman replied.

"But why?"

"I have my reasons."

"We appreciate what you're doing for both us and the baby. . . ." Anna's voice trailed away.

"It's just that we care about you and are concerned," Janet added.

Genevieve's expression softened. "Don't be, I can take care of myself." She offered Janna her little finger and was surprised by the strength with which the baby gripped it. "You're right about her," she said. "Once she finds what she wants in life, there's going to be no taking it away from her."

When Genevieve returned to her cubicle the Countess was asleep, but she'd left the candle burning, and in its fragile light the Frenchwoman once again studied the photographs that stood in glass frames on a small table, comparing the delicate beauty of the girl in the sepia prints with the bloated features of the woman who was snoring on the straw-filled mattress. It seemed impossible that they were the same person. Genevieve experienced a sudden wave of apprehension as she blew out the candle and climbed under her blanket. For a long time she lay with her eyes open, listening to the cacophony of night sounds: vendors hawking their wares; sentries calling to each other; and, just before sleep enveloped her, a terrible scream that rose in a shrieking crescendo before finally being absorbed into the darkness.

The source of this anguish was revealed soon after dawn when the entire camp gathered for roll call on the parade ground and saw Derek Southworth hanging from the wooden door of a building used for storing mattresses. He had been crucified by nails driven through his wrists and ankles but was still half-conscious. The prisoners stared at him numbly. Unwilling to go to his aid and risk the severe punishment that would result from breaking ranks, they remained at attention in the gray light, letting Southworth stay where he hung until the Commandant arrived for the raising of the colors.

He issued orders to the guards, but it took them at least fifteen minutes to get the Englishman down. First they tried to pry out the nails with bayonets, and when that failed they used the butts of their submachine guns. Finally, the Commandant sent one of them to the carpenter's shop for a claw hammer with which they successfully completed the job. But instead of rushing Southworth to the military infirmary just outside the camp's main gate, the Commandant let him writhe in the mud.

While the Englishman suffered, the Commandant gave a rambling speech for almost half an hour and concluded by saying, "The persons responsible for this breach in camp discipline will be found and executed."

Only then did he let Southworth go, but instead of sending him to the infirmary the Commandant told the guards to take the Englishman to the *calabozo,* a stone structure with a corrugated iron roof that was built in such a way as to make it impossible to stand upright or lie down.

"Pauvre homme," Genevieve murmured as Southworth was dragged away.

"Save your pity," the Countess replied. "He isn't dead yet."

15

In the days that followed Southworth's crucifixion, the atmosphere in the camp was strained, as if the prisoners felt angry at having been denied a definitive conclusion to the contest. While both antagonists still lived nothing had really been resolved. Once the Englishman was released from the *calabozo* and recovered from his wounds, the situation between him and Patrón would be exactly as it was before.

This sense of frustration continued for ten days, until Southworth was finally released from his prison and carried by his comrades from the Hangar back to their barracks. He was a terrible sight. Genevieve saw him carried past as she was walking with the Countess near the Promenade des Anglais. He appeared half dead, but when he saw the Frenchwoman he still managed a feeble thumbs-up gesture.

"He's mad," the fat woman muttered.

"But very brave," Genevieve said.

"There's little difference between the two," the Countess replied.

During the weeks in which Southworth was recuperating the fat woman forbade her protégée to appear at the Promenade des Anglais, encouraging her instead to spend her days visiting Anna, Janet, and the baby.

"Sooner or later their embassies will arrange for them to be released," the Countess said, "so you might as well make the best of your time together while they are here. Once they leave, their lives will go in very different directions from yours. War is a great leveler, but when the fighting stops even the closest friendships are forgotten."

"You're wrong, madame," Genevieve countered. "We've been through too much together for that to happen."

"Believe me," the other woman assured her, "you will find I am right. These friends of yours aren't like you or me. Society will embrace them when the war is over, while we will always be considered outcasts. That is why we must be cleverer, and ready to take advantage of whatever opportunities present themselves."

The Countess delivered her words with such fervor that the Frenchwoman couldn't help wondering if they were triggered by a jealousy of her friendship with Anna and Janet. Her mentor had never once made any kind of sexual advance, or expressed even the vaguest emotional attachment, but she had said she expected a return on her investment of time and money. Cash hadn't begun to flow yet, but the Countess clearly assumed it would just as soon as the conflict between Patrón and Southworth was resolved.

This finally occurred sometime during the early hours of Christmas Day, 1943. There had been a pathetic attempt in some barracks to evoke a holiday spirit by making paper chains out of newspaper strips and decorating a few small pine trees the prisoners purchased from guards, but the effort was halfhearted and made even more so by the Commandant's announcement over the camp loudspeaker that he had refused a request by some inmates to sing carols in their barracks.

"There will be no easing of camp rules," he declared. "I expect all prisoners to follow the camp schedule just as they would on any other day."

Even though Genevieve still wasn't producing any income, the Countess provided her with enough money to buy small gifts for her friends. These consisted of milk, smoked bacon, bread, fruit, fresh vegetables, a small cake, and brandy, but the *pièce de résistance* was a doll the Countess dug out of her battered trunk and carefully wrapped in a threadbare silk scarf.

"I've had it a long time," she said. "Now I would like to see it go to another child."

Genevieve tried to persuade her benefactor to accompany her to the other cubicle and give the doll to Janna herself, but she refused. "They are your friends," she said. "This will probably be the last Christmas you will ever spend together. It is not a time for outsiders."

The Frenchwoman sensed that the Countess's loneliness went deeper than merely being on her own: she had learned to accept her isolation from society and wore it with a kind of arrogant pride.

"It's exquisite!" Anna exclaimed when she saw the doll. "I've never seen one so beautifully made."

The porcelain face of the doll was so finely crafted it looked human; with its blue eyes and blond hair, it was almost a replica of the child to whom it was given. Only its clothes differed. They were made of a rich fabric with raised patterns in gold and silver, while Janna wore an ill-fitting garment Anna had fashioned from the tattered blanket that served as their door.

"It's very old," Janet said, examining the doll closely. "Probably from Dresden, although the clothes look Russian."

Genevieve poured brandy into their tin mugs and proposed a toast: "To our friendship, may it endure and grow stronger throughout the coming years."

"To the memory of absent loved ones," Anna added, her eyes suddenly filled with tears.

"And to Janna, whose heritage will be all we can give her," Janet said, looking at the sleeping child.

They raised their mugs, clinked them together, and drank the contents. As Genevieve was pouring more brandy, Anna cut the small cake the Frenchwoman had brought and Janet arranged the rest of the food.

"This is my first Christmas," Anna said.

The others looked at her in surprise.

"It isn't a holiday Jews celebrate," she explained.

"We won't tell anybody." Genevieve laughed.

"And I think God will make allowances," Janet added, her pale cheeks already flushed from the brandy she'd drunk.

By the time they finished the bottle, all of them were light-headed. Despite the Commandant's ruling, they sang carols and told each other stories remembered from their childhoods. When it was finally time for Genevieve to leave, she embraced her two friends, kissing them on both cheeks as she wished them the season's greetings. It was an emotional moment, one that could quickly have turned to tears if the Frenchwoman hadn't quickly departed, leaving the others to finish what was left of the food.

As she walked across the damp stone floor of the barracks, Genevieve remembered the Christmases she'd had as a child, but she couldn't recall a single happy one. She had spent the holidays delivering laundry to her mother's clients, usually to the back doors of houses that were brightly lit and gaily decorated, but into which she could see only by peering through the windows from the street. This time, in spite of her surroundings, at least she hadn't been on the outside looking in.

When Genevieve returned to her cubicle the Countess appeared to be sleeping, but then she noticed the other woman's eyes flicker and guessed she was only feigning sleep. Kneeling next to her mentor's mattress she murmured, *"Merci, madame, et joyeux noël."*

An hour or two before dawn there was a sudden rattle of tin cans, followed by a fusillade of machine-gun fire, shattering the night silence. Searchlights turned darkness into day. The din awakened everybody in camp, but as the curfew was still in effect and the penalty for breaking it was death, nobody dared leave the barracks to investigate the cause of the ruckus. Speculation ran rife—rumors ranged from an attempted escape to trigger-happy guards—but the smart money was on the disturbance's being linked in some way to the bitter feud between Patron and Southworth.

The truth, revealed as the prisoners gathered for their morning ritual on the parade ground, was so gruesome that many of those assembled found it hard to accept. The post-dawn light seeping across the camp fell on the naked bodies of Patrón and *la comadreja,* sprawled across the barbed-wire fence that surrounded the camp. Their corpses were riddled with bullets and still dribbled blood.

It seemed as if they had been shot while attempting to scale the fence, but closer examination established that their wrists and ankles had been tied to the wire with lengths of cord. But the prisoners were puzzled by the many tin cans, each containing stones, which had been attached to the barbed wire alongside each man, and the large metal biscuit tins, such as those that come in Red Cross parcels, which had been attached with electrical tape to each man's stomach. It appeared that Patrón and his enforcer were carrying precious contraband close to their stomachs when they were struck by bullets fired by guards manning the watchtowers.

The real horror of what had happened wasn't established until after the Commandant had performed the morning ceremonies, which he carried out without once glancing in the direction of the two dead men. Even after the flag was raised, he still chose to ignore the spectacle and led the prisoners in singing the Spanish national anthem. When the last echoes of this discordant chant died away, he let the inmates stand in tension-filled silence for another full minute before announcing, "These men broke the rules and paid the consequences. Let it be a warning to you all."

Only after the Commandant had returned to the administration building did four guards cut down the bodies. It was evident from the stiffness of the victims' limbs that rigor mortis had set in, and a French doctor among the inmates whispered that they must have been dead for hours. The manner of their demise only became known some hours later, and its revelation sparked disgust and some words of praise among the prisoners.

Patrón and his enforcer had been enticed to a rendezvous with three prostitutes whose relationship with the guards gave them a free run of the camp, a privilege for which they paid their benefactors—and Derek Southworth—a large percentage of their earnings. These women had let it be known that they were dissatisfied with the way the Englishman was treating them and were looking for protection from the Expatriates. Not realizing they were walking into a trap, Patrón and *la comadreja* were cornered by Southworth and fellow members of the Hangar, silenced by having tape stuck over their mouths, stripped naked, and partially flayed. The skin had been peeled from their stomachs, and tins containing starving rats were secured over the wounds. The victims were then tied to the fence enclosing the camp by silk cords taken from a parachute pack. Tin cans containing stones had then been attached alongside them to the barbed wire, leaving Patrón and his sidekick with the knowledge that the moment they moved the noise would attract the attention of guards in the watchtowers, who were under strict orders to shoot any prisoners attempting to escape.

The agony the two men must have suffered—with rats gnawing at their flayed stomachs, knowing that if they moved the stones in the cans would rattle, immediately attracting fire from guards in the watchtowers—was unimaginable. How long they held out before finally giving in to the pain was anybody's guess, but by then the bullets that killed them must have come as a merciful release.

With their deaths Derek Southworth was acknowleged the boss of all black-market operations in camp, but instead of flaunting his triumph he remained behind the scenes, conducting business as usual, while quietly assuming control of the organization Patrón had previously run. The transition was flawless and Southworth's organizational skills were much admired, even by those whose illegal operations now required them to pay him a percentage for protection. They realized the young RAF officer was a natural leader, a man who, in a single brilliant stroke, had both annihilated his competition and struck terror into the hearts of anybody who nurtured ideas of setting themselves up against him.

After the camp had settled back into its normal routine, the Countess met with Southworth and arranged to pay him a commission on all Genevieve's earnings, but he added an unexpected condition: he insisted on being the first man in camp to sample the Frenchwoman's sexual favors.

When the fat woman told her protégée of Southworth's demands, Genevieve feigned indignation. "*Merde!* First you order me to stay away from him; now you want me to fuck him. What am I to believe?"

"That I am trying to do what is best for us both," the other woman replied quietly.

Genevieve pretended to pout as she put on one of her new dresses, dabbed on perfume, and readied herself to meet Southworth. She'd been attracted to the young Englishman from the moment she first saw him in the jail at Pamplona, not only because of his good looks but because he projected an aura of self-confidence that intrigued her. But when she entered the Hangar, instead of Southworth she found a heavyset man with a huge mustache sprawled on a cot in the Englishman's cubicle.

"You just missed Derek," the man on the cot said. "The Commandant wanted to see him about something, but he shouldn't be long. He asked me to keep you entertained until he gets back."

He poured some brandy into a tin mug and handed it to the Frenchwoman.

"Take a pew," the man with the mustache added, patting the mattress next to where he was lying, "and drink up."

Genevieve sat on the end of the cot and sipped her cognac. She had the uneasy feeling that something was wrong, but she didn't want to offend Southworth by not being there when he returned.

"I can't wait long," she said. "It'll be curfew soon."

"Don't worry about that." The man grinned. "We've got friends in high places among the guards."

He took out a pack of cigarettes and offered her one.

"Thanks, I don't smoke," she said.

"No vices?" He put a hand on her leg and slid it under her dress.

"I'd better go." Genevieve started to get up, but the man grabbed her arm and pulled her to him.

"Won't hurt to get warmed up while you're waiting for old Derek," he said, forcing her back on the cot and cupping her breast with one hand.

"Bastard!" Genevieve started to struggle.

"Come on," the man said, pinioning her under him and ripping the bodice of her dress. "Don't play little Miss Innocent with me."

"I choose who touches me!"

"Not this time, darling. You'll do what I want and bloody well like it."

She tried to fight, but he slapped her hard across the face and tore off her underpants. Unbuttoning his fly, he took out his penis and lowered himself on her. She was dry, and his penetration hurt enough to make her gasp.

"Feels good, eh?"

When Genevieve didn't reply, the man raked her bare back with his nails. She winced.

"So you do have feelings," he said, quickening his thrusts and squeezing her nipples.

The Frenchwoman remained silent, knowing that soon it would be over, but when his body arched, and she felt the hot stream of his semen spurting into her, another voice said, "Not bad, old man. Now let an expert show you how it should really be done."

Another man, thin and bald and wearing an RAF uniform, stepped into the cubicle and began unbuttoning his pants. Genevieve felt his hands on her shoulders as he turned her over and rammed his penis into her ass. The pain made her cry out, but the man thrusting himself into her responded only by slapping her hard across the buttocks.

"Thinks he's a bloody jockey!" The observation was made by one of five men who were peering over the partition that enclosed the cubicle.

"Easy, George, that filly's got a few more races to run yet."

Genevieve closed her eyes and tried to blot out what was happening to her. After the first four men had used her she no longer experienced any pain; it was as though she had entered a dark void where time stood still and all sensory response ceased to exist. How many men took their turn with her, and in what ways, became part of a haze that cleared only when she found herself lying in the mud outside the Hangar, still naked, clothes scattered around her.

"What the hell happened to you?"

She looked up. Derek Southworth was standing over her.

"Your friends entertained me," she answered bitterly.

His eyes blazed. "Don't worry, I'll take care of those bastards."

"It wouldn't have happened if you'd been there."

He didn't answer, but helped gather up her clothes and escorted her to the other side of camp. It was dusk and the lights outside the barbed-wire fence had come on, but even though it was after curfew the one sentry they saw recognized Southworth and turned away without challenging him. Each intake of breath made Genevieve's bruised ribs ache, and blood was caked between her legs, but she gave no evidence of the pain she was suffering as the Englishman helped her to her own barrack block.

"You'll be all right now," he said as they paused in front of the door. "And I guarantee nothing like this will ever happen to you again. Not as long as you are under my protection."

Without waiting for her to answer, he turned and strode away into the darkness.

When the Countess saw Genevieve, she didn't ask any questions, and the Frenchwoman didn't volunteer any information. Both tacitly acknowledged that what had happened in the Hangar was a form of dues that had to be paid, and instead of interrogating her, the fat woman brought a bowl of water and gently wiped away the blood-stained mud and applied salves from bottles with Russian labels that brought cool, soothing relief to the numerous scratches on the Frenchwoman's back.

"Janet was here," the Countess said, when she had completed her ministrations.

"When?" Genevieve asked.

"About an hour ago. She wants to talk with you, says it's important."

"Did she ask where I was?"

The other woman shook her head.

All Genevieve wanted to do was crawl under her blanket and find escape in sleep, but the thought that something might have happened to Janna prompted her to slowly begin getting dressed. The garments she had chosen with such care for her rendezvous with Southworth were now little more than mud-spattered rags, but she put on another silk dress and carefully fixed her hair.

"You're going to get blood on that dress," the Countess cautioned, "and your friend doesn't care how you look."

"I do," the Frenchwoman replied.

It was after midnight when Genevieve went to her friends' cubicle. The baby was asleep, and they spoke quietly so as not to waken her.

"The British Ambassador in Madrid is sending somebody to pick me up tomorrow morning," Janet said. "I got word from the Commandant late this afternoon."

"That's wonderful!" Genevieve exclaimed.

"The best news any of us have had in a long time," Anna added.

"It seems the clerk at the court in Pamplona really did send his reports to our respective embassies," Janet said.

"Then Anna should be hearing something any day too." Genevieve hugged her two friends, trying not to wince as they pressed their hands against her back. "I'm so happy for you both."

"What about you?" Anna asked.

The Frenchwoman shrugged. "The only French government not controlled by the Germans is General de Gaulle's in London, and it hasn't any embassies. Besides, I don't have any papers or powerful friends—except for the Countess, of course."

"There must be something—"

"*Mais non!*" Genevieve interjected, striving to keep her tone light. "This is no time for serious talk. Janet is going home to her family." She turned to the Englishwoman. "They must be longing to see you. How long has it been since you last saw them?"

"Nearly five years."

"*Mon dieu!* Do they know you are coming?"

"The Ambassador cabled my father. It seems they're old friends."

"Then perhaps he can bring pressure to bear on the United States consul in Madrid to get Anna out of here as soon as possible. She's an American citizen, it's their duty to protect her."

"I'll make sure he does everything humanly possible," Janet assured her.

The conversation lapsed, and in the silence they heard the night sounds of camp: low murmurs of conversation; an occasional whimper from somebody crying out in sleep; the splash of a prisoner urinating into the bucket that was kept near the door of the barracks for use when curfew made it impossible to visit the latrines; and the long-drawn-out cries of the sentries shouting *¡Alerta!* to each other. The women knew it might be the last time they would ever be together, and the thought produced a tension that manifested itself in a sudden awkwardness with words.

"We have to make some decisions about Janna," Janet said. "The Commandant allowed me to talk by phone with the British Ambassador, and I asked him if arrangements could be made to take her with me."

"And?" Genevieve asked.

"He wasn't encouraging."

"The British are unfeeling bastards," the Frenchwoman said with unexpected vehemence.

"They had reasons." Janet hesitated. "I made a mistake when I told the clerk in Pamplona that Anna was the child's mother."

"You were only trying to protect Janna," Anna protested.

"True," the Englishwoman said, "but he forwarded a copy of his report to both the British and United States consulates in Madrid, and now my ambassador says the child must remain with its mother."

"Perhaps you will be able to change his mind when you get to Madrid," Genevieve said.

"I doubt it," the other woman replied. "The British are only willing to act on behalf of their own citizens, and because we don't know who Janna's father was—"

"Don't worry," Anna said. "She'll be just fine with me."

"But what if the people at the American consulate aren't willing to believe she's your child?"

"I'll cross that bridge when I come to it," Anna assured her. "Until then, Genevieve and I will see she gets all the loving care she needs."

The Englishwoman looked at Janna, who was sleeping in a blanket-lined basket that served as a crib. "I should leave this with you," she said, taking out the gold medallion and offering it to Anna.

The other woman shook her head. "Keja asked you to keep it until Janna is old enough to wear it," she said. "One day you will give it to her yourself."

"Well, at least you can use this." Janet took out the ruby she had managed to keep from Señor Ortega and gave it to Anna. "I wouldn't use it unless you have to, but at least it'll be handy in case of an emergency."

Once again they seemed at a loss for words.

"I've written my address down so both of you will always know where to reach me," Janet said, handing each woman a scrap of paper. "When I get to London I'll do everything possible. . . . "

"Don't worry about us," Genevieve said. "We'll be all right."

For the first time since either of them had known her, Janet started to cry. "I'm going to miss you both so much!" she sobbed.

"When you get to London I want you to go to the best restaurant and think of me when you order the most expensive item on the menu," Genevieve said.

"And take a long hot bath for me," Anna added.

"I promise." Janet smiled through her tears.

Each knew there was nothing left to say. After another long embrace, Genevieve walked quickly back to her own cubicle. The Countess was still awake and immediately noticed that blood had soaked through the dress from the scratches on Genevieve's back. Instead of commenting on it, she waited until the Frenchwoman was lying under her blanket to say, "Tomorrow we make a new beginning. It will be a long, hard road, but I assure you the rewards will make the journey worthwhile."

"You'd better be right, madame," Genevieve replied quietly, "because I don't know how much more of this hell I can take."

16

At roll call the following morning, Anna stood in a drenching rain with Janna in her arms and experienced a wave of anxiety that was so overwhelming it bordered on panic.

A guard had come for Janet about half an hour before dawn—much earlier than either woman had expected—and hurried her away to the Commandant's office with such haste that there hadn't been time for extended good-byes. In retrospect Anna realized this might have been a blessing in disguise, because the emotional trauma of the parting could have shattered her fragile facade of self-reliance.

As it was, the impact of Janet's departure didn't make itself fully felt until the bugle sounded over the loudspeakers summoning the prisoners to roll call, and for the first time since she arrived in camp, Anna found herself hurrying to the parade ground without Janet. Instinctively, as she had ever since their first day at the camp, she half turned to whisper to her friend, only to find an empty space next to her. Only then did she realize how much the companionship of the Englishwoman had meant and how totally she had come to depend on her friend's good-natured, always dependable presence.

Nor had Anna really envisioned what it would be like to suddenly assume full responsibility for Janna. Neither woman was maternal by instinct, and they'd had to learn by trial and error what was involved in raising a child. But Anna had always felt she could count on Janet's knowing what to do in the event of an emergency because of her training as a nurse.

As the Spanish flag was raised and the assembled prisoners launched into their ragged version of the national anthem, a car displaying Union Jack pennants pulled away from in front of the Commandant's office. When it halted at the main gate, Anna glimpsed Janet looking back through the rear window. Their eyes met for one brief moment before the car moved on.

In the days that followed Janet's departure, Anna's anxiety turned into a full-blown depression, inducing a terrible ennui in which her weariness manifested itself both physically and spiritually. Her joints constantly throbbed, and she was tired from the moment she got up until she went to bed. Even worse was the terrible sense of defeat, the feeling that nothing was worth the effort and that the future offered no hope. She became increasingly withdrawn and remained within the safe confines of her cubicle, only emerging when the camp routine required her to do so, and even then she stayed apart from the other prisoners.

Genevieve saw what was happening, and on her daily visits to supply Anna and the baby with food she did what she could to cheer her friend up. The Frenchwoman was now taking strolls along the Promenade des Anglais both mornings and afternoons, arranging rendezvous with whoever could afford her sexual favors, trysts that were consummated in the Countess's cubicle and paid for in cash given directly to the older woman. Some of Genevieve's regular clients listened to news reports on a radio that had been smuggled into camp, and during their sessions with the Frenchwoman they passed on what they heard.

It was almost the end of January 1944, and the Allied forces were on the move in Europe: the Fifth Army had launched an attack east of Monte Cassino, and there had been amphibious landings at Anzio, south of Rome. On the Eastern Front the Russians had begun an offensive in the Leningrad and Baltic areas and had captured Novgorod after fierce resistance from the Germans.

"Things are beginning to look a lot better," Genevieve told Anna brightly. "There are rumors all around camp that the war will be over in a matter of months."

Anna didn't respond; her emotional state had so deteriorated that the Frenchwoman's ebullience only further deepened her grinding depression, and when Genevieve's nightly visits were imminent she began to feign sleep in order to avoid talking with her.

By mid-February Anna's condition had become so bad that she found the task of caring for Janna overwhelming, and increasingly, when Genevieve arrived at the other woman's cubicle with food, she would find the child needing a bottle or changing, tasks she would undertake herself, even though she was hopelessly unskilled at both.

"This can't go on," the Countess declared after her protégée canceled yet another rendezvous with a prisoner willing to pay the exhorbitant price she was now demanding for her services. "It is interfering with business, and I cannot allow that to happen."

"I'm sorry, madame, but Janna's welfare comes before everything else," Genevieve replied.

"I have invested a great deal in you," the other woman reminded her.

"And you will get it all back, with interest," the Frenchwoman said, "but I'm going to stop taking customers and move in with Anna until she's well enough to care for the child herself."

"As you wish." The Countess shrugged. "But she will rid herself of depression only by learning to stand on her own feet."

During the next week, Genevieve cared for both Anna and the baby. There was little she could do for the former except buy her nourishing food on the black market and let her sleep, only awakening her when camp rules required her to be at such events as the morning roll call. Often Anna stayed in bed for twenty or more hours, seemingly unable, or unwilling, to emerge from the protective cocoon the space under her blanket appeared to provide, and increasingly she would lie in a fetal position, her face to the wall, oblivious to everything happening around her.

The other prisoners observed what was happening to Anna and nodded knowingly; they had seen others get what they called "the sleeping death" and knew of many instances in which inmates had let themselves slide into such deep depressions that they never emerged from them, having completely lost the will to live.

Genevieve was determined to prevent this from happening to Anna, but she didn't know how. She found herself wishing with increasing frequency that Janet was on hand to offer her sage advice.

"There was really good news on the radio today," the Frenchwoman announced excitedly on February 25. "The Allied air forces have bombed every major German city and virtually wiped out the Luft-waffe."

Anna's only response was a blank stare.

The turning point finally came when the Commandant sent a guard to escort Anna to his office in the administration building. At first she didn't seem to understand the orders, but when the guard prodded her in the ribs with the barrel of his submachine gun, she got up from her mattress and let Genevieve help her get dressed.

Carrying the baby in one arm, the Frenchwoman walked with Anna to the administration building and helped her negotiate the shallow steps, but the guard refused to allow Genevieve into the office and ordered Anna to push the door open herself.

The Commandant was seated behind his desk, and to one side was a man Anna had never seen before.

"I'm Mark Hunter," he said, getting up and offering his hand. "Vice-consul at the United States Embassy in Madrid."

His voice sounded to Anna as if it was coming from the bottom of a very deep well.

"Vice-consul?" The words were the first she had spoken in days and they came out blurred, almost as if she were drunk.

"In Madrid," he repeated softly, still holding her hand.

Anna saw the Commandant watching and struggled to gain control of herself, but she couldn't stop shaking.

Mark Hunter saw the state she was in and, taking her arm, gently led her to a leather sofa. "Are you all right?" he asked.

"I assure you the prisoner has not been mistreated," the Commandant announced.

"That may be, but she obviously needs medical attention," Hunter replied.

"No, really, I'll be fine," Anna said slowly. "It's just that . . ." Her voice trailed away. She couldn't find the words to describe how she felt, and when she tried the effort was too much for her.

"Some brandy might help," the vice-consul said, looking at the Commandant.

The other man crossed to a sideboard, took out a bottle of Pedro Domecq, and poured some into a small glass. He handed it to Hunter, who held it to Anna's lips.

"Just a sip," he urged.

The liqueur made her cough.

"Try a little more," the man holding the glass murmured.

This time the liquid warmed her stomach but also went straight to her head, making it even more difficult for her to think straight. Ordinarily she liked brandy, but it was hours since she'd eaten, so the effect of the alcohol was heightened.

"Feeling better?" Hunter asked.

She nodded. Her brain was working sufficiently well for her to notice that her visitor was probably in his early forties. His sandy-colored hair was receding at the temples, and he wore a well-cut tweed jacket, blue checked shirt, striped tie, gray flannel trousers, and brown cordovan shoes. He also smelled pleasantly of pipe tobacco; she glimpsed the stem of a briar in his breast pocket.

"I've been a bit under the weather," she said.

"The prisoner's condition is due in no way to camp facilities," the Commandant stated.

"As you say," the vice-consul replied wearily. "Now, if it's all right with you, Colonel, I would like to spend some time alone with the prisoner."

"I suppose it can be permitted," the Commandant agreed grudgingly.

"You can be sure I will let the Ambassador know of your coopera-
tion," Hunter said.

The other man nodded and left the room. When the door closed the
vice-consul poured more brandy into a glass and swallowed it himself.

"It looks like you needed that more than I did," Anna said.

"Dealing with men like the Commandant gives me a powerful
thirst," he replied.

He spoke with a slight nasal inflection, and the quizzical expression
in his hazel eyes created the impression that his rather formal manner
disguised a more easygoing nature.

"I had begun to think the United States government wasn't interested in my case," she said.

"We're interested, all right," Hunter assured her, "but there was
some kind of snafu in Washington. It seems they checked your records
and couldn't find your father's birth certificate."

"Probably because he wasn't born in America."

"But you were?"

"In Manhattan on July 14, 1920."

"Bastille Day."

"Appropriately."

"I'm sorry. . . ."

"The day celebrates the release of prisoners," Anna said. "Let's hope
it's an omen."

"I'm sure it will be," he replied, "but I must warn you these citizenship claims can drag on. Right now Washington's first priority is winning the war. All nonmilitary matters are put on the back burner until
somebody can find time to get to them. In addition, the administrative
branch of the government is woefully understaffed, and it might be
quite a while before they find a record of your birth."

"Are you telling me I have to stay here?"

"I'm afraid so. Until the Ambassador gets verification that you are
an American citizen, his hands are tied." Anna tried to hide her bitter
disappointment, but it must have shown because Hunter quickly added,
"You can be sure I'll do everything humanly possible to speed things
up, and you can help things along a lot by giving me a few additional
facts."

He took out a small leather-bound notebook and put on a pair of
half-frame reading glasses. They made him look older, almost profes-
sorial. Anna wondered if she hadn't erred on the young side when she
guessed him to be in his forties.

"You were born in Manhattan." He looked at her over the half-rims. "Do you remember the exact address?"

Anna searched her memory but drew a blank. "My parents moved quite a few times when I was still very young."

He wrote carefully in his notebook. "What school did you attend?"

"The Manhattan Academy of Fine Arts."

"Do you have a diploma or anything else that would verify you were a student there?"

"They were destroyed in the ghetto, but my name and photograph were in the yearbook."

"When did you graduate?"

"A lifetime ago." When he looked up in surprise, she added, "In June 1935."

"Well, at least this will give the people back in Washington something to go on," he said. "Now if you'll just give me a few details about your child. . . ."

Anna realized this was her opportunity to extricate herself from the web of lies she'd been caught up in even since Janet deceived the court clerk in Pamplona, but she hesitated because she still didn't know if she could trust Mark Hunter. He seemed nice enough but was still a bureaucrat bound by his government's rules, and that might mean Janna would be categorized as a Displaced Person, which was tantamount to having no official identity, a risk she didn't want to take with Keja's child.

"She's named Janna," she said.

"An unusual name," he observed. "Was it your choice or her father's?"

"Mostly mine."

"And where is he now?"

"Dead."

"I'm sorry."

"He was killed in the ghetto."

"If the reports I've read are even half true, it must have been a living hell."

Anna didn't respond. There was genuine compassion in his voice, and she felt guilty about deceiving him.

"Well," he said, when the silence between them continued, "I think I have enough to get the ball rolling." Then, almost as an afterthought, he asked, "Where was Janna born?"

"Is it important?"

"Not really, at least as far as citizenship is concerned. That's decided on the basis of the nationality of the surviving parent."

"You mean once it's proved I'm an American, Janna is automatically accepted as one too?" When Hunter nodded, Anna experienced the first surge of exhilaration she'd felt in a long time. "She was born at Irati, a small village in the Pyrenees," she said.

"On the Spanish side of the border?"

"Yes. Is it relevant?"

He shook his head. "I was just—"

Before she could press the question, the door opened and the Commandant strode into the room.

"Finished?" he asked the vice-consul.

"For the moment," Hunter replied.

The other man summoned a guard and instructed him to return the prisoner to her barracks.

Hunter took Anna's hand. "Try not to worry. I promise to get in touch the moment I hear anything."

"Thank you," she replied.

Anna could feel Hunter watching her as the guard marched her out of the door. His eyes reminded her of her father's, not in their shape or color so much as in their gentleness. She felt safe in his presence. After what she'd been through, that made him a very rare human being indeed.

In the days that followed, Genevieve observed a radical change in her roommate and realized Anna's depression was finally lifting. Her former lethargy was replaced by a boundless energy, and her withdrawn silence by a need to talk far into the night. She described her meeting with Mark Hunter in great detail, frequently repeating his assurances that it was only a matter of time before her citizenship was proved and she would be freed from camp.

"You'd like him," Anna told the Frenchwoman. "He's so gentle and patient."

Genevieve, who had never known a man that possessed either quality, couldn't help wondering if Anna's assessment of the vice-consul wasn't based more on what she wanted to believe than reality, but instead of spoiling her friend's newfound enthusiasm by raising such doubts, she merely listened and struggled to stay awake for as long as Anna wanted to talk.

Less than two weeks after Hunter's first visit, Anna was once again

marched by a guard to the administration building, where she found
Mark Hunter waiting alone in the Commandant's office. He was obviously pleased to see her again. After telling her that he still hadn't
received any official word from Washington, he added that, thanks to
a quid pro quo relationship he had with a Spanish government official
in Madrid, he'd managed to obtain permission to take her out of camp
for a couple of hours.

"I thought it might do you good to see what the outside world looks
like," he said.

"What about the Commandant, has he approved of the idea?" she
asked.

"Provided I accept full responsibility and guarantee you'll be back
before curfew," he said.

Genevieve was looking after Janna so there was no reason why Anna
shouldn't accept the offer, yet she still found it difficult to make a
decision. After living by rote for so long, taking charge of her own life
seemed impossible. Hunter sensed her dilemma. He gently reassured
her, took her arm, and led her toward the main gate.

"Shall we take a ride?" he asked, motioning to where his car was
parked just beyond the last sentry.

"I'd rather walk," Anna replied. "I've almost forgotten what it's like
to go where I want without being threatened by a guard."

He nodded and, still holding her arm, slowly strolled toward the
center of the town, which bore the same name as the camp. It was
market day and people bustled about the streets, making purchases
from vendors standing behind pushcarts, smiling as they passed and
exchanging pleasantries with Hunter, who responded in fluent Spanish.

"Let me know if you see anything you want," he said. "I just got
paid, and I can't think of a better way to spend the money."

As he spoke Anna caught a reflection in a shop window and barely
recognized the image she saw. Although still only twenty-three years
old, she looked like a woman twice that age, with her hunger-hollowed
cheeks and emaciated body clothed in tattered rags.

Hunter saw what had happened. "I'll get you out of that damned
place if it's the last thing I do," he told her.

Anna was too stunned by the sight of herself to answer and stayed
silent as they continued down the street.

"Tell me what you want to do, anything," he said.

"Anything?" She thought for a moment. "I'd like a hot bath and
some clean clothes."

"I know just the place."

He led her to a store near the center of town and asked that Anna be shown whatever clothes were available in her size. Sensing a big sale, the corpulent owner summoned her assistants, who quickly brought an assortment of dresses, shoes, and silk lingerie. The woman pointedly offered Anna the most expensive garments on the premises.

"Take your time," Hunter said. "While you're making a choice, I'll arrange for your bath at my hotel."

It suddenly occurred to Anna that Hunter's generosity wasn't a simple act of kindness, as she had naively thought it to be, and that he had amorous expectations, but he left before she could confront him. For a long time she sat in the small cubicle that served as a dressing room, surrounded by the brilliantly colored dresses, wondering what to do. She looked at herself in the full-length mirror that hung behind the door. This time her image wasn't softened by the blurred refraction of a shop window, and what she saw was even more shocking than before. She stood naked under the harsh light of a single bulb, her ribs sticking out under skin the color of old tallow. Even her hair, which had once been so lush and dark, now hung in greasy strands. Why, she wondered, was Mark Hunter being so kind to her?

"Is there anything else I can show you?" the owner of the shop asked, peering through a gap in the curtain.

"No, thank you," Anna replied.

"Which do you like?"

She hesitated. "Perhaps the second one. . . ."

"With the same shoes?"

Anna nodded.

"And the lingerie?"

She started to refuse, then thought of Genevieve and realized what a perfect gift the delicate silk undergarments would make for her.

"I'll take the peach-colored set with lace edgings," she said.

"An excellent choice," the other woman assured her. "Señor will be very pleased."

Anna doubted it, particularly once she informed Hunter that she had no intention of going to bed with him. That was why she had deliberately chosen the simplest and cheapest outfit. She didn't want to take advantage of him, but neither did she intend to continue walking around in her prison rags. She decided that the best way to handle the situation was to tell him she considered the money he was advancing for the clothes a loan, one that she would repay as soon as she was repatriated.

"Ready?" Hunter asked from beyond the curtain.

She smoothed the simple cotton dress she had selected and took a last look at herself in the mirror. The new clothes had greatly improved her appearance, except for her hair, which still looked scraggly. Stepping out of the cubicle, she performed a small pirouette.

"You look great," he said.

"What about these, señorita?" the shop owner asked, holding up the peach-colored lingerie.

Anna felt herself beginning to blush. "I got them for a friend," she explained.

"Sure." Hunter grinned, taking a wad of pesetas from his wallet and handing them to the owner of the shop. "Now for that hot bath."

The Casa Grande Blanco was a small hotel, the kind of nondescript establishment frequented by commercial travelers. It possessed only five bedrooms, the occupants of which were required to use a single bathroom that contained a huge tub with massive brass taps.

"They're pretty busy, and I couldn't get you a room of your own," Hunter explained as they approached the bar, which doubled as a reception desk, "but the owner says it'll be okay for you to change in mine, and there is plenty of hot water for your bath."

Anna was disappointed by Hunter's lack of finesse. She'd expected a move that was smoother and more in keeping with the cultured image he projected, but apparently he didn't feel such subtlety was necessary, perhaps because he assumed that after what she'd been through in camp she would gladly settle for anything he offered. This thought triggered a simmering anger in Anna. She resented his thinking he could buy her for the price of a few clothes. If the woman who owned the shop hadn't already taken Anna's filthy rags, she would have returned her new outfit and let Hunter know what she thought of him.

"You'll find my room at the top of the stairs," he said, handing her the key. "The bathroom is at the end of the corridor. You can't miss it. I'll wait down here in the bar until you're finished."

His ingenuousness puzzled Anna, and the bewilderment remained with her as she went upstairs and unlocked the door of his room. She half expected to hear the sound of his footsteps following her, and mumbled excuses that would justify his entering while she undressed, but they never came. Nor was she disturbed by Hunter when, after putting on his robe, she unlocked the door again and hurried down the corridor to the bathroom.

Forewarned by Hunter, the innkeeper's wife had already run a bath and left some clean towels on a small table next to the tub, which was filled almost to the brim with steaming hot water. There was even a small bar of scented soap and a glass jar containing bath salts.

Taking off the robe, Anna slid into the water until it reached her chin, then put her head back against the rounded edge of the tub and closed her eyes. The sensation was so delicious she surrendered herself to it completely; heat permeated her whole body, dissolving away tensions that had been building for months, and she felt herself beginning to relax. Opening the jar of bath salts, she poured the crystals into the water and watched as they melted in streamers of red, orange, yellow, blue, and green. The perfume they gave off stirred memories of spring evenings when she had strolled with her father in Lazienki Park, holding his arm as they walked the gravel paths between beds of daffodils and crocuses. She had been nineteen or twenty then, and the possessor of a fresh beauty that made the heads of young men turn when they passed. Her father had laughed and said, "One day you will find a husband and leave your old father," and she had always assured him that he wasn't old and that she would never leave him. Now he was dead. And she was the one who felt old.

Feeling her initial euphoria beginning to ebb, she turned her attention back to getting herself clean, first shampooing her hair, then spreading a thin layer of suds over her whole body. She rinsed her hair by ducking under the water, then repeated the entire process again until her skin tingled.

But she didn't get out of the tub until the water had finally cooled and there was none left from the brass tap to replenish it. Even then she was reluctant to emerge from the bath, but finally she dried herself with the thick white towel and returned to the bedroom. Putting on her new dress, she fixed her hair and went downstairs to find Hunter seated at a table near the window. He looked up at her and smiled. "You look . . ."

"Like a new woman?"

"Well, let's say a different version of the old one."

"Now I know why you're a diplomat."

He grinned. "Hungry?"

"Starving."

He summoned the waiter and ordered in Spanish. "The food here is very simple," he explained. "I asked him to bring us cheese omelets, green salad, steaks, fried potatoes, and fresh bread with plenty of butter."

"Would you repeat that again, very slowly?"

"Sound good?"

"Perfect."

"White or red wine?"

"Would you mind if I ordered milk?"

"Of course not." When the waiter brought their food, Hunter ordered a jug of milk and two glasses.

"Don't let me stop you from drinking wine."

"Believe me, you aren't," he said. "I attend endless cocktail parties. That's what diplomats do, you know. They spend so much time drinking and socializing that they rarely have time for important problems. I'm glad of any opportunity to give my liver a rest."

Anna appreciated his attempt to make her feel at ease, a consideration he further demonstrated in his conversation. He sensed she didn't want to talk about herself, so he described his own background, establishing that he was born into an upper-middle-class family in Boston, educated at Harvard University, and became a career diplomat shortly after graduating from college.

"Joining the State Department made my parents very happy," he added.

"Why?" Anna asked.

"I'd always loved art, and they were afraid I was going to spend the rest of my life in a garret somewhere on the Left Bank."

"Would that have been so bad?"

"My father thought so. Money and respectability were what mattered to him; art is a profession that seems to promise neither."

"Have you regretted becoming a diplomat?"

"I've hated my job almost from the day I began it."

"Couldn't you have quit?"

"Things weren't that simple," he replied. "I had a wife to support. She was an invalid, multiple sclerosis. It struck early in our marriage and got steadily worse over the next eight years. She had to have a live-in nurse and constant medical attention. Such things cost a lot of money. As a member of the State Department I was covered by an insurance plan, but if I'd changed jobs it would have stopped."

"I'm sorry," she said. "I didn't mean to pry."

"It helps to talk about it." he replied. "She died in the summer of

1940. That's when I applied for an overseas posting and was sent to Madrid. I'd majored in languages at Harvard and spoke pretty good Spanish, so it seemed like a logical assignment. But anywhere would have been all right with me. I just wanted to get away. It isn't easy to go on living as a hypocrite."

"I don't understand."

"When my wife died everybody felt sorry for me. What they didn't know, and I couldn't tell them, was how relieved I felt. She was in constant pain and I couldn't bear to see her suffering. Death was the kindest way out for her. My only regret was that her illness prevented us from having children."

A silence settled between them. Hunter looked at his watch. "It's getting late. I'd better be getting you back to camp. The Commandant strikes me as a man who expects punctuality."

"He demands it," Anna said.

Hunter got up and held her chair. "Well, I don't want to get on his wrong side because I plan to visit you again. Do you mind?"

"I've enjoyed this afternoon," Anna replied, deliberately avoiding a direct response because she still didn't know what he expected of their relationship.

At the main gate he took her hand and said, "I wish to God you didn't have to go back, but it won't be for long if I can help it."

He continued holding her hand a moment longer, then turned and strode to his car. Anna waited until he drove away before checking in with the sentry at the main gate, who reported her return to the Commandant's office and instructed her to go back to her barracks.

Genevieve was waiting when Anna entered the cubicle. The Frenchwoman had already fed Janna and put her to bed, so she was able to give her undivided attention to hearing about her friend's afternoon of freedom. She wanted to know every detail, particularly about the clothes Anna had tried on, and when Anna gave her the lingerie, Genevieve rubbed the silk garments against her cheek. "They're too beautiful to wear in this pigsty, but I promise to put them on the day I'm liberated."

The Frenchwoman assumed Anna had paid for the gifts by having sex with Hunter, and when she heard that the vice-consul hadn't even suggested it she found it difficult to understand why he had been so generous.

"He sounds like a man who hasn't had much love in his life," she said.

"Well, if he thinks I'm the woman to give it to him, I'm afraid he's in for a big disappointment."

"Why?"

"I just don't feel that way about him."

"Who cares about feelings?" Genevieve asked. "The important thing is he likes you, and that gives you power over him. You'd be a fool not to use it, for Janna if not yourself."

Anna didn't respond. She didn't want to accept it, but she knew what the other woman said was true: her primary concern now must be for the child.

"I'm too tired to think about it now," she said.

"Just remember what I told you," Genevieve persisted, carefully rewrapping the silk lingerie Anna had given her. "Mark Hunter could be your way of getting out of here and your chance to guarantee Janna a decent life."

17

During the next five weeks Mark Hunter visited Anna on three different occasions, and each time he arrived with written permission from his counterpart in the Spanish government authorizing her to leave camp with him. The periods of freedom gradually increased from hours to a whole day, and early in April, Hunter presented the Commandant with a document stating that Anna was to be allowed to spend twenty-four hours away from Miranda de Ebro.

"It is very irregular," the Commandant observed. "However, it seems the decision has already been made by my superiors, so I have no choice but to comply. But I must insist that you get her back to camp before curfew tomorrow night."

"I guarantee it," Hunter replied, as the other man countersigned the authorization.

The vice-consul returned to the area beyond the main gate, which had become the place where he always met Anna, and impatiently tapped his fingers on the mudguard of the small Fiat convertible in which he had driven from Madrid, as he studied the groups of prisoners standing in clusters on the parade ground.

He hadn't felt such nervous anticipation for a very long time, not since he went out on his first date when he was sixteen, and that was twenty-six years ago. When he finally saw Anna, she was wearing the simple cotton dress he had bought her the first afternoon they had gone out together.

"I was afraid something might have gone wrong," he said, holding the door as she got into the car.

"I'm sorry," she replied. "Genevieve was late, and I had to feed Janna."

"How is she?" he asked, guiding the car through the narrow, cart-clogged streets.

"Genevieve?"

"Janna."

"They're both fine," Anna replied with a quick laugh. "Genevieve still hasn't worn the lingerie you bought her. She insists she'll only put it on the day she's released."

There was an awkward pause: being freed from the internment camp had become a touchy subject, for despite Hunter's efforts to speed things up, Anna's birth certificate still hadn't been found, and whenever he tried pressuring Washington to make a decision in her case, they stalled by claiming everything possible was already being done.

"It's hard to keep up with Janna now that she's crawling," Anna said, deliberately shifting the focus of their conversation. "I found her halfway out of the barracks the other morning."

"I'll ask the Commandant if you can bring her along on one of our outings," he said. "I'd love to meet her, and she'd enjoy the beach."

"Is that where we're going?" Anna asked.

He nodded. "A village near Ribadeo. Between Luarca and Vivero, about two hundred miles west of here."

"Two hundred miles!"

"Close to it."

"Do we have time for such a long trip?"

"The Commandant has approved your staying away until curfew tomorrow night."

Anna glanced at him but remained silent. Hunter had put the convertible top down, and when she rested her head against the back of the seat she could see puffy white clouds in the sky. It was a perfect spring day with a light breeze and brilliant sunshine that sparkled on the snow capping the peaks of the distant Pyrenees. For one fleeting moment she recalled the horrors she and the others had experienced in those mountains, and the relief she had felt when, after crossing the border, she had gazed out over the plains west of Pamplona. She had wondered then if she would ever reach them, and the fact that she had seemed like a miracle.

It was early evening by the time they reached their destination, and the soft twilight lent a velvety texture to the night sky over the small fishing village. They stopped outside a quaint inn overlooking the harbor and sat for a while watching fishermen unload a fresh catch from their brightly colored, high-prowed boats. Huge lamps on the sterns, used at sea to attract fish into the nets, now provided the illumination by which the men worked.

"We'll be eating some of that catch for dinner," Hunter said.

"You've been here before?"

"Once. It's a lovely place."

Anna realized this was the moment when, if she didn't intend to sleep with Hunter, she should tell him, but she let it pass and followed him into the inn.

The owner was behind a small bar, and when he saw the new arrivals he hurried to greet them. "Señor Hunter! Welcome. It is very good to see you again, and this time I see you have brought your wife. The room is ready, and as soon as you wish it, dinner will be served on the portico."

Hunter led the way upstairs to a bedroom overlooking the waterfront. It contained a large double bed. "I didn't tell him you were my wife," he said. "It was just something he must have assumed. If you'd rather we didn't sleep together—"

"Mark," she interjected quietly, "It's all right."

The look of relief that crossed his face was that of a boy who had plucked up courage to ask for a dance and found himself accepted. It gave him a vulnerability she found endearing, and when he took her in his arms she didn't resist.

"God, I've been wanting to hold you like this ever since that first awful day in the Commandant's office," he murmured.

"Why did you wait so long?" she asked.

"Well—" he paused. "For one thing, I'm so much older than you."

"And the other?"

"I wasn't sure it was what you wanted."

She turned her face and their lips met. He kissed her softly, with great tenderness, and she returned his embrace with warmth but little passion.

"Tomorrow we can go to the beach," he said eagerly. "We'll take a picnic and spend the whole morning exploring the caves. I'll bet you've never seen anything quite like them."

They dined on the veranda of the inn, a roofed-over portico barely wide enough to accommodate their table and one other, which was occupied by a man and woman who finished their meal and left soon after Anna and Hunter sat down to eat. Darkness had fallen, but they could still see the fishermen unloading their boats in the tiny harbor below where they sat, and when the moon emerged from behind a headland its pale light shimmered on the calm surface of the ocean. The air was warm and scented by the fragrance of night-blooming jasmine, its sweetness blended with the more pungent odors of woodsmoke and olive oil. The fishermen called to each other against a background of softly lapping waves, and gulls cried as they wheeled over the boats looking for a chance to feed.

It was the kind of setting Anna had dreamed about when, as a teenager, she had imagined the circumstances in which she would first make love; the sights, smells, and sounds embodied the sort of romance that had always been such an integral part of the fantasies she wove. Only the man was wrong: Mark was a decent, warm, loving person for whom she felt a real fondness, but he wasn't the prince she'd always assumed would be the one to whom she would give herself. Yet she still experienced a mounting tremulousness at the prospect of what so obviously lay ahead; a blend of emotions that incorporated a whole range of feelings from excitement to fear.

When the innkeeper took their order, Anna asked for some wine. Hunter appeared surprised by her request but didn't comment on it and ordered a bottle of Irouleguy. "It's the vin rosé of the region," he explained. "I think you'll like it."

It proved to be delicious, and the food was equally tasty: tiny shrimps potted in butter, a salad of endives and tomatoes in a vinaigrette dressing, grilled sole, and cheese with fruit for dessert. When the innkeeper served coffee he also brought a bottle of Pedro Domecq brandy and some Anis del Mono.

During dinner, in spite of Anna's inner turmoil, she managed to listen attentively as Hunter talked about his duties as vice-consul, a job he described with considerable humor. He told her several anecdotes to illustrate the ludicrous amount of red tape that was involved in any dealings with Washington.

"They want everything in triplicate," he said. "When we asked for permission to refurbish our offices, the government insisted that the paint be shipped from the States, and by the time it reached Madrid it had completely dried out."

"What did you do?" Anna asked.

Hunter smiled. "We sent the stuff back to Washington with a note saying it was the wrong color and had the job done by a local contractor."

Anna found herself laughing a bit too loudly at this story and realized she was getting drunk. She wasn't accustomed to liquor and was only drinking to help overcome the nervousness she had begun to feel. Her trepidation went beyond the fact that she was still a virgin: she was so scarred by events in the ghetto, the rigors of crossing the Pyrenees, Keja's death, and the hardships of life in the internment camp that she was not sure she was capable of responding to Mark, either sexually or emotionally.

"You should have done it yourself," she said, slurring the words slightly. "It was your big chance to become a painter."

This time he laughed. It was the first time she'd seen him so completely relaxed. The tension he had displayed earlier in the evening had gone, and with it his awkwardness. He was no longer hesitant when he touched her, and he frequently placed his hand over hers.

"What about your unfulfilled dreams?" he asked.

During the last four years her fantasies had been limited to mere survival, but she didn't want to spoil the mood of the evening by saying so. Instead, she murmured, "I'm too tired to tell you about them all now, there are so many."

He interpreted her response as a hint that she was ready for bed and led the way upstairs. The innkeeper's wife had lit a small oil lamp and turned down the covers. The shutters were open, and the sound of the waves against the pebbles on the beach provided a background that somehow insulated the room, seeming to exclude the rest of the world with its war and destruction.

Anna stood at the window looking out at the night, her heartbeat quickening as she heard Hunter undress, and when he put his arms around her from behind she began to tremble.

"I want you very much," he whispered, pressing his lips against the nape of her neck. "Come to bed."

She hesitated a moment, and when she turned saw that he had laid out a silk nightgown for her. "It's lovely," she said, picking it up and holding it against herself. "Makes me feel special."

Going into the small bathroom that was attached to the room, Anna undressed by the light of a candle. It cast enough illumination to see herself in the mirror. She looked better than she had the first day Mark had taken her out, but her face appeared pale and there was a strained expression in her eyes that reflected her inner feelings. Now the moment had come, she was more nervous than she had thought she would be. All she could think of was how to present herself in the best possible light. The impulse wasn't a wish to please Mark as much as an urge to lend substance to the fantasies she'd had about the way it would be the first time she made love. In her dreams she had always seen it as a ritual of perfect parts; place, ambience, man, and the way she would look. The fact that in reality it had turned out to be less than she imagined would have saddened her under more normal circumstances, but after the past four years she was undaunted.

Reaching out of the window, which was garlanded with jasmine, she picked a handful of petals, crushed them between her palms, and rubbed them over her body. The delicate perfume enveloped the bathroom as she put on the silk nightdress Mark had bought her and returned to where he was waiting.

"You look beautiful," he said, looking at her from where he was seated on the bed.

He drew her to him and rested his head against her breasts. She looked down at his naked body: it was slender, firm, and more muscular than she would have imagined. The sight of it awed her, not its proportions so much as the fact that it was the first time she had seen a completely nude man. He slid her nightgown off her shoulders and gently pulled it down over the swell of her breasts, letting it fall to the floor around her feet. Standing naked in front of him, she suddenly felt vulnerable and half turned her body in a gesture that was prompted by shyness and apprehension.

"Relax," he murmured, "I just want to taste your sweetness."

She felt awkward and self-conscious and flinched reflexively when he drew her toward him, but when he kissed her breasts and she felt the warmth of his breath against her skin, an unexpected excitement rippled through her. She wanted to give herself up to the sensation but found herself still holding back, and when he pulled her toward him on the bed her body remained rigid.

"I'm not going to hurt you," he whispered.

"It isn't that. . . ."

"What, then?"

"I just don't know how. . . ."

"I'll show you," he breathed, kissing her lips, neck, and nipples, trailing his fingers across her belly and down the insides of her thighs.

Anna lay against the pillows, touched by his gentleness and patience, as he ran the tip of his tongue across her breasts, gradually lowering his head until he reached her crotch, where he touched her clitoris. She shuddered, not from apprehension or fear but from an uncontrolled spasm she had never experienced before.

"Oh Mark!" The words were joined by her quick intake of breath.

He didn't answer but continued moving his tongue backward and forward until the nerve endings throughout her whole body tingled, then moved his tongue slowly down the inside of her calves until he reached her feet and began probing between her toes.

Anna's breathing quickened. In spite of her initial apprehensiveness she found herself savoring her reactions: blood-filled nipples that were swollen and hard; the warm wetness of her vagina; the pressure of his penis pressing against her. Her mind went in and out of focus as her body began to respond with its own rhythms, unreasoned and with a will of their own. When Mark straddled her she grasped his buttocks with both hands and pulled him toward her, arching her pelvis upward, but instead of penetrating her immediately, he rubbed the tip of his penis lightly against the lips of her vagina while he massaged her breasts with both hands. It was a motion that triggered quivering tremors of pleasure, but only when she was on the brink of erupting did he finally press himself downward. She experienced a quick stab of pain, and when she winced, he whispered, "I love you, come to me, now!"

His words were interspersed with short, shallow breaths, and his skin was filmed with sweat. Involuntarily her muscles tensed in a contraction that held and held until she climaxed, and at that precise moment he ejaculated, spurting a pulsating stream of semen deep inside her. Their bodies remained pressed together, each feeling the other's heart pounding, enveloped by the pungent, musky odor of sex. Tears trickled from the corners of Anna's eyes, which was puzzling because she didn't feel sad.

In the silence that followed they held each other tight, hearing the waves roll pebbles up and down the shore, lost in their own reveries: for Anna these included wonderment at her own responses, which had been stronger than she thought they would be; sounds of her mother singing; the laughter of friends at a seder; and the crack of a gunshot as Jacob fired a bullet into her dying father's skull.

"You're shaking," Mark said.

"I'm cold."

He got up and closed the shutters. In the glow of the oil lamp his face looked old, and she realized it did matter that he was almost twice her age. When he returned to bed he drew back the eiderdown and started to get under it, but suddenly checked himself and looked closely at the sheet on which they had just made love. Visibly puzzled, he picked up the oil lamp and held it nearer the bed. Its light fell on a bloodstain that extended from under where she lay, a dark, jagged-edged oblong that was still wet and glistened darkly in the fragile flame from the wick.

"You're bleeding," he said.

Anna had thought the sticky wetness between her legs was the residue of his sperm leaking out of her vagina, but now she realized that the sharp pain she'd experienced when he thrust himself into her had been caused by her hymen being ruptured. Her mother had once told her that many women didn't bleed when they made love for the first time: perhaps she'd wanted to believe herself one of them, because in going to bed with Mark she knew there was a risk of his discovering that it was impossible for her to be Janna's natural mother.

"Do you remember telling me that when people expressed their sorrow about your wife's death you felt like a hypocrite?" she asked.

"Yes, but—"

"That's what I've been living with for months."

"I don't understand. . . ."

"And I want you to, because now it's important that both of us be honest with each other," she said.

Haltingly she described how Keja had died giving birth to Janna; how Janet had lied to the court clerk in Pamplona; why it was necessary to sustain the illusion that she was the mother of the child when they were interned; and the difficulty of continuing to live out the falsehood after getting to know him.

"Why didn't you tell me this before?" he asked.

"I had no way of knowing how you'd react," she said, "and I couldn't take the chance of Janna's becoming a Displaced Person."

"Surely you must have known I would understand?"

"Why should I?" she asked. "My experiences in the ghetto and the internment camp hadn't given me much reason to trust anybody."

"And making love to me, was that part of your hypocrisy?" he asked.

"I was as deeply involved as you," she replied. "If you didn't feel that, we don't stand a chance."

"Is that what you want us to have—a chance?"

"I'm too confused to be sure of anything anymore, except that I'm tired of lying."

"Then let's make a new beginning."

"Can we?"

"I think so."

"How?"

"You could marry me." Even he looked surprised by the abruptness of his proposal.

Anna remembered what Genevieve had told her when they talked after her first outing with Mark: "Who cares about feelings? The important thing is he likes you, and that gives you power over him. You'd be a fool not to use it, for Janna, if not yourself."

"Everything's happening too quickly," she said.

"Then sleep on it. All right?"

She nodded and watched as he got a towel and spread it carefully over the bloodstain. Somehow, she wished he hadn't. When he blew out the flame of the oil lamp, instead of snuggling up to him, she lay with her eyes open trying to order her thoughts, but they were such a welter of conflicting emotions that finally she abandoned the efffort and drifted into a dreamless sleep.

When she awoke the bedroom was flooded with sunlight. She called Mark's name, and he answered from where he was standing on the small balcony beyond the French windows.

"Hungry?" he asked.

"Ravenous."

"Good. I've asked the innkeeper to bring us coffee, rolls, and plenty of honey. How does that sound?"

"Perfect."

After breakfast they walked down to the wharf and watched the fishermen working on their boats. They made light conversation until Mark finally took Anna's hand and led her along the beach to a rocky promontory a short distance away from the village.

"Have you thought about what I said last night?" he asked.

"Yes," Anna replied quietly.

"And?"

"I told you I didn't want to lie anymore, and the truth is I still don't really know how I feel about you. The only way I've been able to get through the past few years is by learning *not* to feel. I hope that changes, but—"

"All I'm asking for is the time to give us a chance."

"Are you sure?" Anna asked.

Instead of answering, he took her in his arms and held her close.

Six weeks later, on May 22, 1944, Anna Maxell-Hunter stood at the rail of the SS *Uppsala,* a Swedish-registered vessel bound from Lisbon to New York, watching the Portuguese shoreline dissolve into the distance. Mark had remained in their cabin, sensing her need to be alone, and busied himself unpacking the clothes they had bought during their three-day honeymoon in Lisbon.

The wedding, a civil ceremony attended by the U.S. Ambassador and a few of Mark's fellow diplomats, had taken place in Madrid, where Anna had arrived after her release from Miranda de Ebro. She had spent her last night at the internment camp with Genevieve; neither of them had slept, preferring instead to spend the hours reminiscing about the times they had shared, and when they talked about Keja's death both of them had cried. Just before the guard arrived to take her to the Commandant's office where Mark was waiting, Anna had given Genevieve the ruby Janet left behind when she was repatriated to England. "You need it more than I do," Anna said, "and Janna will be well cared for from now on." They hugged each other a final time. Anna's last glimpse of Genevieve was through the tears streaming down her cheeks.

When Anna opened the suitcase containing her few personal belongings after she reached Madrid, she found a small package wrapped in tissue paper. It contained the silk lingerie she had given Genevieve months earlier and a note that read, *Wear it for me. Love, Genevieve.*

Now Anna wept again: out of sadness at losing a friend, and relief that the horrors she had lived through were finally over.

"Are you all right?"

She turned and saw Mark holding Janna. Instead of answering, she dried her eyes, took the child, and linked arms with her new husband as together they watched a distant shaft of sunlight break through the layer of dark clouds.

18

LONDON: May 13, 1945

Janet Taylor tried to look as if she was enjoying herself, but she felt like a fish out of water as she helped her parents greet guests at the family's house overlooking Berkeley Square in London's fashionable Mayfair district.

It was Sunday, and the friends they were entertaining had just watched King George VI and Queen Elizabeth ride in an open landau past cheering crowds to attend a special service at St. Paul's Cathedral. The war in Europe had officially ended five days earlier, when Prime Minister Winston Churchill announced to the House of Commons that the Germans had surrendered unconditionally, but the official celebration hadn't taken place until the following weekend.

As she moved among the guests, shaking hands and performing introductions, Janet kept a determined smile on her face and carried out her duties as a hostess with a naturalness that made it appear she was completely at ease among her parent's friends, but in fact nothing could have been further from the truth.

It was over a year since Janet had been released from the internment camp in Spain, but she still hadn't adjusted to life in England. She had been completely changed by her experiences during the previous four years, while her parents' lives had remained very much the same as before the war. There were fewer servants at the family estate in Weston, and the grounds had been cared for by Italian prisoners of war, but meals were still served exactly on time, and formal dress was expected at dinner.

Janet reacted by becoming lethargic and withdrawn. Worried by her condition, her father summoned the family doctor, who, after thoroughly examining his patient, announced that she was suffering a delayed reaction to the stress she had experienced since leaving England in 1939 and needed at least six months of complete rest.

Janet had obeyed his orders and remained in seclusion in the Suffolk countryside, but her enforced inactivity hadn't stopped her from doing everything possible to help the friends she had left behind at the internment camp. Lord Elmhurst, whose connections at the Foreign Office had been responsible for her own early release, lived on a neighboring estate, and Janet pestered him daily to do what he could on behalf of Anna and Genevieve, but as neither were British citizens he could only voice her concern to John G. Winant, the U.S. Ambassador in London. She never discovered whether her efforts bore fruit, and the letters she sent through the Red Cross to the two women at Miranda de Ebro remained unanswered.

"Janet!"

She turned and saw a gaunt-faced, gray-haired man with a livid scar on his left cheek.

"Remember me?" he asked.

There was something vaguely familiar about his eyes, but she couldn't place him.

"George Noble," he said.

Janet remembered the name very well: his family had owned the estate next to theirs in Suffolk, and they had played together as children.

"Of course," she replied, trying not to show how shocked she was by his appearance. "It's been ages. Let's find somewhere quiet where we can talk."

"First I'd like you to meet a friend of mine," he said, leading her to where a Chinese man was standing. He was slightly shorter than Janet, but stockily built, and had penetrating black eyes.

"Chen, I'd like you to meet Janet Taylor," Noble said. "Janet, this is Tak Chen."

"How do you do," she said, offering her hand.

He took it and bowed his head slightly. "Pleased to make your acquaintance." He was wearing a khaki jacket, pants, and shirt made of a lightweight material such as might be worn in the tropics. It made him look out of place among the other guests, most of whom were wearing dress uniforms or ultraconservative Savile Row suits. Immediately after being introduced, Chen politely excused himself, crossed to a glass cabinet in an opposite corner, and focused his attention on a collection of jade ornaments Janet's father had brought back from one of his many prewar visits to the Orient.

"Your friend isn't much of a conversationalist," she observed.

"But the salt of the earth," Noble assured her. "I owe him my life."

Janet listened as her childhood friend described how he had been captured by the Japanese after the fall of Singapore and assigned to work as a slave laborer on the railway line that was being built between Malaya and Burma. He had escaped and been found wandering in the jungle by Chen, who was waging a guerrilla war on behalf of the Allies behind Japanese lines.

"He's got the best military mind I've ever come across," Noble said. "Communist, of course, but a brilliant strategist. He operated a lot like Wingate's Chindits, quick strikes where the Japs least expected it, in and out before they knew what'd hit 'em."

"Why's he in London?" Janet asked.

"To become an Officer of the Most Excellent Order of the British Empire," Noble replied.

"The OBE?"

"A gesture of gratitude for wartime services from His Majesty's government."

Janet looked around the room. Chen was now seated on a chair near the stairs. He had fine, perfectly balanced features and wore his thick, dark hair brushed straight back from his rather prominent forehead.

"He looks so young," she said.

"In his late twenties, I think," Noble said, taking another glass of champagne from a passing waiter and swallowing it in a single gulp. When he immediately called for a refill and spilled half of it down the front of his jacket, Janet realized he was deliberately getting drunk.

"Let's get some food," she said.

Noble started walking with Janet toward the buffet but suddenly collapsed. The other guests took a quick look at him crumpled on the floor, then continued their conversations as if nothing had happened.

Janet had two waiters carry Noble into the library. "Shall I call a doctor, ma'am?" one of the waiters asked.

"That won't be necessary," a voice from the door announced.

Janet looked up. Dr. Parkinson, the family physician, was striding toward where she was kneeling next to Noble. "I'm afraid he's drunk," she said.

"I wish it was that simple," the portly, white-haired doctor replied, "but George has been my patient ever since he got back from Malaya. He's suffering from recurrent malaria with the added complication of the aftereffects of severe hepatitis. I've repeatedly warned him to stay away from alcohol, but he won't listen. Seems the Japs treated him pretty badly." He took Noble's pulse. "He should be all right after a bit of a rest."

"He can stay here," Janet said.

"Your parents won't like—"

"I'll go and tell them what's happened."

She returned to the huge drawing room where the reception was still under way. Her parents were talking to Lord Elmhurst. When Mrs. Taylor saw Janet approaching, she crossed to meet her. "George really is too much—"

"He's ill, Mother," Janet said.

"Not drunk?"

"No. Dr. Parkinson says it's something George picked up in Malaya."

"Not contagious, I hope!"

Her mother's reaction angered Janet, but before she could voice her feelings Lord Elmhurst joined them. "Have you ever heard anything from those friends of yours at Miranda de Ebro?"

"No," she replied.

"Well, I saw a chap at White's yesterday who'd just come back from Madrid, and he tells me the American woman—"

"Anna Maxell?"

"She's Mrs. Mark Hunter now," Lord Elmhurst said. "Married the American vice-consul, it seems. She and her child went back to America with him some time ago, so apparently everything worked out for the best even though our chaps couldn't help."

"What about Genevieve Fleury?" Janet asked.

"Fleury?"

"A French woman."

"He didn't know anything about her."

Janet thanked him and headed for the balcony. She needed air and time to think, but found she wasn't alone on the narrow area beyond the French windows; George's Chinese friend was leaning on the balustrade gazing down at the crowds of revelers who were still gathered in Berkeley Square.

"They don't want to go home," she said. "Some have been celebrating for three or four days with hardly any sleep."

"But the war is not over yet." he said.

"It is for them."

"The Japanese still have not surrendered."

"Surely it's only a matter of time before they do?"

Chen shook his head. "The Japanese would rather die than acknowledge defeat."

Janet was surprised by the fluency of his English. There was hardly a trace of an accent.

"George told me the same thing," she said.

"I have been looking for him."

"He's not feeling very well. Our family doctor is with him. Apparently George has been his patient ever since getting back from Malaya."

"He has malignant tertian malaria," Chen said.

"You know about it, then?"

"He was very sick when we found him. He already had malaria, along with acute dysentery, and four years with my group in the jungle did not improve his health."

"The jungle must be a very hostile place."

"It is indifferent to human life. The real enemy in the jungle is the fear it brings out in a man. If he can conquer this he will find it offers a sanctuary."

After hours of listening to the empty chatter of other guests, Janet was surprised by his carefully enunciated pronouncement and didn't quite know how to respond.

"Are you staying with George?" she asked after an awkward pause.

Chen shook his head. "He was kind enough to offer me accommodations, but I prefer to be on my own."

"You're lucky to have found hotel space with so many people in London."

"I have rented a room in Bermondsey."

"I did my nurse's training near there, at Guy's Hospital," she said.

He looked surprised. "You are a nurse?"

"I was, but it's been some years since I worked as one."

"I would have thought nurses to be in great demand in London during the war."

"They were," she said, "but I wasn't here then."

She didn't volunteer any additional information, and he didn't press her for any. She suspected that Chen had categorized her as another mindless debutante, somebody who hadn't nursed the wounded because it would interfere with her social life, yet she felt no urge to tell him he was wrong. Doing so would only require her to dredge up memories that were too painful, and personal, to share with somebody she would never see again.

"Is the doctor still with George?" he asked.

"I don't know," she replied, "but he wants him to stay here and rest."

"Then I must find out which bus will take me back to Bermondsey."

"Did George drive you here?"

"Yes."

"Then I'd better arrange a lift for you," she said. "You'll never get on a bus with crowds like these all trying to get back to the East End."

"I can walk."

"It would take hours."

He looked at his watch. "There is a meeting I must attend at six o'clock."

"I'll have Parker, our chauffeur, take you."

Janet led him back into the living room and saw her father bidding some guests good-bye. "You met George Nobel's friend, didn't you, Daddy?"

"I don't think I've had the pleasure," her father replied.

She introduced Chen and the two men shook hands.

"I'm going to ask Parker to give Mr. Chen a ride back to where he's staying," Janet said.

"Too late, I'm afraid," her father replied. "Parker's on his way to the Savoy with Lord Elmhurst, and there's no telling when he'll be back, with the streets clogged like they are."

"Then I'll drive him myself," she said.

Chen started to protest, but Janet insisted and led him to a small mews at the back of the house where her 1937 MG had remained locked in a garage throughout the war years. She'd had it overhauled after returning to England and, although petrol was still rationed, Parker always managed to get her enough to keep the car running.

Chen climbed into the passenger seat and Janet eased the car into Charles Street, which was still crowded with people returning from the celebration. An old woman waved at Janet, raised a bottle of beer in a toast, and shouted, "Here's to peace, dearie!"

"Cheers!" Janet called in response.

As she turned down Park Lane another group of revelers, these dressed in the sequined splendor of Pearlies, called out greetings and waved small Union Jacks.

"I didn't know English people could be so emotional," Chen commented.

"Oh, we're a nation full of surprises," Janet answered.

She felt Chen looking at her but kept her eyes on the road, which had been lightly covered with sand along the parade route and was quite slippery to drive on. They turned down Constitution Hill, swung past the Queen Victoria Memorial, and headed east on the Embankment. She'd heard that Somerset House had been bombed early in the war but saw little evidence of damage and wondered where the main impact of the blitz had been felt. The answer became apparent after she crossed the River Thames at Blackfriars Bridge and found herself in the slums of the East End.

The home of dockers and shipyard workers, it was an area where the streets were lined with row upon row of identical houses, almost every one of which showed some signs of the damage that had been inflicted by the thousands of bombs the Luftwaffe dropped on such riverside boroughs as Southwark, Lambeth, Vauxhall, and Bermondsey. The humps of Anderson shelters were visible in patches of garden behind many homes, and children played on the empty sites where houses had been demolished in the bombing.

"It looks like Warsaw," she said, half to herself.

Chen looked surprised. "You were there?"

She nodded.

"George told me he had a friend who survived the Warsaw ghetto, but I had no idea it was you," he said. His voice was edged with a new respect.

"Where can I drop you?" she asked.

He motioned toward a block that was little more than a wilderness of heaped rubble. Following his directions, Janet slowly drove the car past what remained of a low-cost housing estate.

"Here is fine," he said when they came to one of the few buildings that remained standing.

"How on earth did you find this place?" she asked.

"Through Communist Party headquarters," he replied. "Would you like to come in?"

"What about your meeting?"

"It is being held here."

Janet hesitated, then switched off the engine and followed Chen up a steep flight of stairs to a room on the second floor. The seedy house reeked of boiled cabbage and dried urine, but he seemed not to notice as he ushered her into his bed-sitting room.

Eight people had already assembled for the meeting, and when Chen entered they murmured their greetings. A heavyset woman with a deep, almost masculine voice called the meeting to order and introduced Chen. There was a smattering of applause, to which he responded with a slight nod. When it faded, he said, "My father, a coolie, was killed by the British when he joined a strike at a rubber plantation in Pahang four years before the outbreak of World War Two. His only crime was asking for enough pay to keep his family from starving. I was sixteen when it happened, and that is when I joined the Malayan Communist Party."

In a voice that was low but full of restrained passion, he went on to describe how, by infiltrating labor unions and other social organizations, the Communist Party had almost brought the economy of Malaya to a halt by the time the Japanese occupied the country in February 1942.

"Influenced by Russia's decision to support the Allied cause," he told his listeners, "Chin Peng, Secretary-General of the Malayan Communist Party, offered to mobilize his members into resistance units to wage guerrilla warfare behind Japanese lines. The British government agreed to supply him with weapons, ammunition, explosives, and ten thousand Straits dollars a month, which were used to create a group called the Malay People's Anti-Japanese Army. . . ."

Janet found her attention riveted by Chen's story of how fewer than 2,000 Chinese and Malays, aided by a handful of British officers who were parachuted into the jungle, caused so much havoc behind enemy lines that the Japanese had to commit thousands of troops to trying to rout the guerrilla fighters out of the jungle. She was profoundly moved by his deep sense of purpose; it permeated his every word. It was clear that he was totally dedicated to the cause in which he believed.

As Chen continued to speak, Janet began to see the similarities between him and Mordechai Anielewicz, the young commander-in-chief of the Jewish Fighting Organization: the latter had possessed the same calm, deliberate manner and forceful way of speaking; each had been born into poverty and learned early in life to fight in order to survive. For Mordechai it was in the slums of Powisle where his father eked out a bare existence from his grocery store; Chen's father had struggled to support his family first as a tin miner in Kelang and later as a rubber tapper on a plantation south of Seremban. It was an upbringing that had bred in both men a burning desire to improve not only their own lot but also that of similarly deprived people who were the victims of social injustice. But both had quickly discovered they couldn't change the existing order by themselves, and so they had joined groups striving for goals similar to their own: Mordechai, the Marxist-Zionist youth organization Hashomer Hatzair; Chen, the Malayan Communist Party, which was outlawed by the British before World War II. Both had quickly risen to leadership positions and dedicated their lives to striving for social justice and a free homeland.

Now, as Janet continued listening to Chen, she began to experience the same stirrings that had prompted her to become a ZOB courier— a sense of spiritual aliveness she hadn't known since the final days in the ghetto. She realized just how much of an emotional void she had lived in since her return to England.

When Chen finished speaking, the woman who had introduced him asked, "What will happen to the Malay People's Anti-Japanese Army after the fighting in Asia ends?"

"If the British government honors the promises it made to Chin Peng and the Malayan Communist Party, the guerrilla groups will be disbanded," he replied.

"What promises?" the woman persisted.

"Full independence for Malaya," Chen replied.

"Do you think that Britain is just going to hand over a country that provides most of the world's rubber and tin?"

"Those were the conditions they agreed to."

"I'll believe that when it happens," the woman commented wryly.

Chen smiled but didn't answer. He looked tired, but when another woman in the group produced a large thermos of tea and some cold sausage rolls, he politely took some tea.

"You must be famished," Janet observed when the last guest finally left just before midnight. "I haven't seen you eat anything all day."

"I am not accustomed to English food," he replied, poking at the half-eaten remains of a sausage roll left on a paper plate.

"How have you managed since you've been in London?" she asked.

"I cook for myself." He motioned to a small gas ring and sink in the opposite corner. "But even that is not easy because it is so hard to find rice and the other things I enjoy."

"There are some wonderful Chinese markets in Soho," she said. "I'd be glad to show you where they are, if you like."

"That's very kind of you, Miss Taylor."

"Janet."

"If you call me Chen."

"Tomorrow at noon, then, Chen?"

"I will look forward to it," he replied.

She offered him her hand, then turned and hurried back down the stale-smelling stairs to where her car was parked. There were still no streetlights, a residue of the blackout, and a thick mist had come up from the river. After starting the motor Janet glanced up at the window on the second floor and saw Chen standing at it, but when she waved he didn't respond, and moments later the curtain fell back into place.

The following day was the first of many Janet shared with Chen, and the more time they spent together, the more she became attracted to him. He had no interest in seeing London's usual tourist sights, but he loved to go wherever he could observe how ordinary workers lived. They visited Billingsgate, the City's historic fish market, in the gray light of early morning, where Chen talked eagerly with porters who earned a living carrying crates of iced fish on hard-as-rock, thick-brimmed leather hats. On other occasions Janet showed Chen the docks at Limehouse, the West Ham Power Station, the railway marshaling yards at Euston Station, and sewer workers at Eastcheap.

It was a whole new world for Janet, who had never given much thought to how the working class lived, and because she saw it through Chen's eyes it took on a heightened dimension. It was as if she was seeing the society in which she had spent most of her life with real clarity for the first time, and because he was the conduit she found herself more drawn to him each time they were together. And the attraction wasn't only cerebral; she found herself making him the focus of sexual fantasies, looking at his large, powerful hands and wondering what they would feel like on her body. It was nearly six years since Leon Rojak died, and although they'd had an active sex life while they were lovers, Janet hadn't been with another man since his death. Now she felt the urge stirring in her again, but Chen wasn't an outwardly emotional man, and they had been seeing each other almost daily for two weeks before he even kissed her.

They were saying good night when he suddenly took her in his arms and pressed his lips to hers with a passion that surprised her. She responded eagerly, expecting him to invite her up to his room, but instead he explained that he couldn't see her the following evening because he had to attend a Communist Party meeting. He held her car door open and waited at the curb until she drove away.

His lack of sensitivity to her feelings left her frustrated and angry; it was almost as if, having let down his guard for one brief moment, he immediately regretted his display of emotion, considering it evidence of personal weakness. She spent a sleepless night trying to pinpoint a reason for his behavior, but without success. When her parents invited Janet to accompany them to a reception that was being held at the U.S. Embassy the following evening, she accepted. If Chen didn't want her company, she would spend her time in the kind of environment he detested.

Before leaving the house in Berkeley Square, Janet wrote a letter to Anna, telling her friend how she had heard about the marriage and offering congratulations. She also hoped that Janna was well and told Anna to contact her if either she or the child ever needed help. Then, as a postscript, she asked if Anna knew where Genevieve was.

The sealed envelope containing this letter was in her purse when she entered the U.S. Embassy. Ambassador Winant, casual, friendly, and expansive, greeted her and summoned an aide to take Janet in to dinner. Here she found herself seated next to a thin, scholarly-looking man, who admired the single string of pearls she was wearing and introduced himself as Frank Elwood, an under-secretary at the State Department.

"You are just the man I was hoping to meet," Janet announced.

"I am?" He looked puzzled.

"A friend of mine married a vice-consul at your embassy in Madrid, Mark Hunter—"

"Mark! Well, I'll be damned."

"You know him?"

"We were students at Harvard together," Elwood said. "I haven't seen old Mark in ages. Your friend's a lucky woman. He's quite a guy."

"I gather they're living in Washington, D.C."

"Then I may be seeing him, because I'm going back to the States next week."

Janet took the letter out of her purse. "Would you give him this?"

"Not war secrets, I hope." Elwood chuckled.

"The war's over," Janet said.

"For you Limeys, maybe, but we've still got the Japs to beat."

"You'd be doing me a great service," she persisted.

"No problem." Elwood slipped the envelope into his breast pocket. "If I don't see Mark, I'll look up his address and mail it to him."

He turned his attention to a fellow American, a woman with blue-tinted hair who was seated opposite him, and Janet drained her wine-glass. By the time the meal ended and coffee was served, she had consumed enough alcohol to wonder whether she could keep her balance when she got up. When the women left the table, the aide, who had barely uttered a word throughout the meal, asked, "May I escort you to the music room?"

"Thank you, but I can manage quite well by myself," Janet replied, slowly getting to her feet and walking out with careful, very deliberate steps.

When she reached the hallway, instead of crossing to where the other women were busily exchanging gossip, she went into a small library, which had French windows that opened onto a balcony. Stepping out into the darkness she took several deep breaths, but rather than clearing her head the fresh air only made her feel more tipsy, and she grasped the stone balustrade to steady her balance.

"Are you all right?"

Even before turning, Janet recognized the voice as that of George Noble, whom she had seen at dinner seated at the far end of the table.

"My turn to be drunk and disorderly tonight, George," she replied, slurring her words.

"Try some of this," he said, handing her a cup.

"Coffee. Bit out of character for you, isn't it?" She regretted her words the moment she uttered them, remembering too late that his collapse had been caused by illness.

"Not anymore," he said. "The good doctor tells me that if I want to go on living, booze is out from now on."

"Think it's going to be worth the effort?"

He laughed. "Who knows? Not drinking could make me a pariah in the social set we were raised in."

"Surely such a rigid class structure will never survive the war."

"Why not?"

"Because people from all kinds of different social backgrounds have been brought together in the armed forces and made to find a way of getting along together," she said. "Women in particular have found new roles for themselves, as ambulance drivers, ARP wardens, factory workers. They'll never be satisfied just being housewives again. I think the social barriers you describe are a thing of the past."

"Three years ago I would have said you were right," he replied. "I was in Singapore when General Percival surrendered to the Japanese. It was the first time Asians ever saw Europeans utterly humiliated. I would have bet then that the British would never recover the preeminent status they had assumed to be their God-given right before the war, but now I'm convinced I was wrong."

"What changed your mind?"

"Listening to men like Lord Elmhurst," he said. "We are distantly related, on my mother's side, and he says things in front of me that he wouldn't normally reveal to an outsider. He was at a dinner I attended last night where the other guests were mainly high-ranking Foreign Office types. I wasn't drinking, but they were, and when they started talking about the plans they've made to reestablish Britain's presence in Asia after the Japanese surrender, I could hardly believe what I was hearing." He paused and lit a cigarette. "They honestly think they're going to walk back into countries like Malaya and take up right where they left off in 1942, as if the war hadn't happened. I tried to tell them it wasn't going to be that easy, that men like Tak Chen only agreed to fight behind Japanese lines because they were promised independence for Malaya, but they told me not to be naive. They haven't the slightest intention of honoring their word. 'Surely you don't think we're going to hand the country over to the Communists?' Lord Elmhurst said, and when I reminded him that the British government had given its word, he laughingly informed me that the raison d'être for diplomacy is expediency."

The coffee had cleared Janet's head, but she still found it difficult to absorb the enormity of what Noble had just told her. "You mean they've been lying to Chen all this time?" she said.

"Awarding him the OBE is their way of fobbing him off," Noble replied. "Apparently they believe that if they make him a part of the establishment he won't turn against it."

"Have you told Chen?"

Noble shook his head. "What I heard was said in the strictest confidence."

"Why are you telling me?"

He paused a moment, then said, "I understand you've been seeing quite a lot of Chen lately."

"What has that got to do—"

"He visited me this afternoon. We talked at some length, mostly about you. He wanted my advice. It seems he has grown to—well, care for you, and he doesn't know how to handle the situation."

"Why on earth not?"

"He was raised in an environment where relationships between Chinese men and English women simply don't exist." Noble rested his hand on Janet's arm. "I consider both of you my friends, which is why I'm taking the liberty of warning you that nothing constructive can come out of your continuing to see him."

She stepped back. "Is that what you told him?"

"Of course not," he replied. "But I do feel it is my duty to caution you—"

"About what, George? That I belong to a better class? That I should spend the rest of my life going through meaningless social rituals I hate? That I should put my parents before the man I love?"

"I had no idea it had gone that far," he said.

"And now that you know?"

"I'm going to tell you something I hadn't planned to say," he replied. "Chen had a wife. They met before the war when both were members of the Malayan Communist Party. She was a Marxist Leninist who came to believe, after Chen sided with the Allies, that he had put his goals of nationalism before his commitment to the true principles of communism. She began to criticize him openly at the political discussions that were held most evenings when we were behind Japanese lines. Chen warned her that questioning the command of any leader in his guerrilla group could be punished by death."

"I don't see—"

"He had her killed," Noble said.

Janet turned away. After a long pause, she said, "Why are you telling me this?"

"Because I want you to understand that Chen's commitment to the cause of winning independence for Malaya will always come before anything else, including you."

When she didn't respond, Noble turned and walked back inside the embassy, where the evening's festivities were coming to an end.

"Ah, there you are, Miss Taylor," the Ambassador's aide announced from just inside the French windows. "I've been looking for you everywhere. Are you all right?"

"I just needed some air," she said.

"The party's breaking up. Could you use a ride home?"

"Thanks, but I came in my own car," she said.

The aide accompanied her downstairs to where Ambassador Winant was bidding her parents good night. Janet hung back until Parker drove them away in the Rolls-Royce, then thanked the Ambassador for his hospitality and hurried to where she had parked her own car. As she was getting behind the wheel she saw Frank Elwood waving to her.

"I won't forget that letter," he called.

He started toward her but was detained at the last moment by Ambassador Winant, and Janet quickly eased her MG into traffic. She didn't want to get involved in a conversation with Elwood or anybody else. Her brain was too numb from what George Noble had told her. Guiding the car more by instinct than any conscious reasoning, it was only after she had crossed Blackfriars Bridge that she realized she was heading for the seedy house in Bermondsey where Chen was staying.

She parked the car and turned off the engine but stayed behind the wheel, trying to gather her emotions. The alcohol she'd drunk at dinner made it difficult to focus her thoughts. Uppermost in her mind was a deep anger and resentment at the way the British government was tricking Chen, but when an inner voice asked why she should care so much what happened to him, she had no ready answer. George Noble had said Chen had come to care for her and didn't know how to handle the situation, but what did that mean? And what, precisely, were her feelings about him? Conflicting answers whirled in her head, none of them complete in themselves, and she still hadn't reached a conclusion when the door of the house opened and Chen strode toward her.

"I saw you from the window," he said.

"We have to talk," she replied tersely.

"All right." He led her upstairs, seated himself on the edge of the bed, and listened without comment as she spilled out everything George Noble had told her. When she finished he was silent. Then he said, "Can I offer you some tea?"

"You don't seem to understand the importance of what I've just told you," she said, irritated by his restraint.

"I understand perfectly," he replied.

Janet crossed to where he was sitting, knelt in front of him, and put both hands on his knees. "Damn it, they're using you! Don't you see?"

He nodded, but instead of answering he drew her to him and kissed her on the lips. When his tongue probed her mouth Janet responded by curving her lips over it, feeling her pulse quicken as she pressed forward against his body and his penis bulged against the swell of her breasts. When he started to break away, she stood up and held his head against her belly. The emotions she had suppressed from the first day they had spent together suddenly took over; they were far stronger than anything she had ever felt for Leon Rojek.

"Nobody uses me," he murmured, so quietly it seemed he hadn't intended to voice his thoughts out loud.

She felt his fingers moving up under her skirt, grasping her buttocks, kneeding, squeezing, delving first into her anus, then bluntly shifting to part the lips of her vagina. Because of his reticence up to this point, she had thought mistakenly that he would be a tentative lover, sweet but hesitant, and that she would have to take the initiative in order to gain the satisfaction she craved.

He undressed her with a deliberateness that made each item of clothing seem like a layer of shedded skin, a slow peeling away that made Janet sense barriers were being broken down, inhibitions cast aside. When he removed her panties he pressed them against his nose, inhaling deeply.

She watched as he took off his own clothes. His body was lean and hard, with numerous tiny scars across his shoulders and down one arm. When he was naked he stood over where she lay, his huge penis seeming to dominate her. Then, instead of lying down beside her, he grasped her wrists in a vicelike grip and forced her arms above her head, pinioning her as he lowered his head to suck her nipples. The pressure he exerted was so great that it brought the blood racing to her swollen nipples, and she uttered a sound that was prompted partly by pain, partly by ecstasy. Releasing his hold on her wrists, he lifted her legs, placed one on each of his shoulders, grasped her hips, and roughly pulled her to him. His cock pressed against her wet vagina, demanding entry, but when she shifted her body so as to accommodate him, he took hold of his shaft and guided it into her anus. His penetration was not deep, and because the head of his cock was so well lubricated with her own juices it slid into her with ease. Sensing that their mating had become a contest of wills, a joust in which personal combat was being waged through increasingly intimate contact between their bodies, she contracted her sphincter muscle and squeezed his shaft so firmly that he winced.

He slapped her buttocks hard, and she released him. Still supporting her legs with his shoulders, he knelt at the side of the bed and pressed his mouth against her vagina. The firm pressure of his tongue against her clitoris made her quiver. She was losing control but didn't care: now all she wanted was to be totally dominated by him, and when he mounted her she responded by digging her fingers into the flesh at his waist, pulling him even deeper into her.

Stroking, kneading, rubbing, he brought fire to her loins and made her moan with pleasure. Commanding, daring, completely unabashed, he asserted control with a blend of firmness and dexterity that made it evident that his sexual experience far exceeded her own. His every movement reflected the eroticism of the culture in which he'd been raised; she was awed by the number and variety of positions into which he put her body. When she climaxed he still didn't stop making love to her but inserted his fingers alongside his cock, seeming to double its size, constantly moving until she erupted a second time.

"Let me please you," she whispered.

He lay back against the pillows and she took his penis in her mouth, running her tongue repeatedly across its soft underside, at the same time squeezing the tip between her lips. She felt his belly muscles contract and his thighs quiver, but when she sensed he was on the brink of ejaculating, she smoothly shifted her tongue from his penis to his testicles, taking them both in her mouth.

"You do please me," he murmured.

Sitting up, she straddled his chest and slowly moved herself upward until her vagina was inches from his mouth. He put out his tongue and touched the tip of it against her clitoris. Shifting position, she lowered herself until her mons veneris pressed against his shaft, creating a friction against her pubic hair that made him moan. Only when he was almost ready to climax did she finally slip his penis into her vagina and begin a series of undulations that made him squirm.

"Come!" she commanded, squeezing his nipples between her thumb and forefinger.

His body arched, and she felt his semen spurting into her. He grasped her hair and pulled her head back. She gasped, then sank down with her head against his chest as they lay together in each other's arms, wrapped in a silence that was broken only by the distant echoing clatter of freight cars being shunted at Waterloo Station.

It was a long time before either of them spoke, and it was Janet who finally broke the silence. "What are you going to do if the British government reneges on its promise?" she murmured.

"Stay in the jungle and wage war against them until they do grant Malaya the independence they guaranteed us," he replied firmly.

Janet didn't respond, but in her heart she knew she had found a man who brought her both the love she so desperately needed and a cause that gave clear purpose to her life. She wasn't going to let anything keep her from his side.

19

PARIS: Wednesday, December 3, 1947

"Merde!"

Genevieve Fleury uttered the expletive under her breath as the obese French grocer labored over her, his jowled face shiny with sweat, until he finally ejaculated and collapsed on her like a sack of potatoes.

"Mon dieu," he muttered, still breathing heavily. "I am like an animal when I am with you."

"How well I know, monsieur," she replied, squirming out from under him.

"Is it good for you?" he asked.

"The best," she assured him.

He watched her cross to the sink, where she began sponging herself between the legs. "Maybe it's you who should be paying me."

She glanced at his reflection in the mirror over the wash basin and thought, You fool! If it weren't for the fact that you provide free groceries I wouldn't waste a minute on you.

"What time is it?" the man on the bed asked.

"Time you were going, monsieur," she replied.

"Now you want to get rid of me, eh?"

"Of course not." She smiled at him over her shoulder. "But your wife must be wondering—"

"That woman will be the death of me!" He got up, pulled on his pants, and placed some money on the table next to the bed. "This is for you, chérie. I gave the Countess the usual groceries when I arrived."

"Merci, monsieur," she replied.

He slapped her across the buttocks and ambled out of the bedroom, leaving behind a residue of garlic and dried sweat.

"Cochon!" This time the Frenchwoman said the epithet out loud. The grocer had been one of her regulars for nearly two years, almost since the day she and the Countess arrived in Paris after being released from the internment camp in May 1945, but she still felt nothing but disdain for him.

Now, over two years later, the two women still lived in the decrepit apartment in Montmartre they had occupied since their arrival in the French capital. It had been all they could afford to rent with the small amount of money the Countess had been able to save from her protégée's earnings at Miranda de Ebro, a large percentage of which had gone to Derek Southworth for protection. And even though the months immediately after the war ended had been good ones for Genevieve and the Countess—American GI's had eagerly spent their money on a last fling in Paris before returning to the United States—they had fallen on hard times when the boom days ended.

During this bleak period Genevieve gave the Countess the ruby Anna had left her. She sold it for cash, using some of the money to cover their expenses, but investing the bulk of it in steel and coal stocks, which she was convinced would vastly increase in value. As far as Genevieve knew, the investment had never really paid off.

She finished dressing and went into the kitchen, where the Countess was preparing lunch. "I must talk with you, madame."

"First let's eat," the other woman said, pouring a thick creamy sauce over stems of fresh asparagus.

"The grocer is a pig and I can no longer tolerate—"

"You don't have to, chérie," her mentor interjected. "When he left I told him not to come back. Now can we eat?"

Genevieve sat down at the kitchen table and watched as the Countess placed the asparagus alongside a cheese omelet, which gave off a tantalizing aroma.

"I don't understand," she said.

"It is simple enough," the other woman replied, pouring white wine into two glasses. "We have lived this way long enough. It is time for a change."

"If we had money—"

"We have, at last. You remember the stock I bought?"

Genevieve nodded.

"You thought I was crazy, that Germany was finished as a nation," the Countess said, "but I knew that without Ruhr coal, and without the German industrial output that depends on Ruhr coal, the rest of Europe couldn't possibly recover. That is what Stalin wanted, and I gambled on President Truman's being unwilling to let the Communists take over a weakened Europe. He had no choice but to allow Germany to radically increase its permissible level of industry, and that meant steel production had to go up. Now it has, and we've quadrupled our investment."

For the umpteenth time since she met her, Genevieve was astonished by the other woman's acuity. She realized now why she'd pored over the financial section of the paper.

"How much have we got?" she asked excitedly.

"Enough to rent a house on Ile de la Cité," the Countess replied.

Now Genevieve realized why the other woman had so frequently visited the tiny island in the River Seine, one of the highest priced pieces of real estate in the French capital. Many aristocrats and millionaires lived there.

"Does that mean I won't have to work anymore?" she asked.

"On the contrary, chérie, you will sell your favors to the wealthiest men in Paris."

"Why would they want a woman like me?"

"Because I intend to turn you into the kind of sophisticated companion they will pay handsomely to know."

"Even if that could be done, it would take a long time," Genevieve said, "and when you've already proved you can make so much money on the stock market, why bother with me?"

"You are a much surer investment."

"When can we see the house?"

"After lunch, if you stop talking long enough for us to eat it."

When the meal was over they put on their best clothes and rode in a taxi to the Place Dauphine on Ile de la Cité, where a real estate broker was waiting to show them around an Argentine businessman's house that overlooked Quai de l'Horloge and the Right Bank of the Seine. The broker was a distinguished-looking gray-haired man with a haughty demeanor who, despite his threadbare trouser cuffs, made little effort to hide his disdain for the two women, who he obviously thought were wasting his time, and he went to some pains to establish that the mansions on either side were owned by aristocratic families whose titles were among the oldest in Europe.

"It will be nice having them as neighbors again," the Countess observed casually, adding that she and one of the families had owned adjoining estates in Cap Ferrat before the war.

The broker's attitude underwent an immediate change, and he did everything possible to ingratiate himself as he conducted them on a tour of the small but elegant house.

"I will take a five-year lease," the Countess announced when they finished inspecting the premises, "providing the contract contains options specifying that all rental monies will be applied against the purchase price should I decide to buy the property."

"I'm sure that can be arranged, Countess," the broker replied. "The papers will be ready for you to sign tomorrow morning. Where shall I have them delivered?"

"Here will be fine."

The broker looked around at the furniture, which was shrouded by white sheets. "The house needs considerable preparation—"

"I am taking immediate occupancy," the Countess announced. "If you will be good enough to give me the keys, we can formalize our arrangements when you bring the appropriate documents."

He did as she asked, and the fat woman imperiously dismissed him with a wave of her hand.

When they were alone, Genevieve roared with laughter. "You would have made a great actress, madame."

"What makes you so sure I wasn't telling him the truth?"

"Because I know you too well."

"You know almost nothing about my life before we met."

There was a seriousness to the Countess's voice that made the younger woman uneasy. What she said was true: the only knowledge Genevieve had of her mentor's background came from the photographs she kept at the side of her bed, along with bits of information she'd let fall when it suited her.

"Did you have an estate at Cap Ferrat?" she asked.

"Do you think the broker believed what I told him?"

Genevieve nodded.

"Then why shouldn't you?"

Genevieve reflected that the Countess was obviously well educated, spoke numerous languages fluently, and had traveled widely.

"It's certainly possible—"

"I have never been in Cap Ferrat in my life," the other woman interjected.

"You are impossible, madame!" Genevieve exclaimed.

"And you must learn that others measure value by comparison. When I allied myself in the broker's mind with people he knows to be aristocrats, he immediately categorized me as somebody of equal importance. One doesn't *join* the level of society I intend to make you a part of; one is absorbed into it by association."

"I'm not sure I understand what you mean."

"You will, chérie," the Countess assured her.

They returned to their shabby apartment in Montmartre just long enough to pack their few personal possessions. They didn't take any of the clothes they'd worn during the previous two years because the Countess told her protégée they wouldn't be of the slightest use to them in their new way of life.

The house on the Ile de la Cité was sufficiently well-equipped so that it was unnecessary for the two women to buy anything for it. But the Countess still embarked on a shopping spree, which made Genevieve realize that the profit they had made from the sale of their shares must have been greater than she had originally thought; instead of trading her sexual favors with local merchants for food, the Frenchwoman found herself being pampered by designers at some of the most prestigious salons of haute couture in Paris.

Her favorite was Christian Dior, perhaps because she had read so much about him in glossy fashion magazines on rainy afternoons as she passed time between customers, or because she felt his New Look, with its lower hemline, made her appear taller while still accentuating the slenderness of her calves. The Countess shared her enthusiasm and ordered an entire wardrobe from Dior for her, complete with shoes and matching accessories.

Next her mentor took Genevieve to Jacques Tarrier, the leading hairdresser in Paris, who personally styled her hair, cutting it much shorter than it had been, in a way that framed her face perfectly and focused attention on her huge brown eyes.

Every aspect of Genevieve's transformation was carefully supervised by the Countess, who discussed in detail what each expert intended to do before allowing them to effect the changes they proposed. No detail was too small for her attention, and it was surprising how many of the specialists yielded to her suggestions.

The only time she encountered any resistance was at Helena Rubinstein's Salon de Beauté on Faubourg Saint-Honoré, where Madame Giza refused to allow the Countess into the pink-painted room where special skin treatments were given. An hour later Genevieve emerged, skin glowing, eyebrows plucked and shaped. Her makeup was much lighter than it had been, with less mascara and rouge. It was a look that made her appear at once sophisticated and considerably younger than her twenty-nine years.

The Countess showered Madame Giza with compliments but remarked, when she was out of earshot, "That idiot would have done even better if she had let me in to supervise." They were on their way downstairs from the second floor. Before Genevieve could respond, her mentor stopped to greet a solidly built woman with an impassive face whose short neck supported strings of pearls secured by a monumental brooch. She wore all black, and her shiny, form-fitting *tailleur* was topped by a matching bowler hat decorated with a star set in rubies and emeralds. The two women embraced, and the Countess introduced her friend as Princess Gourielli.

"Your little girl has nice skin," the Princess observed. "You must bring her to one of my soirées at Quai de Bethune. You know the address." She patted Genevieve's cheek and continued laboriously up the stairs.

"Madame Rubinstein could prove to be a very valuable social connection," the Countess said when they reached the street.

"Madame Rubinstein?"

"Princess Gourielli and Madame Rubinstein are one and the same," the other woman explained. "What matters is that she thinks you belong with her friends!"

Genevieve's education, the word the Countess used to describe her protégée's transformation, continued into the early weeks of 1948, with frequent trips to Maxim's, the Hotel George V, the opera, fashionable shops along the Rue de Rivoli, and a series of cocktail parties at Madame Rubinstein's. At each of these events the Countess remained at Genevieve's side to make sure she didn't miss anything: "Look how that woman uses her hands . . . see the way that one stands . . . listen to that coquette flirt . . . that is how you should light a man's cigarette."

The Countess kept Genevieve awake far into the night, studying menus or wine lists and explaining how various dishes were made, what foods to order in various seasons, how one paté varied from another, when to question the freshness of vegetables, and the correct way to eat such things as oysters.

The lengths to which the Countess would go in Genevieve's education became apparent when, in the following weeks, an odd assortment of men and women, mostly people whose lives had been disrupted by the war or its aftermath, appeared at the house on Ile de la Cité. They included a British woman whose Italian husband had been killed during the Allied invasion of Sicily, a Frenchman who had been a top official in the Vichy government, and a German, formerly a professor of Fine Arts at Heidelberg University, who was desperate to find any kind of work. Each was an expert in a particular subject, and they tutored Genevieve in everything from etiquette to art appreciation.

Among those hired to assist in the Frenchwoman's transformation was an American named Hank Owens, an ex-GI medical corpsman who, after serving with the U.S. Fifth Army, had remained in Paris after the war ended because he wanted to become a novelist. For him the French capital was the city that had inspired such writers as Hemingway and Henry Miller, and he fully expected it to do the same for him, but while waiting for it to happen he needed a job and had answered the Countess's advertisement in *Paris Soir* hoping to find work.

Her interview with him revealed that he came from a socially prominent family in Boston, had attended Princeton University for a year before being drafted, and was well read, particularly in American literature. The Countess was impressed, and hired him to teach Genevieve enough about Dreiser, Whitman, and Twain for her to carry on an intelligent literary conversation. After all, she pointed out, with the way things were going in postwar Europe, it was more important to impress Americans than anybody else.

Hank Owens was a tall, lanky young man with corn-colored hair, which curled over the collar of the leather flight jacket he perpetually wore. Although only three years Genevieve's junior, he looked much younger than his age, with wide-set blue eyes that projected the guileless, slightly dashed expression of a boy who has just forgotten his lines in a school play. He spoke softly, with a hesitancy that made him appear shy, but once he came to know his new pupil and feel at ease in her company, he readily talked at length about both American literature and himself.

He was obsessed by writers who had settled in Paris between the World Wars and was always seeking out places where they had gathered, such as Harry's New York Bar on the Rue Daunou. He showed her the sawmill on Rue Notre Dames des Champs, over which Hemingway lived when he first arrived in Paris. Hank had underlined passages in *The Sun Also Rises* in which the author described certain areas of Paris, delighting in reading them aloud to Genevieve while they were on the actual spot the book had immortalized. He was also fond of quoting from Fray Luis de León, whom he considered a sage, but whose adages Genevieve frequently didn't understand. It seemed to her that Hank Owens was more interested in knowing about writers than in becoming one, but she enjoyed his company and learned a considerable amount about American literature.

She also sensed that Hank's interest in her went beyond the small fee he received from the Countess for his tutoring services and was flattered by his boyish but obviously genuine attentions, which he expressed with a deference that, although charming, she first found puzzling. It took her a while to realize that Hank had been fooled by the aura of respectability the Countess had so successfully woven around the two of them. He obviously thought that the Countess's title was real and believed her claim that it was one of the oldest in Europe.

His gullibility astonished Genevieve until she stopped to consider herself from Hank's point of view: she always wore dresses bearing designer labels, her shoes were made by Roger Vivier, her hats by Mr. John, and she received weekly skin treatments at Helena Rubinstein's Salon de Beauté. She could order with ease from any menu, discuss wines intelligently, and made casual reference in her conversations to such luminaries as President Vincent Auriol and dapper, London-tailored Foreign Minister Georges Bidault, both of whom she had met at various cocktail parties.

The realization that Hank, while clearly infatuated, was too awed by her breeding to make his feelings known to her, gave Genevieve such genuine pleasure that she did everything possible to sustain the illusion that she was a member of the French aristocracy. Being held in such high esteem was something she had dreamed about for as long as she could remember, and she was secretly delighted by the natural ease with which she wore her invented identity.

While Genevieve spent quiet afternoons being tutored by Hank, the Countess was busy making discreet arrangements for trysts between her protégée and the men whose attention she'd caught at various social functions. These were all individuals the Countess checked very carefully, making sure their credentials, in addition to wealth, included both the right social rank and proven circumspection. The latter she ensured by making certain that the men she chose had more to lose through careless gossip than they cared to risk. With some it was their high rank in government; with others, families they wished to guard against scandal, guarantees against which the Countess included in the exorbitant prices she charged.

Almost every night Genevieve was picked up at the house by a chauffeur and driven to meet her clients at luxurious apartments they kept specifically for just such assignations in various parts of Paris. Invariably, because they didn't wish to risk being seen with her in public, rather than going out to eat they had late suppers delivered from various famous restaurants, establishments whose owners prided themselves on maintaining the confidentiality of their wealthy customers' private lives.

There was nothing sordid about most of these meetings; to her clients Genevieve was simply a very beautiful young woman from an acceptable social background who was attracted to them but was prevented from seeing them in public because their particular situations made such relationships impossible. This was the impression the Countess managed to create in arranging the trysts, and most of the men involved were vain enough to go along with the illusion. They also frequently chose to pretend that the money they gave the Countess was simply a loan she needed to help her through a difficult period that was the result of setbacks the family fortune had suffered during the war. The fact that these loans were interest-free and made without any specified repayment date were details they chose to ignore.

Not all Genevieve's clients were this genteel; a few, the rare ones the Countess misjudged, considered her a high-class whore for whose services they were paying a great deal of money, and from whom they expected to get full value, even when their sexual demands bordered on the bizarre. They never got to meet the Frenchwoman a second time, though, and their names were permanently removed from the list of customers her mentor kept with the meticulousness of an accountant.

The worst of these incidents occurred in the late summer of 1948 when the Countess arranged an assignation with the son of a British lord who was directly related to the Royal Family. The Viscount was in his early thirties, dark-haired and quite handsome in a reserved, rather severe way. His fine features and very pale skin gave him a somewhat somber appearance, and his eyes had a coldness to them even when he smiled, but he was extremely courteous when he picked Genevieve up at the house on Ile de la Cité and ushered her into a chauffeur-driven Rolls-Royce that bore a small replica of his family's crest on the door.

Unlike so many of the other rich men Genevieve had dated, the Viscount wanted to be seen around Paris with her, and he instructed his chauffeur to take them to La Méditerranée, where Jean, the famous restaurant's garrulous owner, welcomed his guests with cries of *"Vicomte!"* while heads turned to see who was commanding such special attention.

Genevieve knew she was meant to feel flattered but sensed that in some perverse way the Viscount was showing her off—not because she was a beautiful woman he was proud to be with but as if she were a specimen he was testing merely to observe her reactions. Consequently, she gave no sign of being impressed and accepted the accolades as her natural right.

They sat in a small alcove in the main dining room that was reserved for celebrities. Before they had a chance to order, a procession came by the greet the Viscount, mostly vague friends and chance acquaint-ances, although he somehow managed to remember all their names. When they were finally alone he ordered cold trout, lobster bisque, and bouillabaisse, explaining the restaurant was famous for its fish.

"I know," Genevieve replied. "I've been here many times."

After cheese and dessert he announced, "I need some air. Let's take a spin."

He told the chauffeur to drive slowly through the Bois de Boulogne, a dark, wooded area favored by prostitutes of both sexes, and he pointedly left the car window open. Blurred faces appeared like Hal-loween masks, calling in harsh voices, *"Tu montes, chéri?"* Each time, rather than answering, the Viscount glanced at Genevieve as if to suggest that, as a professional herself, she was better equipped to re-spond. Again, she had the uneasy feeling that he was deliberately trying to humiliate her, but when she remained silent he became overly solicitous, asking if she was cold and spreading a cashmere blanket across her knees.

By midnight they had gone beyond Les Halles, where crates of vegetables, hunks of meat, and containers of flowers cluttered the sidewalks, finally drawing to a stop in front of an establishment that bore the name Hôtel du Tabon. The jingle of the doorbell brought a man wearing striped pajamas to let them in. His dark eyes glowed from beneath a beret as he conducted them into a room filled with over-stuffed furniture and asked, "Are you here to watch or participate?"

"To chat," the Viscount replied.

"Ah, un cérébral," the other man grumbled.

"We just want to unwind," the Viscount said.

"The best way to relax is to watch."

"Then that's what we'll do."

The man nodded and vanished from the room after requesting that they wait until he could "get things properly arranged." Moments later he reappeared and ushered them into a small cubicle adjoining a larger room into which they could see through a two-way mirror. The tiny space where they sat on hard wooden chairs was in darkness, but the room they looked into was sufficiently well lit for them to see quite clearly what was happening there. An obese man in his sixties knelt at the side of a narrow cot on which lay a girl who couldn't have been more than six or seven years old. He had spread her legs and was lasciviously licking her vagina.

The tableau triggered memories in Genevieve of when she was the same age as the girl and had been seduced by her mother's customers when she returned clean laundry to their homes. Instead of exciting her, the scene only made her feel overwhelmingly depressed, and it wasn't in any way relieved when the Viscount led her through a succession of cubicles where they witnessed everything from a young woman sucking a dog's penis to men sodomizing young boys, to a man she recognized as a prominent member of the French Cabinet being whipped by two thin, hard-looking women wearing leather outfits.

The homosexuality and corporal punishment appeared to excite the Viscount more than anything else he saw, and he was noticably agitated as he paid the man in the pajamas. But by the time he reached the Rolls-Royce he had regained control of himself sufficiently to joke that now he knew why the French government had been so easily brought to its knees by the Germans in 1940. "They've raised submission to the level of an art form!"

When Genevieve didn't respond to his attempted humor, he asked, "Is anything wrong?"

"Just a headache," she replied.

"What you need is a nightcap," he said.

The Viscount owned a house near the Jardins du Luxembourg, and when they arrived he dismissed the chauffeur. Taking Genevieve's arm he led her into an elegantly appointed living room that was filled with exquisite Louis XV furniture, expensive Chinese rugs, and a collection of paintings that included works ranging from Braque to Dali.

"Do you like them?" he asked, when he saw the paintings had caught Genevieve's eye.

"They're beautiful," she replied.

"There's an even more interesting collection upstairs, if you'd like to see it."

She knew it wasn't his art he wanted to show her, but she didn't care; all she wanted now was to end the evening as quickly as possible. She followed him up a graceful, curving staircase to a room on the top floor that had once been an attic but had been converted into a well-equipped gymnasium.

"I learned the importance of keeping fit when I was at Eton," the

Viscount said, dimming the lights. "It requires strict discipline, of course, and considerable suffering."

He undressed and lay face down across a vaulting horse.

"You'll find everything you need in the wardrobe," he added, in a voice that had thickened.

Genevieve opened the door of a large closet. It contained a variety of garments ranging from rubber suits to leather aprons, and a selection of whips hung from a rack behind the door.

"I know I deserve to be punished for the way I have treated you this evening," the Viscount muttered.

Genevieve had whipped men on numerous other occasions and never thought of it as anything more than part of a performance, but now, for reasons she didn't fully understand, the idea of administering corporal punishment to the Viscount sickened her.

"What are you waiting for?" he demanded.

She picked up the whip and brought it down across his naked buttocks.

"Harder!"

She hesitated, then hit him again. Both swipes were halfhearted efforts, and didn't even begin to inflict the degree of pain the Viscount craved.

"What the hell's wrong with you?" he snapped.

"I don't feel well. . . ."

"Don't feel well!" He stood up, his features twisted with rage. "Whores don't get sick after I've paid good money for them."

He grabbed the whip and began slashing her with it. Some of the blows were softened by the skirt of her gown until he pulled it up over her hips and began flaying her legs, thighs, belly, and buttocks. She tried to protect herself, but within minutes her lower body was crisscrossed with welts.

The beating stopped abruptly, and when Genevieve opened her eyes she saw the Viscount had sagged against the vaulting horse. His body was filmed with sweat and he stared with glazed eyes at his penis: its tumescence had gone, and a thin dribble of semen hung from its tip.

"Bitch!" he muttered. "Get out."

Genevieve dragged herself downstairs into the hallway, pulled open the front door, and stumbled out into the street. It wasn't until she was halfway down the block that she realized she had left her purse in the Viscount's living room, which meant she had no money to pay for a taxi or keys to let herself in, even if she forced herself to walk all the way home.

20

It was almost dawn. Genevieve saw garbage collectors emptying trash cans farther down the street, and there was a smell of chicory and coffee in the air, but she was in no mood to appreciate it. As she hurried onward, each step triggered pain in her legs, which finally became so acute that, even though she had no money, she flagged down a taxi.

"Where to?" the driver asked, eyeing the welts on her face and lower arms.

"The Latin Quarter," she replied. "I'll give you directions when we get there."

Her choice of destinations was prompted by impulse rather than reason, and as she gingerly settled back into the seat of the taxi, she wondered how Hank Owens was going to react when he found her on his doorstep at this hour of the morning in such a battered condition. Why, she reflected, was she going to him instead of returning to the house on Ile de la Cité? One good reason was that without a key she would have had to awaken the concierge to let her in, and she didn't want to spark any gossip by letting her see that she'd been beaten up. But she knew that was only a partial explanation: in truth, she wanted to see the only man who had ever offered her kindness without expecting something in return.

"Stop at the next corner," she instructed the driver.

She had visited Hank's tiny studio a number of times and, although she didn't remember the exact address, knew it was over a butcher's shop.

"You sure this is it?" the driver asked, looking at the barred windows of the charcuterie.

"Yes," she replied. "If you'll wait a minute I'll go and get some money."

Before the cabbie could object she climbed out of the taxi and rang Hank's doorbell. It echoed shrilly through the building and started a dog barking. Moments later she heard the bolts being slid open and Hank appeared, wearing cut-off shorts.

"Jesus! What on earth—?"

"Can you pay the driver?" she asked.

He took some francs out of his back pocket and handed them to the man waiting in the cab, while Genevieve climbed the stairs to his cluttered room and sat on the edge of his bed.

"You look like hell," he said when he joined her.

Tears suddenly streamed down her cheeks.

"Hey," he added gently, "I didn't mean—"

"I was with a man who beat me. . . ." She sobbed.

"Hush. You don't have to explain."

"I lost my keys and money. . . ."

"It's all right," he assured her softly.

She eased herself back against the pillows, which were still warm and carried the faint musk of his body odor. Wiping the tears from her cheeks, she watched Hank take a Gladstone bag out of a closet and remove some jars from it.

"Courtesy of Uncle Sam," he said.

Genevieve remembered Hank's telling her he had served as a medical corpsman in the U.S. Fifth Army.

"This is going to hurt," he added.

A sudden burning sensation suffused her whole body as he swabbed her welts with iodine. She whimpered but didn't cry out, and when he asked her to undress so he could treat the abrasions on her belly, she took off all her clothes. He applied the antiseptic wherever there was any possibility of getting an infection, then smoothed on a menthol-based salve that cooled her wounds but still left them throbbing.

"I'm going to give you an injection," Hank said. "It'll ease the pain and let you get some sleep."

"What is it?" she asked.

"Morphine."

He filled a glass syringe from a small vial and inserted the needle into her arm. Seconds later the pain that had racked her body began to dissolve and she was enveloped by a feeling of euphoria.

"It's incredible!" she whispered.

"Try and get some sleep," he replied.

She closed her eyes and drifted into a state somewhere between sleeping and waking. When she came out of it, the afternoon sun was streaming into the room. She felt thoroughly rested, and even though her welts had begun to throb again the pain was nowhere near as bad as it had been.

Instead of putting on the Schiaparelli gown she had worn the previous evening, which was torn and bloody, she donned a pair of Hank's old pants and a sweat shirt bearing the words *Property of the U.S. Fifth Army.* Then, after tying her hair back with a square of blue silk she found draped over a lampshade, she slipped her feet into a pair of well-worn sandals and went into the kitchen.

Hank was hunched over a large black frying pan balanced precariously on a small gas ring that appeared to be his only means of cooking. It was evident from the many cans standing open at the side of the sink that his diet didn't include much fresh produce. Unaware of Genevieve's presence, he tried to turn the steak that was sizzling in the pan, but it slipped off the spatula and slithered across the floor to where the Frenchwoman was standing.

"It's a new way of tenderizing meat," he said sheepishly.

"You should call it steak tombée." She laughed, taking the spatula out of his hand and scooping the meat up from the floor.

"Want an egg on it?" he asked.

"Egg on a steak?"

"It's an old American custom."

"Now I know why you're all crazy."

"Hang around long enough and I'll teach you to like cheese on apple pie!"

They ate at a small table in the other room.

"I might hang around awhile at that," she mused as they were sipping coffee.

"Seriously?"

She shrugged. "I'd rather not be seen around Paris the way I look."

"You're welcome to stay for as long as you want," he said.

"I'd rather get out of Paris for a while. We could both go."

"Sounds great," he said, "but I'm broke."

"Don't worry," she said, "I'll get the money."

The Countess had opened separate accounts at the Paris branch of the Credit Suisse on the Champs-Élysées, and although the bulk of Genevieve's earnings were used to pay their expenses, a small percentage was deposited to her account for miscellaneous purchases. These had been few—the men she dated often bought her expensive gifts—and the money in her account had accumulated.

"What about your aunt?" Hank asked.

Genevieve was momentarily confused, then remembered that the Countess had introduced her protégée to the American as her niece.

"I'll phone her. I don't want her to see me like this."

He nodded. "Where do you want to go?"

"I don't care," she said. "You must know somewhere."

"Switzerland's my favorite country in Europe, particularly the area around Geneva," he said.

"Then we'll go there."

"When?"

"Today."

"You're kidding!"

"I've never been more serious in my life," she said.

That afternoon Genevieve called the Countess, avoiding a confrontation by simply announcing her plans and then hanging up before the older woman could protest. By nightfall she had withdrawn money from her account at the Credit Suisse and purchased a pair of casual shoes, along with an assortment of slacks, shirts, and sweaters, the latter with sleeves long enough to cover the welts on her arms.

The journey between Paris and Geneva was seven hours, and Genevieve had reserved a compartment that converted into double berths, but the sleep she had hoped to get on the journey didn't come. As she lay on her narrow bunk listening to the *click-click* of the train's wheels, her whole body throbbed. Finally the pain became so acute that she switched on a small reading light and tried to distract herself with a paperback novel she had bought before leaving Paris.

"Bad?"

She looked up. Hank was peering down at her from the overhead bunk.

"Very," she replied.

He climbed down the ladder and opened his battered Gladstone bag. "I'm going to give you another shot of morphine," he said, filling a syringe with clear liquid, "but it's the last. This stuff is very addictive. I saw more than one guy in my unit get hooked, and it isn't a pretty sight."

He used his belt as a tourniquet and tapped the inner part of her lower right arm to bring up a vein. She felt a warm flush as he injected the morphine into her bloodstream, and minutes later her pain had vanished. The click of the wheels, which had seemed like a metronome delineating each measure of her pain, now became part of an exquisite order, a total harmony that filled her with tranquillity.

Hank climbed back up to his bunk and not long afterward she heard the deep, even sounds of his breathing. But she wasn't sleepy. Unlike the first time, when the morphine had put her to sleep almost immediately, she lay staring at the underside of the bunk above her, enveloped by a euphoria that seemed to emanate from her abdomen and was like a prolonged orgasm.

She remained in this state until about an hour before dawn, when the train stopped at the border crossing between France and Switzerland for passport inspection. By this time the initial buzz had begun to wear off and she was rapidly sliding into a depression. It wasn't acute and the pain didn't return, but she was irritable, and the ritual of having her papers examined made her unreasonably angry. Hank must have sensed what was happening, because he skillfully pacified the offended passport official, who grudgingly stamped her papers and allowed her to continue on the journey to Geneva.

Genevieve had made reservations through a travel agent at Gare de Lyon to stay in a small hotel near the Jet d'Eau, a man-made geyser spouting from Lake Geneva. Their room had a flower-filled balcony from which they could see a group of sailing dinghies racing across the water in front of the former League of Nations building.

"Welcome to Switzerland," Hank said, plucking a flower and handing it to Genevieve. "What do you feel like doing?"

"Getting some sleep," she said. "I feel drained."

"It's the morphine," he said. "While you're high it's great, but you come down with a crash. Get some rest."

"What are you going to do?"

"Check out some of my old haunts."

He kissed her lightly on the cheek, dug an ancient camera out of his duffel bag, and strolled out of the room. She remained on the balcony and a few minutes later saw him emerge from the hotel. He glanced up and waved. She thought about how young he looked in the bright morning sun, and watched him cross to a promenade that bordered the lake, before wearily getting into bed.

It was early evening when Genevieve awoke. She knew Hank had returned because she could hear the shower running. She felt rested, and her earlier depression had completely vanished. Still nude, she went into the bathroom and slipped into the glass stall where Hank was standing under a stream of hot water. He had his back to her and wasn't aware of her presence until she wrapped her arms around his waist.

"Jesus! You scared me," he said.

"I'll leave if you want," she replied coquettishly.

Instead of answering, he put his head under the stream of water to rinse the shampoo out of his hair, and picking up a bar of soap, she began lathering his chest. He had firm buttocks, narrow hips, and a flat stomach, and his chest was hairless. She ran her nails across his nipples and felt them get hard. Still soaping his body, she moved her hand downward until it brushed against his penis. It was erect and she was surprised by its largeness, but when she began to work her soap-slicked hand slowly up and down his shaft he shied away, pretending to pick up a washcloth that had fallen to the floor.

"I've been in here so long I'm beginning to look like a prune," he said, stepping out of the shower stall and wrapping himself in a large, thick towel.

Puzzled by his abrupt departure, Genevieve remained under the stream of hot water trying to determine why he had so obviously turned her down. It couldn't be because he wasn't attracted to her; ever since they'd first met he'd made no attempt to hide his infatuation. It was she who had kept him at arm's length, but now that she was openly offering herself it seemed he didn't want her.

Getting out of the shower, she gingerly patted herself dry and put on a thick terry-cloth robe the hotel supplied for each of its guests. Dabbing some perfume on, she went into the other room and found Hank lying on the bed smoking a cigarette. She took it out of his hand, crushed it out in an ashtray, and cuddled up to him. Opening his robe she began nibbling on his neck and chest, gradually working her way down until she reached his penis, but it was no longer hard.

"Listen," Hank said, gently easing her upward. "It isn't that I don't care about you—"

"Is it because I'm ugly with all these scars?"

"God, no!"

"What then?"

He hesitated a long time, and then said, "When I was a kid I used to play doctor with a neighbor's little girl who was about the same age as me. All we did was look at each other's genitals, but she told her parents, and the next thing I knew, my father was beating the hell out of me with a leather strap. I didn't understand why, and all he kept saying was that I was no good." He paused. "Years later, when I was a freshman at Princeton, some of the other students got me drunk. They knew I was a virgin and decided it was time I got laid. One of them knew a woman who worked part-time as a prostitute; she was a waitress during the day, but turned a few tricks at night—"

"Tricks?"

"She made love to men who were willing to pay for sex," Hank explained. "It was a disaster. The guys with me insisted on watching, and I couldn't even get an erection. You're the first woman I've been with since then.''

"Have you had men as lovers?''

He averted his eyes.

"It's nothing to be ashamed of,'' she said, taking him in her arms and holding him close. She felt the wetness of tears; then he disengaged himself and hurried into the bathroom. When he reappeared his eyes were still red, but he had regained his composure.

"Let's go out and eat,'' he said. "There are some great restaurants in Geneva. What kind of food do you feel like?''

She shrugged. "Anything's fine with me.''

"Get ready, then, and I'll show you my favorite.''

He took her to a small, little-known café at the Eaux-Vives railway station which specialized in local dishes. The maître d' recognized Hank and, after warmly welcoming him, brought a bottle of Grolsch beer.

"Impressed?'' Hank asked.

"Very,'' Genevieve replied.

He laughed. "It's the only place in the whole of Europe where a maître d' recognizes me. I spent most of my severance pay on meals here after the war ended.''

Genevieve started to open the menu, but he took it out of her hands.

"Let me show off,'' he said. "Their sauces are exceptional, particularly on the trout, and we'll have a bottle of Rivas. It's a good wine and surprisingly cheap.''

Genevieve remembered that when she visited the Credit Suisse in Paris they had suggested that, rather than traveling with a large amount of currency, they could arrange for her to withdraw money from her account through their main office in Geneva.

"I must go to the bank first thing in the morning,'' she said. "Will you remind me?''

"I wish I could afford—''

"It doesn't matter,'' she assured him. "I was the one who wanted to get away.''

"Even though I can't—''

"Real friendships are rare.''

They lingered over coffee and cognac, then walked hand in hand along the promenade flanking the lake, stopping to watch the constantly changing colors of light on the four-hundred-foot plume of the Jet d'Eau, and that night they slept together in each other's arms, without making love. For Genevieve it was an unfamiliar but welcome experience.

After breakfast the following morning, while Hank visited a travel agency to make reservations at the various places in Switzerland he wanted to show her, Genevieve took a taxi to the Credit Suisse at the Place Bel-Air, an imposing building filled with a churchlike silence. The customers talked in hushed tones to tellers who listened discreetly. As the Frenchwoman stood in line, she had the uneasy feeling that she was waiting for confession instead of just withdrawing money from her account.

This trepidation was heightened by the awareness that she was standing in the bank to which she and the other couriers would have delivered the treasure from the Warsaw ghetto if it hadn't been buried with Pan Halevi under the ruined farmhouse in Austria. Or at least that was where she assumed the jewels had ended up. There was always the faint possibility that Halevi could have escaped seconds before the German tank opened fire, but it was a chance in a million: he had been in the cellar when the shelling started, and none of the women had seen him get out. But what if, by some miracle, he hadn't been killed? The idea hadn't occurred to her before, but now she found herself intrigued by the possibility, faint though it was, that Halevi had somehow managed to deliver the jewels to Josef Kandalman's personal banker. His name was engraved on her memory: Pierre Chambord.

"May I be of assistance?" the teller asked.

"I'd like to speak with Monsieur Pierre Chambord," she said.

The teller summoned a clerk. "This lady is asking for Monsieur Chambord," he said. "I think it is a matter that should be handled by the manager."

Genevieve followed the clerk to a glassed-in area at the rear of the bank where a dark-haired man was seated at a desk.

"I am Jacques Demmard," he said, standing up and offering his hand. "Can I help you in some way?"

"I was wondering if I might speak to Monsieur Chambord," Genevieve said.

"I am afraid he is no longer with the bank," the manager said. "Perhaps I will do in his stead?"

"It is a matter that goes back some years. . . ."

"Monsieur Chambord left very complete records."

"I believe Josef Kandalman was his client."

"May I ask you for identification?"

She showed him her passport, which he examined carefully before turning his attention to a huge Rolodex file. He stopped at a listing under the initial K, then crossed to a metal filing cabinet and took out a manila folder, the contents of which he studied for a full minute before looking up. "You know, of course, that we have very strict banking laws here in Switzerland. Under normal circumstances I am forbidden to reveal any information about our clients. However, there is a letter here that was written in May 1943, which lists the names of those Josef Kandalman authorized to make deposits on his behalf, and yours is one of them. Is that why you are here?"

"No," she replied. "I just wondered if any of the other four made any deposits."

"Can you name them?" the manager asked warily.

"Anna Maxell, Janet Taylor, Pan Halevi, and Keja. She only had the one name."

Apparently satisfied that he wasn't breaching a confidence, he said, "There is no record of any of the people you mention making a transaction at this bank. Is there anything else?"

"I'd like to make a withdrawal from my own account."

"The teller will take care of that for you." He summoned the clerk who had escorted her to his office. "It was a pleasure meeting you," he said. "If I can be of further assistance at any time, please don't hesitate to get in touch with me."

They shook hands and Genevieve returned to the teller's cage, where she withdrew the funds she needed. Outside the bank, she thought about Halevi, who obviously hadn't survived, and about the treasure that was still buried under the farmhouse in Austria. Perhaps it had been discovered by a lucky farmer who, on uncovering the cellar, had come upon wealth beyond his wildest dreams. In any event, it was an episode in her life that had come to a close.

Hank was waiting when Genevieve arrived back at the hotel. He had spread a dozen brochures across the bed and excitedly described the arrangements he had made to show her "his" Switzerland.

"You're going to love it," he enthused. "And there's so much to see. When do you want to leave?"

"As soon as possible."

He took her face between his hands and said, "You're special."

Genevieve smiled, kissed him lightly on the cheek, and turned her attention back to the brochures.

Hank had rented a Volkswagen and almost drove it into the ground during the next three weeks. At Interlaken they joined in a celebration of folk dancing and alpine sports, spending nights at the Baren Hotel and days wandering through streets ringing with music. In Bern they attended a staging of *Faust* at the Flein Theater on Kramgasse, a former coal cellar furnished with church pews, and afterward ate a late supper at a small inn on the banks of the River Aare.

Their days were so filled with activity that Genevieve began to lose track of time, and she was glad when Hank announced that he had arranged for them to spend two days at the hideaway hamlet of Foroglio on the southern doorstep of the Swiss Alps. It was a break she needed, a pause during which she walked alone in the high meadows while Hank worked on the engine of the car, which had been misfiring because of a clogged carburetor. Here the first blaze of autumn had turned the leaves bright yellow and rust, making the farm where they stayed, built of hand-hewn granite, seem like a gray ship afloat on a sea of vibrant colors.

She knew their idyll was almost over and wondered what was going to happen after they returned to Geneva. They had slept together throughout the trip but there hadn't been any sex between them, and she couldn't help noticing the frequency with which Hank went off with young men he met during their travels. She wasn't offended; if anything, it was a relief to know that his infatuation with her was only a passing phase. Far more worrying was the awareness that they couldn't live for long on the money in her account at the Credit Suisse, and that sooner or later they were going to have to return to Paris.

In another few months she would be thirty years old. She knew her days as a courtesan were numbered. She might get by for another two or three years, but after that she would no longer be able to command the same prices. Rich men liked their women young, and there was always an endless supply of newcomers eager to make them happy. It was a depressing prospect. As the years passed she would either have to resort to walking the streets or try finding a new profession. But doing what? Her only talents apart from sex were those she had mastered under the tutelage of the Countess, and being an expert on etiquette, ordering food and wine, and carrying on witty conversations weren't exactly marketable skills.

Genevieve and Hank spent the last day of their trip sharing a picnic on a mountain slope high over Bern, watching the rays of the setting sun turn the snow-capped peaks of the Jungfrau and the Eiger a delicate pink. By the following afternoon they were once again ensconced at the same hotel they had stayed at when they first arrived from Paris. Hank showered, put on a clean shirt, and announced that he was going to take a walk around town "to check things out." In fact, Genevieve knew he was going to meet a young Austrian student he had met in the lobby while they were checking in, and when she went out onto the balcony she saw them walking together along the lakeside promenade.

Rather than spend the rest of the day alone in the hotel room, she boarded a bus that left hourly for Montreux, where she wandered down a narrow path that led to the water's edge and sat on a grassy bank overlooking the castle of Chillon. Hank had told her it was a view that had stirred Lord Byron to write "The Prisoner of Chillon," a poem he had read aloud to her during their first day in Geneva, and now she identified with the prisoner, who must have peered up through his barred windows at the serrated, snow-crowned peaks of the Dents du Midi. In her own way she also was a prisoner, but of her past, and she saw no way of escaping it.

She thought about Anna and wondered how her life had worked out. She had written her after being released from the internment camp, and received a response from New York, where Anna was living with her husband. He had left the State Department and opened an art gallery on Fifth Avenue that specialized in the sale of eighteenth-century European paintings. While Janna was at nursery school in the mornings, Anna had begun using her spare time to study jewelry design and planned to set up her own studio in the basement of her husband's gallery.

It seemed, according to what Anna wrote, that her life with Mark Hunter was better than she could ever have imagined. Genevieve knew that when Anna married Mark she didn't love him, but that had changed. By being kind, gentle, loving, and infinitely patient, Mark had slowly won Anna's deepest devotion. *He has given me the security I needed in order to become myself,* the other woman wrote in her letter, *and I'll always be grateful to him for it.*

As Genevieve gazed out over the shimmering water of Lake Geneva, she tried to imagine what it must feel like to have a secure foundation in life. The concept was so far from anything she had ever known that she found it impossible to comprehend. There was the Countess—but not much else. Getting up, she continued her walk, lost in thought, and it wasn't until the path came to an abrupt end at a stone wall that she saw the villa.

Set back from the lake, the large white structure had once been elegant but was now empty and abandoned, except for an old man who was trimming a hedge near where Genevieve stood. The golden light of evening flooded the scene with a hue that gave it the look of a Vermeer painting.

"It's the most beautiful place I've ever seen." She wasn't aware that she had spoken aloud until the old man stopped his work and looked in her direction.

"It used to be magnificent," he said, wiping sweat from his forehead with the back of his hand, "but now it's all weeds and decay."

"Who owns it?" Genevieve asked.

He shrugged. "An Italian woman used to live here, but she died, and because of the war they're finding it difficult to trace her heirs."

The Frenchwoman continued to gaze at the villa long after the gardener, who was employed by the dead woman's lawyers to keep the grounds from getting completely overgrown, had packed up his implements and ridden off on his bicycle. In her mind's eye she saw the house as it could be, cracks plastered over and newly painted, gardens tended, freshly mowed lawns sweeping down to the water's edge. It would make a perfect home for somebody wealthy enough to afford its restoration, she thought, or perhaps an exclusive boarding school.

Then it struck her! It could be a finishing school where daughters from rich families would come to learn the social graces, such things as etiquette, posture, art appreciation, gourmet cooking, the art of conversation—all skills she had mastered at the hands of the Countess and her other tutors.

Genevieve felt as if a curtain had been lifted, and suddenly what had been a void became a world filled with possibilities. She knew that achieving her goal wasn't going to be easy—it would mean going back to work for the Countess until she had saved enough capital to finance her new venture—but the prospect of returning to Paris was no longer forbidding because now she had a worthwhile objective. Even if this villa was no longer available when she was ready to embark on her new endeavor, it wasn't important, because she would find another place. What mattered wasn't the building so much as a way of life that offered two things she'd always wanted more than anything else: security and respectability. It would be like beginning again with a clean slate, where nobody knew about her past and she could be accepted on her own terms.

On the bus back to Geneva she tried to think of what to say to Hank, but still hadn't decided on the right words by the time she reached the hotel and went up to her room. She hesitated before putting the key in the door, searching for a way to tell him that she was returning to Paris. The last thing she wanted to do was hurt his feelings; he had been a good friend, and cared for her when she needed it most, but it was time for her to go back to a world where sentiment was a dangerous emotion.

When she entered the room she heard the shower running and poked her head into the bathroom. It was filled with steam, and she saw the outline of two nude bodies in the shower, both male, pressed together in anal intercourse. Tiptoeing back into the bedroom, she quickly packed her bags and went down to the lobby.

At the front desk she paid what was owing on her bill, plus another two weeks in advance so Hank would have a place to stay until he returned to Paris. She sat down at a writing desk to compose a farewell note, but nothing she wrote seemed quite right, and it wasn't until she'd torn up half a dozen sheets of hotel stationery that she suddenly remembered a phrase Hank had taught her when he first became her tutor. It was from Fray Luis de León: *What matters most is that each should act in conformity with his own nature.* She signed it *Your loving friend, G.*

21

NEW YORK: November 25, 1963

There was an air of expectancy in the crowded courtroom at the Federal Court Building in Foley Square, almost like that of a first-night theater audience awaiting a much-anticipated performance, but the excited stir of conversation among the spectators, many of whom had stood in line for hours to be assured a seat, abruptly ended as a court officer announced, "All rise," and the judge entered from his robing room.

"Hear ye, hear ye. All people having business with this court, draw near, give your attention, and you shall be heard. Federal District Court Judge Fisher presiding."

Judge Fisher, a rotund, white-haired man in his sixties, took his place on the bench, glanced at the court calendar his clerk handed him, and announced to the spectators, who had resumed their seats, "The government of the United States versus Mark Hunter, charged with illegal transportation of stolen goods and forgery."

Anna looked at Mark, who was seated at the defendant's table next to his attorney, Dave Wilson, and saw a muscle at the side of his mouth twitch. It was his only display of emotion, but he appeared haggard and much older than his sixty-two years.

The prosecutor, a slender, balding Assistant U.S. Attorney who was half Mark's age, rose and began his opening statement.

"If it please the court"—he turned to the jury—"and you ladies and gentlemen of the jury, the government intends to prove that the defendant, Mark Hunter, while serving as vice-consul at the United States Embassy in Madrid, Spain, arranged with certain unscrupulous art dealers to purchase works by various seventeenth- and eighteenth-century European painters, which he knew to have been stolen by the Germans from individuals and museums in countries they occupied during World War Two."

The prosecutor looked toward the defendant's table, as if half expecting Dave Wilson to make an objection; when the other attorney made no move, he turned his attention back to the jury.

"The government further intends to prove," he continued, "that the defendant used his privilege of diplomatic immunity to illegally transport these stolen paintings into the United States as undeclared items, which he then resold at an immense profit through the art gallery on Fifth Avenue in the city of New York that bears his name."

He paused again just long enough to glance at the yellow legal note pad on top of his briefcase and allow the murmur that had stirred through the spectators to settle.

"Finally," he added, "the government will establish that on many other occasions since the end of World War Two, some as recently as this year, the defendant arranged for purchases in Europe of art works he knew to be forged, illegally transported them into the United States as undeclared items, and sold them as originals to numerous museums and private collectors. . . ."

Anna tried to concentrate on the prosecutor's words, but they bore so little relationship to the truth that she found herself thinking back, retracing in her mind each step of the journey she had taken since marrying Mark, in an effort to relate the accusations she was hearing with what really happened.

After the SS *Uppsala* completed its crossing from Lisbon to New York they had taken a train to Washington, D.C., where Mark resumed his duties at the State Department while Anna looked after Janna in the small two-bedroom apartment in Georgetown that became their new home. It was a period of adjustment for all three of them, and although it was difficult to determine what effect the transition had had on Janna, who was still less than a year old, both Anna and Mark had quite distinct reactions.

For Anna, who was born in America and spent the first fifteen years of her life in New York, returning to her own country after the horrors she'd endured throughout the war years was a cathartic experience. She felt free for the first time since the Nazis invaded Poland in 1939. She relished being able to come and go as she pleased without the feeling that at any moment she might be arrested. For months, though, she would regularly awake from nightmares of the Warsaw ghetto, her parents' death, her escape across the Pyrenees, and the weeks she spent in the internment camp, drenched in a cold sweat, waiting to hear the ring of hobnailed boots and the guttural cries of *"Juden raus!"*

Whenever this happened Mark was always on hand to comfort her; patient, understanding, gentle, loving, he held her in his arms and soothed her until she went back to sleep. Not once did he become irritable with her, even though he was experiencing the turmoil that resulted from continuing to do a job he hated. Finally, after about a year in Washington, Anna persuaded her husband to quit the State Department and gamble everything they possessed on opening an art gallery in New York.

Both of them knew it was a risky venture, but Anna was determined to see it succeed and played her part to the hilt, helping maintain the facade of success so necessary in the art business. During times when they could barely afford to pay the rent, she shopped at sales, searched the classified ads for bargains in clothes, and carefully furnished their apartment with items she purchased at bargain prices at estate sales. When they were required to entertain, she spent hours in the kitchen doing the cooking, yet always managed to emerge just before the guests arrived, elegantly dressed, to play hostess to Mark's business associates.

It was a constant juggling act, but one Anna enjoyed. The results were rewarding, not only the gradual success of the gallery, which slowly became accepted by the art establishment as a prime source for collectors of seventeenth- and eighteenth-century European painters, but also in the change it precipitated in her husband. Despite the difficulties of being in business for himself, Mark was happier than Anna had ever known him. He changed rapidly from the serious, rather shy diplomat who had visited her at the internment camp to a relaxed, outgoing, self-assured man who was proud to be acknowledged an expert in his chosen field.

The focus of his life was his family. He and Anna tried to have children but, after repeated failures, were informed by a gynecologist that she was infertile, possibly because of the severe emotional trauma she had experienced during the war. Although disappointed, Mark did everything possible to alleviate his wife's sense of failure and concentrated his paternal affections on Janna, whom he treated as his own daughter. They spent weekends playing in Central Park, visiting the zoo, buying cotton candy on the boardwalk at Coney Island, and going shopping for toys at F.A.O. Schwarz.

As the years passed, Anna and Mark frequently discussed ways to tell Janna the truth about her extraordinary heritage. They both agreed that it should be done as soon as she was old enough emotionally to cope with the information, but neither was sure what this age was. Although not an orthodox Jew, Anna had regularly attended services at a synagogue on the Upper West Side out of respect for her parents and had often taken Janna with her to these assemblies, but only as an observer. Anna explained the traditions of Judaism to the child she considered her daughter, but she insisted that Mark, who was Episcopalian, take her to services at his church also and familiarize her with Christian beliefs. Neither parent wanted to foist a religion on Janna, believing that she should make her own choice after she was old enough to learn about her natural heritage, but as she approached her teens Keja's child had enough girlfriends who were Jewish that she begin asking when she would have a Bas Mitzvah.

Anna and Mark realized the time had come to tell Janna the truth, and on her thirteenth birthday they explained everything they knew about the child's background. Anna described Keja, emphasizing the bravery she had shown in crossing the Pyrenees, her death in the village of Irati, and the ways in which Janet Taylor and Genevieve Fleury had contributed to Janna's care as a very young child. Janna listened, asked questions, and appeared to accept the trauma of discovering that the two people she loved most weren't her real parents; her equanimity was astonishing for a girl her age.

Anna had the uneasy feeling that the shock of discovering she was different from all her friends affected Janna far more profoundly than she was willing to admit, but she so completely internalized her emotions that it was impossible to gauge her precise reaction. Anna took advantage of every opportunity to talk with Janna about Keja, always stressing the pride she should feel in her natural mother, and while she was going through her early teens Janna showed an insatiable curiosity about her heritage, but she was so protective toward the two people who had raised her that it was hard for either of them to know whether or not she harbored any resentment toward them.

The only indication that Janna's equanimity was a facade that hid confusion, even hurt, came in a gradual pulling away from Anna and Mark. When Janna enrolled at Barnard College, even though the school was located within walking distance of the apartment where she had been raised, she elected to share a loft with three other girls on the Lower East Side, an expense she insisted on paying for herself by taking a part-time job at Macy's. Anna had been worried, aware that it wasn't the safest area of Manhattan, but Mark cautioned his wife against raising any objections, stressing that it was important for Janna to do whatever was necessary to discover her own sense of identity.

Now Anna looked at where Janna was seated in the front row of spectators just behind the defendant's table, her eyes fixed on the prosecutor as he continued to address the jury in his opening statement. At five feet six inches, she was much taller than Keja had been, and her body, although curvaceous, was longer-limbed and more slender. She also had a very different personality. Far from being the introvert Keja had been, Janna was outgoing and quite aggressive, particularly when it came to asserting her independence.

It was difficult to know from observing Janna how she was bearing up under the pressures that had begun with Mark's arrest. Six weeks ago, two plainclothes U.S. Customs agents had appeared at the door of the apartment on Riverside Drive soon after dawn, handcuffed Mark, and driven him to the Federal Court Building. The judge had set bail at $350,000, a sum Anna had raised by putting up everything they owned, including the gallery. Mark had been released before the end of the day, but the shock of what happened to him had taken its toll. He looked drained and his hands shook. For a long time he refused to talk about what had happened, and when he finally did it was in such a disjointed way that she thought he had suffered a minor stroke.

A thorough medical examination established that he was suffering from shock, and his condition wasn't helped by the way in which the media reacted to his arrest. It had all the elements of a good story: the glamour of Fifth Avenue, the intrigue of the inner machinations of the art world, the scandal of an ex-diplomat accused of abusing his position of trust, the mystery of forgery and international smuggling. Reporters had hounded Mark from the day he was arrested, through the hearing before the Federal grand jury, to the trial that was now taking place, and they hadn't limited their efforts to him alone—Anna and Janna had both become objects of their probing.

To Anna it had been a continuing irritation, but for Janna the consequences were more serious, because reporters followed her onto the campus at Barnard and waylaid her between classes in attempts to get interviews. The Dean of Students had finally called Anna to report that Janna's teachers felt she wasn't concentrating on her studies, and suggested that it might be better for her to take the semester off and return to classes when she was under less pressure, but Janna refused.

Anna had maintained a correspondence with both Janet Taylor and Genevieve Fleury. Janet, who was now living in a small village in Malaysia, had frequently offered advice as to how Janna should be raised, and when the Frenchwoman learned of Mark's dilemma she immediately responded with an invitation for Janna to spend a year at the finishing school Genevieve now owned in Montreux, but Janna had rejected the offer because she felt Mark needed all the support he could get.

"The government's case will be based not only on circumstantial evidence but also on the testimony of a witness who, in return for immunity from prosecution, has agreed to describe for the jury how he assisted the defendant in his schemes to defraud. . . ."

The prosecutor's words snapped Anna's attention back to the courtroom. Mark's already-pale face had turned ashen. Her heart ached for him as she watched him whisper something in Dave Wilson's ear, but the defense attorney appeared unruffled and smiled reassuringly at his client.

It was almost noon by the time the Assistant U.S. Attorney finished his opening statement, and the judge recessed the court for lunch. While spectators streamed out of the dreary, high-ceilinged room, their voices raised in an excited buzz as they discussed the prosecutor's closing remarks, Anna made her way to the defendant's table. Janna was already standing next to Mark's chair, her arm across his shoulders.

"What's this stuff about a witness?" she asked worriedly.

"They must have worked out a deal with somebody," Dave Wilson replied.

"But who?"

"They don't have to reveal that until he's called," the attorney replied. "But it doesn't mean that what he says is going to stand up under cross-examination."

"I thought the prosecution made a voluntary disclosure of their evidence to you before the trial started," Anna persisted.

"They did," Wilson said. "But they're not required to tell us where they got it. Now, instead of playing guessing games why don't we all go and get some lunch?"

"I don't think I can face those reporters," Mark murmured.

Anna leaned down and kissed him on the cheek. "You'd don't have to, darling," she said. "I brought some sandwiches and coffee. We can eat right here."

"I've got to call my office," the attorney said. He snapped his briefcase closed and strode down the aisle toward the door.

"I've got to go too," Janna said. "I'm already late for work, and I have a biology class after I finish at Macy's." She kissed Mark and Anna, and they watched as she was absorbed into the mob of reporters waiting outside the courtroom.

"God, I wish she didn't have to go through all this," Mark said.

"You know how she feels about leaving," Anna said, spreading a napkin on the table and opening a plastic bag containing the sandwiches.

"Can't you change her mind?"

"I tried," Anna replied, "but she's stubborn—and she cares about you a great deal."

Mark put his hand over Anna's and held it for a moment. "I don't know what I would have done without both of you," he said.

They had finished eating their meal by the time Dave Wilson returned from making his telephone calls. When the trial resumed, Anna took the seat Janna had vacated near the defendant's table, listening intently as Mark's attorney delivered his opening statement.

In a firm but quiet voice, he began by characterizing his client as an honorable, trustworthy citizen and by detailing his upbringing, education, and years of service to the nation as a diplomat. He followed this with a brief mention of the care and attention Mark had lavished on his first wife during her tragic illness. Then, in a tone that slowly increased in volume, he denied all the charges the prosecution had claimed it intended to prove, concluding by saying, "Under the laws of this State it must be established beyond any reasonable doubt that Mark Hunter committed the acts with which he is charged, and before this trial is over I will demonstrate to the jury that the evidence cannot support any contention other than the simple truth that my client is innocent and should be found not guilty."

When court adjourned, Anna took Mark's arm and helped him to his feet. Flanked by Dave Wilson, they forced their way through the reporters who were waiting for them outside the Federal Court Building, but only after the attorney had made a statement into the battery of cameras and microphones were they able to find sanctuary in the back seat of a taxi.

As the cab crossed Foley Square and merged with traffic flowing west, Mark sat hunched in the corner with his eyes closed. He looked on the verge of collapse. It was apparent from the way Dave Wilson kept glancing at him that the attorney was worried.

"How are you feeling?" he asked.

"How do you expect him to feel?" Anna asked, when her husband didn't answer. "There wasn't a word of truth in what that damned prosecutor claimed."

"That's what I intend to prove," the attorney replied.

"The dates he specified in the early part of 1944, when he claims Mark was buying paintings from the Germans, are pure inventions."

"The prosecution claims its witness can substantiate them."

"Well, they're lying," Anna snapped. "On at least two of the occasions he named, Mark was visiting me at the internment camp."

"As his wife you won't be able to testify."

"The Commandant must have kept records of when I was allowed out with Mark, for God's sake!"

"I talked with the Spanish Embassy and they checked with their people in Madrid," Wilson said. "It seems the Commandant died about ten years ago and they haven't been able to find any of his records."

"Surely other inmates at the camp could testify to having seen us together," Anna persisted.

"After the war, most of the detainees were either sent back to their own countries or put in Displaced Persons camps. It would be impossible to find them, and even if we could they aren't going to remember what happened twenty years ago."

"I had two friends there who could," Anna said.

"So you've told me," the attorney replied wearily, "but Janet Taylor is currently living in Malaysia as the mistress of a Chinese Communist for whose capture the British are offering four hundred thousand dollars, and Genevieve Fleury—"

"—owns one of the most expensive finishing schools in Switzerland."

"But she earned the money to open it by working as a high-class prostitute," Wilson said. "That kind of background isn't going to lend credibility to what she says."

"Whose goddamn side are you on?" Anna asked angrily.

"I'm doing everything humanly possible to see that Mark is cleared of these charges," the attorney said patiently, "but it's important that you both understand what we face. They have a pretty strong case. Quite a few of the paintings Mark purchased in Europe have indeed turned out to be forgeries. I'm sure he had no idea they were anything but genuine, yet the fact remains that a great many people have lost a lot of money, and they're looking for blood. Mark is the only person they can finger, so they're making him their target."

When the taxi stopped at the corner of Seventy-seventh Street and Riverside Drive, Wilson helped them out and said to Anna, "I think you should have a doctor look at Mark. The pressure's going to get a lot worse before the trial is over."

Anna did as the attorney suggested and called an old friend, Dr. William Hansen, who stopped by the apartment on his way home from his office. He examined Mark, diagnosed exhaustion, and ordered his patient to bed.

"How is he?" Anna asked anxiously when the doctor returned to the living room.

"Not so good. He's the kind of man who takes these kinds of things very hard. I've known Mark a long time, and he's always been ultra sensitive to what people think about him. Having his integrity questioned in public, as well as his professional competence, is a devastating blow," Dr. Hansen replied. "And his worry about the way Janna's life is being disrupted only makes things worse. I think he's more upset about her than what's happening to him."

"A friend of mine invited her to spend a year in Europe," Anna said, "but she wouldn't go. She feels she needs to be here."

"Leaving New York would probably be the kindest thing Janna could do for Mark," the doctor said. "Anyway, I've left a sedative that should give him a good night's sleep. If there's any change don't hesitate to call me, day or night. You have my home number?"

Anna nodded. "Thanks, Bill, you're a good friend."

Alone, Anna stood at the window overlooking the Hudson River and reviewed the charges the prosecutor had told the jury he intended to prove. The evidence against Mark was so detailed that whoever provided it—the U.S. Attorney's mystery witness—must have gone to great lengths to give it a veneer of truth. The dates and places corresponded very closely with Mark's movements during the specified periods and had been skillfully used as a foundation to support an overlay of half-truths and outright fabrications. Somebody obviously wanted very badly to destroy him, and they were succeeding. Even if the case didn't stand up in court, Mark's reputation had been irreparably damaged. The gallery was already closed, and Anna knew it would quite possibly never reopen: business in the art world was conducted on the basis of personal trust, and after the publicity her husband had received it was highly doubtful that he would ever be able to redeem himself.

The ring of the telephone jolted Anna out of her reverie. It was Janna's voice on the other end of the line.

"Where are you?"

"At school," Janna replied. "I've got one more lecture, but I thought I'd call and see how it went this afternoon."

"Well, Dave Wilson made his opening statements."

"Was Mark pleased?"

Anna hesitated. "Dr. Hansen just left. He says Mark is emotionally exhausted."

"I'll come by and see him after class."

"He's taken a sedative, and I'm rather worn out myself. . . ."

"In the morning, then."

"Fine. We love you."

As she replaced the receiver, Anna caught a glimpse of herself in a mirror and saw how tired she really did look. Her face was pale, and there were dark circles under her eyes, but the weariness wasn't entirely attributable to the pressures of the last few weeks. She was forty-three years old, and time was beginning to take its toll. Her once-black hair was now streaked with gray, and the lines at the side of her nose had deepened. It was as if all her features had become smudged. The only blessing was that without the glasses she now needed to read with, the aging process wasn't as visible to her as it was to others.

Turning away, she went upstairs to check on Mark and was surprised to find him awake. "I thought Bill had given you a sedative," she said, rearranging the comforter that had slid to one side of the bed.

"I haven't taken it yet," he replied. A small plastic bottle stood next to a glass of water on the bedside table.

"How are you feeling?"

"Worried."

"Bill says all you need is rest—"

"About Janna."

"She just called. I told her you were asleep. She's coming by in the morning."

"Isn't there some way of getting her to accept Genevieve's invitation to spend some time in Switzerland?"

"I've told you how Janna feels about it."

"It would be a load off my mind."

Anna didn't answer but handed him the sedative and watched him swallow it. She held his hand until he fell asleep. Only then did she go downstairs to the living room, pick up the phone, and give the overseas operator the number of Genevieve Fleury in Montreux, Switzerland.

Janna lay in bed listening to the sounds of her three roommates as they ate breakfast and got ready for the day. Two of them were fellow students at Barnard College, while the third was an actress who worked in the basement at Macy's during the day and appeared at night occasionally in off-off-Broadway plays.

The apartment they had shared for almost two years had once been a warehouse, and signs stenciled on the walls still indicated where crates of fruit and vegetables once stood. Janna's room had been a small office over the storage area. The loft had been converted into living quarters by a painter who was now in the south of France. He had leased it to the four women on condition that he could reoccupy the premises whenever he chose. So far the only times they'd heard from him were once a month when he wrote a note from St. Laurent d'Eze, acknowledging receipt of their rent check.

"You awake, Janna?" The voice belonged to Susan, one of her fellow students at Barnard. When Janna didn't respond, the other woman called, "If you miss another sociology class you're going to be in deep trouble!"

Still Janna remained silent.

"Okay, it's your funeral," Susan said. "Kathy and I are leaving, and Melinda's already gone to work. The coffee's still hot and there are some doughnuts in the 'fridge. See ya."

The sound of footsteps crossing the hardwood floor was followed by a metallic clang and a loud whirring sound, as the ancient freight elevator that was their only way in or out of the loft moved slowly downward. It was the signal that Janna had been waiting for ever since she awoke an hour earlier. It meant she was finally alone.

This desire for solitude wasn't a natural part of Janna's emotional makeup. Normally she was a gregarious person who enjoyed nothing better than sitting around with her roommates, gossiping over coffee about work, school, and whatever else was happening in their lives. But in recent weeks, ever since Mark's arrest had made her the focus of so much publicity, she had avoided everyone, even the friends with whom she shared the loft, and rather than get up when they did she feigned sleep in order to avoid coming in contact with them. They knew what she was doing, and why, and had tried to lessen the tension by pretending it didn't matter, but Janna sensed their patience was growing thin.

Reaching up to a shelf over her bed, she flicked on a small record player and leaned back against the pillows with her eyes closed as the sound of Django Reinhardt's rendition of "Troublant Bolero" flooded from speakers set against the wall. It was a recording he had made with Stephane Grappelly at a Rome recording studio in 1949, a classical example of his virtuosity as a jazz guitarist, but the reason she'd bought it wasn't his technique so much as the fact that he was one of the few Gypsies whose music was available on records.

She had purchased the album soon after her thirteenth birthday, in the vague hope that by listening to Gypsy music she would learn something about her past. It was one of many such quests: she had spent hours in the New York public library looking at books that described the lives of European Gypsies, searching the photographed faces in vain for some trait she might share. They were, almost without exception, a dark-complexioned people, with black hair, while she was fair-skinned with hair the color of golden wheat. Nor was there anything in their customs, beliefs, or lifestyle with which she could identify. The more she read, the harder Janna found it to discover a kinship on which to build an identity for herself.

She never let either Anna or Mark know of her research—instinctively she wanted to protect them from hurt, which is why she hadn't cried when they told her about her heritage—but she had wept frequently when she was alone, and after her thirteenth birthday she seemed filled with an unacknowledged yearning to discover not only her birthright but also the identity of her father.

Discovering that the two people who had raised her, and whom Janna had always thought of as parents, weren't even blood relatives had shattered her life completely. She felt set apart, not only from Anna and Mark but also from the friends with whom she'd grown up, and even the environment in which she'd been raised. It was as if a carpet had been abruptly pulled from under her, and in the years that followed she still hadn't regained her balance. She loved Anna and Mark, and did everything possible to make them believe that their revelation hadn't altered the way she felt about them, but within herself Janet knew that she would never rest easy until she learned more about her natural parents and discovered the identity of her real father.

Because of this need, which had gradually become a compulsion, Janna had found it more difficult to refuse Genevieve Fleury's offer than Anna ever imagined. Genevieve had roomed with her real mother for almost four years and knew more about her than either Anna or Janet Taylor, which made the thought of spending a year at the finishing school in Switzerland an enticing one, but Janna felt duty-bound to stay at Mark's side.

Thinking about Mark made Janna remember her promise to visit him, and getting out of bed, she put on a robe and climbed down the steep wooden steps to the main living area. The shower was located in what had once been a checker's booth at the far end of the loft, closer to where the other girls slept, and because it was next to an uncurtained window she didn't take off her robe until she was in the stall and had closed the plastic curtain. She stood under the needle-thin streams of hot water, wondering what she could say to Mark that would ease his suffering, but the question remained unanswered as she dried herself off and began to get dressed.

When Janna entered the kitchen she found a thermos containing hot coffee standing next to two newspapers. The first one she picked up was the *Wall Street Journal,* to which she'd subscribed for almost a year, and instinctively she turned to the pages listing the previous day's stock prices. She'd become interested in the market through an M.B.A. student at Columbia University, an occasional suitor, who claimed that the average investor could pick stocks by throwing darts at the listings in the *Wall Street Journal* as well as by heeding the advice of a broker. To illustrate his point, he named ten stocks at random. Soon afterward Janna had stopped seeing him, but she continued to follow the stocks he had chosen and was intrigued to discover that they did indeed out-perform the Dow Jones industrial average.

Putting the *Wall Street Journal* aside, she picked up the *New York Times* and glanced at the front page. It featured stories relating to President Kennedy's assassination, which had taken place in Dallas four days earlier. She flipped to the inside pages. A headline reading MARK HUNTER—MAN & MYTH carried a Madrid dateline and had been written by a member of the paper's bureau in the Spanish capital. Her first instinct was not to look at it—so much had been written about Mark in recent weeks that she doubted if there could possibly be anything new to say about him. But her interest was piqued by the length of the piece, and before she knew it she had begun to read.

It was an in-depth profile of Mark, with particular emphasis on the period he spent as vice-consul in Madrid. The research was the most thorough Janna had yet seen. Every aspect of his life was recorded in minutest detail, starting with his upbringing in Boston by middle-class parents and continuing through the first day of his trial. Drawing on interviews he had taped in Spain, the writer reconstructed how Mark first met Anna at the internment camp, and the course of their romance during the months that followed. Janna read the piece through to the end, not only because it was the most thorough piece of reporting she had seen so far, but out of a driving need to discover any fragment of information, however infinitesimal, that might shed light on the identity of her father. There was none. When she put the paper aside, she was left with the same restless yearning that had haunted her since she was thirteen.

An hour later, she let herself into the apartment on Riverside Drive. Anna was in the living room; Janna saw she'd been crying. A copy of *The New York Times* lay open on the sofa at the page containing the in-depth profile of Mark, and It was obvious that Anna had just finished reading it.

"Hey," Janna said gently, putting her arms around Anna, "Don't let it get to you."

"It just brought back so many memories."

"I know, but we've got to be strong for Mark."

"You don't know what it's like to sit in court and listen to that prosecutor tell the jury lies about him," Anna sobbed.

"I was there, remember?"

"I'm sorry, it's just that I'm so frustrated by not being able to do anything—"

"Has Mark read the article yet?" Janna asked.

Anna shook her head and dried her tears. "He's still asleep. The sedative Dr. Hansen gave him still hasn't worn off—"

Her sentence was cut short by the ringing telephone. She spoke briefly and hung up.

"That was Dave Wilson. He wants to spend time with Mark tomorrow."

"Is he well enough to start answering a lot of questions?"

"I don't think so," Anna said, "but Dave insists it's important that they talk before Mark testifies."

"I'll try and be in court," Janna said.

Anna nervously twisted her wedding ring. "I talked with him last night, and he asked me to try and persuade you to accept Genevieve Fleury's offer."

"But I thought we'd already agreed—"

"Bill Hansen says Mark is more worried about you than about the trial. He feels responsible for getting you involved in this mess, and feels that a year away from it—"

"Why a year?" Janna asked.

"The trial could drag on for months," Anna said. "And you know the Dean of Students at Barnard thinks it would be best for you to make a complete break, get away from the distractions, and make a new start next fall—"

"But twelve months!"

"It's the kindest thing you could do for Mark."

Janna crossed to the window and looked out at the traffic streaming along Riverside Drive. "Is that really true?"

"Bill Hansen thinks so."

"And you?"

Anna crossed to where Janna was standing and put her arms around her from behind. "Not having you here is going to hurt terribly, but if it's best for Mark . . ."

"You really feel it would ease his mind?"

"He's worrying himself sick."

Janna experienced a slew of contradictory emotions. Rather than trying to make sense of them, she said, "All right, if it'll help him get through this nightmare, I'll go."

"I hoped you would say that," Anna replied. "I telephoned Genevieve last night and told her I was going to ask you to change your mind. She's expecting you."

"When?"

"I said you'd leave tonight. I made a flight reservation, just in case."

"Tonight!"

"The sooner you go, the better Mark's chances of surviving this ordeal without breaking down."

"Is there any chance of that happening?"

"Bill Hansen's very worried about him."

"But it hardly gives me time to pack."

"You don't have that much stuff. I'll help you," Anna said.

They barely exchanged a word in the taxi on the way down to the Lower East Side, and they were still silent as they rode the ancient freight elevator up to the loft. Janna felt drained. It was as if she'd been existing on a reserve tank of nervous energy from which the plug had suddenly been pulled. It left her aching inside. When the packing was finished, she tore a sheet from one of her notebooks, found a pen in her purse, and asked, "What shall I tell my roommates?"

"I'll talk to them," Anna said. "They'll understand. And I'll call Macy's and the Dean."

Janna took out her checkbook and started to write a check.

"What's that for?" Anna asked.

"The balance of my rent."

"I can take care of that."

"Thanks, but it's my responsibility," Janna said.

After a last look around the loft, they went back down to the street. Janna hailed a taxi.

"I'd like to see Mark before I go," she said.

"I'm not sure the sedative's worn off."

"Still . . ."

Anna leaned forward and asked the driver to take them to Riverside Drive. "I'll wait for you," she said, when the cab stopped.

Janna let herself into the apartment and tiptoed into the bedroom. The drapes were still drawn, but there was enough light seeping through for her to see Mark propped against the pillows. His eyes were closed and his face was deathly pale. For a moment she thought his breathing had stopped, but then she saw the shallow movement of his chest and realized he was still drugged by the sedative. She leaned down and kissed his forehead. His eyes flickered open, and he smiled weakly.

"I came to say good-bye," Janna murmured, tears welling in her eyes.

"Good-bye?" His voice was little more than a whisper.

"I've decided to accept Genevieve's offer."

"I'm so glad." He sounded infinitely relieved. "It's going to be lonely around here without you, but it's the best thing to do. When this nightmare is over—"

"We'll all be together again."

He nodded, and his eyes began to water.

"I love you," Janna said, pressing her cheek against his and holding it there. She knew if she didn't go quickly she wasn't going to leave at all.

When Janna returned to Anna in the waiting cab, her cheeks were wet.

"Was he awake?" Anna asked.

Janna nodded but didn't trust herself to say anything. She suddenly felt overwhelmingly weary.

They picked up Janna's ticket at the Air France counter in the airport lobby. "Your passport is valid through the middle of next year," Anna said, "but you should go to the U.S. Embassy in Geneva and get it renewed before . . ."

The rest of her sentence was drowned out by an announcement over the loudspeakers requesting all passengers for Janna's flight to Paris to board the plane immediately.

"You'll have a two-hour layover at Orly and another hour's flying time before you reach Geneva," Anna said as they headed down the tiled corridor. "I'll call Genevieve and let her know what flight you'll be on."

Janna sensed Anna was talking in an effort to control her emotions, and when they reached the departure gate tears began to stream down the older woman's face.

"God, I'm going to miss you!" Anna sobbed.

Janna felt herself beginning to cry, too, and wrapped her arms around her mother. "Not as much as I'll miss the both of you."

They remained locked in each other's embrace until the final boarding call; then Anna watched as Janna disappeared down the ramp to the plane. The anguish the older woman felt seemed unbearable, like having a part of herself ripped out of her. She continued to weep as she stood at the observation window, her eyes fixed on the plane as it taxied toward the runway. Only after it finally lifted into the air and vanished into the darkness did Anna turn away, but she continued to cry throughout the ride back into the city.

It was after 10 P.M. when she let herself into the apartment. Instead of going upstairs immediately, she sat in the darkness of the living room, trying to dispel the feeling of emptiness that Janna's departure had created. She didn't want Mark to see her grief. When she heard him moving around upstairs, she went into the kitchen and poured some milk into a pan. Late at night, there was nothing her husband enjoyed more than a cup of hot chocolate. While the milk was heating she rummaged around in the refrigerator for the makings of a sandwich. All she found were some eggs, so she set about making him an omelet. Although it was late for a meal, it was almost eighteen hours since he had eaten.

When it was ready she put the omelet and the hot chocolate on a tray and carried it upstairs to the bedroom. The bed was empty, its comforter thrown back, and a pillow lay on the floor. Anna set down the tray, reached for the pillow, and saw a sheet of notepaper on the floor. It was unlike Mark, who was compulsively neat, to leave whatever he'd been writing where it lay, even to go to the bathroom—which is where he must have gone, because she could see the light was on. She picked up the paper and read:

> *Darling,*
> *Our life together*
> *has meant everything to me*
> *. . . you gave it meaning . . .*
> *but I can't go on.*
> *I love you . . .*

"Mark!"

Anna ran to the bathroom door and pushed it open.

"Oh, God!" she gasped.

Mark's body hung by a short length of cord from the steel pipe to which the shower head was attached. His eyes bulged from their sockets, and his grotesquely swollen tongue protruded from between his lips. He had taken off his pajama top but left the pants on, and they were soiled with excrement.

The telephone in the bedroom started to ring, but Anna couldn't bring herself to move. She was too stunned to avert her eyes. The phone continued ringing for another full minute and then stopped, leaving the apartment shrouded in a heavy, deadly silence.

22

MALAYSIA: November 26, 1963

Janet Taylor knew she was being watched, but she kept her eyes closed as the ramshackle bus, little more than a garishly painted wooden frame on a converted truck chassis, bumped along the rutted dirt road that was the only link between Kuala Lumpur, the new Federation of Malaysia's capital, and the tiny jungle village of Bukit Mekan in the state of Selangor.

Jammed onto the hard wooden seats around her was a near-solid mass of Chinese and Malay peasants—twice the number of passengers the vehicle had been designed to carry—and most of them had baskets containing live ducks, pigs, or chickens. Some of the items they had purchased in the open market at Kuala Lumpur were wrapped in sheets of the *Straits Times* bearing the previous day's date, November 25, the front page of which carried headlines announcing the killing of a leading Communist terrorist. Janet had glimpsed it earlier in the journey, but when she saw the dead man wasn't Chen, she breathed a sigh of relief and decided to get some sleep.

But a squalling child soon made rest impossible, so Janet abandoned the effort, turned to the woman holding the little girl, and, speaking in Malayan, offered to hold her while the mother fed an even younger baby she was carrying. Coming from any other European the offer would automatically have been rejected, but Janet had lived in Bukit Mekan for so many years that everybody on the bus knew who she was, and the Chinese woman smilingly handed over her little daughter.

Janet, who was wearing a baggy white cotton shirt and pants identical to those worn by most peasant women on the bus, used the gold medallion she wore around her neck to amuse the child by letting her see her own reflection. At the same time the Englishwoman used the highly polished surface of the talisman Keja had entrusted to her as a mirror in which to observe the faces of the passengers seated behind her. One was Chinese, the other Malay; they had followed her from the moment she stepped off the train in Kuala Lumpur, after her arrival from Singapore, and she guessed both were plainclothes members of the Malayan Police. Even in Singapore their men watched her around the clock, and whenever she journeyed upcountry at least two of them were assigned to shadow her.

It was no secret that she was Tak Chen's woman, and even though she had left Bukit Mekan when Malaya was granted independence in 1957, they still kept track of her every move in the hope that sooner or later she would lead them to the man they considered, after Chin Peng, to be the most dangerous Communist terrorist left in the jungle.

Janet twirled the medallion and smiled at the baby's wide-eyed wonder as the talisman reflected the afternoon sun. Being the object of scrutiny by undercover policemen wasn't a new experience for Janet. From the first day during the early months of 1946 when, following instructions she'd received from Chen, she had settled in the village of Bukit Mekan, the British authorities had kept her under constant observation. They knew her reason for being in the country was so she could be close to her Chinese lover, and after the nationalist revolt became a grim half-war that was dubbed the "Emergency," they maintained a particularly close vigil, assuming that sooner or later she would make contact with the man for whom the British government was willing to pay a reward of 400,000 Straits dollars, alive or dead.

They could have arrested Janet at any time, or sent her to live in one of the quasi-concentration camps called "resettlement centers," where over 500,000 men, women, and children had been relocated from outlying villages in an effort to stop them from supplying the Communist guerrillas with food. Instead, they tried to use her as bait to lure Chen into their trap.

Janet had continued this cat-and-mouse existence for eleven years, supporting herself by working for a Chinese herbalist in Bukit Mekan who was widely respected for his medical skills, and whose patients included many whom doctors qualified in traditional Western medicine had failed to cure.

At first Janet had considered Chu Kai, the soft-spoken, white-haired doctor and herbalist—who had practiced his profession for over forty years in China and Thailand before settling in Malaya—a lovable old fake. Nothing she had learned in her nurse's training in London or in her experience working with Dr. Maxell in the Warsaw ghetto had prepared her to acknowledge the curative powers of seal kidneys (for potency), powdered crab (for open wounds), four-legged ducks (a tuberculosis cure), or gorilla blood (for female ailments). Nor was she willing to believe that wine made from fermenting tiger bones could give those who drank it the strength they needed to recover from debilitating illnesses. But the longer she worked for Chu Kai, and the more she witnessed at first hand how effective his cures were, the greater became her desire to learn from him.

As Janet came to understand Kai's methods, she began to realize that her initial doubts had been rooted in the way she had been conditioned to perceive illness. In the West, doctors started with symptoms and searched for underlying causes, while Chu Kai directed his attention to the complete physiological and psychological condition of his patient. In order to discover the imbalance in the sick person's "pattern of harmony," his diagnostic techniques included close visual inspection, listening, smelling, questioning, and palpation. He could deduce a great deal merely by studying the patient's face; the color and temperature of the bridge of the nose, Kai taught Janet, could indicate a great deal about the lungs, spleen, and stomach.

When Janet expressed interest in learning more of Kai's skills, he invited her to move into a spare room over his simple wood-frame shop, explaining that the only way for her to understand Chinese medicine was to watch while he treated patients. She accepted his offer, and in the months that followed Kai spent hours every evening imparting his knowledge.

The British had imposed a 6 P.M. curfew, and anybody found on the streets after that time was arrested. Under the Emergency regulations they could be held indefinitely without charges being brought; paragraph 4-C made the death penalty mandatory for anybody found carrying weapons or Communist propaganda. So the people of Bukit Mekan, like those of every other village in Malaya during the Emergency, had to find ways of filling the long hours of tropical darkness without leaving their homes.

This wasn't a problem for Janet; the sessions she spent with Chu Kai lasted far into the night. He taught her that the Chinese perceive the universe as a vast indivisible entity, within which no one thing can exist without others. By violating this harmony, a person brought sickness on himself. "If a man wishes to remain healthy," Kai repeatedly declared, "he must attune himself and his actions to this ever-moving cycle." Precise instructions on ways to achieve this were contained in a 2,000-year-old book called *Lu Chih Ch'un Ch'iu* (Spring and Autumn Annals), a copy of which he insisted Janet read until she knew it almost by heart.

Her education in the arts of Chinese medicine continued under Chu

Kai's nightly tutelage throughout most of the eleven years she lived in Bukit Mekan. In that time she became highly proficient in acupuncture, moxibustion, therapeutic massage, correct breathing techniques, simple orthopedic treatments, and the use of talismans. These last were ideographs similar to the characters used in Chinese writing, painted in black on a background of red or yellow paper—a different symbol for each disease—which were either tied to the patient's bed or burned and the ashes swallowed.

She mastered the use of Chinese pharmaceuticals, many of which involved the use of the same animal parts she had thought so bizarre when she first saw Chu Kai's shop. Experience taught her that elephant skin was useful for slow-healing wounds; boys' urine for lung disease (swallowed warm it also soothed inflamed throats); ground turtle shells worked well to stimulate weak kidneys; boiled swallows' nests, because of the high mineral content of bird droppings, helped cure vitamin deficiencies; and the ink from cuttlefish, mixed with vinegar, ameliorated heart conditions.

But the one area in which Janet really excelled was in the use of curative herbs. Ginseng, which the Chinese called *jen-shen,* was considered by most of Chu Kai's patients to be a panacea for all ills, and one of the first things she had to learn when she started working for the Chinese doctor was how to incorporate it into numerous prescriptions. Other herbs were equally effective: wild ginger for head colds, curcuma root to heal wounds, ephedra for treatment of pulmonary diseases, weeping forsythia to destroy intestinal worms, barberry to mitigate toothache. Lotus leaves healed eczema, rippleseed plantain increased fertility, knotweed helped in treating cancer, common dandelion often cured mammillary ulcers, and verbena worked well as an antiperiodic for malaria.

At first Janet was puzzled by Chu Kai's willingness to spend so much time teaching her his healing arts, but the longer she remained with him, the clearer it became that it was all part of an elaborate plan Chen had conceived to make it possible for them to meet even though he was a wanted man and she was watched around the clock by the British. When Chu Kai was called out to attend patients too sick to visit him, Janet accompanied her teacher to the villages and frequently helped administer treatments. Over a long period of time her watchers grew accustomed to seeing her walk alongside the old, frail-looking Chinese doctor, often carrying the basket containing his various potents and herbal remedies, and they became less vigilant. Little did they realize that many of the "villagers" Chu Kai and Janet treated were actually Chen's comrades, wounded in skirmishes with British, Malay, and Gurkha units or stricken by illnesses that would have proved fatal if they'd had to remain unattended in the jungle.

For the one thing Chen's guerrilla groups lacked were doctors. Life as a fugitive in the jungle was simply too harsh for the few who supported the Communist cause, and the situation was aggravated even further by the fact that the British authorities kept careful track of all medicines in an effort to stop them from being used to treat injured terrorists. Every doctor who practiced Western-style medicine in Malaya was required to account for all the pharmaceutical supplies he ordered, but there was no way the authorities could control the manufacture of remedies used by such practitioners as Chu Kai. The animals and plants that went into his cures were readily available throughout the country and easily obtained at a moment's notice from the ever-present jungle.

It was while Janet was with Chu Kai, who was an ardent supporter of the fight for Malayan independence, that she met Chen for the first time since they had become lovers in London. She had gone to a village on the fringe of the jungle with her teacher to treat a woman who was close to death from acute colitis, when a young Malay girl suddenly appeared at Janet's side and beckoned her to follow. Thinking there was some other villager who needed attention, she accompanied the youngster to a palm-thatched hut on the edge of the jungle and went inside to find Chen waiting for her.

It was months since she had last seen him, and although they had exchanged frequent messages with each other through the Min Yuen —a network of Chinese and Malay coolies, servants, and lower-level office workers who demonstrated their support of the Communist cause by supplying the jungle fighters with food, money, and intelligence reports—they had never found a previous opportunity to meet. Chen looked haggard and very thin. His faded green battle fatigues hung on him, and when they embraced, Janet could feel the protrusion of his ribs.

"Oh, God," she murmured, resting her head against his chest, "I've missed you so much."

"I tried to arrange for us to meet before, but something always came up at the last minute that made it too dangerous," he said.

Janet raised her head and looked into his eyes. They were harder than she remembered, but when he pressed his lips against hers she felt the same tremor of anticipation she had experienced the first time they made love. He undressed her and took off his fatigues. Janet lay on a mat woven from palm fronds, but instead of joining her Chen stood looking down at her body as if he was memorizing every part of her.

"I want you," she said, reaching toward him with her open arms.

He knelt next to where she was lying and trailed the tips of his fingers across her breasts and down her belly. "You don't know how many times I've dreamed of you," he said, his voice so soft it was almost as if he were speaking to himself. "At night in the jungle I keep remembering the way we were together in London, and wondering if you still feel the same. . . ."

"I do," Janet whispered.

Chen lowered his head and kissed her nipples, then slowly ran his tongue downward until it reached her crotch. Janet felt the warmth of his breath against her pubic hair, and a tingle of anticipation as he straddled her waist. He didn't enter her immediately, but knelt with his rigid penis resting against her belly, and once again she sensed he was imprinting a picture of her in his mind's eye.

"I love you," he said.

"Show me. . . ."

He spread her legs and slowly lowered himself into her. She felt his firm shaft probe deep and responded with rhythmic undulations of her pelvis, slowly but surely quickening the pace until they came simultaneously. For a long time Chen lay on her without moving, his head pressed in the crook of her shoulder, and only after his penis slipped from her of its own volition did he finally roll to one side.

"You're still my woman," he murmured.

"Did you think I wouldn't be?" Janet asked.

"I didn't know."

"And now?"

"I wish I could stay here with you forever."

"But you can't. . . ."

He shook his head. "It's risky for me to have been here this long."

"Will that ever change?"

"The moment Britain honors its promise to grant Malaya independence," he answered, getting up and putting on his green fatigues.

Janet didn't answer, just held him in her arms. Even after he picked up his Sten gun and silently disappeared back into the jungle, accompanied by the two young Chinese comrades who had kept watch while their leader was inside the hut, she remained where she lay, still naked, savoring the pungent, slightly musky odor that lingered in the humid air. She could feel his semen trickling out of her vagina. Impulsively, she wet her fingers with it and touched it to her tongue. Then she repeated the gesture, this time smearing the still warm milky fluid over her breasts, belly, face, and hair.

It was the first of many such meetings Janet had with Chen during the eleven years she lived in Bukit Mekan, and they invariably followed the same pattern. When she least expected it, usually on a visit with Chu Kai to some outlying village, her Chinese lover would appear like a specter out of the jungle, and they would spend a brief time in each other's arms before he would disappear into the almost solid wall of foliage. Each time he left her Janet was convinced she would never see Chen again—the anguish was so intense it made her wonder if the pain of such love was worth the suffering—but then Chen would reappear, and for an hour, perhaps less, all her doubts would disappear.

But as time passed Janet began to notice changes in him. It was imperceptible at first, but over the years it became more obvious, and she had to acknowledge that he was no longer the man she had fallen in love with in London. The physical differences were attributable to his lack of food and the perpetual tensions of living for so long like a hunted animal in the jungle. Although almost the same age as Janet, he began to appear much older; his skin, under constant assault by leeches, had become a mass of constant sores, and the whites of his eyes took on a permanent yellowish hue as a result of frequent attacks of malaria. She kept him supplied with herbs to treat both conditions, but because it was necessary for him to constantly remain on the move, he often wasn't able to carry them with him, and both afflictions grew worse.

But the greatest change was a psychological one, which manifested itself in a callousness that she hadn't seen when they first met. He seemed to have developed a total disregard for human life. He talked about British soldiers he had killed in jungle ambushes with a lack of feeling that made Janet realize he had come to rely on the same primitive instincts that enabled other animals in the jungle to survive. The ideals he had talked about so convincingly in the bed-sitting room in Bermondsey seemed to have been abandoned in favor of killing for the sake of violence itself, and he seemed to have totally lost sight of the ideals that originally prompted him to return to the jungle and declare war on the British. He no longer talked of achieving independence for Malaya; he was far more concerned with prevailing over rival factions that had sprung up within the Communist party—groups he was convinced were trying to usurp his authority.

When Chen decided to remain in the jungle with Chin Peng, who began his third campaign of insurgency, this time against the new state, immediately after Malaya was finally granted independence in 1957, Janet confronted her lover at a meeting he'd arranged in a village north of Bukit Mekan.

"Communism is no different from colonialism," she charged. "They both have the same rigid inequities."

"You don't understand the problems," Chen countered.

"That may be true," the Englishwoman acknowledged. "But the freedoms you talked about in London as worth fighting for, which were why I came here to share the struggle with you, now look to me like the exchange of one autocracy for another."

"Then why stay?" he asked.

"Because I love you," she answered. "But that's not enough of a reason anymore. My belief in your ideals, as well as our love, made the last eleven years bearable, but you've lost sight of what they were. I have no faith in what you seem to want now, which is just power itself."

Not long afterward Janet moved to Singapore, where she supported herself by practicing the skills Chu Kai had taught her, but she never stopped caring about Chen and still made periodic trips back to Bukit Mekan on the pretext of delivering herbal supplies to her old mentor that weren't available to him locally. Alerted to these visits by the Min Yuen, Chen continued to appear unexpectedly. During these interludes they would talk and sometimes even try to rekindle their old passions, which still lingered despite the widening chasm between them. . . .

The sudden squirming of the child she was holding brought Janet out of her reverie and made her realize that she had dozed off. It was late afternoon and still very hot on the bus. Although the direct rays of the sun failed to penetrate the lush walls of jungle that pressed in on both sides of the dirt road, the air was suffocatingly humid, and sweat drenched Janet's body. She had been in Malaya for seventeen years but still hadn't adapted to the sweltering heat and found herself longing for the rains, which swept in from the ocean toward the end of each day during the monsoons. They never lasted long, but they were torrential and mercifully cooled the air before nightfall. The odor of the jungle—heavy with the smell of perpetually damp earth and rotting leaves—blended with the stench from passengers jammed on the bench seats beside her, their breaths fetid from the durian fruit they had eaten during the long journey, to create a redolence that was nearly suffocating.

When the little girl Janet was holding began to cry again, she handed the child back to her mother and glanced toward the rear of the bus where the two plainclothes police officers were seated. One was asleep with his mouth wide open, but the other, whose teeth were heavy with gold inlays, had his eyes riveted on her, and she knew her guess as to his identity had been correct.

An hour later, as the ramshackle bus turned into the single street along which the village of Bukit Mekan was strung, it began to rain. There was no preliminary drizzle: one moment it was unbearably hot and humid, the next a near-solid sheet of water had started to fall. It thundered on the corrugated iron roofs of the bamboo huts in which most of the villagers lived, and within minutes the dirt road became a fast-flowing stream.

The weathered sheets of canvas that had provided the passengers with shade from the sun earlier in the day did little to protect them from the downpour; streams of water cascaded through tears in the worn fabric and a tumult ensued as passengers pressed against each other to avoid being soaked. Their protests and laughter melded with the raucous screech of ducks, pigs, and chickens to create a cacophony that continued until the bus slowed to a stop at the far end of the village. There was a momentary lull as each person weighed the prospect of stepping out into the deluge, but it quickly resumed when, realizing they had no other option, the passengers climbed down from the chassis of the converted truck and immediately were soaked to the skin.

Janet was among the last to leave the vehicle. She waited, hoping the two policemen would get off before her, but when they didn't she picked up the two baskets containing the pharmaceuticals she had brought for Chu Kai and lowered herself from the bus.

It was like stepping under a waterfall: the impact of the huge raindrops was so great that they stung her skin, and the force of the water streaming down the road was almost enough to sweep her along with it. Blinded by the rain and struggling to maintain her balance, it wasn't until Janet reached the shelter of a nearby corrugated iron roof that she saw Chu Kai's granddaughter waiting for her.

Amy Chuong was now nearly fourteen years old, with a slender body that showed the first swell of small breasts, and exquisitely delicate features that lit up with a shy smile when she saw the Englishwoman. Janet had assisted at Amy's birth and had watched the youngster grow up, but it was some months since she had seen the girl and she was surprised by the obvious changes Amy's transition to young woman-hood had wrought.

"My grandfather sent me," Amy said in English, a mark of respect toward the woman who had taught her the language.

"It is good of you to come," Janet replied in fluent Cantonese as she warmly embraced the girl.

"He is waiting," Amy said, picking up one of Janet's baskets and stepping out into the street.

The rain stopped as suddenly as it started, and the swift torrent that had turned the roadway into a stream drained away, leaving a residue of gooey mud. Amy waded through it barefoot, and Janet struggled after her, trying to keep up but finding the going hard. By the time she reached Chu Kai's shop her legs were caked with mud. Pausing by a huge barrel, she scooped out handfuls of rainwater and cleaned herself off before going inside.

The shop was filled with villagers patiently waiting in line to purchase herbs or be treated. They recognized Janet and murmured polite greet-ings in Chinese and Malayan. Making her way to the back room, which Chu Kai used as his surgery, Janet held aside the beaded curtain across the doorway and looked inside. Chu Kai, unaware of her presence, continued examining a young Chinese woman who was lying on a wooden examination table under a single lightbulb that provided the only illumination in the tiny room.

"*Chi mai* or *shu mai?*" Janet asked.

Chu Kai looked up, adjusted the wire-rimmed glasses that always slipped down his nose when he performed an examination, saw who had spoken, and smilingly beckoned her forward. "You tell me," he said, placing the patient's wrist in the Engliswoman's hand.

Janet placed her middle finger parellel to the lower knob on the posterior side of the radius and let her index finger fall on the woman's wrist, palpating her pulse at three levels of pressure.

"*Hua mai,*" she said.

"Which is a sign of?"

"Excess mucus."

"And your diagnosis?"

"She's pregnant."

"For how long?"

"About two months."

He nodded, visibly pleased with his student's performance, and turned his attention back to the patient.

"There are many others waiting to see you," Janet said. "I will go upstairs and unpack the things I have brought."

Chu Kai was too busy to respond; he was describing to the woman how she should take a potion made from white peony. Janet knew it might be hours before he finished with his last patient.

She went into the front part of the shop, where those still unattended were waiting. Years of experience had taught her that quite a few of the older men who sat silently smoking cigarettes, inhaling through half-clenched fists, were seeking such herbs as longspur epimedium and Malay-tea scurf pea to enhance their sexual potency. Chinese love philters constituted a large part of her own business in Singapore, and even her younger clients frequently requested potions they had heard about from their fathers and grandfathers.

When Janet entered the small upper room directly over the shop, which she had occupied throughout most of her eleven years in Bukit Mekan, she saw that Amy had already brought the wicker baskets upstairs. Crossing to the window, she pushed open the shutters and looked out into the street, hoping to see the young Chinese girl, but there was no sign of her. Darkness had fallen as it always did in the tropics, with the abruptness of a lowered curtain, but the villagers still sat in small groups in front of their flimsy bamboo houses, talking and smoking. Women cooked over open fires. The night air was heavy with the smell of fried coconut oil, which mingled with the sweet scent of night flowers blooming in the surrounding jungle to produce an odor that embodied the essence of everything she loved about Malaya. She stood at the window for a long time as memories filtered through her mind.

She tried to recall the specific convictions that caused her, in 1946, to abandon the comforts of life in England for the rigors of living in Bukit Mekan, but she could no longer pinpoint exactly what they had been. At the time she had lumped them all under the heading of communism because it seemed to be the antithesis of everything she detested about the world of power and privilege in which her parents lived. Now she realized that had been a mistake. She was not a political creature. What she'd really been seeking was a sense of purpose, and she'd tried to find this through relationships, first with Leon Rojek, then the ZOB, and finally Tak Chen. She had believed that, merely by being close to somebody with dedication, some of it would rub off on her. It hadn't worked out that way. The men whose causes she adopted had all believed they could achieve their goals through violence, and in the end the violence had become all that mattered to them. In London Chen had talked about his dreams of independence for Malaya, but now he was obsessed with bitter dissension among his Communist comrades. Two major factions were engaged in a grim competition of death and destruction: if one group blew up a bridge, the other group, to prove it was stronger, blew up a train; if one assassinated a policeman, the other killed two policemen.

Such pointless and seemingly endless brutality had finally made Janet understand that all dogma was nothing more than a trick done with mirrors—a slight shift in position gave a totally different illusion of reality—and in the end none of it was worth the sacrifice of a single human life. That was why, after moving to Singapore, she had dedicated herself to caring for the poor, whether they could pay for her services or not. And that was why this trip to Bukit Mekan was different from all the others.

She had anguished for weeks before making up her mind, and even now she knew it was going to take all the willpower she could summon to go through with it, but she had finally decided that she must stop seeing Chen. The love she had once felt for him had lost its urgency, and her belief in his cause was dead. She still cared for him deeply, but only as somebody she had once loved. It was time for them to let each other go. This is what she intended to tell him if they established contact.

When Janet turned away from the window her sleeve brushed against a small framed photograph, a snapshot one of the villagers had taken of her soon after she arrived in Bukit Mekan, when she was twenty-seven. Now, at forty-four, her once smooth, soft skin had turned leathery from constant exposure to the sun, and tiny liver spots mottled the back of her hands. There were more strands of gray than brown in her hair, and the years of worry and stress had etched deep furrows in her brow. Yet, strangely, she felt more complete within herself than she had when the photograph was taken and felt no regrets about her loss of youth.

As she replaced the frame on the window ledge, Janet saw one of the men who had kept her under surveillance on the bus standing in the shadows of a wood-frame building across the dirt road, one shoulder propped against a wall, smoking a cigarette. There was no sign of his companion, but Janet knew he would be waiting somewhere close by to relieve the other man when it was his time to watch Chu Kai's shop. She was so accustomed to being watched that it was almost reassuring to see the plainclothesman playing his allotted part in the ritual. From past experience, she knew that his presence would in no way deter Chen from making contact with her if he wished.

She undressed and lay on the bed, a simple wooden frame held together by crisscrossed leather thongs, and closed her eyes. Her body ached and she felt feverish. Keeping her rain-drenched clothes on so long hadn't been wise, but she'd had no choice; every spare inch in her baskets was taken up with the herbs and pharmaceuticals she knew Chu Kai needed.

Instead of sleeping she thought about Anna and Genevieve. How were they coping with middle age? she wondered. They were in their forties too, and even though their experiences after leaving the internment camp had been very different from hers, she guessed they'd been faced with the common problems of getting older. She heard from Anna two or three times a year and treasured the photographs of Janna the other woman had sent. The most recent had arrived about six months ago and showed that Keja's child had grown into a very beautiful young woman. Anna had also mentioned in one of her letters that Genevieve had opened a finishing school near Montreux. The thought of the Frenchwoman, who had spent most of her life selling sexual favors, teaching wealthy young women the fine points of etiquette made Janet smile, but knowing Genevieve's infinite capacity to adjust to any situation, she was sure it was something her old friend would do with aplomb.

"Wake up!"

Janet opened her eyes and saw the faint outline of Amy Chuong leaning over her.

"Tak Chen wishes me to take you to him," the girl whispered urgently.

Glancing at the window, Janet saw that night had begun to dissolve into the first muted colors of dawn. She must have drifted into sleep. Getting up as quietly as possible, she reached for her clothes, which were still damp, and quickly put them on. Then, after stuffing some fruit and strips of dried meat in her pocket, she silently followed Amy downstairs to the street.

There was a stillness just before dawn broke that made it Janet's favorite time, and as she hurried after the young Chinese girl she marveled at the freshness with which each new day began. The air was cool and smelled sweetly of flowering jungle plants. It was as if the oppressive heat and wilting humidity of the previous afternoon were marks on a slate that had been wiped clean, and even though she knew they would come again by midmorning, Janet still relished the moment by taking a series of deep breaths that dispelled what cobwebs of sleep still remained.

Amy Chuong kept up a brisk pace as she led the way along a narrow path into the jungle. Before entering the dense foliage, Janet looked back over her shoulder, half expecting to see a policeman following her, but all she glimpsed was a half-starved dog slinking behind a row of bamboo huts in search of food.

"We must hurry," her young guide called softly. "It will be light soon."

Within minutes they were in jungle so thick that it cut their rate of progress in half. The ground was covered with a carpet of seedling trees and dead leaves that completely obscured the bare earth. Up to a height of about ten feet a dense undergrowth of young trees and palms hid the roots of giant tree trunks, which rose like pillars in a dark and limitless cathedral with no apparent decrease in thickness. A hundred and fifty feet up, a solid canopy of green burgeoned, entirely cutting out the sky. The undergrowth was so thick that at one point they clambered over a solid mat of flowering rhododendron scrub without once touching the ground, an achievement that was applauded by a loud chorus of grasshoppers, cicadas, and tree frogs.

By midmorning Janet was nearly exhausted by the constant exertion, and the damp, clinging heat was causing her to sweat away what little reserve of strength she still possessed. Even Amy showed signs of fatigue but insisted they move on, seemingly intent on reaching her destination by a deadline known only to her. Janet forced herself to keep up, her movements now mechanical as she forged on through the jungle. The total absence of sunlight and color seemed unreal. It was as if they were walking beneath the canopy of a gigantic tent that housed only death and decay. The air smelled stale and the earth rotten. The only visible signs of life, of another, sunlit world, were far above in the matted treetops, where flowering creepers and orchids hung like butterflies fluttering in permanent semi-darkness.

Barely conscious of where she was going, Janet followed Amy along an upward-leading ridge until they reached a summit above the tree line.

"He is waiting for you in there," the Chinese girl announced, pointing to a large hole in a rock face pitted with small caves.

"Aren't you coming?" Janet asked.

Amy shook her head. "I will wait for you here."

Janet started toward the cave, suddenly realizing that her arms and the backs of her hands were a mass of scratches and her white cotton pants and shirt were badly stained from brushing against the dead bark of fallen trees. Moving cautiously, she stepped into the darkness. "Chen!"

"Over here," a voice replied.

As her eyes adjusted to the gloom inside the cave, Janet saw Chen seated on the floor, his back propped against the wall. When she drew closer she saw he was shivering. His skin was mottled with purple splotches from hundreds of leech bites, and his shins, which were bare above his rotting, rubber-soled sandals, were covered with suppurating sores.

Her heart went out to him. "Amy should have told me you were ill," she said, kneeling in front of him.

"She didn't know," Chen replied, gently resting his hand on hers.

His skin was hot. Janet knew he was running a high fever.

"Do you still have any of the herbs I gave you last time we were together?" she asked.

He shook his head. "They were lost when we were ambushed five days ago."

"The passengers on the bus talked about a Gurkha patrol—"

"Gurkha?" He shook his head. "Our attackers were Communists."

Both were silent for a long time. Then Janet murmured, "How long can this insanity go on?"

"Until Malaya is free."

"But it's had independence for over six years—"

"That is a sham!"

Janet knew he was referring to Malaysia's new constitution, into which policies favoring Malays had been written, guaranteeing that by 1990 they must control at least 30 percent of the economy. It was a provision that had bred bitter resentment among the Chinese, many of whom, like Chen, had been born in Malaya. The animosity between the two races had reached a stage where many believed that if the Communist terrorists didn't destroy the country, the smoldering conflict between Malays and Chinese would.

"You need medical treatment," she said, deliberately shifting the focus of their conversation.

Chen shrugged. "A few sores and a bit of fever aren't going to kill me."

Janet tore a strip off the bottom of her cotton shirt and used it to wipe the sweat off his forehead. He was probably experiencing an attack of the most severe form of malaria, and the only things that would really help him were antibiotics or quinine, both of which could only be obtained illegally.

"I'll come back tomorrow—"

"I have to move on," he said.

"Will you ever stop running?" she asked.

"Do you care?"

She averted her eyes, aware that this was the moment for her to tell him she wasn't ever going to see him again, but when he put his arms around her all she could do was cry.

"No tears," he whispered, stroking her hair.

A sudden burst of gunfire shattered the silence. Chen grabbed his Sten gun, "Stay here!" he ordered.

He inched cautiously toward the mouth of the cave but paused before reaching it, and looked back at where Janet was crouched on the floor. Their eyes met and the flicker of a smile crossed his tired face. He continued gazing at her a bit longer, then pulled back the bolt of his Sten gun and began firing as he stepped from the cave.

The answering salvo came from three or four different directions, all short bursts from automatic weapons, but they ended quickly and left a silence that was broken only by the echo of the shots bouncing from the walls of the limestone cave. It was a long time before Janet moved, and when she finally walked outside, the blazing afternoon sun was so intense that for a moment she was blinded. When her eyes finally adjusted to the glare she saw Chen's body lying less than three yards from where she stood. That of Amy Chuong lay sprawled in the dirt a short distance away. Both had been riddled with bullets fired by six Gurkhas wearing the drab green fatigues and red-banded jungle hats of the Malaysian police. Standing with them were the two plainclothes policemen who had tailed her from the moment she stepped off the train in Kuala Lumpur.

They were smiling broadly.

23

MONTREUX: September 27, 1963

Genevieve Fleury gripped the telephone and tried to absorb the meaning of Anna's words from the other end of the line in New York.

"Did you hear me?" Anna asked. "Mark has hanged himself!"

"Oh, God!" The Frenchwoman searched for the right words to
express her sympathies, but none came.

"I want you to tell Janna before she hears about it from somebody
else. She's on an Air France flight that had a two-hour layover in Paris,
which means she should arrive in Geneva about ten fifteen your time."

"I'll be there to meet her," Genevieve said, "and I'll make sure she
calls you the moment we get here. Do you want her to go back to New
York?"

"Not now," Anna replied. "The press has turned this whole thing
into a circus. It's better if Janna stays away."

"Until things quiet down?"

"That could take a long time. The gallery is closed and Mark left a
lot of debts. . . ." The other woman's voice trailed away, but then she
added, "I'd like to stick with our original plan, if it's still all right with
you."

"I'll love having her," Genevieve said. "And of course you needn't
worry about her board or tuition."

"That's kind of you." Anna paused. "Tell her I'll be waiting for her
call. . . ."

When the line went dead, Genevieve continued to hold the receiver
against her ear for a time before finally replacing it in its cradle. Her
hand shook, and sweat beaded on her forehead, but only partially
because of the shock of what Anna had just told her.

Genevieve's suffering had begun some hours before Anna called,
when the first pangs of withdrawal had made themselves felt: cramps
in her stomach and spasms in her legs that were so severe she could only
control them by wrapping herself in a blanket.

"Bastard!" she muttered as her guts churned again and sent her into
the bathroom to relieve her diarrhea for the fourth time in the last hour.

She was thinking of Dr. Pierre Brassard, who had promised to visit the school the previous evening to give her the injection of morphine she now needed at least twice a day. She had exhausted the supply he left her on his last visit two days ago, but when she called his office in Geneva his secretary had informed her that Dr. Brassard was in surgery and wouldn't be able to see her until the following day.

But he hadn't come and Genevieve knew why: she still hadn't paid him for the morphine he had supplied during the previous month, and making her wait was his way of reminding her just how much she needed him. The Frenchwoman knew that if he weren't dependent on her for his job as medical consultant to the school—a perquisite that allowed him to milk high fees from the parents of girls he treated for minor ailments—he would have stopped supplying morphine the moment she couldn't pay for it. Instead, he had decided to make her suffer by giving her diluted doses of the drug, gambling that the owner and director of the Fleury École de Perfectionnement would come up with the money she owed him sometime in the near future.

When Dr. Brassard failed to keep his appointment, Genevieve's first instinct had been to call his private number and plead with him for the drug, but instead she perversely decided to wait him out and show him she wasn't as dependent on morphine as he thought. She had forced herself to sit through dinner with the forty-three girls who comprised the student body and had even managed to keep a sharp eye on their table behavior. Although she hadn't been able to eat anything, she appeared ebullient and sustained a spirited conversation until the meal ended. But instead of joining the girls for coffee, which was always served in the huge living room overlooking Lake Geneva, she excused herself, saying that she had a lot of paperwork to do, and went upstairs to her private suite of rooms on the second floor.

Normally, the elegantly furnished little apartment—one of the first major alterations she'd made to the villa after buying it in 1954—was her refuge from the frenetic chatter and the loud music the girls liked to play, but this evening it seemed more like a prison.

Unable to sit in one place for more than a few seconds, she had paced the room, her mouth dry, trying to focus on anything that would take her mind off her growing craving for the drug. She tried to sleep but was immediately hit by convulsions, and her diarrhea became so acute that she had to twist her legs and roll over in an attempt to hold it back. Her nose started to run and her eyes burned. She vomited until only bile came up, then gagged and choked out blood. Her head got wobbly and she began to see crazy things: quick flashes of scenes she remembered from the Warsaw ghetto, but this time she was inside the burning buildings and the flames were licking at her flesh.

She stifled her moans by burying her head in the pillow; the last thing she could afford to do was let the girls know of her suffering. Suddenly, as if in response to her half-remembered prayers, the anguish stopped, but within minutes it returned, this time with renewed fury. She began to twist and tear at the sheets. Finally, she threw them off, ran into the bathroom, and pressed her naked body against the cold tile floor in an attempt to cool her burning fever.

The torture went on all night: seizures, vomiting, hammer blows in the stomach, and a fitful period of exhausted sleep from which she awoke every ten or fifteen minutes drenched in sweat.

About five in the morning, when it seemed she was finally beginning to come out of her suffering, the telephone rang and Anna was on the line from New York telling her about Mark's suicide. The other woman's words seemed to be an extension of the nightmare she had suffered through during the previous hours. Even now, after hanging up, it was impossible to separate the two because the pain she thought had exhausted itself suddenly hit her again, worse than ever, with a series of cramps and spasms that set her whole body writhing. Then, as suddenly as the assault began, it ceased.

"Please God, no more," she moaned.

She waited, cursing the day fourteen years earlier when Hank Owens had given her that first dose of morphine. He had intended it as an act of kindness, and she remembered his warning: "I've seen guys get hooked, and it isn't a pretty sight." Now she knew what he'd been talking about, but it was too late to stop. It was no longer a question of seeking pleasure, merely survival.

When Genevieve returned to Paris from her brief sojourn with Hank and resumed working for the Countess, the only way she was able to tolerate the men with whom she had to have sex was by continuing to inject herself with morphine. The drug made the next five years bearable and enabled her to go through whatever perverse acts her customers requested. Her detachment was so complete that she felt like a voyeur watching a complete stranger going through motions she found, in her euphoria, oddly amusing. Her only anxiety was that she would run short of morphine, but in the decade after the war it was readily available on the black market in Paris for anybody who could afford it.

And money was no problem for her then. Within five years she had managed to save enough to buy the villa in Montreux, have it converted into a school, and do the advertising necessary to attract daughters of wealthy families. Her break with the Countess had been bitter. The other woman wanted her to continue working, arguing that it was silly to terminate an arrangement that had proved so lucrative for them both, but Genevieve was firm; she'd had enough of her old life.

It had gone well at first. The Credit Suisse Bank in Geneva, impressed by the business she'd done with their branch in Paris, approved a line of credit that provided her with the operating capital she needed to make the school financially viable, and after the first year she was able to raise the tuition fees to a level that made the venture almost self-sustaining. The success of the initial twelve months also gave her confidence in what she was doing. She discovered she had a natural ability for the task she had undertaken: her instinctive knowledge of people, allied with the various social skills she had learned, made her a good teacher. The girls liked her, as did their parents, who were impressed by the education and experience she listed in her brochure—credentials they never bothered to check out—and when they visited the school they were charmed by her personality and gracious demeanor.

She had succeeded in making a clean break with her past in all respects except one—she still needed morphine. It wasn't hard to find an accommodating doctor in Geneva who, for a price, was willing to keep her supplied with the drug, but when, two years previously, the Credit Suisse, for no apparent reason, suddenly terminated her line of credit, she'd been beset by problems.

So far, in spite of repeated attempts, she had failed to find another bank that would loan her money. The school seemed doomed until, at the very last minute, she received an offer of assistance from the least likely person in the world: the Countess de Cabo. She had simply appeared at the school one day, unannounced, and made her a proposition: she was willing to guarantee the school a line of credit at a bank of Genevieve's choice in return for two things—half ownership in the school and the right to recruit its graduates for an international job placement agency she had opened in Paris after her protégée had left her.

Genevieve's initial reaction to the latter part of the proposal was skeptical. She knew the other woman well enough to suspect that the jobs the Countess planned to offer her graduates would be exploitive in one way or another, but as she listened to her describe the idea behind the agency, Genevieve reluctantly acknowledged that it made a lot of sense.

It was based on a concept whereby girls from good families, specifically trained in the social graces, were matched with wealthy business tycoons who needed personal assistants who could move with ease in the highest levels of society. "Good secretaries are easy to get," the Countess said, "but where do extremely successful men look for a woman who is not only intelligent but accustomed to wealth and can be counted on not to let him down whatever the social occasion?"

Genevieve knew there was a certain logic in the Countess's reasoning: most of the young women wealthy enough to attend her finishing school weren't going to bother learning the skills that would equip them for jobs after they graduated. A few would go on to universities, but most were too spoiled even for that—they wanted positions that would give them an immediate sense of importance while allowing them to continue living the privileged life to which they had been accustomed since birth—and what the Countess was offering appeared to be a perfect solution.

The first girls to be recruited had been selected from the class that graduated two years ago. The Countess had sent them all over the world for interviews with prospective employers who guaranteed them first-class round-trip plane tickets, plus generous expenses, in return for the opportunity of talking to them in person about the duties they would be expected to perform. Not all of them had gone with the first employer they met, but each ultimately found a job as personal assistant to an extremely wealthy man, and in reports Genevieve received from the girls' parents they were more than satisfied with the services rendered by the Countess's placement agency. It was also clear to Genevieve that she didn't have much choice but to accept the other woman's proposal, because without a new line of credit the school would go bankrupt.

The shrill ring of the telephone startled Genevieve and made her realize she must have fallen asleep. Dawn had broken and the gray light, although still barely enough for her to see across the room, seemed unendurably bright. Her eyes wouldn't focus properly, she was drenched with sweat, and her heart was pounding.

When the phone rang again she started to reach for it but stopped when a sudden cramp knifed through her belly. The ringing continued, and when she finally managed to lift the receiver, the voice of her assistant principal said, "Dr. Brassard is downstairs, madame."

"All right, Helga," Genevieve murmured weakly. "Send him up."

"Are you ill, madame?"

"Just a slight cold."

"Do you still wish me to order the car to take you to the airport in Geneva?" the German woman asked.

"Yes, Helga," she replied in a firmer voice. "Tell the driver I am meeting a flight that arrives from Paris at ten fifteen, and that it is important for me to get there in good time."

A few minutes later Dr. Brassard entered the room, took out a syringe, filled it with morphine, tapped up a vein on the inside of her left arm, and slowly injected the drug into her bloodstream.

24

Janna looked down on the green patchwork of countryside as the small Air France Caravelle gained altitude over the farmlands outside of Paris and headed south to Geneva.

When clouds obscured her view she closed her eyes and tried to sleep. The eight-hour flight from New York had been packed with Europeans returning from a bus tour across the United States, and they had stayed awake all night exchanging experiences in a stream of chatter that got louder with each drink they consumed. The noise had made it impossible for Janna to get any rest, and although she had tried to doze during the layover in Paris, she had been prevented from doing so by a young Frenchman who persistently tried to engage her in conversation.

Now she felt completely drained, both physically and emotionally, not just from the rigors of travel but also from the strain of what she'd been through before she left. Everything had happened so quickly that it wasn't until she was in flight over the Atlantic that she realized the enormity of the step she was taking, and for the first time since she agreed to leave New York, she experienced real anxiety.

Her only previous trip out of the country had been a three-week vacation with Anna and Mark to Bermuda soon after her seventeenth birthday. It had been an idyllic time, during which they'd come even closer together as a family, and thinking about it now made her realize just how much she was going to miss the two people who had raised her. Mark had seemed particularly happy during those three weeks. He had taught Janna how to snorkel, and they went for long bicycle rides around the island. She had never seen him so relaxed. The recollection of how he'd been then, compared with the way he'd appeared when she kissed him good-bye in New York, a few hours ago, made her heart ache.

She loved Mark and Anna more than anybody else in the world and couldn't bear to see them suffer. Yet she was also conscious of a flicker of excitement at the prospect of spending a year with Genevieve Fleury, who knew more about Keja than anybody else. The journey from New York to Geneva was more than a matter of crossing from one continent to another; it was the beginning of an odyssey of self-discovery. In uncovering her natural heritage, Janna was convinced she would be able to make whole again that part of herself which had been fragmented by the revelation that Anna and Mark were not her real parents.

The plane banked over Geneva. In the brilliant morning sunlight, the lake looked like a huge, shimmering aquamarine, and she experienced a quickening of her heartbeat, despite her fatigue. She was one of the last passengers to disembark, and when she entered the airport terminal she was surprised when a thickset man wearing a raincoat hurried toward her. "Miss Maxwell-Hunter?"

Assuming him to be somebody Genevieve Fleury had sent to meet her, Janna replied, "Yes, I have some other bags—"

"My name is Anders, George Anders," the man said, taking a notebook from his pocket. "I'm with United Press. My New York editor cabled me overnight to say you'd be arriving in Geneva this morning. I wondered if I might ask you a few questions about Mark Hunter?"

"I came to Europe to get away from you people," Janna said tersely.

"Just a few quotes—"

"Please leave me alone."

Janna turned and started walking away, but stopped when she saw a woman aiming a camera at her.

"If you'll just talk to me for a minute," the reporter persisted.

"Listen, Mr.—whatever your name is," Janna snapped, "Mark Hunter is on trial, not me."

"Not anymore."

"What do you mean?"

"Mark Hunter killed himself last night."

"Is this your idea of a game?" Janna demanded.

"It was on both wire services this morning," Anders replied.

Uncertain whether or not to believe him, Janna remained rooted where she stood as the photographer took a series of flash pictures, the sudden explosions of which momentarily blinded her, and when she turned she lost her balance.

"Okay?" the reporter asked as he helped Janna to her feet.

"Let go of me!" she said, angrily shaking herself free.

"What are your plans now?"

"To scream if you ask one more question."

"Will you be going back to New York for the funeral?"

Janna opened her mouth and let out a shriek. It echoed from the glass walls of the cavernous terminal and caused a momentary lull as bustling passengers paused to look in her direction. Aware that she was the focus of their attention, but not caring, Janna shouldered her way through the crowd until she found sanctuary in a women's rest room, where she sat on a toilet seat, tears streaming down her cheeks.

Mark dead by his own hand? It was inconceivable. When she kissed him good-bye less than sixteen hours earlier she never dreamed it would be the last time she would see him alive. Sobs racked her body, and she was too lost in her grief to hear the door of the rest-room open.

"I saw what happened out there and recognized you from pictures Anna sent. I can't tell you how sorry that I didn't get to you first."

Janna looked up. The person who had spoken was a petite, auburn-haired woman with a trim figure and strikingly attractive features. She was wearing a simple but beautifully tailored suit that made her look both elegant and distinctly feminine. She appeared to be about Anna's age and spoke with a French accent.

"I'm Genevieve Fleury," the newcomer said.

"That man out there, the reporter, he told me Mark is dead!"

"I'm afraid it's true," the other woman said gently. "Anna called me . . . she so wanted me to be the one to tell you. . . ."

Janna buried her face in her hands. "How did it happen?" she asked when her crying subsided.

"I'm not sure this is—"

"Please, I want to know."

"He hanged himself."

Janna shook her head from side to side. "Why, in God's name?"

"People under extreme pressure sometimes just crack."

Janna sat numbly on the toilet seat, then slowly got up and splashed some cold water on her face. "Anna's going to need me," she said. "I've got to get back to New York."

"She asked me to try and persuade you to stay here with me," the Frenchwoman said.

"I can't!"

"It's what Mark would have wanted. . . ."

Janna's first instinct was to argue, but then she realized that Genevieve was right. It was Mark who had suggested she come to Switzerland in the first place, and the circumstances that prompted him to make the decision hadn't changed. His suicide would only add fuel to the already raging blaze of publicity. If Anna didn't want her to be in New York, she must have her reasons.

"I guess that's true," she said.

Genevieve looked around the washroom. "This isn't quite the setting I'd planned for our first meeting, but welcome anyway." She embraced Janna and kissed her on both cheeks, then added, "You wait here while I go and see if it's safe for us to leave."

Before Janna could answer, the other woman hurried from the washroom. She was gone about five minutes, long enough for Janna to dab some more cold water on her eyes and run a comb through her hair. When the Frenchwoman reappeared she said, "That reporter is still hanging around, but if we move fast I think we can give him the slip."

"What about my luggage?" Janna asked as she followed Genevieve through the crowded terminal to where a chauffeur was waiting behind the wheel of a black Mercedes-Benz limousine.

"Give the driver your tickets. He'll pick up your bags."

They waited in the back of the car as the chauffeur collected her two suitcases and loaded them into the trunk. As he eased the limousine away from the curb, Janna glimpsed the UPI reporter hurrying toward them, but a group of passengers suddenly emerged from the terminal, and by the time he could elbow his way through the Mercedes was already on the road to Montreux.

"I'm sorry about my display of hysterics in there," Janna said.

"You had every reason to be upset," the woman next to her replied.

"It's kind of you to invite me—"

"Please," Genevieve interjected, "thanks aren't necessary. I've been waiting a very long time to meet you agaain."

Janna had thought she wouldn't be able to wait to ask the other woman questions about Keja, but now all she could think about was Mark. Outside the window, the sun was glistening on Lake Geneva, and it reminded her of the leisurely afternoons she and Mark had spent together sailing a toy boat on the pond in Central Park. He may not have been her real father, but no other man could possibly have been as kind or given her as much love. Not since she had learned about her natural mother had she experienced such a terrible sense of loss.

It came as a shock to discover that she had been so emotionally dependent on him; in her own mind it had seemed that once she moved away from home, got a job, and shared an apartment she was standing squarely on her own two feet, but now that conviction had been revealed as an illusion.

She glanced at the reflection of Genevieve in the rearview mirror. The Frenchwoman's eyes were closed, and she appeared to be sleeping, but her hands trembled and perspiration glistened on her forehead. As the limousine turned into the long curving driveway that led to the school, the other woman suddenly uttered a gasp and clutched her side.

"Are you all right?" Janna asked.

After a long moment of silence the Frenchwoman replied, "Just a cramp. I often get one when I sit too long in the wrong position."

When the chauffeur opened the door Janna saw Genevieve grimace again as she stepped out of the car.

"Shall I take the young lady's bags upstairs, madame?" the driver asked.

"Yes, Helga will show you her room." Turning to Janna, she added, "I'll place a call to New York after lunch, which will be in about half an hour. Why don't you take a look around the grounds until then?" Without waiting for a response she hurried inside and up the stairs.

Surprised by the abruptness of Genevieve's departure, Janna walked slowly across the sweeping expanse of lawn to the edge of the lake. Sitting on a stone bench, she watched a flock of white-winged sailboats skittering across the silvered surface of the water, then shifted her gaze to the serrated snow-capped peaks of the distant mountains that were vividly etched against the blue sky.

It was picture-postcard pretty, but the awesome beauty was lost on Janna. She felt rejected by Genevieve. Ever since hearing about the Frenchwoman, Janna had woven fantasies around her in which she filled in the blanks about Keja, but now it seemed Genevieve didn't even like her.

"Mademoiselle Maxell-Hunter?"

Janna turned and saw a tall, slender girl with blue eyes and long blond hair and a fresh, wind-blown beauty that was heightened by her fair, lightly tanned skin.

"I'm Elke Kruger," the newcomer said. "Madame Fleury asked me to show you around the Taj Mahal."

"Taj Mahal?"

"Our nickname for the school."

"It's an odd choice."

"You'll see, this place might be beautiful, but it's as much fun as a mausoleum," the other girl replied.

In spite of herself, Janna found herself smiling as she followed Elke on a tour of the school grounds. They included grass tennis courts, an Olympic-size swimming pool, and an equestrian ring flanked by stables housing horses that some of the students were grooming. In the course of their walk, Elke explained that although both her parents were German she had been raised in Buenos Aires, spoke five languages, and was spending a year in Montreux to perfect her French. She was very witty and possessed a quiet but staggering sophistication that must have come from years of traveling abroad with her parents. She talked vaguely of one day working as a translator at the United Nations in New York, but at the same time she conveyed the impression that it was something she would do only if it didn't interfere with her social life.

Genevieve appeared at lunch looking as fresh as when Janna first saw her at the airport. Gone was the ashen complexion, the sweat-beaded forehead, the trembling hands, and in their place was an exuberance which manifested itself in lively conversation and quick outbursts of spontaneous laughter. She paid particular attention to Janna, showing a warmth toward her that dispelled the young woman's feelings of not being welcome, and after lunch took her upstairs to her private apartment so she could call Anna in New York.

". . . from a reporter?" Anna said.

"At the airport."

"But I specifically asked Genevieve to tell you."

"It wasn't her fault," Janna replied.

Genevieve observed how upsetting the telephone call had been to Janna, and tried to take her mind off it by showing her some of the classes that were being conducted in various parts of the villa. They included flower arranging, drills in the four basic methods of food service, posture, dress, conversation, languages, wines, menus, and etiquette. Girls were also encouraged to participate in sports. In addition to swimming, riding, and tennis, the school also offered sailing, sculling, and water skiing on Lake Geneva.

Janna tried to appear interested, but she was still so shaken by her telephone conversation with Anna that it was hard for her to respond with any real enthusiasm, and she was glad when Genevieve suggested she make it an early night.

The Frenchwoman had assigned her to share a room with Elke Kruger, but the German girl was still involved in a rowdy game of poker downstairs when Janna got ready for bed at about 10 P.M. She learned a lot about her roommate just by looking at her side of the room: dresses bearing the labels of Dior, Balenciaga, and Schiaparelli were in a heap on the floor; three or four stylish ski outfits had been stuffed under the bed; a huge alligator handbag hung from a nail in the wall and was apparently being used as a laundry basket for filmy lingerie. Posters across the doors of her closet showed race driver Peter Revson standing next to a Formula One car, Elvis Presley gyrating in a sequined outfit, and a downhill ski racer in goggles and helmet crossing the finishing line. On the table next to Elke's bed there was a silver-framed photograph showing a man and woman, both blond-haired and blue-eyed, in the cockpit of a huge yacht that bore the name *Kruger IV.*

Janna was sleeping when, soon after midnight, she was awakened by the sound of the window being opened. She glimpsed Elke climbing out over the sill and onto a trellis, but Janna was too tired to investigate and didn't stir again until the wake-up bell sounded at eight thirty the following morning.

During the days that followed, Janna's body slowly adjusted to the six-hour time difference, but her mind could not conform to the established routine of the finishing school. Although she dutifully attended the various classes, she never felt a part of what was going on around her. She was always conscious of the difference between herself and the other girls, almost all of whom were from families that possessed not only wealth but distinguished lineages, which gave them a strong sense of personal identity. When they asked Janna about her origins, she found herself sidestepping the questions or, even worse, resorting to half-truths that left her feeling as if she'd betrayed Anna and Mark.

It was a difficult period of adjustment, which didn't escape Genevieve Fleury's notice, and after dinner one evening the Directrice invited Janna to her private rooms for coffee.

"I'm sorry I haven't been able to spend more time with you," Genevieve said, "but there's always so much for me to do during the school year. How are you getting along?"

"Truthfully?" Janna asked.

"Of course," the other woman replied.

"Not great."

"A lot of girls get homesick. . . ." the Frenchwoman said.

"It isn't just that."

"What then?"

Janna hesitated. "When I was thirteen, Anna told me as much as she knew about my real mother, but ever since then I've wanted to know more. . . ."

"And you think I'm the person to tell you?"

"Well, you knew her longer than Anna or Janet."

"I did share living quarters with her for almost four years, but that doesn't mean I was close enough to her to know her innermost secrets."

"Such as the identity of my natural father?"

Genevieve nodded. "Keja never revealed that to anybody."

"But you were with her daily in the months when I must have been conceived."

"I spent most of my time on the Aryan side of the wall, arranging for the purchase of arms on the black market, and during those final weeks Keja worked as a courier for Josef Kandalman."

"Anna told me about him," Janna said.

"He gave Keja a job and a place to live after the Nazis decimated her tribe."

"Was she in love with him?"

The Frenchwoman shrugged. "Perhaps. She cared enough about him to give him a gold talismen he always wore around his neck."

"Were they lovers?"

"I doubt it. The Gypsy tradition under which Keja was raised forbid premarital sex."

"But it was possible?"

"I suppose so. She often slept over at his bunker in the ghetto, but even if Keja had been willing to compromise her rigid moral code I doubt if Kandalman would have been interested. His sexual appetites were—" She checked herself.

Janna sensed that Genevieve was hesitant to discuss this further, so instead she said, "All Anna was able to tell me about my mother was the escape across Europe with Tibere, crossing the Pyrenees, and her death giving birth to me."

"That must have been enough to convince you that she was a very special woman."

"Everyone keeps saying that, but it's all so vague."

Genevieve chose her words carefully. "Keja was shy . . . withdrawn . . . as unsure of herself as you seem to be now." The Frenchwoman's voice trailed away. "I wish I could be more specific, but it's so hard. Maybe another time. Now go to bed, it's getting late."

25

The conversation with Genevieve left Janna feeling uneasy, with an even greater desire, now that she knew more about her mother, to find out who her father was. She was preoccupied to the point that she found herself unable to concentrate on classes, or much else of what was going on around her. Her roommate, Elke, noticed it and suggested that what Janna needed was a change of pace.

That night, after the Assistant Director had checked out each room to make sure all the students were in bed, Elke led Janna out of the window and down the trellis. Moving cautiously, they made their way to the rear of the villa and followed a path that ran alongside the lake in the direction of Montreux. When they came to a farm between the school and the town, Elke told Janna to wait and disappeared into the courtyard.

When she was alone Janna realized she hadn't brought any money: the small amount she'd had when she arrived from New York—meager savings from her job at Macy's—had been lost to Elke in a poker game, and Janna knew she couldn't expect any additional funds from Anna. When they talked on the phone the day after Janna arrived at the school it was evident from the conversation that the other woman was going through an extremely difficult period. Mark's estate had been frozen by the courts until claims against it by creditors could be settled, and the contents of the gallery had been impounded by the government in lieu of import duties they said were still owed on the paintings. Anna had been forced to give up the apartment on Riverside Drive, find a cheaper place to live, and take a job designing wholesale jewelry on Seventh Avenue.

An engine roared into life and Elke rolled into view behind the wheel of a red Porsche convertible.

"Get in," she called. "We'll have to hurry if we're going to get a drink before everything closes."

The moment Janna climbed into the passenger seat, Elke stepped on the accelerator and sent the Porsche careening over deep ruts in the dirt road.

"I didn't think students were allowed to own cars," Janna shouted over the high-pitched whine of the engine.

"They're not," Elke replied, her long blond hair streaming in the wind as she shifted smoothly into top gear. "That's why I pay the farmer to let me keep mine in one of his barns."

Janna tried to appear at ease as the car hurtled around sharp twists in the road along the edge of the lake, but she was only able to relax when Elke slowed to a stop outside a small bar and restaurant overlooking the lake between Vevey and Lausanne.

"I'd hate to be with you when you're in a hurry," Janna said.

"You must come soaring with me sometime." The other girl laughed, running her fingers through her wind-tangled hair as she led the way into the Café Pully where a jukebox was playing Bob Dylan's "Blowin' in the Wind."

It took a moment or two for Janna's eyes to adjust to the dimly lit interior, and before they did she stumbled into a table where a group of men and women in their early twenties were seated.

"Watch it, man!"

The speaker was compactly built and not much older than Janna, with dark, curly hair and an angular face. His white ski sweater was stained with red wine that had spilled from his glass when she stumbled into his table. "I'm sorry," she said, "the light in here—"

"American, huh?"

"Yes."

"Where from?"

"New York." Janna looked around for Elke and saw her talking to a man at the bar.

"It's the pits, man."

"I'm not a man," Janna replied coolly, "and it takes somebody with taste to appreciate New York."

"Hey, loosen up, okay?" He grinned. "I'm Joe Dawson, who are you?"

"Janna."

"Janna who?"

She hesitated. "Maxell-Hunter."

"Sounds like one of those fancy old cars—Pierce Arrow, Maxell-Hunter. . . . Grab a chair and join us."

His brashness irritated Janna.

"What are you drinking?" Dawson asked.

"Just Coke," she said.

He placed the order. "What are you doing over here, anyway?"

"Going to school."

"The Taj Mahal?"

Janna nodded.

"Sounds like a real square joint from what Elke tells me," he said, "but she doesn't let it stop her from getting kicks. That's one real crazy lady."

"Why are you in Switzerland?" Janna asked.

"You serious?"

"It's a simple enough question."

"You really don't know who I am?"

"Should I?"

"And I thought the stumbling bit was just an excuse to meet me."

"I think I'll join Elke," Janna said, infuriated by his ego, but when she started to get up he put his hand on her arm.

"Nothing personal," he said. "It's just that when you're a top skier over here most people know you. It's like being a star pitcher in the States."

Janna was relieved to see Elke approaching the table with the man she'd been talking to at the bar.

"I see you've met Joe Dawson," the German girl observed.

"He's hard to avoid."

"Been telling you how great he is?"

"Number one in World Cup isn't bad," Dawson protested.

"At downhill he's good, maybe the best American ever," Elke said, "but in bed he's—well, let's just say average."

"Thanks a lot," Dawson said, feigning hurt.

"But I do have somebody really interesting I'd like you to meet." Elke turned to the man at her side. "Fritz Demmer, this is the friend I've been telling you about: Janna Maxell-Hunter."

"I am very pleased to meet you," Demmer said, enunciating his words carefully with a slight accent.

"He is Swiss, a banker, and single," Elke added, "which makes him eligible in any language."

"Elke likes to make jokes," he said. "It is true that I am Swiss and single, but I only hold a minor position at the bank."

"He's senior enough to trade the bank's stock on the Zurich exchange," Elke said.

"In Switzerland bankers also function as stockbrokers," Demmer explained.

Janna liked the fact that he was shy, if only because it was a welcome contrast to Joe Dawson's braggadocio. He was also the complete opposite of the young American skier in both appearance and manner. Where Dawson was lithe and well-muscled, Demmer was stocky and soft-looking, with a pale face and ordinary features that included eyes the color of washed-out denim. His thinning hair was a nondescript hue somewhere between blond and brown. This made him look older than he probably was, which Janna gauged to be about thirty. The dark gray suit he was wearing also set him apart from Dawson, who had on jeans and a ski sweater.

"How has the assassination of President Kennedy affected the market here in Europe?" Janna asked.

Demmer appeared nonplused. He grinned as if expecting to find himself part of a joke. "Do you really wish to know?" he asked hesitantly.

"Yes," Janna replied. "I used to follow the market when I was in New York."

"As a trader?" Demmer asked.

"Just a make-believe one," she replied, telling him how she had followed the activity of the stocks her boyfriend had picked at random.

"Boring!" Dawson announced loudly, suddenly aware that he was no longer the focus of attention.

Because it was hard to make himself heard over the noise of the jukebox, Demmer suggested to Janna that they go out onto the deck overlooking the lake. She agreed and for the next hour listened intently as the Swiss banker described his job, the intricacies of his country's banking laws, and how trading was done on the Zurich exchange. He had a precise, careful manner and a deference that created the impression of subservience.

"I go to Zurich two or three times a week," he said. "Why don't you come along with me sometime?"

"Sounds like fun," she replied, "but I don't think I could get away from school."

He took out his wallet and handed her his card. "In case you find a way, I can usually be reached at this number."

The jukebox had stopped playing and the lights inside the Café Pully were beginning to go out.

"It looks like they're getting ready to close," Janna said.

"I will drive you back to school if you wish," Demmer offered.

"Thanks, but I think Elke is expecting me to go back with her," Janna replied.

When they went back inside the club there was no sign of either Elke or Dawson, and Demmer said hopefully, "They must have left."

Janna thought the same thing until she went outside and saw her roommate half undressed inside the Porsche with Joe Dawson. "Maybe you'd better give me a lift back to Montreux after all," she told Demmer.

He took her arm and led her to where his car was parked. It was a small Fiat sedan, which he drove cautiously back along the road skirting the lake, following Janna's directions, until they reached the farmhouse where Elke kept her Porsche.

"I can walk the rest of the way from here," she said.

There was a moment of awkward silence after Demmer switched off the engine. "I would very much like to see you again," he said hesitantly.

"If I can get away I'll give you a call," Janna said.

"Please try," he said.

His shyness was agonizing and made Janna feel vaguely guilty. Impulsively, she kissed him lightly on the cheek, then got out of the car and hurried toward the school.

The villa was cloaked in silence and each step she took on the gravel driveway echoed through the darkness, yet she managed to climb back up the trellis to her room without being detected and minutes later was safely in bed.

When Elke returned just before dawn she was still half drunk, and the noise she made climbing over the windowsill was more than enough to awaken Janna.

"God, I feel like hell," the German girl groaned. "Joe and I did too much cocaine. . . ."

"I don't know what you see in him," Janna said, helping her friend undress.

"He has his points," Elke replied, studying herself in the full-length mirror behind the door. Her breasts were covered with bite marks and her back was a mass of scratches. "What about Fritz?"

"He's nice."

"And that's all." Elke yawned. "Like most Swiss men, nice—but dull."

"He wants to show me the stock exchange in Zurich."

"For him, that's high excitement."

"It sounds fascinating," Janna said.

"So go."

"It would mean getting away on a weekday."

"Nothing easier. We're going to Davos for the World Cup downhill next week. All you have to do is wait until the last minute and then tell Madame Fleury you're sick," Elke said.

Janna thought about the scheme all day; she really was interested in seeing the Zurich exchange, and the thought of getting away from school for even a brief time was equally appealing. The next morning she called Fritz Demmer, told him she could go with him to Zurich the following Thursday, and suggested he meet her at the farmhouse where he had dropped her off the previous evening. He sounded surprised to hear from her so soon, but eagerly agreed to the arrangements.

On Thursday morning all the students got up early to get to Davos in time for the skiing events, where Joe Dawson was favored to win the downhill. A bus had been chartered, and they boarded it immediately after eating breakfast. At the very last minute Janna announced that she had a sore throat and a high fever.

"Why on earth didn't you tell me earlier?" Genevieve asked sharply.

"It only came on during the night," Janna said with faked hoarseness.

"There won't be anybody to look after you," the other woman warned. "I've given the whole staff the day off."

"I can look after myself," Janna insisted.

Genevieve hesitated. "Dr. Brassard's number is posted on the bulletin board," she said. "If you feel any worse, I want you to call him immediately."

"I will," Janna promised.

She managed to keep up her facade of being ill until the bus was out of view. Then she rushed up to her room, exchanged her slacks and heavy sweater for a beautifully cut two-piece suit that Elke had first loaned her, then insisted she keep, and hurried to the farm, where Fritz Demmer was waiting in his car.

The drive to Zurich took about four hours. When they arrived, noontime shoppers thronged Bahnhofstrasse, the street leading from the lake to the railway station. As Fritz guided the Fiat through slow-moving traffic, Janna glimpsed displays in beautifully decorated shop windows, and when the Swiss banker noticed her interest, he said, "I'll show you around after the market closes."

They entered the ancient stone building that housed the stock exchange, to be greeted by the strident voices of traders shouting out the prices of stocks they wished to buy or sell. Huge screens built into the walls displayed the prices, and traders in small glassed-in cubicles sat watching them with telephones glued to their ears as they relayed information to customers. The atmosphere was highly charged. Janna found herself exhilarated by it.

"There is some business I must take care of," Fritz said, "but when I get back I will show you around and explain how everything works."

She watched him greet traders as he made his way onto the floor of the exchange and was surprised by the transformation he underwent. His shyness had vanished. Instead, he exuded a confidence that made it evident he was in his element.

Turning away, Janna slowly walked around the perimeter of the exchange, observing the furious activity going on around her. It was as if many auctions were being conducted simultaneously in a variety of languages, including French, Italian, German, and English. In the foreign exchange section, teletype machines chattered while a dozen traders with direct lines to London, Rome, and New York bargained for blocks of pounds sterling, lire, and dollars. On electronic calculators they quickly computed rates to six decimal places while continuing to talk with customers thousands of miles away.

Janna had often heard of the gnomes of Zurich, but never expected to watch them at work. She knew from faithfully reading the *Wall Street Journal* that the decisions they were making could help prop up or undermine the currencies of entire nations. This was real power, she realized. It intrigued her, as did the whole concept on which trading was based: deducing a course of action and putting it to the test by gambling money on it. Mark had once taken her to Aqueduct racetrack and shown her how to place a two-dollar bet, but this was different. Luck was essential in picking a horse, but knowing what stock to buy at what price, and when to sell it, required a kind of skill.

She found her attention focused on the activities of one man in particular. He appeared to be in his late forties, had thick dark hair that was graying at the temples, and was wearing a well-tailored dark blue suit. Other traders watched his every move, straining to hear the orders he placed so they could immediately duplicate them. He seemed to sense he was being watched, because he looked up, smiled, and crossed to where she was standing.

"Do you like Abbott Laboratories or Hoffman-La Roche?" he asked.

"Abbott Laboratories," she replied.

He nodded, returned to the floor, and came back several minutes later holding a thick wad of Swiss francs.

"Your commission," he said.

"For what?" she asked.

"Telling me about Abbott Laboratories. I was holding both stocks, but after what you said, I sold Hoffman-La Roche. It just went down two points. You saved me a lot of money. This is your commission."

"But I don't know anything about Abbott Laboratories." She laughed. "I thought you were playing some kind of game."

"I was. It's called trading. Now take the money."

"But it was just a lucky guess, I couldn't possibly—"

"Then let me show you around the exchange."

Janna suddenly felt flustered.

"I'm with somebody."

"Another time, perhaps." He handed her his card. "If I can ever be of service, please don't hesitate to call me."

He turned and went back to the floor, leaving Janna flushed.

Fritz Demmer appeared at her side a few minutes later. "Sorry to keep you waiting," he said. "I hope you haven't been too bored."

"Tell me," Janna said, glancing at the card she was holding. "Who is Felix Ervin?"

"A lot of people would like to know that," Fritz replied. "He's made millions trading here in Zurich, as well as in Paris, London, and New York, but so far nobody has been able to discover very much about his background. Why?"

"It's just that I couldn't help noticing how all the others seem to watch his every move," she replied.

"That's because they want to capitalize on his trades," Fritz explained. "He always has the most accurate inside information."

"Where does he live?"

"Anywhere there's money to be made," Fritz said.

Janna looked across at where Felix Ervin was watching the screen. Once again, he seemed to sense he was being observed, because he broke off in the middle of a conversation and gazed directly at Janna. Their eyes met and held. She felt almost as if he was challenging her and turned away.

"I've got to get back to Montreux," she said.

"But I thought you wanted me to take you shopping!"

"If I'm not at school when the other girls get back from Davos there's going to be real trouble," Janna said.

Fritz didn't talk much during the drive back to Montreux. Janna knew he had expected her to stay over in Zurich, and she felt guilty about having deceived him, but she justified the lies she had told by reasoning that they were saving him from further hurt. She liked him, but only on a platonic level, and she sensed his interest went beyond simple friendship.

"Will I see you again?" Felix asked as he parked the Fiat outside the farmhouse.

"If you can settle for us just being friends," Janna said.

"Maybe when you get to know me better your feelings will change. . . ."

"I want to be honest about the way I feel now," Janna replied.

He sat holding the wheel, his eyes fixed straight ahead. "I would like to be your friend," he said.

"I hoped you would say that," Janna said, kissing him on the cheek and hurrying down the path toward the school.

In the months that followed, Janna settled into the routine of the École de Perfectionnement and developed a pattern of visits with Genevieve that quickly became a twice-weekly ritual. After dinner on Tuesdays and Thursdays the two women would return to the Directrice's private rooms, have coffee, and talk late into the night. Initially their conversation focused on the past, as Janna continued to probe for details about Keja, but after that subject had finally been exhausted and all possible clues as to the identity of her real father explored, they began to discuss the present and the future.

Janna enjoyed these meetings with Genevieve and learned a great deal from the Frenchwoman. The social functions that were such an important part of the school year, however, such as dances and garden parties attended by parents and friends, as well as students from various nearby exclusive boys' boarding schools, brought Janna far less joy. She didn't have either clothes or jewelry to match those of the other girls, which made her feel like a poor relation, and even though Elke generously shared everything she owned with her roommate, the functions only served to remind Janna that she was very different from the rest of the young women at the school. But whenever she felt too sorry for herself, she found herself thinking how much more difficult it must be for Anna.

Janna knew that Anna's financial situation, which kept her from making a visit to the school, was not going to improve. If this was ever going to change, Janna knew it would be because of her. In order to learn more about the financial world, she subscribed to the *Wall Street Journal*. If she had bought one hundred shares of the stock her old boyfriend had picked at random two years earlier, she would have made a profit of around $7,000. Encouraged by this, she read every copy of the newspaper scrupulously, paying particular attention to articles about smaller companies that had just gone public. Using the information she gleaned from these stories, she drew up her own list of stocks, all priced at less than five dollars, and persuaded Elke that instead of constantly losing the $500 monthly allowance her parents sent her at poker, she might like to try a different kind of gamble.

When she responded enthusiastically to the idea of backing her roommate's plan to play the market, Janna warned that there were no guarantees of making a profit.

"So what?" the German girl shrugged. "Let's do it."

The following morning, a week after an Easter party she'd attended in an evening dress Genevieve had given her for Christmas, Janna called Fritz Demmer and asked him to purchase one hundred shares of Burke International for her.

Obviously delighted to hear from her again, the banker said, "It's selling at a fraction under five dollars."

"I'll send you a check in the morning," Janna told him.

She had picked Burke International because of an article in *Forbes* magazine that described a new fastening device the small California company was manufacturing which was being tested by such major aircraft manufacturers as Hughes and Boeing. A week later it was announced in the *Wall Street Journal* that both companies had entered into a multimillion dollar contract with Burke International to use the fasteners on all their new planes, and the value of the stock zoomed to $12 a share.

"You've more than doubled our money!" Elke exclaimed when she heard the news. "This is more fun than poker. Now let's try for something bigger."

"We could sell Burke, leave the money with Fritz, and use it as collateral to buy some other stock on margin," Janna said.

"Margin?"

"We use the one thousand dollars to buy fifteen hundred dollars' worth of stock."

"Can you do that?"

Janna nodded. "Fritz told me how it's done."

"Sounds great."

"It is, provided the stock goes up in value. If it goes down beyond the point where we have cash equity, we'll get a call notice."

"What's that?"

"Fritz will want more money from us or he'll sell the stock he's holding to protect himself and the bank against possible losses."

"Is it risky?" she asked.

"Very."

"Great! Let's do it."

After studying all the research material she'd been able to assemble, Janna picked Opto Products, a firm that manufactured lenses which were widely used in copying machines sold by such giants of the office products industry as IBM and Xerox. She had read in an article in the *Wall Street Journal* that Opto Products had developed a system that not only improved the quality of copies but also simplified the maintenance of copying machines, and decided it was a promising stock. When she placed her order for one hundred shares they were selling at $15, but by the time she sold them six weeks later their value had risen to a fraction over $22.

"You really have a feel for the market," Fritz Demmer told Janna when she called asking him to sell.

"Beginner's luck, I guess," she replied.

"I'm not so sure," he said. "You were interested enough to want to visit the exchange in Zurich and have obviously read a lot of business publications. It seems to me you should credit your skill."

Janna began to believe Fritz might have been right because almost every stock she picked immediately went up in value. In a matter of months she had parlayed Elke's original $500 dollars into a portfolio of stock worth in excess of $8,000.

"Do you want us to cash it in?" she asked her roommate.

"I think we should gamble it all on one really big play," the German girl replied.

"Well," Janna said hesitantly, "there's a company called Arctico that I really like. It's a Canadian firm that makes oil drilling equipment. They've developed a drilling bit that a lot of oil experts think is better than the one made by Hughes Tool Company. It's still in the testing phase, but if it proves out the price of the stock is going to go through the roof."

"Sounds good to me," Elke said.

"Shall I buy on margin?"

"Why not?" the other girl said. "There are only two months left before graduation. We might as well have a last fling."

Janna placed an order with Fritz Demmer for $12,000 worth of Arctico stock, using the $8,000 she already had in her portfolio as collateral and leveraging it fifty percent. Within a week the stock had risen three points, but then an article appeared in the *Wall Street Journal* which revealed that a judge in Dallas, where the Hughes Tool Company had brought suit against Arctico, had ruled that Hughes's patents had been infringed by the other company, and overnight the value of Arctico stock plunged seventeen points.

The following morning Janna received a telegram from Fritz Demmer demanding payment of a further $4,000. She telephoned him and he explained that the telegram was a formality, a way of legally putting her on notice that unless she came up with the additional cash her stock would be sold to cover the $4,000 she had borrowed on margin.

"I don't have four thousand dollars," she told him.

"Then I'm afraid I must sell your stock for whatever price I can get," he said.

"How much will I have left?" she asked.

There was a brief silence as he made a calculation. "About a thousand dollars," he said.

"Would you send me a check?"

"Of course, it will be in the mail today." He paused, then added, "I'm sorry, Janna, it seems your luck ran out."

Janna was stunned, and felt nervous about telling Elke, but when she did so after dinner that evening, the German girl just laughed and said, "Well, we had some fun while it lasted."

For Elke investing had just been another lark, a new kind of excitement that was no more important to her than any of the numerous other distractions with which she filled her life. But it had meant something very different to Janna: her share of the money would have given her a nice nest egg, a reserve on which she could live after her year at the finishing school was over and allow her time to look around for a job.

She had kept in touch with Anna through weekly letters and twice-monthly telephone calls, which Genevieve allowed her to charge to the school, and knew that things in New York weren't going well. Anna had suggested that it might be wise for Janna to make use of the contacts she had made in Montreux to line up a job in Europe, but with less than eight weeks left before graduation, she didn't even have the slightest idea where to begin.

The solution came unexpectedly with the arrival of the Countess de Cabo. She appeared one morning during the last week in April, her corpulent body wrapped in a garment that looked like a cross between an oriental cheongsam and a tent, and was introduced by Genevieve Fleury to the assembled students as the owner of an international employment agency. She was a striking figure with her hair drawn in a tight chignon, dramatizing the imperial line of a commanding nose curving over flaring nostrils. Her mouth, a slash of crimson, was set over a strong jawbone, and her eyes shrewdly assessed her audience. Janna had the impression that, in a single glance, the Countess had picked out the students who interested her.

"Madame Fleury has been kind enough to invite me here this morning, as she did last year, and the year before that, to describe a unique opportunity in which some of you will undoubtedly be interested," the Countess announced.

She went on to describe her program, whereby the young women she selected were carefully matched with potential employers throughout the world.

"These men need personal assistants who are well versed in the social graces," the Countess said. "It is more important to them that you carry on a witty conversation at a business dinner than that you type or take shorthand."

A murmur of interest stirred through the room. Janna saw that Elke Kruger, for one, was listening intently.

"Your duties will vary," the Countess continued, "but generally they will involve such things as arranging formal dinners, entertaining your employer's business associates, and keeping his social schedule running smoothly. The remuneration will be commensurate with your responsibilities. Before any of you decide whether or not you want to accept the position being offered, you will be given a first-class round-trip air ticket to wherever your potential employer is located. After an interview, should you decide not to work for him, you will be flown back to Paris and reimbursed for any out-of-pocket expenses."

One of the girls in the audience raised her hand. "How do you match applicants and employers?"

"First I conduct personal interviews while I am here," the Countess replied. "Then those I select will be invited to Paris, where my offices are located, for a week of observation—where my staff and I can mingle with applicants in a wide variety of social circumstances so as to determine who will best meet the needs of different employers."

"It sounds like the men we'd be working for would also expect bedroom privileges. How has it worked out for girls you recruited in previous years?" another student wanted to know.

"Last year I selected eight girls, and five the year before that," the Countess replied. "Not all stayed with the first employer who interviewed them, but each ultimately found jobs to their liking in a wide range of businesses on three different continents. Only one of them is no longer employed. She married her boss and just had his baby." She paused, slowly scanned her audience, and added with much pomposity, "I am a Countess, not a madam."

Loud laughter greeted her declaration.

"I assure you it is a unique, and completely legitimate opportunity for the few who are chosen," the Countess assured her listeners, "and guarantee that any of you who put yourselves in my hands won't ever regret it."

26

Genevieve Fleury was worried, but she tried not to show it as she smoothly shifted to a lower gear and followed the chartered bus up the narrow, steeply winding road from Chur to St. Moritz.

The trip to the ski slopes of the Upper Engadine Valley was the last outing the students would take together before graduating in mid-June, and they had been in high spirits when they left the school in Montreux earlier that morning. A World Cup ski event was scheduled to take place during the afternoon, and plans had been made for them to remain overnight at the pension where Genevieve stayed with her students every year.

As the girls were boarding the bus, Genevieve, who was driving up to St. Moritz in her own car, had invited Janna to travel with her. "It'll give us a chance to catch up on things before you leave next month," the Frenchwoman said, but in fact she had quite a different motive.

Janna had been among the first to raise her hand, when the Countess asked which students wished to be considered for jobs, and had spent at least an hour being interviewed in private. Genevieve hoped to discover what had transpired at this meeting by talking with Janna during the long drive from Montreux to St. Moritz, but Janna had slept throughout most of the journey up to the mountains.

It was early afternoon when Genevieve parked her car in front of the pension in St. Moritz where she and her students were to spend the night. Madame Croz, the wife of the owner, a heavy, florid-faced woman who spoke with a thick German accent, was expecting them and showed the girls to the rooms where they would be sleeping.

"You must hurry," she told her guests. "The downhill races have already started. The Swiss team is doing very well, both Aloys Perren and Simon Biner were still in the running when I left the slopes about twenty minutes ago."

"How's Joe Dawson doing?" Elke asked.

"He hasn't made his run yet," Madame Croz replied.

Chattering excitedly, the girls left their knapsacks on their bunks and hurried away to the ski slopes—all except Janna, who stayed behind to buy a postcard from a rack on the reception desk. "For Anna," she said. "Are you ready for the slopes?"

"Not yet," Genevieve replied. "I'm still a bit tired from the drive up here."

"I'll see you up there, then." Janna tucked her long hair under a woolen hat, zipped up her nylon parka, and hurried off in the direction the other girls had taken. A group of young men, their hair bleached by the sun, whistled as she passed them.

"Oh, to be that young again!" Madame Croz sighed. When Genevieve didn't answer, the other woman added, "You look worn out."

"The drive up here seems to get longer each year."

"Would you like some coffee?"

"Thanks, but I think I'll just go to my room and rest for a while."

Madame Croz watched as Genevieve pulled herself out of the chair and started slowly upstairs. She had known the Frenchwoman for five years, ever since she first started bringing her students for an overnight stay at St. Moritz, and was startled by the physical changes the other woman had undergone since the last time she saw her. She was rail thin and her eyes seemed to have sunk into their sockets; there was also a slight lack of coordination in her movements that made her wonder if Genevieve was sick.

The Frenchwoman felt Madame Croz watching her—and knew why. She thinks I'm ill, she reflected as she entered her room, and she's right, I am ill, but in a way she couldn't even begin to understand. She had felt the symptoms coming on toward the end of the drive from Montreux, but couldn't give herself another injection because Janna had been with her.

Carefully locking the door, she opened her overnight bag and took out a small leather case that contained a syringe, needle, rubber tourniquet, and a vial of morphine that Dr. Brassard had delivered about half an hour before she left for St. Moritz. Instead of injecting herself immediately, Genevieve held the vial to the light and studied its contents. The clear liquid, lit by rays from the afternoon sun, turned the color of gold, forming a background against which she saw her own reflection. Narrowed and elongated, her face appeared as it might in the mirrors of a funhouse at a fairground, a caricature in which her normal features were so grossly distorted as to be barely recognizable.

The waiting game: that is what she secretly called the deliberate pause she always made before injecting herself with morphine. By denying herself the drug, even for a few minutes, when she actually had it in her hands, she experienced a jumble of conflicting emotions: fear, anxiety, desire, hope, despair, apprehension, dread, even dismay. But towering over them all was certainty. The next fix was assured, which was all that mattered.

But this time a shadow hovered over the waiting game. An essential part of the ritual was lining up other vials, her whole week's supply, so that at a glance she could see the guarantee she needed to get her through the upcoming days, but they were missing. Dr. Brassard had delivered only a single ampule. "You must understand, madame, the school year is coming to an end and you still haven't paid what you owe. From now on I must have cash or you will get no more morphine from me."

Wrapping the rubber tourniquet around her upper arm, she tapped for a vein but failed to find one. Over the years most of them had collapsed, retreating back to the bone to escape her probing needle. For a while she had used arteries—deeper than veins and harder to hit, and which required special long needles. She rotated from arms and hands to veins in her feet, but this time couldn't find one, and after fifteen minutes of poking and cleaning the needle out each time it clogged with blood, she finally abandoned her search and shot the morphine under her skin.

Almost immediately the cramps she had experienced during the drive went away, to be replaced by a euphoric sense of well-being. Putting on a parka and fleece-lined boots, she went downstairs. Madame Croz, who was behind the reception desk checking the register, looked up in surprise.

"I thought you were resting," she said.

"I promised the girls I would join them on the slopes," Genevieve replied brightly, "and I don't want to disappoint them."

Before the other woman could answer, the Frenchwoman hurried into the street and headed into the town she had come to know so well over the past years. She felt gloriously alive as she made her way past hotels and pensions, teahouses and restaurants, pharmacies and groceries, the post office, the Roman Catholic church, and the ski school. She loved St. Moritz, particularly at night under a full moon when, standing on a hilltop beyond the town, she could look down on the lighted windows of the hotels and pensions and feel herself wrapped in the peaceful silence that settled on the glittering snow mantle of the surrounding mountains.

Her ebullience continued as she searched the crowd lining both sides of the steep, snow-packed ski slope for some sign of Janna, but when she finally spotted her, Genevieve's good humor was replaced by panic. Talking to Janna was a tall, ruggedly handsome, fair-haired man whom the Frenchwoman immediately recognized as Derek Southworth. What in God's name was he doing here? It seemed impossible that his presence could be mere coincidence. Even though it was nearly twenty years since she last saw him at the internment camp, there was no mistaking the ex-RAF pilot. Now in his late forties and considerably more mature looking, he still exuded the same virile dynamism that had so attracted Genevieve when she first saw him being dragged away by guards at the jail in Pamplona.

"The next competitor is the current leader in World Cup points," a booming voice announced in French over the loudspeaker. "From the United States, Joe Dawson!"

As the crowd roared in applause, Janna half turned to say something to Southworth, glimpsed Genevieve, and called to her, but her voice was drowned out by excited shouts from the crowd as Joe Dawson flashed into view. The young American was traveling at over sixty miles an hour, yet he still managed to maintain a low crouch that put his head over the tip of his skis. Suddenly he lost his edges and his legs slid out from under him. For one long moment he floated in midair, etched in silhouette against the azure sky; then his body slammed down onto the hard-packed snow with a thud loud enough to be heard above the astonished cries of those watching. The force of his forward motion was so great that he continued to slide down the steep slope, his skis torn loose, until he was finally stopped by a pile of straw bales.

"Oh, God!" Janna gasped, her eyes fixed on Dawson, who lay sprawled like a rag doll as two course marshals stood over him. "Why aren't they helping him?"

"It's dangerous to move somebody with internal injuries unless you know what you're doing," Southworth said. "But it doesn't look good . . . it's the worst fall I've seen in the five years I've been coming here."

A figure Janna recognized as Elke broke through the crowd and ran to where Dawson lay. The German girl tried to cradle the fallen skier's head in her lap, but the course officials pulled her away, holding her back as two men wearing Red Cross armbands carefully placed him on a stretcher. Dawson was still unconscious, and one of his arms trailed limply in the snow until a medic strapped it to the side of his body. They attached nylon ropes to the stretcher, which was on a sled, and skied slowly down the mountain, followed by Elke, stumbling after them on foot.

"Is he a friend of yours?" Southworth asked.

"My roommate's, the girl who ran to him," Janna replied.

"Well, don't worry, he's in good hands," he said. "I'd take you down to the first aid station if I didn't have an appointment I can't break. But I'd like to see you again," he added. "Will you have dinner with me tonight?"

"I'm not sure I can get away. . . ."

"Try. The Palace Hotel, eight o'clock."

He smiled and without waiting for her to respond walked briskly to a parking area at the bottom of the hill, got into a red Ferrari, and roared away toward the center of town.

When Janna returned to the pension, she was surprised to find the other girls already seated at a long wooden table, dining on sausages and noodles, thick soup, and Fendant, a white wine from Valais.

"We're eating early so Madame Croz can visit her ailing sister," Genevieve explained.

As soon as the girls finished eating, Genevieve organized a game of charades and insisted that everybody take part.

"Come on, Janna, it's your turn," the Frenchwoman declared as a cuckoo clock on the wall of the lobby chirped the hour of seven.

"I really don't feel up to it," Janna said.

"Is anything wrong?"

"Just tired. I think I'll go upstairs and write that card to Anna."

Janna looked around the room for Elke. There was no sign of her, so Janna guessed that she must have accompanied Joe to the hospital. Upstairs in her room she lay on her bunk and tried to think of a way to keep her date with Derek Southworth. She wanted to see him again, but she couldn't figure out how she was going to do so with Genevieve keeping such close tabs on everybody. At 7:45 P.M. she peered downstairs, saw that she was still supervising the game of charades, and realized it was going to be impossible to leave the pension without being seen. Just before 8 P.M. she telephoned the Palace Hotel and asked to be put through to Derek Southworth.

"It's me," she said when he came on the line. "I'm afraid I can't make our dinner date."

"What happened?" he asked.

"I got—delayed. . . ."

"Well, I'm going to be here all evening, so try and join me for a nightcap. I'm counting on it."

There was a click and the line went dead. Replacing the receiver, Janna lay back on her bunk and tried to pinpoint why, when he could be so abrupt, she was so attracted to him. He was handsome, urbane, funny and charming, and had a way of listening that made her feel as though whatever she said was extraordinarily interesting. When he first spoke to her on the slopes it was to comment on the grace of the skier, and she had reacted peremptorily, but he hadn't seemed to be daunted by her manner, and she soon found herself warming to him. She was smiling to herself at the recollection of his description of his first attempt to ski when the door opened and Elke came into the room looking pale.

"Is Joe all right?" Janna asked.

"He's still in surgery," Elke reported. "He's broken his collarbone and an arm, but the doctors are more worried about internal injuries, something to do with his spleen."

"It happened right in front of where I was standing."

"I know, I was across the other side of the course just before Joe fell. By the way, who was the man you were with?"

"Somebody I met on the slopes. Derek Southworth. He's English—"

"And attractive," the other girl said.

"He invited me to dinner."

"And?"

Janna shrugged. "I was to meet him at eight o'clock, but Madame

Fleury is watching everybody like a hawk. I had to phone and tell him I couldn't make it."

"What did he say?"

"That he'll wait up."

"Sounds sure of himself. You should go."

"I don't see how."

Elke opened the door, tiptoed to the top of the stairs, and looked down into the large room that served as a lobby and sitting room. Genevieve was sitting in front of the fire reading a newspaper. "It isn't like her to stay up this late," Elke whispered. "Maybe she guesses you're going to meet him."

"She did see me with him," Janna acknowledged.

"So we'll improvise," the German girl said.

Stripping the sheets off both bunks, she knotted them together and opened the window. There was a full moon, and its pale light glistened on the thick blanket of snow that coated the roof of the pension. It had two levels, and the lower one, immediately below the girls' bedroom, angled down to a point less than five feet from a large snowdrift that had piled up against one side of the chalet. Throwing one end of the knotted sheet out of the window, Elke secured the other to a wooden post supporting the bunks.

"I don't know . . ." Janna hedged.

"I do," Elke replied firmly. "When something you want comes along you've got to grab it with both hands."

"But how am I going to get back?"

"The same way you're leaving. It shouldn't be any harder than climbing the trellis back at school. Now go!"

Janna hesitated a moment longer, then climbed out of the window. The snow on the roof was covered with a thin layer of ice, enough to support her weight as she slowly lowered herself across it, using the knotted sheet to stop herself from sliding. She was wearing tight-fitting ski pants and a heavy sweater, both of which quickly became caked with snow and finally ceased to provide any friction to slow her descent. Just before reaching the end of the knotted sheet Janna's numbed hands lost their grip and she slid over the edge of the roof. She landed in the snowdrift, but the impact still knocked the breath out of her.

"Now I suggest you go back upstairs the easy way," a voice announced sternly.

Janna looked up from where she was sprawled to see Genevieve standing on the balcony in front of the pension. Angered by her failure as much as the other woman's tone of censure, Janna snapped, "I wish you'd stop treating me like a child."

"I'd be glad to," the Directrice replied, "just as soon as you stop behaving like one."

"I have a perfect right—"

"Not while I'm responsible for you."

"When I graduate—"

"Then you can make your own decisions. But now you will do as I say. Go back to your room."

Janna knew it would be futile to argue. Gathering her bruised pride, she walked stiffly past Genevieve and went back upstairs.

Elke, who had witnessed the scene from the window, shook her head. "That woman doesn't miss a trick."

"There's no way I'm going to get out of here now," Janna said.

"Why don't you call him again?"

"And say what?"

"Maybe you can arrange to see him after you graduate. It's only a few weeks away."

"I'm not sure he's interested enough to want that."

"There's one way to find out," Elke said, picking up the phone and handing it to her friend.

Janna put the receiver to her ear. "The line has been disconnected," she said.

"Madame Fleury must have pulled the plug from the switchboard downstairs," Elke muttered. "Like I said, she doesn't miss a trick."

Realizing she'd been outmaneuvered made Janna even angrier, and the following morning she sullenly informed Genevieve that instead of riding back in her car she would travel with the other girls on the bus.

"As you wish." The Directrice shrugged.

After checking to see that all the girls were aboard the bus, Genevieve put her key in the door of her Peugeot and was surprised to find it unlocked. Compounding the mystery was her discovery of a broken matchstick on the driver's seat.

Perhaps, she thought, as she drove her car through the center of town, a little ahead of the bus carrying her students, somebody had broken into the Peugeot during the night and failed to start the engine. The car was equipped with an anti-theft device on the steering column which, although not enough to frustrate a professional car thief, might have deterred an amateur.

Despite the logic of this explanation, Genevieve's unease lingered as she entered the first of the S-turns on the steep mountain road linking St. Moritz with the town of Chur. Dawn was beginning to break, but a mist shrouded the surrounding peaks and visibility was poor. She caught a glimpse of the steel rail guarding the outer edge of the road —a barrier to protect motorists from the sheer drop to the valley floor —and realized she was nearer to it than she should have been. She braked, to slow down, but nothing happened. She tried again, this time harder, and heard a metallic screech. The pace of the car quickened until, within seconds, it was careening out of control toward a steep S-curve.

Frantically wrestling the wheel, she tried to guide the car into a narrow turnoff designed specifically for just such emergencies, but the Peugeot was moving too fast and missed the entrance. Moments before the car slammed into the steel barrier Genevieve knew what was going to happen, but she also realized there was nothing more she could do to prevent it, and instead of screaming she closed her eyes, rested her forehead on the steering wheel, and waited for the end to come.

Three days later, Captain Otto Stube was driven by his sergeant from police headquarters in Lausanne to the Montreux École de Perfectionnement, where he questioned each one of the students separately.

Janna was one of the last to be interviewed. As she waited outside the library, where the interrogations were taking place, she listened to the sound of each girl's footsteps as she emerged and crossed the tiled hallway. They echoed hollowly, a sound that seemed heightened by the atmosphere of desolation that had settled on the school since Genevieve's death.

Janna couldn't rid herself of the feeling that she was responsible for what had happened to the Frenchwoman: perhaps if she'd behaved more maturely, and journeyed in the car from St. Moritz back to Montreux, Genevieve would still be alive. Janna had watched through a window of the bus as the car went out of control, and it seemed to her that Genevieve had momentarily lost concentration on her driving. Had she been crying? Did tears blur her eyes just long enough for the accident to happen?

Janna knew that she would never know for sure, and she was haunted by the feeling that she had been to blame for the death of the woman to whom she'd become so close.

"We seem to be jinxed," she said to Anna when she called immediately after getting back to the school to let her know about Genevieve.

"First Mark, and now this. . . . I wish I could be there with you," Anna said.

Janna's memory of the phone conversation was interrupted by the police sergeant saying, "Captain Stube is ready for you now."

He took her to the library and held the door open. Captain Stube was seated behind a desk. He half got up as Janna entered the room.

"I'm sorry to keep you waiting so long, mademoiselle," he said in lightly accented English, motioning her to take a seat. "I know this must be a very difficult time for you."

"The whole school's very upset," Janna replied.

"But I gather you were closer to Madame Fleury than any of the other students?"

Janna nodded. "She and the woman who raised me were friends during the war."

Captain Stube glanced at a file that lay open on the desk in front of him. "The woman who raised you?"

"Anna brought me up after my real mother died."

The police officer slid a sheet of paper from the file. "I see. Yes, it is all here in the report my office received from Interpol, but there is no mention of your real father."

"I don't know who he was," Janna said tersely.

"Did Madame Fleury?"

"No."

"When was the last time you discussed the matter with her?"

"A few days before we went to St. Moritz," Janna replied. "We often spent whole evenings talking together."

"About your natural mother?"

"That and other things."

"And you rode in Madame Fleury's car on the journey up to St. Moritz?"

Janna nodded.

"And yet you chose to return with the other students on the bus. Why was that?"

"Madame Fleury and I had . . ." Janna paused. "We had an argument the night before the accident."

"About what?"

"She caught me climbing out of a window at the pension."

The trace of a smile flickered across Captain Stube's somber face. "And where, may I ask, were you going at that late hour?"

"I'd made a date earlier in the day."

"And the name of the man you were going to meet?"

"Derek Southworth."

Captain Stube picked up a pencil and made a careful notation on the sheet of paper in front of him. "What can you tell me about—er, Derek Southworth?"

"Not much, except that he's English. . . ."

"During the time you were with Mr. Southworth did he speak to Madame Fleury?"

"No," she replied. "They never met."

Captain Stube gazed at the documents in front of him. "An autopsy has established that Madame Fleury had a considerable quantity of morphine in her system at the time of her death," he said. "Do you have any idea where she might have obtained it?"

Janna tensed. She remembered Genevieve's frequent mood swings, but she said, "I imagine her doctor prescribed it."

"Dr. Brassard denies having provided her with the drug."

"Was it the effects of the morphine that caused the accident?" Janna asked.

"It was not an accident, mademoiselle. The brake cylinders on all four wheels of her car had been drained before she left St. Moritz, probably sometime during the night."

Janna's reaction was a mixture of horror and relief. It was inconceivable that anybody would have wanted to kill Genevieve, but if somebody else was responsible it lifted the guilt from her own shoulders.

"Why is God's name would anybody do such a thing?" she asked, her voice mirroring her shock.

"Somebody who wanted her—or you—dead."

Janna was stunned. "Me!"

Captain Stube shrugged. "Why not? You had ridden up to St. Moritz in Madame Fleury's car. It was therefore perfectly reasonable to assume that you would also be her passenger on the journey back to Montreux. My purpose in asking these questions is not to determine the cause of an accident, mademoiselle, but to try and understand why the Directrice of this school was murdered."

27

Janna sat on the balcony of her room at the Hotel George V in Paris watching early evening traffic stream along the Champs-Élysées. It was the end of the second week in June 1964, over two weeks since her interview with Captain Stube, and yet she still hadn't been able to rid herself of the shock of discovering that Genevieve's death hadn't been an accident, and that whoever killed her might also have intended herself as a victim.

She had been so shaken by the revelation, combined with the terrible sense of grief she experienced when Genevieve died, that for a while she had seriously considered abandoning her plans to find a job through the Countess's placement service, and returning to New York so she could be with Anna. It was an instinctive reaction, one born of a need to be with somebody she loved at a time when she was feeling scared and vulnerable, but when she discussed the idea with Anna on the phone, the other woman encouraged her to go through with her original plan.

"You know I'd love to have you with me," Anna said, "but if there's a chance of your getting a decent job, I'd take it if I were you. I know it's what Mark would have wanted too."

Anna had spoken very little about her own situation, but from their many conversations Janna had realized that the other woman was having her own problems. The charges against Mark had been dropped after he died, but the cost of mounting a defense had left Anna in dire financial circumstances. She was now living in a one-bedroom apartment in a converted brownstone on the Upper West Side of Manhattan and working as a jewelry designer. The job provided enough income to keep her head above water, but her standard of living was a far cry from what she had enjoyed while Mark was alive. She didn't even have enough money to make the trip to Switzerland for the funeral.

Genevieve was buried in the cemetery of a small church overlooking Lake Geneva. The simple ceremony was conducted by a young priest, who, although he had never met Genevieve, still spoke eloquently of her high moral character which had been a source of inspiration to her students. Captain Stube told only Janna about the real cause of Genevieve's death, and the other girls continued to believe it was an accident. As official graduation ceremonies had been canceled, when the graveside services were over most of the students returned to their families, and by week's end the only girls still in residence at the Montreux École de Perfectionnement were the eight who had been selected by the Countess for job placement, a group that included both Janna and Elke Kruger.

The following Monday they left for Paris, where rooms had been reserved for them at the George V for their week of observation. For Elke and the other girls, all of whom came from wealthy families, the considerable cost of these accommodations was inconsequential. Nor were they short of funds with which to enjoy the city, and their days were spent shopping on the Rue de Rivoli and the Faubourg Saint-Honoré for clothes and other items they intended to take with them on their trips abroad for job interviews.

They were led on these expeditions by Elke Kruger, whose parents had sent her a graduation present of $10,000, the bulk of which she had already spent in the salons of such designers as Christian Dior, Schiaparelli, and Balenciaga. She also bought a solid gold Piaget watch, which she left under Janna's pillow with a note, saying, *For my best friend in the whole world.*

Even though Janna appreciated the sentiment behind the gift she was embarrassed at not being able to reciprocate. Anna had sent her a check for $100, and when Janna called to thank her for it she hadn't mentioned Captain Stube's conclusion that Genevieve had been murdered, or that she herself might have been an intended victim. Anna had enough worries of her own.

On the third day after Janna arrived in Paris, the Countess sent for her. "I know you can't afford the George V, but I'd be happy to advance you—"

"Thank you, madame," Janna countered, "but I'd rather pay my own way."

That afternoon Janna took the watch Elke had given her and pawned it for a sum that was more than enough to pay the cost of her week in Paris. The Countess accepted the money without comment, but privately the gesture aroused her interest and admiration.

As the purple evening shadows settled over the Champs-Élysées, Janna looked down at the crowds sauntering along the sidewalks of the broad avenue, among whom were many young American college students. Most of the ones she had talked with in cafés and parks had come to France seeking respite from the violence that had recently swept the United States. They were still shocked by President Kennedy's assassination and, having grown weary of protest, had come to Paris to immerse themselves in a different culture.

Listening to the experiences of these young people, most of whom were her own age, made Janna aware of the vacuum she'd been living in during the months she had spent at finishing school.

"Aren't you ready yet?"

Janna turned. Elke Kruger was standing at the open French windows. She was wearing a pale blue dress she had bought that afternoon at Christian Dior's, and her hair was held back from her face by a ribbon of the same color.

"You look beautiful," Janna said.

"I never know what to wear for Prince Gozini's parties."

"Who is he, anyway?"

Elke shrugged. "I met him last summer in Saint-Tropez. He had a party on his yacht. I think he's Italian. Very rich and rather eccentric, but quite amusing. I met him again when we were in St. Moritz. It was the day Joe was injured, and I was too preoccupied to spend time with the Count, but he invited me to the party he's having tonight."

"His invitation didn't include me," Janna said.

"He won't mind."

Janna wished she could think of an excuse so she wouldn't have to go. "I don't know—and I haven't the right clothes. . . ."

"I've got more than enough for us both," Elke interjected.

She led the way into the bedroom, where newly purchased clothes were strewn across the bed along with an assortment of shoes, hats, handbags, and accessories. Janna picked up a simple white dress bearing the label of Jacques Fath and said, "This is nice."

"But too virginal," Elke said.

"It should suit me then."

"A virgin at twenty? It's hard to believe. Are you sure you've been telling me the truth?"

Janna's cheeks flushed. "We're talking about dresses, not my sex life." She laughed. "Should I wear this little number or not?"

"Go ahead," Elke said, "but hurry, we're late."

It was almost eleven by the time they reached the Prince's house on Ile Saint-Louis. Elke had sold her Porsche before leaving Montreux, so they took a taxi to the island in the River Seine where many of the wealthiest people in Paris lived. In the darkness it looked dismal, dank, and deserted. The gray shapes of eighteenth-century buildings lined narrow, poorly lit streets that were shrouded in mist. When they rang the bell at the address the Prince had given Elke, a porte-cochere opened, allowing a thin shaft of light to slice through the darkness, and an angular old woman in a black head shawl appeared. When Elke gave her name the concierge checked a list. "The invitation was for you alone, mademoiselle. I must talk with the Prince before I can admit your friend."

The old woman slammed the porte-cochere, and they heard the sound of her footsteps disappearing down a stone corridor.

"I told you he wasn't going to like me turning up uninvited," Janna said. "Why don't I walk back to the Pont de la Tournelle—"

"It'll be all right, you'll see," Elke assured her.

Moments later the porte-cochere opened again, wider this time, and the concierge beckoned them inside. "The Prince wishes to meet your friend," the old woman said, holding open the door of a small elevator.

"I told you he wouldn't mind," Elke said.

Janna was less sure. She felt awkward, but it was too late to change her mind. When the elevator door opened the two young women stepped out into a hallway that epitomized the glittering thirties, with its incredible construction of Lalique glass and chrome plating. There was Greek statuary, African masks, Louis XVI sideboards, opaline glass, Samarkand rugs, and mirrors everywhere reflecting the scene. But what surprised Janna more than the contrast between the dingy exterior of the house and the opulent furnishings was the fact that the guests filling the numerous rooms were all wearing costumes.

It was like stepping backward in time, for the outfits mostly reflected the period when Louis XIV ruled France: men wore ornate brocades with long stockings and silver-buckled shoes, while women paraded in dresses of heavy silk that swept the floor when they walked. Sprinkled among them were a few guests wearing priest's chasubles, nun's habits, and costumes representing the devil, and each person was wearing a mask.

The man waiting in the hallway to greet them was wearing the scarlet robes of a cardinal, a liturgical headdress, pendant rubies in the lobes of each ear, and heavy pancake makeup.

"Darling!" he exclaimed in a thin, high-pitched voice as he lightly brushed Elke's cheek with moist, petulant lips. "I thought you were never going to get here. Do introduce me to your mysterious friend."

"This is Janna," Elke said.

"Quite extraordinary," the man in cardinal's robes observed, standing back to study Janna through a lorgnette. "Marvelous bone structure, rather boyish legs, but I like that. Does she speak?"

"Janna, I'd like you to meet Prince Gozini," Elke said.

"How do you do," Janna murmured.

"Rather well, and quite often," the Prince answered puckishly.

"Behave yourself," Elke chided.

"Why? It makes life so boring."

He winked slyly at Janna and hurried away with mincing steps into a ballroom where scores of other guests milled around against a background of music from a trio on a small stage.

"I think this was a mistake," Janna said.

"Don't be such a pessimist," Elke chided.

"We're the only ones not wearing costumes."

"Who cares?"

"I think the Prince might."

"That wasn't what interested him about you."

"I got the impression he doesn't like women."

"Women, men, animals—he's very democratic for an aristocrat."

"He sounds bizarre to me."

"But rich enough to only be described as eccentric." Elke picked up two glasses of champagne from the tray of a passing waiter, handed one to Janna, and led the way down a corridor filled with ornately carved and brightly painted masks.

"I like his choice of art," Janna observed.

"A lot of his stuff is in the Louvre's African collection."

"It's hard to believe that a man like that has any of the finer instincts."

Elke suddenly swung around and faced her friend. "Why don't you stop being so snide?" she demanded.

Janna was too taken back by the tone of her voice to answer. "I've had enough of your goddamn moralizations. Who the hell are you to sit in judgment?"

Elke turned and strode back toward the crowded ballroom, leaving Janna stunned by her roommate's outburst. They'd had a few minor disagreements in the past, mostly over Elke's chronic slovenliness, but none as unfounded as the outburst that had just occurred. Still puzzled, Janna went into a room where lush plants spiraled upward to a domed glass ceiling, sat down on a richly brocaded sofa, and pensively sipped her champagne.

"There you are!" a voice announced breathlessly. "Elke tells me you need a little help getting into the party spirit, and I've got just what the doctor ordered."

Janna looked up and saw Prince Gozini holding a small jeweled box containing a white powder. He took a pinch and sniffed it up each nostril, then offered her the box.

"Thank you, but I'd rather not," she said. In an effort to bridge the awkwardness of the moment, she added, "I was admiring your collection of African art."

"Particularly the phallic objects, eh?" The Prince chuckled, took her arm, and led her back in the direction of the ballroom, where he went in search of more champagne.

The trio had stopped playing. After Janna adjusted to the light, which had been dimmed, she saw that the costumed guests who had been sedately dancing with each other were now engaged in a full-scale orgy. Bodies writhed together on the polished parquet floor: women with multiple partners; men engaged in oral and anal intercourse with each other; an Alsatian dog hungrily licking meat paste that had been smeared on the vagina of an elegantly coiffed young socialite who squatted on all fours in the midst of a group of voyeurs. It was a Bosch-like tableau that perfectly illustrated the vacant lives of the participants, and Janna experienced both pity and disgust.

Then she saw Elke. The German girl, completely nude, lay on the small stage that had been occupied by the trio, accepting multiple sex partners. She saw Janna watching and grinned at her with defiance in her eyes that sent shivers through her friend. Janna started forward, instinctively wanting to protect her, but then checked herself, turned away and hurried to the elevator.

"Janna?"

The man who had spoken was wearing a black cape, pants, and shirt, a feathered hat, high-heeled boots, and a sword. His face was partially covered by a mask. When he removed it, she recognized Joe Dawson.

"I thought you were still in the hospital," she said.

He drew back his cape to reveal a cast that covered the upper part of his left arm, shoulder, and ribs. "I could have come as a mummy." He grinned.

"Elke said you also suffered internal injuries?"

"My spleen isn't where it used to be." He tried to sound nonchalant.

"Did Elke know you were going to be here?" Janna asked.

He shook his head. "I thought I'd surprise her." He glanced toward the ballroom. "She beat me to it."

Janna sensed his anguish and her heart went out to him as they rode together in the elevator down to the ground floor and were ushered out by the sullen-faced concierge. They stood together on the sidewalk in awkward silence.

"I feel drained," Janna said.

"Coke'll do that to you."

"It isn't that," Janna said. "The Prince offered me some, but I don't use drugs."

"You must be the only guest who doesn't," Dawson said. "The Prince always has the best stuff and everybody knows it. He was handing it out like candy to the racers up at St. Moritz. I was dumb enough to take a toot before I went out of the starting gate, and you saw what happened."

"Was Elke high tonight?" Janna asked.

"Tonight, last night, last week, she's always high on something."

"I tried to talk with her about the drugs she was using, but she always said she could handle them."

"She isn't fond of admitting the truth about herself," Dawson said. "There's a lot you don't know about that little lady."

"You really care about her, don't you?"

Dawson averted his eyes. "Let's get a cup of coffee."

"It's late."

"Please?"

For the first time since she'd met the young skier she sensed his vulnerability. "All right," she said, "let's find a taxi."

The mist that hung over the river had moistened the sidewalks, which reflected the light cast by ancient, cast-iron streetlamps. They walked toward the Pont de la Tournelle. The river flowed dark and silent, reflecting the myriad lights of the city like diamonds on black velvet. They found a taxi in front of the Tour d'Argent but spoke very little until they were seated over coffee and cognac at Les Deux Magots.

"Will you be able to ski again?" Janna asked.

"The doctors don't think so."

"What will you do?"

Dawson shrugged. "I was accepted at UCLA Law School a couple of years ago," he said, "but I didn't go because I was earning too much money on the pro ski circuit. Now I might give it another shot."

"I didn't know you were interested in becoming a lawyer."

"Pale stuff compared with being number one in the world at downhill, huh?"

"I'm impressed."

"Elke wasn't. She liked being the girlfriend of a winner."

"I know she cares for you."

"She's got one hell of a way of showing it."

"From what you've told me, it sounds like she needs help," Janna said.

"More than you know," Dawson replied, moodily dipping a cube of sugar into his coffee.

There was another strained silence, which Janna finally broke by asking, "Why did you pick skiing?"

"I grew up pretty wild. Never knew my old man. My mom was a waitress in a greasy spoon in Los Angeles and she was always working. I got into stealing hubcaps, shoplifting, dealing a little grass. I got busted when I sold some to an undercover narc at high school. They assigned me a Public Defender, a real nice guy, who really got me interested in how the law works. The judge was impressed by my demeanor in court and gave me a choice, a year in juvenile hall or eighteen months in a court-ordered placement. I went for the placement and ended up working for a guy who ran a snow grooming business in Mammoth. That's where I learned to ski. I guess you could say crime paid off for me."

"When are you going back to the States?"

"In about six hours."

"Does Elke know?"

"I was going to tell her tonight and ask if she wanted to go with me, but now I don't give a damn whether or not I ever see her again."

"She'll be leaving Paris herself in a few days." Janna told him about the Countess's job placement agency.

"Sounds like the perfect setup for Elke," he commented. "Plenty of kicks and not much work. I can see why she's interested, but what's in it for you?"

"I need the work."

"I thought all you girls at that fancy finishing school were from rich families."

"You're looking at the exception."

"Shit!" He shook his head. "Elke told me your father is one of the wealthiest art dealers in the States."

"Why on earth would she lie like that?"

"Who knows? Logic doesn't apply to people like Elke. There have been times when I wondered if she was sane."

The waiter brought the check and a few customers smiled at Dawson's costume as they went outside.

"Where are you staying?" he asked.

"The George Cinq."

He gave the taxi driver instructions and settled into the seat next to her. A light rain had begun to fall, and the Champs-Élysées glistened under a panoply of lights.

"I wish I'd been smart enough to talk straight with you when we first met," he said.

"Me too," Janna replied.

When the taxi stopped in front of the hotel, Dawson said, "Don't tell Elke I saw her up there tonight. She'll probably pretend it never happened anyway; that's part of her paranoia. And be kind to her. She needs to be loved. She's a lot more fragile than most people think."

He leaned over and kissed Janna lightly on the lips. She waited on the sidewalk until the taxi carrying Dawson disappeared from view and then hurried into the hotel. As she lay in bed watching the play of shadows on the ceiling, she thought about what Dawson had told her about Elke and tried to remember if there had been any warning signs she should have picked up on that would have indicated her roommate's mental instability. She couldn't pinpoint any. She was high-spirited and constantly searching for new kinds of excitement, but there had been little to indicate that she was bordering on insanity, as Dawson suggested.

It was almost noon by the time Janna awoke. She looked across at the other bed and saw Elke sleeping as peacefully as a child. In repose her features possessed a singular innocence. The only evidence of the previous evening was the smeared makeup she had failed to remove. Janna went into the bathroom and turned on the shower. As she stood under the jets of hot water, she thought about Joe Dawson. How ironic it was that she should discover he was a man who interested her, perhaps somebody for whom she could genuinely care, when it was too late for a relationship between them to be possible! When she reentered the bedroom, Elke was seated in front of the dressing-table mirror rubbing the last traces of makeup off her face with cold cream and paper tissues.

"Where did you go last night?" she asked innocently.

Janna remembered what Dawson had said about Elke's pretending the orgy had never happened and was tempted to confront her with it, but because she had no way of knowing just how close to a breakdown her friend might be, rather than risk upsetting her, she said, "I got tired and left early."

"You should have stayed." Elke replied lightly. "It turned into a great party."

The Countess had scheduled a meeting for all the girls at her house that afternoon to announce where she was sending them for job interviews. Janna and Elke shared a taxi, and throughout the short journey from the Hotel George V to the Ile de la Cité the German girl bubbled with excited speculation as to where she would be going. As she listened to her chatter, Janna wondered how she could help Elke. Perhaps, she thought, when the right opportunity presented itself, she could hint that Elke might benefit from talking with a psychiatrist. She would have to be very tactful.

"How do you think the Countess decides where to send us?" Elke asked.

"It beats me," Janna said.

Supposedly the decisions were based on conclusions the Countess had made by observing the girls during their stay in Paris, but she hadn't once put in an appearance, and although each of the applicants was required to telephone her each evening with a description of how she had spent her day, most of them invented scenarios they thought would impress her.

When the Countess announced her selections in the elegantly furnished living room of her house, Janna was surprised at how astutely she had matched each girl with a prospective job. After spending so much time with them at the finishing school Janna knew all the girls well enough to be aware of their various personalities and was astonished at how accurately the Countess had gauged them.

The assignments ranged from working for a Bolivian tin mining millionaire in La Paz to a Greek shipping tycoon in Monte Carlo who lived on a yacht even bigger than that owned by Aristotle Onassis. Elke was being sent to Beverly Hills for an interview with a financier whose interests ranged from cosmetics to the ownership of a major motion picture studio.

Janna's destination was the last to be announced, and it evoked a murmur of surprise from the other girls.

"I'm sending you to Singapore, my dear," the Countess said. "You will be interviewed by a Chinese gentleman named G. K. Wong. He is one of the wealthiest men in Asia and operates businesses that include hotels, newspapers, shipping lines, rubber plantations, real estate, and a host of others I can't even remember. I think you will find it a position for which you are admirably suited."

Janna was stunned. Not even in her wildest imaginings had she ever dreamed of being sent to Asia. She felt both apprehensive and excited, but before she could say a word the Countess had turned back to the rest of the applicants and repeated the rules of her agency. Each girl would be provided with a first class round-trip air ticket to her destination, where she would stay at the best hotel available while being interviewed by her would-be employer. Should she decide not to accept the job being offered, she was free to return to Paris, where the Countess promised to make every effort to find something more to her liking.

"However," she added, "should you accept the position, I will negotiate a contract on your behalf directly with your employer, a service for which I will receive a commission of six percent of your first year's salary. Does anybody have any questions?"

Elke raised her hand. "I've arranged a little party at Maxim's this evening, and I would like you to join us, madame."

"That's very kind of you," the other woman replied, "but I think you girls should share this occasion without me. I just want to say that I've received reports on all of you during the past week and am most impressed by what my assistants have told me. I know you are all going to make me proud of you."

There was a spontaneous burst of applause and the Countess warmly embraced each of the girls as she handed out envelopes containing plane tickets, expense money, and specific directions on what to do when they reached their destinations.

"I know you are going to love Singapore," she told Janna when it was her turn to leave. "Of all the jobs I think yours will be the most challenging, and from what Madame Fleury told me about you before her tragic murder, I have every confidence that you will do it well."

Janna tensed. How did the Countess know Genevieve had been murdered? Captain Stube had told Janna she was the only person to whom he had revealed the truth about how the Frenchwoman died, and newspapers had reported her death as an accident.

The other woman's words continued to gnaw at Janna throughout the rest of the day and remained with her when she joined the other girls in a private room at Maxim's for the farewell dinner Elke was hosting. The German girl had spared no expense, and the banquet, which included smoked trout mousse, Beluga caviar, and veal stuffed with truffles, was served with Château Margaux and jeroboams of Bollinger champagne. By the time coffee was served, all the guests, including Janna, were extremely light-headed.

Tapping the rim of a wineglass with a spoon to get everyone's attention, Janna announced, "I propose that all of us meet here at Maxim's a year from today, when I'll be the hostess. . . ." The rest of her words were drowned out by a loud chorus of assent.

After their meal, Elke led her guests on a tour of bars on the Left Bank. But gradually the group dwindled, as girls who had early flights returned to the hotel for a few hours of sleep, and finally only Elke and Janna were left.

"It was a great party," Janna said.

Elke nodded. "I think everybody had a good time."

"A week from now we'll be on different sides of the world. Hard to believe, isn't it?"

"When you've traveled as much as I have, one place begins to look pretty much like another."

"You sound burned out."

"I feel burned out."

"Have you ever thought about talking to someone about it?"

Elke's eyes narrowed. "What are you getting at?"

"Just that sometimes people who are trained to listen—"

"When I need your goddamn advice I'll ask for it," Elke snapped.

"I was just trying—"

"Well, don't!" There was a long strained silence, during which each avoided the other's eyes. Then Elke drained her glass and said, "Come on, let's get out of here."

Dawn was breaking as they walked with uncertain steps along a path bordering the Jardins du Luxembourg, their only company a group of garbage collectors who were just beginning their rounds.

"I'd better be getting back to the hotel. My plane leaves in less than four hours, and I've still got a lot of packing to do." Janna said.

Elke nodded but didn't reply and, when Janna flagged down a taxi, made no attempt to get into it. "Go ahead," she said, "I don't have to be at Orly until late afternoon."

"But you've got to get some rest."

"Plenty of time for that on the plane."

"Sure you'll be all right?"

"You know me," Elke said wryly. "If trouble doesn't turn up I'll go looking for it."

There was an awkward pause, and then they embraced. Tears spilled down their cheeks.

"I'm going to miss you like hell," Janna murmured.

"You won't have to pick up after me anymore. . . ."

"I'll miss that, too."

"You are my best friend, maybe my only one. Please don't lose touch. . . ."

"I won't. I'll let the Countess know my address as soon as I have one. You do the same, and we'll write each other often."

The driver, who was growing impatient, tooted his horn.

"Better be going," Elke said.

Janna nodded. "Take care of yourself."

She got into the taxi. As it pulled away from the curb, she caught a last glimpse of her friend, standing alone in the gray morning light.

28

Suddenly turbulence hit the UTA French Airlines Boeing 707 as it banked over Singapore, a lush green island linked by a mile-long causeway to the peninsula of Malaysia. Janna couldn't relax until the plane that had brought her on the eighteen-hour journey from Paris finally settled onto the runway.

It had been a tiring trip, broken only by brief stops at Muscat and Columbo for refueling, and there had been plenty of time for her to think about the conversation she'd had with Anna about an hour before taking off from Orly airport. The other woman had been surprised and delighted to hear that Janna was going to Singapore. "It'll give you a chance to meet Janet Taylor. I'll write and tell her you're going to be there. She gets her mail through a post office box, so I don't know her street address, but I'll tell her you'll be staying at Raffles and ask her to get in touch with you. It's been twenty years since I last saw her and she's been through a great deal since then, but she loved you as a baby and I'm sure her feelings haven't changed."

As the plane winged its way high over the Indian Ocean during the final hours of its flight to Singapore, Janna reflected on what she knew about the Englishwoman who, according to everything Anna had told her, had nurtured her through the first six months of her life. Janet had traveled with Keja across wartorn Europe and over the Pyrenees and had helped deliver Janna in the village of Irati. For years now she'd been living in a small village in northern Malaya as the lover of a Communist guerrilla fighter with a huge price on his head.

Janet's history was intriguing to Janna in and of itself, but especially because she knew this woman was the last link with her past. Perhaps Janet Taylor could help her to discover the identity of her real father. If she couldn't Janna knew that the mystery would remain unsolved forever.

As Janna stood in the aisle of the plane with the other passengers waiting to disembark, she felt especially vulnerable. She was half a world away from Anna, Genevieve was dead, and Elke Kruger was on the edge of a breakdown.

A stewardess with a bright smile said, "Thank you for flying UTA," as it was Janna's turn to leave the plane.

She nodded and stepped out onto the mobile stairs, where she was immediately assaulted by a wall of hot, suffocatingly humid air heavy with the odor of raw rubber, fried peanut oil, diesel fumes, and the fetid stench of rotting excrement. The impact was so overwhelming that she felt faint and leaned against the rail of the stairway to steady herself.

"Are you all right?" the stewardess at the door asked worriedly.

"It's the damned humidity," a florid-faced man announced loudly. "I've been living in Singapore for over twenty years, and I'm still not used to it."

"I'll be fine," Janna said, suddenly conscious that she was blocking the way for others who were waiting to get off the plane.

"Sure?" the stewardess persisted.

"Yes, really, thanks," Janna replied, climbing slowly down the stairs and entering the passenger reception area. Wearily, she went through passport control and customs, a ritual from which she emerged bathed in sweat.

"Miss Maxell-Hunter?"

A man in a white linen suit was looking at her inquiringly. She experienced a moment of déjà vu that took her back a year to Geneva, when she'd been greeted by a reporter telling her about Mark's suicide. When she nodded, the man said, "I'm Gerald Foster, Mr. Wong's personal assistant. He asked me to meet you."

Janna followed him outside the terminal to where a Rolls-Royce waited, its engine running, and handed her baggage tags to the Chinese driver, to whom Foster spoke rapidly in his own language. The air-conditioned interior of the car was exactly the refuge Janna had yearned for from the moment she stepped out of the plane.

"It feels so good in here." She sighed.

"I wish I could offer some reassurance by telling you it cools off at night in Singapore," Foster said, "but I'm afraid it doesn't."

Janna luxuriated in the refrigerated air, watching as Foster pulled open a panel in the burled walnut liquor cabinet that was built into the back of the front seat. He was a thin, sharp-featured man with receding hair and a weak chin. His skin was the color of old tallow, and there was a slight cast to his eyes that made him appear vaguely Oriental.

"This should cool you down," he said, handing her a gin and tonic. He tapped the rim of her ice-filled glass with his own. "Welcome to Singapore. G.K. knew you'd be tired after your flight, so he set aside some time to talk with you tomorrow morning."

"G.K.?"

"Mr. Wong. Everybody calls him by his initials."

Janna heard the chauffeur loading her luggage into the trunk, and when he got in behind the wheel Foster spoke to him again in Chinese.

"Does it take long to learn to speak the language that well?" she asked.

"Not when you're raised speaking it," Foster replied. "My father was English, my mother Chinese. But you shouldn't find bazaar Malay too hard, and that's what most people speak here in Singapore."

"I thought they spoke Malaysian."

He took a long swallow from his glass and said with the forced patience of the reluctant teacher, "Malay is a language, Malays are a race, and Malaysians are a national group that includes Chinese and anybody else who is a citizen."

"I understand there isn't much love lost between Malays and Chinese," Janna said.

"That's an understatement," Foster said, fixing himself another drink. "We had serious rioting here a few months ago, and it won't take much to spark another racial explosion."

While they talked the chauffeur smoothly guided the Rolls-Royce through streets crowded with trishaws and crossed a narrow bridge over the Singapore River. Its clogged banks were lined with godowns bulging with goods being held for transshipment: bales of rubber, palm oil, Oriental woods, tin ore, spices, and hemp. A motorized sampan towing nine barges chugged its way under the bridge, sending up clouds of diesel smoke that was drawn in by the car's air conditioner and penetrated the cool elegance of its interior.

"I didn't mean to lecture you," Foster said as the Rolls glided across St. Andrew's Square toward the Raffles Hotel.

His words were slightly slurred. Janna realized that the gin and tonics he'd consumed during the ride from the airport were taking their toll.

"G.K. wouldn't like me suggesting there are going to be more riots. It isn't the kind of things that instills confidence in a newcomer."

"He won't hear about it from me," she assured him.

Foster looked relieved. "The chauffeur will pick you up at ten o'clock tomorrow morning," he said, "and if you don't mind me making a friendly suggestion, wear your most modest dress. G.K. may be Genghis Khan with other businessmen, but when it comes to women, particularly Europeans, he's rather a prude."

Janna thanked him for his advice and went into the lobby of the hotel. The famous hostelry, which Somerset Maugham had described as representing all the fables of the exotic East, made a disappointing first impression on her. A white, three-story building with a red tiled roof, it had an oddly located main entrance at one corner and a ballroom that appeared to have been added as an afterthought.

The Indian desk clerk, a thin man with a preoccupied expression, informed Janna that a room had been reserved for her and that she was to sign for anything she needed. He summoned a turbaned porter, who led her to a room on the third floor that was spacious but somewhat barren, with a large ceiling fan that turned lazily, keeping the humid air in constant motion. After unpacking she took a long, cool shower, put on a light cotton dress, and went down to dinner in the Palm Court Grill, which was located outdoors on a lawn around which the hotel was built. The menu was in English, and the waiter patiently described the dishes to her. She ordered papaya, fish, and water chestnuts marinated in an aromatic liqueur for dessert. While she ate, a string quartet played a selection of Noel Coward tunes, and she felt herself beginning to relax.

When she returned to her room, Janna stood at the window and looked out over the sweltering city, wondering when Janet Taylor would contact her. The view was mesmerizing: there were pinpricks of light from kerosene lamps on food vendors' stalls, Mah-Jongg players were shuffling their pieces in the doorways of shops which were still open even though it was almost midnight, and the pungent odor of sewage in the Singapore River blended with the smell of latex and the scent of night-blooming jasmine. After the sterile cleanliness of Switzerland, Singapore was like being wrapped in a sweaty embrace.

At exactly 10 A.M. the following morning, Wong's Chinese chauffeur arrived in front of the main entrance to drive Janna to her interview. Taking Gerald Foster's advice, she wore a well-cut but simple white linen suit that was part of the wardrobe Elke had insisted on buying her as a going-away present. The drive to Wong's took them through the crowded streets of Chinatown, which were teeming with people. The narrow thoroughfares were lined with curbside vendors selling everything from fruit to motor oil, and bamboo poles holding laundry sprouted from hundreds of windows like the banners of a ragtag army. Once again, even though insulated from it by the luxurious interior of the Rolls-Royce, Janna was struck by the intimate ambience of the city, where Chinese, Malays, Tamils, Indians, and a host of other different nationalities lived cheek to cheek in rooms that served as both home and shop.

The headquarters of G. K. Wong International with its distinctly American architecture and ultramodern decor provided a stark contrast to the ramshackle buildings of Chinatown. The carpeted lobby, which contained chrome furniture upholstered in Italian leather and walls decorated with works by Rouault, Matisse, and Chagall, possessed the same sepulchral quiet that Janna had observed in most Swiss banks. It served to heighten the trepidation that had already caused a hollow feeling in the pit of her stomach, and she was glad to see the familiar face of Gerald Foster, who was waiting in the lobby.

"Not quite what you expected, eh?" He motioned to the paintings. "G.K. is a walking paradox: he admires Western technology but still believes that a daily dose of pulverized dragonflies intensifies his sexual vigor."

"Is that why you warned me to wear a chaste-looking dress?" Janna asked.

"You're pretty sharp for somebody who's meant to still be suffering from jet lag." Foster grinned as he ushered her into an elevator.

"I slept very well," she said.

"That's good, because you're going to need all your wits about you in there." He nodded toward huge double doors beside which a pretty Chinese secretary sat behind a desk.

"Mr. Wong is still speaking long-distance," she announced demurely. "He shouldn't be long. Please make yourselves comfortable."

Foster looked at his watch. "I've got to be down at the docks soon," he said.

"Go ahead, I'll be fine," Janna assured him.

He hesitated. "I'd better wait. G.K. won't like it if I'm not there to perform introductions."

Crossing to a huge plate-glass window, he gazed down at the scene below, where various passenger ships and freighters were leaving the docks or waiting to berth. Hundreds of Chinese coolies unloaded cargo into waiting trucks, while farther along the coastline thousands of others labored on building a massive housing development.

"Quite a sight," Janna observed.

"Even more so when you realize that G.K. owns almost everything you can see from here." Foster replied. "Ships, warehouses, trucks, hotels, and the project that's under construction over there." He pointed to the housing site. "It will have its own mosque, temple, shops, theaters, markets, and schools. Light industries will be established nearby to give residents work."

"Who will live there?" Janna asked.

"Thousands from over there." Foster gestured to an area that lay just behind the main business buildings in downtown Singapore. "You're looking at the most densely populated square mile in the whole of Asia."

"G. K. must be quite a man."

"See for yourself." Foster patted a life-sized bronze statue which stood against a wall. "Not quite in the flesh, but a good likeness."

The statue was of a man of short stature in a Chinese coolie hat and pajamalike trousers. Across his shoulders was a long pole supporting two buckets.

"What's he carrying?" Janna asked.

"Night soil."

"What's that?"

"G.K. started out collecting human waste and selling it as fertilizer," Foster explained. "He gave credit to poor farmers who couldn't afford to pay cash and charged exhorbitant interest on the loans. When they fell behind on payments he claimed their land and leased it back to them. Then, using the land as collateral for loans, he expanded into buying farm machinery, equipment he then rented out on a time-sharing basis to the owners of small farms who couldn't otherwise have afforded such expensive machines." He touched the statue again. "Muck to multimillionaire in two decades. Not bad, eh?"

Before Janna could answer, the Chinese secretary announced that Mr. Wong was ready to see them, opened the huge double doors, and ushered them into the room beyond. It occupied almost the whole floor and was furnished in the same modern style as the lobby, but instead of walls supporting modern art, three sides of the office consisted of floor-to-ceiling panes of plate glass through which the panorama of the city was visible on one side, the waterfront on the other.

G. K. Wong was seated behind a massive oak desk that was bare except for a single folder he had placed directly in front of him. The immensity of the desk dwarfed everything else in the room and made the man behind it appear even smaller than his statue.

"May I present Miss Janna Maxell-Hunter," Foster said. "Miss Hunter, this is G. K. Wong."

The man behind the desk didn't speak or move, but examined Janna through unblinking, almond-shaped eyes with an intensity that was unnerving. He was squat and solidly built, with a completely bald head and unwrinkled skin. His age was hard to determine; Janna guessed somewhere in his late fifties but wouldn't have been surprised to find herself off either way by more than a few years.

"Pleased to meet you," Janna said, offering her hand.

He made no attempt to take it but continued to study her a moment or two longer, then motioned her to sit in a deeply cushioned leather chair in front of his desk. "Did you have a pleasant journey?" he asked in lilting, heavily accented English.

"Yes, thank you," she replied. "It was kind of you to send Mr. Foster to meet me."

G.K. nodded and looked across at his personal secretary. "You must have work to do, Gerald. . . ."

"I do, sir." He patted his pockets nervously. "I'll be seeing you later, then, Miss Hunter."

Janna nodded and watched him back out of the office, surprised by the abruptness of the change he had undergone in the presence of his employer.

"Will you join me in some tea?" G.K. asked when the door closed.

"I'd love some," Janna said.

He summoned his secretary, ordered tea, and continued to talk in generalities until she returned carrying a beautiful lacquer tray on which were two translucent porcelain bowls and a simple, exquisitely crafted teapot.

"The Countess is a very thorough woman," he said, after his secretary finished pouring the tea and left the room. "She sent me detailed information about your background and talked with me a number of times on the telephone. I understand she first met you at the Montreux École de Perfectionnement?"

Janna nodded. "She came to recruit some girls for job placement through her agency."

"When was that?"

"About six weeks ago."

"Before Madame Fleury was murdered," he murmured, glancing down at the file.

Janna stiffened: first the Countess, and now G.K., both privy to information she had thought was known only by the Swiss police and herself. She was tempted to ask how he knew but resisted the impulse. This was an inappropriate moment. "During the last week in April," she replied evenly.

"I also understand that Madame Fleury was a friend of the woman who raised you?"

Again Janna tried to hide her shock at his accurate description of Anna. She suddenly had the uneasy feeling that G. K. Wong knew a great deal more about her background than she had ever confided in the Countess.

"They knew each other during the war," she replied cautiously.

The man behind the desk slid a sheet of neatly typed notes out of the dossier and scanned them carefully. "I see they were both prisoners at an internment camp in Spain, and that an Englishwoman called Janet Taylor was with them when they were arrested. Do you know her?"

"Anna kept in touch with her."

"Are you aware she's now living in Singapore?"

"So I understand."

"Will you be seeing her while you are here?"

Irritated by his probing, Janna replied brusquely. "When I talked with Anna before leaving Paris, she volunteered to drop a note to Janet Taylor informing her of my arrival and asking her to contact me, but whether we meet will depend on whether I decide to accept the job you are offering, about which I still know very little."

"You must excuse the directness of my questions," G.K. said, his manner turning solicitous as he got up from behind his desk and settled into a chair opposite where Janna was seated. "I am not a cultured man and sometimes my bluntness offends people. Because I speak English quite well, others assume that I also understand the etiquette of Europeans, but regretfully that is not true. This is why I have great need of somebody like yourself who has been educated in these niceties. Should you decide to accept the position as my personal assistant, which I very much hope you will, your primary duty will be to act as liaison between myself and the many European businessmen who come to see me here in Singapore."

He refilled Janna's cup with tea and handed it to her with a smile that revealed extensive gold bridgework. "They will expect to be entertained and shown the many places of interest in the city," he continued. "It will be your job to arrange this and to make sure they know where to find the facilities they need to conduct their business. You will have to learn which restaurants serve what food, where various banks are located, how transshipments of cargo can be arranged and local transportation hired. I would also expect you to frequent places where Europeans like to gather, such as the Singapore Swimming Club, and make yourself available as a dinner companion for men who are my guests." He paused and sipped his tea. "In return for these services," he said, "I will pay you a generous salary, all your expenses, and provide you with a car. During the first three-month probationary period you will continue to live at the Raffles Hotel, at company expense, after which, should you decide to complete your year's contract, you will be provided with an apartment in a building I own, which overlooks the ocean on the outskirts of the city."

"It sounds interesting," Janna said.

"It would also be a wonderful learning experience if you intend to continue in business."

"Sounds even better."

"Does that mean you accept?"

"I'd like to try it for three months."

"The Countess was right when she assured me I would be pleased with you, and the timing is perfect." G.K. beamed. "I have scheduled a particularly important meeting for the end of the month. Bankers and financiers from all over the world will be coming here to discuss underwriting an industrial park I am building. It is of the utmost importance to me. At least a dozen of these visitors are European, and I know they will appreciate having somebody like yourself to make their stay enjoyable."

"I'll do what I can," Janna assured him.

"But first you must familiarize yourself with Singapore," he said. "My guests will expect you to show them around, and you can't do that if you are still a stranger to the city yourself. I suggest you spend the next week getting to know the island. Do you drive?"

"Yes."

"Then I will tell Mr. Foster to lease you a car and make arrangements to get you a license. If there is anything else you need, don't hesitate to let him know. I want you to enjoy being here."

As Janna took the elevator down to the lobby and was driven back to the hotel in the Rolls-Royce, she reflected on the interview and tried to pinpoint why it was that she had the uneasy feeling G. K. Wong was manipulating her. She still hadn't isolated the cause of her worry when the phone in her room rang.

"You must have worn the right dress," a voice she recognized as that of Gerald Foster announced without preamble. "G.K. was impressed. I'd like to buy you dinner this evening to celebrate."

Janna hesitated, remembering Foster's drinking during their ride from the airport. "I'm really tired and—"

"I have a surprise I think you'll like."

"You're being very mysterious."

"I'm an inscrutable Oriental—or half a one, anyway."

She laughed. "Well, all right. . . ."

"I'll pick you up at eight o'clock," he said.

When Gerald Foster arrived in front of the hotel he was driving a green MG sports car. Instead of opening the passenger side door for her, he handed her the keys and said, "Here's your surprise. You drive."

Janna could hardly believe what he was saying. "You mean it's mine?"

"Leased."

"But I don't even have a license."

He handed her a card bearing an official-looking insignia. "You do now. It's only a temporary, but it will do until you get a regular one."

"How on earth did you get it at such short notice?"

"Friends in high places."

Janna settled in behind the wheel. It felt strange to be sitting on the right side and even odder to be driving on the left side of the street, but by the time they had crossed St. Andrew's Square she was beginning to get used to it.

"Why an MG?" she asked, shouting to make herself heard over the roar of traffic.

"Just a hunch." He grinned. "Was I right?"

"It's great, but would you mind telling me which way to go?"

Following Foster's directions Janna wove in and out of the London-like traffic, past double-decker buses, and guided the little sports car down streets bearing such names as Mountbatten, Lavender, and Victoria. Its convertible top was down, and warm, moist air, heavy with the pungent odors she was beginning to accept as an integral part of Singapore, sent her hair streaming back. She experienced a surge of adrenaline each time the car responded to her foot on the accelerator. It was quick, cornered well, and had good brakes—which were constantly tested as trishaws and pedicabs crisscrossed through traffic, often missing her bumper only by inches.

"Don't worry about bumping a few backsides," Foster shouted after one particularly near miss. "It's the only way you get respect out here."

Janna realized he had been drinking again, but as they toured the city he kept up a commentary that was unusually witty. He obviously knew Singapore extremely well. Because he spoke fluent Malay as well as Chinese he was able to translate a lot of things Janna would otherwise not have understood, such as when he took her backstage to see how a shadow play was performed.

Flat painted figures cut from parchment served as actors, and bamboo sticks moved jointed arms as light reflected from a flickering oil lamp cast shadows on the screen, to the vast amusement of the audience out front. The star of the show was a puppeteer and storyteller from Kota Bharu who, employing bass or falsetto, recited the lines of scores of characters, male and female, breathing life into his cast while orchestra members tooting flutes and beating cymbals laughed at every joke even though they'd heard them a thousand times. Janna found herself laughing with them, not at the jokes, which Foster translated and she didn't understand, but rather at the obvious good time all the participants were having.

After the show Foster directed Janna toward Bugis Street, where, he assured her, they would find the best food in Singapore. Parking the car, they wandered past rows of stalls lit by kerosene lamps and fronted by cloth-covered tables, eyeing prawns as big as bananas, gray-pink on glittering ice, pyramids of cockles, heavy clawed crabs in truculent rows, naked chickens glistening with oil, and streaky pork hanging from hooks where ruddy sausages twined.

When they sat at a rough wooden table, a young Chinese crossed the littered street carrying hot scented towels with wooden tongs, and while Janna wiped her hands he recited the delicacies offered by all the stalls. He himself was in the roast duck business, but he didn't push his own wares and showed no surprise when Foster ordered in fluent Cantonese.

"I think I'm going to like Singapore," Janna said.

"Just pray it doesn't explode while you're here," Foster replied, draining his glass and ordering another beer.

Janna looked at the passing people: young Chinese women sporting skin-tight brightly colored pajamas; a few Chinese men wearing Western dress; a Malay farmer squatting on a stool beside a basket of live chickens; a coolie trotting along the crowded street under an over-loaded shoulder pole—she found it hard to believe that Foster was so convinced these people were capable of violence.

When the food came Janna ate slowly, aware that Foster wasn't touching the dishes he had ordered, preferring instead to continue drinking, and she found herself growing increasingly apprehensive.

"It's getting late," she said when the meal was finished. "I think I'd better be getting back to the hotel."

"There's one more place I want to show you," Foster insisted, slur-ring his words.

"I don't think—"

"Oh, come on," he urged. "G.K. told you to get the feel of the city, didn't he?"

"Yes, but—"

"The place I'm going to take you is the kind of spot the Europeans you'll be entertaining will love." He paid the bill, left a generous tip, and took Janna's arm as they walked back to the car. "You should be paying me for the insights I'm giving you, for Christ's sake!"

Against her better judgment Janna followed Foster's directions and drove the MG down North Bridge Road, a neon-lit avenue lined with small stores. Although it was after midnight, late shoppers darted in and out of open doorways from which merchants called loudly and beck-oned. The mingled music of East and West from radios and record players poured from the glassless windows of every building.

"Turn left here," Foster said.

Narrowly missing a trishaw, Janna turned the car into an alleyway that was illuminated by garish neon signs bearing such names as *Palace of Joy* and *Lotus Gardens.*

"Listen," she said after Foster told her to stop and she parked along-side a six-foot-deep monsoon ditch half filled with rotting garbage, "I'm really not sure—"

"Come on, let your hair down," Foster urged.

"All right," she said hesitantly, "why not?"

"That's the spirit," Foster said. "You're going to love this."

He led the way into a dimly lit, smoke-filled club where a Chinese hostess greeted Foster by name and led them to a table in front of a small stage. He ordered two bottles of Tiger beer, said something to the hostess that made her laugh, and pointed to where half a dozen exquisitely beautiful Eurasian girls were clustered to one side of the stage.

"What's the joke?" Janna asked.

"You'll see." Foster grinned.

The lights dimmed even more and loudspeakers blared atonal music as a single spotlight illuminated the stage. It was bare except for a large screen on which shadows appeared, like those they had seen earlier in the evening at the puppet theater, except that these images represented mythological figures, animal and human, and moved with a rhythmic cadence which, although not syncopated to the discordant music, still possessed an almost hypnotic quality. Janna found her gaze fixed on the screen until the Eurasian girls came on stage and began a dance that emulated the movements the shadows behind them were making.

They moved in figures, like American square dancers, and then paired off in undulating duos as Malay men wearing colorful silk outfits entered from the other side of the stage and joined the girls as partners. Their bodies never touched even though they came within inches of each other in a seemingly effortless motion that called for faultless timing and rhythm.

"Glad you came?" Foster whispered.

"They're incredible!" Janna answered.

"It gets better," her companion assured her.

The heat in the narrow confines of the club was almost unbearable, and Janna was quickly covered with sweat. Without taking her eyes off the stage she reached for the glass of beer Foster had ordered and took a long swallow. It tasted bitter, but it was ice cold, and she drained the glass. Foster ordered refills as Janna continued to focus her attention on the stage. The pace of the dancers had quickened and the movements of the shadows on the screen had undergone a subtle but distinct change.

Instead of fierce, warlike gestures, the motions of the puppets took on a sensuality that made them appear more like lovers than adversaries. Laughter stirred through the audience as the performance of the shadow figures changed from a portayal of mythological events to the enactment of pornographic vignettes. Instead of dancing, swordplay, and battle scenes, there was a series of explicit sexual tableaus.

As Janna watched, the dancers, still emulating the movements of the shadows on the screen behind them, duplicated their poses. Their grace was such that at first it seemed like no more than an extension of their earlier effortless motion, for their bodies still didn't touch, and their timing continued to be faultless. But then they began to undress: first the men, who shed their pajamalike costumes with such dexterity that they didn't miss a step; then the women.

The women seemed deliberately to remain half a beat behind their partners, as if taunting them, and each time they removed an item of clothing it was with a coyness that was part denial, part submission. First the sarongs they wore over their cheongsams were removed, then their delicate silk blouses, and finally their loose-fitting chemises. Suddenly each male dancer grabbed his female counterpart and ripped away the last pieces of clothing.

The audience roared its approval when this final act established that the women were really young men artfully made up, and the applause continued as the dancers engaged in an orgy of oral copulation and sodomy.

"I think I've seen enough," Janna announced.

"Relax, for Christ's sake," Foster said.

Janna got up and strode out of the cabaret. Angry, embarrassed, and humiliated, all she wanted to do was put as much distance between herself and Gerald Foster as possible. Getting into the MG, she gunned the engine and slammed into gear, sending the car surging forward with an abruptness that almost toppled it into the monsoon ditch.

It wasn't until she was well down North Bridge Road that Janna realized she wasn't sure how to get back to her hotel. She had followed Foster's directions all evening, and because he wanted to show her various parts of the city they had taken numerous detours through side streets. Her first instinct was to get directions, but after two attempts to question trishaw drivers riding alongside her in the unending flow of traffic almost resulted in accidents, she decided to try and find her own way back.

Seeing a shop she thought she remembered having passed earlier, Peking Lace Ltd., Janna turned right and drove slowly down a narrow street she believed would take her to St. Andrew's Square, but instead found herself in the old Chinese quarter. Here the houses lining both sides of the street were decrepit and old, and instead of the bright lights that turned night into day on North Bridge Road, there was only a ghostly luminescence cast by hissing kerosene lamps behind half-shuttered windows. Nor was there the same milling crowd of people, just a few night watchmen who had placed primitive wooden beds across the doorways of the shops they guarded so they could sleep while they worked.

Janna felt as if she'd suddenly crossed an invisible barrier separating one world from another. She was frightened. This was an alien place of dark shadows and quick, fleeting movements in the deep recesses beyond stinking monsoon ditches. She saw an old Sikh watchman squatting on his charpoy, a half-starved dog at his side, and stopped to ask him directions, but he didn't understand English and it was all he could do to keep his snarling dog from attacking her.

The ruckus started a score of other dogs barking along the street, and the darkness echoed with metallic clanking sounds as iron shutters across shop doorways were pulled up. Within minutes dozens of people appeared on the street, apparently believing a robbery was in progress. Most of them were young Malay and Chinese men, and some of them carried knives.

When they approached the car threateningly, Janna slammed the gearshift into reverse and attempted to back up so she could turn the car around. The abruptness of the movement took a Chinese boy in his teens by surprise, and in trying to get out of the way he toppled into a monsoon ditch. His cries for help were amplified by the smooth concrete walls of the six-foot-deep trench and set up an echo that was loud enough to awaken the few people on the street who still slept.

Already sensitized by the bloody racial riots that had taken place in Singapore a few months earlier, when fighting between Malays and Chinese had shattered the peace of the city, people poured out of shabby buildings jabbering at each other in an effort to find out what had happened.

Janna jammed the gearshift into first and tried to move the car forward. It was an instinctive reaction, but one that proved to be the worst she could have made, because in the eyes of the few who had seen what happened it appeared she didn't care about the Chinese youngster who had fallen into the ditch and was trying to escape. As she inched the car forward the crowd closed in around it, forming a solid wall and forcing her to stop. She began to tremble as a cacophony of voices screamed at her in a mixture of languages, and hands reached down to lift her from behind the wheel.

She struggled as the crowd raised her in the air. Then the human support suddenly gave way and her body hit the ground, slamming the air out of her lungs and sending a searing pain through her ribs. She was still conscious, but barely so, and when a young Malay boy jabbed at her with his knife, she felt little more than a slight stinging sensation as the tip of the blade sliced across her belly. Before her attacker could strike again, a Chinese man grabbed him and tried to wrestle the knife from his grip, starting another melee as others joined in. Within seconds a small riot had begun.

Using fists, bottles, pieces of iron, wooden stools, and whatever else they could lay their hands on, Chinese and Malays fought each other along the entire length of the street. In the midst of the fracas, momentarily forgotten, Janna lay on the ground feeling consciousness slowly ebbing away. The pain in her ribs had turned to a dull ache, and although her dress was drenched with blood from the knife slash, the wound didn't hurt. She possessed neither the will nor the strength to get up; everything around her seemed to be happening in slow motion as the crowd around her parted to reveal a white woman wearing Chinese coolie clothes. Her graying hair was pulled tightly back from a broad face with plain features, and she looked down at Janna with deep-set, brownish-green eyes that commanded attention.

"Your mother had more sense in her little finger—" The woman shook her head and left the sentence unfinished as she issued orders in Chinese to two men, who picked Janna up.

As they carried her through the angry crowd, Janna saw faces looking at her that were filled with hate, and when unconsciousness finally enveloped her she gladly surrendered herself to it.

29

When Janna opened her eyes she saw a gorilla, three tiger skulls, a two-headed turtle, and a duck with four legs. She thought for a moment that she was hallucinating until a voice said; "Keep still!"

She raised her head slightly from where she was lying and saw, hunched over the table, the woman who had saved her from the rioters.

"I told you not to move!" she admonished.

The only illumination in the small room came from a single bulb, which hung on a length of dusty cord directly over Janna, but it gave enough light for her to see the wound on her stomach, which the woman was closing with neat sutures. The cut didn't appear deep but was maybe four or five inches long and ran horizontally just below her belly button. The upper part of her pubic hair had been shaved and the area around the wound swabbed with a brownish-colored liquid that glistened under the light. She looked around at the glass jars that lined each wall and tried to determine where she was, but her brain was still numb.

"I'm almost finished," the woman leaning over her murmured. "Just hold steady another minute."

Janna watched the woman wielding the needle and wondered why the procedure didn't hurt.

"You can sit up now," the woman announced.

Janna lowered her legs over the side of the table, but the moment she tried to raise the upper part of her body a shaft of pain stabbed through her chest, making her gasp.

"Easy does it," the woman said, helping Janna into a sitting position. "Your ribs are badly bruised, but I don't think they're broken."

Janna saw that the area immediately below her breasts was tightly wrapped with broad strips of linen.

"That's just a precaution," the woman said. "Anna would never forgive me if I left anything to chance."

"You know Anna?" Janna asked, barely able to believe what she'd just heard.

"Very well indeed, even though I haven't seen her for twenty years." The other woman's face creased into a broad smile. "I'm Janet Taylor."

It was a moment before Janna fully absorbed the other woman's words, but then she experienced a surge of excitement that swept all thoughts of injuries out of her head.

"You delivered me," she said.

"I assisted a doctor at your birth—"

"And were with my mother when she died."

"Yes. She was one of the bravest women I've ever met."

"I want you to tell me everything you know about her," Janna said. "I've been looking forward to meeting you so much! Anna told me she was going to write and let you know that I was coming to Singapore, but I didn't think you had gotten the letter yet."

"She cabled me that you would be staying at the Raffles Hotel," Janet said. "Ever since I got the news I've been wondering just how to contact you. I'm not very popular with the European community in Singapore."

"The man I'm working for, G. K. Wong, is certainly interested in you. He was very persistent in trying to find out whether or not we were going to be in touch."

"So that's his game," the other woman said, musing to herself. "Well, we found each other."

"And just in time."

"You can thank Mr. Soong. It was he who alerted me to what was happening out there on Hock Lam Street."

Janet motioned to a wiry-looking Chinese man who stood behind where Janna was sitting. As he stepped out of the shadows, light shimmered from the lenses of his gold-rimmed glasses. "I am pleased to have been of service," he said softly.

"Mr. Soong is my lawyer and very dear friend," Janet explained. "We've been neighbors since I moved to Singapore some years ago."

Janna started to offer her hand to the Chinese man but stopped when the movement triggered a spasm of pain in her abdomen.

"It's going to start hurting now," the Englishwoman said, putting some herbs into a mortar and crushing them with a stone pestle.

"I guess the Novocain is wearing off."

"Novocain?" Janet pointed to where nine extremely fine steel needles, all slightly different in shape, lay on a folded towel. "There's the only anesthetic I used on you. Inserted at specific points along certain meridians, they completely block pain."

"Is it a new procedure?" Janna asked.

"Far from it." The Englishwoman laughed. "Acupuncture has been used for over two thousand years in Asia. Western doctors are just taking longer to catch on."

She poured a powder from the mortar onto a square of tissue paper and handed it to Janna along with a glass of water.

"What is it?" Janna asked.

"Curcuma root and Chinese chaulmoogra." When Janna hesitated, she added, "Trust me. I really do know what I'm doing, and it will ease your pain."

Janna poured the powder into her mouth and washed it down with a swallow of water. "Will my injuries immobilize me?" she asked.

"They shouldn't."

"It's just that I'm meant to be spending the next week familiarizing myself with the city."

"If what happened tonight is anything to go by, I'd say you're going to need a guide." Janet chuckled. "Why don't you stay here with me for a few days? That way I can keep an eye on how well you're healing, and you can get the feel of the island by accompanying me on my rounds."

"I'd love to," Janna said, "but I'll have to let G.K. know where I am and go back to the hotel and get some clothes."

"We can arrange all that tomorrow." The Englishwoman turned to Mr. Soong, who was still standing silently in the shadows. "Would you ask Teo Kah to put Janna's car in a garage? It'll be stripped before morning if it's left where it is."

When the Chinese lawyer left, Janet pulled a steel grille across the front door, locked it, and led the way up a narrow flight of stairs to a small room. No more than 20 by 30 feet, it contained a sleeping space, a cooking alcove, and a few pieces of bare wooden furniture. Everything was spotlessly clean. Books on a shelf included Sartre's *L'Être et le Néant,* Conrad's *Under Western Eyes,* and a textbook on cardiovascular symptomatology. Above the books on a narrow ledge were a few personal possessions: a worn-looking stethoscope, a collection of smooth pebbles, and a gold medallion that caught Janna's eye because of the uniqueness of its design.

"It's beautiful," she said. "Leonardo da Vinci's Divine Proportions of Man. . . ."

"Very similar," Janet agreed, "but actually it's back-to-back K's."

Janna looked at the medallion more closely. "What do they stand for?"

"Kandalman."

"Josef Kandalman?"

"You know about him, then."

"Anna told me about the war years on my thirteenth birthday, and Genevieve filled in a lot of blank spots during the time I spent with her in Switzerland. He was the man you all worked for as couriers, wasn't he?"

Janet nodded. "I took this from his neck. He had been horribly burned by acid, and Anna and I had to treat him. The medallion left a scar on his chest."

"Was he dead?" Janna asked.

"Not the last time I saw him. He stayed behind with the other ZOB fighters, and they held out against the Germans for quite a few more days, but it was a hopeless struggle." She reached out and hung the medallion around Janna's neck. "I've kept this for over twenty years," she said. "It was originally a gift from your mother to Kandalman."

"Genevieve told me she didn't think they were lovers."

"She would have known better than I about that. I only really got to know Keja after we escaped from the ghetto. She was a very special person. How she endured the terrible crossing of the Pyrenees in her condition is something I'll never understand. The only thing that kept her going was the urge to see you safely born." The Englishwoman's voice faltered. "Keja believed the medallion had magical properties. She gave it to me just before she died and made me promise that I'd keep it for you. . . ."

"I wish I could have known her," Janna murmured.

Janet picked up a small photograph in a tarnished silver frame that showed four women posed in front of a wagon piled with logs. "This was taken in 1943 in Austria," she said. "We were traveling with a gypsy named Tibere who needed photographs for false documents he had obtained. The blond woman is Keja and the swelling under her work shirt is you, although we didn't know it at the time."

Tears welled into Janna's eyes as she looked at the old black-and-white picture. "It's the first time I've ever seen what she looked like."

"She was very beautiful."

Janna continued to gaze at the picture, tears streaming down her cheeks, trying to summon up courage to pose the question to which she'd sought an answer for over seven years. Finally she asked, in a voice that was barely more than a whisper, "Did she ever tell you who my father was?"

The Englishwoman gently wrapped her arms around Janna and said, "It's a secret Keja took with her to the grave. I'm sorry. . . ."

The two of them stood together in the spartan room until Janna's crying finally stopped. Janet took a glass vial from the shelf and poured a brown liquid into a cup. "Take this," she said, "it'll help you sleep.

This time Janna swallowed the potion without any hesitation and helped the other woman prepare an extra sleeping mat on the floor. Janet checked her guest's wound, spread a light cotton sheet over her, and blew out the oil lamp.

"You know that Genevieve's dead, don't you?" Janna asked.

"Anna told me about the accident in a letter."

They continued to talk until the potion began to take effect.

When Janna awoke it was midmorning and sunlight was streaming into the room through open shutters. There was no glass in the windows, and street noises flooded in: discordant Chinese music from many radios, the shouts of merchants urging customers into their shops, the cries of vendors hawking their wares from handcarts, and the chatter of women gossiping as they cooked over charcoal braziers in the street.

Janna looked over to where Janet had slept, but there was no sign of the Englishwoman and her straw mat had been neatly rolled up. Raising herself on one elbow she looked around the sparsely furnished room and remembered that less than a week ago she had been living in the luxury of a suite at the Hotel George V. She thought about Elke. Was her friend settling down in California? Perhaps having a job and being required to behave responsibly would be good for her, although it seemed from the way she'd been in Paris that her problems stemmed from more than just a lack of self-discipline.

A sheet of notepaper had been propped against Conrad's *Under Western Eyes*. Janna got up slowly, expecting to feel pain from the injuries she had suffered the previous night, but there was only a dull ache in her ribs and a slight throbbing sensation in her belly. Picking up the note, she read, *Thought I'd let you sleep. There's rice and tea in the cooking alcove. Come on downstairs when you're ready.*

Janna crossed to the small alcove, where charcoal smoldered under an iron brazier, and put a pan of rice on to heat. Hearing a murmur of voices, she crossed to the stairs and looked down into the room below. It was filled with patients waiting to buy herbs or receive treatments from Janet. They included both young and old Chinese men and women, along with a sprinkling of Malays. From where she stood, Janna could also see into the back of the shop, which was used as an examination room.

Janet spent a considerable amount of time talking to her patient, an elderly Chinese woman, observing her carefully as if gleaning from her expression and tone of voice clues that were important in making a diagnosis. After taking the woman's pulse three different times, she kneaded a thick paste into a small cone-shaped lump and set it on the back of the woman's hand between the middle and index fingers. This she lit with a match and left it to burn down to the skin, after which the old woman left, apparently well pleased by the treatment she had received.

It was impossible to ignore the near-veneration shown by Janet's patients, both Chinese and Malay. Some paid with crumpled bills, and others left baskets containing fruit or chickens; more than a few offered neither, and yet she treated them with the same care and concern she gave to the others.

It was early afternoon by the time Janet finished with her last patient, but instead of resting she announced that she must begin her rounds to visit patients who were too ill to leave home and invited Janna to go with her. Leaving the apothecary shop in the hands of a young Chinese man who was serving an apprenticeship with her, Janet ordered a trishaw and, with Janna squeezed in next to her, rolled off down Hock Lam Street to join traffic flowing along North Bridge Road. First they went to Raffles Hotel to pick up Janna's things and telephone a message to G.K.'s secretary letting her new employer know where she would be staying.

Then they jounced northeastward, past the great green Holy Sultan Mosque and squalid rows of houses, until they finally came to the Kalang River's stinking tidal basin. Janet directed the trishaw driver down a dusty lane, paid him, and headed for a narrow boardwalk that was the only access to Kampong Kuchan, a community that was built on pilings above the tidal flood.

A young village watchman with an easy smile but wary eyes appeared out of a thatched hut. He recognized Janet and eagerly shook hands, but only nodded at Janna before leading them down swaying planks to a cluster of palm-roofed huts where babies swung in suspended cradles and women in sarongs stood over charcoal fires from which rose the smells of fish and curry.

"This place got a bad name during the riots earlier this year," Janet said. "Most Europeans won't come near it."

"They seem pleased enough to see you," Janna observed.

"That's because they know I was Tak Chen's woman. He died fighting for a cause they still believe in. Because of that, they seem to think I've got magical powers, but the patient I've come to see needs more than I can offer."

She went into a palm-thatched hut where an old Malay man lay on a wood-frame bed. His face was ashen and each of his breaths was labored. Speaking to him in Malay, Janet gently felt his pulse and carefully studied his eyes. Then she took out a leather case containing acupuncture needles and skillfully inserted them at various points on the old man's body.

"Malignant melanoma," she murmured. "All I can do is ease his pain."

"Shouldn't he be in the hospital?" Janna asked.

"They wouldn't take him," the other woman replied. "He's so poor his relatives probably won't even be able to afford a funeral."

When Janet finished treating the old man, she went outside to where a circle of men sat talking in low voices. They acknowledged the Englishwoman with grave nods and questioned her about the patient, and she replied in their own tongue. As the conversation continued, a young Malay man carving a tholepin stared at Janna with such hostility that she had to turn away. Instead, she watched a small girl who was smelling flowers in a tiny garden on the shore, where bougainvillea, jasmine, and hibiscus grew in earth-filled cans.

"There are times when I wonder if I'll ever understand these people," Janet said wearily when they were once again seated in a trishaw and headed for the village where her next patient lived. "They know the man I just treated is going to die and can't understand why I continue to visit him."

"Why do you?" Janna asked.

The other woman looked at her in surprise. "To ease his pain."

"I couldn't help noticing that many of your patients can't pay you."

"I'm not doing it for the money."

"Anna used to talk about you a lot when I was growing up in New York. She said you chose to stay with her father in the ghetto—"

"Tell me about Anna," Janet said, deliberately shifting the focus of their conversation. "We've managed to keep in touch over the years, but most of her letters were filled with news about you."

Janna described Anna's life in New York before the trial, and how it had been shattered by Mark's suicide. "She's living in a tiny apartment now, working as a designer for a wholesale jeweler."

"It's a far cry from the way she was raised." Janet talked about Anna's parents, stressing how cultured both of them were, while Janna listened intently, absorbing details she was hearing for the first time.

They stopped to treat a Chinese woman who had cut her foot badly. She lived in a one-room dwelling situated next to a rubber grove where half a dozen young children were collecting latex from cups attached to furrows cut into the rubber trees.

"They're a happy-looking bunch," Janna remarked when the other woman emerged from treating her patient and got back into the trishaw.

"Don't let their smiles fool you," Janet said. "They earn about thirty-three cents a day for ten hours of work."

"How can they live on that?"

"They can't. That's why so many young Chinese join the Communist terrorists in the jungle."

"Do you think an armed insurrection is the answer to Malaysia's problems?"

The Englishwoman shook her head. "Communism is no better than colonialism, or imperialism, or any other *ism*, but when you've got nothing, any promise of hope sounds good."

As Janet tended her patients in outlying villages, she talked at length about her life in Bukit Mekan and her experiences as Chen's lover. Janna was fascinated by the story, but as she listened to Janet she realized her life was far from the romantic odyssey the younger woman had always imagined it to be.

It was late afternoon when they finally returned to the apothecary shop on Hock Lam Street. Rather than cook, Janet took Janna to a nearby market, where they ate hot noodles with pork and prawn gravy.

"What are your own plans?" Janet asked, while they waited for the food to cool.

"I've told G.K. I'll stay for the three-month probationary period—"

"I mean, what do you really want to do with your life?"

Janna shrugged. "I haven't given it much thought."

"You should. We have less time than most of us think, and it's a pity not to use it well." The Englishwoman was silent for a moment. "I've often wondered what would have happened to Keja if she lived."

As they ate she continued to reminisce about the past, recalling what it had been like to live through the final days of the Warsaw ghetto; the perils she and Anna had faced in escaping through the sewers, and details relating to their endless trek across war-torn Europe.

"Your mother underwent a remarkable change during that long journey," Janet said. "She rediscovered her Gypsy heritage. When we left Warsaw she was withdrawn and very unsure of herself, but by the time we reached Tarbes she'd really come into her own."

During the days that followed, Janna accompanied the Englishwoman on her rounds and was continually impressed by her dedication. This was nowhere more evident than when they visited a Chinese squatter's farm about seven miles east of Singapore, located in a lovely stretch of old coconut trees standing in clean, sandy soil. Rain clattered in palm fronds as they entered the house, and they were welcomed by a sweet-faced woman who was crippled by arthritis.

After treating her patient, Janet showed Janna a pigsty roofed with corrugated iron near a tidal marsh. "This is the only legal structure here," Janet said. "The farmer is like hundreds of others; he rents space for agricultural purposes, hence the legitimate pigsty, and builds a hut because he has nowhere else to live. That makes him a squatter, and he can be evicted at any time."

"I thought the government was building new housing for the poor," Janna replied, when they were back in the trishaw.

"You mean places like Queenstown and Jurong?"

"I don't know their names, but G. K. Wong is putting one up on the outskirts of Singapore."

"Have you seen it?"

"Only from a distance."

"Well, now's your chance to get a closer look, because that's where I'm going on my next call," the other woman said.

As they approached the massive high-rise buildings Janna had first seen while she was waiting outside G.K.'s office, they passed an area where hundreds of Chinese coolies were carrying baskets of earth on their heads, an operation that was supervised by a handful of Europeans, among whom was Gerald Foster. He looked up as Janna went by in the trishaw and their eyes met, but instead of greeting her he quickly turned his attention back to a pile of blueprints.

"He won't waste any time phoning his boss," Janet commented.

Janna was surprised the other woman knew who Foster was and had noticed the mute exchange between herself and G.K.'s personal assistant. "To tell him where I am?"

"To confirm that G.K.'s plan is working."

"Plan?"

Janet pointed to where a group of Chinese and Malay children were playing kickball on a large piece of ground that was flanked on three sides by the towering high-rise buildings. "That piece of land is probably why G.K. brought you to Singapore," she said. "I bought it long before he started putting up these monstrosities. It was cheap, and I wanted a place for the local children to play. G.K. needs it now. Without clear title to my land, he's finding it increasingly hard to get the financing he needs to complete his project. That's why he's been pressuring me almost daily to sell."

"But what has that got to do with his bringing me to Singapore?" Janna asked.

"My guess is you're just a pawn in an elaborate game he's playing," the other woman replied. "I don't know what he's got up his sleeve, but he probably thinks he can get to me through you."

"I can't believe he'd go to such extremes."

"Then you have a lot to learn about your employer," the English-woman declared. "He's tough, devious, and will go to any lengths to get what he wants."

30

When Janna returned to the hotel late on Sunday afternoon it was like finding herself transported to another planet: after the constantly blar-ing radios and noisy traffic of Hock Lam Street, where she had felt a part of the crowds that lived as much on the sidewalks as in the cramped interiors of the shop/houses, the cool elegance of Raffles seemed sterile.

She wrote a postcard to Elke Kruger in care of the Countess, giving the German girl her address and saying how much she looked forward to hearing from her. Then she settled down to write a letter to Anna detailing events that had happened during the past week. The task was harder than she had thought it would be. To explain the impact of her visit with Janet Taylor went beyond merely describing things they had done together.

As Janna sat with her pen poised over the hotel notepaper trying to find the right words to describe for Anna what it had been like to get to know the Englishwoman, she realized that an essential part of it was attributable to the vast disparity between the way she'd been raised in New York and the world Janet Taylor had chosen to inhabit. It seemed there was no common bond, and yet, on reflection, Janna realized one did exist: without the loving care of all three women, Janna would never have survived after Keja gave birth to her, and each of them had continued to contribute in their own way as she grew to maturity.

These three women, who had shared so much during the war, had gone in very different directions. What kind of life would Keja be living now if she had survived? It was a rhetorical question, yet Janna knew that whatever course her natural mother might have taken would have profoundly affected her own life. As things were, if Janet Taylor hadn't lied to the court clerk in Pamplona about Anna being her mother, it was quite possible Janna would have been left in the internment camp with Janet and been raised by her.

Janna put down her pen and picked up the gold medallion that had once belonged to Keja. She ran the tips of her fingers over its glistening surface as she tried to separate her feelings for the mother she had never seen from the deep caring she felt for Anna and, to a lesser extent, for Genevieve and Janet.

Putting the unfinished letter aside, she went to the window and looked out over the sweltering city. In the distance she could see the housing development G.K. was building, its high-rises standing end on end like dominoes, twenty stories tall, glittering white against the azure skyline. Janet's warning—"My guess is you're just a pawn in an elaborate game"—triggered other thoughts: of G.K. and the Countess both knowing that Genevieve had been murdered; of Captain Stube's suspicion that Janna might also have been an intended victim; of the way Mark had been framed. Maybe the Englishwoman was right about her being manipulated, but why?

The question continued to nag at Janna throughout the night, making sleep fitful. When she reported to G. K. Wong's office at 9 A.M. the following morning it was with a feeling of considerable apprehension, but his manner was just the same as it had been when they talked the first time. He expressed the hope that she'd been able to familiarize herself with the city and briefed her on an upcoming meeting of bankers that was scheduled to begin later in the week.

"It is most important that during the time they are my guests you show them around and do what you can to make their stay comfortable," he said. "The bankers from Hong Kong and Tokyo will be arriving a day earlier than those from Europe. I will be having a formal dinner for them at my house which I would like you to attend."

He didn't say whether he expected her to go alone or as somebody's date, and rather than ask Janna returned to the lobby.

"Have a good week?" a voice asked archly. Gerald Foster was standing near the reception desk.

"Very," she replied coldly.

"Ready to show our VIPs fakirs and snake charmers?" He grinned and strolled away before Janna could answer.

She had expected him to comment on seeing her with Janet, and when he made no mention of it she felt vaguely uncomfortable. The sense of unease stayed with her during the following days as she arranged hotel accommodations for the expected bankers and personally checked out their rooms to make sure they were satisfactory. She also visited several restaurants in an effort to determine which served what kinds of food, where there were bands for dancing, and what kinds of entertainment were available.

On the day of G.K.'s dinner, his secretary called her to say that she would be picked up at 7:30 P.M., and she was waiting on the hotel steps when the Rolls-Royce arrived. She wore a white Balenciaga evening dress and carried a small, beautifully embroidered purse. Her hair was tied in a ribbon at the nape of her neck, and the only makeup she wore was a touch of lipstick, yet she still looked radiant.

When she glimpsed her reflection in a window of the car, Janna found it hard to believe that a week ago she had been sleeping on the floor over a Chinese herbalist's shop in a decrepit building on teeming Hock Lam Street, but as she got into the car the pain in her ribs was a sharp reminder. They were still tightly bound and the knife wound, from which Janet had removed the stitches, was still sore.

Settling back into the deep leather seat, Janna tried to prepare herself mentally for the upcoming evening, but she had no idea what to expect. It was highly unusual for a high-ranking Oriental to entertain an unescorted single European woman in his home, and even more so for G. K. Wong, who was known to guard his privacy very carefully.

The drive to his villa, which was located on a secluded stretch of oceanfront on the outskirts of the city, took Janna down North Bridge Road, where she saw coolies hunched on the sidewalk scooping rice into their mouths from cracked plastic bowls. Remembering Janet, she experienced a pang of guilt that was exacerbated when the Rolls-Royce reached its destination and an armed guard motioned the driver past heavy iron gates to a driveway that led in a series of graceful curves to an elegant white villa on the crest of a hill overlooking the ocean.

On either side of the driveway were beautifully landscaped gardens, lit by hidden lamps, which displayed a wide variety of plants, including the most brilliantly colored orchids Janna had ever seen. Scattered among them were fountains and ancient Chinese statues set in fish-filled reflecting pools.

When Janna stepped from the car onto the marble floor of an ornate portico fronting the villa, she was surprised to find G. K. Wong himself waiting to greet her. Ushering her inside, he first introduced her to his wife, a beautiful Chinese woman who looked half her husband's age, and then escorted her across a spacious teak-paneled living room to meet the other guests.

All of them were either Chinese or Japanese except for one man. When he turned, Janna recognized Felix Ervin, the man who had so intrigued her at the Zurich stock exchange. She must have showed her surprise because he laughed and said, "I've been expecting you."

"How on earth did you know I'd be here?"

"When G.K. told me he had hired a European woman as his personal assistant, and mentioned your name, I told him I would only come to dinner if he invited you too."

"I didn't think the financiers from Europe were arriving until tomorrow," Janna said.

"Most of them aren't," Ervin replied, "but I have another meeting in Kuala Lumpur so I came a day early."

A servant announced that dinner was served, and Mrs. Wong led her guests into an ornate dining room. Felix Ervin took Janna's arm, escorted her to an enormous circular table, and insisted that she sit next to him.

He was still just as attractive as Janna remembered him, and impeccably dressed in a superbly tailored white silk dinner jacket. She was glad she had worn her Balenciaga dress and wished she had a string of pearls to go with it. Instead, she had worn the gold medallion Janet had given her. Felix Ervin continued his bright, witty conversation while they were waiting for the first course to be served, but she noticed his eyes constantly shifting to the medallion. He didn't question her about it, but he was obviously intrigued.

The other guests, although overly polite, seemed uneasy at having a young European woman at the table, but their stiffness toward her softened as they consumed glass after glass of rice wine. The guest on Janna's left, a grossly overweight Chinese man from Hong Kong who had drunk more than the others, was sufficiently light-headed by the time a servant brought a tureen of soup for him to fish out a chicken foot with his chopsticks and deposit it in her bowl.

"It is the best part," he assured her.

Janna felt everybody at the table watching her, waiting to see how she would react. After a moment's hesitation, she scooped up the chicken foot in a porcelain spoon and placed it in Felix Ervin's bowl, saying, "As an honored guest, you should have the pièce de résistance."

The others, appreciating her adroitness, roared with laughter and complimented G.K. on his sagacity at having hired such a clever woman, but when the next course was served they continued to watch

Janna closely. How would she cope with the challenge of a whole pompano steaming in its own broth when her only utensils were chopsticks and a spoon?

Janna picked up her chopsticks without much conviction, trying to determine how to go up against a fully assembled six-pound fish without a knife and fork. She poked at the fish but nothing came loose.

"Like this," Ervin said after Janna's repeated attempts produced no results. With chopsticks in one hand and spoon in the other, he dislodged a large piece of flesh from the pompano's plump side. Following his example, Janna performed the same feat on her own fish and found it worked.

"You wouldn't make kidnappers very happy," declared the Chinese banker who had given her the chicken foot.

"I wouldn't?" Janna looked at him, puzzled.

"Years ago when there were many pirates along the China coast, they frequently held captives for ransom. Their problem was finding out how much to ask, so they'd starve their victims, then serve pompano and watch what part of it was eaten first. Those who were used to the best always went for the head or underbelly. The less privileged usually started with the area closest to the dorsal fin. Those who went for the side of the fish, as you did, were hardly worth ransoming."

"What happened to victims who weren't worth a ransom?" she asked.

"They were killed and thrown to the sharks," G.K. answered before the other man could reply.

The guests laughed loudly and the dinner party, which had begun on a restrained note, quickly became boisterous.

"Keep this up and you can ask for a raise," Ervin said, masking his remark behind a napkin.

Janna realized she should have felt pleased at being accepted by the other guests, but G.K.'s words, although seemingly uttered in jest, had frightened her.

She struggled to remain calm and concentrated on her food. After the remains of the pompano were cleared away, servants set empty platters in front of each guest and removed an elaborate display of orchids which had occupied the center of the table. It immediately became evident that the bowl holding the flowers had covered a small circular hole, through which now appeared the head of a monkey. It was terrified and made pathetic, childlike whimpers as it looked frantically around at those seated at the table. Its dark, slightly bulbous eyes widened with fear as a servant holding it from below, who had remained hidden under the cloth-draped table since the meal began, positioned a white cloth around its neck and gripped it so it couldn't move.

Janna watched in horror as G.K. accepted a long silver knife from a servant and split the monkey's skull. He administered the blow with the practiced skill of an executioner, stopping the blade a split second after it sliced through the cranium and then giving it a quick twist to spread the two halves of the skull apart. The blow hadn't killed the monkey, and it looked around in stunned bewilderment through glazed eyes as the guests, led by G.K., used their chopsticks to pick out pieces of its brain, morsels they ate with obvious relish. The last to partake of the grizzly dish was the obese Chinese banker who had offered Janna the chicken's foot; now he proffered a piece of brain.

She tried to refuse gracefully but felt vomit rising in her throat and, pressing a napkin to her mouth, quickly rose to her feet and hurried out through open French doors into the garden. The night air was heavy with the scent of jasmine, but its sweetness only made her feel worse, and she threw up into a thick stand of bougainvillea. When her retching finally subsided, she knelt by a reflecting pool and used her napkin to moisten her face.

"Are you all right?" a voice she recognized as Felix Ervin's asked quietly.

She nodded but didn't look up.

"Do you want to leave?" he asked.

"I wish I could," she murmured, "but after what just happened—"

"I've already made your excuses to G.K., so don't worry about him. You aren't the first European to react that way. He enjoys shocking them."

"Why, for God's sake?"

"Others rubbed his face in it when he was a night-soil collector; now it's his turn."

Taking her arm, he led her to where his rented Cadillac was parked on the gravel driveway in front of the house. Janna still felt too sick to attempt much conversation as Ervin drove back along the coast road toward Singapore, but when he suddenly turned the car down a narrow dirt trail flanked on either side by jungle she asked, "Where are we going?"

"You've had quite a shock," he replied, parking alongside a small bar and restaurant that overlooked the ocean. "A stiff brandy should do you a world of good."

After a momentary hesitation, Janna got out of the car and followed him through the restaurant to a deck that was built over the water. It was a warm night, but there was a cool breeze coming in off the ocean, and she found it a blessed relief. They were seated by the owner, a sallow-faced European with a heavy German accent, who obviously knew Ervin and made a considerable fuss over him.

"I gather this isn't your first trip to Singapore," Janna said when they were seated.

"I've been here a lot on business," Ervin replied.

"Then you won't need me to show you the sights."

"If I didn't have to leave for Kuala Lumpur first thing in the morning, I'd take you up on your offer." He smiled, pausing as the waiter brought coffee and cognac. "That's why I got here before the other European financiers. I was able to spend this afternoon alone with G.K., discussing the financing he's trying to raise to continue construction of the low-cost housing estates he has contracted with the government to build."

"I've seen them," Janna said.

"Then you know it's a huge undertaking. They're going up at the rate of one new apartment every forty-five minutes. He's aiming to complete over a hundred thousand of them in the next five years."

"Do you think he'll achieve his goal?"

"I did at first, that's why I came out here, but now I'm not so sure."

"Why not?"

"Because of increased inflation since the project started. The Singapore Housing and Development Board has upped the amount of the bond they want G.K. to post against any losses they may incur if he fails to complete construction on schedule. That's why he's invited all these bankers to the meetings this week. He desperately needs to establish new lines of credit."

"Will they go along?" Janna asked.

Ervin shrugged. "I don't know."

"What about you?"

"The Board is more than satisfied with what G.K. has done so far, but I've discovered it's a riskier proposition than I first thought," he replied, sipping his brandy. "G.K. led me to believe he owned all the land he intends to build on, but now it turns out that isn't quite true."

"You mean the lot that's being used as a children's playground?"

Ervin appeared surprised. "You know about it?"

"A woman I know owns it. Janet Taylor. She gave me the medallion I'm wearing."

"I saw it earlier." He reached over and took the medallion between his thumb and forefinger. "It's an interesting design."

"Back-to-back K's."

"K's?"

"The initial of the man to whom it was first given, Josef Kandalman," Janna explained.

"A friend of Janet Taylor's?"

"Somebody she knew in the Warsaw ghetto. He died there during the final days of the Jewish uprising."

"And she is living here in Singapore?"

"She owns a Chinese herb shop on Hock Lam Street." Janna felt so completely relaxed with her companion, an ease that was partly due to having finished her brandy, that she went on to describe what Janet had said about G.K.'s ruthlessness.

"She might be right," Ervin commented. "G.K. has his own way of doing things, and he really needs that land."

"Well, Janet's determined not to let him have it."

Janna, who was beginning to feel quite light-headed, found herself attracted to him, and after the way Ervin had behaved toward her in Zurich she half expected him to make a pass, but instead, after they finished their coffee, he drove her back to the hotel.

"See you next time I'm here," he said.

"I may be gone by then," she replied, miffed by his apparent disinterest. "The first three months of my contract are a probationary period, and after the way I behaved tonight—"

"Don't worry, G.K. will want to keep you here as long as possible," Ervin assured her. "He needs your friend's land very badly, and if he thinks the only way to weaken her resolve not to sell is by keeping the pressure on you, that's exactly what he'll do."

He took her hand, held it for a moment, then lightly kissed her on the cheek before saying good night and driving away. Janna was puzzled by his behavior toward her. She was still thinking about it an hour later as she lay in bed, unable to sleep, her eyes fixed on the slowly turning fan, which cast eerie shadows on the walls of her room. Why had Felix Ervin been interested in her in Zurich and not now?

In the days that followed she tried to decide whether or not to stay in Singapore after her probationary period was over, but there was little time for introspection as she busied herself entertaining the European bankers who arrived for their meetings with G.K. She took them to all the best restaurants; to the ballroom at Raffles, where they watched nimble-footed Malays entertain with their traditional dances; to the Chinese opera, where she took them backstage to watch actors apply their fierce tiger makeup; to Tiger Balm Gardens, where the unique stone sculptures attracted those taking photographs; and through the streets of the old Chinese section, to watch displays by spirit mediums who cast away demons by searing their chests with flame, driving daggers through their tongues, and twirling hoops while standing barefoot on a throne of knives.

When the conference ended and the bankers returned to their respective countries, G.K. summoned Janna to his office and congratulated her on a job well done. The reports he had received unanimously extolled the efforts she'd made to ensure that the visitors enjoyed their stay, and G.K. suggested that, instead of waiting until her three-month probationary period was up, Janna agree to remain in Singapore for the balance of her one-year contract. As an inducement he offered to double her salary and provide a luxury apartment overlooking the ocean at company expense.

Janna hesitated before responding to G.K.'s offer, remembering what Felix had said. G.K. seemed to be going out of his way to be friendly, so she decided to accept. Later in the day Janna loaded her suitcases into the MG and drove out along the coast road to the apartment complex G.K.'s company owned overlooking the offshore island of Blakang Mati.

Her apartment was on the top floor and consisted of two bedrooms, a bathroom, a tastefully furnished living area, and a fully equipped kitchen. As she unpacked her bags she came across a postcard that had arrived from Elke the previous day: it showed the German girl with her arms around Joe Dawson on the beach at Malibu, and bore the inscription: *See you at Maxim's in nine months. Don't forget! Love, Elke (and Joe).* When she first read the message Janna had studied the card, made from a photograph, to see if there was anything about her ex-roommate's appearance to indicate her state of mind, but she was smiling broadly and seemed delighted to be with Joe again.

Also in the suitcase were two small tape recorders and a collection of blank cassettes Janna had bought so that she could exchange messages with Anna. She had taken one of the units on her twice-weekly visits to Janet Taylor's shop on Hock Lam Street, and the Englishwoman had joined Janna in sending greetings to her old friend in New York. Now, as Janna played back portions of the tape and listened to what they had said, she realized how much she had come to care about Janet. As Christmas approached she found herself counting the days until she could be with her again.

G.K. gave Janna a week off at the end of the third week in December, and she immediately headed for Janet's shop on Hock Lam Street. The Englishwoman was clearly delighted to see her again and they talked long into the night, mostly about Anna, with whom both had kept in frequent touch by mail. It was clear from the tone of her letters that Anna's life in New York was still difficult, and there didn't seem to be any promise of change. Just before going to sleep, Janet asked Janna if she might use the tape recorder to send a private message to Anna, and went downstairs to record it. Janna heard the soft tones of her voice but couldn't identify the words, and before the Englishwoman returned she had fallen asleep.

When Janna awoke on Christmas morning she found a small package wrapped in orange tissue paper lying next to her sleeping mat. It contained the silver-framed photograph of Anna, Genevieve, Janet, and Keja that she had seen during her first visit to Hock Lam Street.

"I love it!" she exclaimed, getting up and hugging Janet. "It must be the only picture of my mother in existence."

"That's why I wanted you to have it. Now get dressed and come on downstairs, we've got some visiting to do."

Janna assumed the Englishwoman was getting ready to make her usual rounds, but when she entered the shop she saw Janet had filled her basket with food and milk instead of the medical potions she usually carried. Without offering an explanation, the older woman led the way briskly down Hock Lam Street and Janna followed, hurrying to keep up. The sidewalks were even more crowded than usual, and one or two shops even displayed artificial Christmas trees for the benefit of their few Christian customers. The heat was unbearable.

"How much farther?" Janna panted.

Instead of responding, the Englishwoman suddenly turned into a doorway on Sago Lane. Outside the building, flower-decked trucks were parked alongside the garbage-filled monsoon ditch and musicians stood around with woodwinds, cymbals, and drums, seemingly awaiting a signal to start playing. Inside on the ground floor Janna saw a sad little group of Chinese men and women praying before a half-open coffin, and as she started up the littered stairway to the second floor a turbaned Sikh barred her way. "Foreign visitors are not allowed," he told her gruffly.

"It's all right, Adnan," Janet said, "she's my friend."

The Sikh grudgingly stepped aside but continued to glare at Janna as she followed Janet upstairs and then down a short corridor that opened into a large room, the floor of which was littered with sleeping mats. On them, like flotsam, lay a score of Chinese children, the eldest of whom couldn't have been more than eight years old. Some were too sick to move and lay with their glazed eyes fixed on a point only they could see.

Janna remained near the door and watched Janet as she went from one child to the next, murmuring words of solace in Chinese, using a wooden spoon to feed them milk. The stench was overpowering: many of the children lay in their own vomit and excrement. One little girl must have thought Janet had come to take her away, because when the English-woman leaned over her she put her skeletal arms around her visitor's neck, preparing herself to be lifted. Janet let them remain there, speaking quietly to the child, until the girl's arms finally fell away.

Badly shaken, her vision blurred by tears, Janna went back downstairs.

"As I told you," the Sikh at the doorway said as she passed, "it is not a place for foreigners."

When Janna reached the sidewalk, a group of Chinese carrying a cheap wooden coffin emerged from the room on the ground floor and the musicians struck up a discordant melody. About fifteen minutes later Janet came downstairs and summoned a trishaw.

"Are you all right?" she asked.

Janna, who still felt devastated, nodded.

"I probably shouldn't have taken you into a death house."

"Why did you?" Janna asked.

"For the same reason that I took you with me on my rounds," the other woman replied. "So you could see for yourself how poor people live and die."

A silence settled between them. Janna's first instinct had been to challenge Janet's assumption that it was a lesson that needed to be taught, but she checked herself when she realized how fatuous such a statement would sound. Finally she asked, "Doesn't anybody feed them?"

"Poor Chinese call the young who are dying 'short-life persons,' and parents often don't even go to their children's funerals," the English-woman replied. "In their culture juniors mourn seniors, not the other way around. The child of a poor family who is terminally ill is sent to a death house."

"And left to starve?"

Janet shrugged. "They believe that because death is inevitable, it doesn't much matter what form it takes."

"Why do you go there?" Janna asked.

"Because life itself is what matters, and so long as there's a spark of it left I try to sustain it."

The trishaw stopped. Janna saw they had come to the outskirts of the city, where G.K. was constructing the massive low-cost housing complex. Because it was a holiday for the European supervisors, no work was taking place, but dozens of children were playing on the land Janet owned. When they saw her approaching they stopped their games and clustered around her as she handed out the food that was still in the basket.

"Most of the children at the death house were too ill to eat," she explained. "There's no point in wasting it."

Janna waited until the children had finished eating and returned to their play before saying, "I don't understand why you won't sell this plot to G.K. He's offered you a good price. With that kind of money you could buy an even larger piece of land for the children."

"I don't care about the money!"

"Why are you continuing to hold out, then?"

"Because somebody has to take a stand against men like G.K.," Janet replied. "To them, human beings are just units to be shuffled about at will. The dignity of the individual doesn't mean a damned thing to him. That you should even suggest I knuckle under to him disappoints me terribly."

She picked up her empty basket and strode angrily back to the trishaw, leaving Janna to follow along behind her.

31

New Year's came and went, and as the months merged into each other during the first half of 1965 Janna saw little of Janet. They quickly made up after their differences at the building site, but with the constant pressure of Janna's work and G.K.'s endless flow of visitors from all over the world, mostly financiers from whom he desperately sought backing, she was constantly busy. There was almost never a day when she got back to her apartment before midnight, and even though much of what she did appeared undemanding, it still left her so exhausted that it was all she could do to put a tape in her portable recorder and listen to the latest message from Anna.

The sound of her voice was a comfort, even though what she had to say suggested things were still far from easy for her in New York. She talked about her work and tried to make it sound interesting, but Janna, remembering the fine jewelry Anna had once designed while Mark still had his gallery, knew how disheartening it must be for her to turn out items for mass production. Although she had plenty of friends, Anna never mentioned that she was seeing any particular man, and Janna sensed her loneliness. She felt guilty for not having returned to New York after her year in Montreux, even though Anna had urged her not to.

By early May, when G.K. had arranged another conference of Asian and European venture capitalists, Janna realized she was catering to the needs of a very different group from those she had entertained soon after her arrival in Singapore. Although a few still arrived in their own private jets, they were frequently accompanied by bodyguards, and from bits of conversation she overheard, she got the distinct impression that they represented the kind of money that didn't come from legitimate sources. G.K. also alerted her to the fact that these men were not much interested in seeing the usual tourist sights, preferring instead to be taken to clubs that featured shows with a strong sexual content.

The only club of this kind that Janna knew was the one to which Gerald Foster had taken her, and she hadn't liked it, but rather than admit the distaste she felt for her assignment, she stubbornly searched out places that specialized in sexually oriented entertainment.

Her best sources of information proved to be trishaw drivers, who knew every inch of the city, and Janna hired them to take her to nightclubs that presented erotic shows, frequently paying them twice their normal fare to wait outside for her until the show was over.

One such place, the Scorpion Club, was situated on a side street off North Bridge Road. The show was already in progress when she arrived. The small stage was occupied by two women, both Orientals, one in her late forties, the other no more than thirteen or fourteen. Each wore sheer, loose-fitting robes through which their bodies were faintly visible. Their hips were gyrating to the accompaniment of a steady drum beat, and the women exhibited neither a sense of rhythm nor any emotion. Janna found their performance ludicrous, but the two women had obviously succeeded in exciting their audience, for a number of men, both Chinese and Malay, shouted drunken encouragement.

When the performers shed their robes, the spectators roared their approval, which the older woman, whose face was ravaged with pock-marks, acknowledged by striding to the edge of the stage and standing with her legs wide apart. She intended it as a sensuous pose, but to Janna it seemed merely obscene.

As she strapped on a rubber dildo the audience began to chant, repeating words Janna didn't understand. The woman responded by kneeling in front of the younger girl and licking her thighs, then slowly raising her head until she was probing the other woman's clitoris with her tongue. Closing her eyes the girl uttered a series of low moans. It seemed to matter little to those watching that these sounds of ecstasy were obviously feigned.

Realizing she had seen enough to be aware of the kind of show presented at the Scorpion Club, Janna stood up and tried to reach the door, but the audience, angry at having its view blocked, forced her back into her chair. She looked at the stage and saw the tableau had changed. The older woman had bent the girl over a low table and was poised behind her holding the dildo inches away from the younger woman's buttocks. With tantalizing slowness she slid the artificial penis deep into the girl's anus, at the same time reaching an arm around her partner's waist so she could finger her clitoris.

The older woman was still pumping away when Janna once again attempted to reach the door, prying a path through the onlookers, many of whom had climbed on chairs and tables in order to get a better view of what was happening on stage. Furious at being disturbed, they cursed Janna in three or four different Chinese dialects, kicking at her with their heels as she tried to squeeze past. One man, a fleshy Chinese who was very drunk, grabbed Janna's arm and tried to pull her down on his lap, but he let go abruptly when a hand suddenly reached in and grabbed his shoulder in a vicelike grip.

"You'd better get out of here before the shit hits the fan," a man's voice warned.

The light was too dim, and the crowd around her too dense, for Janna to determine who had come to her assistance, and she didn't wait to find out. It wasn't until she had stumbled through the door and was trying to compose herself on the sidewalk that she saw the man who had come to her aid was Derek Southworth.

In an attempt to distract attention from the blood she could feel flooding to her cheeks, she asked, "What on earth are you doing here?"

"I could ask you the same thing." He grinned.

"It's part of my job to check out places like this."

"A likely story."

"Honestly," she insisted. "The man I work for, G. K. Wong, has business associates who like these kinds of clubs, and it's my duty to keep them happy."

"Then that includes me," Southworth said.

"You?"

He nodded. "I got in from London this afternoon and am meeting with G.K. tomorrow."

"You must know Singapore awfully well to have found this place your first night in town," she said as a frenzy of applause echoed through the open door of the club.

"It's my first visit," he said. "And this place wasn't my choice. I'm staying at the 'Cockpit' and just asked the trishaw driver to take me somewhere I could get a feel of the city's night life."

"Well, if there's anything you need—"

"My meetings with G.K. should be over by Friday," he said, "and I was thinking about staying on over the weekend if I could see some rain forest."

"There isn't much of it left in Singapore," Janna said. "But the government has preserved a few thousand acres in the center of the island."

"Would you show it to me?"

"It's part of my job."

"I'd like to think it was more than that," he interjected, "and after the way you stood me up in St. Moritz . . . "

"There was a reason."

"Why don't you tell me about it over the weekend?"

Janna hesitated. Southworth was just as virile and attractive as she remembered him. "All right," she said.

"I'll rent a car and pick you up."

"I have a car. Maybe it would be easier for me to collect you at the 'Cockpit.' Can you be ready by eleven o'clock Saturday morning?"

"I'll be waiting for you."

During the trishaw ride back to her apartment Janna wondered if Derek Southworth had believed her explanation of why she was at the Scorpion Club. After the willingness she'd shown to meet him for dinner after their meeting in St. Moritz he must already have formed the impression that she was free-spirited, and the encounter she'd just had with him must have confirmed it. She smiled to herself at the irony of appearing to be an experienced woman of the world when, in fact, she was anything but, and still a virgin, but she couldn't deny deriving a certain pleasure from the illusion she had created, particularly as it was one that Southworth obviously found attractive.

When Janna arrived at work the following morning, the receptionist in the lobby handed her a brightly wrapped package. It contained a doll, exquisitely outfitted in Malay national dress, to which was attached a note that read: *To keep you company until Saturday. Derek.* She was both amused and touched. It wasn't the kind of gesture she had expected from Southworth.

"There's also a telephone message for you, mem," the receptionist said, giving her a small yellow sheet.

It was from Janet, reminding her that they had arranged to spend the weekend together and that the Englishwoman was expecting her on Friday evening. The fact that she was going to have to choose between the two nagged at Janna all day, and when she returned to her apartment that evening, having decided in favor of Derek Southworth, it was with a considerable feeling of guilt that she telephoned Janet to inform her that she wasn't going to be able to meet her. As an excuse she offered a half-truth: that she had to entertain one of G.K.'s business associates, and the understanding Janet expressed only made Janna feel worse about the deception. But, she thought after hanging up, what could she have said if she'd been completely straightforward—that she'd met a man who interested her? All she knew for certain was that Derek Southworth excited her, much more than any other man she had dated.

On Saturday morning Janna discovered that the battery in her car was dead, and by the time a mechanic arrived to replace it she was more than an hour late. Derek Southworth was waiting for her in his hotel lobby, holding a bunch of flowers that had wilted. "They looked better an hour ago," he said, feigning moroseness.

"I'm terribly sorry," Janna said, explaining what had happened.

"What about the flowers?" he asked as she led the way to where she'd parked.

"We'll give them a decent burial," she said, taking them out of his hand and putting them behind the seat. "It's the thought that matters, and I'm grateful, for them and for the doll. It was beautiful."

"I thought it looked a lot like you."

"Except for the dress, hair, and skin color?"

He grinned. "Same shape nose, though."

Janna offered him the keys. "Want to drive?"

"You trust me?"

"After your Ferrari this should be easy."

He got behind the wheel and gunned the engine. "You saw it at St. Moritz?"

She nodded and climbed in beside him.

"I really hoped you'd come. What happened?"

Interrupting herself several times to give Southworth directions, Janna told him about her attempt to sneak out of the pension and how her efforts were frustrated by Genevieve Fleury.

"It sounds like she suspected you were meeting somebody," he observed.

"I thought the same thing. It wasn't like her to be so diligent."

"Did you know her well?"

Janna described the relationship between Genevieve, Anna, and Janet, including mention of the months they had spent together imprisoned at Miranda de Ebro, and the fact that the Englishwoman was now living in Singapore.

"Did Madame Fleury ever tell you about her experiences at the internment camp in Spain?" he asked idly.

Janna shook her head. "It seemed to be a period of her life she wanted to forget."

"Being imprisoned like that can be a traumatic experience. I was caged up in a German prisoner-of-war camp for nearly three years and found it to be the worst kind of hell."

"What branch of the service were you in?" Janna asked.

"The Royal Air Force. I was shot down on a bombing mission over Germany."

"Is that where you got those scars?"

They were visible on both wrists as he gripped the steering wheel, but when Janna asked him about them Southworth instinctively inched the cuffs of his long-sleeved shirt over them.

"I was trapped in the wreckage," he said. "My wrists and ankles were broken pretty badly. The German doctor at the POW camp set them but botched the job, and they had to be operated on after the war."

She sensed his tenseness and changed the subject. As they talked they had driven northeast and come to a tree-covered rise of almost six hundred feet.

"Bukit Timah," Janna announced. "The highest point on the island."

They parked and walked together along the paths that wound through the carefully preserved few thousand acres, which was all that remained of the rain forest that once covered the whole island. It was a world of jade-green twilight where pythons twined undisturbed among lianas as serpentine as themselves. On both sides of the path the undergrowth was impenetrably lush. The noise of birds, like bells and flutes, sounded from deep shadows, while monkeys chattered in their lofty galleries.

"It's so eerie in here," Janna said, surprised to find herself whispering.

Southworth didn't answer. His head was tilted back, tightening the line of his jaw, and his eyes were riveted on the matted treetops where flowering creepers and orchids formed islands of brilliant color. There was an intensity to his expression that belied his usual easy, charming manner. Janna sensed he was lost in a private reverie from which she was excluded.

As he went along the paths deeper into the rain forest, she slipped her arm through his, feeling some measure of protection in his touch. It was as if they were journeying through a demi-world where the creepers were the torn rigging of sunken ships and where time no longer existed. From somewhere close came the raucous call of an argus pheasant, the braying of hornbills, the gibbering of gibbons, and the trills of other birds high in the branches of an ironwood tree. He must have sensed her fear, because he put his arm across her shoulder and led the way back toward the car.

"All right?" he asked when they finally emerged into the sunlight.

"It was silly of me," she said, "but I was always afraid of the dark as a child."

"Me too," he said.

"Really?"

"Terrified. Maybe that's why the rain forest had such an effect on me. There's a certain fascination in fear."

When he didn't elaborate she asked, "Where to now?"

"How about showing me some more of the island?" he said.

Following the coast road, this time with Janna behind the wheel, they drove past miles of palm-fringed beaches: heart-shaped weirs and Malay fishing craft dotted the waters; rivers snaked past villages nestled among coconut groves. Southworth spread his arm across the back of the seat and occasionally touched Janna's shoulder as he asked about

various places they were passing, and when she stopped to make way
for a procession wearing the colorful Malay dress he idly trailed his
fingers through the ends of her hair.

"What's going on?" he asked.

Janna, who had learned enough Malay during her months in Singapore to make herself understood, spoke to a local official standing
under a temporary lean-to where a dignified village headman was preparing to cut a ribbon that had been strung across the road.

"They're celebrating the opening of a new bridge," she said. "Spirit
mediums are going to banish demons so the structure will stand up
when the monsoons bring flooding. And tonight there's going to be a
festival. It should be worth seeing."

"Is there anywhere we can get something to eat?" he asked.

Janna spoke to the local official, who told her there was a small hotel
on the beach about half a mile down the road. They found it at the end
of a dusty lane: a ramshackle wooden building that had once been
white, but from which the paint had peeled so completely it looked
more like bleached driftwood.

There was a battered piano in the lobby, and a dilapidated reception
desk, but nobody was behind it, and only after repeated bell-ringing did
the owner appear. He was a middle-aged, pot-bellied Malay wearing
a loose-fitting robe.

"If you want a room," he announced, smiling broadly at his guests,
"I have a very nice one overlooking the ocean."

"We're here for food," Janna said. "Can we get something to eat?"

"I have promised to help the villagers prepare *sati* for the celebration
tonight," he replied, "but my wife will take care of you. Please sit at
any table you wish."

They went out onto a wide veranda built on stilts over the beach and
sat at a table with places already laid. Southworth asked for some beer.

"God, that was good!" the Englishman exclaimed after taking a long
swallow from the bottle. "This moist heat really gets to me."

"I couldn't stand it either when I first got here," Janna said, "but you
get used to it after a while. The trick is to wear loose clothes and drink
plenty of liquids."

"Yes'm," Southworth said, draining what was left in his bottle.
When the hotel owner's wife appeared with the food, he ordered
another beer.

The tiny woman, who wore her long black hair in a single plait,
served them huge prawns with hot, spicy sauce, glazed duck, crisp

vegetables, broiled beef strips, and mounds of steaming rice. Later she returned with Southworth's beer and a large bowl of fruit.

While he ate Southworth talked about his years as a pilot in the RAF, in which he had served as a Pilot Officer and been awarded the Distinguished Flying Cross. After the war he had built a business, Regent Securities, Ltd., that specialized in what he described as "gap financing."

"If a bank is willing to put up sixty percent of the financing for a deal," he explained, "there are a lot of investment houses that will invest an additional thirty percent. That means the deal is still ten percent short of becoming a reality. That's where I come in with venture capital. It's where the real risks are taken, because there's no collateral a lot of the time, but the profits can be substantial."

"Are you going to invest in G.K.'s project?" she asked, but when he tensed, she quickly added, "Not that it's any of my business."

"It is as long as you work for him."

"I didn't mean to probe."

"I know." He was silent for a moment, then added, "It's just that the deal isn't as clean as I first thought."

"Because of Janet Taylor?"

He nodded. "If she doesn't sell G.K. her land, nobody in their right mind is going to come up with the backing he needs. It was a mistake for him to even begin construction when he didn't have clear title to all the property he intended to build on. Now he's backed himself into a corner."

"I've tried to talk Janet into selling . . ."

"And?"

"She won't listen."

"Why not, for Christ's sake?"

Janna looked at where a group of Malay children were using a long stem of bamboo to vault from the gunwale of a fishing boat into the shallows. "She has these principles . . ."

"Principles or not, she must be mad to try and stand up against a man like G.K."

"He represents everything she hates."

"Either she's very brave or unbelievably stupid. G.K. can be very dangerous if he feels himself trapped."

"You mean he might hurt her?"

"He's quite capable of more than that," Southworth replied. "He knows the moment she's dead her land is going to be put on the auction block, and you'd better believe he's going to be the highest bidder."

"I've done everything I know to persuade Janet to change her mind."

"Why worry?" he asked. "It isn't your problem."

"Maybe not now. . . ."

Taking his beer, he went inside and sat at the battered piano. At first he just tapped different keys and listened to its out-of-tune, tinny sound; then he launched into a mixture of ragtime, boogie woogie, and blues. Finally, after draining his glass, he embarked on the opening chords of Rachmaninoff's Concerto No. 2 but abandoned it only minutes after he started.

"Don't stop," Janna said. "You play beautifully."

"It's meant to be played in C minor, and this piano doesn't have a C minor."

"Maybe the owner's wife can find us one."

"I'll ask her." He grinned, disappearing into the kitchen.

After paying for the meal Southworth took Janna's hand and led the way down some steps from the veranda to the beach. "The lady innkeeper told me we can get to the celebration by walking along the sand," he said.

Slipping off his shoes he tied the laces and slung them over his shoulder, while Janna took off her sandals and slipped them into a tote bag she was carrying. It was late afternoon and the sun had sunk low enough in the sky to cast shadows along the palm-fringed beach. The tide was going out, and each step they took formed a fresh imprint in the cool, moist sand. After the shimmering heat of the day, Janna relished walking through shallow tide pools, as low waves created by the lazy swell of the ocean lapped over her feet.

"I used to do this at the Jersey shore when I was a kid," she said. "Have you ever been to America?"

"Many times," he replied.

"New York?"

"And Los Angeles."

"Which do you like best?"

"If I had to choose I'd take—London."

"Bloody Limey!" She laughed, kicking wet sand at him.

He picked up a handful to retaliate and she ran, but he tackled her before she'd gone more than a few yards and they tumbled together in the sand. When she tried to escape he locked her in his arms, playfully at first, but more tenderly as their lips came together in a long, passionate kiss.

"I've been waiting for that ever since St. Moritz," she murmured.

"No more than I have," he answered, pressing his mouth against her neck and lightly sucking her earlobe.

"We're being watched," Janna whispered.

Southworth pulled back and followed her gaze to where a monkey was looking down at them from the top of a palm tree. It was attached by a long rope to a young Malay boy on the ground who, through voice commands, was able to instruct the animal to throw down coconuts from a tree that had already been denuded of its fronds by local villagers, who used the broad leaves for thatching. Aware it was being observed, the monkey held on with its feet and, working upside down, hurled a shower of coconuts that landed dangerously close to where Janna and Southworth were lying in the sand.

"He reminds me of a bombadier I had when we started flying missions over Berlin," the Englishman said. "His aim was about as bad."

"Let's move before it improves." Janna laughed.

They got to their feet, waved to the Malay boy, who was grinning broadly, and continued along the beach toward the music they could hear from the festival. The predominant sound was a deep booming, which continued with hypnotic regularity, only to suddenly stop, then start again with a slightly different tempo. It matched the beat of Janna's heart, which had been irregular ever since Southworth kissed her, and she had the feeling that in some strange way she was participating in a ritual that was even more primal than the one they were about to see.

When they reached the clearing where the celebration was under way they saw men and boys jumping up and down in a near frenzy as they pounded *rabana* drums, made of buffalo hide stretched over hollow tree trunks. They spelled one another without missing a beat and when they stopped, exhausted, others squatting nearby continued the rhythm by thumping small coconut drums.

Malay families in holiday garb had flocked in from miles around, and the fat Malay hotel owner was busy behind a booth handing out *sati*, cubes of spicy, barbecued meat skewered on sticks. Not far away nimble-footed boys thrust and parried in the Malay kris dance, a stylized version of the duels that settled village disputes long ago. They were accompanied by the drummers and a few musicians, playing simple stringed instruments, who set the pace, first furious, then slow and rhythmic.

But the event that attracted the most attention was the top-spinning contest, strictly a man's sport, where the motions of the players were like those of a baseball pitcher throwing sidearm as they hurled a ten-pound top wound with rope. Using split-bamboo scoops, helpers lifted the whirling disks from the ground and transferred them carefully to metal-capped poles, where they continued to spin while onlookers laid bets on which top would rotate the longest.

"Pick one," Southworth said. "Blue or red?"

"Blue," Janna said.

"You're on!"

"What does the winner get?" she asked.

"We'll think of something," he replied, trailing the tip of one finger lightly over the mounds of her breasts. Her nipples stiffened and, feeling herself beginning to blush, she tried to hide her sudden agitation by asking a nearby spectator, in Malay, how long the tops were likely to spin.

"The record is one hour and twenty minutes," the Malay answered in perfect English.

Holding hands they wandered through the clearing. Many played *sepak raga,* a game where the participants kept a rattan ball from touching the ground by using all parts of their bodies except their hands. Others flew huge colorful kites, which skittered about in the early evening offshore breeze like leaves caught in thermal updrafts, with those holding the strings constantly tugging in an attempt to win by flying the kite as near to 90 degrees overhead as possible. Janna stopped at one stall, where an old woman was selling fragrant oils, and purchased a small bottle that contained an amber-hued liquid that smelled of sandalwood.

The sound of a fisherman calling his crew with a buffalo horn drew Janna and Southworth to the palm-bordered crescent beach, where they stood with the villagers watching the local fishing fleet arriving home. As they neared the shore, patched sails were dropped and the crafts caught long, swollen combers that hurled them shoreward while the fishermen, holding their paddles aloft, shouted excitedly as they deftly maneuvered each boat to a perfect landing.

"How far do they go out in those boats?" Southworth asked.

Janna repeated the question in Malay to a fisherman. "He says the length of time it takes to smoke a cigarette after the palm trees disappear below the horizon."

"I'm glad my navigator wasn't that vague."

She laughed. "You'd be surprised how well they find their way around these waters without a compass."

"You're going to miss all this when you leave Singapore," he said.

"If you'd told me that a year ago I would have said you were crazy," she replied, "but now . . . "

"Where will you go?" he asked when her voice trailed away.

She shrugged. "Back to New York, I guess. I really miss Anna."

He seemed about to say something, but checked himself at the last minute and led Janna back to where the tops were still spinning. As they watched, the blue one fell.

"My lucky day," Southworth said.

Janna didn't answer, but as they retraced their steps toward the hotel she experienced a mounting excitement. She was more and more conscious of the man beside her, making a mental inventory of his physical parts: the size and strength of his hands, the firm set of his mouth, his muscled arms, the lithe grace with which he walked, the way his blond hair blew in the light evening breeze, the bulge at his crotch. It was as if there was a tacit understanding between them. When they entered the dilapidated lobby, Janna wasn't surprised when Southworth leaned over the reception desk, took down a key from a board, and led her to a room on the second floor. When he had disappeared into the kitchen to pay for their meal she had suspected he was also arranging for them to spend the night, but she hadn't questioned him because it was what she wanted.

Nor did she now as Southworth took her in his arms and kissed her. She wanted him and made this clear in the passion of her response, but when he began to undress her, she eased herself out of his arms, whispered, "I'll be back in a minute," and went into the small bathroom. It was illuminated by orange-gold light from the rapidly lowering sun, which, when she took off her dress, gave her body the sheen of wrought bronze. She looked at herself in a cracked mirror that had the words *Tiger Balm* stenciled across it: this was the moment she had anticipated since she reached puberty, and in the years between then and now she had tried to imagine what it would be like the first time she made love. Her excitement was tinged with nervousness, and a measure of fear. Derek was older and experienced, and she was afraid she wasn't going to live up to his expectations.

Taking the small bottle of oil out of her skirt pocket, she poured some in the palm of her hand and smoothed it on her body. The delicate sandalwood scent filled the small room. For a moment she was afraid the smell was going to be overpowering, but it quickly dissipated when a gust of wind blew in through the unshuttered open window, leaving a beguiling trace on her skin.

When she returned to the bedroom in just her pants and brassiere, Southworth was lying on the bed. He had removed his shirt and shoes, but still had his pants on. "You look beautiful," he said, smiling up at her and reaching out his arms.

Janna walked forward, and when she leaned forward he raised himself up to kiss her breasts, but when he started to pull her down next to where he lay, she held back, murmuring, "Let me undress you."

She unbuckled his belt and unzipped his fly. When she eased his pants down over his narrow hips, his penis suddenly emerged, huge and erect, unconstrained by undershorts. Lowering her head, she kissed the throbbing shaft, surprised at its softness and warmth. She didn't know whether he expected her to take it in her mouth or not, and she hesitated just a moment too long.

"This is the first time for you, isn't it?" he said.

She nodded.

He took her head between his hands and pulled her down alongside him. Taking off her panties and brassiere, he traced the outline of her body with his tongue, lightly biting her neck, shoulders, and nipples. When he came to her stomach, where the scar from the knife wound was still visible, he put his cheek against it and said, "So I'm not the only one with wounds."

"At least you got yours fighting a war," she said.

"And you?"

"I just got in the way."

He didn't press for details, but moved his head downward and pressed his lips into her pubic hair. His hot breath made her tremble, and when he touched her clitoris with his tongue her body stiffened. Putting both hands behind her buttocks he pulled her even closer, until his face was buried between her legs, licking until she was on the brink of an orgasm, then moving away, deliberately prolonging her ecstasy.

"Turn over," he said.

She obeyed and felt him straddle her waist. His rigid penis pressed hotly against the small of her back as he began manipulating her shoulder blades with his hands, skillfully easing out tension as his fingers worked their way down her spine.

"Relax," he murmured. "I'm not going to hurt you."

Janna no longer cared if he did; the pleasure was too great for it to matter. She felt completely at ease with herself as a sexual being for the first time in her life.

When he finished massaging her she kissed him, probing his mouth with her tongue, then slowly moving down over his chest and across his belly until she reached his penis. Putting the quivering shaft in her mouth she pressed her lips over its tip.

"Harder!" he said.

She felt his body tense as she pressed her teeth into his flesh, and heard his breath quicken when she worked her tongue along its underside.

"Put me inside you," he muttered hoarsely.

Straddling his hips, she slid his penis into her vagina. There was a quick stab of pain but it quickly vanished. She began to moan, and after she came she couldn't stop herself from shaking.

He held her close for a while, his head on her breasts, then made love to her again, this time so slowly and tenderly it was as if he was relishing a new-found discovery. The touch of his fingers on her lightly oiled skin made her tingle.

"You're exquisite," he sighed.

Janna lay back and closed her eyes, abandoning herself to his caresses. The sound of his breathing merged with the soft sigh of wind coming in from the ocean and the cry of a bird calling to its mate from the branch of some distant tree. When he mounted her there was none of the fervor or pain that had been there the first time, only a steady pressure that began inside her vagina and steadily increased as it spread through her whole body. She felt herself enveloped by his presence: the salt taste of his skin as she kissed his chest, the film of sweat that linked their bodies wherever they touched, the lightly pungent odor of his sperm in her hair, and his low moans of pleasure as he pulsed deep inside her.

He lay on top of her for a long time. Only when his penis lost its tumescence did he finally pull away and lie back on the pillows next to her. Even though the shutters over both windows in the room were open it was unbearably hot, and their bodies glistened damply in the fragile illumination cast by the rising moon as it was reflected from the shimmering, silvered surface of the sea. Reaching for a towel that lay on the bedside table Janna first dried Southworth off, then herself.

He raised himself on one elbow, watching her with a half smile, and when he saw the bloodstain on the sheet under where she had been lying he touched it with his index finger, which he then raised to his tongue. It was a simple gesture, but one that gave Janna inestimable pleasure. At that moment she knew she loved Derek Southworth.

Still without speaking, they lay together in each other's arms listening to the distant noise of the *rabana* drums, which still throbbed in the darkness. It was like muted thunder heralding a storm, and when it suddenly began to rain the abrupt onslaught seemed almost expected. Huge drops pattered on the corrugated iron roof, setting up a counterpoint to the drums, a cacophony that created an eerie, otherworld effect. It reminded Janna all too vividly of the strange, subterranean demi-monde of the rain forest at Bukit Timah, and when Southworth slept her eyes remained open until the first pink light of dawn seeped into the room.

32

Janna returned Derek Southworth to his hotel early the following afternoon, in plenty of time for him to catch his flight back to London. She offered to drive him to the airport, but he refused, saying there were one or two bits of business he had to finish up before leaving Singapore and that it would be easier for him to take a taxi. Somehow, though, she sensed this wasn't his real reason.

During the ride back from the ramshackle hotel where they had spent the night, he had fallen into an introspection even deeper than that manifested while visiting the rain forest at Bukit Timah. Although Janna tried to snap him out of it by maintaining a flow of conversation, he limited his responses almost to monosyllables and managed to create the impression that her attempts to alleviate his somber mood were little more than intrusions.

She was deeply hurt but determined not to show it, and when he kissed her good-bye in the car before going into the hotel, she kept the moment light, wished him a safe trip back to London, and avoided any mention of when they might see each other again. If their lovemaking had been nothing more to him than a pleasant way to spend a weekend she was damned if she was going to let him know, by word or gesture, that it had been one of the most important moments of her life. But when she drove away and was finally alone, tears welled into her eyes.

Puzzled, Janna felt a desperate need to talk to somebody, and instead of returning to the solitude of her apartment, she instinctively guided her car down North Bridge Road toward Janet's apothecary shop. But when she turned into Hock Lam Street she was surprised to find it deserted: metal grilles had been pulled down across shop windows, not a single garment hung from the bamboo laundry poles, and there was no sign of any of the street vendors whose stalls normally cluttered the thoroughfare. The entire street was shrouded in an unnatural silence at a time of day when the mingled music of East and West usually blared from dozens of radios and record players.

When she came to Janet's shop she saw a barricade had been set up around the entrance: yellow sawhorses supported an orange tape on which was printed, in Chinese, Malay, and English, NO ADMITTANCE TO UNAUTHORIZED PERSONS. Standing in front of it were two Malays wearing uniforms of the Singapore Police Force. When Janna got out of her car, one of them stepped forward and said, "Sorry, mem, nobody can be permitted through."

"My name is Janna Maxell-Hunter. I'm a friend of Janet Taylor's. What on earth's going on here?"

A slender white man in his late thirties wearing a khaki shirt, the epaulets of which bore the insignia of a captain in the Singapore Police Force, appeared at the door of the shop. "Let her through. I've been expecting Miss Hunter."

"What's all this about?" Janna asked as the Malay constable lifted the orange tape to let her past the barricade.

"I'm Captain Oldham," the man in uniform said. "Would you mind if we talk inside?"

He led the way into the dark confines of the shop, and when Janna followed him she was astonished to see that all the glass jars containing herbs had been cleared from the shelves, leaving the room bare except for the stuffed gorilla and a few tiger skulls.

"Where is Janet?" she demanded.

"I'm afraid she's dead," Captain Oldham answered quietly.

"Dead!" Janna repeated the word out of shock more than disbelief.

"She was murdered sometime between midnight Friday and two o'clock Saturday morning." He moved a chair toward Janna. "Please sit down."

Numbed, she sank into the chair to save herself from collapsing. "How?"

"Her throat was cut." Captain Oldham took off his peaked cap and wiped sweat from his brow with the back of his hand. "Sorry to be so blunt, but after enough years as a policeman one forgets how to be subtle. We still don't know why she was killed."

"Simple greed seems the most obvious motive," Janna said bitterly.

"Would you mind elaborating?"

"It's no secret that my employer, G. K. Wong, desperately needs a plot of land Janet Taylor owned and had repeatedly refused to sell to him."

"We know all about that, Miss Hunter, and have checked Mr. Wong's whereabouts at the time the victim died. He was with business associates, a group that included Derek Southworth, until the early hours of Saturday morning."

"Have you questioned Mr. Southworth?"

"At about ten thirty Saturday morning."

The realization that Derek must have known about Janet's death all weekend but failed to say a word about it made Janna feel as if she'd been kicked in the stomach.

"Where is Janet's body?" she asked.

"At the death house on Sago Lane." Captain Oldham replied. "She had no relatives, and when somebody dies in a climate like this . . . "

"Do you need me for anything else?" Janna asked coldly.

Captain Oldham took a large manila envelope out of his battered briefcase and handed it to Janna. "This contains her personal possessions. Normally we pass them along to next of kin. I thought you might like to have them."

Oldham walked out of the shop and issued orders for the police barrier to be removed. When she was alone Janna felt the sparseness of her surroundings and realized how much of its former fullness had come from the presence of Janet Taylor. She was the life force; the herbs and other artifacts of the Chinese healing arts were only adjuncts. Now that she was gone, there was only a residue of dust and emptiness.

Still carrying the envelope, she slowly climbed the stairs to the upper room, which had also been stripped by Captain Oldham's men. Even Janet's few books had been taken, as had her clothes, and virtually every other movable object. The only items left were the charcoal brazier, sleeping mats, and a few eating utensils. It was as if a deliberate attempt had been made to erase everything that could be linked with the woman who had become a legend among Chinese and Malays as Tak Chen's lover. Perhaps, Janna thought, because the British didn't want anything left that could turn the small upper room into a shrine. Now that Janet was dead, an irritating thorn in the side of the European establishment in Singapore had finally been removed. The last thing they wanted was for her to be remembered, let alone revered. Captain Oldham hadn't said as much, but Janna sensed from his attitude that the Singapore police weren't going to devote much time or manpower to seeking her killer.

When Janna entered the cooking alcove she saw the walls were stained with dried blood. It had spattered everywhere, creating Rorschach-like patterns that established beyond a doubt that this spot was where Janet had been killed. No attempt had been made to wipe the walls clean, and even though it was two days old the blood still attracted a constant stream of flies.

She stood motionless, imagining how Janet must have struggled, even after her throat was cut, blood spurting as she twisted and turned, until she finally fell to the floor, the life having seeped out of her. Instinctively she looked at the place where the Englishwoman must have lain as death settled on her: there was a bloody handprint and a broken matchstick on the stone floor. When she picked it up, Janna saw the sulfur tip was still intact but the other end was splayed as if it had been chewed. She wondered if it could have been a clue that Captain Oldham's investigators had somehow overlooked, but realized their search would have been too thorough for such an obvious oversight. The matchstick must have been dropped by one of the policemen collecting evidence.

Turning back into the main living area, Janna opened the envelope Captain Oldham had given her and emptied its contents onto a bare tabletop. Janet's personal possessions consisted of a worn-looking stethoscope, a collection of smooth pebbles, the tape recorder containing a cassette that Janna had left with her after their Christmas visit, and a tarnished silver-framed photograph showing Janet as a young girl, standing with her family in front of an imposing-looking mansion. Janna remembered that Janet had also displayed a picture of Chen, but it wasn't in the envelope.

Gazing at the determined, unsmiling face of the child that was Janet when she was eight or nine years old, Janna saw that her stubbornness had been present even then. It was the trait she most admired in Janet, that and her selfless concern for the well-being of others. Tears rolled down Janna's cheeks: if only she'd made more effort to spend time with her . . . if only she'd listened more intently to what she'd said about Keja . . . if only she'd spent the weekend with her instead of going off with Derek Southworth . . . if, if, if. She was racked with guilt at knowing that had she kept to her original plans and stayed with Janet over Friday night, the other woman might very well still be alive. Instead she had lied in order to be with a man who only wanted a convenient bedmate!

She pressed the PLAY button on the tape recorder and immediately heard Janet's voice: *". . . Christmas reminds me of the one we spent together at Miranda de Ebro. Remember the beautiful doll Genevieve gave Janna? I wonder where it is now. Well, at least Janna is with me, and I want you to know how proud I am of the way you and Mark raised her. She's a credit to you both. I always wanted a child of my own, and now I feel I have one. . . ."*

The player stopped as the tape came to an end. Before Janna could turn the casette over, she heard the sound of footsteps on the stairs. "Who's there?" she called nervously.

"Mr. Soong," a voice answered softly.

Janna recognized the wiry Chinese lawyer who was also Janet's friend.

"My neighbors told me you were here," he said, adjusting his gold-rimmed glasses. "They wish me to express our sadness at the death of your friend."

"Thank you," Janna said. "I just found out."

"It is a terrible thing," Mr. Soong murmured. "We all respected her greatly. She and I had been associates and friends for a long time. It is a loss I feel very deeply."

"I gather they've taken the body to a death house on Sago Lane."

"We offered to make other arrangements," the Chinese lawyer said, "but Captain Oldham insisted that since she had no relatives living here that is where she must be taken."

"And the funeral?"

"It is about to take place," Mr. Soong replied. "That is another reason why I came. I knew you would want to be there, but we must hurry."

When they reached Sago Lane, Janna realized why Hock Lam Street had looked deserted, for the crowd that had gathered outside the death house included many faces she recognized: Janet's neighbors, patients, and hundreds of others with whom she'd come in daily contact. The coffin had been loaded onto a flower-decked truck that stood ready with its engines running as Chinese musicians lined up with their instruments on the sidewalk. Numerous paper objects had been piled around the coffin: the replica of a house, a trishaw, spirit money, and scrolls representing books—symbolic replicas of things Janet's friends felt she would need in the afterworld.

"It is customary for the family of the deceased to wear these," Mr. Soong explained, offering a garment made of sackcloth. "But as you are not a blood relative, perhaps . . . "

Janna took the rough-textured robe and put it on, along with a tall hat made of the same material.

"These will chase evil spirits away," the frail-looking lawyer added, handing Janna a porcelain container holding a cluster of smoldering joss sticks.

The muscians began their discordant playing and the truck carrying the coffin slowly moved forward, leading the procession through the streets of Chinatown toward a graveyard on the outskirts of the city. The tailgate of the truck carried a gaudy altar at which dancing priests worshipped, turning in time to the musicians' wailing rhythm. The ceremony seemed to submerge in noisy bustle the frightening mystery of death, insulating Janna by sound, color, and ritual from the pain of her loss.

Even after the burial itself was over, and Janet's simple wooden coffin had been lowered into the ground, covered with earth, and garlanded with wreaths of orchids and frangipanis, there was no pause in the proceedings in which to grieve. Instead, the scores of Chinese who had flocked to her funeral, a rare mark of respect when the deceased was neither family nor Asian, returned en masse to Hock Lam Street, where they sat eating and drinking at small tables arranged alongside the moonsoon ditch until the early hours of the morning.

Only when they went to bed, or finally drifted away—a few of them drunk from having celebrated with too much rice wine the entry of Tak Chen's woman into the spirit world—did Janna break down. It was as if she had teetered for hours on the brink of a void, then suddenly lost the strength to maintain her precarious balance and abruptly fallen into the abyss.

Mr. Soong saw her tears and murmured in his barely audible voice, "This is not a good time for you to stay alone. I think it is better if you spend the night at my house."

He led the way through a maze of lanes and alleyways until they came to an ancient, decrepit house that was almost identical to Janet's, except that its lower floor was equipped with desks and the shelves lining the room supported dusty-looking law books.

"I am a bachelor," the lawyer explained, "and it would not be proper for me to sleep in the same room as you, but you will find a bed upstairs."

"What about you?" Janna asked.

He motioned to a pile of papers on a desk. "I have much work to do, and at my age one requires little sleep."

"I feel I'm imposing on you. . . ."

"On the contrary," he answered, "it is an honor for me to have a friend of Janet Taylor's as my guest."

After her months in Singapore Janna knew enough about Chinese customs to be aware that Mr. Soong was risking severe censure from his neighbors for allowing an unmarried European woman to spend the night under his roof when he was the only occupant of the house, but she sensed it was his way of showing his respect for Janet, and rather than risk offending him by refusing his offer, she went upstairs and lay fully clothed on the wood-frame bed.

A feeling of abject isolation descended on her; it was similar in many ways to the sensation she'd experienced after Anna and Mark revealed the truth about her past. She felt separate from others and herself, suspended in a vacuum of uncertainty, not sure of her future or her past. Janet had suggested she learn to use time well, because in the end that's all we ever really possess, but without the other woman's sage counsel Janna wasn't sure she knew how. . . .

She wasn't conscious of falling asleep, but when she opened her eyes the room was bathed in sunlight, and a steady clicking sound emanated from the room below. She got up, crossed to the sink, and turned on a large brass faucet. The water that dribbled out was tepid, warmed in the pipes by the already hot sun, and when she washed out her mouth the liquid tasted brackish.

"I have brought you some tea," Mr. Soong announced, appearing at the head of the stairs with a black lacquer tray containing a white porcelain bowl from which a cloud of steam rose. "And some noodles from the street vendor."

"Thank you," Janna said, taking the tray and setting it down on a table near the window.

"If you would not consider it impolite of me to speak while you eat," he said hesitantly, "there is a matter of some importance I would like to discuss."

"Go ahead, please," Janna replied.

"As I have told you," Mr. Soong said, glancing down at some papers he had taken out of his pocket, "I was not only Miss Taylor's friend but also her lawyer. I acted for her when she purchased the land that is now being used as a children's playground."

"Then you must have known the pressure she was under from G. K. Wong?"

"Mr. Wong made her frequent offers, all of which she refused, despite my advice to the contrary, but as you know she was a stubborn woman with a very strong will."

"She wouldn't listen to me either," Janna said. "And in the end I believe it cost Janet her life."

"That is quite probable," the lawyer agreed. "G. K. Wong is not the kind of man to let anybody stand in his way."

"I told Captain Oldham the same thing," Janna said, "but he claims G.K. had an alibi."

"It is far more likely that Captain Oldham wishes to close the books on Janet Taylor with as little fuss as possible. She was not appreciated by the European community here, and the sooner she is forgotten the better they will like it." He spoke with a vehemence that gave a hard edge to his normally soft voice. "But if G. K. Wong did have Janet killed in order to gain control of her land, he failed to achieve his goal."

"I thought that since the land was part of her estate and she had no family or will, it would be auctioned off—"

"But she did leave a will," the Chinese lawyer said quietly. "I made it out for her soon after the two of you first met. It is in my safe downstairs, but I can tell you that under its terms you are her only heir and, as such, possess legal title to everything she owned, including the land G. K. Wong wants so desperately. . . ."

Janna began to laugh, quietly at first, then louder. "I'm sorry," she said when she saw Mr. Soong's alarmed expression, "it's just that the irony of the situation—"

"I understand." He took off his glasses and wiped them. "Will you let me know what you wish to do with the property?"

"As soon as I've had time to think," Janna assured him.

The clerk typists looked up from their work when she walked by, obviously puzzled by the sounds they had heard from the room overhead, but soon turned their attention back to their ledgers. Her car was still parked where she had left it the previous night in front of Janet's place on Hock Lam Street, and because she knew she would never find her way back through the maze of narrow streets and alleys, she hired a trishaw driver to take her there.

The traffic along North Bridge Road was already heavy by the time

Janna turned her MG into it and headed out along the coast road to her apartment. She felt physically drained, yet strangely exhilarated, as if the grief she had experienced at Janet's death had been a catharsis for a deep-rooted anger that had been smoldering for months and was ready to erupt.

When she entered her apartment the telephone was ringing. It was Gerald Foster. "Where the hell have you been?" he demanded. "G.K.'s been trying to find you all weekend."

"Really?"

"He wants you here immediately."

"I'll be there when I'm ready and not a moment sooner," she replied.

After Foster hung up, Janna placed a call to Anna in New York. When she heard her voice on the line, she said, "I wish there was a gentle way of telling you what's happened, but I can't think of one, so you might as well know the truth right off. Janet is dead. She's been murdered—"

"Oh, God!" Even though separated by half a world, the emotion in the other woman's voice was clearly audible.

"It happened sometime Friday night or early Saturday morning," Janna said.

"Why didn't you call me yesterday?" Anna asked.

"I didn't find out until late afternoon, and what with the funeral—" She paused, feeling guilt flooding over her again. "They don't know for sure who did it or why, but I think the man I work for might have been behind it."

Janna told Anna as much as she knew and promised to call her again.

"The quicker you leave Singapore the happier I'll be," Anna said. "It's time for you to come back to the States."

"I think you're right," Janna agreed. "We've been apart too long. I love you. . . ."

It took her an hour to shower, change into clean clothes, and drive the relatively short distance to G.K.'s office.

Gerald Foster was anxiously pacing the floor when Janna walked through the revolving door. Although perfectly groomed, as always, he still managed to look frazzled. "I don't know what makes you think you can just vanish like that," he snapped as they entered the elevator.

"I didn't vanish," Janna said. "My guess is G.K. knew exactly where I was every minute of the weekend."

When they reached the top floor Foster hung back, and when the elevator doors slid shut he was still in it.

"Mr. Wong is expecting you," the secretary announced. "Please go right in."

For a brief instant Janna recalled the moment, almost a year ago, when she stood in this very same place trying to imagine what her new employer was going to be like. She had been nervous then and eager to please, but now she was just angry, and it showed in her posture as she strode purposefully into G.K.'s office.

He was standing behind his enormous desk and there was a cold edge to his voice as he asked, "Where have you been?"

"I think you know," Janna answered calmly.

Her self-confidence seemed to throw him off balance. "I have been trying to contact you in order to express my condolences on the death of your friend Janet Taylor—"

"Bullshit!" Janna snapped. "You had Janet killed to get her land, and now you've discovered that she left a will naming me her sole heir, right?"

G.K.'s face remained impassive. "I am willing to pay you twenty million Straits dollars for her property," he said.

Janna shook her head.

"Thirty million."

"No way."

"Forty million. That is nearly ten million American dollars."

"I don't do business with murderers," Janna said, turning and starting toward the door.

"You are wrong to believe I had anything to do with Janet Taylor's death," G.K. announced before she could leave his office. "It is true that I wanted her land, but not desperately enough to have her killed. If you think I am lying, ask yourself why I would offer you a small fortune for something that I could get by merely disposing of you in the same way."

Twenty-four hours later, as Janna sat in a UTA Boeing 707 waiting to take off from Singapore on her way to Paris, G.K.'s words still rang in her ears. She wanted to believe his final statement had been a bluff, but she couldn't rid herself of the undeniable logic it contained: he could just as easily have had her killed, too, instead of offering to buy Janet's property.

The unease remained with her as the jet lifted off the runway and circled the city. It was early evening, and hundreds of feet below lightermen maneuvered their motorized tonkays from Singapore River's crowded quays between wharves and ships anchored in the roads. Beyond them the city's harsh neon glitter blended with the softer pastels of waning daylight to form a halo of light against the darkened sky. But long after the island disappeared from view, and the Boeing 707 was winging its way west across the Indian Ocean, the question continued to nag at Janna: If G. K. Wong hadn't killed Janet Taylor, who had—and why?

33

"Weston, luv?" The ticket collector tugged at his ear. "Reckon you'll have to change at Ipswich and take a local train from there. Will you be wanting any tea?"

"No, thank you," Janna replied.

"If you're hungry they'll be serving refreshments in the dining car for another fifteen minutes," he said, punching her ticket and sliding the door shut behind him as he stepped out of the compartment.

Janna settled back in her corner seat and looked out the window as the train rolled through the lush green Suffolk countryside. It was early afternoon and the sun filtered through high, broken clouds, turning the tranquil setting into a landscape by Turner. It was her first visit to England, but she felt as if she already knew it from the canvases of eighteenth- and nineteenth-century British painters that Mark had displayed in his gallery. During the years she was growing up she had spent hours gazing at portrayals of the very same vistas she was now observing from a first-class compartment. She had boarded at London's Liverpool Street Station a short time after her flight from Paris touched down at Heathrow Airport, and she experienced an odd sense of déjà vu as she now looked at the countryside that had inspired such great art.

She was alone in the compartment and glad of it; making polite conversation would have required effort, and after the long flight from Singapore, and a two-day stopover in Paris, she felt utterly drained. All she wanted to do was rest. Her initial plan had been to stay in the French capital a few days before going on to New York, but when she telephoned Janet Taylor's parents to say she had a few of their daughter's personal possessions that they might like to have, they had invited her to visit them at their country estate in Suffolk, urging her to try and get there for the weekend.

Now she was beginning to wonder if accepting their invitation had been a wise decision. She was much more tired than she originally thought, not just physically but also mentally. The year in Singapore had been one of unrelenting pressure, and the way it ended had left her emotionally spent. Janet's murder had been shattering enough, but when added to Derek Southworth's odd behavior after their night together, and his deception in not revealing that he knew about Janet's death, it had taken a toll that was only now beginning to make itself felt.

And the two days she had spent in Paris hadn't lessened the strain. After checking into an inexpensive pension in Montmartre she had walked the streets for hours trying to put the events in her life in proper perspective. It was anything but easy. During the twenty-four hours between her bitter confrontation with G.K. and her departure from Singapore, she had met again with Mr. Soong, who informed her that he had managed to find a prospective buyer for Janet's apothecary shop, the cash from which he promised to transfer to her bank in Paris. But when Mr. Soong asked Janna for instructions as to the disposition of the land Janet had left her, she had been indecisive; she knew that if it was sold to anybody in Singapore, G.K. would immediately acquire it from them, and Janet's struggle to keep it as a children's playground would have been for nothing. By leaving the land untouched and thereby continuing to frustrate G.K., it would become a monument of sorts to Janet's ideals. Janna told Mr. Soong to leave it the way it was, at least for the time being. It would take months for the paperwork transferring title to Janna's name to be completed, and perhaps by that time she would be better equipped emotionally to give more explicit instructions.

Even though she owned land worth ten million dollars, Janna realized that until it and the shop were sold she was going to be extremely short of cash. She also wasn't sure how hard it would be to find a job after she arrived in New York, and decided that one way of making the right kind of contacts would be through the Countess's placement agency. She telephoned to request an interview, and the Countess invited Janna to visit.

Her appointment had been for three o'clock the following afternoon but the Countess kept her waiting almost an hour, and when she finally did appear it was immediately evident that she had aged considerably in the twelve months since they last met. She had lost weight and walked uncertainly with the aid of a silver-headed cane. Her black hair was liberally sprinkled with gray, and when she offered her hand Janna noticed it trembled.

"You must forgive me for keeping you waiting, my dear," she said feebly. "It seems to take me a little longer to do everything nowadays. You had a good flight back from Singapore?"

"I've still got jet lag," Janna replied.

"Jets!" The Countess raised her eyes in supplication. "Before they existed it was possible to enjoy travel. Now getting from one place to another has become a test of endurance. How was your year with G. K. Wong?"

"Another test of endurance," Janna said.

The Countess smiled thinly. "But I see you survived."

"A friend of mine wasn't so lucky."

"You mean Janet Taylor?"

Janna nodded. She was surprised the other woman was so well informed and assumed she must have heard the news from Wong. "Did you know her?" she asked.

"Not personally," the other woman replied after a brief hesitation, "but I understand from people who did that she was a misguided but well-intentioned woman—"

"There was nothing misguided about Janet Taylor," Janna interrupted defensively.

"Then I was misinformed," the Countess replied smoothly. "Which makes me wonder about the validity of the rest of the information I received."

"Which was?"

"That you inherited land from her worth in excess of ten million dollars."

"At least your informant got that right."

"Forgive me," the Countess said, fluttering her hands, "but I don't understand why somebody with that much money needs my help in finding them a job."

"Until the land is sold I have virtually nothing to live on," Janna said.

"But surely it is only a matter of time—"

"If I decide to sell the land."

"You may not?"

"I still haven't decided."

"I see." The Countess was silent, lost in her own thoughts, but roused herself when a maid brought a trolley containing a Georgian silver teapot, cups, and a platter of petits fours. She waited until the maid had served them and left the room before saying, "There are plenty of interviews I could send you on in America, of course, but it would be absurd for me to do so because it is I who need a personal assistant more than anybody."

She paused and sipped her tea.

"As you may have observed," she continued, "my health has deteriorated in the past year and I find it increasingly difficult to cope with the constant demands I receive for cultured young women. It appears the time has come when I must find somebody to help me run the business, and nobody is better equipped to do that than you."

"But I don't have the qualifications—"

"Nonsense!" the other woman chided. "You attended one of the finest finishing schools in Switzerland, have first-hand experience working as a personal assistant, and have demonstrated sufficient strength of character to endure the undeniable hardships of working for a man like G. K. Wong."

"What would my duties be?" Janna asked.

"Mainly recruiting," the Countess explained. "There are a number of very good finishing schools in the United States where you could explain the benefits of my program and interview girls who express interest in it."

"I'm not sure—"

"Perhaps I should add," the other woman said, "that what I am offering is not so much a job as a potential partnership. You will receive a salary, of course, and a generous expense account, but when you realize the funds from your inheritance I propose to offer you the opportunity of purchasing a share of ownership in my agency."

Her offer took Janna so completely by surprise tht all she could say was, "I'd like to think about it."

"I am in no hurry," the other woman said. "My offer stands until you make a decision." She struggled to her feet with the help of her cane. "Now I must let you go so you will have time to get ready for the party this evening."

"Party?"

"Ah!" The Countess put her hand to her mouth. "I let the secret out. Never mind. The girls who have completed their contracts are gathering at Maxim's."

Janna suddenly remembered the night a year ago when, after drinking too much champagne, she had suggested that they should hold a reunion when their first year abroad was over.

"I'd completely forgotten," she admitted.

"The other girls haven't," the Countess assured her. "They were planning to surprise you, but now that you know I am sure you won't disappoint them."

Three hours later Janna entered Maxim's wearing her Balenciaga dress, now well traveled and the wrong length, but nobody seemed to notice this in the private room where the other girls had already gathered. Elke Kruger was in the midst of telling them about her experiences in Beverly Hills.

"Janna!" the German girl exclaimed, rushing to her former roommate and embracing her. "You look fantastic."

Janna wished she could return the compliment, but Elke looked far from well. Rail-thin and haggard, she appeared deathly pale, and her ebullience seemed more forced and harder-edged than it had a year ago. "It's great to see you again!" she replied, trying not to look surprised at Elke's appearance.

"How was Singapore?" Elke asked.

"Hot and humid."

"And probably very sensual." The German girl raised her glass. "Well, now you're back and I couldn't be happier."

The other girls joined in the toast. Janna could see from their eyes that they were already quite drunk, but that didn't account for the change she saw in them all. In some indefinable way, their experiences during the preceding twelve months had transformed them from spoiled adolescents into world-weary adults; the dew of youth had been replaced by a jaded cynicism.

During dinner, which Elke had ordered, Janna listened as each of the girls described with considerable wit how she had spent her year abroad. Eugenie Schiele, an attractive brunette, had worked as personal assistant to a Bolivian tin mining millionaire with whom she had traveled throughout South America.

"A charming man, but a closet homosexual," she said. "My job was to help him create a macho image by appearing to be his mistress and sex slave. This enabled him to add to his facade of masculinity by loaning me out to his business associates."

"That's one way to learn the angles." The girl laughed.

"And a lot more," Eugenie said. "I was surprised at how much confidential information they were willing to divulge. The president of Mato Grosso Explorations revealed that his company has made the largest discovery of tin ore ever found in Brazil, a fact he's keeping a secret for at least another month or two so he can manipulate the futures market. I told my boss, of course, and he stands to make millions."

"I hope he rewarded you," Elke said.

"He was very generous," Eugenie replied, fingering a huge diamond pendant that was hanging on a platinum chain around her neck, "and I received a lot of stock in his company to ensure my silence."

Solange Perauer, a French girl who had worked as a personal assistant to a shipping tycoon in Athens, Greece, had fallen in love with her employer, even though he was married and nearly thirty years her senior. "He's getting a divorce," she assured the other women, "and it had better come through quickly because I'm going to have his baby in about five months."

While the other girls clustered around Solange, Elke excused herself and went to the toilet. Her mood had undergone an abrupt change from forced ebullience to a nervousness that made it hard for her to sit still, and Janna wondered if she was ill. But just as she was about to go and find out, the German girl returned to the table, once again in high spirits.

As the evening progressed and more of the girls described their experiences as personal assistants to some of the world's wealthiest and most powerful men, Janna realized that each of them had gleaned bits and pieces of information which, in the right hands, could be invaluable. Eugenie Schiele's information about the tin discovery in Brazil was a commodity trader's dream; Solange Perauer's revelations about how her Greek shipping tycoon planned to finance the building of his newest fleet was worth its weight in gold to competitors; even Elke Kruger's discovery, confided to her by the head of a major motion picture studio, that a large part of the back lot at 20th Century-Fox was going to be converted into a complex of office buildings and condominiums to be called Century City, was the kind of information that could make a real estate speculator rich.

The gossip continued until well after midnight, when, one by one, the guests departed, until once more only Janna and Elke were left at the table.

"What about a nightcap somewhere else?" Elke asked.

"I'm worn out," Janna said.

"Oh, come on, we can go to that bar in Montmartre where we got drunk the night before you left for Singapore," she urged.

Janna sensed her friend's desperate need for company. "All right, but just one quick cognac."

Before they left, Elke again excused herself and went to the washroom. It was her fifth or sixth visit of the evening. Janna was puzzled but assumed the other woman must have an upset stomach. Realizing she could no longer delay the moment she had been dreading, Janna summoned the maître d' and asked him to bring the bill.

"But it has already been paid," he said. "Mademoiselle Kruger took care of it this afternoon."

Janna heaved a sigh of relief. It had been her idea to hold the reunion, and when she drunkenly issued the invitation a year ago she had also declared she would foot the bill. She had been wondering all evening how much it was going to be, and whether the check she was going to have to write would be accepted by Maxim's and covered by the meager funds in her account at the Banque Paribas.

When Elke still hadn't returned after twenty minutes, Janna sensed something was wrong and went to find her. She opened the door of the washroom, only to hear a loud tirade in a mixture of French and German; Elke was engaged in a heated argument with the woman attendant.

"This bitch tried to steal money from my purse!" Elke exclaimed.

"Liar!" the attendant, a solidly built, gray-haired woman countered angrily.

The two of them lapsed into German and Janna heard both frequently utter the word *Juden.* At one point it seemed Elke was about to hit the other woman but restrained herself when the attendant suddenly burst into tears and buried her face in her hands.

"Let's get out of here!" Elke declared.

She grabbed her purse, which was standing open next to one of the sinks, but only grasped one strap. The contents spilled onto the floor. A small glass vial containing white powder shattered, sending up a tiny cloud of dust.

"Shit!" Elke exclaimed, getting to her knees and trying to scoop up the cocaine with her fingers, but abandoning the effort when a sliver of glass pierced her skin. Picking up her wallet but leaving the rest of the items on the floor, she got up and strode out of the washroom.

"What was that all about?" Janna asked when they were in front of the restaurant.

Instead of answering, Elke summoned a taxi, instructed the driver to take them to the Café Picone in Montmartre, and settled into a brooding silence. Her face was ashen, and she repeatedly clenched and unclenched her fists. Only when they were seated at a table in the seedy bar and had been served their drinks did Elke respond, and even then her body remained coiled tight as a steel spring.

"It was nothing, forget it," she said.

"You were awful to that poor woman—"

"She deserved worse."

"But it's so unlike you—"

"Unlike me? What the hell makes you such an expert about me?" she demanded harshly.

There was the same wildness in Elke's eyes that Janna had first seen at Prince Gozini's party.

"I think it's time I got you back to your hotel," Janna said.

"Don't patronize me," Elke replied angrily. "I had enough of that from Joe."

"Joe? Joe Dawson?"

"So there is something you don't know." She drained her brandy and ordered another glass. "I met him when I was in Los Angeles. He was at UCLA law school. We got together again. I was burned out after a month of partying in Acapulco and he wanted to marry me. . . ."

"Did you?"

Elke nodded. "I thought it might be good for me. He quit law school because he was too proud to let me support him. He joined the Los Angeles Police Department. Can you imagine me trying to live on a policeman's salary?"

"How long did it last?"

"About three months. He kept telling me how I should live my life and I got tired of hearing about it. The producer I'd worked for earlier in the year was starting a new movie in the Caribbean, and he wanted me to go with him."

"How did Joe take it?"

Elke shrugged. "I never saw him again after I left."

"Are you divorced?"

"Maybe he's divorced me by now, I don't know. . . ."

For a long time she remained motionless, her eyes fixed on her brandy, as if seeking answers in its amber depths. Suddenly her shoulders hunched and she began to cry.

"Come on, it's time you got some rest," Janna said, taking her friend's arm.

The other woman allowed herself to be led outside, but when Janna summoned a taxi she shook her head. "My mother is here in Paris from

Buenos Aires. She's staying with me at the George Cinq. I don't want to go back there, not yet. . . ."

It was still raining, but Elke seemed unaware of it as she started down the cobbled street clutching a bottle she'd carried with her out of the bar, the brandy she used to wash down three or four different-colored pills. By the time Janna caught up with her both of them were drenched, but they continued together in silence until they came to a pathway along the banks of the River Seine.

"Everything that has gone wrong—the fact that I'm not settled, that I don't want to do anything with my life, that my marriage to Joe Dawson didn't work—all of it's because of the lie under which I was raised."

"Lie?"

"You wouldn't understand."

Sensing her friend was on the brink of a breakdown, Janna flagged down a passing taxi and helped Elke into it. The German girl sat slumped with her chin on her chest, her head swaying from side to side as the driver guided his vehicle through the twisting streets that led to the Hotel George V. She appeared only half-conscious, and when Janna helped her out of the taxi, she threw up in the gutter. The doorman, who recognized Elke, helped Janna get her to her room.

"Tell the hotel doctor it's an emergency," Janna instructed the doorman, "and have somebody inform Mrs. Kruger that her daughter needs her."

When they were alone, Janna undressed Elke and got her into bed. She trembled so uncontrollably that instead of drying herself off with a towel, Janna held her in her arms until the hotel doctor arrived.

"What happened?" the plump, red-faced man asked, taking out his stethoscope and listening to Elke's heartbeat.

Janna described what had taken place over the course of the evening and, believing he needed to know about it in order to make an accurate diagnosis, included the fact that her friend had taken a number of pills and snorted a lot of cocaine.

"You are mistaken, mademoiselle," a voice announced brusquely from behind where Janna was standing. "My daughter doesn't take drugs."

Janna turned and saw a tall, attractive-looking blond woman wearing a silk robe.

"She is very ill, madame," the doctor announced gravely. "With your permission I will summon an ambulance and get her to the hospital immediately—"

"A private clinic," Mrs. Kruger countered, patting her daughter's hand. "And call Dr. Frenay. He is familiar with Elke's case and will know what to do." When the doctor hurried from the room, she turned to Janna and said, "I appreaciate your help, mademoiselle, but my daughter is in good hands and I think it best if you leave us together now."

Realizing she was being dismissed, Janna took a last look at Elke, but her friend's eyes were glazed and there was no sign of recognition in them.

Janna snapped out of her reverie as the train entered a tunnel, its whistle shrieking. Moments after it emerged into daylight the door of the compartment slid open and the ticket collector poked his head inside. "Ipswich in about ten minutes," he announced. "I checked the schedule, and there's a local train that should get you into Weston by four-twenty."

As the ticket collector had predicted, the local train from Ipswich arrived at Weston at exactly 4:20 P.M. A chauffeur was waiting to meet Janna. He had no difficulty in recognizing her because she was the only passenger to get off the train, and he loaded her suitcase into the boot of an elegant but slightly dated Bentley with a brisk efficiency that suggested military experience in his background.

"You may need this, ma'am," he said, offering Janna a fur wrap. "It gets chilly around these parts at this time of year, and the heater isn't working as well as it should."

Janna allowed him to tuck the wrap around her legs, but the moment he got in behind the wheel she freed herself of its encumbrance. Staying awake was already difficult enough without the sleep-inducing warmth of the wrap, and in a further attempt to remain alert she gazed out at the passing scenery, deliberately forcing herself to try and envision how it must have looked to Janet when she was growing up.

Weston was the kind of picturesque village frequently used on post-cards to portray the quaintness of English country life: a Norman church surrounded by moss-covered headstones in a graveyard filled with wildflowers; two pubs marked by weathered signs; thatch-roofed cottages surrounded by carefully tended rose gardens; and a few shops whose windows displayed goods ranging from groceries to the kind of unfashionable clothes only country lovers would wear. Ancient, placid, timeless, it exuded an aura of comfortable well-being and was the last place in the world she would have thought would have spawned a woman with a social conscience as intense as that of Janet Taylor.

Janna could easily have mailed Janet's few possessions back to her parents, but she had decided to deliver them in person because she wanted to discover as much as possible about the Englishwoman's background.

Her body swayed as the Bentley turned in through a pair of ornately wrought iron gates and headed up a long driveway to a massive gray stone mansion set in the midst of fields of rolling grasslands. Janna recognized the residence as the same one she had seen in Janet's silver-framed photograph, and experienced the strange feeling of coming face-to-face with a reality which, until now, had been only an image in a faded picture.

She half expected to see Janet waiting in front of the house but instead found an elderly couple on the steps whom she recognized from the picture as Janet's parents. Mr. Taylor was a tall, stoop-shouldered man, with thin features and steel gray hair, while his wife, Adele, was a plain, frail, petite woman with flawless skin. Both welcomed her warmly, but it was Mrs. Taylor who insisted on climbing the wide, curving staircase to show Janna the room that had been readied for her on the second floor.

"It used to be Janet's," she said. "The last time she used it was after she came back from the internment camp in Spain. It was a difficult time for her. She just couldn't seem to settle down. I used to hear her at night pacing the floor like a caged animal. It worried me a great deal."

Janna opened her suitcase, which one of the footmen had brought upstairs, and took out the silver-framed photograph. "Your daughter kept this with her wherever she lived," she said. "I know she would have wanted me to return it to you."

The older woman looked at the picture for a long time, then held it against her breast. "You look tired, my dear," she said. "Why don't you take a little nap? I'll see that you are awakened in plenty of time for dinner."

When she was alone, Janna unpacked, then lay on the canopy-covered four-poster bed. It was a comfortable room with an ornately molded ceiling, oak-paneled walls, and a large fireplace, but the only indication that it had once belonged to Janet were two photographs: one showing her on a horse, and the other of her wearing a mortarboard and gown. Again Janna tried to understand what it was about Janet's upbringing that had caused her to turn her back on such a comfortable life, but she had reached no conclusion when she drifted off to sleep.

A maid awakened her in time to take a bath and dress for dinner. By the time she arrived downstairs Mr. and Mrs. Taylor were waiting for her in the large drawing room, and a butler was serving cocktails.

"What will you have?" Mr. Taylor asked.

"Vodka and tonic would be nice," Janna answered.

After the butler mixed the drink, Mr. Taylor handed it to her and the three of them sat around a huge fireplace, talking about everything but Janet.

"We are having guests down for the weekend," Mr. Taylor said. "Just a few old friends and business associates. I hope you don't mind. It's something we'd arranged before you called from Paris and thought you might enjoy. Do you ride?"

"Not very well."

"Then we'll have to find you a nice placid mount so you can join us in the hunt."

The small talk continued through dinner, which was served in a massive dining room furnished with Louis XVI chairs, green damask curtains, and wall mirrors that reflected dozens of crystal objects scattered about on ebony display stands. There were treasures everywhere: Gainsborough portraits smiled down from leaf-green walls onto enigmatic Egyptian sculptures; silver ashtrays threw sparks at the massive Empire crystal-and-bronze chandelier; and Persian carpets added a field of muted hues. The oblong table at which they ate was big enough to seat at least thirty guests, and the three of them occupied only one end of it where Irish linen place mats, Waterford crystal, and solid silver utensils glistened in the flickering light cast by candles in gold candelabras.

Henry Taylor, a soft-spoken man, dominated the dinner conversation, displaying a quick wit and considerable charm as he questioned Janna about her upbringing in New York, debated the merits of country versus city life, and amusingly described his duties as master of the local hunt. Although he was in his late sixties or early seventies, he displayed a keen mind and an astonishing memory for detail, which made it easy for Janna to understand how he had parlayed the wealth he inherited into one of the great fortunes in England. But he never once mentioned his daughter, and when his wife fleetingly broached the subject by mentioning a portrait Graham Sutherland had done of Janet after she graduated from Oxford, he deftly switched the conversation to a more general discussion of contemporary art.

Janna finally retired to her room just before midnight. She was in bed and ready to turn out the light when there was a tap on the door and Mrs. Taylor entered the room, carrying a riding habit over her arm.

"I thought you might like to have these now," she said, putting a black jacket and gray twill jodhpurs over the back of a chair. "They were made for Janet when she was about your age, so they should fit. I've told the butler to leave a selection of boots outside your door."

"That's very thoughtful of you," Janna said.

"The hunt is meant to get under way at nine thirty, but it never does, so it won't matter if you're a bit late."

"Did Janet ride to hounds?" Janna asked.

The other woman shook her head. "She loved horses but detested all blood sports. It was something her father never understood about her. One of many things. . . ." Her voice faltered. "You must forgive him for so obviously not talking about her at dinner. He found it hard to understand the way she chose to live and even harder to accept the manner of her death."

"Why was he so insistent that I come, then?"

"It was more my idea that his. I just couldn't bear being left in the dark. The Singapore Police merely informed us that Janet had been murdered."

"Didn't Janet keep in touch with you?"

"We haven't heard from her since she went to Malaya," the other woman replied quietly. "I tried to get in touch with her many times, but she never responded to my letters. I don't even know if she received them, particularly during the Emergency. . . ." Her words trailed away, and Janna saw the anguish on her face.

"I'd be glad to tell you whatever I know," she said.

"I would be so very grateful," Mrs. Taylor said quietly.

It was late by the time Janna finished describing how she met Janet and the events that took place afterward. Mrs. Taylor remained seated on the edge of the bed, listening intently, and when she heard that her daughter had willed her estate to Janna, she nodded approvingly. "When Janet came back from the internment camp she told me about you. She spoke of you almost as if you were her own child," she said.

"Then you know about my real mother?"

The other woman nodded. "Janet told me how she died in a mountain village."

"Did she ever say anything about the identity of my father?"

"She told me it was a secret your mother had never revealed."

Janna tried to hide her disappointment but it must have showed because Mrs. Taylor put her arms around her. "You've got your whole life ahead of you. You must learn to look forward, not back."

She held Janna a moment longer, then walked to the door and quietly closed it behind her. Janna switched out the light and lay in the darkness, listening to the night sounds of the surrounding countryside and thinking about the other woman's words. Perhaps it was time to stop worrying about her past and begin carving out her own identity. This is what Janet had done; the path she had followed had been circuitous, and might not have led where she planned to go, but the level of self-awareness that she had attained must have made the journey worthwhile.

The maid, a rosy-cheeked girl, woke Janna at eight with a strong cup of tea, but it was well after nine thirty by the time she dressed herself in Janet's riding habit, pulled on a pair of riding boots, selected from half a dozen pairs that had been left outside her room, and made her way downstairs.

She heard dogs baying long before reaching the cobbled courtyard where the hunt had assembled. Twenty-five or thirty riders, men and women, impeccably dressed in hunting pinks or black habits, milled around on magnificent horses in the brisk morning air.

"There you are!" a voice called heartily.

Janna saw Henry Taylor, resplendent in scarlet jacket, white jodhpurs, and brown riding boots, smiling down at her from the back of a gray stallion.

"I've asked the stable to send you Lisa's Fleet," he said. "She's a solid horse. You shouldn't have any trouble with her. If the going gets too heady, just cut out of the pack and follow at your own pace. A lot of the chaps are pretty keen and the chase can become a bit of a scrimmage, so don't feel you have to keep up."

He raised his crop to the peak of his cap and trotted off to where huntsmen were readying a pack of hounds. Moments later a groom approached, leading a beautiful mare with a chestnut coat that glistened in the pale morning sun. He cupped his hands and knelt to give Janna a leg up onto her mount. It was the first time she had sat an English saddle, and she wasn't at all sure she liked the sensation. She had learned to ride at a school in upstate New York where everybody used Western saddles, which were much larger than the one she now found herself in, and the absence of a pommel made her feel as if she would slide too far forward. But she was determined not to embarrass herself, and when Henry Taylor sounded his horn and the hunt clattered out through the gate at the far end of the courtyard, she moved with it.

It was an exhilarating sensation, like being caught up in a sea of brightly bobbing floats propelled along by a current that carried her out of the meadows surrounding the house, through a stand of oak trees so thick with foliage that sunlight came through only in dappled patches, onto higher ground where the terrain was more rugged. As the pace of the hunt quickened, Janna began falling back, and by the time the main body of riders disappeared over the crest of a hill her horse had slowed to a walk. She made no effort to catch up; being present at the kill held no fascination for her.

When the mare stopped on a high ridge, Janna loosened the reins enough for her to graze, content to watch the progress of the others from a distance. They streamed across open ground at a gallop, jumped gates and stone walls, hurtled over fast-flowing streams, constantly vying with each other to lead the pack. Their sounds rose in the crisp morning air: thundering hooves, barking dogs, and the thin wail of the hunting horn.

Suddenly, less than three yards away, a pheasant broke cover from a gorse bush and rose in flight with a clatter of wings. Her startled horse reared, and only quick reflexes enabled Janna to stop herself from being thrown, but as she struggled to keep her balance the horse bolted, pulling the reins from her hands. Grabbing the mane, she held on as the terrified animal plunged down a steep slope, almost slipping on the scree, then continuing at a full gallop across broken ground toward a narrow stream, beyond which rose a hedge of tangled thorns topped by strands of rusted barbed wire. The saddle started to slip; Janna guessed the girth had snapped. Feeling the mare's withers tense, she sensed the animal was about to take the hedge, and rather than risk falling in mid-flight and landing on the rusty barbed wire, she threw herself clear a split second before the horse jumped.

She hit the ground hard and somersaulted into the shallow stream. Icy water swirled around her body. Still dazed, she felt herself being lifted up and heard a vaguely familiar voice say, "You won't find the fox in there!"

Janna opened her eyes and found herself looking into the face of Derek Southworth, who gently laid her on the grass bank and loosened the collar of her riding habit.

"I saw what happened," he said. "You're damned lucky you fell off when you did."

"I threw myself off."

"If that's the way you prefer I tell the story—"

"I don't give a damn what you say!" Anger brought Janna to her senses, and she forced herself into a sitting position.

"Want a ride back?" he asked with a grin.

She saw his horse grazing nearby and realized her own must be long gone. It was at least a three-mile walk back to the Taylors' and the way she felt it seemed an impossible distance. "I don't have much choice, do I?" she said.

"You can always wait until some other good Samaritan passes this way."

Janna, who had climbed to her feet, suddenly dashed for his horse, mounted it, and dug her heels into its flank. The animal broke into a gallop, and by the time she looked over her shoulder Derek Southworth was barely visible next to the stream.

It was late afternoon when she saw him again. The hunt had made its kill and returned for a lavish buffet that had been set up in the courtyard. While servants handed out glasses of champagne, the guests wolfed down roast beef, lobster, and caviar. Janna, who had changed from the riding habit into slacks and a silk blouse, was nibbling a stalk of celery when Southworth, spattered with mud, strode toward her.

"What kind of a damned silly game—"

"Not a game," Janna interrupted coldly. "Just an old grudge I wanted to settle."

"Grudge?"

"For not telling me you knew Janet Taylor had been murdered."

"I didn't know."

"Captain Oldham told me he questioned you before I picked you up at the Cockpit Hotel."

"He did," Southworth acknowledged, "but he never said why. The first time I knew about Janet Taylor's death was when I read about it in the *Straits Times* on my flight back to London."

"It seems very odd that you didn't even mention that Captain Oldham had questioned you," Janna persisted.

"Why should I?" Southworth asked. "Men like G.K. don't get to be multimillionaires without bending a few rules. It wasn't the first time I've been questioned by the police about a man with whom I've done business. Besides," he added, "it was the farthest thing from my mind during the time we spent together. That weekend meant a great deal to me. I've been thinking about it ever since I got back from Singapore. Why else do you think I'm here?"

"For the hunt, like everybody else."

"Only because I knew you'd be present."

"Who told you?"

"Henry Taylor. We're business associates. He invited me down for the weekend, but I wasn't going to come until he told me who would be here, and mentioned your name. I hate hunting."

"At least we have that much in common."

"We have a lot more."

Janna's anger began to dissolve. "How long are you staying?" she asked.

"Long enough to take a shower and change my clothes. I drove down and have to get back to London tonight. What about you?"

"Only the weekend," she said.

"Then where to?"

"Paris first, then probably New York."

"Why not break your journey when you pass through London and have dinner with me?"

"I don't—"

"Eight o'clock Monday evening at Claridge's grill?"

"It isn't as easy—"

"Try. I hate eating alone." He kissed her lightly on the lips and strode away toward the house, leaving Janna flustered.

After what Captain Oldham had told her, she had been convinced Southworth had deceived her, but now she didn't know what to think. On the surface his explanation sounded rational enough, and he had obviously gone to considerable lengths to see her again, yet she still felt uneasy.

"I hear you took a nasty spill," Henry Taylor said, walking toward her carrying a glass of champagne.

"A pheasant startled the horse and it bolted," Janna said. "It was my own fault. I'd let go of the reins."

"Odd," her host remarked. "Lisa's Fleet is usually such a docile creature. Any damage done?"

"Just a few bruises."

"Well, drink up," he said, handing her the champagne. "Nothing like a drop of bubbly to cure what ails you."

He strolled away to talk with some other guests, and Janna went to the stables to check on the condition of the horse she had been riding. The cobbled area was a hive of activity as grooms rubbed down horses before loading them into trailers, and it took her ten or fifteen minutes to find the stall where Lisa's Fleet had been placed. The animal was being hosed off by a groom.

"How is she?" Janna asked.

"Not too bad considerin' what she's been through, ma'am," the groom replied, tipping his cap. "Bolted, she did."

"I know, I was riding her. A pheasant suddenly broke cover—"

"Aye, that'll do it. She went over some barbed wire, from the look of the scratches on her belly."

"I couldn't stop her," Janna said. "The girth had come loose and the saddle started to slip. All I could do was throw myself clear before she jumped."

"Lucky you did, miss. If you'd 'ave stayed on you'd 'ave been 'urt bad." The groom put down his hose and crossed to where a saddle had been placed on a stand at the rear of the stall. "Take a look at this 'ere," he said, holding up the girth. "Somebody cut it half through."

"The man who brought me the horse should have checked the girth when he saddled the horse."

"That he should, ma'am, but on hunt days things get pretty 'ectic around 'ere, what with folks bringing their own grooms an' all. 'Course," he added, scratching the gray stubble on his chin, "somebody could 'ave cut the girth after 'e put the saddle on, too. But whoever done it wasn't just after getting you hurt, miss. If you'd been on when old Lisa took off over that barbed wire, you'd have been lucky not to have been killed."

34

"Where to, miss?" the taxi driver outside Liverpool Street Station asked.

Janna hesitated a moment. "Claridge's Hotel, please."

The cabbie reached back to open the door for her, pulled down the flag on his meter, and turned his boxy, diesel-engined vehicle into traffic flowing south along Bishopsgate.

As he skillfully wove his way through the congestion near the Bank of England, Janna sat back and wondered if she was doing the right thing in meeting Derek Southworth for dinner. She knew it was tempting fate to see him again. Even if she dismissed her reaction to him in

St. Moritz as a schoolgirl's crush, it wasn't so easy to ignore what she'd felt during the time they spent together in Singapore. For her they had been moments of the deepest caring, and when it seemed as if he didn't feel the same she had been devastated. The last thing she wanted was to be hurt like that again, and throughout a long sleepless night at Weston she had tried to decide what to do. Logic cautioned her that with a man like Southworth she was out of her depth, but an inner voice urged her to follow her heart and in the end it had won out. Yet she still experienced a flutter of apprehension when the taxi stopped in front of Claridge's, at the corner of Brook and Davies streets in London's fashionable Mayfair district.

"'Ere we are, miss," the cabbie announced cheerfully. "Not much to look at, but when the Queen 'ad 'er coronation eleven royal families stayed 'ere."

To Janna the legendary hotel, one of the most exclusive in the world, looked very ordinary: six stories of faded red brick, a front door set flush against the sidewalk, and a small canopy bearing its name in discreet letters.

A doorman, resplendent in a chocolate brown uniform with glittering brass buttons and top hat, held the door of the taxi open for Janna and regally ushered her through the bare marble foyer to the hotel's dignified lobby.

Janna felt thoroughly intimidated. The air, rarefied and tinged with a gracious mustiness, seemed difficult to breathe. Behind the reception desk, men in pinstriped trousers and morning coats watched her with carefully averted eyes while waiters wearing knee breeches and brocaded coats moved about the bleak-looking lounge like frog footmen from *Alice in Wonderland*.

"May I be of assistance?" a man wearing a morning coat asked solicitously.

"I'm to meet Mr. Southworth."

"Ah, yes, he has reserved a table in the grill for eight o'clock. He hasn't arrived yet. Perhaps you would like to wait in the lounge?"

He led Janna to a table in front of an all-woman string quartet and asked if the waiter could bring her a drink. She refused his offer and glanced nervously at a gilt clock to one side of the reception desk. It was 8:10 P.M. Her flight back to Paris was scheduled to leave Heathrow Airport at midnight. She decided to give Southworth ten minutes and leave if he hadn't arrived by then. Glancing around the lounge she saw a number of people she recognized: Merle Oberon was seated with Sir

Alexander Korda at a table in one corner; Stavros Niarchos, the Greek shipping tycoon, was engaged in animated conversation with a woman in a group that included Greer Garson, David Niven, and Noël Coward.

When there was still no sign of Derek Southworth by 8:20 P.M., Janna decided to extend his deadline by ten minutes and ordered a gin and tonic. She had almost finished her drink when she saw Southworth enter the lobby, accompanied by a man she recognized as Felix Ervin.

"Sorry I'm late," Southworth said, "you can blame it on Felix here. I was in a business meeting with him, and he wouldn't let me get away. Janna, I'd like you to meet—"

"We're old friends," Ervin said, taking Janna's hand. "Janna, how are you?"

"Surprised to see you," she replied.

"Like the proverbial bad penny, I keep turning up." He laughed.

"It's good to see you again," Janna said. "Are you joining us for dinner?"

"Unfortunately not."

"He has a plane to catch," Southworth said.

"As do I," Janna said.

"You're going somewhere?" Ervin asked.

"Back to Paris," she said.

"But not until midnight," Southworth added.

"How do you know that?" Janna asked.

"Because that's when coaches turn into pumpkins and princesses lose their glass slippers."

"I can see it's high time I left you two alone." Ervin laughed again.

"Really, Felix," Southworth said, "if you can take a later plane you are more than welcome to join us."

"I would if I didn't have to be in Los Angeles for a meeting on Wednesday morning."

"I've never been to California," Janna said.

"If you ever get there you must look me up." Ervin reached in his pocket and took out an engraved business card, which he handed to her. "Fate has brought us together twice, but we can't keep depending on her. She can be very fickle."

He took her hand and held it for a moment, said his good-byes to Southworth, and strode back to the lobby, where Mr. Van Thuyne, the youthful-looking manager of Claridge's, was waiting to walk him to the door.

"He's quite a man," Southworth remarked. "By far the most successful financier to emerge since the end of World War Two. Nobody knows much about his background, but he's got a finger in so many pies it's staggering. Where did you meet him?"

"At the Zurich stock exchange," Janna said.

"Zurich?"

"Before I met you in St. Moritz," she explained, "a Swiss friend took me to the stock exchange in Zurich to show me how things worked in the real world."

"Felix is certainly an expert at that," Southworth said. "Did you learn anything from him?"

"A lot."

"About trading?"

"Among other things," Janna replied, sensing a hint of jealousy in Southworth's voice and deliberately making her answer vague.

"All right, be coy!" Southworth leaned forward and rested his hand on hers. "I'm glad you came. It means a lot to me. Hungry?"

"Starving."

He escorted her to the grill, where they were greeted by Luigi Donzelli, the silver-haired restaurant manager who obviously knew Southworth and welcomed him with a perfect blend of friendliness and deference.

"Luigi is the quintessential diplomat," Southworth said, after the restaurant manager had seated them at a corner table. "He treats heads of state like movie stars, and movie stars like heads of state. I've seen him handle the King and Queen of Greece with the same easy charm as Bulganin and Khrushchev."

"They stayed at a capitalist bastion like Claridge's?"

"In the royal suite."

"You're a mine of information," Janna said.

"I should be." Southworth grinned. "I've been coming here most of my life. Wealthy British families list their children with Claridge's at birth, the same way they are entered at Eton and Harrow. That's why I can always get a reservation. It used to bother the hell out of a friend of mine when I was in the RAF." He chuckled. "The poor chap tried for weeks to get a New Year's Eve reservation for himself and his mother but was always told there was nothing available. I suggested that next time he call he identify himself as the Maharaja of Peshawar —a title I made up—and he was immediately promised a table."

"How did he pull it off?"

"He dressed his mother—the dowager maharani—in a mauve silk sari, and he put on a gray-and-gold brocade jacket and a turban made from a silk bedspread. They darkened their faces with wood stain and received the royal treatment from everybody at Claridge's."

Janna laughed. "You made that up!"

"It's true, I swear," Southworth declared, "and nothing compared with what I could tell you."

"Don't stop now."

"Well, I remember a story the head housekeeper, Mrs. Huggett, told me before she retired. . . ." He paused as the sommelier displayed a dusty bottle of Château Mouton, uncorked it, and poured a small quantity in a glass for Southworth to taste.

"Don't leave me hanging," Janna said after the sommelier had served them and left.

"On second thought, maybe it isn't appropriate dinner conversation," he said with exaggerated propriety.

"Oh, come on!"

"Well"—he leaned forward conspiratorially—"it seems an exceedingly rich, middle-aged female guest sent for Mrs. Huggett, locked the door as she entered the room, and announced, 'I'm bored. I've been everywhere and done everything, experienced almost every sensation —except strangling someone.' "

"What happened?" Janna asked when Southworth paused to sip his wine.

"For once Mrs. Huggett declined to serve," he said. "Instead, she ducked for the door, opened it with a passkey, and later had the guest removed in a straitjacket."

"Now I know you're pulling my leg."

"Don't let Claridge's staid facade fool you," he said.

"You really do know where the skeletons in this place are hidden."

"My parents first brought me here when I was barely old enough to hold a spoon."

"Are they still alive?" she asked.

He shook his head. "They were both killed during the blitz."

"I'm sorry."

"A lot of people died on the night of September fifteenth, nineteen forty. Four hundred German planes dropped over a thousand bombs on London. . . . One of them hit my parents' house in Grosvenor Square."

Janna lightly touched her fingers to his. "I shouldn't have asked. . . ."

"I don't mind," he said. "I want you to know everything about me."

"Were you an only child?"

He nodded.

"What did your father do?"

"He ran the family estates in Devon. By the time I got back from the war, they were sold to pay taxes. The land had been in the family for over three hundred years."

As he talked, and the waiter served truffled *coquilles foie gras* with chives, Janna found herself captivated. Not only because of the deprecatory way in which Southworth managed to make being born into a privileged class sound humorous, but also because the warmth he emanated made her feel she was someone he trusted enough to share his innermost secrets. It was an experience she'd only had once before with a man, and that was Mark Hunter. When they talked, the communication went beyond words. Now it was happening again.

"I'd always heard English food is terrible," she said, sipping Napoleon brandy after finishing a serving of *gratin de fruits aux liqueurs* for dessert, "but after this evening I'll never believe anybody who says that again."

"Why not stay a few days and try some more?" he asked.

"Because I have to work, and I've been offered a position with the employment agency through which I got the job with G.K. The woman who runs it, the Countess de Cabo—"

"The Countess!"

"You know her?"

"Her name's familiar," Southworth replied after a split-second pause. "I think I've received some of her mailings."

"She specializes in recruiting young women who graduate from finishing schools and placing them with top business executives around the world."

"What would your duties be?" he asked.

"Helping the Countess run the agency. She isn't getting any younger and needs somebody to represent her in the United States."

"Is it a way of life you'd enjoy?"

"After my experiences with G.K. I'm not sure, but it's a good job, and I'd be able to spend time with Anna."

"When do you have to make a decision?" he asked.

"Whenever I'm ready."

"So there's really nothing to stop you from staying in London long enough for me to show you the city?"

The idea appealed to Janna a great deal, but prudence cautioned against it. "I don't think I should," she said.

Rather than trying to convince her, he nodded, paid the bill, and, taking her arm, led her toward the door of the grill.

"Was everything satisfactory?" Luigi Donzelli asked as they approached.

"As always," Southworth said. "And the 'fifty-nine Château Mouton is a classic."

The restaurant manager bowed slightly and escorted them to the lobby where Mr. Van Thuyne was waiting to bid them good night.

"How does he manage to appear like that at exactly the right moment?" she asked.

"It puzzled the hell out of me for years." Southworth laughed. "Finally I asked, and Van Thuyne showed me how the system works. There are two lights in his office, one green, the other red. The green light flashed once by the doorman means a guest is arriving and the assistant manager should be in the hall to extend proper greetings. Three flashes of the green light means a guest will expect to see Van Thuyne personally.

"And the red light?"

"That means a guest is departing to whom farewells must be said."

"Felix Ervin must have got a red light because I saw Van Thuyne in the lobby to see him off," she said.

"All the lights probably went off simultaneously when he left!"

"Taxi, sir?" the doorman asked.

"Thanks, Jack," Southworth said, "we're going to walk."

"If I'm going to make the midnight flight I've got to be getting to the airport," Janna said.

"And I'm going to drive you there," he replied, "but my house is just around the corner, and that's where my car is parked."

"I guess a little exercise won't hurt, particularly after gorging myself on that dessert." Janna slipped her arm through his. "If I had more willpower I would have resisted."

"It's good to spoil yourself now and then."

"The trouble is I could easily make a habit of it."

They crossed Berkeley Square and continued down Hill Street until they came to where an E-type Jaguar was parked outside an elegant townhouse.

"I'll just go in and get the keys," Southworth said. "Why don't you come inside while I find them?"

Janna hesitated a moment. By the time she entered the house Southworth had switched on lights that cast a muted pink illumination, reflected in floor-to-ceiling mirrors that covered the whole of one wall. She watched as he went upstairs in search of the car keys, then turned her attention to a group of paintings hanging over an Italian leather sofa. Two by Pierre Bonnard showed nude women in bathtubs. They were extraordinary works which, although giving equal pictorial value to everything on the canvas, still seemed almost transparent: osmotic, colored ghosts that allowed the passage of light around and through them. The other, by Egon Schiele, was a distorted, yet oddly provocative portrait of a nude female, so stylized it seemed only half finished.

Janna, who was still light-headed from the wine and brandy she had drunk at dinner, found herself strangely moved by the paintings. Their sensuality triggered her own. Reaching out her hand, she ran the tips of her fingers over the canvases. There was an intimacy to this touching that sent shivers through her body and constricted her throat. Swallowing dryly, she moved from object to object in the room, feeling the cool smoothness of crystal cones and carved jade; listening to the measured ticking of an antique gilt clock on the mantel over the fireplace; pressing a sweater she found draped over the back of a chair against her cheek, deeply inhaling its odor. She was dizzy from the overwhelming sense of his presence. The room seemed to be spinning, and only stopped when the sounds of Beethoven's Sixth Symphony drifted from somewhere upstairs. She looked at her watch. It was almost 11 P.M. The drive to Heathrow Airport would take at least forty-five minutes, and her plane left for Paris at midnight.

"Derek!" she called. "It's getting late."

When there was no response, she assumed he hadn't heard because of the volume of the music and started upstairs in search of him. Her head was still far from clear, and she was conscious of being propelled onward by an impulse that was more instinctive that reasoned. Following the music, she came to a partially opened door and looked inside. Steam was billowing from a bathroom, which served to diffuse the scene, and when Southworth emerged with a towel wrapped around his waist she experienced the same urge that had prompted her to touch the paintings. She crossed to where he was standing and kissed him on the lips. Their tongues touched, and she felt the pressure of his erection against her belly.

"I want you," she murmured.

He didn't answer, but slowly lifted her skirt and cupped her buttocks in his hands. The pressure of his fingers increased as he pulled her firmly against his still-wet body and trailed the tip of his tongue down the side of her neck. She felt herself enveloped by him, merged into one whole entity that throbbed as his fingers probed under her panties into the cleft of her buttocks. Her breathing quickened, and blood thundered in her ears as the pressure against her anus steadily increased. There was pain when he slowly inserted his finger inside her, but it was a hurt she wanted and she pressed back to force him even deeper. His other hand slid across her belly, resting for a moment in the mat of her pubic hair before sliding between her legs to spread the lips of her already moist vagina. A flash of blinding white light erupted under the lids of her closed eyes as he ran his nail over the tip of her clitoris, and the swollen strains of Beethoven's Sixth Symphony ebbed and flowed to a rhythm that seemed dictated by her thundering heart.

Piece by piece he took off her clothes, then lifted her in his arms and carried her to the bed. Taking off his towel he stood over her, his cock rigid and pulsating. She felt dominated by it, and submissively raised herself until the shaft pressed against her lips. The vein on its underside bulged darkly under its veil of pale skin, and she ran her tongue along its full length, conscious each moment of the desire to taste the blood she could feel flowing through it. When she took his penis in her mouth he smoothed a strand of hair away from her cheek, rested his palms against the ridges of her jawbone, and traced his fingers over her lips. Gently parting her lips he inserted his finger alongside his cock. The immensity of both was so overwhelming that for a moment she felt near suffocation, yet when he started to withdraw she held him fast with her teeth.

She felt him wince and tasted a sticky sweetness she knew was blood. Whether from his finger or penis was something she didn't have time to determine before he forced her back against the pillows and began sucking her nipples. Constantly moving from one to the other he created a suction that swelled them to twice their normal size, and made them so tender that tears welled up in her eyes, but she made no effort to pull away.

"Make love to me, please!" she whispered.

Instead of answering he touched, stroked, and fondled, seemingly intent on making her wait as he explored every inch of her body with his tongue. She felt his hot breath against her neck, smelled the scent of the soap he had used in the shower, and tasted the saltiness of his sweat as he moved with tantalizing slowness, caressing her breasts, nipples, inner thighs, even the soles of her feet. When he raised his head and rested it against her mons veneris she ran her fingers through his hair, then squirmed free, straddled him, and taking his penis in one hand guided it into her vagina as she lowered herself on him.

"God, you feel good!" He sighed.

A dog barked somewhere out on the street, and Janna experienced an unaccountable flicker of solitude, but the void was filled by the hard certainty of Southworth deep inside her. She contracted her vaginal muscles and felt the stiffness of his cock.

"Move!" he said.

Slowly at first, then with quickening undulations, she brought him to the brink of ejaculation, but when she sensed he was about to erupt waited motionless until the moment passed. With him inside her she felt complete, and she didn't want the sensation to end. Again and again she stopped just short of his coming, and when it finally happened their release was simultaneous. Their bodies arched and Janna felt herself suspended in a vacuum where she hung weightless, no longer conscious of self or place. A wind rustled from a great distance, swirling leaves that fluttered against an azure background before exploding into fragments that gently settled over the length of her naked body, brushing her exposed nerve endings with a light friction that made her skin quiver.

Still trembling, she lay on top of Southworth, his penis deep in her, her head resting against his chest. She could hear his heart thumping and feel the firm, comforting warmth of his arms around her, but it was a long time before her tremors subsided.

"All right?" he whispered.

She nodded.

"It was even better than last time," he said.

Janna remembered how it had been then, in the dilapidated hotel on the beach north of Bukit Timah. There had been passion but later an emotional detachment on his part, as if his involvement had been purely physical. Afterward, as she had listened to the booming of *rabana* drums, she had felt herself separate from him, while now, with Beethoven's *Pastoral* softly playing in the background, she was no longer alone.

When the record finally ended and silence settled on the house, Janna lay awake wondering how the man sleeping in her arms would react to their lovemaking when he awoke. Please God, she prayed silently, not like last time. I couldn't stand that.

35

In the morning Janna eased herself out of Southworth's arms, careful not to wake him, put on a dressing gown she found hanging on the bathroom door, ran a comb through her hair, and tiptoed back in to the bedroom to study him as he slept.

His body was firm, without a trace of fat on it, even though she guessed he must be well into his forties. Broad-shouldered, deep-chested, narrow-hipped, he was a strikingly handsome man. What once might have been almost too-perfect features had become more rugged with time. His only visible blemishes were the scars on his wrists and ankles. For the first time she was able to examine them closely. Their symmetry puzzled her; she couldn't understand why each of the scars was circular, almost as if a spike of some kind had been driven in.

Seeing the injuries evoked a feeling of genuine anguish in Janna, almost as if, for one fleeting moment, she was instinctively sharing his pain, and kneeling next to the bed she brushed her lips over one of the scars. Southworth stirred but didn't open his eyes, and his steady breathing resumed. Watching him sleep, Janna experienced an intimacy that was even greater than anything they had shared during their lovemaking. The intensity of the moment made her feel as if she might suffocate. Quickly getting up, she crossed to the window, opened it, and took a series of deep breaths. The cold, damp morning air revived her, but when she turned away from the window her robe brushed against a cluster of framed photographs standing on a small table, and some of them fell.

Janna picked them up. They showed Southworth in a variety of poses: in front of an RAF Lancaster bomber; on a polo pony; in evening dress with a beautiful woman on each arm. But the picture that most interested her was of a young woman in a wedding dress, with long dark hair and exquisite features. It was inscribed: *Together, always, my love—Angela.* Janna experienced a quick stab of jealousy as she replaced the photograph on the table and quietly made her way downstairs.

Her intention was to surprise Southworth by making him breakfast, but on her way to the kitchen, she explored the whole lower floor of the house. In addition to the living room there was a formal dining room, inner hallway, and library. This last room contained, in addition to shelves of leather-bound books, another painting by Egon Schiele, a gruesome work showing a dead woman holding a bright pink infant inside her black, womblike cloak. Its heavy symbolism made the theme inescapable: emergence and separation. It evoked revulsion in Janna, and yet she continued to examine it, mesmerized by its visceral impact. It made her think of Keja. Finally, feeling oddly depleted, she turned away and hurried to the back of the house, where she discovered the kitchen.

It was neater than she had expected of a bachelor and extremely well equipped. The refrigerator was fully stocked. She took out eggs, bacon, mushrooms, and tomatoes. Southworth was awake, propped up against a pile of pillows smoking a cigarette, when she entered the bedroom carrying breakfast on a tray.

"I like a woman who takes care of her man," he said.

"Does Angela?" Janna asked.

Southworth glanced quickly at the photograph and grinned. "I'd still be married to her if she had."

Janna was immensely relieved. "How long have you been divorced?" she asked.

He shrugged. "About eight years."

"And you still keep her photograph next to your bed?"

"Why not?" he asked. "We weren't good at being married, but that doesn't mean I don't have fond memories."

"Do you still see her?"

"I think you're jealous!" Southworth chuckled.

Janna blushed and started to get up from where she was perched on the side of the bed, but he grabbed her arm and pulled her down next to him. He kissed her and stroked the inside of her thigh, at the same time lightly rubbing the stubble of his unshaven chin over her nipples, and when they swelled he pressed her breasts together in such a way that he was able to suck both nipples at once.

Even though her nipples were still sore, Janna felt a tremor in her belly and, lying back against the pillows, surrendered herself to the pleasure she could feel mounting within her. Their lovemaking was different from the previous evening; then it had possessed a fervent intensity, while now there was almost a childlike sense of play about it. Each gesture seemed an arch reminder of something that had happened the evening before, which both could now look back on with relish. When he spread her legs and entered her, the tray at the end of the bed tilted to one side, sending its contents clattering to the floor, but instead of letting it distract them, they just laughed and continued their undulations until both of them climaxed.

"There's nothing to be jealous about," he said when they were resting in each other's arms. "Angela and I were married for three years. She wanted children and I couldn't oblige because of internal injuries I suffered when I was shot down. The doctors said it was a permanent condition and that we might as well forget about having children. Angela was determined to be a mother, so we went our separate ways."

"Did she marry again?" Janna asked.

"About a year after our divorce became final."

"Does she have children now?"

"Twins."

"Any regrets?"

"About getting divorced?"

"That, and not having children. . . ."

"There's not much I could do to alter either situation, so why have regrets?"

"I guess you're right."

"I know I am."

"What makes you so sure?"

"Meeting you."

Her pulse quickened. "Really?"

"Stay a few days and I'll prove it," he replied, pulling her to him.

For Janna, the next three days were everything she'd hoped for after their weekend in Singapore. He was warm, loving, and attentive as he showed her the sights of the British capital. He took her to a pub across the Thames from St. Paul's Cathedral where its architect, Sir Christopher Wren, was reputed to have stayed while his famous dome was being completed; for an Elizabethan dinner at the Gore Hotel, where they ate a huge meal with their fingers as had been the custom during that period in history; and to the Tower of London, where they posed for pictures next to a bizarre helmet, a gift from Maximilian I to Henry VIII, that had spectacles fitted in a narrow slot alongside the nosepiece.

Southworth clearly loved London and went to considerable pains to ensure that Janna experienced its full flavor. They spent hours in rare book shops along Charing Cross Road; attended Covent Garden Opera to hear a performance of *Tosca;* journeyed by barge along the little-

known canals that make it possible to travel from Little Venice to
Regent's Park; and watched buskers as they entertained queues waiting
outside theaters along Shaftsbury Avenue. Janna was entranced, both
by the sights and the man who showed them to her. He made her feel
the way Mark had: protected, appreciated, extra-special.

Although he was a member of White's and various other exclusive
private clubs, she soon discovered that Southworth didn't limit his
social life to Mayfair. He was perfectly at ease on all levels of society.
This was particularly evident the evening he took her on a tour of the
pubs in the East End of London, where people whose families had been
poor for generations entertained each other by singing songs in rhym-
ing Cockney slang. Southworth joined them in rousing choruses with
an enthusiasm that was contagious and tried to teach Janna the words.
Her attempts to mouth them evoked good-natured laughter from the
locals, who vied with each other to give her examples of the rhymes
that were an integral part of their language: jam-jar (car), rub-a-dub
(pub), sausage roll (Pole), and Kangaroo (Jew).

By week's end Janna realized that Southworth was a man whose
personality had an infinite number of subtle shadings, a person who
could render a Cockney song in an East End pub with the same intensity
he demonstrated in explaining the intricacies of commodities trading.
Nor was he a predictable lover: one moment he would be gentle and
understanding, the next firm and demanding. Janna relished both, and
after a week in his company she knew she was in love with him. So sure
was she that, when Southworth announced he had to go to Yorkshire
on business and invited her to accompany him, she readily accepted.

Before leaving he took Janna on a shopping spree on New Bond
Street, in the Burlington Arcade, and at Liberty's on Oxord Street,
where she selected a well-cut skirt, four different-colored blouses, two
sweaters, and a pair of slacks, which Southworth assured her would
come in handy in the cold, damp climate of northeastern England.

She wore her skirt on the drive up to York, which was Southworth's
destination, and was glad she did, because on the long journey from
London in Southworth's Jaguar he frequently slid his left hand up the
inside of her thigh to her crotch, resting it there for long periods at a
time, during which he inserted his finger into her vagina. It was a
gesture that brought Janna sustained excitement and an immense sense
of bonding. She lay with her head propped against the back of the seat,
eyes closed, legs spread apart, feeling him inside her, hearing the
flip-flap of passing cars, smelling the musky odor of her own juices,

lulled by the vibration of the powerful engine, which somehow seemed transmitted through Southworth's arm to the very depths of her being. He didn't strive to arouse her, but the friction of his hand against her clitoris brought her to multiple orgasms.

York possessed one of the finest cathedrals in Great Britain, a magnificent structure that was visible from thirty miles away and towered over the ancient city like a huge white monolith. While Southworth was completing his business, Janna explored the Minster, the city walls, and the great gates known as Bars. She was intrigued by the quaintness of narrow streets such as Shambles and looked at sumptuous materials at York Weavers. The city reeked of history. She could almost hear the tramp of Roman legions along its cobbled streets and feel its Tudor elegance as she examined the gabling of St. William's College. But it was all just a way of filling time before she could be with Southworth again.

When he finished his business meeting, instead of remaining overnight in York he drove another fifty or sixty miles northwest, through bleak but ruggedly beautiful countryside, to the small village of Carperby, where he had reserved a room at a tiny, graystone inn called the Wheatsheaf. From the outside it appeared ordinary, but once inside Janna discovered it was a cozy place. The two women who ran it appeared to know Southworth from previous visits and were determined to ensure him a comfortable stay.

That night, although they made love, Southworth seemed tense and distracted, but the following morning he appeared much more relaxed when he described over breakfast how, as a boy, he and his parents had frequently spent summers in this part of Yorkshire, a time during which he had learned to love the countryside.

During the next three days, Southworth conducted Janna on a tour of nearby scenic places that made her realize why he had developed such an affinity for the North York moors and Yorkshire dales. It was a rugged, unforgiving environment whose bleakness might have been too much for most people, but it struck a chord in Janna. Each new sight was a revelation: the valley of Swale with its muted purple and burnt-umber hues melting into a background of green so subtle it had an infinite number of gradations; the ruins of Whitby Abbey etched against the darkening night sky; shafts of sunlight slicing through storm clouds over Cloverdale; and the upper falls of the Ure River at Aysgarth, where peaty water roared over worn gray shelves of stone softened by moss.

It was a setting as alien to her as the surface of the moon, and yet she felt at one with it because of the man showing it to her. His love of the place was contagious, and because she saw it through his eyes the discoveries she made were as much about Southworth as the location in which she found herself. He evidenced a sensitivity that hadn't been apparent during the time they spent together in Singapore, and a love of simple beauty that belied the contorted complexity of the two Egon Schiele paintings he owned. The startling image of the dead woman holding a baby in her womblike cloak had stayed in Janna's mind and made her wonder if it mirrored a hidden part of Southworth, but after being with him on the North York moors she dismissed the notion from her mind. It was simply inconceivable that a man who could marvel at walls made of piled stone, zigzagging up dizzying gradients that seemed to meld with the sky, could also possess the dark side she had imagined; she wondered why she'd even thought it possible in the first place.

As they walked hand-in-hand through the dales, Southworth talked about himself as a boy. "I always liked being alone," he said. "It's funny, but for me solitude was perfect freedom. Can you understand that?"

"I'm not sure," Janna said.

"That's probably why I loved it up here so much. It was almost as if I could give myself up to the elements." He pointed to a high mountain pass. "There's a place up there, between Wensleydale and Swaledale, called the Buttertubs, where I used to lie with my ear to the gound and listen to the earth. It has a distinct sound, you know. I can't describe it, you'll just have to hear it for yourself."

"I'd like to. Can we go up there?"

"Tomorrow," he said. "We'll take a picnic and spend the whole day. You'll be the only person to whom I've ever shown it."

He put his arm around her shoulders and pulled her to him, holding her close as they walked slowly back to the Wheatsheaf Inn.

"There was a telephone call for you while you were out, Mr. Southworth," one of the women who ran the inn announced. "They said it was important and left a number. I said you'd call them back just as soon as you got in."

Janna was seated in front of the fire in the bar when Southworth returned from making the call. The change in his mood was immediately apparent. "Is anything wrong?"

"Just business," he said. "The people I met with in York wanted some more details about a deal we've been discussing."

She sensed his reluctance to confide in her and felt disappointed. She had thought they'd reached a stage in their relationship where they could share secrets, but it seemed she'd been wrong. Was that all she'd been mistaken about?

That night in bed, she found it hard to let herself go. If he sensed it he didn't say anything, but next morning there was a strained feeling between them as they set out on their picnic. Southworth's introspection reminded Janna of that which had enveloped him after they spent their first night together.

They parked the car at Thwaite, a typical dales village with a hump-backed bridge, and set out on foot for Buttertubs Pass. Southworth walked slightly ahead, carrying the picnic basket, packed by the women at the inn, deliberately putting enough space between them so they couldn't carry on a conversation. The road rose steeply and Janna found herself breathing hard long before they reached their destination. After continually dropping farther behind, she stopped trying to keep up and paused to rest. A cold wind had come up, bringing with it a canopy of dark, rain-laden clouds. Taking shelter on the lee side of a stone wall, she took out a bar of Cadbury's chocolate and chewed on it as she looked down at the panorama spread out below.

It was staggeringly beautiful. The land fell steeply away to a deep gorge, through which ran a thin ribbon of a stream. Crisscrossing the wild moorland, walls of piled stones made crazy-quilt patterns similar to the one that now protected her from the wind. She could taste salt in the wind and hear the bleating of sheep as sudden gusts carried the sound up from the valley.

For the first time since dining with Southworth at Claridge's, Janna felt lonely and isolated. The feeling settled in the pit of her stomach like a cold stone, making her realize just how much she had come to depend on his company. What had she expected from the relationship? She and Southworth were from different worlds, he was twice her age, there was no possibility of their having children, and yet she loved him. That was the simple truth.

Getting up, she continued her trek to the summit. Southworth was gazing into a deep, menacingly dark chasm of fluted rock faces. Caused by centuries of rainwater dissolving the limestone, they descended into seemingly bottomless depths that were made even more ominous by glistening black surfaces where miniature waterfalls tumbled out of fissures and disappeared soundlessly into the gloom in gossamer clouds of shimmering spray. The atmosphere was one of malevolence, which was heightened when rain started to fall.

"Are you all right, Derek?" she asked.

For a moment it seemed he hadn't heard her, then he nodded. "We'd better make a run for it. These rocks get slippery when they're wet."

Taking her arm, he hurried toward a broken-down stone structure. It had been built to provide shelter during winter for cattle grazing the high, wild moorland but was now little more than a ruin.

"That chasm's a frightening place," Janna said breathlessly as they took shelter under a section of roof that hadn't caved in.

"It's just an unusual rock formation," he replied, putting his arm around her. "There are lots of them around here."

"That's the first loving gesture you've made toward me since you got that phone call," she said.

"I'm sorry." He kissed her neck. "I've got a lot on my mind."

"Personal or business?"

"Hey," he said, pressing his lips against her ear. "I've never been happier with anybody in my life."

She cradled her head against his shoulder. "I suddenly felt so alone," she murmured.

"You're not and never will be."

"Do you want to talk about it?" she asked.

He hesitated. "The meeting I had in York was with some bankers I'd borrowed heavily from to invest in tin futures. They're getting nervous about the way the market seems to be going."

"Is it serious?"

"I'm in way over my head," he said, "and they're threatening to pull the rug out from under me."

"What would convince them to change their mind?"

"Some solid information about the supply side."

"Such as prior knowledge of a major new discovery?"

"I'd sell my soul for that kind of tip."

"How about your body?"

"That, too." He grinned.

"Do you know a company called Mato Grosso Explorations?" she asked.

"They've been looking for tin in Brazil for years."

"And they've found it," Janna said. "The largest deposits ever discovered in South America."

"How do you know?" he asked skeptically.

"One of the Countess's girls has just finished working as a personal assistant to Rafael Ortega—"

"The Bolivian tin tycoon?"

Janna nodded. "Her duties included escorting Ortega's business associates, one of whom was the president of Mato Grosso Explorations. He told her about the discovery."

"There hasn't been a word about it, and news like that travels fast."

"It's being kept a secret so the futures market can be manipulated."

"When did you hear about this?"

"About a week ago." Janna described the reunion she had attended at Maxim's. Southworth listened intently. When she finished, he could barely contain his excitement.

"Do you realize what information like that is worth to anybody who trades in stocks or commodities?" he asked.

Janna nodded again. "Unfortunately, it's a one-time thing—"

"It doesn't have to be," Southworth interrupted. "If women like the ones you describe could be strategically placed as personal assistants to men whose decisions influence business on the highest levels, there's no limit to the kind of inside information that could be obtained. Instead of stumbling across bits and pieces of news, future applicants for placement through the Countess's agency could be briefed in advance on what to look for. They could then feed the information back to us."

"Us?"

"The two of us could run the operation together."

"What about the Countess?"

"You told me she's already offered to sell you part of the business. Why not buy her out completely?"

"That would take a lot of money," Janna said. "If you're under pressure financially, finding capital wouldn't be easy."

"You could get it," he said. "The land you inherited from Janet Taylor must be worth at least ten million dollars."

His statement surprised Janna. She hadn't told him about her inheritance and could only assume he'd learned about it from G. K. Wong or Janet's family. "That property is a symbol of everything Janet believed in," she said. "Selling it would be a betrayal—"

"You don't have to sell it," he said. "Use it as collateral for a loan."

"I wouldn't know where to begin."

"You don't have to," he assured her. "Just leave everything to me. I'll get the papers drawn up and you sign them. It's the chance of a lifetime. We could both make a fortune."

"How would I participate?" she asked.

"As my wife you'd be an equal partner," he replied, taking her in his arms and kissing her. "I love you, darling, and want you to marry me. Will you—please?"

36

In New York, Anna smiled as she listened to Janna's excited voice at the other end of the telephone in London.

"Derek's asked me to marry him. I haven't given him an answer yet, because I want you to meet him first. He left this morning for California, but after he finishes his business there, he'll be in New York. I've booked a flight on TWA that arrives at Kennedy at eleven forty-five tonight—"

"I'll be there to meet you," Anna interrupted. "I can't offer you your own room, but my sofa awaits you."

"I can't wait to see you!" Janna enthused. "It's been almost two years, and I've got so much to tell you—"

"Well, before you hang up, maybe you'll let me know the full name of the man you're so crazy about. All I know so far is Derek."

Janna laughed. "I guess I got carried away. It's Southworth. Derek Southworth."

The name triggered an indelible memory: a young, fair-haired man in a tattered RAF uniform nailed to the door of a building overlooking the parade ground at Miranda de Ebro. But before Anna could respond, Janna had hung up.

Anna's first impulse was to call back immediately and warn Janna against the man she was planning to marry. It was inconceivable that the girl she and Mark had raised, the one person in the world she loved more than anybody else, should commit herself to an utterly ruthless profiteer. Anna had never forgotten the vengeance Southworth had taken against Patrón and his enforcer; the sight of their ravaged bodies still haunted her dreams. But she resisted the initial urge to telephone Janna. They would soon be together, and she wanted to be quite sure she was doing the right thing before revealing information that could irrevocably change Janna's life.

Sitting alone in her tiny living room, Anna tried to determine where her responsibilities lay. Her gut feeling was to protect Janna against Southworth at all costs, but then she considered the context in which Derek had been operating.

The camp was a microcosm of the larger conflicts that had turned Europe into a war-ravaged wasteland. It was filled with an eclectic group of people—half starved and subjected to pressures that stripped them of dignity—who had learned to do whatever was necessary in order to stay alive. Southworth had merely been better at ensuring his own existence than the other inmates.

Anna pictured the final days of the Warsaw ghetto, remembering how Jews had betrayed Jews in attempts to save their own skin; how even the Judenrat had assisted at selections in the deluded hope that, by collaborating with the Germans, others would be spared their wrath; how even decent, honorable people like Janet Taylor, who had dedicated their lives to healing the sick, had been willing to kill in a last futile stand against the Germans. If Anna hadn't been arrested after her parents were slaughtered, she would have destroyed Nazis with impunity and felt herself justified in doing so. Could she now, in all honesty, risk ruining Janna's possible happiness with Derek Southworth by holding him accountable for things he had done at a time when the world had gone mad?

Reaching out, she picked up a photograph Janna had sent her from Singapore in one of the many letters she had written. It showed her behind the wheel of the rented MG. that she had mentioned so often in her telephone calls and tapes. Although Janna's features still resembled those of Keja, they had undergone a subtle change. They possessed a maturity that made Anna suddenly conscious of her own forty-five years and sparked an awareness that Janna was now an experienced young woman who was more than capable of making her own decisions. Anna decided that her sole obligation was to tell Janna what she knew about Southworth and let her decide what to do with it.

The phone rang, jolting Anna out of her introspection, but when she picked up the receiver the line was dead. It had happened to her frequently in recent months, and she found it unnerving, but dismissed it as just another of the many irritations women who lived alone in New York had to endure. Such things had never happened when Mark was alive. How she missed him! For a long time after his death she hadn't dated anybody; the memory of her husband was simply too strong, and she had compensated for her loneliness by frequently visiting friends, and working extremely long hours. Only recently had she begun to go out again, but so far she hadn't found anybody who came even close to matching the qualities Mark possessed.

The phone rang again. This time it was Dave Wilson, the attorney who had represented Mark at his trial and had remained Anna's friend.

"I was just going over some paperwork and saw that my secretary mailed you a receipt for money you sent. We've talked about this before. I wish you would stop—"

"Thanks, Dave," Anna interrupted, "but I want to pay off Mark's debts. It's what he would have wanted."

There was a brief silence. "Are you all right?" the attorney asked.

"The best I've been in a long time," Anna replied. "Janna's arriving at eleven forty-five tonight on a TWA flight from London. I can't wait to see her."

"That's great news," Wilson said. "Give her my love."

At eight thirty Anna left her apartment, walked down five flights of stairs to the street, and began looking for a taxi to take her to the Port Authority, where she could get a bus to the airport. Janna's flight wasn't due for over two hours, but Anna knew how bad traffic could get and didn't want to risk being late. When three or four cabs passed without stopping, she returned to the lobby of the apartment building, intending to use the public phone to call a taxi, but it was being used by a big man who had his back to her.

Rather than climb the five flights of stairs to her apartment, she decided to wait and checked her mailbox. It contained an envelope with Dave Wilson's name and address in the upper left corner. She guessed it contained the receipt he had mentioned on the phone and stuffed it unopened into her pocket. The attorney had told her long ago not to feel obligated to continue paying off Mark's sizable legal bill, but doing so was a matter of pride with Anna, even though she could only afford to send small amounts each month.

Glancing over at the phone, Anna saw it was still being used by the man with his back to her. She saw he had dark hair, but she couldn't get a good enough look at his features to determine if he was a tenant of the building or not. When he showed no sign of ending his conversation, she decided not to wait any longer and headed down 96th Street toward the subway entrance on Broadway.

It was a hot, muggy evening, and Manhattan was still blanketed by the usual odors of exhaust fumes and rotting garbage. A group of young blacks were clustered at the entrance to the subway. "Wanna suck cock, bitch?" one of them called. The others laughed, but Anna's scalp tingled. There had been a lot of muggings in the area, and some of the victims had been killed. She pretended not to hear, put a token in the turnstile, and hurried down the platform, which was crowded with people waiting for the next train.

Anna looked around to see if the black youngsters had followed her and glimpsed a figure that appeared to be that of the man who had been using the phone in the lobby of her apartment building. He was wearing dark glasses, which obscured his features, but she thought she recognized him. She turned back to face the track as a muted thunder and sudden waft of hot, stale air signaled the approach of a train. The crowd around her surged forward, and Anna felt herself propelled toward the edge of the platform. The roar of the oncoming train grew louder as it emerged from the tunnel at the far end of the station, and Anna instinctively pulled back, as did the near-solid mass of people next to her, but at the last moment somebody planted a hand between her shoulder blades and forced her forward.

There wasn't time for her to see who was responsible or whether the act was intentional or not; all Anna knew for sure was that she was losing her balance and beginning to fall into the path of the oncoming train. Everything seemed to be happening in slow motion as she teetered on the edge of the platform: the approach of the train; her own flailing efforts to remain upright; the frantic reaching of those nearest to her in the crowd who saw what was happening and tried to grab her before she fell. A young woman wearing patched jeans and a T-shirt caught hold of Anna's arm and held on long enough for the young man with her to snag the falling woman's jacket. Neither had a good grip and couldn't have held on if they hadn't been aided by other waiting passengers who grabbed her so forcibly she was slammed to the platform.

The impact left her grasping for breath. She saw faces peering down at her and heard a murmur of voices, but they were like waves lapping on a distant shore, and she couldn't distinguish any words. Her heart was pounding and there was a terrible pain in her chest. It felt as if a fist were crushing down between her breasts with a force that threatened to collapse her lungs. Her body was drenched with sweat and she couldn't stop herself from shaking. White light exploded behind her closed eyelids and she felt consciousness fall away.

Janna braced herself as TWA flight #187 finished its approach and touched down on the runway at Kennedy Airport. She was tired but excited, especially because Anna would be waiting to meet her. Throughout the journey across the Atlantic she had mentally reviewed all the things she wanted to tell her—about the year at the finishing school in Montreux, Genevieve's death, the time she had spent with Janet in Singapore and the visit to her parents—but uppermost in her mind was Derek Southworth's proposal.

It had taken Janna completely by surprise, and when he asked her to marry him she hadn't immediately accepted. There was no doubt in her mind that she loved him, but the difference in their ages and the fact that he couldn't have children were factors she wanted time to consider. Her first instinct had been to call Anna and discuss it with her, but when she mentioned this to Derek he suggested a better alternative: "I'm scheduled to meet Felix Ervin in California in a couple of days," he said. "Why don't you fly to New York, visit with Anna, and I'll join you there when I finish my business on the West Coast? If she approves of me we could even get married in New York."

It had been a perfect solution, and the understanding he demonstrated in suggesting it had gone a long way toward helping Janna make up her mind that she wanted to be his wife.

"Miss Maxell-Hunter?"

Janna looked up. One of the flight attendants, a slender, dark-haired woman, was leaning over her seat.

"Yes?" Janna said.

"The pilot received a message from the tower that there's been some kind of emergency, and arrangements have been made to get you through customs and passport control as quickly as possible."

"What on earth's happened?" Janna asked, feeling her pulse quicken.

"I don't know," the flight attendant said, "but if you'll follow me I'll show you where to go."

She led the way to the door, edging past the other passengers, who were already standing in the aisle waiting to disembark. As soon as the door of the aircraft opened, Janna was led down a ramp and through a series of subterranean passageways that brought them to an immigration inspector seated at a desk. He examined Janna's passport, quickly stamped it, and waved her through to customs, where her carry-on bag was passed without being opened, and she was informed that, if she wished, they would hold her other luggage for pickup at a later time.

"Janna!"

Hearing her name called, she turned and saw Dave Wilson waving to her from beyond a barrier.

"Where's Anna?" she asked. "Is something wrong?"

"I'm afraid so." Wilson took her arm and led her outside the terminal to where his car was parked. "Anna's had an accident."

"Oh, God!" Janna felt a sick sensation in the pit of her stomach. "What happened?"

"She almost fell in front of a subway train."

"Is she badly hurt?"

"Some people grabbed her before she fell," Wilson said, turning his car into traffic flowing toward Manhattan. "The train never actually struck her."

"What then?"

"The shock of what happened triggered a stroke. The paramedics took her to the emergency room at Columbia-Presbyterian Medical Center. A doctor found a letter in her pocket with my name on it, gave it to the police, and they contacted me. I'd talked with her earlier in the day, so I knew she was planning to meet you. . . ." His voice trailed away and silence settled between them.

Each of them made attempts at conversation during the ride to the hospital, but they were too preoccupied with their own thoughts to succeed.

"I'll wait for you down here," Wilson said when they entered the lobby.

Janna nodded and followed a nurse to the doorway of a semiprivate room where a doctor was examining an electrocardiogram. When she introduced herself and asked how Anna was, he said, "It's hard to make a prognosis at this stage. All we know for sure is that she's had a stroke and it's paralyzed the whole of her upper body. She can't speak or move either of her arms. It'll be a day or two before we can determine whether there's been any permanent brain damage, but even if there hasn't I'm afraid it will be a long time before she recovers her verbal and motor abilities."

"Can I go in?" she asked.

"Of course," the doctor said. "But I must warn you that she probably won't recognize you."

The other bed in the room was empty, and the one Anna occupied was flanked by a metal stand holding an IV unit, oxygen tanks, and a wheeled trolley supporting a mobile EKG device. Plastic tubes sprouted from her lower arms, and wires from electrodes attached to her chest lay across her body. They made her seem smaller and infinitely fragile, like a delicate, bewildered child, and Janna's heart went out to her.

"Anna," she said, "it's Janna. . . ."

The woman in the bed didn't respond. Her eyes were open, but they remained fixed in an unblinking stare on the ceiling. Janna choked back the emotion she could feel rising in her throat, leaned over Anna, and kissed her gently on the cheek. "I'm going to take care of you," she whispered, her voice cracking.

Anna's eyes slowly turned toward Janna, and tears trickled down her cheek.

37

In the weeks that followed, Janna's only concern was caring for Anna. She sat at her bedside for hours at a time, holding her hand and talking to her even though she couldn't respond. Derek had arrived in New York two days after Anna suffered her stroke, but he didn't stay long. After having Janna sign some documents authorizing him to borrow money using her land in Singapore as collateral, he returned to London at the end of the week without pressuring Janna about an answer to his proposal.

Janna appreciated his sensitivity. She was so upset about Anna that she couldn't think about anything else. After Anna had been at the hospital for almost a month, Bill Hansen, Anna's personal physician, told Janna there was nothing to be gained by keeping her there any longer.

"What she needs now is intensive physical and speech therapy," the doctor said, "and she can get that as an outpatient."

When Janna asked him for a long-range prognosis of Anna's condition, he was hesitant to give one. "A lot depends on what happens in the next few months," he said. "If she responds to therapy there's a good chance of substantial recovery, but the longer her verbal and motor capabilities remain impaired, the less likely it is she'll improve."

Dave Wilson had informed the superintendent of Anna's building that Janna would be using the apartment while she was making her daily visits to the hospital. But when Bill Hansen suggested it was time his patient went home, it became obvious to Janna that she had to find another apartment for the two of them. The only way Anna could be moved was in a wheelchair, and that made her apartment, a fifth-floor walk-up, out of the question.

Derek solved the problem. Through a contact he had at a leading real estate company, he found and leased a ground-floor apartment on Fifth Avenue opposite the Metropolitan Museum of Art. When Janna questioned its expense, he told her to consider it payment for the information she had given him about Mato Grosso Explorations, data he had been able to use to make a tidy profit.

He established a regular pattern of commuting across the Atlantic in order to spend weekends with Janna, visits during which he revealed in considerable detail how he was investing the money he had borrowed, using Janet's land as collateral. He had contacted the Countess in Paris and worked out a deal with her whereby he purchased a controlling interest in her agency but kept her on to run it for him. The only change in its operation was that Southworth now told her where he wanted girls placed as personal assistants and what kinds of information he expected them to glean from their employers. He had named the holding company Star Industries and registered it in London under both his name and Janna's. "Like it or not," he told Janna, "you are director of a company that's already beginning to be looked at with interest by more than a few respected investment bankers in the City."

He also described various stock purchases he had made, on the basis of inside information provided by the Countess's girls, all of which had turned out spectacularly well. "Everyone's trying to guess how I do it," he said, "but so far none of them have come even close."

Janna's feelings about what Southworth was doing were mixed: one part of her reacted with instinctive unease, while the other justified his actions with the argument that without his success, and the generous way in which he shared it, it would be impossible to foot the considerable bills that resulted from caring for Anna. She needed twice-daily speech and physical therapy sessions, the constant attention of neurological specialists, and a private nurse to care for her whenever Janna wasn't able to. Anna's expenses had been partially covered by a group health insurance program at the firm where she worked, but it only paid minimum rates, and Southworth insisted that no expense be spared when it came to anything Anna needed.

Janna became increasingly dependent on him, not only financially but emotionally. She had been shattered by what happened to Anna and had focused all her energies on caring for her. There had been nothing left for her to give Derek, and when they were together during his first few visits from London, all she could do was lie in his arms and cry. She knew that other men might have grown tired of this, but he wasn't one of them: patient, reassuring, gentle, understanding, he seemed quite content merely being with Janna, which endeared him to her more than he could ever have imagined. In many ways his behavior reflected Mark's best characteristics—a fact that wasn't lost on Janna— and each time he returned to London she found herself feeling increasingly more lonely without him.

It must have shown, because about three months after Anna's stroke, Dave Wilson invited Janna to meet him for cocktails at the Plaza and told her it was time she started looking after herself. "There are no guarantees where's Anna's concerned," he said. "Bill Hansen tells me she might be the way she is for a long time, possibly forever."

"I can't accept that," Janna said.

"You might have to," the attorney replied. "Meanwhile, life goes on, and Derek Southworth isn't going to wait forever."

"Has he talked to you?" Janna asked.

"Only to ask about the technicalities involved in getting married in New York."

"Could you arrange it?"

"With pleasure."

"Somewhere Anna can be present?"

"I know a judge who will be happy to perform the ceremony in your apartment."

That night Janna called Derek in London and told him she had decided to accept his proposal. Two weeks later they were married in the apartment on Fifth Avenue. Anna witnessed the ceremony, mute and still paralyzed, from her wheelchair. When the judge pronounced the couple man and wife, Janna looked at the woman who had raised her and saw what appeared to be the first physical response Anna had demonstrated since her stroke. Her mouth opened and it seemed she was desperately trying to speak, but when no words came she sagged back in her wheelchair with tears streaming down her cheeks.

Leaving Anna in the care of a nurse, Janna returned to England with Derek for a three-week honeymoon, at the end of which he insisted on going through a second marriage ceremony, this time in a beautiful church with an octagonal tower at Coxwold, a village in north Yorkshire. After the ceremony, at which she wore a white dress Derek purchased for her in York, they drove across the moors to Carperby and spent the night at the Wheatsheaf Inn.

"I had the banns posted when we were last up here," he said as they lay in each other's arms. "I've loved that church at Coxwold since I was a boy and always dreamed that one day I would get married there. Thank you for making me a very happy man."

Janna was so deeply moved that instead of trying to put her feelings into words she kissed Derek with a passion she hadn't felt since Anna's stroke. It was like a dam suddenly breaking. Derek responded with equal intensity, sucking her nipples and then lowering his head to her crotch and probing her vagina with his tongue.

"Don't stop," she whispered.

Her voice sounded hoarse as she pressed her lips against his cock. Its veined surface felt like live tendrils as she ran her tongue along its underside, tasting its saltiness and deeply inhaling its pungent, musky odor. When she opened her eyes his shaft loomed like a corded limb, white and pulsating against the darkish-blond mat of his pubic hair.

She felt herself transported to another dimension, floating weightless in a vacuum where droplets of water, tearlike in shape, refracted light in a galaxy of colors that shimmered in ever-expanding brilliance, slowly swelling until they exploded in fragments that formed and re-formed in an infinite variety of patterns.

She took his fingers in her mouth and sucked on them with the urgency of a child seeking sustenance, and when he entered her she pressed his palm over her nose and lips, momentarily making it impossible to breathe. It was a moment of ecstasy she wanted to suffocate her, a swollen tide undulating through her body, her being, deep, forceful, so all-embracing that she wanted to give herself up to it forever.

"My love!"

His voice came like an echo from a far-off sphere, a soft repetition of another place and time when she was surrounded by love and warm understanding. There had been laughter and music then; a melody she had moved to in the secrecy of adolescence and now repeated to a rhythm that began with slow undulations and gradually built to a crescendo which vibrated at the very core of her being.

She was full of him: cock, fingers, mouth, tongue, all moving at once, sucking, probing, clawing, biting, her juices, his juices, and pain that made her cry out in pleasure. She dug her nails into his buttocks as something inside her was torn. Veils parted, mist-fine vapors of blood settled over her, and her body arched, pressing against his in an unreasoned spasm that held and held for what seemed like all eternity.

"Oh, God, how I've missed you!" he said.

She put her fingers alongside his penis inside her vagina and felt the sperm pulsing in hot spurts. It came with the measured regularity of a heartbeat, seeping over her skin before dripping into deeper recesses. When he sagged against her, fully spent, she withdrew her fingers and put them in her mouth, savoring the chalk tartness of his viscous milk.

Her thighs were still open and trembling. He remained buried deep within, but as his tumescence faded a trickle of fluid made its way into the crack of her anus. Night sounds brought back the world that had been so briefly stopped: the creak of the house like a ship's rigging under strain, a quick patter of rain driven by a gusting wind against the windowpanes, a dog whining, the query of a curlew's call.

She lay silent, feeling the slow retreat of his shrinking penis. She contracted her vaginal muscles in an effort to keep it in her and succeeded momentarily, but its retraction resumed and this time was unstoppable. No longer joined, Derek slid off her and rested his head against her breasts. She trailed her fingers through his hair, trying to pinpoint the cause of her anxiety, finally attributing it to the awareness that even though his lovemaking had exorcised all thought from her mind for a little while, her concern for Anna lingered like a banished spirit, waiting in the shadows to reestablish itself.

"I wish I knew what to do," she murmured.

"About what?" he asked.

"Anna."

"She's in good hands."

"I mean in the future. I want to be near her, but we aren't going to have much of a marriage if I'm in New York and you're in London."

"There's one way we could solve both problems," he said, propping himself up on his elbow. "My visits to Los Angeles have convinced me we should open an office there. California is booming, and there are all kinds of business opportunities. Felix Ervin is making a fortune, and we could too, but one of us would have to be there to run things. Most of my contacts are in London, but there's no reason why you shouldn't supervise our operation in Los Angeles."

"What about Anna?"

"The University of California has one of the best stroke rehabilitation units in the world. You could be with her and learn to run the business at the same time."

"But you'd be in London—"

"I'd commute: two weeks in America, two weeks in England."

"Do you think our marriage can stand that kind of separation?"

"Others do," he replied. "Short periods apart will make us appreciate the time we spend together all the more."

He started to make love to her again, and she responded, but her mind was focused more on what he had said than what he was doing. Maybe what he had suggested would work. It was less than perfect, and the idea of running the company on the West Coast filled her with apprehension, but if it was the only way to be married and look after Anna she was willing to try it.

In the months that followed, the experiment proved more successful than either of them could have imagined. Derek had already rented office space in Century City and purchased a condominium in Beverly Hills, to which Janna moved with Anna at the end of November 1965. Each day a private nurse arrived to drive Anna to the UCLA Medical Center for therapy at the stroke rehabilitation clinic, leaving Janna free to supervise the running of Star Industries, a job that initially required her to do little more than implement Derek's instructions and prepare reports on various investment possibilities, which he checked during his semimonthly visits to Los Angeles.

In spite of their frequent separations, the time Janna spent with her husband was so full of joy it more than compensated for their being apart: he was tender, loving, funny, charming, and endlessly patient in teaching his wife the intricacies of investing venture capital. She proved to be an apt pupil and quickly learned the techniques of real estate syndication, how to buy stock in companies that were going to be involved in mergers, how to leverage buyouts, where to invest capital in gap financing, and how to trade in commodities. Almost all Southworth's moves were dictated by the information he received from the girls the Countess had placed as personal assistants. It proved to be data that quickly made Star Industries an envied part of the financial community in both Europe and America.

He developed a reputation for having an uncanny ability to know when to buy and sell stock, which companies needed infusions of capital to replace drained resources, where land was being considered for large-scale development, how to trade profitably in futures on the commodity market, where new products were in development, and which shifts in key management personnel could alter the fortunes of an industry. The late sixties and early seventies were times when the financial world was a never-never land in which a will-o'-the-wisp rumor was all that was required for a stock to run rampant. Equity Funding, which was headquartered in Century City, became one of the most successful mutual funds in America by setting up boiler rooms where employees wrote up phony insurance policies as collateral for nonexistent investments. And another corporation, one not even in the aviation industry, announced a plan to refurbish surplus transport planes into Guppies and Super-Guppies that would be capable of generating enormous profits from their increased load capacity, a story that was enough to cause the company's stock to zoom from 10 to 65 in a matter of a few months before further investigation revealed that no aircraft had actually been purchased.

Star Industries became the most closely watched company on both sides of the Atlantic. When Derek Southworth made a move in the market, others instinctively followed, even though much of the time there was no evidence warranting them to do so. It was sufficient that they made a profit, and this they did most of the time. Nor were Janna's perceptions ignored, particularly when it came to investments she made in the purchase of television stations, at which she became an acknowledged expert. What nobody knew was that because Derek Southworth's lack of U.S. citizenship prevented him from buying such businesses, owing to a ruling by the Federal Communications Commission, he used his wife as a front to acquire the properties.

In the course of these transactions, Janna got an on-the-job training that was far more effective than the education she could have received at the Harvard Business School or any other university, and by the mid-1970s she was more than capable of supervising the operations of Star Industries within the United States. As Chairman of the Board and Chief Executive Officer, titles she shared equally with her husband, Janna ran a company that occupied five floors of a skyscraper on the Avenue of the Stars in Century City, the high-rise complex that had been built on the old back lot of 20th Century-Fox studios. It was a structure that also housed the offices of Felix Ervin, who, even though he lived on a ranch in the Santa Ynez mountains overlooking Santa Barbara, still made the daily 200-mile round trip at the controls of his private helicopter, which he landed on a pad on top of the building.

The financier played an active role in helping Janna learn the intricacies of her business, particularly during the years after she first moved to California with Anna, and became a close friend on whom she felt she could always depend for advice. He remained a very private man, who never invited Janna to his ranch or revealed anything about his background before their first meeting in Zurich, but he was always friendly and supportive. They frequently met for dinner at La Scala or Chasen's, occasions during which Janna talked freely about whatever problems she might be facing, both personal and business, and he offered what usually proved to be sage counsel. As Janna became more experienced and Star Industries flourished, Ervin proposed various enterprises she might like to undertake as joint ventures with him, endeavors that frequently proved immensely profitable and made her realize that it was possible to succeed without relying on inside information.

As Anna's health improved and she slowly regained her speech and the use of her arms, Janna made frequent trips to London for consultations with her husband, who ran the European operations of the firm from their offices in an elegant mansion on Threadneedle Street in the heart of the financial district. During these visits she stayed at Derek's house on South Audley Street, and for the first six or seven years of their marriage made a determined effort to be his devoted wife as well as his business partner. She bought numerous cookbooks and learned how to fix the dishes he liked, even though they had a cook-housekeeper come in daily, and she went to considerable lengths to arrange a social life they could share. He appeared to appreciate her efforts and was always an attentive lover, but the confrontations between them over the issue of continuing to rely on inside information brought a strain to their personal relationship that finally began to pull them apart.

"Every organization has its research-and-development arm," he argued. "Ours is just better than anybody else's."

"What we're doing is not only unethical," she countered, "it is illegal."

"You managed to overlook that when we started out."

"Things were different. Anna needed help, and I didn't know as much about business as I do now."

"And you think, because you've had a few successes with deals Felix Ervin has arranged, that you can do it without having an edge on the competition?"

"I'd like us to try. . . ."

He shrugged. "Go ahead, but experiment on your turf, not mine!"

As the rift between them widened, Janna began to see her husband in a new light. He seemed to have changed a lot in the ten years they'd been married. Now that she was thirty-one years old and he was in his early fifties, the differences between them were more pronounced: he was less sensitive to her needs as a woman, not sexually but emotionally, and their lovemaking had become more mechanical. His humor took on an edge of cynicism, and he showed increasing disinterest in Janna's efforts to make their home a place where both could seek refuge from the storms that beset them almost daily in the business world. He also began to drink more, and he stayed away longer on the frequent trips he took to the Continent. His early success with Star Industries had been so great, and achieved with such ease, that he began to assume he would triumph whether or not he invested the care and energy each different deal required. This attitude produced a sloppiness in detail that resulted in an increasing number of bad investments, which Janna was frequently required to cover out of profits from the company's American division.

The worst of these occurred in late August 1975, when Southworth initiated the takeover of a major European hotel chain by acquiring a large block of its stock and threatening a proxy fight to gain control. Rather than caving in, as Derek had thought they would, the directors of the hotel chain decided to fight Southworth by letting it be known that they would like to strengthen their financial base by merging with a friendly backer. They found one but refused to disclose who it was, preferring instead to play a waiting game by delaying the date on which the issue would be put to the stockholders. It was a clever ploy, because Southworth had borrowed heavily to buy the stock necessary for a takeover, and the delay was costing him a great deal in interest. Then a sudden unexpected downward movement in the market depressed the value of the stock he had purchased, leaving him in a situation where if he sold it would be at a huge loss.

Janna was aware of the problem but, sensitive to the fact that it pertained to European operations of the company, which were strictly her husband's domain, refrained from getting involved until the banks from which he had borrowed brought pressure to bear on Star Industries (USA) for repayment of the loan. Janna was in California when this happened, and even though she could easily have authorized the transaction, which would have been written off as a loss against her division of the company, she sought the advice of both Anna and Felix Ervin before doing so.

By this time, Anna had almost fully recovered her speech and the use of both arms and was working part-time as Janna's assistant. She still spoke haltingly and suffered occasional pain in her right arm, particularly when she became overtired, but she could function enough to arrange Janna's daily schedule and screen telephone calls.

The older woman had been aware of growing tension between Janna and her husband, but she hadn't commented on it because she felt it was something that should be worked out between the two of them. Having regained her ability to communicate, she had deemed it prudent not to reveal what she knew about the Englishman's past. What was to be gained by it? They were already married by the time Anna regained her speech and, for the first six or seven years at least, seemed very happy. Even when Janna told her that they were having problems, Anna decided not to disclose anything that might come back to haunt her if Janna and Southworth were able to work things out. Instead she listened, offered solace, and suggested that if Janna did decide to take steps toward a permanent separation from her husband she should talk with Dave Wilson.

Felix Ervin limited his advice strictly to the business side of the problems Janna faced, specifically the dilemma Southworth found himself in regarding the abortive takeover of the European hotel chain.

"It's the opportunity you've been looking for; to prove yourself in his eyes," Ervin said over dinner at Scandia Restaurant on Sunset Boulevard.

"By paying off his debts?"

"By showing Derek that a situation he thinks is hopeless can not only be saved but turned into a hugely profitable venture."

"How?" Janna asked. "They've called his bluff and hung him out to dry."

"That's the way he sees it, but you've got a trump card he doesn't have."

"What's that?"

"Me." Ervin grinned. "I knew they were looking for a white knight, so I guaranteed the backing they needed to call Derek's hand." He shrugged. "I've already loaned them twenty million dollars and guaranteed an unlimited line of credit, but that can be withdrawn at any time, and when that happens they're not going to have a leg to stand on."

"Wouldn't they just look for another white knight?" Janna asked.

"Probably," Ervin acknowledged, "but if I demand immediate repayment of the loan, nobody's going to invest capital in a firm facing a problem like that."

"And you'd do that for me?"

"It makes good sense all around," the financier replied. "They're going to be vulnerable to a takeover, and it might as well be us as your husband. My only condition is that you go to London and handle the deal in person. You've been living in Derek's shadow long enough. Spreading your wings is one thing, but seeing if you can fly is another. This is your chance to find out."

38

LONDON: September 3, 1975

"That's my final offer," Janna told the four men seated in front of her desk.

One of them, Joseph Bonventre, a middle-aged Italian with silver-streaked hair, was president of the hotel chain. Throughout the two-hour meeting he had said very little, preferring to leave the bargaining to his three lawyers. Now they looked at him, aware that only he could respond to Janna's ultimatum. The atmosphere in the elegantly furnished room on the top floor of Star Industries' London headquarters grew tense. The roar of early evening traffic barely penetrated the heavy velvet drapes, forming a background hum that seemed to further heighten the silence inside the office.

Janna kept her eyes fixed on Bonventre's face. He was a handsome man whose features showed signs of yielding to too much of the good life, but he masked his emotions well, and it was hard for her to determine what thoughts were going through his head. He had come expecting to meet with Derek Southworth, and the discovery that the Englishman's wife was to be his adversary instead had thrown him off balance. He accepted Janna's explanation that, as her husband was still abroad, she would be substituting for him, and acknowledged that as co-owner of Star Industries she had the power to make the necessary decisions, but he still seemed uneasy about dealing with a woman. Only after the meeting had been under way for about an hour did he begin to realize that she was much cleverer than he first thought, and by then it was too late.

Bonventre had played a cool hand, and for a while Janna had let him believe it was a winning one. The Italian had made it appear he was negotiating from a position of strength: Derek Southworth had made a mistake in thinking he could make an unfriendly takeover of the hotel chain by threatening to wage a proxy battle, the long delay had cost him high interest on loans, the downturn in market conditions had made it impossible to sell the block of stock he had acquired, and Bonventre had gained the support of a white knight who had infused huge amounts of new capital that enabled him to stall indefinitely. "Your husband has been caught in a trap he himself baited," Bonventre concluded. "The only question remaining is what we wish to do with him."

Janna's face remained impassive, but inwardly she smiled at the Italian's bravura performance. She knew he was bluffing: Felix Ervin had withdrawn the line of credit he had extended to Bonventre just hours earlier and was pressing for immediate repayment of the entire twenty million dollars, but rather than let Bonventre know she was aware of the perilous position he was in, she had let him play out his hand until there were no cards left in it. Only then did she announce that, far from backing down and selling the stock Derek had acquired at a loss, she had purchased enough additional shares to give Star Industries control of the hotel chain without fighting a proxy battle, a transaction that had taken place just before the market closed that day.

"I happen to think that hotels are best run by those who have a lifetime of experience in the business," she added. "Which is why I'm willing to sell all the shares I now own back to you and guarantee that no further takeover attempts will be made by us, provided you meet my price."

Janna named a sum that would give Star Industries a seven-million-dollar profit and stated that she wanted a letter of agreement signed before the meeting concluded. To emphasize her point, she slid a document across the desk for the Italian to examine.

Bonventre was dumbfounded. He started to get up, making it appear that he was going to storm out of the room, but then he slowly sank back down into his chair, shaking his head. He had spent his whole life building the hotel chain that now spread across half of Europe, and the thought of losing control of it was more than he could bear. Somehow he would raise the extra seven million dollars; it was worth it to get Star Industries off his back so he could reestablish a sense of permanency in his organization. After four or five minutes of whispered conversation with his lawyers, he took out a pen, reached for the letter of agreement, and signed it.

When the Italian and his entourage left, Janna sat back in her chair, closed her eyes, and savored her triumph, but her exhilaration was tempered by the uncertainty of not knowing how her husband would react when he learned what she had done. Southworth, who was in Spain for meetings with bankers who were financing construction of a resort on the Costa Brava, had known Janna would be meeting with Bonventre, but he had assumed she would merely arrange to sell him the shares Derek had acquired, at a loss to Star Industries. Thanks to Felix Ervin, Janna had turned defeat into victory, but she wasn't at all sure her husband would see it as one.

Although Janna was nominally in charge of Star Industries' operations in the United States, Derek had expected to continue calling the shots, and whenever she had acted alone, frequently in ventures that had proved enormously profitable, he seemed to resent it. She had the impression that her successes somehow threatened his sense of self. This had been particularly evident in recent years, when her triumphs were more than matched by his failures. It had resulted in a strain between them that threatened their marriage to the point where Janna was no longer certain she wanted it to continue.

Before leaving California, she had called Dave Wilson on the pretext of needing to know about the apartment on Fifth Avenue, the purchase of which the New York attorney had handled. Then she had casually mentioned that next time he was in London it would be great if they could have a drink together. She hadn't asked him outright about the technicalities involved in getting a divorce from Derek because she still wasn't sure that was what she wanted: ten years of marriage was a long time, and she was reluctant to abandon the relationship if there was still a chance of its working, but she was equally determined to resolve matters one way or the other. Dave Wilson had telephoned her that morning to say he was in London, and they arranged to get together at the Savoy at 8 P.M.

Getting up from behind her desk, Janna switched off the lights in her sumptuous office and took a private elevator down to the lobby, where her chauffeur was waiting for her. "I'd like you to drop me off at the Savoy," she told him, "then go and meet Mr. Southworth at the airport. His plane gets in at ten thirty: Iberian Airlines, Flight One Thirty-two. I can take a taxi home."

She looked out at the passing traffic as the driver guided the Rolls-Royce smoothly down Ludgate Hill into Fleet Street. It was the same route she had taken ten years earlier when, after spending the weekend with the Taylors at Weston, she had gone to meet Derek Southworth at Claridge's. How different her life would have been if she hadn't accepted his invitation, and yet there was no guarantee it would have been better. The early years of her marriage had been good, she had derived a great deal of satisfaction from the successes she had achieved in business, but they weren't enough to justify the compromise her relationship with Derek had become.

Dave Wilson was waiting for her in the lobby of the Savoy. He had aged considerably in the years since she last saw him. "Good to see you," he said, kissing her cheek and leading her to a table in the lounge. "On you the years look good; with me they've settled in all the wrong places."

"I'm glad you called," Janna said.

"I'm in and out of London quite often," he said. "A lot of my clients have business interests here, and they like me to keep an eye on things for them."

There was a lull in their conversation as the waiter brought drinks, and it grew into a strained silence when they were alone again.

"How have you been?" he asked.

"I'm fine," Janna replied, "but I can't say as much for my marriage. . . ."

When her voice trailed away Wilson said quietly, "Remember, I'm your friend as well as Anna's lawyer."

"I've been thinking about getting a divorce, and Anna thought I should talk things over with you."

"And?"

"The trouble is, I don't know if it's really what I want. . . ."

"Have you talked with Derek about it?"

"No."

"Wouldn't that be a logical first step?"

"It isn't that easy."

"Confrontations never are, but sometimes they're the only way to get things out in the open," he said. "Is there anything specific you'd like to tell me?"

After a moment's silence, Janna said, "About six months ago Derek had a minor operation, something to do with his bladder, and while he was recovering the surgeon assured me that what he'd done wouldn't in any way impair Derek's ability to father children."

"I would have thought that was good news."

"It would have been the best in the world if Derek hadn't told me before we got married that he was sterile because of an old war wound."

"Did you ask him about it?"

Janna nodded. "He denied ever having told me he couldn't have children."

"Was that the only time he lied to you?" the attorney asked.

"I don't know," she replied. "That's what makes it so difficult for me to confront him. There have been a lot of small things, half-truths, but nothing I can pinpoint. He always seems to have a plausible explanation for everything."

"Can you give me an example?"

"I inherited some land in Singapore—"

"Anna told me about it."

"When Star Industries became successful I asked Derek to arrange for a playground to be built on it as a memorial to the woman who left it to me, but every time I've pressed him for details he's hedged."

"Anything else?"

"He told me his parents owned estates in Devon, but whenever I've suggested we visit them just to see where he was raised, he says they were sold for taxes ages ago and he doesn't want to stir up old memories."

"Have you been under a lot of pressure recently?" Wilson asked.

"Derek and I both have," Janna admitted.

"Maybe all the two of you need is to spend some time together away from work. Marriage isn't easy under the best conditions, and sometimes you have to make a real effort to get the romance back into it." He looked at his watch. "I've got a plane to catch, but I do a lot of work with an English solicitor, Basil Matson, who handles quite a few divorce cases which often require him to use a private investigator."

"Oh, I don't think—"

"Divorce is a big step, particularly when both of you are involved in the same business," the attorney said. "Splitting up could cost you a great deal, both emotionally and financially, which would be tragic if there's no real reason to do so. Wouldn't you feel more comfortable knowing your suspicions are groundless?"

"I suppose so."

"Then I'll ask Basil to get his men to do a bit of digging. Don't worry, it's all done very discreetly. Your husband won't even be aware that anyone is checking up on him. When Matson knows the full story I'll ask him to give you a call, okay?"

"Thanks, Dave," Janna replied. "You're right about my having been under a lot of pressure recently. Maybe I'm making a mountain out of a molehill."

It was almost 10 P.M. by the time Janna's taxi arrived at the house on South Audley Street. Although she stayed there whenever she was in England, the decor hadn't changed much since the night she first returned to it with Derek ten years earlier. After their early successes had made them millionaires, Janna had tried to persuade her husband to buy a new house, a place where they'd be making a new beginning together, but he resisted the idea, arguing that it was silly to go through the disruption of moving when there was plenty of room in the house he already owned. One of the few concessions Janna had been able to wring out of him was to replace Egon Schiele's bizarre painting in the library with another Pierre Bonnard, bought by her as a gift on their first anniversary.

Nor had he wanted live-in staff, whose presence would infringe on his privacy. Janna had had to arrange for a cook to come in daily, along with cleaning women. And whenever they entertained, maids and butlers were supplied through a Mayfair employment agency.

Going into the kitchen, Janna saw that the cook had left some dishes in the refrigerator: salmon in aspic, cold roast chicken, and a chocolate mousse. She fixed herself a tray, opened a bottle of Pinot Chardonnay, and took the meal upstairs to the bedroom.

Putting on her nightgown, she climbed into bed, positioned the tray across her lap, and reached for the latest issue of *Time* magazine.

"Doing your homework?"

Janna looked up. Derek was standing at the doorway of the bedroom. He looked tired, and it was apparent from his bloodshot eyes that he'd had quite a few drinks on his flight back from Madrid.

"Good trip?" she asked.

"Not bad." He took off his jacket and loosened his tie. "The bankers were bastards, as usual, but it looks like the deal will go through and we should end up with twenty percent of it. How did your meeting with Bonventre go?"

"I told him we'd sell his shares back."

"We can write the loss off against our American earnings."

"We didn't take a loss."

Southworth looked up from untying his shoe. "What?"

"I heard that Bonventre had lost his white knight and was under pressure to repay the money he'd borrowed to fight off a takeover, so

I bought additional stock, enough for us not to need to wage a proxy battle, and told him we'd absorb his company if he didn't buy back our controlling—"

"That's greenmail!"

"Something you taught me."

She tensed, anticipating her husband's angry response, but instead he just laughed. "How much did we make?"

"About seven million dollars."

"Not bad, Mrs. Southworth. You've learned more from me than I thought. I think this calls for a small celebration."

Janna watched as he crossed to a small mahogany cabinet containing a tiny refrigerator where three or four bottles of Dom Perignon were stored. She was puzzled by his acquiescence. She had the uneasy feeling that, for reasons known only to himself, he had deliberately avoided a confrontation. When he started to pour a second glass of champagne she said, "Not for me."

"Come on, you deserve it," he urged, raising his glass. "To my star pupil. Here's hoping our next ten years together are as good as the last."

"Do you honestly feel they're still good?" she asked quietly.

"Business has never been—"

"For us, I mean."

"What are you getting at?" he asked, sitting on the edge of the bed.

"Let's be honest, Derek, our marriage is falling apart."

"After ten years you can't expect it to be all hearts and flowers."

"But there should at least be some real love between us," she said.

It seemed he was about to answer, but instead he picked up the tray, put it down on the floor, and lay next to her on the bed. Putting his head against her breasts he held it there for a long moment, then slowly raised himself and kissed her. His breath smelled strongly of whiskey and the stubble on his chin felt like sandpaper.

"The trouble is we've been spending too much time apart," he said.

"It's more than just that."

"What else?"

"There is no more trust—"

"That damned sterility thing!" he said angrily. "I thought we had that out months ago."

"There have been so many . . ."

"Yes?"

"Half-truths."

"Only in your imagination."

Janna didn't respond. Maybe he was right. Perhaps her frustrations had been triggered by the awareness that she was almost thirty-two and still childless. "Let's talk in the morning, I'm worn out," she said wearily.

"We've both been working too damned hard," he said, his voice taking on a gentler tone. "What we need is time together somewhere, a second honeymoon. Why don't we spend a few days up in the Hebrides?"

"I can't. There are all those meetings I've lined up in California."

"Now it's you who is putting business before our relationship."

Janna closed her eyes and put her head back against the pillows. She really did feel drained. It was a tiredness that went beyond physical fatigue, an emotional emptiness that left a void encompassing her whole being. When her husband climbed in bed next to her she felt his erect penis press against her buttocks, and when he fondled her breasts, even though his touch irritated her, her nipples got hard.

"Please," she murmured, "I don't feel—"

Ignoring her protest he continued to caress her. She felt herself coming alive, as if her senses existed apart from the rest of her and weren't concerned with her emotions. They responded to a greater and more urgent life force that overcame her reluctance and started her body moving in a series of undulations that culminated in an orgasm which left her trembling.

Afterward, as they lay in each other's arms, Janna tried to understand why she'd let Derek make love to her and realized that she still needed him. Perhaps a second honeymoon would help. Yet she couldn't rid herself of the unease that had prompted her meeting with Dave Wilson, and when the first light of dawn brought the gray hues of a new day into the bedroom her eyes were still wide open.

39

Soon after the ferry left Oban, the mist melted and the sun broke through the heavy overcast. Because it was the second week in October, the tourists who flocked to the islands off Scotland's west coast during summer had mostly gone, and there were few passengers aboard the small ferry that was the only link between the mainland and the Inner Hebrides.

Standing near the bow of the boat, Janna saw the dark, brooding mass of the Ross of Mull, an eroded remnant of a once-great volcano, and experienced a quick flutter of foreboding, but it was rapidly dispelled by the sound of a harmonica, played by a craggy-faced islander who had attracted a small audience when he got up to perform.

Derek and Janna had driven up from London in his new Mercedes convertible. It was a great deal more comfortable than the Jaguar he had owned ten years earlier, when they had made the trip to the Yorkshire moors. Janna remembered that time with nostalgia, as she did the two-week holiday the following year, when they had explored the islands of the Inner Hebrides for the first time. Was it possible to recapture the feelings she'd had then? If not, she reflected, it wouldn't be for want of effort on Derek's part. He had telephoned ahead to make reservations at the same hotel near the Ross of Mull where they had stayed on their earlier trip, and carefully planned a schedule for each day that virtually duplicated their first visit.

As the ferry continued its short crossing, Janna began to feel herself enveloped by the ambience of the Inner Hebrides. It was a place where nobody hurried, and queries as to the time were as likely to be answered by the day or month as the hour. The setting was mountains and wind, clouds and sea, all in awesome abundance. The clouds suddenly cleared, revealing a blue sky that seemed to magnify the sun, bringing unearthly visibility and a luminous glow that only wild untainted lands could know. The dark threat of distant peaks melted away before the clean sea wind and the radiance from the sky, where gulls wheeled in lazy circles uttering endless cries. Crossing to where her husband stood watching the harmonica player, she slipped her hand into his and lightly squeezed it.

"He's celebrating a profit of nearly fifty pounds that he made on the sale of his lambs," Derek said.

"Almost enough for dinner at Claridge's."

"He's already spent a good part of it," Derek said, nodding toward a paper bag containing several bottles of whisky, "and I don't think he's too interested in food."

They continued holding hands until the ferry docked at Mull. Then Southworth drove the Mercedes over a shaky ramp to the quayside and headed it along the road that dissected the island from Craignure to Fionnphort. Janna put her head back against the seat and looked out at the rugged beauty of the countryside through which they were passing. Hardy Blackface sheep, flecks of white against rock-torn turf, spilled across the hillsides seemingly untended; at one point they had to stop the car while two or three hundred of them leisurely crossed the narrow road. To the north, the crags of Ben More stood etched in sharp relief against the sky, where ragged tatters of cloud had begun to gather, threatening to plunge Mull into shadowed melancholy.

Such quick shifts in the weather were typical of all Scotland, but even more so of the Inner Hebrides. Near the southern end of Loch Na Keal, which almost divided the island into two parts, Janna saw an old farmer and his wife, both seemingly well into their seventies, repairing wind-damaged stacks of hay. They looked like topknotted loaves but were the islanders' customary way of storing winter fodder for the handful of cows they kept in dilapidated sheds, buildings that were hard to distinguish from the croft cottages in which the farmers lived.

The Skellig Arms Hotel was a welcome sight after the long drive from Craignure. Set on the northern tip of the Ross of Mull, it overlooked Iona, the sacred island where the Irish saint Columba established his first church in Scotland, and where a fine medieval abbey still stood. The owners of the small hotel, Colin and Jean Macneill, a young couple from Glasgow who had turned an old manor house into a comfortable inn, were waiting to welcome them and had prepared a meal for their guests.

"Will you be with us for a while?" Colin MacNeill asked in his soft, lilting Scottish accent.

"A week or ten days if the weather holds," Southworth said.

"Ah, it's been bonnie in these parts," the hotel owner assured him. "We've had no more than half a dozen showers in the last two days."

Janna laughed. She remembered that it had rained almost every day during their last visit to Mull, but it was a fine mist rather than a steady downpour, and not unpleasant to walk in provided the wind wasn't blowing. "Have you many other guests?" she asked.

"Just four couples," MacNeill replied. "We were full until a week ago, but most tourists are gone by this time of year, which goes to show how little they know about the climate up here."

It was true. Most visitors didn't realize that the Inner Hebrides were warmed by offshoots of the Gulf Stream which made them more temperate than the mainland.

"We plan to do some hiking," Southworth said.

"Aye, it's grand country for that," the other man said, "and my wife will be glad to make picnics for you."

When they finished dinner, which consisted of fresh salmon and raspberry tart drenched in thick cream, Janna and Derek sat together on the sofa sipping Drambuie in front of a roaring fire. For a long time neither of them spoke, but it was an easy silence, in which each was aware of the other's closeness, yet engaged in personal reflections. Janna's thoughts lingered on Anna, Genevieve, and Janet: the three women had all influenced her, and yet she had followed such a different path from theirs. But where was it leading her? She felt Derek's hand on hers and was reassured by his touch. When Mrs. Macneill cleared away the dishes she switched off the overhead light, leaving the room illuminated by the soft glow of an oil lamp, which cast flickering shadows that merged with those given off by the fire to form constantly dancing images on the walls.

"They look like the figures in a shadow play I once saw in Singapore," she said.

"Remember the ramshackle hotel where we first made love?" he asked.

She nodded. "That was so special."

"So is Mull. Our being here together again is going to bring back the magic," he said, kissing her gently on the lips.

Janna experienced the tingle of excitement her husband had always aroused in her during the early years of their marriage and responded eagerly to his embrace.

Their bedroom overlooked the narrow stretch of water between the Ross of Mull and Iona, a ribbon of glittering silver in the light of the full moon. As they lay together in bed listening to the soft lapping of waves on the shore, Derek murmured, "I love you, Mrs. Southworth."

When he made love to her, it was with a tenderness that had been missing from their relationship for a long time. Janna surrendered herself to it completely. He kissed her neck, breasts, thighs, and belly, before spreading her legs and resting his rigid penis against her vagina, but instead of entering her he slowly trailed the head of his shaft over her clitoris until the juices seeped from her, making a slippery trough that he lightly plowed again and again, slightly fuller each time until he was deep inside her. She shuddered as his thrusts quickened, and she felt herself enveloped by a warmth that grew in intensity until she was sweating from every pore. The echoing darkness seemed filled with wind that sighed from an infinite distance away, a turbulence that brought the scent of musky body odors and the salt taste of tears; she felt it against her sweat-filmed skin, and when she opened her eyes saw her pelvis arch as they climaxed together. They slept in each other's arms, like children protecting each other against an unknown darkness, and when they woke they were still locked together.

The days that followed made Janna wonder why she had ever questioned the worth of her marriage. Derek was funny, attentive, loving: the man she had fallen in love with ten years earlier. They recaptured the feelings they had shared during their first trip to Mull as they happily explored the islands together. They visited the High Cross of Kildalton on Islay in early morning when the still-veiled sun gave the eastern sky the cold cast of iron. A doe, startled from her bracken bed by Janna and Derek, stood silhouetted against the gray background, watching without fear, as they walked hand-in-hand toward the object that was a milestone in early Hebridean history. As the muted morning brightened, details of the cross stood out: Irish twined vines, Pictish coiled snakes, Northumbrian figures—a blending of ancient designs within the simple sign of the eastern religion that had blessed the west.

Standing before it in silence, Janna felt she could reach out and touch its aura of timelessness. It was a moment in which past and present seemed to merge. Unaccountably she felt a burden lifted, and when she finally turned away the mist had dissolved, revealing a clear view of Loch Gruinart. Now the sun found jewels in the dew-drenched bracken and glittered greenish-gold in the twisted branches of wind-bent trees.

From Islay, they went on to Jura, an equally large island which, although all but a continuation of Islay, still differed from it in almost every way. It was not green and grassy but dark and mountainous. The name, of Norse origin, meant "deer island," and five or six thousand of the animals still grazed its hills. They were the most numerous creatures on the island, whose human population was little more than 200. After World War II George Orwell had lived here. They went in search of the farm where he wrote *1984* but were driven back by swirling clouds and icy rain and returned to the pier drenched to the skin.

They were late for the ferry, but its captain saw them coming and delayed the departure of his boat until they boarded. When they reached the mainland they drove north to Oban, crossed in another ferry to Mull, and arrived back at the Skellig Arms Hotel in time for another of Mrs. Macneill's sumptuous dinners.

After they finished eating, at Colin Macneill's urging, they attended a *ceilidh* that was being held to celebrate a neighbor's wedding. It was an informal party where people entertained each other by singing, playing various instruments, and drinking a great deal. Around midnight the dancing began: Eightsome Reels, the Gay Gordons, and the Dashing White Sergeant. Janna didn't know the steps, but when the islanders invited her to dance, she did her best to follow their lead, while her husband shouted encouragement from the sidelines.

When the evening finally ended, Southworth accompanied a drunken local farmer to his car, where he sat behind the wheel singing at the top of his voice. "Are you sure you can make it home?" the Englishman asked worriedly.

"As full as I am, ye mean?" the farmer asked with a sly grin. "Don't worry about me, laddy, as long as I can sing I'll find my way home."

When Southworth joined Janna, who was preparing for bed, she asked, "Do you think he'll be all right?"

"Probably," her husband replied. "These island folk can drink more than anybody I ever met. He told me something interesting while you were dancing. It seems there are some caves just south of here that contain pictographs which are believed to have been carved by the monks who accompanied St. Columba here from Ireland. The theory is that the group lived in the caves while they were building their church on Iona."

"I'd love to see them," Janna said.

"Let's go tomorrow. It'll be our last chance for an outing because I have to be in Paris for meetings with the Countess on Monday morning."

"All right." Janna paused. "I've been thinking about the Countess. She's in her seventies now and must have made more than enough to retire."

"Retire?"

"You know I've never liked the way we've used her services."

"Let's not go through all that again," Southworth said wearily. "We're up here to have a good time, not fight with each other."

Janna sensed from the tone of his voice that it would be useless to argue, and rather than spoil what had so far been an idyllic holiday she decided not to force the issue.

That night was the first they didn't make love since arriving on Mull. Long after her husband fell asleep, Janna remained with her eyes open, listening to the night sounds of wind and water, sheep and sea birds, trying to pinpoint why, despite the success of their holiday, she still felt apprehensive. Perhaps it was because they must soon leave the Hebrides, with its special magic that was so conducive to romance, and return to the harsher realities of the outside world, where their newfound closeness would be tested under the pressures that had eroded their relationship in the first place.

Janna was still apprehensive the following morning as she waited in the car while her husband, who had stayed behind to collect a picnic basket, talked with the hotel owner and his wife.

"What was all that about?" she asked as Southworth loaded the picnic basket into the trunk.

"You know how these islanders are," he replied. "Time means nothing to them. They both wanted to gossip about last night's party."

"Did your drunken friend get home all right?"

"We'd have heard about it if he didn't. People around here aren't the kind who keep secrets."

It was a surprisingly warm day for early October, and the sun shimmered on the foam-streaked sea as they drove through Fionnphort. They stopped to buy a bottle of wine at an off-license shop near the post office, before continuing to a spot close to where the Ross of Mull met the water's edge. Parking on the grass shoulder, Southworth unloaded the picnic basket and led the way along a narrow path to a steep decline down which they scrambled to the beach. The sand was rippled and firm enough to make walking easy. Janna took off her shoes and was surprised to find that the shallow pools of water, warmed by the sun after they were left behind by the retreating tide, were almost tepid.

They rounded a headland and came to a crescent-shaped indentation the sea had carved into the basaltic rock of the towering Ross of Mull. It was as if a huge bite had been taken out of the place where the mountain met the water, creating a semicircle composed of two jutting headlands encompassing an inlet, invisible from the road, that was backed up against a sheer rock face pockmarked with dark openings marking the entrances to caves.

The place felt ominous, and Janna hesitated when her husband suggested that they enter the largest of these openings and start looking for the pictographs. Despite the brilliance of the day, with its warm sun and blue skies, she experienced an involuntary shiver as she looked up at the glistening rock. It was perpetually damp from underground water seeping out of the fissures that patterned its surface like cracks in glacial ice. No birds were visible, even though the ledges seemed to offer perfect nesting places, and as they got closer to the caves Janna became aware of an eerie sound, a kind of echoing whisper created by the wind blowing through the hollowed-out spaces.

"Ready?" Southworth asked.

"I don't know about this, Derek."

"You're not going to back out now, are you?"

"We won't be able to see a thing in there."

"I brought a torch." He opened the picnic basket and took out a large flashlight. "I always keep one in the trunk in case I have to change a flat at night. The batteries are new and should last for hours."

He flicked the torch on and shone it into the entrance of the largest cave. Its beam sliced through the darkness with a reassuring brightness as he led the way inside, leaving the picnic basket where he had placed it on a rock ledge. After a moment's hesitation, Janna followed her husband into the cave.

She was surprised to discover that, near the entrance at least, it wasn't as dark as she thought it would be. Refracted sunlight, mirrored by the wet sand, cast a pale illumination that was sufficient for her to see where Southworth had positioned himself at the entrance to a gallery that led from the main part of the cave.

"Look at this," he called, motioning her to where he stood.

His voice echoed in the cavern, bouncing off sheer rock surfaces until it dissolved into a murmur and finally disappeared into the subterranean depths. The dark air smelled of rotting seaweed and was tangy with salt. Moving cautiously, feeling loose pebbles crunching underfoot, Janna crossed to her husband's side and looked at where he was pointing his torch.

The markings on the wall were little more than blurs, indistinct smears that could easily have been formed by ferrous oxide leaking from the pores of the rock during thousands of years.

"What do you think they are?" she asked.

He shrugged. "Damned if I know, but the ones over there look a lot like a primitive cross."

Janna studied the markings carefully and had to agree that they did bear a striking resemblance to the High Cross at Kildalton, but she was also aware they might well have been caused by minerals dissolving in the rock.

"If St. Columba's monks did do these, why would they put them in such an inaccessible place?" she asked.

"Maybe the floor of the cave was higher in those days," her husband replied. "It was over a thousand years ago, and from the dampness around here I'd say it fills with seawater at high tide. Let's go in a bit further and see if we can find anything more definitive."

They made their way along the gallery leading away from the main cave, using the beam from the flashlight to search the walls, until they came to a place where the subterranean passageway split into half a dozen other tunnels.

"I think we'd better be getting back," Janna said nervously.

Southworth didn't answer but aimed the light from his torch down one of the long narrow openings, where its beam rested on what appeared to be a group of figures painted on an area of stone that had been smoothed. As he moved toward them with his flashlight they took on distinct shape and definition: primitive portrayals of men in helmets carrying long, curling banners. They were scratched into the rock, rather than painted on it, but color had been added to the shallow furrows after they were carved, and scraps of it still remained.

Janna traced the markings with the tips of her fingers, feeling the roughness of their edges and the slime that had accumulated in the furrows over the centuries. "They're beautiful," she said.

"Hold this while I take a look farther down the tunnel," Southworth said, handing her the torch. "There may be some more."

"Shouldn't we be getting back?"

"It'll only be a few minutes," he said.

He moved off down the tunnel, his way lit by the beam from the torch Janna was holding, peering at the walls as he continued along the narrow passageway until he reached the outer perimeter of the light, where he paused and glanced back at Janna for a moment before stepping beyond the illumination and vanishing into darkness.

She waited a few minutes and, when he didn't return, called his name, but her voice bounced off the wet walls of stone, and all she heard in response was the echo of the word she had spoken. After another brief pause she shouted his name again, but he still didn't answer. Confused and frightened, she tried to decide whether to turn back or go in search of him. Her first instinct was to do the former, but she wanted to know why Derek wasn't responding. It couldn't be because he hadn't heard her; the sound of her cries must have been audible for a considerable distance in every direction. Perhaps he's been injured, she thought, hit his head on a jagged protrusion of rock and been knocked unconscious. This thought spurred her to action and, moving forward cautiously, she inched her way down the tunnel. It continued for a distance of about fifty yards, then split into four other passageways which, although smaller than the one in which she stood, were still big enough for a man to pass through.

"Derek!" She called his name frantically. A wave of panic was beginning to envelop her, and she had to will herself not to lose control. "Easy," she muttered half out loud, "he couldn't have gone far. . . ."

Shining the beam of her flashlight down each of the narrow galleries in turn, she saw nothing but empty space until she came to the last one. It was slightly wider than the others, with a sandy floor, and she saw footsteps leading down it. Following them along the passageway, stooping as the tunnel height lowered, she continued on for what seemed an eternity but was, in fact, only about seventy or eighty yards, to a point where the sandy floor was replaced by slime-covered rock and the imprint of footsteps was no longer visible.

Yet another junction of tunnels brought her to a halt. She now realized there was a labyrinth of passageways, some of which fanned out deep under the Ross of Mull, while others twisted and turned at odd angles, a few even doubling back on themselves.

"Derek!"

Her voice now was little more than a plaintive whisper, yet it still produced an echo, and she heard the word repeated again and again. It was as if hidden presences were mocking her, and she suddenly felt she was being watched. Terrified, she swung the beam of the flashlight back and forth, half expecting to see hideous faces grinning back at her, but there was nothing except empty darkness and the distant noise of gurgling water.

She began to tremble. In an effort to prevent herself from succumbing to hysteria, she concentrated on reviewing her options: she could continue searching for her husband, whom she was now convinced was lying unconscious somewhere in the maze of tunnels, or she could try and find her own way back and get help. Her attempts at the former had so far proved fruitless, so she decided to retrace her steps and seek out somebody better equipped than herself to look for him.

Once the decision was made she felt more in control; simply having an attainable goal gave her a renewed sense of purpose and, aiming the beam of the flashlight a few feet ahead of her, she followed the imprints she had made on the lightly sanded floor of the tunnel, using them to guide her back in the direction from which she had come. As she moved forward, the gurgling sound she'd heard earlier got louder, and moments before she reached the place where she and Derek had seen the pictographs a trickle of water entered the periphery of light cast by her torch.

At first it was little more than a thin gentle stream, just sufficient to obliterate the tracks in the sand that she had been following, but within minutes it had become a flood that lapped at her ankles, and quickly rose to her knees. Retreating before it, she backed down one gallery after another, quickly losing all sense of direction as she struggled to keep ahead of what she now realized was the incoming tide. For a while it seemed she was succeeding, and the water remained at waist level, but then it began to rise faster than she could force her legs through it, and the power of the current swept her off her feet.

Even after she was caught in the flood of seawater and propelled down the tunnel along which she'd been trying to escape, the flashlight continued to work, and she was able to see sharp rocks in the jagged roof passing scant inches above her head, but then she slammed into a protrusion of the gallery and the torch was knocked out of her grasp, plunging her into darkness.

If there had been time to think she would have panicked, but everything happened so quickly that she reacted by reflex. Somehow she managed to stay afloat. Instead of struggling she allowed the current to carry her with it, concentrating all her efforts on just keeping her head above water. A pocket of air trapped in her clothes increased her buoyancy. Floating on her back, she expected at any moment to feel the jagged rocks in the roof of the tunnel tear into her face, but miraculously this didn't happen, and moments later she realized why.

The rising tide had swept her into a cavern that was about as big as two good-sized rooms, dimensions she was able to determine because it was illuminated by a fragile shaft of sunlight coming through a funnel-like opening high in the roof. Numbed by the bitterly cold water, she kept her eyes on the source of the light, half-conscious that she was being lifted ever closer to it by the rising tide. But she could also feel her strength ebbing away, and knew it could only be a matter of minutes before she was too weak to keep herself afloat.

Suddenly the water under her surged, and she felt herself being propelled upward. The force with which she was lifted was so great that it squeezed the air out of her lungs, and for a long moment she was unable to breathe. The next seconds were a blur in which the smooth surface of the funnel flashed past her eyes, merging with images in her mind's eye, kaleidoscopic fragments of memory that were jumbled together without any connecting links. It was as if she were lying under a waterfall, face upward, as the torrent thundered into her mouth and nostrils. Reason had fled, but an inner voice still warned that unless she tried to breathe her lungs would burst.

Finally, when the pressure inside her was unbearable, she inhaled deeply, aware that it might be the last breath she would ever take, yet no longer caring: all she wanted now was for the anguish to end. Water filled her mouth and nose. She felt as if she was being suffocated. Then even that sensation ended as consciousness slipped away and she was enveloped by darkness.

40

Every day of the year, regardless of the weather, Hamish McKinnon met the ferry from Oban at Craignure, loaded mail into his van, and set out to make deliveries throughout the island of Mull.

It was a job he had done since he returned from World War II as a young man of twenty-four, and in the thirty years since that time he had never missed a day's work or failed to meet the ferry when it arrived on its first trip of the day at 8:10 A.M. Hamish had become an institution among the islanders, who relied on him both for mail and the small grocery items he carried in his van, which he sold to them for the same price they would have paid if they'd made the long journey to Tobermory, Ulva, or Fionnphort. It was a convenience on which they had come to depend, and the profit he made, meager though it was, enabled him to stay on Mull, the island he'd fallen in love with as a teenager on a day trip from Glasgow.

Jobs were scarce on Mull and many of the islanders had been obliged to leave and take up employment on the mainland, but Hamish McKinnon had managed to hang on and carve out a niche for himself. Although he was now in his mid-fifties, he had the smooth cheeks of a young boy and sandy hair just beginning to thin on top. His good-natured manner and thoughtfulness had made him well-liked by the taciturn islanders, who also depended on him for island gossip, which he delivered with a relish that made his arrival an event most of them eagerly awaited each day.

Hamish made his own schedule and always allowed time for stops at various points on the island to admire its spectacular views: Torosay

Castle through the mists of early morning; Loch Na Keal when the afternoon sun shimmered like beaten gold on its smooth surface; Ben More silhouetted against an azure sky. But the sight he never tired of seeing daily was the blowhole south of Fionnphort, where the Ross of Mull plunged to the sea.

Tourists from the United States had told him it resembled the geysers in Yellowstone National Park, but this meant very little to Hamish, who, except for the war years which he spent as a medical orderly at a naval base on the Clyde, had never traveled farther away from Mull than an occasional visit to what remained of his family in Glasgow. To him the blowhole was a wonder of nature that ceaselessly amazed him, and each day as he came to the end of his rounds he would park his van off the road and walk the few hundred yards across broken ground to where, when the tide was high, a fountain of water spurted up through a hole in the rock to heights of thirty or forty feet. He knew it was caused by incoming tides traveling at high speed over extremely flat sands and surging through subterranean tunnels, until they reached a hollowed-out chamber where the churning water was forced up through a narrow funnel-shaped opening to create a jet that spurted high into the air, but he preferred to believe the legend that the phenomenon was caused by spirits who lived inside the mountain and wallowed playfully inside the caves at high tide.

This day Hamish was surprised to discover that the flotsam ejected through the blowhole included what appeared at first sight to be the body of a harbor seal. It wasn't until he looked closer that he realized the shape he had spotted on the spume-flecked rocks to one side of where the column of water pulsated skyward was that of a young woman. At first he thought she was dead, but when he knelt next to her he saw she was breathing and, drawing on training he had received in the Royal Navy, he applied artificial respiration. At first it appeared to have little effect, but then the woman began coughing up water and, turning her head to one side, suddenly vomited. She opened her eyes but they were glazed, and it was apparent that she was barely conscious.

"Rest easy, now, lassie," McKinnon murmured as he lifted her in his arms. "I'll have you in good hands in no time at all."

Moving as quickly as he could over the uneven ground, McKinnon gently loaded the woman into the back of his van, got in behind the wheel, and started the engine. Twenty minutes later he stopped in front of Dr. Ramsay's house in Fionnphort and rang the bell. The door was opened by a rotund man smoking a briar pipe, who smiled broadly and said, "Good morning to you, Hamish, have you brought my medical journals?"

"Aye, doctor, and a patient along with 'em."

He led the other man to the van and opened the rear doors. Dr. Ramsay, displaying unexpected agility for a man of his bulk, climbed inside and examined the young woman lying among the undelivered groceries.

"She's in a bad way," he said. "We'd better get her inside."

The two men lifted her out of the van and carried her upstairs.

"Is it an emergency, John?" called the doctor's wife, a plump, sweet-faced woman.

"Aye, Flora," her husband replied. "A poor woman who's half drowned. I'm putting her in the spare room. Will you bring some hot water bottles as soon as you're able?"

Flora Ramsay, accustomed to having emergency cases under her roof, there being no hospital on the island, disappeared into the kitchen and put a huge copper kettle on the stove.

"Will she live, doctor?" McKinnon asked after they had covered the woman with blankets.

"She's in shock," the other man replied. "Where on earth did you find her?"

"Down by the blowhole. She must have got too close."

The doctor shook his head. "This woman's been under water a lot longer than that."

"I gave her artificial respiration," McKinnon said. "Was it the right thing to do?"

"If you hadn't she'd have died, Hamish," Dr. Ramsay replied, looking into the woman's eyes with a tiny flashlight.

The pinprick of light burned into Janna's retina, then abruptly went out. She heard a voice say, "She's coming to."

Opening her eyes, she saw the blurred outline of faces, then the light came again, even brighter than before, and this time it remained. As her vision came into focus, Janna found herself looking into the glare of a tiny flashlight which, when it suddenly clicked off, left a reddish-orange halo that took a long time to dissolve.

"Can you hear me?" the man leaning over her asked.

Janna heard his words but didn't have the energy to attempt a response; instead, she looked up at the man, whose pale eyes seemed strangely enlarged by the thick-lensed spectacles he was wearing, then turned her gaze to the pink-cheeked woman standing next to him.

"How are you feeling?" the man asked.

"I . . ." Janna's words trailed away, but she tried again and managed to say, "My husband is dead. . . ."

"No, lassie, he's waiting downstairs. I'm Dr. Ramsay and this is my wife, Flora. You've had an accident. The man who delivers mail on the island found you down by the blowhole near the caves at the foot of the Ross of Mull. Can you recall how you got there?"

"Derek, alive?" Janna muttered the words half to herself.

"Your husband told the local police you were missing," the doctor said. "That's how we discovered who you are. We let him know you were safe immediately, of course, and he's been waiting three days to see you."

"Three days?"

"Aye, that's how long you've been unconscious," Dr. Ramsay said. "Your husband tells us you were lost in the caves, and we've been wondering how you got out when they are completely flooded at high tide."

When Janna didn't answer, Mrs. Ramsay said to her husband, "She's still very weak, John. I'll tell her husband to come back later."

"No," Janna protested in a hoarse croak, "I want to see him."

Dr. Ramsay took her temperature, and while the thermometer was in her mouth, put his stethoscope to her chest.

"You're in surprisingly good condition considering what you've been through," he commented when he finished his examination, "but are you sure you're strong enough to talk with your husband now?"

Janna nodded.

"All right," the doctor said, "but only a short visit. I don't want you having a relapse."

Janna closed her eyes. Her whole body ached. She felt as if a short circuit had occurred somewhere deep inside her brain that made it impossible for her to connect with the present. Her recollections of the moments before she'd been engulfed by the tide were hazy, and each time she attempted to remember what happened, all she could recall was that Derek had vanished.

"Hello, darling."

She opened her eyes and saw her husband smiling down at her. He leaned forward and kissed her lightly on the cheek. "God, you don't know how glad I am to see you," he said. "I've been waiting downstairs for days. How are you feeling?"

"Confused."

"I'm not surprised. Dr. Ramsay says you hit your head pretty hard and thinks you may have suffered a concussion."

Janna raised her hand, felt her head was bandaged, and wondered why she wasn't feeling any pain. "I tried to find you."

"Lord, what a nightmare!" Southworth shook his head and sat down on the edge of the bed. "After I left you I went a short distance down the tunnel and came to a junction of galleries that fanned out in all directions. When I turned back I got lost."

"But I kept shouting your name, surely you must have heard me?"

"I was out like a light." Southworth turned to display a gauze pad held in place by strips of adhesive tape at the back of his head. "I lost my footing on those damned slime-covered rocks and slammed my head against something."

"But how did you manage to get out when the tide was coming in?"

"Sheer luck." He shook his head at the recollection. "When I came to I started looking for you but got hopelessly lost in that maze of tunnels and ended up in the main chamber at the entrance to the cave. The tide still hadn't turned, and I had to decide whether to try finding you myself, without the flashlight, or get help. I thought it would be at least an hour or two before the incoming tide reached the caves, so I drove back to Fionnphort and told the local constable what had happened. He arranged a search party, but by the time they got to the caves they were flooded. If I'd known the tide came in that fast . . ."

He left the sentence unfinished and brushed away a strand of hair that had fallen across Janna's cheek. She closed her eyes and tried to focus on what her husband had told her. It all sounded completely logical, yet she couldn't rid herself of the feeling that his explanation was too pat.

"Didn't the man who told you about the caves warn you about the tides?" she asked.

"If he had, do you think I would have left you in them?" he asked in an injured tone.

"I guess not," Janna murmured.

"You look tired out," he said. "I think the kindest thing I can do is let you get some rest. Dr. Ramsay wants to keep you here until you're back on your feet. I suggested that it might be better to take you to a regular hospital, in Oban or Glasgow, but he didn't seem to think that was necessary. He feels you'll get more peace and quiet here on Mull than you would in the city."

"Will you come and see me tomorrow?" she asked.

"I wish I could," he said, taking her hand, "but I've got to talk with the Countess in Paris, and after that there are half a dozen meetings I've lined up with bankers in Geneva."

"Can't they wait?"

"You know how bankers are, they don't like broken appointments."

Janna wanted to weep. Derek didn't seem to understand how utterly vulnerable she felt. His lack of sensitivity made her realize that the dreams she had woven about rekindling the romance in their marriage had all been illusions, but pride prevented the display of her hurt. "When are you leaving?"

"This afternoon," he replied.

"Are you taking the car?"

"I'd better," he said. "You aren't going to be in any condition to make a drive of that distance alone, and the flight from Glasgow to London only takes about an hour."

All Janna wanted was to be left alone. For a full minute neither of them spoke, then Derek put his arms around her shoulders, kissed her on the lips, and smiled. "Take care of yourself," he said. "You're in good hands, and we'll be together when I get back from my trip."

Janna listened to the sound of his footsteps disappearing down the stairs and tears welled into her eyes. She was still sobbing when the door opened and Mrs. Ramsay bustled into the room.

"Now, lassie, don't go fretting yourself," the doctor's wife said. "It's a sad thing your husband has to leave, but you'll be well enough to join him in no time at all."

"How long will I be here?" Janna asked, wiping her cheeks with a handkerchief the other woman gave her.

"That's for my husband to say, but I don't think it'll be more than a week or so at the most. Just long enough for you to get your strength back."

"Can somebody bring my things from the hotel?" she asked.

"Och, I've already arranged that. Jeannie Macneill's coming over this very afternoon. . . ." Mrs. Ramsay paused as the sound of the doorbell echoed through the house. "That'll be her now, more than likely."

She went downstairs and appeared minutes later with the wife of the owner of the Skellig Arms Hotel, who was carrying a suitcase and a large paper bag.

"Well, now, and how is the patient feeling today?" Mrs. Macneill asked, setting her load down at the end of the bed.

"A lot better, thank you," Janna replied.

"And looking much bonnier than when I last saw you, which was the day Hamish McKinnon found you down by the blowhole," the other woman said in her soft, lilting voice. "Although how you got there is still puzzling us all."

"I'm not sure myself," Janna said. "The last thing I remember was being in a cave that was rapidly filling with seawater, and then being propelled upward."

"So Hamish was right," Mrs. Ramsay said. "He's been blathering to everybody who'll listen that you were forced up through the blowhole. We all took it with a pinch of salt, but from what you say it sounds like that is what happened."

"You're a very lucky woman," Jean Macneill said. "And I thank the Lord you've been spared, but I still can't understand what you were doing in those caves at all after the warning Andrew McDonald gave your husband."

"McDonald—warning?"

"Do you remember the man at the *ceilidh* who told your husband about the pictographs?"

"The one Derek helped to his car?"

"Aye, that's Andrew right enough. He swears he warned your husband about the tides being treacherous. It's the flatness of the sands, you see. Once the tide turns and starts coming in, a galloping horse couldn't outrun it."

"And Mr. McDonald warned Derek?"

Janna's two visitors glanced at each other. "So Andrew says," the hotel owner's wife replied, "but he's a terrible drunk and no good at all at remembering his own name half the time."

There was an awkward silence. "Didn't your husband say anything about it?" Jean Macneill asked.

"I don't remember."

Again silence settled on the room.

"I'd better be off, then, or my husband's going to begin wondering where I've got to," Mrs. Macneill announced briskly. "You'll find all your things in the suitcase, and there's a wee cake I baked for you in the paper bag."

"Thank you," Janna said.

"You're more than welcome. I'll just look in tomorrow to see how you're getting along."

The two women left the room together. Alone, Janna desperately tried to piece together in her mind the exact sequence of events that had led to her getting trapped in the cave, and to recall any mention Derek might have made about the danger of incoming tides. But she couldn't recall anything. She was left with the nagging suspicion that what happened to her had not been an accident.

During the days that followed, Janna tried unsuccessfully to erase these thoughts from her mind. They were still there a week later when Dr. Ramsay finally declared her well enough to travel. And they continued to gnaw at her during the taxi ride from Fionnphort to Craignure, the ferry to Oban, and the train to Glasgow, where she boarded a British Airways jet to London.

She had telephoned her chauffeur from Glasgow, telling him what flight she would be on, and he was at Heathrow to meet her. When she entered the house on South Audley Street the telephone was ringing, and when Janna picked up the receiver she heard a voice say, "This is Dave Wilson, I've been trying to reach you for hours. Your secretary told me you were on holiday in Scotland and gave me the number of the hotel where you were staying on Mull, but the owner said there had been some kind of accident and that you were under the care of a Dr. Ramsay. I called him this morning, but you'd just left for Glasgow. Are you all right?"

"Still a bit bruised. . . ."

"What happened?"

Janna hesitated. "It's a long story."

"I'd like to hear it," the lawyer said.

"Not on the phone."

"Can you meet me?"

"When?"

"As soon as possible," he said, adding quickly, "It's very important."

"Where are you?" she asked.

"At Basil Matson's office on Chancery Lane." Wilson gave her the address. "I have a plane to catch in a couple of hours, so come as soon as you can."

"You're beginning to make it sound like a matter of life and death," she said.

"It may very well be," the attorney replied.

After Janna hung up she noticed there was something different about the room, and realized that the Bonnard she had bought Derek as a gift on their first anniversary had been replaced by Egon Schiele's bizarre portrait of a dead woman holding a child inside her black cloak. It had always triggered a feeling of revulsion in Janna. The pink-faced infant stared out at her wildly, pupils centered in their whites, mouth agape in wonderment and horror. It appeared to be trapped and yet unwilling to separate itself from the corpse of the woman inside which it crouched. Outsized hands cupped and clawed at the darkness surrounding it, one finger projected beyond its natal sack into the void beyond.

Hurrying upstairs, she showered and changed into clean clothes. Her body was still badly bruised from where she had been battered against the rocks in the cave, and the wound on her head, which had required a dozen stitches to close, still hadn't healed, although it was hidden under her hair.

Instead of summoning her chauffeur, Janna took a taxi to Chancery Lane and got out at the address Dave Wilson had given her. It was a gray stone building that appeared as if it might once have been a private dwelling, but now it housed the offices of solicitors and barristers whose names were listed on a brightly polished brass plate to one side of the front door.

"May I help you, ma'am?" a uniformed doorman asked.

"I'm looking for Mr. Basil Matson."

"Second floor," the doorman said, ushering her into an antiquated elevator. "Turn right when you get out, and you'll find his offices at the end of the hallway."

Following these instructions, Janna found herself in front of a glassed-in door on which gold letters spelled out the names of Basil Matson and his associates. It opened before she could knock, and Dave Wilson took her hand. "The doorman called to say you were on the way up," he said, looking at her searchingly. "How are you?"

"Still quite weak," she replied.

"From what Dr. Ramsay told me on the phone I gather Derek didn't travel back with you?"

"He left Mull a week ago. There were some meetings he had to attend in Paris and Geneva."

"When will he be back in London?"

"It's hard to say; Derek makes his own schedule. Maybe a week or ten days, why?"

Instead of answering, he ushered her into an oak-paneled office that was furnished with overstuffed leather chairs, a sofa, a partner's desk, and gilt-framed replicas of etchings by Hogarth portraying chaotic mob scenes inside eighteenth-century courtrooms. Standing with his back to the window was a tall thin man wearing a morning suit, white shirt, and black tie.

"I want you to meet Basil Matson," Wilson said. "Basil, this is Janna Southworth."

"Pleased to meet you," the British solicitor said. "I've followed reports of your business successes during the last decade with great interest. May I offer you some tea?"

"No, thank you," Janna replied, sitting in a leather chair in front of the partner's desk.

"David?"

"Not for me, either," Wilson said. "I'm cutting things pretty fine, so if it's all right with both of you I'd like to get down to why we're here."

"What on earth's all this about?" Janna asked.

"You remember our conversation at the Savoy a couple of weeks ago?"

"Of course."

"Well, I contacted Basil before I went back to New York and asked him to arrange for somebody to make a few discreet inquiries into your husband's background."

"I do a lot of divorce work," the British solicitor explained. "It's a much more complicated business here than it is in America, and often requires my using a private investigator to get the evidence the courts need."

Dave Wilson opened his briefcase and took out a manila folder. "Basil had this material waiting for me when I arrived in London yesterday," he said. "And before leaving New York I called Anna—"

"What has she got to do with this?" Janna asked.

"I'll get to that in a minute," Wilson replied. "But before I do, I want you to know that she made me promise I would only reveal the substance of her conversation if I thought the situation serious enough to warrant it." He tapped the manila folder. "After reading what's in here, I decided it is."

"Would you please tell me—"

"I gather Derek told you his parents were dead," Wilson said, cutting her short.

"They were killed in the blitz," Janna said.

He handed her a glossy photograph, showing an elderly couple seated on a park bench. "This was taken a week ago. The people in it, both obviously very much alive, are your husband's mother and father.

As for the family estates—well, they live on a small pension in a council house at Clapham Junction. But that's only the tip of the iceberg. Derek Southworth married three women prior to you, all wealthy, and he's fathered children by them all."

Janna felt her stomach churn. "So he isn't sterile," she murmured.

"Obviously not," Wilson said, "and neither was he ever an officer in the Royal Air Force. Basil's investigator actually talked with a man who was part of the crew in Derek's plane when it was hit over Berlin. It seems the pilot was able to land in an open field moments before dying from loss of blood. Your husband changed uniforms with him, apparently because he wanted the Germans to put him in a prisoner-of-war camp for officers."

"It seems to have marked the beginning of his propensity for inventing identities for himself," Matson remarked.

"Why, for God's sake?" Janna asked.

"It would take a psychiatrist to answer that," the British solicitor replied.

"But he had nothing to gain from marrying me—"

"Wrong." Wilson interrupted. "His firm, Regent Securities, was on the verge of bankruptcy when he married you. He was desperate to raise capital, and you provided him with the very thing he needed."

"The land I inherited from Janet Taylor?"

Wilson nodded. "But he didn't use it as collateral for a loan, he sold it outright to G. K. Wong."

Janna experienced a terrible sinking sensation as she remembered the documents Derek had asked her to sign. Because at that time she knew so little about business and trusted him completely, she hadn't checked them over thoroughly. He assured her they were in order, and she simply took his word for it. Ever since then, whenever she had asked about the land, he had assured her that all the money he had borrowed against it had been repaid and that it was still being used as a children's playground. The revelation that he'd really sold it outright to G. K. Wong made her angrier than anything else she had heard so far. She was shattered by the realization that Janet's stubborn pride in holding out against G.K. had all been for nothing. She felt betrayed, and it was only with great difficulty that she managed to control her emotions sufficiently to hear the rest of what the two men had to tell her.

"Now I want you to know what Anna told me when I talked with her on the phone before leaving New York," Wilson said.

Janna listened numbly as the man who had been Mark's attorney repeated what he had heard from Anna about Derek Southworth's activities at Miranda de Ebro: how he had been crucified and the terrible revenge he had taken against his tormentors; the ruthless means he had employed to take control of all illegal operations inside the camp; the profits he had made through extorting money from inmates.

"Why didn't Anna tell me all this before I married Derek?" Janna asked. "I know they didn't meet, but surely she must have recognized his name—"

"You're right," Wilson admitted, "and she was planning to tell you everything when you arrived to stay with her in New York before you were married, but her stroke made that impossible. By the time she regained her speech and the use of her arms, you'd already been married to Derek for some time and appeared to be quite happy, and she didn't want to risk destroying your relationship when it seemed to be working out so well. She feels you should know now because she's convinced that your husband is a very sick man. I agree with her wholeheartedly."

Janna stared out of the rain-streaked window. After what happened in the caves on Mull she had suspected that Derek had tried to kill her, but now that she'd heard Dave Wilson's revelations her suspicions were more than confirmed. Derek had been in St. Moritz when Genevieve died, in Singapore when Janet was murdered, and could have been in New York when somebody tried to push Anna in front of a subway train. When she confided these thoughts to Wilson and Matson, they exchanged glances as if to suggest that what she had told them only confirmed possibilities they had already discussed.

"I've got to get away from him," she said.

"I gather you were married in England as well as America," Matson observed.

"At Derek's urging," Janna replied.

"I'm afraid getting a divorce here won't be easy," the British solicitor said. "Chances are he'd fight it, which means you'd have to prove adultery, and that's one of the few indiscretions my investigator wasn't able to uncover."

"What options do I have?" she asked.

"After a five-year separation, divorce would be more or less automatic."

"You can stay in California and run the American side of the business," Wilson added. "I don't think it'll be too difficult for me to

convince Derek that splitting Star Industries into two distinct and separate halves will be for his own good, particularly when I let him know
what we've uncovered about his past. And the sooner you leave for Los
Angeles the happier I'll be, because I'm convinced that Derek is not
only a pathological liar but a cold-blooded killer, as well.''

41

LOS ANGELES: August 10, 1984

The helicopter, a Bell 206 Jet Ranger, shivered as the pitch of its
engines rose to a shrill whine and its rotors slowly lifted it clear of the
pad on top of the skyscraper in Century City.

It was an ascent Janna had made many times with Felix Ervin at the
controls of the craft he used to commute between his isolated hilltop
ranch overlooking Santa Barbara and his offices in the same high-rise
that housed the headquarters of Star Industries in Century City. She
also knew him to be a skilled pilot, but her body still tensed as the
aircraft rose from its minuscule perch and she found herself suspended
in midair with nothing between herself and the space below but the thin
plastic from which the bubble of the cockpit was made.

"All right?" Ervin shouted over the roar of the engine.

She nodded, but her fists were still clenched as she gazed down at
the view unfolding below. It was almost nine years since she had made
her departure from London at Dave Wilson's urging, a period during
which she had prospered beyond her wildest imaginings, thanks in
large part to the advice and encouragement she had received from Felix
Ervin. Since he first encouraged Janna to join him in various projects
after she took over supervision of Star Industries in California, they had
invested heavily together in numerous undertakings, including financing much of the construction that had converted the back lot at 20th
Century-Fox into the canyons of steel and glass skyscrapers she now saw
like stalagmites below her.

The profits from these enterprises had turned Star Industries into one
of the richest privately held venture capital firms in the world, but in
recent years its assets had been severely strained through losses incurred by the European division of the company, which was still ope-

rated out of London by Derek Southworth. After Janna sought sanctuary from her husband in California, Dave Wilson had drawn up documents that legally established that she would be solely responsible for running the firm in the United States, while Southworth's domain would encompass the British Isles and Europe, with the rest of the world divided equally between them. Initially Southworth had contested the arrangement, but when confronted with what the New York attorney knew about the Englishman's past, Derek had signed, yet he still stubbornly refused to agree to a divorce. Janna would have preferred the complete separation the latter would have ensured, but she was also aware of the damage Star Industries would suffer if it was split up as community property, so she had learned to live with the arrangement.

Under the terms of the agreement, although still legally married to Southworth, Janna was free of him in all respects except that she couldn't remarry, and as that was the least of her desires, it had seemed a small price to pay for her otherwise complete liberation.

But she and Southworth were still linked by Star Industries, which they jointly owned, and the losses incurred by the European division were debited against profits the company accrued in the United States. For a while this had proved to be a workable situation, for even though Southworth continued to make bad investments, Janna had accomplished such spectacular gains that Star Industries was rich enough to absorb the losses. But recently the situation had reached a point where Southworth's repeated ineptness had resulted in losses so huge they threatened the stability of the company, and Janna realized that something drastic must be done, and done quickly.

The situation had deteriorated after the Countess died and the operations of the job placement agency she had been running for so many years came to an abrupt halt. Janna had accepted the Countess's death as a blessing in disguise, but Southworth, who had become totally dependent on the inside knowledge he received from the Countess's girls, was shattered. He made one bad investment after another and, like an unskilled gambler, tried to recoup his losses by doubling up on his stakes, rapidly getting Star Industries deeper and deeper into debt.

Finally, after years of bailing Southworth out of one disaster after another, Janna sought Felix Ervin's help in resolving the dilemma. He had advised her to try and buy out her estranged husband's share of Star Industries. "It's the only logical thing you can do," he told her. "If you file for divorce he will claim the firm is community property and probably be awarded fifty percent of its assets. Then there will be nothing to keep him from selling his share, and you will have lost control of your own business. As things stand he's deeply in debt and will probably accept any reasonable offer. Pay him a lump sum up front and a small percentage of the firm's profits over a long period of time. That way he won't be tempted to do anything to shake investor confidence in Star Industries. But make everything contingent on his signing a quitclaim deed to any future rights, title, or interest in the firm. Wait a year or so, then file for a divorce, and you end up maintaining control as well as getting your freedom."

Janna realized it was brilliant advice and lost no time implementing it. But rather than having Dave Wilson or one of the other half-dozen lawyers she kept on retainer deliver the proposal—and risk Southworth's responding through his attorneys, which could only result in an endless round of negotiations that would probably produce a stalemate—Janna decided to make the offer to Derek in person. Under the guise of calling a Board of Directors meeting, at which his presence was required, she had telephoned him in London and asked him to fly to Los Angeles to attend the meeting she had scheduled for 10 A.M. on Monday morning. Her stomach churned at the thought of the upcoming meeting, a feeling that was heightened when the helicopter hit an air pocket and fell two or three hundred feet before Felix Ervin steadied the craft.

"Sorry!" he shouted. "The heat makes for a bumpy ride at low altitudes."

Janna glanced at the altimeter and saw it registered almost 3,000 feet, high enough for her to see the whole of Century City spread out below, flanked on one side by Westwood, and on the other by Beverly Hills. To the east stood the Los Angeles Coliseum, where the track and field events of the XXIII Olympiad were still under way, and in the west she saw matches in progress at the new tennis center on the campus of the University of California. But what caught and held her attention was an overhead view of the section of Wilshire Boulevard between Westwood and Beverly Hills that had become known as the "Golden Mile."

"There's what I really brought you up here to see," Ervin said.

Janna looked at where he was pointing and saw Wellington House, dominating all the other high-rises because of its size and the uniqueness of its design. Rising like a huge fluted column of burnished bronze, it stood glistening in the bright morning sun, its glass-sheathed exterior appearing more the work of a sculptor than an architect.

"It looks even better from up here than it does from the ground," Janna said, raising her voice to make herself heard over the flap of the rotor.

Ervin nodded and busied himself at the controls as he readied the helicopter for a landing on the pad on top of Wellington House. To Janna it seemed an impossibly small target, and in an effort to hide her anxiety she mentally reviewed the various stages through which she'd seen Wellington House go before reaching its present state of near-completion.

First had been Felix's conviction that extremely rich people no longer wanted to live in sprawling mansions in Bel Air or Beverly Hills. "Individuals with that kind of wealth live in constant fear," he told Janna when he initially proposed that they become partners in building Wellington House. "They know they're walking targets for all kinds of crazies. What they really want is a luxurious environment that is built from the ground up to guarantee them absolute security."

With this as his principal objective, Ervin had commissioned Charles Billson, one of America's leading architects, to come up with a concept for a high-rise building that would incorporate both the ultimate in luxury and the latest state-of-the-art security devices. The latter were specifically designed for the project by Honeywell and included infra-red, microwave, and ultrasonic detection systems; access control through coded passcards; voiceprint locks; closed-circuit surveillance cameras with low-light lenses and automatic zoom controls; computerized central monitoring stations; perimeter shock detection systems; and panic buttons in every room that would immediately alert guards on twenty-four-hour duty in the lobby in the event of an emergency. There was even a centralized computer programmed to keep on file the medical data of every tenant, including the name and phone number of doctors, medications, and special precautions to be observed in emergency treatments.

As an added security measure, Charles Billson had also included a design feature that made Wellington House unique among the luxury condominiums along the Golden Mile: private elevators, big enough to accommodate cars, into which tenants could drive directly from Wilshire Boulevard and remain behind the wheel as they and their automobiles were whisked to the level on which they lived.

Because these elevators were the only ones of their kind in the world, Wellington House had attracted considerable media attention. In a local paper, one columnist had suggested that people who purchased condominiums there were motivated more by fear than the desire for luxury. "The truth is," he had written, "that today's super-rich treasure one thing above all else: the promise of personal security. They demand anonymity because they live in constant fear of being kidnapped, robbed, extorted, even killed. The sad fact is, more often than not, that people able to afford millions for a place to live have accumulated their wealth by means that are both ruthless and beyond the law. There is blood on the fortunes they have secreted away in numbered Swiss bank accounts, and the path leading to their luxurious existences at such sanctuaries as Wellington House is littered with the corpses of those they have exploited for profit. The occupants of the opulent bastions along the Golden Mile have good reason to live in fear, for they know better than anybody else that vengeance has a far reach and a long memory."

The engine pitch increased to an even shriller whine as Felix Ervin skillfully settled the helicopter onto the landing pad and released the controls. Although now in his late sixties, he was still a handsome man with a quiet, forceful presence that somehow belied his age. His left cheek and jaw were marked by small patches of whitish scar tissue, but they had been there two decades ago when Janna first met him at the Zurich stock exchange, and they in no way diminished the aura of supreme masculinity he emanated. Nor had age slowed him down; he maintained a schedule that would have exhausted a much younger man and still managed to find time to indulge his various hobbies.

A main interest of his was building a library that contained some of the best documentary footage shot during World War II, including films from German and Japanese as well as Allied camera crews. Many of the sequences had been taken by official cameramen assigned to record military endeavors which had received little publicity during the actual hostilities and so portrayed happenings that weren't well known. In order to write his hobby off as a tax deduction, Ervin had created a firm that specialized in renting the footage to producers making films using World War II as a background and had reinvested the profits in hiring experts to develop special effects, particularly holography, that had been used in a number of top-grossing feature movies.

As Janna watched him take off his headphones, she remembered how, the first time they met, he had made a pass at her, but ever since then their relationship had been strictly platonic. In the decade since Janna had been legally separated from Derek Southworth—a period during which she had resumed her maiden name—Felix Ervin had not only been her partner in numerous business ventures but had also become her most trusted confidant and friend. Their offices were in close proximity, and they frequently dined together at Spago or Ma Maison. Now they were equal partners in Wellington House, a venture in which they had jointly invested almost $100 million.

"Keep your head down," Ervin cautioned, holding the door of the cockpit open for her.

Even though he had switched the engine off, the rotor was still turning slowly, and Janna moved at a crouch as she followed her partner across the landing pad to where some steps led down to the rooftop.

Taking a plastic card from his wallet, Ervin inserted it into a slot at the side of the door and punched a numbered code into a panel with buttons. There was a brief pause as the information he had entered was checked by the computerized central monitor located in the lobby thirty-five stories below; then the lock clicked back, allowing the door to open automatically. Inside was a small elevator they used to travel one floor down to the lobby of the penthouse.

Janna had visited it on numerous other occasions during the course of construction, yet she was still impressed by what she saw when she entered the huge double doors. Its 9,000 square feet looked even larger because the penthouse was still without carpets and drapes, but it didn't require much imagination for her to see in her mind's eye how wonderful the place would look when it was finally completed: the foyer filled with paintings; ten bedrooms equipped; twelve bathrooms marbled; the climate-controlled wine cellar fully stocked; crystal chandeliers gleaming; the private screening room furnished with plush seating; video-stereo entertainment console; and a kitchen outfitted with equipment that would delight the most discerning chef.

"What do you think?" Ervin asked.

"I doubt if there's a condominium like it in the world," she said. "When will it be finished?"

He shrugged. "You know what it's like trying to get an architect or builder to make a firm commitment about completion dates, but the last I heard was about another week or so."

"For the whole building?"

"That might take longer, but at least they've promised to have the penthouse ready," Ervin replied.

"Have you fixed an asking price?"

"Twenty million."

Janna gazed around the sunlit expanse. "It's going to be a spectacular home for somebody. I just can't help wondering who has that kind of money to spend on a condominium."

"How about Janna Maxell-Hunter?" he asked. "You're one of the wealthiest women in America, although you're having a hard time accepting the fact."

Janna knew Ervin was right: on paper she was worth millions, yet in her mind she was still the only girl at Genevieve Fleury's finishing school who didn't have a regular monthly allowance, who had to borrow clothes from friends whenever there was a social occasion that required a formal outfit, who had tried so hard to remedy the situation by playing the stock market. Acquiring wealth was one thing, she now knew, but feeling rich quite another. It was an adjustment she still hadn't been able to make.

"I guess you're right," she admitted.

"I know I am," Ervin said. "There's no reason in the world why you shouldn't live here."

"You're beginning to sound like a real estate salesman." She laughed.

"That's exactly what I am, and so are you, until we get rid of all the units in Wellington House," he replied.

Janna walked out onto the enormous landscaped balcony and stood looking at the view. To the south she could see jets lifting off the runway at Los Angeles International Airport, which had been newly remodeled to accommodate the flood of visitors who had arrived for the Olympic Games, and beyond that the outline of Catalina Island etched like a bank of clouds against the azure sky. In the west was a curve of beach linking Santa Monica with Malibu, and behind that the sweep of mountains extending from the Pacific Ocean to downtown Los Angeles. Thirty-five stories below, traffic snaked along the Golden Mile like a brightly speckled serpent slithering between glistening canyons of concrete and glass.

"Maybe when I get this business with Derek settled," she mused, turning back into the penthouse, "I'll give some more thought to—"

She stopped in mid-sentence, suddenly aware that Felix Ervin was nowhere to be seen. Assuming he had gone into one of the other rooms while she was on the balcony, she went in search of him, but without success. Puzzled, she went back into the lobby and walked down the short passageway that led to the garage, an area that had been incorporated onto the same floor that the penthouse occupied. The huge elevator that was designed to raise cars from street level was still being installed, and when Janna peered down the open shaft she could see straight down for thirty-five floors to where workmen were welding steel girders to the roof of the lift.

Hearing a sound behind her she swung around and saw Felix Ervin standing immediately behind her. He was highly agitated. He was breathing rapidly, his cheeks were flushed, and there was an expression on his face that Janna had never seen before: intense, strained, eyes slightly glazed.

"You scared the daylights out of me!" she exclaimed. "Are you all right?"

He nodded. "There's nothing to be frightened about up here," he replied. "You're standing in one of the safest places in the world."

"I looked all over for you," she said.

"I went up to fasten the tie-downs on the helicopter. A sudden gust of wind could blow it off the landing pad."

"Wind on a day like this?"

"It doesn't take much," he assured her, "and I'd rather be safe than sorry."

They walked back to the penthouse in silence, and by the time they reached it Ervin was once again his usual calm, controlled self.

"What about our meeting with the construction supervisor?" Janna asked. "I thought that's why we came."

"I just talked to him on the house phone," Ervin said. "He'd planned to come up on the automobile lift because the other elevators aren't working yet, but they're still welding beams to it, and there's no other way of getting here."

"So we've had a wasted trip."

"Not really," he replied. "You saw Wellington House from the air for the first time."

"I guess that made coming worthwhile," she admitted, "but I've got to be getting back."

"Why so soon?"

"I've got a lot of contracts to read before Derek arrives on Monday morning."

"Is that when he's coming?"

She nodded. "And I can't say I'm looking forward to seeing him."

"It's a confrontation that had to happen sooner or later," Ervin said. "Better that you get it over with before he drags Star Industries into more bad investments."

"What if he refuses my offer?"

"He won't," Ervin assured her. "I've dealt with men like Derek Southworth all my life. When the pressure's on, they roll over and play dead."

"I hope you're right," Janna said, "because if he doesn't let me buy him out I'm in trouble."

"There are ways to make him change his mind," Ervin observed, as they rode the small elevator that was separate from the main bank of lifts and only connected the penthouse with the roof.

"Such as?" Janna asked.

"Let's cross that bridge when we come to it," he replied. When they reached the helicopter, he climbed immediately into the cockpit and strapped himself into the seat behind the controls.

Puzzled, Janna clambered in beside him and tensed herself for the lift-off. She remembered what Ervin had said about the tie-downs and wondered why he hadn't unfastened them, but before she could ask the craft rose in the air, fell away from the roof, and headed in the direction of Century City.

It was a journey of less than ten minutes, and throughout it Janna's unease continued to mount. Normally she would have attributed her anxiety simply to being in a helicopter, which always caused her considerable distress, but this time she knew it was triggered by Felix's strange behavior at the penthouse. She couldn't rid herself of the weird expression on his face when she turned and saw him standing behind her at the open elevator shaft. Nor could she account for the mystery of the tie-downs. She wasn't sure how tie-downs worked, and it was possible they automatically released themselves, but if this wasn't the case then Felix Ervin had deliberately lied about his abrupt disappearance, and she couldn't for the life of her think why.

42

When they landed on the roof of the skyscraper housing Star Industries, Janna climbed out of the helicopter and ran at a crouch until she was clear of the rotor, but Ervin remained behind the controls and immediately took off again, this time heading north toward his ranch in the Santa Ynez mountains, close to where President Reagan lived when he wasn't at the White House.

She watched as the helicopter climbed into the clear blue sky and disappeared in the sea haze over the ocean near Malibu. Ervin had never invited her to his ranch, even though they had been close for so long. Whenever they met it was either in one of their offices or at a restaurant. In fact, Janna realized, she knew little more about Felix Ervin's private life than she did after their first meeting in Zurich, when Fritz Demmer had provided a few details. She knew Ervin was unmarried, and he never mentioned any children. On the rare occasions when he had confided in her about his experiences, they always related to events that had taken place after 1963, the year she first met him, and invariably dealt with matters pertaining to business. She still hadn't the slightest idea where he was born, how he had spent the war years, or the means by which he originally acquired his great wealth. He was already a very rich man by the time she met him in Zurich, but she had never been able to discover the source of his fortune, and whenever she probed he always managed to cleverly sidestep her questions.

Still deep in thought, Janna took the elevator from the roof down to the twenty-fifth floor where her company headquarters was located. When she entered the luxuriously appointed reception area, an attractive young receptionist handed her a sheaf of telephone messages that had come in during Janna's brief absence. Barely glancing at them, she continued toward her office, which occupied a corner, but before she reached it a Yorkshire terrier raced toward her, his long silky hair blowing back as he ran yelping along the corridor.

"Come on, Shep, there's a good dog," Janna said, kneeling and catching the tiny animal in her arms.

Anna appeared at the door of the office next to the one Janna occupied. "He must have heard you coming," she said. "I just dropped by to pick up some papers, and rather than leave him at home I thought I'd bring him with me."

"I'm glad to see him," Janna said.

"I'm about to leave," Anna said.

"Shep can stay with me. I haven't any meetings scheduled for this afternoon, and it'll be nice having him for company."

"Sure?" Anna asked.

Janna nodded. Anna looked tired. The stroke she had suffered two decades earlier had taken its toll: even though she had regained about eighty percent of her movement, her speech was still slightly slurred, and the trauma of the experience had left her looking much older than her sixty-four years. As Janna looked at her she was filled with love.

How hard it must have been for Anna to sit mutely at Janna's wedding, knowing what she knew about Southworth but being physically unable to express it! Obeying a sudden impulse, she put her arm over the other woman's shoulder and lightly kissed her on the cheek.

"How did Wellington House look from the air?" Anna asked.

"Incredible," Janna replied. "Felix is trying to persuade me to buy the penthouse."

"Seriously?"

"I don't know." Janna laughed. "But it would be a wonderful place for us both to live."

As they talked the women walked together into Janna's office. It had floor-to-ceiling windows, which gave her a 180-degree view that included the perfectly manicured fairways of the Los Angeles Country Club as well as the sound stages at 20th Century-Fox studios, and was tastefully furnished in a contemporary style. The walls were paneled in bleached oak, and shelves of books occupied the area behind Janna's desk. The effect was one of simple elegance, with just the right number of personal touches, such as vases of flowers, and a selection of paintings that included works by Renoir, de Kooning, Derain, Rouault, and Picasso.

"You look worried," Anna remarked, speaking with the slow precision she had learned from her speech therapist. "Is it Derek?"

Janna nodded. "I'm dreading the meeting on Monday."

By careful planning Janna had managed to keep her path from crossing that of her estranged husband during the nine years they had been legally separated. The few times each year that Southworth visited Century City, Janna had always arranged to be at her beach house in Big Sur, a rugged stretch of coast overlooking the Pacific Ocean about 300 miles north of Los Angeles, and whenever it had been necessary for somebody to attend meetings in London, she had told a senior staff member to go rather than make the journey herself.

"You won't be alone with him," Anna said. "Dave Wilson is flying in from New York, and he'll make sure everything goes smoothly."

"I know it's silly of me to feel anxious," Janna admitted, "but there's a lot at stake."

"Just don't get involved in emotions," the other woman warned.

"Believe me," Janna replied, "any feelings I might once have had for Derek died a long time ago."

A buzzer sounded and Janna flicked a switch on the intercom. "Lieutenant Dawson is on the line, ma'am," her secretary announced. "Do you want to speak to him?"

"Go ahead," Anna said. "I've got an appointment with my speech therapist."

"Put him through," Janna told her secretary, and when Anna had left the room, picked up the receiver. "Joe?"

"Hi." The voice at the other end of the line had an echo to it. "I called earlier, but your secretary told me you were out."

"I went over to Wellington House with Felix Ervin."

"That guy uses a helicopter like us LAPD minions use cars," Dawson remarked.

"Is that envy I hear?"

"Damn right. That and fatigue. I'm still down at the Coliseum and have just been told that we have to go on a stakeout tonight."

"There goes our dinner date," Janna said.

"But we can still see each other if you'll settle for a crepe and a cup of coffee." he said.

"When?"

"About five o'clock. We can meet at the Magic Pan."

Janna hesitated a moment, looking at the pile of documents on her desk that required her attention. "All right," she said, "I'd love to."

"Great," he said. "See you at five."

Janna replaced the receiver and turned her attention to an artist's rendering of how the penthouse would look after it was finished. With its twelve-foot-high ceilings and spacious interior halls, it was made to look even larger by mirrored walls that brought the reflection of the landscaped terrace into the living room. The color scheme, white-on-white, wasn't what she would have chosen, but her familiarity with the penthouse was such that she could easily envision how it would look with the light pastels and earth tones that were her favorite colors.

What didn't show in the renderings were the spaces recessed into the ceiling of the living room for special projection equipment, or the hidden alcoves in the walls of each room that were designed to house speakers. It was Felix Ervin's contention that whoever occupied the penthouse would prefer to be entertained in the security of their own home, rather than risk going out to public theaters, and he had worked closely with the architect to ensure that facilities were built in to accommodate state-of-the-art audio and video equipment.

Janna looked up from where she was seated at her desk and gazed through the window, across the lush green golf course of the Los Angeles Country Club, to the Golden Mile, where she could see the bronze column of Wellington House glistening in the late afternoon sun. But her mind wasn't on the renderings, or the high-rise in which she had invested so much of Star Industries' capital, but rather on the telephone call she had received from Joe Dawson.

They had met six months earlier when Janna attended a reception for President Reagan at the Century Plaza Hotel, and Joe Dawson, now a lieutenant in the Metro Division of the Los Angeles Police Department, had been present to supervise the added security that was always necessary whenever the nation's Chief Executive visited the city. Although he was now in his early forties, Dawson still had the athletic body that had made him a top skier, and he had changed relatively little in appearance since Janna first met him in Switzerland. His face was fuller, and his curly hair had started to thin, but he still possessed the same brashness that had once so irritated her but which she now found a refreshing contrast to the smooth, characterless personalities of the men by whom she was surrounded most of her working day.

Their encounter at the Century Plaza Hotel had resulted in their arranging to have lunch together, a meeting at which they had caught up on what had happened in their lives since they were last together in Paris. After his skiing accident at St. Moritz ended his career on the professional circuit, Joe had returned to law school at UCLA but had quit, when he married Elke Kruger, and begun a career in the police force, which he continued after she left him.

Janna described her meeting with Elke in Paris, the depression the other girl had been suffering from and how she'd been dismissed by Elke's mother after taking Elke back to the hotel. "I called the George Cinq before leaving for England the following day," she added, "but was told that Madame Kruger and her daughter had checked out without leaving a forwarding address. I remembered Elke's mother mentioning Dr. Frenay, so I telephoned him, but he was very up-tight about telling me anything, and wouldn't even say whether Eke was his patient. The only address I had for her was in Buenos Aires, and I wrote at least half a dozen letters, but I never received an answer. I was worried sick about her."

"She died in September 1971," Dawson said. "An overdose of drugs. They found her with a needle still in her arm at a fleabag hotel in downtown LA."

Janna was shattered. She went into the rest room and cried her eyes out. For several weeks afterward she frequently lunched with Joe and listened to him describe how he had coped with his grief. He hadn't remarried, preferring instead to bury himself in his work, and over the years had worked himself up to the rank of lieutenant commanding a

SWAT team. Because of his expertise in terrorist techniques, Janna had asked him to check out the security systems that were being built into Wellington House, something he had done on his own time. He had declared it the best-protected building of its kind he had ever seen.

Suddenly, Janna picked up Shep, who had been a gift from Felix Ervin the previous Christmas, and strode from the office. As she passed the front desk the receptionist said, "Mayor Bradley is on the line."

"Tell him I'll call back," Janna said.

It was a little after 4 P.M., almost an hour before she was due to meet Joe Dawson, and the sun was still warm as she crossed the pedestrian bridge that spanned the Avenue of the Stars. The skyscrapers of Century City rose like monoliths around her, their offices filled with thousands of workers, and yet the landscaped walkways between the high-rise buildings were virtually deserted. Shep, delighting in his unexpected freedom, made frequent stops to sniff at bushes in hopes of detecting the scent of other dogs, but failed to find any, for Century City wasn't a place where people walked their pets.

As Janna headed along Little Santa Monica Boulevard toward Beverly Hills, she felt like a child playing hooky from school: for years every minute of her working day had been carefully prescribed, and even now her desk was piled with legal documents that had to be studied before her meeting with Derek Southworth on Monday morning, but she didn't care. They could wait. All she wanted to do now was squander a few hours and feel herself in contact with the real world again.

She looked in at Grimmett's Automotive Service, the garage that had serviced her car ever since she settled in California, and saw the brothers who ran it, Tom and Glenn, talking with customers in the tiny office next to the repair shop. The walls were covered with photographs of celebrities whose vehicles they had cared for over the years, Janna's among them, and when Tom spotted her passing he waved.

On Lasky Drive she stopped in at Schreiner Pharmacy, the most exclusive in Beverly Hills, and spent a few minutes chatting with its owner, Dave Powells, a charming man who had filled her prescriptions for years but almost always had them delivered to her home or office.

"Did Dr. Pearlstein call something in?" he asked, obviously puzzled by her appearing in person in the middle of the afternoon.

"Just taking a break, Dave," she replied.

"If people would do that more often, they'd live a lot longer," the pharmacist said.

"And you wouldn't sell nearly as many tranquilizers," she replied.

He laughed and turned to serve a customer. When it became apparent he was going to be busy for some time, Janna continued on across Wilshire Boulevard into the main part of Beverly Hills, where she stopped into Church's Shoes to ask Carl Waxberg, the manager, about a pair of slippers she had ordered as a Christmas gift for Felix Ervin.

"I'll just go and see if they're in yet," Mr. Waxberg said, disappearing into a back room.

"Janna!"

She turned and saw David Wolper. "I saw you from outside and just had to say hello," the producer said, giving her a big hug.

Janna congratulated him on the opening ceremonies he had staged at the Coliseum to mark the beginning of the XXIII Olympiad.

He laughed. "If you think that was good, wait till you see the closing ceremonies. They're *really* going to be something!"

David Wolper had left by the time Mr. Waxberg returned to say that the slippers Janna had ordered from England still hadn't arrived but were expected any day. She thanked him and continued on to Rodeo Drive, where she idled away the time looking at window displays in Gucci's, Cartier's, and Georgio's.

It was a little after 5 P.M. when Janna entered the Magic Pan, but there was no sign of Joe Dawson, and after being seated she ordered a glass of wine. It was half empty by the time Dawson finally arrived and stood in the reception area where a cluster of customers were waiting to be taken care of by the hostess. He was wearing jeans, sneakers, a sports shirt, and a windbreaker. It was an outfit that gave him a rumpled look and made him appear out of place among the fashionably dressed people standing around him. Janna smiled as the hostess, a slender, elegantly coiffed woman, approached Dawson with an expression that seemed to suggest she had spotted a panhandler and was going to have to ask him to leave.

"Joe!" Janna waved as she called his name.

He grinned as he strode to her corner table. "Hi. Sorry I'm late." He sat down next to her. "Did you order yet?"

"Just wine."

"Don't you want anything to eat?"

She shook her head. "I've still got a lot of work to do, and now that we aren't having dinner I'll probably stay late at the office."

"Jesus, I'm really pissed about standing you up, but there isn't a hell of a lot I can do about it," he said. "We got a tip that some Libyan terrorists are cooking something up out in Carson, and that means an all-night stakeout. Have you ever been in Carson?"

"Not that I can remember."

"It's an easy place to forget, believe me. Spending the night there is not my idea of a good time."

"What is?" Janna asked.

"Taking you to McDonald's for a double quarter-pounder—"

"With a large order of french fries?"

"Only if you'll settle for a small Coke."

She laughed. "You'd better eat some hot food. It sounds like you've got a long night ahead of you."

Dawson studied the menu, which consisted of crepes with various fillings, and ordered a combination of spinach and chicken curry. When he handed the menu back to the waitress his windbreaker opened wide enough for Janna to see that he was carrying a revolver in a shoulder holster.

"Have you ever had to use that thing?" she asked after the waitress left.

Instinctively, Dawson zipped up his windbreaker and sipped a glass of water a busboy had brought. "Now and again," he said.

"To kill?"

"Once."

"I don't know how you could do that."

"You would if you'd seen some of the situations I've been in."

"What goes through your head before you pull the trigger?" she asked.

He shrugged. "It's an instinctive thing."

"Even though somebody's life is in the balance?"

It was a moment or two before Dawson answered. "In the end we all have to make choices. All you can do is hope to God they're the right ones."

She sensed it was a subject he didn't want to pursue and let it drop. Throughout the rest of the meal they talked about the Olympic Games, to which he'd been assigned in plain clothes so he would be inconspicuous as he mingled with the crowds. Finally, he said, "I get a few days off after the Games are over, and one of the guys has offered me the use of his cabin down in Baja, near Cabo San Lucas. He has a boat and there's great fishing. How would you like to join me?"

"I don't know if I can get away," Janna said.

"Think about it over the weekend," Dawson said. "We'd have a great time together."

An unmarked police car was waiting outside the restaurant to pick him up, and after he'd gone Janna collected Shep at Church Shoes, where Carl Waxberg had taken care of the dog while she was with Joe. As she walked back along Little Santa Monica Boulevard toward Century City, Janna thought over Joe's invitation: they weren't lovers yet, but they had seen enough of each other to be aware that it was the next logical step. The trip to Cabo San Lucas would mark a turning point in their relationship one way or another. She liked Joe Dawson a great deal and found him physically attractive, but she wasn't sure if she wanted anything serious to develop between them.

It was nearly six thirty when Janna returned to her office. Most of the employees had left for the day. Shep curled up on the sofa and promptly went to sleep, while Janna sat behind her desk reading the legal documents with which she needed to be familiar before meeting Derek Southworth the following Monday.

At first she kept thinking about Joe Dawson and found it difficult to concentrate, but gradually she managed to focus her attention on the papers so completely that she lost all track of time, and it wasn't until she heard footsteps in the corridor outside her office that she looked at the digital clock on her desk and saw it was almost 11 P.M. Assuming the sound she'd heard to be the security guard making his nightly rounds, she turned back to her reading, but when Shep suddenly began to growl, then bark, she looked up again and saw a figure standing in the doorway. It was lit from behind, and because the only illumination in her office came from the desk lamp, Janna couldn't see the features of the intruder.

"What do you want?" she asked, trying to veil the nervousness she felt.

"Is that any way to greet your husband?" The words were slurred, but Janna immediately recognized the voice.

"Our meeting isn't until Monday," she said brusquely.

"Thought I'd get here a few days early and see the closing ceremonies of the Olympics on Sunday," he said.

As he spoke Southworth entered the pool of light cast by the desk lamp and slumped down in a chair to one side of the desk. She could see his eyes were bloodshot and knew he'd been drinking. It was almost ten years since she'd last seen him, and he had aged. At fifty-three he'd still been attractive, but the decade between then and now had taken its toll, turning his face into a puffy caricature of what it once had been.

"Why did you come here?" she asked.

"To talk about us."

"That's what we're meant to be doing on Monday."

"I mean you and me, not business."

He got up and ambled to a glass-fronted liqueur cabinet.

"I think you should go," Janna said coldly.

"No you don't." He grinned, half filling a snifter with Napoleon brandy. "You didn't invite me to come seven thousand miles just to talk shop. Now why don't you relax, have a drink, and tell me what is really on your mind?"

"I don't—"

"You could begin by saying how much you've missed me."

Christ, Janna thought, he really believes I want a reconciliation! Her first instinct was to laugh, but knowing that he could quickly become violent when he was drunk, she managed to control the impulse.

"How did you get in?" she asked.

"Through the front door."

"It's just that the guard in the lobby usually—"

"Aren't you forgetting that I still own half this firm?"

Janna didn't answer. It was true that Derek had been coming to Century City for board meetings three or four times a year for the last decade, gatherings from which she'd always managed to absent herself, and his name was listed on the directory in the lobby as president, a title he shared with her.

"Stop sitting tight-assed behind that big desk of yours and join me in a drink." he said.

"I don't think so," she replied.

He shrugged and slumped down on a leather sofa. "Here's to us and new beginnings," he muttered, raising his glass in a toast and swallowing the contents in a single gulp. Putting his head back he closed his eyes, and for a moment Janna thought he had passed out, but then he opened them again, and she was astonished to see they were filled with tears. "God, I've missed you," he said thickly. "We had a good life together, and could again."

"That's not true. Right from the beginning it was built on a lie."

"You've never given me a chance to explain."

"It wouldn't have helped. The simple truth is I trusted you, and all you gave me in return was years of deception."

"There were things I was ashamed to tell you. Those lawyers told you only the facts, not my feelings. . . ." He paused. "When I was a kid growing up in the slums of London's East End I used to walk miles into Mayfair just so I could study how the toffs carried themselves, what they wore, how they smoked a cigarette . . ."

"Please don't."

"All I needed was the chance to prove I could be like them. . . ."

"Whatever we once had has been gone for a long time."

"When I took that dead pilot's uniform, men who had been educated at Eton and Harrow automatically assumed I was their equal. . . ."

"Stop it!"

"All it took was a thin blue stripe on an epaulet—"

Anger suddenly welled up inside Janna. "I want you out of my life completely! That's why I asked you to the meeting on Monday, to make a clean break."

He closed his eyes again, and his head lolled to one side. Thinking he had passed out, Janna got up from behind her desk and tiptoed past where he was sprawled as she made her way toward the door. Suddenly, his hand shot out and, grabbing her arm, he pulled her down next to him on the sofa. She tried to squirm free but he kissed her hard on the mouth. "For Christ's sake!" she gasped. Ignoring her protests, he tore away the front of her blouse and pulled up her skirt. She struggled to free herself as he pressed his fingers into her vagina, clumsily probing for her clitoris.

"Come on," he muttered, loosening his belt and unzipping his fly.

Janna abruptly twisted to one side, pulled herself free, and stumbled down the corridor leading to the reception area, followed by Shep, who had barked nonstop from the moment Southworth first laid hands on her.

Reaching the elevators, she pressed the call button and waited for the door to open. She saw Southworth emerge from her office and begin running down the corridor, but he was forced to stop when his pants slid down to his knees. Janna looked up at the panel over the elevator, and saw the indicator was rising, but the lift was still three floors away. Southworth had hurriedly fastened his belt and had reached the reception area by the time the elevator doors finally opened. Stepping inside, Shep in her arms, she pressed the CLOSE button, but it was seconds before the doors began to slide shut. They were still inches apart when Southworth jammed his foot between them, and when they automatically opened again he half fell into the small area where Janna was standing.

"Bitch!" He slapped her hard across the face, sending her reeling into the opposite corner as the elevator began its descent, and when Shep barked furiously he kicked the dog hard in the ribs.

"You bastard!" Janna raked his cheeks with her fingernails.

"That's more like it." Southworth grinned, oblivious to the blood seeping from the deep scratches. "You were always sexier when you were angry."

He grabbed her hair and forced Janna to her knees. "Suck it!" he commanded, pressing her face against his erect penis.

She twisted her head away, but he used her hair to turn it back and forced his shaft against her lips. When she refused to part them he dug his fingers into both sides of her cheeks until the pain finally forced her to open her mouth, but when he forced his cock down her throat it penetrated so deep that she retched. Stepping back, he looked down at his vomit-covered penis, but before he could react, the doors he had been leaning against suddenly opened, and he fell backward, dragging Janna with him, and slammed into a huge man wearing work clothes who was waiting for the elevator in the subterranean garage area.

"Help me!" Janna pleaded.

The man, who was carrying a metal toolbox, looked down at where Southworth was sprawled and said, "Leave me out of it, lady."

"For God's sake . . . !"

Ignoring Janna's plea, the man, apparently part of a maintenance crew, stepped into the elevator moments before the door closed. Janna pressed the call button, hoping the doors would open, but saw from the light on the floor-indicator panel that the elevator had already begun its ascent. Her only chance now lay in reaching her car before Southworth, who was still sprawled on the garage floor, could regain his feet. Her Rolls-Royce was parked in a private stall on the far side of the elevator shaft and she ran toward it, feeling in her pocket for the keys, but moments before she reached the vehicle Southworth lunged past her to grab the door handle.

There was a bluish-white flash as his hand touched the metal. His body jerked in a series of spasms, and his skin began to smoke. Janna watched in horror as his eyeballs bulged and his skin cracked. She tried to turn away, but was transfixed by the sight of her estranged husband's electrocution.

She screamed and looked around frantically for somebody who could help, but the garage was empty. She ran back to the elevator shaft, saw a glass-fronted fire alarm, and used a small metal hammer hanging next to the box to smash its protective covering. When she pressed the button inside a siren blared through the underground garage in a wail that continued unbroken as she hurried back to where Southworth lay writhing on the grease-slicked concrete floor. His mouth opened and shut as he tried to speak, and finally he managed to utter in a low whisper, "Insane . . . kill you . . ."

Two cars with flashing red lights mounted on their roofs screeched down a ramp at the far end of the garage, but they still hadn't come to a stop when Southworth expelled a long last breath and his head lolled lifelessly to one side.

43

Point Lobos, described by Robert Louis Stevenson as the most beautiful meeting of land and sea to be found anywhere in the world, is a rocky peninsula 300 miles north of Los Angeles. It was obscured by a thick wall of mist as Janna turned off Highway 1 onto a rutted dirt road leading to the beach house she'd built three years earlier.

Designed by Jack Lionel Warner, a friend who was also one of the most distinguished architects in the United States, it was a deceptively simple-looking structure planned in such a way that it appeared to be an extension of the rocky bluff on which it stood. So complete was this illusion, particularly now that the elements had weathered its exterior, that passengers in cars driving the coast road, who eagerly searched the shoreline for a glimpse of the harbor seals that basked on the rocks offshore, usually failed to see it.

Janna had christened the dwelling Casa de Oro. It was a name she had chosen on first seeing the rocky promontory after spending a weekend in Carmel, when rays from the setting sun had suddenly pierced a bank of dark clouds, sending down a shaft that bathed the headland in golden light. She knew from that moment it was a setting in which she had to build a hideaway, a sanctuary to which she could escape whenever the pressures of running Star Industries became too intense for her.

After parking the car inside a garage that had been blasted out of living rock, Janna remained behind the wheel and tried to collect her emotions. She had been so badly shaken by Derek's death that when the homicide investigators arrived at the garage she was too numbed by what she had witnessed to answer their questions. Only after they took her back up to her office and allowed her to rest was she finally able to describe what had happened. She told the investigators how the man in the garage had refused to help, but when they pressed her for a description of him the only outstanding characteristics she could recall were his enormous size and pronounced foreign accent.

The investigators had fired questions at her with a rapidity that made her head swim. Why was she still married to Southworth when she hadn't seen him in ten years? Was his visit to Century City his idea, or had she invited him? If he was already drunk when he appeared in her office, why hadn't she summoned a guard? What happened to her estranged husband's share of ownership in Star Industries now that he was dead?

Her interrogators had allowed Janna to telephone Henry Jones, her personal attorney, when they began their questioning, but they were almost finished by the time he arrived from his home in Marina del Rey, and all he could do was inform the investigating officers that he was advising his client to remain silent until they specified whether any charges were being brought against her. "She's free to go any time she wants," one of the officers replied. "Just keep us informed as to her whereabouts if she leaves town."

As the police were leaving, the telephone had rung, and Janna had heard Joe Dawson's voice on the line. "I heard what happened. It just came over the car radio," he said. "Are you all right?"

"I'm still pretty shaky," Janna replied.

"I wish to hell I could be with you, but I'm liable to be at this stakeout for quite a few hours. The media is going to turn the whole thing into a circus. Is there anywhere you can go to lay low until the dust settles?"

"My beach house in Big Sur."

"Perfect," he said. "The sooner you take off the better."

"Whoever killed Derek was after me, Joe. . . ."

"That's another good reason to get away."

"But I'm not sure I want to be alone, particularly in such a remote area as Big Sur."

"You won't be," he assured her. "The minute I get off duty I'll drive up there. Okay?"

He hung up before Janna could answer, but his words were sufficiently reassuring for her to be on the road soon after dawn. The police had impounded her Rolls-Royce as material evidence, so she took a company car and, after calling Anna to tell her what had happened and assure her she was all right, drove for five hours straight through to Big Sur. During the trip she heard frequent mention of Southworth's death on radio news programs that identified him as "the husband of the richest woman in America," but it was obvious from their brevity that, apart from the grotesque manner of his death, the police still hadn't released many details of the previous night's events. Even Janna still didn't know how her Rolls-Royce had been rigged so that Derek was electrocuted when he touched it, and when she'd asked the homicide investigators they had told her the matter was still being studied.

She got out of the car and walked up the narrow, winding path holding Shep in her arms. Unlocking the door, she went inside the house and opened the wooden shutters that barred the windows whenever she left the place for any length of time. The sea mist had begun to burn away, and the slopes of the Santa Lucia Mountains were bathed in brilliant sunlight. Features of the surrounding landscape took on shape and form: gnarled trees, their trunks twisted into anguished shapes by the constant wind, stood on nearby cliffs; waves pounded on the rocks below with a force that sent spume floating high in the brisk morning air; the crescent sweep of sandy beach fronting the Carmelite monastery arched past Carmel to the exclusive, gated community of Pebble Beach.

As Janna watched, the whole panorama was unveiled, a canvas of such beauty that she felt her spirits lift and the tensions she'd brought with her from Los Angeles begin to dissolve away. "Come on, Shep," she announced to her Yorkshire terrier, who was still moving gingerly from the bruises he had suffered when Southworth kicked him, "we're going for a nice long walk."

Going upstairs to the master bedroom, she changed into a pair of faded jeans, pale blue work shirt, and rubber-soled moccasins. Then, picking up Shep, she returned to the car and backed down the narrow driveway. The cliffs on which Casa de Oro stood were three or four hundred feet high, a headland sculpted by the constant lapping of turbulent waves into a series of sharp-edged ridges where, in the fractured rock, flocks of gulls had built their nests, but the drop was so sheer that it was impossible to reach the beach from above.

The nearest access was located in front of the Carmelite monastery, less than a ten-minute drive away. Here was a magnificent curve of white sand which, because the sun had only just burned away the mist that had blanketed it since before dawn, was still virtually deserted.

Parking on the edge of the road opposite the monastery, Janna put a leash on Shep and walked down a path that led through beds of purple ice plants to the powder-fine sand.

She took off her moccasins, tied the leather laces together, slung them over her shoulder, and started out barefoot along the beach toward Carmel. Excited by his new surroundings, Shep forgot about his bruised ribs and kept tugging on the leash until Janna finally unfastened it, letting him run free. She knew it was against the law, but as the only people in sight were a father playing Frisbee with his young daughter, she decided to allow her pet the same sense of freedom she was experiencing.

The dog ran barking toward the father and daughter, leaping high in the air in vigorous but futile efforts to grab the whirling disk of orange plastic. The girl, who must have been twelve or thirteen, tried to stroke Shep, but he was more interested in playing, so she tossed the Frisbee to her father on a trajectory low enough for the dog to have a chance of reaching it. Watching the game from a distance, Janna experienced a moment of déjà vu as she remembered the happy times she had spent with Mark, playing in Central Park. It evoked sadness that was so overwhelming she had to sit down cross-legged on the sand to maintain her equilibrium.

It was as if something inside her had suddenly ruptured. A thin protective membrane had given way, drenching the whole of her inner being with grief: not just a mental sorrow but a physical ache that brought with it an indescribable sense of desolation. Mark, Genevieve, Janet—all gone. A mother she had never known, a father whose identity would remain a mystery forever. She was almost forty-one, had failed at marriage, and bore no children. And never would. After leaving Derek she'd gone to a specialist who had informed her that she was sterile. The irony of it all had plagued her. Tears streamed down her cheeks.

"Is this your dog?"

Janna looked up and saw the young girl holding Shep. "Yes," she muttered.

"It's just that my Dad and I are leaving now and we didn't know if you wanted him running around on the beach without a leash."

"Thanks." Janna reached up and took Shep. "I know he enjoyed playing with you."

"He's cute." The girl laughed. "See ya."

Janna watched as the girl clambered up a steep embankment to where her father was waiting in a car. Father. Was that what Derek had really represented? Christ! She could feel the bitterness welling up inside her and made a conscious effort to fight it back. Derek Southworth was a bastard, a pathological liar, but a murderer? Janna had been willing to believe it possible until he died in front of her eyes, the victim of somebody who obviously wanted her dead. But who? Why? When would another attempt be made on her life?

Getting up, she walked along the beach searching her memory for anybody who would want to kill her: Derek was the only person who had stood to profit by her death—he would automatically have assumed outright ownership of Star Industries—but it was obvious he didn't know her Rolls-Royce had been wired.

"Hey, lady!"

Janna had sunk so deep into introspection that she hadn't noticed she'd reached the section of beach at the end of the main street that ran through the center of Carmel. Nor had she been aware that a young, flaxen-haired lifeguard had been watching her and Shep as they approached his white watchtower.

"That your animal?" he asked.

"Yes," Janna replied.

"Dogs are meant to be kept on a leash at all times."

She scooped Shep up in her arms and strode up the path that led into the small picturesque town, similar in many ways to those along the Maine and New England coasts. It was a Saturday in the middle of August, and Carmel was crowded with tourists. She glanced in the windows of shops that sold everything from expensive silk dresses to bric-a-brac curios masquerading as antiques, and paused in front of a patio restaurant where a crowd had gathered to watch Carl Lewis, on television, anchor the U.S. 4×100-meter relay team to an Olympic victory in world record time. It was the last day of track and field competition at the Los Angeles Coliseum. Was Joe Dawson on his way up to Big Sur?

It mattered to her a great deal. Yesterday, when he invited her to share his vacation in Cabo San Lucas, she hadn't been sure of her feelings. But after Derek's horrible death, she really needed Joe's caring.

By the time she reached her car, the weather had undergone a sudden change and dark rain clouds filled the previously clear blue sky. A cold wind blowing in off the ocean had also brought back the sea mist, which settled over the coastline with such rapidity that by the time she turned onto the dirt trail leading to her house on Point Lobos, the slopes of the Santa Lucia Mountains were obscured by banks of swirling mist.

When she headed the car across the natural rock bridge that linked the headland with the promontory of rock on which Casa de Oro was built, she experienced a quick flutter of excitement as she saw a beat-up old Porsche parked in front of the garage. Joe Dawson was slumped behind the wheel, a newspaper covering his face, seemingly asleep. She started to honk her horn, then decided to surprise him and tiptoed to the side of the other vehicle.

"Never sneak up on a cop, lady," Dawson drawled, his face still covered by that morning's edition of the Los Angeles *Times*. "Particularly one who spent the whole night in Carson staking out a house that was meant to be housing Libyan terrorists but turned out to be the home of two gay florists."

Janna laughed. "God, I'm glad to see you," she said, leaning down and nuzzling his neck.

"You okay?" he asked, pulling the paper aside.

"I am now." As Janna spoke large drops of rain began to fall. "You'd better put the top up," she said.

"It doesn't have one, but the guy I bought it from told me it floats."

"You'd better put it in my garage."

"I'd like to see if he was right."

"You were crazy when I met you, and you haven't changed one bit!" She led the way into the house and put a match to a gas pipe under some logs that were piled in the fireplace.

"Are you really all right?" he asked, kneeling behind her and putting his arms around her shoulders.

"It was a nightmare. I keep seeing Derek's face. . . ."

"I talked with the guys who questioned you."

"The way they behaved, I got the feeling they suspected me."

"Guys from homicide aren't too subtle."

"Do they really think I was involved?"

Dawson shook his head. "Even they aren't dumb enough to believe you'd attach a live wire from the elevator circuits to the frame of your own car in the hope that Southworth would touch it before you did."

"Do they have a suspect?"

"Not yet, but they're real interested in the guy who refused to help you, particularly because he was carrying a toolbox."

"He looked like a maintenance man."

"They've checked the building's maintenance crew, and none of them even remotely resembles the man you described." He paused, then added, "But headquarters checked with Interpol and did come up with some interesting background on Southworth."

"I could have told them most of it, but my lawyer instructed me not to," Janna said, getting up from where she'd been kneeling in front of the fireplace.

"Like what?" Dawson asked.

She told him everything that Dave Wilson and Basil Matson had uncovered about her estranged husband's background.

"There's more," Dawson said. "Southworth had a criminal record going back to the end of World War II. He was involved in a whole slew of rackets, mostly black market operations, but by 1948 he was in Vienna, buying penicillin from doctors in the Royal Air Force, watering it down, and selling it for use in children's hospitals."

"Christ!" Janna exclaimed, "I had no idea!"

"With the profits from that little scheme, which resulted in a lot of kids dying, he started smuggling foreign currencies the Germans had forged during the war, including five-pound notes that were such good quality that the Bank of England had a tough time detecting them." Dawson stopped speaking and cocked his head, listening to the roar of the storm churning its way south from Point Cyprus.

"Go on," Janna said quietly.

"In 1963 he was arrested by U.S. Treasury Agents and charged with smuggling works of art stolen by Göring and other high Nazi officials into the United States. One of the dealers he sold them to was Mark Hunter."

Janna's body tensed. "Are you sure?"

Dawson nodded. "Southworth was part of a much larger operation that the Justice Department had been after for years," he said. "They offered him immunity from prosecution if he would testify as a government witness at Hunter's trial. He agreed and gave them enough names, dates, and places to fill half a dozen filing cabinets."

"I can't believe Mark would . . ." Janna's voice trailed away.

"He didn't," Dawson said. "Because the trial ended after Hunter's death, Southworth's evidence was never tested in court, and as the Justice Department had agreed not to prosecute they had to let him go. It wasn't until months later, after other key members of the ring were arrested, that the U.S. Attorney's office discovered Southworth had invented most of the evidence he had given them against Hunter."

"So Mark was innocent?"

"Completely."

Janna remembered the anguish that had driven Mark to take his own life, and for a long time was silent, struck mute by the revelation that the man she had loved so much had been deliberately framed—by another man she had loved. Darkness settled over the room. Finally, she got up and flicked on the light switch, but nothing happened. "The power must be out," she said dully. "It often happens during a storm."

Dawson picked up the phone. "It's dead, too."

"The lines are probably down between here and the road."

"I promised to check in with my boss at Metro."

"You can walk up to the Highlands Inn when it stops raining. The cable is underground, to that point, so their phones will probably be working and it's less than half a mile from here." Janna put a match to an oil lamp. "Are you hungry?"

"Starving," he said. "I was going to take you to Nepenthe. . . ."

"I can fix something here. The stove works on propane, and I always keep a supply of canned foods."

"I'll help you."

"You cook?"

"Best short-order chef Ship's ever had during the time I was at UCLA."

"Do you knit too?"

"I can learn."

She laughed, more glad of his presence than he knew, and felt the depression she'd sunk into beginning to dissolve. They prepared a makeshift meal together consisting of Anderson's split pea soup, baked beans on matzos, English plum pudding, and glazed petits fours that came in a sealed tin imported from France, which they ate at a circular oak table in a small alcove off the living room. It jutted out on a spur of rock, and they could watch the storm-tossed sea angrily swirling below them as they sipped red wine that was a product of a small vineyard Star Industries owned in Napa Valley, and reminisced about the two decades that had passed since their first meeting at the Café Pully on the shores of Lake Geneva.

"Elke really hated Switzerland," Janna mused. "Everything about it bored her."

"She tired of things very easily," Dawson replied tersely.

"Maybe you'd rather we didn't talk about her." Janna said, remembering how the German girl had left him.

"It doesn't matter." He shrugged.

"There is one thing that's always puzzled me."

"What's that?"

"How a young beautiful woman, with all the money she could ever need, ended up dead from an overdose of heroin in a skid row hotel."

Dawson gazed out of the rain-sheeted window. "You never knew that both her parents were Jews, did you?"

"Jews?"

He nodded.

"That's impossible!" Janna exclaimed.

"Because she had blond hair and blue eyes?"

"Elke was the most typically Aryan woman—"

"Her father owned a clothing store in a small town east of Munich," Dawson said. "The whole family escaped arrest because of their Aryan appearance. Elke was born after her parents emigrated to Argentina. There was already quite a large group of ex-Nazis living in Buenos Aires, who wielded a lot of power because of the huge amounts of money they'd been able to smuggle out of Europe before Germany surrendered. They used it to look after their own kind, including the Krugers, who invented a background for themselves as loyal Nazis."

"Did she know her parents were Jews then?" Janna asked.

Dawson shook his head. "They'd done everything possible to hide it from her."

"How did she find out?"

"Guilt must have got to Elke's father because he had a breakdown and began openly declaring his Jewishness."

"It must have torn Elke apart."

"It did. She left school, and not long afterward was raped by a gang of German university students. That's when her mother decided to send Elke to Switzerland."

Janna remembered the tall, slender blond woman who had imperiously dismissed her from Elke's room at the George V after denying that her daughter used drugs. Now that she knew about the terrible schism in the German girl's life, Janna understood more clearly why she'd been driven by such self-destructive demons. Poor, funny, beautiful, proud, tragic Elke, carrying that secret around with her for so long. "When did you find out about her background?" Janna asked.

"About a year before she died," Dawson replied. "She'd been in and out of three or four institutions, but none of them did her any good.

They'd given her electric-shock therapy at one place. I saw her for the last time not long after that. The incredible thing was she still looked the same: all the drugs and booze hadn't destroyed her beauty, but her eyes were dead. She wanted to come back to me. That's why she told me the truth about her upbringing. I guess she figured that if I understood why she'd fallen apart . . ."

Tears welled in his eyes as his voice trailed away, and when Janna held him in her arms he buried his face against her breasts.

"It's all right," she murmured. "We both did everything we could."

"Do you really believe that?"

She shook her head.

"Neither do I," he said. "That's what has been haunting me ever since she died. . . ."

Janna took his hand and led him upstairs to the master bedroom where, after undressing him and herself, they lay in bed wrapped in each other's arms. She wanted to lose herself in him, be so completely enveloped that, for a moment at least, she would cease to exist. When, after a long silence, they finally made love, Janna felt herself falling into a warm, moist void where the wind whispered and sighed.

44

Janna's eyes were open when the first gray light of dawn seeped into the bedroom. She hadn't slept much because the hours of darkness had been filled with memories: of Mark and Anna when she was growing up in New York; of Genevieve the day she had met her at the airport in Geneva; of Elke, her hair streaming in the wind as she careened her Porsche around the hairpin turns from Montreux to Lausanne; of Janet visiting children at the death house in Singapore; of the vacant expression in her German friend's eyes the last time she saw her in Paris.

She had shared these moments with Joe, and he had responded with details about his own life, as they lay in each other's arms after making love. It had somehow deepened their intimacy, touching levels of feeling that transcended sex, and when he finally slept Janna knew she had found the man with whom she wanted to spend the rest of her life.

Moving carefully so as not to disturb him, she got up, put on a robe, and went downstairs to clear away the dishes they had used at dinner. The storm seemed to have slackened, and even though the wind was still strong, the gusts were no longer of gale force. The fire had gone out, but she lit the gas jets, and putting her head back against the cushions, closed her eyes and listened to the spatter of rain against the window. She tried to remember how she had felt twelve hours ago, but it seemed far away.

"Am I that hard to sleep with?"

Janna opened her eyes and saw Joe looking down at her.

"I didn't want to disturb you—" The rest of her words were smothered as he leaned down and kissed her on the lips.

"Hi," he said, when they finally broke apart.

"Hi, yourself," she replied.

"The power's still out, and the phone isn't working. I'm going to walk up to the Highlands Inn."

"But it's still raining."

"Not too heavily. I've got to let my boss know where I am."

"Why don't you drive over?" she asked.

He hauled her upright and guided her to the window, through which she could see his battered Porsche—which, because it had no top, now looked like a full bathtub on wheels.

She laughed. "Take my car."

"It isn't that far."

"All right," she said, "Go and make your call, and I'll have breakfast ready when you get back."

"Baked beans again?"

"On matzos."

He grimaced, zipped up his parka, and went outside. Janna watched through the window, smiling as he opened the door of his Porsche to let the water that had flooded it cascade out, and waited until he disappeared from view in the thick, swirling fog. Going through to the kitchen, where Shep was curled up in his basket, she filled the kettle with water, put it on the stove, then opened a can of dog food and emptied it into a feeding bowl before returning upstairs to the bedroom.

She had showered and was toweling herself off when the dog began to bark. "Quiet, Shep!" she shouted, and moments later the animal became silent. But when she finished dressing and went back down to the kitchen, she saw the back door had blown open, and Shep was nowhere to be seen.

"Shep!" Her voice echoed in the stillness of the house. Crossing to the door she peered out into a thick wall of fog. She thought she heard Shep barking, but the sound was drowned out by the moan of a foghorn from Point Pinos lighthouse. She heard the barking again and decided it was coming from somewhere beyond the bank of mist. She strained to see beyond the opaque wall, which seethed and billowed with each shift in the wind. After what had happened to Derek she was jumpy and suspicious about anything that was even slightly out of the ordinary, but she couldn't help feeling paranoid. Surely, Joe had left the door unlatched, the wind had blown it open, and Shep had simply gone exploring. It wasn't the first time she'd had to go looking for her pet when they were staying at the beach house.

"Here, boy!"

She clapped her hands and whistled, but the fragile sound was whipped away by the wind the moment it left her lips. The barking came again, this time from the direction of the cliffs that fronted the house, and when it continued unabated, she stepped out into the fog and slowly felt her way through it in the direction from which the sound was coming.

The path she followed was very narrow. It led to a small patch of lawn, which occupied the only flat piece of ground on the promontory and separated the house from a sheer rock face that descended in a series of steep ledges hundreds of feet to the raging sea. Pebbles crunched under her shoes until she reached the edge of the muddy grass, where her footsteps became muffled.

"Shep!"

This time her call was answered by a burst of frantic barking that seemed to come from below where she was standing. Peering over the edge of the cliff, she saw Shep crouched on a ledge of rock midway down the steep slope. The dog must have seen Janna, because he attempted to climb back along the ridge down which he must have wandered, which stood out from the cliff face in a natural ramp that was at least two feet wide. But his legs were too short for him to bridge a section where the rock had crumbled, and his repeated attempts to jump the gap kept him teetering on the brink, inches away from falling hundreds of feet into the raging sea.

Relieved at having found the dog, and equally glad to discover that her early suspicions had been unfounded, Janna lowered herself onto the ramp and began edging her way to where Shep was trapped. The descent was steep, and the rocks slippery from rain, which was still falling in a fine mist. "Easy, now," she said to herself as she inched her way down, "just take it nice and slow. . . ."

There were plenty of clefts in the rock for her to hold on to, and the angle of the ramp was sufficiently gradual for her rubber-soled moccasins to maintain a good grip. Sporadic gusts of wind, remnants of the storm that had almost blown itself out, tore at her body, but by remaining motionless until they died away she managed to maintain her balance and continue edging down to where Shep, his little body quivering, was watching her progress with wide-eyed anticipation.

When Janna finally reached him, she carefully grabbed the dog under the belly and scooped him up in her arms. Shep gratefully licked her face and whined repeatedly. As she was trying to quiet him, a shower of rocks tumbled down from high above her, cascading within inches of where she stood on the ledge. She pressed her body against the cliff, one hand holding Shep, the other lodged in a cleft in the wall. Assuming it to be scree loosened by the wind, she hung on, waiting for the mini-avalanche to end, but as the minutes passed the size of the rocks careening down on her got bigger, and she was gripped by fear. Her first thought was that the cliff itself had begun to crumble, or that a major slippage similar to the one that had wiped out the road south of Point Lobos the previous winter was taking place, and she closed her eyes, expecting at any moment to be swept into the sea, but gradually the debris falling from above lessened, and then finally stopped.

Fearful of getting dirt in her eyes by looking up, she clung to the cleft in the rocky wall and hugged Shep, who had scrambled inside her sweater. Her left hand, the one that was jammed into the V-shaped fissure, was bleeding from a deep gash, and blood trickled down her forearm into her sleeve. Her joints ached, and the rest of her body was numb from the buffeting it had taken by the bitter wind. After four or five minutes, when there were no further rock falls, she eased herself back from the face of the cliff far enough to see over a small ridge that had been deflecting the falling stones. At first the swirling mist was too thick for her to see far above where she crouched, but then a sudden wind shift parted the opaque veil, allowing her a clear view all the way to the top of the cliff. Somebody was peering down at her: a large man whose features she suddenly recognized as those of the person who had refused to help her when she was trying to get away from Derek in the garage.

She tried to scream, but the only sound she could muster was a noise that was part strangled fear, part hopeless moan. The man above her grinned as he reached down and pried loose a boulder that was wedged in the earth just below where he lay at the edge of the cliff. It teetered for a moment, held by the suction of the rain-sodden clay, then toppled free and tumbled bouncing down the rock face straight at Janna's head. She yanked herself against the cleft to which she was clinging, and the boulder hurtled past, missing her by inches as it careened hundreds of feet through midair into the turbulent sea.

Janna attempted another scream and this time there was nothing fractured about the sound she uttered; it was loud enough to be heard over the screech of gulls, the roar of the ocean, and the wail of the foghorn. Hugging her body against the cliff so tightly that she could feel Shep's tiny frame being squashed against her breasts, she waited for the next onslaught from above, knowing that all it would take to dislodge her precarious hold was one direct hit by even a small rock. For two or three minutes, earth loosened by the falling boulder continued to shower down over the ledge above her, but it gradually subsided, and finally stopped.

Too petrified to do anything but remain frozen where she stood, Janna felt a numbness spreading down her legs and knew it was only going to be a matter of minutes before they gave way under her. Images flashed through her mind, kaleidoscopic fragments of shapes and colors that were completely unrelated to each other, and when the veins in the rock just inches from her eyes appeared to throb, she knew she was beginning to hallucinate.

"Oh, God. . . ." Her face was pressed so close to the rock that when she uttered the words her lips came into contact with the slick wet surface of the cliff and she tasted its saltiness.

"Janna!"

The call seemed to come to her from the bottom of an empty well.

"Where the hell are you?"

This time the voice sounded closer. She waited a moment, then willed herself to lean backward and look up. The wind had blown the fog back from the top of the cliff, and she saw that the place where her attacker had crouched was now occupied by Joe.

"Down here!" Her fear-parched throat turned Janna's cry into a barely audible croak, but Dawson saw her, waved, and lowered himself onto the narrow ledge down which she had originally descended.

Moving with the practiced ease of a man whose job required that he keep in top physical condition, he edged his way down to where Janna was crouched and grasped her arm. "Hang on to me," he instructed.

She tried to respond, but her muscles refused to obey the commands from her brain. "I can't," she muttered.

"Yes you can," he assured her, putting his arm around her waist for support. "It's okay, I've got you, now let go of the rock."

Janna looked through glazed eyes at where her left hand was jammed into the V-shaped fissure; it was covered with blood and the skin had turned a bluish-black color. She had clenched her fist to act as a wedge, but when she tried to loosen her fingers they wouldn't move.

"Christ!" She began to tremble.

"Easy now," Dawson murmured, "just keep looking up and let me do the work."

He reached up and pried her fist open, then slowly lifted her hand out of the fissure and took the full weight of her body against his shoulder. "I want you to start edging toward me," he said with practiced calm.

"My legs are too numb. . . ."

"You can do it," he urged, like a father coaxing a child.

Janna glanced down at her feet and saw they were scant inches from the edge of the ledge, beyond which, far below, the storm-swollen ocean crashed against rocks at the base of the cliff.

"Up!" Dawson snapped. "Keep looking up, and move your left leg toward me."

She obeyed, edging herself sideways and keeping her eyes fixed on the top of the cliff.

"Now the right leg, good, keep moving. . . ."

Still with one arm around her waist, he started back up the ledge, encouraging her constantly, until they finally reached the top of the cliff. It took them less than twenty minutes, but to Janna it seemed an eternity, and even after they were standing on the small grassy area in front of the house she couldn't stop shaking.

She started to cry, silently at first, then with an intensity that racked her whole body with sobs. "It's okay," Dawson consoled, "let it all out." He took off his parka and wrapped it around her shoulders. In doing so his body brushed against the bulge under Janna's sweater, and Shep's face appeared at the neck.

"He's why I was down there," Janna said.

"You've got to be kidding!" Dawson exclaimed. "A dog wanders down the side of a cliff and you risk your life—"

"Shep didn't wander down there," she said. "He was put on that ledge."

"Come on," Dawson said, taking her arm and leading her toward the house, "you're in shock."

"But you must have seen him!"

"Who?"

"The man who was in the garage when I was trying to escape from Derek Southworth."

"What you need is a hot bath."

Janna pulled away from him, ran into the house, and hurried upstairs. Angry and hurt, she rubbed Shep dry with a towel, then stripped off her wet clothes and stood under a steaming hot shower. Its pulsating jets dispelled the cold that had numbed her limbs, and washed away the blood caked on the back of her left hand, but did little to ease the bitter frustration she felt at Joe's lack of understanding. Still nude, she returned to the bedroom in search of a dry towel and saw him standing just inside the doorway.

"Feeling better?" he asked.

"No thanks to you," Janna replied curtly, rummaging in a drawer for a large bath towel which she draped around her breasts.

"You were right," he acknowledged. "Somebody did try to kill you out there."

"My word wasn't enough?"

He shrugged. "I'm a cop."

"First, last, and always."

"Skepticism is an occupational hazard."

"What changed your mind?"

"I found an impression where somebody very tall and heavy lay in the grass at the edge of the cliff."

"Who the hell was it, Joe, and why is he after me?"

"I don't know," Dawson said, "but you'd better believe I'm going to find out."

"Meanwhile, I'm a walking goddamn target!"

"Which is why I want you to start taking some real precautions."

"Like what?" she asked.

He put his arm around her shoulders. "The best first step I can think of would be to move into the penthouse at Wellington House. With its state-of-the-art security, you'll be safer there than in Fort Knox."

45

LOS ANGELES: June 3, 1985

Anna Maxell-Hunter sat alone in the library of the penthouse at Wellington House, her eyes fixed on the place where the intruder had scrawled a swastika on the wall. Although it had been painted over by the building's maintenance crew, the outline of the Nazi symbol was still faintly visible and would require two or three more coats before it was totally obliterated. Even then, she thought, it would remain etched in her mind, as ineradicable as all the other memories of the odyssey that had taken her from the horrors of the Warsaw ghetto to the night of terror she had just endured.

She had told the story to Joe Dawson in utmost detail, and he had listened without interrupting until she had said everything she remembered, and then, after asking a few brief questions, he had returned to Metro headquarters at Central Station in downtown Los Angeles. It had been impossible for Anna to gauge from his reaction whether or not what she told him had provided any clues to the identity of the person who was stalking Janna, but he had made pages of notes during her painstaking recreation of the forty-two-year time span.

The files she had received earlier that morning from the Wiesenthal Center still lay on a small desk next to where she was seated, plain manila folders whose well-thumbed covers seemed out of place in the elegantly furnished library, with its antique Chippendale furniture, hand-cut Waterford crystal vases filled with fresh flowers, and exquisitely hued Aubusson carpet.

She rested her hand on the files, remembering the day she had watched from the window of the vacated hospital building overlooking Umschlagplatz as thousands of Jews were piled into boxcars waiting to transport them to concentration camps. The recollection was as vivid now as it had been forty years earlier. She could still hear the furious barking of guard dogs and the plaintive cries of people lost in the melee trying to find their loved ones.

The telephone rang, jolting Anna out of her reverie. When she picked up the receiver the switchboard operator in the lobby said,

"There's a call for you from the County Hospital, ma'am, they say it's an emergency."

Immediately thinking of Janna, Anna's heart skipped a beat. "Put them through," she said.

There was a click as the connection was made, and another woman's voice asked, "Is that Anna Maxell-Hunter?"

"Yes," Anna replied, her pulse racing.

"My name is Mrs. Stevens," the other woman said. "I'm a nurse in the Medical Intensive Care Unit at Los Angeles County-USC Medical Center. We have a patient in emergency who has given us your name, a Mr. Al Levy. . . ."

Anna was so relieved to hear it wasn't Janna that she could barely concentrate on what the woman was saying. "Al Levy? I'm afraid I don't know anybody by that name," she said.

"His relationship to you isn't specified on the admitting card," Mrs. Stevens said, "but the doctor who treated him says he's somebody you knew years ago in Poland."

Anna searched her memory again for some recollection of a man called Al Levy: there had been a lot of people in the ghetto with the name Levy, and during the turmoil of the final days it was quite possible her duties as a courier had brought her into contact with the man who was now in the hospital. Perhaps he had been a member of the Jewish Fighting Organization, one of the few who survived, and had become ill while attending the annual gathering of the Holocaust survivors. It was even possible that he possessed information about the identity of Janna's real father, which she'd failed to find on her visit that morning to the Simon Wiesenthal Center. "I'll get down there as soon as possible," she said.

Half an hour later, Anna walked down the short corridor to the garage, where her chauffeur was waiting, and was helped into the back seat of the car. As the giant elevator smoothly lowered the vehicle to Wilshire Boulevard, she continued culling her memory for some recollection of an Al Levy. But by the time they reached Lincoln Heights, where the County-USC Medical Center was located, she still hadn't been able to remember anybody by that name and was puzzled as to why a complete stranger would specify her as his next-of-kin.

The receptionist in the hospital lobby used a computer to verify that Al Levy was still in the Intensive Care Unit and then summoned the young intern who had treated him when he was admitted to the emergency room some hours earlier.

"He suffered multiple stab wounds and has lost a lot of blood," the intern told Anna as they rode in the elevator to the sixth floor.

"How did it happen?" Anna asked.

The intern, who spoke in a monotone that reflected abject fatigue, shrugged. "The police found him in an alley off Third and Main. He could have been hit by a gang or just mugged. Hell, people down there kill each other for exercise."

He led the way down a corridor with a highly polished linoleum floor and paused outside a door marked MEDICAL INTENSIVE CARE UNIT. "We don't normally allow people to visit patients in here, but Levy's in bad shape so I've authorized your going in. I'm not sure he'll recognize you, but it's worth a try."

Without waiting for Anna to reply, the intern retraced his steps and disappeared into the elevator. Anna hesitated, then eased the door open and found herself in front of a desk behind which television monitors displayed the images of each patient in Intensive Care. She identified herself to the nurse, who was obviously expecting her and who showed her into a room containing four beds, only one of which was occupied.

The man in it was propped against a pile of pillows, an IV tube in one arm, his chest and belly swathed in bandages. Wires connected him to a unit at his bedside that monitored his heartbeat with blips on a luminous green screen. He had a large head, eyes that were half-closed by scar tissue, and the splayed nose of the professional fighter.

"Hello, Anna," he said in Polish, "it's been a long time."

She still didn't recognize him, but the distinctive sound of his low, guttural voice triggered memories buried deep in her subconscious, and she realized that she was looking at a man she had believed dead for over forty years, entombed under tons of rubble when a German tank shelled the farmhouse where she and the other women couriers had taken refuge. His name wasn't Al Levy but Halevi—Pan Halevi!

Janna heard the metallic clang of the street-level doors closing and felt a slight pressure in the pit of her stomach as the giant elevator began its ascent from Wilshire Boulevard to the penthouse at Wellington House. It was a sensation to which she had never become fully accustomed in the year she had occupied the penthouse, and she was still awed by the experience of sitting behind the wheel of her Mercedes 380-SL and looking down through the slats in the outer walls of the shaft at traffic streaming along the Golden Mile far below.

She had decided to make the penthouse her home after being attacked on the cliffs at Point Lobos—an incident that had been sufficiently terrifying to convince her that Joe Dawson was right in suggesting that she avail herself of the protection that was built into Wellington House —and her decision was enthusiastically endorsed by Felix Ervin. But after the terrors of the previous night, when an intruder had gained access despite the many security devices, she realized both men had been wrong in assuming the penthouse to be the ultimate sanctuary.

She had phoned Ervin at his isolated ranch in the Santa Ynez Mountain the moment she arrived at her office that morning and told him what had happened.

"God, I'm glad you weren't hurt!" he exclaimed. "I'd never have forgiven myself. I mean, if it hadn't been for me you wouldn't have bought the place."

"Neither would most of our tenants have purchased their condominiums for millions of dollars if we hadn't guaranteed them an unbreachable security system," she replied. "If they find out what happened in the penthouse last night, we're in deep trouble."

"I'll fly down this afternoon," Ervin said. "Meet me at the penthouse and ask Anna to join us. I want to see for myself what happened. The firm that installed those security devices assured me they were foolproof. The way things look they're going to have a lot of explaining to do to my lawyers."

A slight jolt made Janna aware that the elevator had reached the garage area next to the penthouse. She looked at the digital clock in the dashboard and saw it was 2:47 P.M. Her meeting with Ervin was scheduled for 3 P.M., and he was always punctual. Getting out of her car, she walked down the short corridor linking the garage with the spacious private foyer fronting the penthouse, used her coded passcard to operate the electronic lock, and opened the thick, copper-sheathed door.

She paused in the art-filled entrance hall, puzzled by the unusual silence, and then realized it was because Shep wasn't there to greet her. In the past he had always come rushing to meet her, alerted by a sixth sense of her arrival even before she left the garage area, and she had grown accustomed to hearing his excited barking, but now she remembered his dismembered body and shuddered.

"It's me," she called, not wanting to startle Anna by her unexpected arrival. "I talked with Felix and he's meeting us here at three o'clock."

Unconsciously fingering the gold medallion that Janet Taylor had given her in Singapore, which hung from a fine gold chain around her neck, she waited for a response, and, when none came, called again. "Anna?"

Her voice echoed through the penthouse, but there was still no reply. Assuming the other woman hadn't heard, or was sleeping, Janna checked Anna's bedroom, the balcony, the living room, and finally the library. There she saw the manila folders Anna had picked up at the Wiesenthal Center earlier that morning, but there was no sign of Anna herself.

The folders reminded her that Anna had planned to attend the annual gathering of Jewish Holocaust survivors, so, assuming that was where the other woman had gone, Janna went in search of Sarah to ask her to have some refreshments ready to serve when Felix Ervin arrived.

Pushing open the door of the kitchen, she looked inside and froze. The black woman was sprawled on the floor, face up, her eyes staring sightlessly at the panels of neon lighting in the ceiling. Blood oozed from a gaping wound in her throat and trickled down the side of her neck into a widening pool that had formed around where her head rested.

"Oh, God!" Janna gasped, kneeling next to the black woman's side and feeling for a pulse. There was none. Willing herself not to panic, she got up and reached for the wall phone next to the refrigerator, but when she put the receiver to her ear the line was dead. Nor were any of the other phones in the penthouse working, and when Janna pressed the button that was meant to alert the guards, there was no response. She ran to the front door and tried to open it, but her coded passcard wouldn't operate the electronic lock. She was trapped.

She was still frantically searching her mind for some other means of escape when every television screen in the penthouse suddenly came alive with bizarre images: concentration camp inmates hurling themselves onto high-voltage fences; hundreds of skeletal corpses dumped in common graves; a storeroom piled with thousands of eyeglasses; a prisoner being castrated with a bayonet; eight naked old men writhing as they were hung by piano wire from a scaffold; a young Jewish girl being ravished by an Alsatian dog; tattoed skin being peeled from the chest of a man while he was still alive.

Sickened by the scenes, Janna went from room to room unplugging television sets. When she couldn't locate the cord supplying power to the monitor in the custom-built audiovisual console in the den, she shattered the screen with a heavy crystal ashtray.

Silence shrouded the penthouse for two or three minutes, and then Janna heard hushed voices coming from Anna's bedroom. She knew it was unoccupied, yet there was no denying the noise that now issued from it. Her first instinct was to remain where she stood, but when the volume grew louder, and she heard a woman weeping, Janna ran to the room and threw open the door. It was empty, but the murmuring shifted to a succession of other bedrooms, the library, and the den. Janna checked each out in turn but failed to find anybody in them, and each time she entered a room the voices began again somewhere else.

No sooner had she returned to the living room than the electrically operated drapes slid across the picture windows, plunging the penthouse into darkness, and when Janna tried to turn on the lights nothing happened. Suddenly a guttural voice shouted, *"Alle Juden herunter!"*

The words were repeated again and again, each time louder than the last, until Janna screamed, "For God's sake, stop it!"

There was a moment of absolute silence, then the voice resumed, this time with cries of, *"Juden, raus! . . . Juden, raus! . . ."*

Before Janna could scream again, half a dozen narrow beams of light sliced through the gloom, emanating from panels that had slid open in the ceiling, and the entire living room came alive with pictures—projected on walls, floor, drapes—accompanied by sounds amplified to near-deafening levels by speakers hidden in the walls.

She found herself enveloped by burning buildings; a synagogue exploding in a fiery cloud; tanks rolling along cobbled streets; strutting German soldiers; children impaled on the spikes of iron railings; barking guard dogs; whip-wielding SS troopers; bloated bodies floating in excrement-filled sewers.

The air was filled with the chatter of machine pistols; fleeing Germans shouting, *"Juden haben Waffen!"*; women screaming; children pleading for food; a girl's sweet voice tremulously singing a Zionist song.

The volume was so loud that the floor vibrated, and when Janna reached out to support herself against a wall, her body reverberated with tremors running through the plaster, as Laser beams knifed through the darkness like streams of tracer bullets.

As abruptly as it had begun, the terrible cacophony suddenly ended, leaving the huge room illuminated by the images that continued to be projected through openings in the ceiling, many of them holograms which created three-dimensional images. So real was the effect that

Janna, who had slumped to the floor in a corner of the room, could almost feel them touching her.

Moments later, all but one of the beams vanished and only a single image remained. It was of a man in his late sixties wearing a tattered, blood-stained shirt, torn pants, and boots caked with dried mud. He was carrying a Mauser pistol, and two grenades hung from his wide leather belt. His head was wrapped in filthy bandages, making it difficult to see his features.

Janna watched the image, waiting for it to disappear like the rest, but this one remained and began moving toward her. At first she thought it was a particularly realistic hologram, but as it came nearer and she was able to get a closer look at the partially obscured face, she realized with horror that she'd been wrong, for the man staring down at her was no trick of light, but rather a being of flesh and blood she had known —and trusted—for a very long time.

It was Felix Ervin.

In the Medical Intensive Care Unit on the sixth floor of County-USC Medical Center, Anna Maxell-Hunter stared at Pan Halevi and struggled to control her emotions.

"Thought I was dead, eh?" Halevi said in a hoarse whisper.

Anna nodded.

"Well, if the doctors are right, my number's up this time," he said weakly. "That's why I gave them your name. . . ."

In short, halting sentences, interspersed with frequent pauses during which he struggled to draw on his rapidly failing strength, he told Anna what had happened to him after they became separated at the farmhouse in Austria. Rather than being buried, as Anna and her three companions had thought, Halevi had escaped from the cellar moments before the German tank began its shelling and managed to flee with the knapsacks containing the jewels. When he was attempting to cross a frozen lake near Oberriet on the border between Austria and Switzerland, the ice under him had broken, dumping him in the freezing water, and he'd had seconds in which to choose between saving the treasure and himself; the weight of the knapsacks was dragging him under, and if he hadn't let go of them he would have drowned. He chose to save his own skin, let the jewels sink to the bottom of the lake, and escaped to Switzerland, where he spent the rest of the war.

"After the Germans surrendered, Josef Kandalman, who had survived both the Jews' last stand in the ghetto and imprisonment in

Dachau, tracked me down and demanded to know why the jewels had never been delivered to the Credit Suisse bank in Geneva," Halevi said, in a voice that was now a labored wheeze. "I was afraid to tell him the truth. I'd seen what he could do to anybody he felt had crossed him. So I told him you women had stolen them. He swore to spend the rest of his life getting revenge, and ordered me to kill each of the couriers. . . ."

Genevieve Fleury had been his first victim, then Janet Taylor in Singapore, and finally Anna, whom he had tried to push under the subway train in New York. He had made an attempt to kill Janna, too; first by cutting the girth of the horse she was riding when she was a guest of the Taylor's at Weston, and later in Big Sur, but had failed both times.

"But what in God's name has Kandalman got against Janna?" Anna asked, utterly stunned by Halevi's revelations.

"It was enough that her mother betrayed him," the dying man whispered.

"Janna isn't my daughter. . . ."

"He's known that for years," Halevi breathed. "He and Keja were lovers. She slept with him whenever she stayed overnight at his bunker in the ghetto. The medallion he always wore, the one she gave him—"

"Back-to-back K's?"

"Keja and Kandalman. It was an amulet she believed would protect him."

"Janet took it after he was burned with acid."

"It left a scar on his chest," Halevi murmured. "After the war he underwent extensive plastic surgery to remove the scars and completely change his appearance, but he refused to let the surgeon touch that brand. In his own twisted way he loved Keja."

"Did he know she was pregnant?"

Halevi nodded. "That's why he kept urging her to leave Warsaw. He didn't want his child to—"

"His!" Anna exclaimed.

"He knew that from the moment Keja conceived."

"Yet he still ordered you to kill Janna?"

"He believed Keja had betrayed him by helping to steal the treasure."

"But his own daughter!" Silence settled on the room, which was heavy with a fetid stench. "I don't understand why you are telling me all this now," Anna said, finally ending the strained quietness.

"I served my purpose," Halevi muttered bitterly. "He was afraid I would talk and wanted me out of the way. It was Kandalman who arranged to have me knifed last night. Telling you everything is my only way of getting back at the bastard!"

"When were you attacked?"

"Just after ten o'clock."

"Then it wasn't you who vandalized the penthouse."

"It was him. Kandalman designed Wellington House from the beginning as a trap."

"But that building was Felix Ervin's concept."

"Kandalman, Ervin, they're one and the same, a man who feels he failed the thousands of Jews who trusted him with their last earthly possessions, who has never stopped feeling guilty that he lived and they died . . . it has festered for forty years, slowly driving him insane. . . ."

Halevi closed his eyes and sank back against the pillows. Talking had drained every last ounce of strength from his huge, once powerful body, and it was evident to Anna, from the rattle each intake of breath caused in his throat, that death wasn't far away.

She didn't wait for the end to come but hurried out of the ward, past the desk where the duty nurse, who had witnessed Halevi's collapse on a television monitor, was urgently summoning a doctor, and down a long polished corridor to where a public telephone was located. Taking coins from her purse, she dropped them in the coin box and dialed the operator.

"This is an emergency," Anna said. "Put me through to Central Police Station."

"What department?" the operator asked.

"Metro."

"That number is 555-4091. I'm putting you through."

When Metro answered, Anna asked to speak with Joe Dawson. There were a series of clicking sounds before a voice said, "Lieutenant Dawson. Can I help you?"

Anna identified herself and quickly relayed what she had just learned from Pan Halevi.

"Did you tell Janna?" Dawson asked.

"Not yet," Anna replied. "I thought you should know first—"

"I just called her office," he said. "Her secretary told me she'd gone to meet Felix Ervin at the penthouse!"

◇

As the police helicopter lifted off its pad at Parker Center in downtown Los Angeles, Joe Dawson, wearing the black jumpsuit of a SWAT leader, shouted over the high-pitched whine of the engine as he briefed his partners. "The target is Wellington House on Wilshire Boulevard between Beverly Hills and Westwood," he told them. "A hostage is being held in the penthouse. I have first-hand knowledge of the building and know it is inaccessible from anywhere but the roof. Luckily, it has a helipad, and that's where we'll land. Any questions?"

"How big is the group we're up against, Lieutenant?" asked Sergeant Paul Escove, a dark-haired, clean-shaven man in his late twenties.

"One man," Dawson replied.

"What kind of weapons has he got?" Officer Ken Warren, a lithe, well-muscled man whose youthful appearance belied his extensive experience as a member of a SWAT entry team, wanted to know.

Dawson hesitated. He had no idea whether Felix Ervin—or Josef Kandalman, which he now knew to be the financier's real name—was even armed. After listening to what Anna had told him when she called from County-USC Medical Center, he had immediately telephoned Frank Kershaw, the manager of Wellington House, in an attempt to have Janna intercepted before she could keep her rendezvous with Ervin, but learned it was too late: a guard in the lobby had seen her Mercedes as it entered the private elevator just before 3 P.M. The only other means of access to the penthouse was by a much smaller passenger elevator in the lobby, but it required a coded passcard to operate, and it too was locked in place thirty-five stories above street level. After talking with Kershaw, Dawson knew the penthouse was completely secured against entry from anywhere but the roof, and even then the only point of access was through a steel fire door that was kept shut electronically at all times. Repeated attempts to reach Janna by phone had proved fruitless as the main cable to the penthouse had somehow been cross-circuited. Dawson realized that unless he moved fast he was going to be too late to save the woman he loved.

"I don't know," he said, replying to Officer Warren's question about weapons, "but the guy we're after is a psycho, so I don't want either of you making any quick moves without my say-so."

The three men had worked together on SWAT operations many times in the past and had learned through experience to trust each other. Hundreds of hours of training had turned them into well-oiled machines whose job it was to smoothly resolve any situation that appeared to be life-threatening. For Officers Escove and Warren, accessing Wellington House was just another routine operation, but for Joe Dawson it was the most important mission of his life.

As the helicopter continued its flight across the mid-Wilshire district, he thought about some of the other hostage situations he'd been involved in, more than a few of which had resulted in deaths, and he began to wonder whether his personal stake in the outcome of the mission would ultimately prove to be a liability. Experience had taught him that once things started happening they moved extremely fast, split-second life-and-death decisions had to be made, and there was no time for sentiment. If it had been one of his team's loved ones who was being held captive, Dawson would automatically have excluded him from the operation on the grounds that he could prove to be a weak link when the action started. He felt guilty at not having applied the same criterion to himself.

He looked at the other two men: their black jumpsuits clung to their lean, tough bodies like second skins, and they both nursed Uzi automatics against their bulletproof vests, even though each was also equipped with .45-caliber pistols. They had been trained to use the weapons only as a last resort and both were top marksmen, but this was one mission on which Dawson hoped they weren't going to be required to prove their shooting ability.

"Hey, Joe, looks like somebody got there before us," the pilot shouted, motioning downward.

Dawson peered through the clear plastic bubble of the cockpit and saw the landing pad on top of Wellington House was already occupied by another helicopter. "Get me a readout on its I.D. numbers, will you?" he said.

The pilot nodded and radioed the markings on the fuselage of the other craft into the communications room at Parker Center, and moments later he put his mouth next to Dawson's ear. "Its registered owner is Felix Ervin, and as long as that baby's on the pad there isn't a damned thing I can do to land you guys on top of Wellington House."

"I'm going down on the cable," Dawson said.

"You're crazy! With wind shears like this I can't keep her steady. . . . "

Dawson ignored the other man's protests, slung a rope around his shoulders, and buckled on a harness that was designed to be used to lower one man at a time at the end of a short-armed boom.

"We'll follow you down," Sergeant Escove said.

"It'll take too long to retract the cable," Dawson replied. "I'll do this solo. Once I reach the roof I'll rappel down the outside of the building to the penthouse balcony.''

Before Escove could respond, Dawson stepped out of the open hatch and, with Officer Warren at the controls of the winch, issued instructions over the walkie-talkie that was strapped to his harness for the other man to begin lowering him. "Keep her steady, for Christ's sake!'' he shouted when, after descending forty or fifty feet, a sudden swirl of hot air sent the helicopter bucking upward.

"It's the goddam updrafts,'' the pilot replied, wrestling with the controls.

Sergeant Escove lay on his belly at the open door looking down at where Joe Dawson was swinging wildly back and forth above the roof of Wellington House. "It's the first dumb move I've ever known him to make,'' he muttered. "If he hits the side of that building . . .'' He left his sentence unfinished as the helicopter hit another pocket of turbulence that sent the man at the end of the steel cable careening in a wide arc.

"Give me more cable,'' Dawson yelled over the walkie-talkie.

"You've got all there is,'' Officer Warren answered.

Dawson looked up at the Jet Ranger hovering above him and saw the expression of concern and disapproval on Sergeant Escove's face. He knew it reflected the feelings of the pilot and Officer Warren that he was taking unnecessary risks, but he didn't care.

"Get me lower!'' he instructed.

The pilot steadied the helicopter and had almost lowered Dawson to the roof when the craft suddenly veered, sending him slamming into the concrete balustrade that surrounded the top of the building. The impact left Dawson fighting for breath, and he guessed from the shooting pain in his right shoulder that he had broken his collarbone, an injury that would make it impossible to rappel from the roof to the balcony.

"You okay, Joe?'' the pilot asked over the walkie-talkie.

"Yeah,'' Dawson answered, "but I changed my mind about going down from the roof. It's gonna take too long. I want you to keep decreasing altitude until I'm on the balcony.''

"You crazy?'' the pilot replied, "it's way too risky.''

"I'm not asking your opinion,'' Dawson snapped, "I'm giving you a goddamn order. Now do it!''

Inside the darkened penthouse Janna crouched trembling in a corner of the living room, realizing as she looked up into Felix Ervin's crazed

eyes that some fragile mechanism deep inside his brain had snapped.
His hand holding the machine pistol trembled, and his facial muscles
twitched. When he spoke, it was in an oddly pitched voice that quav-
ered and was so low as to be barely audible.

"Get up," he instructed, keeping the gun pointed at her head.

Janna experienced the copper taste of fear under her tongue as she
swallowed dryly, struggling to control her rising panic, and willed her
tone to remain calm as she murmured, "Easy now, Felix. . . ."

Reaching out he grabbed the gold medallion that was hanging on a
gold chain around her neck, yanked it free, tore open the front of his
shirt to reveal a scar on his chest, and pressed the talisman against his
skin. The two matched perfectly. Janna remembered Janet Taylor's
telling her that the gold ornament had been around Josef Kandalman's
neck when he was burned with acid in the ghetto and realized with
shattering clarity that she was looking at Keja's employer, a man everybody had assumed to have perished in the ZOB's courageous last stand
against the Germans.

"Yes," he muttered, nodding his head as he saw from the expression
on her face that she had made the connection, "it belongs to me. . . ."

"A gift from Keja."

Her statement seemed to surprise him, and for a moment the wildness in his eyes was replaced by a vacant stare. "She believed it would
always protect me. . . ."

"Were you lovers?" Janna asked, aware that her best chance of
staying alive lay in keeping him talking.

He grinned slyly. "Nobody knew except Halevi. He survived, too,
but now he's dead. . . ."

"Did you make her pregnant?" Janna's already wildly beating heart
raced even faster as she waited for him to answer.

He fixed her eyes in a searching gaze and slowly nodded his head.
"I am your father," he said.

Although she had anticipated his answer, Janna was still stunned by
it. It was as if the shock of discovery had short-circuited her central
nervous system, and when it slowly came alive again, instead of relief
or joy, she was only conscious of a terrible anger that rose up inside
her with such force that it overwhelmed her earlier fear. "Why didn't
you tell me, for Christ's sake?"

"Your mother betrayed me. . . . I trusted her, but she was no better
than the other women . . . they stole a treasure that represented the only
heritage the Jews in the ghetto had to leave. . . . That's why I ordered

Halevi to kill Genevieve Fleury and Janet Taylor . . . it was my solemn duty to seek atonement. . . ."

"For a crime they didn't commit?"

"The jewels never arrived. . . ."

"Because they were buried by German shelling under the ruins of a farmhouse in Austria!"

The intensity of her outburst seemed to throw him off balance, and he sounded confused as he muttered, "Halevi said they stole the treasure. . . ."

"Then he lied," Janna countered. "Genevieve, Janet, and Keja, like Anna, carried out your orders to the letter. Without them I would never have survived. . . . They gave me the only parental love I've ever known, something you chose to deny me! Now put down the gun."

The insane intensity in his eyes was replaced by flickers of doubt, and spasms shook his body so violently that the weapon he was holding wavered erratically back and forth, pointing one moment at Janna's head, the next at her reflection in a mirrored wall. He appeared utterly disoriented, on the verge of cracking, and his confusion was audible in his voice as he whispered, "Why would Halevi lie?"

"To protect himself. He had the jewels; if he survived, so did the treasure. God knows what he did with it; we can talk about it if you put down your gun. . . ."

He remained motionless, frozen in a schism somewhere between sanity and madness, but finally he lowered his Mauser and let it fall to the floor.

"Now freeze!" a voice commanded from behind where the two of them were standing.

Instead of obeying, Ervin threw an arm around Janna's neck, pulled her to him, and whirled around to face Joe Dawson, who was standing just inside the curtains that had been drawn across the entrance to the balcony. He was holding an Uzi automatic, and it was aimed at Ervin, but both men knew it was impossible for him to fire without hitting Janna.

"Let her go and nobody gets hurt," Dawson announced.

Ervin remained motionless, his body like a coiled spring. Janna felt her windpipe being squeezed shut as he tightened his hold around her neck.

"Back off, Joe!" she gasped, her voice little more than a hoarse croak.

Dawson hesitated, then lowered his Uzi but still kept it at the ready, holding it across his body.

"Drop it!" Ervin ordered.

When the other man didn't obey immediately, Ervin extended his left hand to reveal that he was holding a grenade from which the pin had been pulled. Aware that only the pressure of Ervin's fingers on the detonator lever was keeping the grenade from exploding, Dawson carefully laid his Uzi on a glass coffee table and stepped back from it. "Okay," he said, "now let Janna go."

"I'm giving the orders here," Ervin snapped.

"Right," Dawson replied placatingly.

"Back up!"

Joe moved backward until he reached the drapes.

"Hold them open," Ervin instructed.

Dawson pulled back the curtains and held them as Ervin edged past him, holding Janna around the neck with one arm, the grenade in his other hand. His grip was so tight that Janna had to fight for each breath, and the blood supply to her head was so diminished that she felt herself on the verge of fainting as Ervin backed across the balcony until he reached the stone balustrade.

"Easy," Dawson said in a tone he might have used to calm a frightened animal.

Janna felt Ervin shaking and saw his fingers beginning to ease up on the detonator lever of the grenade. His lips were so close to her ear that they brushed her lobe as he muttered, "Traitors, all traitors. . . ."

Convinced that she only had seconds to live, Janna suddenly twisted her shoulders and pulled away with an abruptness that sent her sprawling to the floor. Her unexpected movement caught Ervin unaware and knocked the grenade out of his hand. Live now that the spring on its detonator lever had been released, it hit the base of the stone balustrade and ricocheted toward where Janna was lying. She watched transfixed as it rolled nearer, conscious that Joe Dawson had taken a step forward but aware that he was too far away to reach her before the grenade exploded. It was only inches from her when Ervin sprang from where he'd been standing, grabbed the grenade, and, with it clutched to his stomach, ran to the balustrade and launched himself into space.

Dawson helped Janna to her feet, and together they hurried to the spot where Ervin had disappeared, but before they reached it there was a muffled explosion, and when they peered down all they saw was a cloud of roiling smoke midway between the balcony and the sidewalk below.

"Oh, God!" Janna gasped, her whole body shaking.

"It's all right," Dawson murmured, putting his arms around her and holding her close. "It's over now."

They stood together for a long time, wrapped in a silence that was finally broken by the wail of a siren from a police car snaking through traffic flowing along the Golden Mile. It was a sound that echoed and reechoed from the smooth facades of the towering high-rises long after Dawson took Janna's hand and led her back into the penthouse.